Henry Callaway

Nursery tales, traditions and histories of the Zulus in their own words

With a translation into English: Vol. I

Henry Callaway

Nursery tales, traditions and histories of the Zulus in their own words
With a translation into English: Vol. I

ISBN/EAN: 9783337137571

Printed in Europe, USA, Canada, Australia, Japan

Cover: Foto ©Andreas Hilbeck / pixelio.de

More available books at **www.hansebooks.com**

NURSERY TALES,

TRADITIONS, AND HISTORIES

OF THE

ẔULUS,

IN THEIR OWN WORDS,

WITH

A TRANSLATION INTO ENGLISH,

AND NOTES.

BY

THE REV. CANON C̱ALLAWAY, M.D.

VOL. I.

NATAL:

JOHN A. BLAIR, SPRINGVALE;
DAVIS AND SONS, PIETERMARITZBURG.

LONDON:

TRÜBNER AND CO., 60, PATERNOSTER ROW.

1868.

NATAL:

PRINTED AT SPRINGVALE MISSION STATION.

NATAL:

PRINTED AT SPRINGVALE MISSION STATION.

PREFACE TO THE FIRST VOLUME.

On completing this First Volume of Zulu Native Literature,—if we
may be allowed to apply such a term to that which has hitherto been
stored only in the mind and imparted to others orally,—I feel there is
something due to the Reader and to myself.

When the First Part was issued in May, 1866, I had no idea
what the First Volume would be; much less, when I wrote the Pre-
face to Part I. in the preceding January. I had collected a certain
amount of material from natives; enough to make me feel that it was
worth printing, even though at the same time I felt sure that it was,
for the most part, very fragmentary, and to be regarded rather as a
help to others to collect fuller and more perfect materials, than as
being complete in itself. But I had no idea how really poor comparatively the materials I then possessed were; or how abundant a store
of Popular Tales might be found among the Natives of Natal. The
issue of the First Part aroused a spirit of enthusiasm among the
natives of the village who were able to read, and several came and
offered themselves as being capable of telling me something better
than I had printed. From this source of information thus voluntarily
tendered I have obtained by far the best part of the contents of this
Volume,—the tale of Ukcombekcansini, which one of my reviewers
describes as being " as beautiful and graceful as a classic idyll,"—Umbadhlanyana and the Cannibal,—The Appendix on Cannibalism,—
Ugungqu-kubantwana and the Appendices which follow,—Umkxakaza-wakogingqwayo,—The Two Brothers,—Ubongopa-kamagadhlcla,
—The Appendices to Umdhlubu and the Frog,—Unthlangunthlangu
and the Appendices which follow,—Untombi-yapansi,—Umamba,—
Unanana-bosele,—The wise Son of the King, and some of the smaller
pieces with which the Volume is ended.

Thus the Work has to a great extent been collected, translated,
and arranged whilst passing through the press. This must be my
apology for the many imperfections which will be found in it; the
absence of order, and occasional repetitions. I have been feeling my
way all along; and have discovered that there exists among the people
a vast store of interesting traditional tales, which may yet be collected; and it is possible that I have only just learnt the way of collecting them. I have already several of considerable interest, which
will appear, it is supposed, in a Second Volume.

I must here state that I regard the Work in its present form as

THE STUDENTS' EDITION: the student whether of the Zulu language, or of Comparative Folk-lore. There are therefore some things retained in it which are not fit for the public generally; but which could not for the student be properly suppressed. The very value of such a work depends on the fidelity with which all is told. To be a trustworthy exposition of the native mind it must exhibit every side of it. I have felt what so many other collectors of such legends among other people have felt before me, that I have had a trust committed to me, and that I can only faithfully execute it by laying every thing before others.

But it would be quite easy to prepare a POPULAR EDITION, which with a few alterations in the tales, and a condensation and modification of the phraseology, might become an interesting and not uninstructive book for the people generally and especially for the young, with whom it would become as cherished a favourite as any which is found in nursery literature.

And now for the worth of the Work itself. Those

> " Who love a nation's legends,
> Love the ballads of the people,"

will not look upon it as a mere collection of children's tales. They will not banish these legends to the nursery; but will hear them,

> " like voices from a distance
> Call to us to pause and listen."

To such as these every thing human is valuable. The least incident which can throw light on the nature and history of man, especially his nature as he was in the now hoary past; and his history, as he has been moving upwards in an ever progressing development, or sinking lower and lower in an ever increasing degradation, becomes a treasured fact to be placed among that ever accumulating mass of materials from which hereafter a faithful record of man as he was in the past, and of the causes which have influenced him, and the varying states through which he has passed to the present, shall be compiled. Regarded from such a point of view, these simple children's tales are the history of a people's mind in one phase of its existence. The tales of olden times collected from the people by Grimm, or Thorpe, or Campbell, or Dasent, are of a very different character, and speak of a very different society from that which takes so much pleasure in the compositions of Hans Christian Andersen.

We know not yet what shall be the result of such collections of children's tales. Children's tales *now;* but not the invention of a child's intellect; nor all invented to gratify a child's fancy. If carefully studied and compared with corresponding· legends among other people, they will bring out unexpected relationships,[1] which will more and more force upon us the great truth, that man has every where

---

[1] An ingenuity similar to that which the Rev. G. W. Cox has exercised on the ancient literature of Greece, would readily convert many of these tales into *Solar Myths,* and thus connect the Greek with the Zulu, or both with a period anterior to either of them.

thought alike, because every where, in every country and clime, under every tint of skin, under every varying social and intellectual condition, he is still man,—one in all the essentials of man,—one in that which is a stronger proof of essential unity, than mere external differences are of difference of nature,—one in his mental qualities, tendencies, emotions, passions.

Elizabeth Cookson has remarked in her Introduction to the Legends of Manx Land :—

"What Fossil Remains are to the Geologist, Customs and Creeds are to the Historian—*landmarks* of the extent and progress of intelligence and civilization.

"Popular Tales, Songs, and Superstitions are not altogether profitless; like the fingers of the clock, they point to the time of day. Turns and modes of thought, that else had set in darkness, are by them preserved, and reflected, even as objects sunk below the horizon are, occasionally, brought again into view by atmospheric reflection.

"Fables are facts in as far as they mirror the minds of our less scientific Ancestors.

"That man should have solemnly believed in the existence of Fairies, Spectres, and every variety of Superstition, but testifies the vivid impression physical and mental phenomena made upon his mind. Placed in a world of marvels, he questioned the marvellous—questioned until Dark Diviners, Interpreters, arose—bewildered and bewildering, yet striving after the light—striving to solve the enigma of LIFE,—striving to fling from the soul the burden of an unexplained existence."

In reflecting on the tales of the Zulus the belief has been irresistibly fixed upon my mind, that they point out very clearly that the Zulus are a degenerated people; that they are not now in the condition intellectually or physically in which they were during "the legend-producing period" of their existence; but have sunk from a higher state. Like the discovered relics of giant buildings in Asia and America, they appear to speak of a mightier and better past, which, it may be, is lost for ever. But though by themselves they may be powerless to retrace the footsteps of successive generations, yet is it unreasonable to suppose that under the power of influences which may reach them from without, they are not incapable of regeneration ? Far otherwise. For it appears to me that this Zulu legendary lore contains evidence of intellectual powers not to be despised; whilst we have scattered every where throughout the tales those evidences of tender feeling, gentleness, and love, which should teach us that in dealing with these people, if we are dealing with savages, we are dealing with savage *men*, who only need culture to have developed in them the finest traits of our human nature.

And it is in bestowing upon us the means of bringing this culture to bear upon them, that we may see the chief practical use of this collection. We cannot reach any people without knowing their minds and mode of thought; we cannot know these without a thorough knowledge of their language, such as cannot be attained by a loose colloquial study of it.   What Sir George Grey felt was requisite for the rightful government of the people of New Zealand,—not only a thorough knowledge of their language, but also of their traditional lore,—the earnest and intelligent missionary will feel in a tenfold degree as necessary for himself, who has to deal with questions which require a much nicer and more subtle use of words than any thing affecting man in his mere external relations.   For myself I must say that scarcely a day passes in which I do not find the value of such knowledge.   Whilst the lighter study of these children's tales has prepared me to handle with a firmer and more assured grasp the graver task of translating the Bible and Prayer Book into the native tongue.

I would take this opportunity of telling such readers as are interested in the Work, that the means at my disposal are very inadequate for the easy or rapid completion of all I have in hand.   We calculate that at our present rate of proceeding it would take little less than ten years to print the materials already collected.   And I would earnestly ask their assistance in some practical manner.   This may be rendered in various ways :—By increasing the circulation of the Work ; it has reached about four hundred copies, quite as large, I admit, as might have been anticipated, but quite insufficient to cover expenses ; or by aiding to raise for the Work a special printing fund. The loan or gift of books on kindred subjects would also be a great assistance.

I must now for some time take leave of the reader.   I purpose at once to commit to the press the part of the Work on the Zulu notion of the Origin of Things,—in other words, what I have been able to collect of their traditional religion.   It is already prepared for the press ; but it is very undesirable to issue it in parts ; it must be read as a whole, carefully and thoughtfully, in order to form any just conclusion as to its real meaning.   It will probably be about one hundred and twenty pages, unless it should swell under my hands, as have the Nursery Tales.

I would now, in conclusion, take this opportunity for heartily thanking those friends who have interested themselves in the Work, and expressing my obligations especially to Mr. John Sanderson for the much valuable assistance he has rendered me.

HENRY CALLAWAY.

Springvale, Natal,
  March, 1868.

PREFACE.

Twelve years ago, when I commenced the study of Zulu, with the exception of a short, but valuable, paper by Mr. J. C. Bryant, on "The Zulu Language;" and another by Mr. Lewis Grout on "The Zulu and other Dialects of Southern Africa," in the First Volume of *The Journal of the American Oriental Society*, there was not a publication to which a student could refer for a knowledge of the rudiments of the language. In the Kxosa dialect, indeed, there were the *Grammars* of Appleyard and Boyce; and the small *Vocabulary* of Ayliff. But these were of little use to one engaged in the study of Zulu, and tended rather to confuse than to help. I was therefore, from the first, thrown on such resources as I could myself develop.

At a very early period I began to write at the dictation of Zulu natives, as one means of gaining an accurate knowledge of words and idioms. In common conversation the native naturally condescends to the ignorance of the foreigner, whom, judging from what he generally hears from colonists, he thinks unable to speak the language of the Zulu: he is also pleased to parade his own little knowledge of broken English and Dutch; and thus there is a danger of picking up a miserable gibberish, composed of anglicised Kafir, and kafirised English and Dutch words, thrown together without any rule but the caprice and ignorance of the speaker. But whilst such a compound might answer for the common relations between whitemen and natives, yet it must be wholly insufficient to admit of any close communication of mind with mind, and quite inadequate to meet the requirements of scientific investigation.

Very different is the result of writing at the dictation of a native. The first impression immediately produced is of the vast difference between the best translations and the language as spoken by natives. A native is requested to tell a tale; and to tell it exactly as he would tell it to a child or a friend; and what he says is faithfully written down. We have thus placed before us the language as nearly as possible such as it is spoken by the natives in their intercourse with each other. And, further, what has been thus written can be read to the native who dictated it; corrections be made; explanations be obtained; doubtful points be submitted to other natives; and it can be subjected to any amount of analysis the writer may think fit to make.

Such is the history of the mode in which the original Zulu, here presented to the public, has been obtained. Very many different natives have taken part in the work. There will be, therefore, found here and there, throughout, personal and dialectic peculiarities; but for the most part the language is pure Zulu. It was clearly no part of the work of the collector to make any change in the language with a view of reducing it to one imagined standard of purity.

The materials, which at first I sought to collect merely for my own instruction, gradually accumulated. As my ear became more educated, and the natives more intelligent, and able to comprehend the object I had in view, I could write with greater facility, until at length there was no subject on which I could not obtain the most accurate information possessed by the natives themselves.

Thus, as the materials increased they began to have another and somewhat different value ; they became not merely a means of learning the Zulu language, but also a means of obtaining a knowledge of Kafir customs, histories, mode of thought, religion, &c.   And what was commenced as a mere exercise-lesson was soon pursued with the further object of discovering what was the character of the mind of the people with whom we are brought into contact ; and of endeavouring to trace out their connection with other nations by the similarity which might exist in their traditions and myths, their nursery tales and proverbs.

The result of this investigation has been quite beyond my own most sanguine expectation ; and it is probable that very much remains to be added which may help us in many ways to understand the past history of the Zulus, and to connect them with other people.

For some time it has appeared to me hardly right to allow so vast a mass of materials, full of interest to the missionary, the philologist, the ethnologist, and antiquarian, as well as to a large portion of the general public, to remain on my shelves, useful to myself alone, or to some few friends who might see it in MSS. Others whom I consulted were of the same opinion ; and after much consideration, and overcoming many difficulties, I have at length entered on the task of preparing it for the press.

At first I intended to print the Kafir only, with a few explanatory notes. But so many have expressed the opinion that a Zulu book would have but few attractions, and a very limited sphere of usefulness, that I have, at the moment of going to press, concluded to print, side by side with the original Zulu, a translation.   It will thus become available both to English and Kafir scholars, and can be used as a class-book to teach the English Zulu, or the Zulus English.

The translation, without being absolutely literal, will be found to be a true representation of the original.   An absolutely literal translation, on the Hamiltonian system, would be almost as unintelligible to a person unacquainted with the language, as the original Zulu itself.   My object has been to give idiom for idiom rather than word for word, and at the same time to preserve, as far as possible, the characteristic peculiarities of the original.   Hence the translation will necessarily present a quaint and somewhat unenglish character, which will not, however, be urged against it as an objection.

Whilst on the subject of translation, it may be as well to remark that among the natives, as among all uncultivated people, there is great freedom of speech used in allusion to the relations between the sexes, &c.   Whenever I could soften down such expressions, to suit our own more refined taste, I have done so.   But, perhaps, there will still be found instances of what some may regard as too great outspokenness.   I would, however, deprecate the thought that such outspokenness is to be construed into an evidence of a want of purity among the natives, or that our reticence on such subjects is a proof of purity in ourselves.

Writing and Spelling.—The principles which have guided me in writing and spelling claim a few remarks in this place.

There are two modes of writing—one adopted by Dr. Colenso and Dr. Bleek, in which a number of small words is run together ; and the other, that adopted by the American missionaries and others, in which there is, perhaps, the opposite mistake of unnecessary division.

As regards the first, I am quite unable to see anything to recommend it, or even to conceive the reason of its adoption.   Why should we write *ngabebabopa*, "they ought to bind them ;" and not *nga be ba bopa*, "ought they them bind ?" Why should we run the Zulu words together, when we write the English ones apart ? How strange it would appear, and how difficult it would be to understand, a sentence of this kind, written in English as one word, Theyoughttobindthem ! But it is not less difficult or strange in Zulu than in English ; and tends, as it would, indeed more than it would, in English, to produce confusion and obscurity.   A person thoroughly acquainted with the language gets over the obscurity by means of the context, and has little difficulty in determining whether he is to understand *ubuya* as *u b' u ya*, "you were going," or as *u buya*, "you are coming back."   So in the following sentence, *Nembala ateti gulugudu ukungena*, "so then he hastens inside ;" he may see at once that *teti* is not the negative form of *teta*, to "chide :" but it requires a ready knowledge of the language to separate a sentence so written into its elementary words, and catch at once the meaning of *a t' e ti* in *ateti*. One could multiply instances *ad infinitum* of the confusion which arises from writing by sentences instead of words.

Who that has ever attempted to decipher old manuscripts, in which the words are all run together, has not felt a wish that the writers had adopted the modern system of writing each word by itself? The Cuneiform inscriptions appeared but as a mere "conglomerate of wedges" to those who first discovered them, about which a doubt might exist whether they were writings at all, or "mere arabesque or fanciful ornaments." In attempting to decipher these inscriptions a sign was discovered by which the words were separated; on which Max Müller remarks:—"Such a sign is of course an immense help in all attempts at deciphering inscriptions, for it lays bare at once the terminations of hundreds of words." (*Lectures on the Science of Language. Second Series, p. 4.*) Being then practically acquainted with the difficulties and obscurities occasioned by the ancients having run their words together, why should we, in reducing a savage language to writing, introduce similar difficulties?

I need not say much on the system I have adopted of writing the words apart. It is substantially the same as is found in other Zulu and Kxosa works. But in some instances, where a sentence has become petrified, as it were, into a word, although its etymology is still evident, I have written it as one word, as *ngani*, not *nga ni*, "why;" or *kangaka*, not *ka nga ka*, "so much." So, perhaps arbitrarily, I have written prepositions with the nouns they govern as one word, regarding the combination as a case of the noun, as *kuye*, not *ku ye;* *nami*, not *na mi*. By doing so I jump over, rather than solve, some questions which arise as to the proper method of writing certain words, as *kwiti, bakwetu.*

Again, I do not separate what is called the possessive particle from the noun. In most instances they are necessarily blended, forming the possessive case. It therefore appears consistent to write them together under all circumstances; and as we have *umntwana wenkosi* (wa-inkosi), "the child of the chief," I also write *umntwana kampande*, "the child of Umpande:" that is, I regard *kampande* as the genitive of *Umpande*, just as *wenkosi* is the genitive of *inkosi*. I also write *umuntu waselovo, umuntu wakwazulu;* and not *wa s'elovo, wa kwa Zulu;* regarding these as genitive cases, and examples of the mode in which the genitive of places is formed.

A difficulty, too, has been felt as regards the capital letters; and we find consequently in printed books some ugly anomalies, such as a capital in the middle of a word, and paragraphs beginning with a small letter. This has arisen apparently, in part, from the error of not regarding the prefix as an essential part of a noun, and so giving the nominal root an undue prominence; and, in part, from our not being accustomed to those *initial* changes upon which grammatical inflection so much depends in the Zulu language. But to use the capital letters to distinguish nominal roots is a novelty in writing; and it appears to have been overlooked that when, as a mark of eminence, the capital is placed at the beginning of the root in such words as *nKosi*, "Lord," *Kosi* has no personal meaning, indeed, no meaning whatever; and that therefore the mark of eminence is thrown away on a meaningless combination of letters, which can only assume a living sense by having combined with it the requisite prefix. These nominal roots doubtless had, originally, determinate meanings well understood; but the prefix was always necessary to specialise the fundamental root-meaning.

I have, therefore, very much reduced the number of capital letters, and use them only to mark paragraphs, and proper names in the nominative case.

The orthography of the language presents much greater difficulties. We profess to write it phonetically; but then we are at once met by the objection that the same letters have a different phonetic value in different European languages, and even in one and the same language. The desirability of a uniform orthography is very generally felt. But if it be ever attainable, we are as yet very far from the adoption of a "universal alphabet." The practical difficulties in the way of using that of Lepsius are insuperable, even if we were prepared to admit the soundness of all the principles on which it is founded. I have therefore departed as little as possible from the mode of spelling already in use;

for it appears better to continue for a time some things which are felt to be unsatisfactory, than to introduce new characters, according to one's private fancy, which may not be adopted by others, and which would only have the effect of removing to a greater distance the attainment of a uniform orthography. The system of Max Müller is more available for missionaries; and mentioning only that I have, as far as possible, followed his principles, as laid down in his *Survey of Languages*, it will not be necessary to allude in detail to anything but the clicks, the aspirates, and the aspirated linguals.

The Clicks.—It is generally supposed that the sounds called clicks are a modern intrusion into the alliterative class of languages, arising from intercourse with the Hottentots. Dr. Bleek remarks :—"The occurrence of clicks in the Kafir dialects decreases almost in proportion to their distance from the Hottentot border. Yet the most southern Tekeza dialects and the Se-suto have also (probably through Kafir influence) become to a slight extent possessed of this remarkable phonetical element." *(Bleek's Comparative Grammar, p. 13.)* Be this as it may, the natives scout the idea of having borrowed anything from the Hottentots. It is certain, however, that there are tribes speaking an alliterative language, the Amanganja and Ajawa on the Shire for instance, in which there are no clicks. And Kolben, whose observations were made early in the eighteenth century (his work was published in 1731), speaking of the natives of "Terra du Natal," says :—"There is nothing of the Hottentot stammering or clashing of the tongue in speaking among them." *(The Present State of the Cape of Good Hope. Vol. I., p. 81.)* Whether other tribes have driven out these "non-clashing" people who then inhabited Natal, or whether the "clashing" has been introduced since, we have no data at present which would enable us to determine with certainty. The question may be some day solved by researches in the comparative philology of South African languages, so happily begun by Dr. Bleek. The view that the clicks are not native to the alliterative languages is quite in accordance with the theory I have formed of their nature.

Dr. Bleek remarks :—"There is this distinction between the Hottentot and Kafir clicks, namely, that the latter are only found in the place of other consonants, and are used like consonants at the beginning of syllables, whilst in the Hottentot a guttural explosive consonant *(k, kh,* or *g),* the faucal spirant *h* and the nasal *n,* can be immediately preceded by a click, and form together with it the initial element of the syllables." *(Bleek's Comparative Grammar, p. 13.)*

My own conclusions as to the clicks do not accord with the view here expressed. The clicks in Zulu are never heard without an accompanying consonantal sound. The *c, q,* and *x* were adopted to represent "this remarkable phonetic element," simply because they were not needed for other purposes, in reducing the Zulu language to writing on phonetic principles. It is customary, in some instances, to write these letters alone, not only to represent the click, but at the same time the combined consonantal sound. But this is a merely arbitrary mode of writing; for when there is not an accompanying consonant expressed, the *c, q,* and *x* are supposed to have *an inherent k sound,* and are to be pronounced accordingly. The consonantal sounds found with the clicks, and, with the exception of *k* already mentioned, expressed in writing, are *g, k,* and *n ;* the *g* may be nasalised, *ng ;* and it, as well as *k* and *n,* is often found in combination with *w.* Thus we have *g, ng, ngw ; k, kw ; n,* and *nw,* in combination with the clicking sound.

A difference of opinion exists as to whether the *click* precedes or follows in pronunciation the associated consonantal sound. Lepsius *(Standard Alphabet. Second Edition, p. 81)* and Dr. Bleek *(Comparative Grammar, p. 13)* consider that the click precedes the consonantal sound, and that therefore the sign for the clicking should precede the associated consonant. Grout and Döhne, on the other hand, do not concur with this opinion, but write the click sign after the consonant.

The true explanation of the clicking sounds appears to be, that they are impediments coming in the way of the free enunciation of the consonants with which they are combined, and which they modify. The organs of speech assume the position for uttering *g, ng, ngw ; k, kw ; n,* or *nw,* and find a bar to the utterance, which is leaped over, giving rise to the click sound ; and then the consonantal sound is uttered. If this view be correct, there is an unsuccessful, but quite perceptible, effort to pronounce the combined consonant *before* the click, but its full utterance takes place *after* it. *In fact, the sound is one ;* and it is immaterial whether the click sign precedes or follows the consonant with which it is associated.

But what shall the click signs be ?

As the click sounds are new sounds, for which our alphabet has not provided, they seem to demand new signs, not found in that alphabet ; especially as *c, q,* and *x,* though not wanted in Zulu, are wanted when the Zulus are taught to read English or other languages.

If the clicks are an intrusion into Zulu of a foreign origin, and the sounds be a mere modification of previously existing consonantal sounds, it would appear that the best way of indicating them would be by a diacritic mark written with the consonants thus modified.

These two principles being laid down, it would not be difficult to determine a diacritic sign. The form of that sign is absolutely unimportant : it demands only that it should be distinct in print, and of easy adaptation to writing. If these two requisites are ensured, all that is required further is that writers generally should agree upon one sign. If we cannot yet have a uniform orthography in other respects, we ought to have no difficulty in determining what shall be the sign for a new sound, not provided for in any known alphabet.

Mr. Lewis Grout has adopted Lepsius' characters for the clicks. And I would have willingly followed his example, but that the characters suggested by Lepsius do not present the two requisites above mentioned, distinctness in print, and easy adaptability to writing ; defects which, as it seems to me, must be fatal to their being generally used. Further, they do not provide for the consonantal sounds with which the clicks are pronounced.

Whilst this subject was under my consideration, being desirous of carrying out the principles above alluded to, and at the same time very unwilling to introduce novelties on my own responsibility, I corresponded, through a friend, with Max Müller. He suggested the employment of *k, t,* and *l,* either with a dot under each, or to be printed in Italics in Roman type, and *vice versâ.*

To follow such a suggestion appears to me calculated to increase the present difficulties without any corresponding advantage : *k, t,* and *l* have already in Zulu their known and acknowledged phonetic value : to introduce them as the signs of the click sounds, even though distinguished by being written as Italics, or with a diacritic dot, would be confusing. All that can be said, on the other side, is that *k, t,* and *l* dimly intimate the parts of the organs of speech where the several clicks are formed.

I have therefore concluded, until something better can be determined, to continue to use *c, q,* and *x,* which are already used, which are well known to the natives, and which have no other phonetic value in the Zulu language. But in order to impress on the eye the fact that they are not letters but *diacritic marks,* I so far adopt Max Müller's suggestion, that I write them in Italics in Roman type, and *vice versâ.* And as these letters, thus used as diacritic signs, have no inherent consonantal value, I always write the consonants before them with which they are combined in pronunciation.

I should prefer diacritic marks written with *g, k,* and *n.* But having stated my own opinions, I leave the matter to the consideration of others, and would express the hope that before very long, on this subject at least, there may be a uniform orthography.

The Aspirates.—There are at least four aspirates—the common aspirate *h,* a "lateral fricative," and two guttural fricatives.

The aspirate *h* requires no remark ; the lateral fricative will be spoken of presently.

The letter *r,* not being used in Zulu orthography (although the sound of *r* does actually occur in one onomatopoetic word, *ukuti dri,* "to whir"), has been used for the guttural fricative. It is absolutely necessary to cease to use *r* for this purpose ; for it is continually needed to express its own proper sound in the names of persons and places now being rapidly introduced into the Zulu language. There may be something said in favour of the Greek χ, recommended by Lepsius, and adopted by Bleek and Grout. But I have preferred on the whole, at the suggestion of Max Müller, to use *hh*. We cannot use *kh*, because that will be required for the aspirated *k*, which is a wholly different sound from the guttural fricative. The guttural fricative in many Zulu words is interchangeable with the simple *h ;* the double *h*, therefore, seems a very appropriate sign for the guttural fricative.

The second guttural fricative is extremely difficult to pronounce ; and as I can only approximately pronounce it myself, I speak with some diffidence on the subject. It is the sound alluded to by Dr. Colenso in his *Zulu Grammar*, as a "sound peculiar to Zulu-Kafir, which may be pronounced either as a guttural from the bottom of the throat, or as a click in the ordinary way. Happily it occurs in only a very few words. *(Elementary Grammar of the Zulu-Kafir Language, p. 6.)* The sound certainly does somewhat resemble an imperfect faucal click. But it is not a click. Dr. Colenso uses the italic *x* to represent it. Mr. Grout uses for this sound the Greek χ with a diacritic mark (which Lepsius proposes for a different purpose). He describes it as "a peculiar, hard, rough guttural sound, which seems to be made by contracting the throat, and giving the breath a forcible expulsion, at the same time modifying the sound with a tremulous motion of the epiglottis." *(Grammar of the Zulu Language, p. 16.)* Dr. Bleek, who apparently has not heard the sound pronounced, calls it a "faucal explosive ;" but acknowledges that he is "as yet at a loss regarding this sound," from the description of Colenso and Grout. *(Comparative Grammar, p. 17.)*

I should propose to call it *the lateri-guttural fricative*. Natives, and those who can pronounce it as the natives, have one idea of the mode in which the sound is produced : it is this,—the anterior portion of the tongue lies flat and relaxed in the mouth ; its base is curved upwards, so as to close the centre of the faucal region, and the breath is forcibly expelled on each side. It generally has a *k* sound with it ; and in many words is interchangeable with the guttural fricative. I shall therefore use for this sound the Italic *hh* in Roman type, and *vice versâ.* When it is combined with a *k* sound, *k* will of course be written before *hh.*

The Aspirated Linguals, or more properly the aspirated l.—This sound occurs under at least two forms, usually spelt by *hl* and *dhl.* The aspirate heard in either case is not the common aspirate *h.* Dr. Bleek says :—"The aspirated lingual *hl* sounds in Kafir as if the guttural fricative (like the German *ch* in "suchen") was pronounced in combination with and at the same time as *l.*" *(Comparative Grammar, p. 16.)* The aspirate, however, is a *lateral fricative*, as stated by Lepsius, who compares the Zulu aspirated *l* (that is *dhl*) with the Welsh *ll.* *(Standard Alphabet, pp. 172, 270, 272.)* The sounds produced by the aspiration of *l* are difficult to pronounce, as is evident from the sounds which are uttered by colonists instead of the true native pronunciation, such as *shla*, or *thla*, the *t* being too much pronounced. To my own ear, the first aspirated *l (hl)* has always somewhat of a *t* sound more or less audible, especially where it follows a vowel, as in *lahleka.* But it is probable that the aspirated *l* occurs in three forms—simply aspirated, and preceded by *th* and *dh ;* the aspirate being not the common *h*, but a lateral fricative. I think it will help English readers to the pronunciation if they try to pronounce *hl*, as in *hlala*, as though the *l* were preceded by the *th* as heard in *thigh*, or, better still, the *th* as heard in *breath.* Lepsius, indeed, tells us that *t* must not be the basis of this sound. *(Standard Alphabet, p. 65.)* And no doubt *thigh* can be pronounced, or a sound very like it, without a *t*, in the same way as *hla.* The *dhl*, as in *dhlula*, may be pronounced by supposing the *l* to be preceded by *th* as heard in *thy*, or better as in *breathe.* The difference of the sounds in *thigh* and *thy*, or in *breath* and *breathe*, appears to me very exactly to distinguish the difference between *hl* and *dhl.* And it may well admit of discussion whether we should not use *thl* and *dhl* for the aspirated *l* sounds as heard in Zulu ; for I feel sure that no one who has never heard the sound would be guided to anything like a correct pronunciation by the ordinary spelling, *hl.* In translations I have used *thl.* At the same time I would have it understood that the *t* must be as little audible as possible. I do not think that *k* is ever heard in Zulu with the aspirated *l*, as it appears to be in other dialects of South Africa. *(Bleek's Comparative Grammar, p. 16.)* As it appeared desirable to distinguish the lateral fricative from the common *h*, I have determined to use for this purpose the Italic *h* in Roman type, and *vice versâ :* thus, *h*lala, d*h*lula ; h*lala,* dh*lula.* We shall thus have a uniformity and distinctness without any real change in the spelling, and without the introduction of new characters. The four aspirates, therefore, are thus written :—The common h, or faucal spirant, h ; the lateral fricative, only found with l, *h ;* the guttural fricative, hh ; the lateriguttural fricative, *hh.*

It does not appear worth while to mark by any sign the long and short vowels, as the organs of speech seem naturally to use the short vowels in the proper place. Neither have those few instances in which *u* is pronounced as in French been distinguished by any diacritic mark.

In conclusion, I would remind those who may read the following pages that "he who first undertakes to bring into form the scattered elements of any subject can only accomplish his task imperfectly." No one will be more sensible of the many imperfections which mark my work than I am myself. If, however, the result of my labours be to lead others to a deeper study of the Kafir language, and so to a deeper knowledge of the Kafir people ; and by their own investigations to fill up the gaps which exist in many subjects here brought before them, I shall be satisfied. If others will continue and perfect what I have begun, I shall not have begun in vain.

H. C.

Springvale, Natal,
      January, 1866.

IZINGANEKWANE.

(NURSERY TALES.)

IZINGANEKWANE.

INTRODUCTION TO THE ZULU NURSERY TALES.

LIKE most other people, the Zulus have their Nursery Tales. They have not hitherto, so far as I know, been collected. Indeed, it is probable that their existence even is suspected but by a few; for the women are the depositaries of these Tales; and it is not common to meet with a man who is well acquainted with them, or who is willing to speak of them in any other way than as something which he has some dim recollection of having heard his grandmother relate. It has been no easy matter to drag out the following Tales; and it is evident that many of them are but fragments of some more perfect narrative. One cannot but feel that one has here put together a great deal of what is supremely ridiculous, and which considered by itself may well be regarded as utterly unworthy of being perpetuated. Yet ridiculous and worthless as it is in itself, it will have its use in many ways. It will, I think, help us to find unsuspected points of contact between the Zulus and other people; and may even give us a clue to their origin. It will also give them a claim to be reckoned as an integral part of our common humanity, by showing that they have so many thoughts in common with other men, and have retained in their traditional tales so much that resembles the traditional tales of other people. It will form a book, too, which the young Kafir will greedily read, whilst he pores, not without loathing, over translations which he understands with difficulty, which relate to subjects that are new and strange to him, and which he does not readily comprehend; to which, it may be, he has a repugnance. It would be a great mistake to teach an English child to read solely from the Bible or books of devotion: yet this is what hitherto we have been doing, with scarcely any exception, for the Zulu. We want to teach the young Kafirs to read. We must, then, give them some inducement to read; and where can we find a greater than by giving them the traditionary tales of their forefathers, in the same words as they have heard them around their hut-fires?

The first Tale in the Series is the History of the Travels and Adventures of Uthlakanyana, a kind of Tom Thumb, the Giant

Killer. Not that his cunning is exerted on giants alone. All is fish
that comes to Uthlakanyana's net ! Uthlakanyana is not a common
man : he is a cunning, malicious dwarf; and is possessed of magical
powers. There are in these Tales, too, accounts of gigantic cannibals,
who can carry a man in a sack, or swallow him at a gulp, as the
Guzzler, in Uthlakanyana ; whilst the ogress Uzwanide, or Long-toe,
is evidently a mighty magician, and capable, like Heitsi Eibip, of the
Hottentots,[1] of rising from a succession of deaths. We have, too,
various animals introduced, not exactly as in Fables, but talking
freely and, as it were, naturally, and holding intercourse with man.
The leopard, the hare, the iguana ; doves, swallows, pigeons, and mice
play their part on the stage, sometimes in their own characters, sometimes rather as forms assumed by magical powers ; as the swallow in
the Tale of Uzwanide, and the striped mouse in that of Ubabuze.
All these Tales allude more or less distinctly to the magical, and a
contest going on between good and malicious genii ; and it is remarkable that nothing is said of the use of medicines, so much talked of
now among the natives, and which they imagine can produce such
marvellous results—love or hatred ; beauty or deformity ; prosperity
or ill-luck ; bravery or cowardice. This would seem to give the Tales
an antiquity of origin, referring them back to a very different social
condition from that now existing. There are two Tales in which a
Magical Tree is introduced ; and there is the Rock of Two-holes,
which opens and closes at the voice of those who know the secret,
reminding one of " Open Sesame " in the Forty Thieves. Huge fabulous monsters, the existence of which has not been suggested by the
fossil bones of extinct animals,[2] are introduced ; the Isikqukqumadevu,
which was as big as a mountain ; the Isitwalangcengce, or Isidawane,
which carried people away on its head, and fed on their brains, and to
this day is the nursery bogy, with which noisy Zulu children are
silenced ; and the huge River Tortoise, which is mistaken for an
island. And then there is what is probably a modern " Myth of
Observation," in which is gravely related, as a fact, the existence of a
Fiery Serpent five hundred yards long !

I have combined with the Nursery Tales the few Fables I
have met with, and some other Narratives, which do not properly
belong to them, but which could not so well be arranged with any
other subject.

<hr>

[1] Bleek's Hottentot Fables and Tales, p. 75.
[2] See Tylor's Researches into the Early History of Mankind.

PREFACE TO THE TALE OF UTHLAKANYANA.

Uhlakanyana umuntu ohlakanipile kakulu, omnçinyane kakulu, ngangekcakide. Lo 'muntu wa deleleka ngezikati zonke kulabo 'bantu, a e ba kohlisa, a vela kubo; ngokuba ba be ti, ba nge kohliswe umntwana; ba nga kohliswa umuntu o ngangabo. Ku ngaloko ke ngoku nga m kçondi, ukuba ka kulanga nje ngokusindwa ubukçili nokuhlakanipa, wa za wa batsha, wa ba imbatshelana yokudelelwa, ba zinge be m delela njalo. Kepa a kohlise umuntu e nga bonakalisisi ukuba u yena impela o fanelc ukukohlisa. Kwa tiwa futi u Ukcaijana-bogconono, Mahlab'-in-doda-i-s'-emi. Lelo 'gama lokuti Ukcaijana inyamazane encinyane ebomvana, i nomsila omnyama, isihloko sawo. Kepa leyo 'nyamazane inyamazane ehlakanipe kakulu kunezinye, ngokuba ubukçili bayo bukulu. Ku ti, uma ku tiywe insimba, i fika masinyane endhlwaneni, i tate umjonjo[4] o bekelwa insimba, i godele yona kukçala; i ya fika insimba, i fika umjonjo se u dhliwe ikcakide.

Uthlakanyana is a very cunning man; he is also very small, of the size of a weasel. This man was despised constantly among those people, whom he used to deceive, and from whom he sprang; for they thought they could not be deceived by a child—they could be deceived by a man as big as themselves. Therefore, through not understanding him, that he had not grown because he was overweighted by cunning and wisdom, and so was undersized, and became a contemptible dwarf, they habitually despised him at all times. But he deceived a man, through his not being clearly seen to be, in fact, the very man to deceive. He was called also Ukcaijana-bogconono, Mathlab'-in-doda-i-s'-emi. The word Ukcaijana signifies a little red animal, which has a black-tipped tail. And this animal is cleverer than all others, for its cunning is great.[3] If a trap is set for a wild cat, it comes immediately to the trap, and takes away the mouse which is placed there for the cat: it takes it out first; and when the cat comes, the mouse has been already eaten by the weasel.

[3] As we say in English, "You must be pretty deep, to catch weasels asleep."

[4] *Umjonjo.*—This name is given to the mouse only when it is used as a bait. Its meaning is uncertain. But it is an *ukuhlonipa*-word, that is, a term of respect. The natives say that if they give a mouse the name of *impuku* when used as a bait, it will not catch anything, because it has been treated with contempt! It is also called *injova,* and *umvuzane.* The same notion appears below, where it is said that when a weasel has been caught, it stands in the way of other animals, that is, exerts an influence adverse to the trapper's success.— The same remarkable custom of speaking of numerous animals, and even of inanimate things, by euphemisms, instead of by their proper names, prevails in the north of Europe. (*Thorpe's Northern Mythology. Vol. II., p.* 83.)

Futi, i *hlup'* abantu; ngokuba uma i nga tandi ukusuka end*h*leleni, i ti i nga bona umuntu 'eza, i k*c*ezuke kancinane end*h*leleni, i bod*h*le, y etuse umuntu; nembala umuntu a ze a gweme lapo, e ti i vinjelwe isilwane. Kanti ik*c*akide. Kumbe ku ti, lapa e se hambele kude, e hamb' e bheka, a bone se li suka, li gijima; umuntu a jambe, a pel' amand*h*la, ngokuti, "O, ind*h*lela *le* ngi i shiyiswe i lesi 'silimana!" A buyele end*h*leleni.

Futi, li ya zondana kakulu nezinyoka; ngokuba li ya zi d*h*la. Ku ti lapa li bona kona imamba y ejwayele, li i linde, li ze li bone ukuba i pumile, y alukile; li sale li ngene kuk*c*ala emgodini wayo, ukuze i t' i fika, i fike se li pambili; li i bone i s' eza njeya; li be li lunga, li *h*lale emgodini, se li bh*c*kene nen*h*loko, ukuze i ti i sa ngena imamba, loku i ngena pela emgodini wayo a y azi 'luto, li i bambe ngen*h*loko, li pume nayo; se li bod*h*la li i bulale; li d*h*lale, li i d*h*lalela, ngokuba li i bulele. Li zinge li y ek*c*a ekupeleni, li i d*h*le.

Futi, ik*c*akide li nesisila esikulu; ngokuba uma abatiyi be tiyile izinnyamazane, kwa banjwa ik*c*akide, lowo 'muntu k' etembi ukuba izinnyamazane u ya 'ku zi bamba; u y' azi ukuba ik*c*akide li ya landula;[5] umva walo mubi. Noma u *h*lan-

It also is a trouble to men; for if it does not choose to get out of the way, if it see a man coming, it just quits the path a little, and growls and frightens the man; and, sure enough, at length he goes round, thinking the path is obstructed by a wild animal. And it is a weasel, forsooth. Perhaps, when he has gone to a distance, he going and looking, he sees it depart and run away; so he is ashamed, and his heart sinks, and he says, "O, I have been made to quit the path by this piece of deformity!" And he returns to the path.

Again, it is at great enmity with snakes; for it eats them. If it sees a place to which an imamba habitually resorts, it watches it, until it sees that it has gone out to feed; it then goes into the hole of the snake first, that when the snake comes, it may come, it being there beforehand; it sees the snake coming at some distance, and prepares itself; it remains in the hole altogether intent on the snake's head, that as soon as the snake enters,—for it enters the hole without any suspicion,—it may lay hold of its head, and go out with it; and then it growls and kills it: it plays with the snake because it has killed it. At last it jumps backwards and forwards over the snake, and eats it.

Again, the weasel is an animal which occasions very bad luck; for if trappers trap wild animals, and a weasel is caught, that man has no confidence that he shall catch any animals: he knows that the weasel stands in the way; evil

---

[5] *Landula,* "stands in the way," that is, not by actual presence, but by a kind of magical influence. The meaning of *Umuva* is, "that which follows in order after, or as the result of something." Its force may be understood by comparing it with antecedents. As we say, "his antecedents are bad;" so here, if we may coin a word, "the succedents of the weasel are bad;" that is, that which follows in order after, or happens as a result of its entering the trap, is bad luck. Or it may be rendered the "leavings."

gene nalo end*h*leleni, l' ek*q*a in-d*h*lela, a u tembi ukuba lapa u ya kona u ya 'ku ku fumana ukud*h*la; u ti, "Ngi *h*langene nomtakati, nokud*h*la a ngi sa yi 'ku ku tola."

Ukcaijana u lingana nekcakide; ku nga i lolu 'lu*h*lobo impela; ngokuba e bizwa ngegama lekca-kide, ku nga u 'lu*h*lobo lunye nekcakide; ubun*c*inane bake bu ngangobalo; nobuk*q*ili bake bu ngangobalo: u lingana nalo ngako konke.

Amanye amabizo okuti Bogco-nono, Ma*h*lab'-indoda-i-s'-emi, izi-bongo zake zokutshenisa ubuk*q*awe bake; u wezwa[7] ngazo. Lapa ku tiwa Bogconono, ku tiwa uma si kumusha, "owabogconono," isiswe sakubo esi pambili. Ogconono elinye ilizwi eli nga *h*langani kakulu nelokuti Uma*h*lab'-indoda. Li lodwa lona, ngokuba li ti "amakcakide." Uma si kumusha Uma*h*lab'-indoda-i-s'-emi, li ti, u i *h*laba kuk*q*ala, i sa delele, i bona emn*c*inane, i ti, innganyana nje; a i bulale, i nga ka m enzi 'luto.

follows it. Or if you have fallen in with it in a path, it crossing the path,[6] you no longer expect to get food at the place where you are going; you say, "I have fallen in with a wizard, and I shall no longer get any food."

Ukcaijana is like the weasel; it is as though he was really of that genus, for since he is called by the name of the weasel, it is as though he was of the same genus as it; his smallness is like its, and his cunning as great as its: he resem-bles it in all respects.

The other names, Bogconono, Mathlab'-indoda-i-s'-emi, are his praise-giving names, which set forth his bravery: he is lauded by them. When we say Bogconono, it means, when interpreted, "one of the weasel family," the nation from which he sprung. Ogconono is a word which has a different mean-ing from Umathlab'-indoda; it has its distinct meaning, for it means "weasels." If we interpret Uma-thlab'-indoda-i-s'-emi, it means that he stabs a man first, whilst he still despises him, seeing that he is so small, and regarding him as a mere infant; he kills the man before he has done anything to him.

---

[6] So in other countries it is considered a bad sign if a *hare* cross the way. (*Thorpe, Op. cit. Vol. II., p.* 274.)

[7] *Ukuweza*, "to help to cross a river," or *ukuweza ngamazibuko*, "to help to cross over by the fords," is used of celebrating the praises of braves, by recounting one after another their praise-giving names, which they have gained by great actions. *Amazibuko* is used metaphorically for the difficult things they have accomplished. Thus, if a man has interfered between two fighting bulls, or between two contending parties, and so has obtained the praise-giving name, *Umulamula-'nkunzi-zi-lwako*, "He-separates-fighting-bulls," they pass him over the river by this name.

UHLAKANYANA.

—◆—

Uthlakanyana speaks before he is born.

Kwa ti umfazi w' emita. Kwa ti ngensuku wa kuluma umntwana esiswini, wa ti, "Ngi zale masinya; inkomo zikababa za pela abantu." Wa t' unina, "Ake ni ze 'kuzwa; nanku um*h*lola; umntwana u ya kuluma kumi esiswini lapa." Ba ti, "U ti ni na?" "U t' 'A ngi m zale masinya;' u ti, 'Inkomo zi ya pela esibayeni.'"

A certain woman happened to be pregnant. When her time was fully come, the child spoke in the womb, and said, "Mother, give birth to me at once; the cattle of my father are devoured by the people." The mother said, "Just come and listen. Here is a prodigy. The child is speaking within me." They asked, "What does he say?" "He tells me to give birth to him at once; he says the cattle in the kraal are coming to an end."[8]

The father calls the people together.

Kwa ku *h*latshiwe inkabi uyise. Ba fika abantu, ba butana, ba puma namadoda esibayeni, ba ti, "Woza ni 'kuzwa; nank' um*h*lola, umntwana e kuluma." Wa tsho uyise, wa ti, "Ka kulume ke umntwana njengokutsho kwako." Wa kuluma umntwana, wa ti, "Yebo; ngi ti, ka ngi zale umame, ngokuba inkomo zi ya pela esibayeni; nami ngi ti, a ngi ye 'kuzi-*h*linzela inyama." Ba ti manga abantu, ba ti, "Ku za 'kwenziwa njani na?"

The father had slaughtered some oxen. The people came together, and left the cattle-kraal with the men, crying, "Come and hear. Here is a prodigy, an unborn child speaking!" The father said, "Let the child speak according to your saying." The child spoke, and said, "Yes, indeed, I say, let my mother give birth to me; for the cattle in the kraal are coming to an end. And, I say, let me go and get ready flesh for myself." The people wondered, and said, "What is going to happen?"

---

[8] How utterly absurd and far-fetched! exclaims the English reader. Yet a no less wonderful thing happened, according to Mabillon, towards the end of the fifth century. He informs us that "St. Benedict sang eucharistic hymns in his mother's womb." (*Stephen's Ecclesiastical Biography.*) To whom shall we award the palm of originality—to Pope Gregory the First, Mabillon's authority, or to the inventor of the Tale of Uthlakanyana? The Pope intended his "pious fraud" to be believed; the author of Uthlakanyana intended his fiction to produce laughter. The authors of fiction are allowed some license; but those who invent "pious frauds" should be careful to state, as facts, such things only as are within the bounds of possibility.

All the people are put out of the hut, and Uthlakanyana is born.

Wa ti uyise, "A ku punywe endhlini: a u zalc, si m boue ukuba umuntu ini na ? Ku 'mhlola lo." Ba puma ke bonke. Wa ti uyise, "A ku nga hlali 'muntu. Bonke abantu ba pume, ngokuba u kqale ukukuluma e yedwa unina." Ba puma ke. Wa puma umntwana esiswini. Wa ti e sa puma, w' ema. Wa ti unina, "Woza lapa, ngi ku nqume oku lengako." Wa ti umntwana, "Kqabo. Musa uku ngi nquma, ngi za 'kuzinquma; nami ngi ndala; ngi indoda yebandhla." Wa tata umkonto woyise, wa zinquma, wa lahla pantsi. Wa tabata unina amanzi, wa m geza.

The father said, "Let all go out of the house. Do you give birth to him, that we may see if it is a man or not. It is a prodigy, this." All went out. The father said, "Let no man remain. But all go out, because he began to speak when his mother was alone." So they went out: and the child was born. As soon as he was born, he stood up. His mother said, "Come here, and let me cut off that which is hanging from you." The child said,[9] "No, indeed. Don't you cut me; I am going to cut myself. I too am old. I am a man of the council." He took his father's spear,[10] and cut himself, and threw it down. His mother took water, and washed him.

Uthlakanyana goes out, and the people run away.

Wa puma ke nomkonto; wa m amuka pandhle unina; wa u shiya, wa ngena esibayeni; ibandhla la baleka; wa hlala eziko, wa dhla imbengo e b' i dhliwa libandhla.

He went out with the spear; his mother took it from him outside: he left it, and went into the cattle-kraal. The men ran away. He sat down by the fire, and ate a strip of meat, which the men had

9 In 1623 a report was extensively circulated in Europe, that information had been received from their spies by the "brothers of the Order of St. John of Jerusalem, in the isle of Malta," of the birth of a child "on the 1st of May, 1623," near Babylon, which "said child, incontinent on his birth, walked and talked perfectly well." The child was supposed to be Antichrist. (*Englishman's Magazine. Vol. II., p. 116.*)

10 The word *Umkonto*, usually translated assagai, is applied to any weapon which is used in fighting, slaughtering, or hunting. (A gun or a knife is so called.) There are various kinds; all two-edged and sharp-pointed. The *isinkemba* or *isijula* consists of a broad and long blade, with a short strong shank, which is set entirely into a strong stick. They use this as an axe, when necessary, or to dig up roots. It is a deadly weapon, and would make a wound between two and three inches long. *Inqcawe:* A short blade, about as long as the finger, and slender; the shank is very long, and is often twisted, or otherwise ornamented; its stick is slender and short. It is used for hunting, either by throwing or stabbing, and in slaughtering. The *inhlenhla* or *izakha* is barbed, with shortish shank, and is used in hunting. The *ikebezana* has a short light blade; it is used for carving, skinning, and eating. *Ikhhwa:* Has a long blade, about as wide as two fingers, short shank and stick; it is used as the *inqcawe.* These are the chief genera of *imikonto;* there are many other names, which are used to specify more slight peculiarities.

La buya, la ti, "Indoda kanti; umuntu omdala: si be si ti umntwana." A buza amadoda, a ti, "U yena umntwana na o be kuluma kuwe na esiswini sako?" Wa ti unina, "U ye."

been eating. The men came back, and said, "So then it is a man! an old man! We thought it was a child." The men enquired, and said, "Is this the very child which was speaking within you?" The mother said, "It is he."

The men praise his wisdom, and propose that he shall be the great child.

Ba ti, "O, si ya bonga, nkosikazi: u si zalele umntwana ohlakanipile e sa zalwa. A si bonanga si bona umntwana e njengalo 'mntwana; lo umntwana u fanele ukuba a be umntwana omkulu kubo bonke abantwana benkosi, ngokuba u si mangalisile ngokuhlakanipa kwake."

They said, "O, we thank you, our queen. You have brought forth for us a child who is wise as soon as he is born. We never saw a child like this child. This child is fit to be the great child among all the king's children, for he has made us wonder by his wisdom."[11]

Uthlakanyana proposes a test of manhood.

"Yebo!" wa ti umntwana. "Baba, lo ni ti ngi umntwana (ngi ya bona ukuba ni ti ngi umntwana, nina), tata umlenze wenkomo, u u ponse lapa ngenzantsi kwesibaya, si bone ke ukuba u ya ku tatwa ngubani na? B' esuke bonke abantu bako, nabafana namadoda, si ye 'ku u tata umlenze, si ze si bone ke, o indoda; u ya 'kuba ngu ye o indoda, o ya 'kutata umlenze." Wa u tata ke uyise, wa u ponsa ngenzantsi kwesibaya. Ba ya 'kukcinana ngasesangweni bonke, eli ngasenhla; yena wa puma ngase-

"Yes, indeed," said the child. "Father, since you say I am a child (I perceive that you, for your part, think I am a child), take a leg of beef, and throw it below the kraal, that we may see who will get it first. Let all your people, both boys and men, and me, go to fetch the leg, so at length we shall see who is the man. He shall be the man who gets the leg." So the father took the leg, and threw it below the kraal. They all crowded together at the opening, at the upper part of the kraal;[12] but he

[11] In the Basuto Legend, Litaolane grows to the stature and wisdom of manhood as soon as he is born. But Uthlakanyana is a destroyer, Litaolane a deliverer. On the day of his birth he kills the monster Kammapa, the devourer of the world. Some things are said of him that are said of Uthlakanyana; but Litaolane's skill is used only in self-defence. (*Casalis' Basutos, p.* 347.) In the Arabic Legend, Abraham is nourished by food miraculously supplied from his own fingers, and in fifteen months attains the size and semblance of a youth of fifteen years. ("Arabic Legends." *Englishman's Magazine. Vol. II., p.* 246.)

[12] Among the natives of these parts, the opening of the cattle-kraal looks downwards. Among the Amakxosa, Amapondo, Amabakca, &c., it looks upwards.

nzantsi kwesibaya, e kcusha; wa *h*langana nabo e se buya nawo umlenze. Wa ti, "Mame, yamukela ke; nantsi inyama yami." Wa ti unina, "Ngi ya jabula nam*h*la, ngokuba ngi zelc indoda e *h*lakanipile."

went out at the lower, creeping through the enclosure; and met them when he was already returning with the leg.[13] He said, "Mother, just take it. Here is my meat." His mother said, "I am glad this day, because I have given birth to a wise man."

Uthlakanyana practises hypocrisy, and appropriates the property of other people.

Wa buya wa ya esibayeni: kwa piwa omunye umuntu, o indoda, uyise. Wa ti, "Leti kwimi, ngi ye 'ku ku bekela end*h*lini yako." Wa ti, "Yebo ke, mntwana wenkosi." Wa i tabata inyama, wa ngena end*h*lini; w' etula isitebe nepini, wa bukca igazi esitebeni nasepinini; wa puma nayo, wa ya kunina nayo inyama; wa ti, "Mame, yamukela; nantsi inyama yami." Wa bonga kubo bonke beband*h*la; wa buya wa bonga ke. Wa buya w' enza njalo na kwenye indoda, wa i tata njalo, wa ti,

He returned to the cattle-kraal. His father was giving another man some meat. He said, "Hand it to me, that I may put it for you in your house." The man replied, "Yes, certainly, child of the king." He took the meat, and went into the house; he took down the eating-mat and stick, and smeared blood on them, and went out with the meat, and took it to his mother, and said, "Mother, take it; here is my meat." He gave thanks to each of the men (as he took the meat from him); and gave thanks again on his return. Again, he did the same to another man; he

[13] How deep a descent from the grand and poetical to the petty and practical, when Uthlakanyana's exhibition of strength on a leg of beef is compared with that of Magni, a son of Thor and Jamsaxa, who, when only three days old, removed the giant Hrungnir's foot from the neck of Thor, which all the gods had been unable to do! (*Northern Mythology. Vol. I., p. 71.*) Or that of "Odin's son Vali, who though only one day old, unwashed and uncombed, slew Höd," to avenge the death of Baldur. (*Id., p. 77.*) Or that of Hercules, who when eight months old boldly seizes and squeezes to death the snakes sent to destroy him. Or with the Basuto Legend, where Litaolane kills the monster Kammapa on the day of his birth. But in Rabelais' political satires imagination is carried further than in either, both as regards coarseness and exaggeration. He represents the birth of "the gigantic despot" Gargantua as miraculous. He springs from his mother's left ear; and at once, instead of uttering the infant's ordinary cry, shonts with a loud voice, "A boire, à boire, à boire; comme invitant tout le monde à boire." (*Book I., ch.* 6.) And his son Pantagruel far exceeded his father; and the youthful feat of Hercules was as nothing compared with that of Pantagruel. At each meal he sucked in the milk of four thousand six hundred cows; and whilst yet in his cradle one day seized one of them by the hind leg, and eat into the bowels and devoured the liver and kidneys. The attendants summoned by the cow's cries, took it away, but not before he had got possession of the leg, which he eat up like a sausage, swallowing the bone as a cormorant would a little fish; and then cried, "Good, good, good!" And when bound with large cables to prevent a repetition of such voracity, he snapped the cables asunder with as much facility as Samson the withs with which he was bound. (*Book II., ch. 4.*)

"Leta kumi, ngi ye 'ku ku bekela endhlini yako." W' enza njalo njengokuba 'enze njalo nakweyokukqala; wa bukca isitebe nepini, wa shiya njalo, wa i sa kwabo; wa ti, "Mame, yamukela; nantsi inyama yami." Wa bonga unina, wa ti, "Ngi zele indoda namuhla." Kulo lonke ibandhla a ku banga ko namunye owa i funyana inyama yake. Ya pelela kwabo yena lowo umfana, o zelwe ngelanga lelo eli hlabile inkabi zoyise. La tshona ilanga; ba m buza bonke bomuzi, be nga i funyani. Wa ti, "Bheka ipini nesitebe, ukuba a ngi i bekanga na esitebeni, ng' etula ipini, nga i hloma pezulu, njengokuba inyama i ya hlonywa pezulu." Ba ti, "Yebo; si ya si bona isitebe sibomvu, nepini libomvu. Kepa y' etulwe ini na?" Wa ti ke, "Lo, nasi isitebe sibomvu nje." Bonke ke kwa njalo, kubo bonke ke kwa njalo; wa banga ngesitebe kubo bonke abantu bomuzi woyise.

took his meat in the same way; he said, "Hand it to me, that I may put it for you in your house." He did with that as he had done with the first; he smeared the feeding-mat and stick; he left them in the same way, and took the meat to his own house, and said, "Mother, take it; here is my meat." His mother thanked him, and said, "I have given birth to a man this day." In the whole company there was not one who found his meat. The whole of it was in the house of the boy, who was born on the day the oxen of his father were slaughtered. The sun set. All the people of the village enquired of him when they did not find the meat. He said, "Look at the stick and the feeding-mat, whether I did not place it on the mat, and take down the stick and hang it up, as meat is hung up?" They said, "Yes, we see the feeding-mat is bloody, and the stick is bloody. Then has the meat been taken down?" So he said, "(Yes), for there is the mat really bloody." All made the same enquiry; and he answered them all alike. He persisted in making the feeding-mat a witness to all the people of his father's village.

The women express great doubt as to Uthlakanyana being a real man.

Abafazi bomuzi ba kala, ba ti, "Namuhla ku zelwe ni na? Ku zelwe umuntu onjani na? A bonanga si ku bona loku. Nina ni be ni m tumela ni, lo ni ya bona nje, ukuba Uhlakanyana lo na? Ni ti umuntu na? Ni ti umuntu

The women of the kraal cried out saying, "What is this that has been born to-day? What sort of a man is this that has been born? We never saw the like. Why did you send him, since you clearly see that this is Uthlakanyana? Do you say he is a man?[14] Do you say

[14] It is a pity these women were not acquainted with Ellen Leah's specific for testing the fact of Uthlakanyana's being a real man or a "fairy substitute." Mrs. Sullivan had "a healthy, blue-eyed baby, which in one night shrivelled

wa ka wa nje na, 'azi ukukuluma kaugaka e se umntwana, a kǫine kangaka 'aḥlule amadoda a amadala? Ni be ni nga m boni ini na ekutateni kwake umlenze wenkabi? Ni nga ni kǫondile lapo, ukuti lo there ever was such a man, who knew how to speak thus whilst a child; and who was so strong that he could get the better of old men? Did you not see him when he took the leg of beef? You might then have understood that this man was

into almost nothing, and never ceased squalling and crying." Of course Mrs. Sullivan believed, and her neighbours helped her in the belief, that fairies had taken a fancy to her baby, and had placed one of themselves in its stead; and it was nothing but the strong resemblance which still lurked under the shrunken features, that saved the changeling from being griddled alive, or having some other equally merciful experiment tried upon it, which was sure to settle the child's identity by proving the possibility or impossibility of destroying it! But Ellen Leah was a more sensible and cautious woman; she recommended Mrs. Sullivan to make a "brewery of egg-shells," and she would see what she would see; and then if the "squalling, crying" thing turned out to be a fairy, and not till then, the red-hot poker was to be crammed down its throat. Mrs. Sullivan determined to try Ellen Leah's specific, and the following is the result, no doubt in the authentic words of Mrs. Sullivan herself, duly attested:—

"Home went Mrs. Sullivan, and did as Ellen Leah desired. She put the pot on the fire, and plenty of turf under it, and set the water boiling at such a rate, that if ever water was red-hot—it surely was.

"The child was lying for a wonder quite easy and quiet in the cradle, every now and then cocking his eye, that would twinkle as keen as a star in a frosty night, over at the great fire, and the big pot upon it; and he looked on with great attention at Mrs. Sullivan breaking the eggs, and putting down the egg-shells to boil. At last he asked, with the voice of a very old man, 'What are you doing, mammy?'

"Mrs. Sullivan's heart, as she said herself, was up in her mouth ready to choke her, at hearing the child speak. But she contrived to put the poker in the fire, and to answer, without making any wonder at the words, 'I'm brewing, a vick' (my son).

"'And what are you brewing, mammy?' said the little imp, whose supernatural gift of speech now proved beyond question that he was a fairy substitute.

"'I wish the poker was red,' thought Mrs. Sullivan; but it was a large one, and took a long time heating: so she determined to keep him in talk until the poker was in a proper state to thrust down his throat, and therefore repeated the question.

"'Is it what I'm brewing, a vick,' said she, 'you want to know?'

"'Yes, mammy: what are you brewing?' returned the fairy.

"'Egg-shells, a vick,' said Mrs. Sullivan.

"'Oh!' shrieked the imp, starting up in the cradle, and clapping his hands together, 'I'm fifteen hundred years in the world, and I never saw a brewery of egg-shells before!' The poker was by this time quite red, and Mrs. Sullivan seizing it ran furiously towards the cradle; but somehow or other her foot slipped, and she fell flat on the floor, and the poker flew out of her hand to the other end of the house. However, she got up, without much loss of time, and went to the cradle, intending to pitch the wicked thing that was in it into the pot of boiling water, when there she saw her own child in a sweet sleep, one of his soft round arms rested on the pillow—his features were as placid as if their repose had never been disturbed, save the rosy mouth which moved with a gentle and regular breathing." (*Croker's Fairy Legends and Traditions of the South of Ireland.*)

For the various methods for detecting an imp which has taken the place of a child, see *Thorpe, Op. cit. Vol. II., pp. 174—177.*

'muntu ka mitwanga; u ngene nje lapa kuy' inkosikazi; u ngene, ka mitwanga; nenkosi le ka si ye wayo. Si y' ala manje tina sonke, tina 'bafazi; nani nina 'madoda ni za 'ku m bona ngenye imini; u za 'kwenza izinto ezinkulu, ngokuba e kulumile esiswini. Nantsi inyama yenu e n' amukile ngomlomo, ni 'badala nonke; wa za wa ko*h*lisa noyise ngomlenze wenkabi yake. U za 'kwenza imi*h*lola, ngokuba naye e ng' um*h*lola, isibili som*h*lola."

Ya pela ke inyama leyo.

not produced in a natural way. He got into the queen; he got in;[15] he was not produced in a natural way; and as for the king, he is not his son. All we women deny it now; and you men will see it some other day. He will do great things, for he spoke before he was born. There, he has taken away your meat from you by his mouth, and you all old men too; and he circumvented even his father about his leg of beef. He will do prodigies; for he, too, is a prodigy, a real prodigy."

Thus, all that meat was finished.

Uthlakanyana goes a hunting, and takes birds out of other people's traps.

Wa hamba, wa ya 'uzingela ngasemfuleni; wa funyana izitiyo, ziningi kakulu, zi babisile izinyoni, izind*h*lazi, zonke izitiyo; zi ngambili na ngantatu. Wa zi koka ke zonke, wa zi bopa umfunzi, wa goduka nazo. Wa fika ekaya, wa ngena kunina, wa ti, "Mame, ng' etule, ngi ya sindwa." Wa ti, "U twele ni na?" Wa ti, "Ngi twele izinyoni zami, e ngi be ngi ye 'ku zi zingela." Wa bonga unina, wa ti, "Umfana wami u indoda, u *h*lakanipile. Wena u ya

Uthlakanyana went to hunt by the river. He found very many traps: all the traps had caught birds, izindhlazi, by twos and by threes. So he took them all out, and made them into a bundle, and went home with them. On his arrival he went in to his mother, and said, "Mother, take off my load; I am weighed down." She said, "What are you carrying?" He said, "I am carrying my birds, which I went to catch." His mother returned thanks, saying, "My boy is a man. He is wise. You

[15] Luther believed in some such thing as this, which he speaks of not as a possibility merely, but as fact, which had come under his own observation. He says that, under certain circumstances, the offspring of women is "oftentimes an imp of darkness, half mortal, half devil;" and adds, "such cases are peculiarly horrible and appalling." *(Michelet's Life of Luther. Bogue. p. 325.)* Such belief was not peculiar to Luther. He held it in common with his countrymen and the rest of Europe. In the Danish Traditions there is the legend of a demon who, under the form of "Brother Ruus," succeeded in corrupting, and almost in handing over to absolute perdition, the good brethren of Esrom; but having been detected, was "conjured into the form of a horse" by the abbot, and on promising to do no more harm, and swearing eternal obedience to him, was allowed to go free. The demon then passes over to England, and "*enters the king's fair daughter.*" When no wise man could be found sufficiently wise to expel the intruder, at length the demon himself exclaims, "I am Brother Ruus. No one can expel me from this fair vessel, save the abbot of Esrom, to whom I have sworn obedience." *(Thorpe's Northern Mythology. Vol. II., pp. 269.)*

d*h*lula amadoda onke noyi*h*lo, na-
bangane bako." Wa tu*k*ulula ke.
Wa ti, " Zi peke zonke ; u zi nameke." Wa zi peka ke unina. Wa
ti umfana, "Nam*h*la ngi za 'kupuma lapa end*h*lini, ngi ye 'kulala
kwabanye ; u ze u nga zibukuli
inyoni zami lezi ; ku ya 'kufika
mina kusasa, kona zi ya 'kuba
mnandi kusasa."

surpass all the men, and your
father, and your friends." So she
untied the birds. He said, "Cook
them all; lute them down with
cowdung." So his mother cooked
them. The boy said, "I am going
out of this house to-day, and shall
sleep with the other boys. Do
not take the cover off these my
birds. I shall come in the morning; they will be nice then."

The boys object to have Uthlakanyana as a bedfellow.

Wa puma ke, wa ya 'kulala
kwabanye. Ba ti, " U ya pi na
lapa na? A si tandi ukulala nawe." Wa ti, "Ini na ukuba ngi
nga lali kwini, loko nami ngi
umfana nje na? ngi intombazana
ini na?" Ba ti, "K*q*a! u *h*lakanipile kakulu. Wa ko*h*lisa obaba
ngenyama yabo, be i piwe inkosi.
Wa ti, u ya 'ku ba bekela ezind*h*lini
zabo; a i bonwanga namunye kuwo wonke umuzi lo wenkosi. Nati
si ya bona ukuba ku si ye owenkosi." Wa ti, "Ngi ng' okabani
na?" Ba ti, "A si kw azi; a ka
ko owenkosi o njengawe nje. Wena u ng' um*h*lola impela. I kona
into o ya 'uze u y enze ; a ku 'kupela nje. U um*h*lola impela."
Wa ti, "Loku ni tsho, ngi za
'kulala ngenkani." Ba ti, "Ngenkani yani, u umfana nje na? U
ti namand*h*la u nawo okulwa? u
namand*h*la kodwa omlomo nama-
zwi ako; u nga s' a*h*lula ngomlomo ; amand*h*la wona ku nawo,
ngokuba u s' and' ukuzalwa;
manje si ya kw azi ukuba u
umntwana impela. Amazwi ubu-
*h*lakani bako; bu ya s' a*h*lula

He went out to go to sleep with
the other boys. They said, "Where
are you going here? We do not
like to sleep with you." He said,
"Why may not I sleep with you,
since I too am a boy indeed? Am
I a little girl?" They said, "No.
You are very wise. You deceived
our fathers about their meat, which
the king gave them. You said
you would put it in their houses
for them. There was not even one
in the whole village of the king
who saw anything more of his
meat. And we see you are not
the king's son." He said, "Whose
son am I?" They said, "We
don't know. There is no child of
the king like you. You are a
prodigy, that's a fact. You will
be up to some mischief. It is not
ended yet. You are a prodigy,
that's a fact." He said, "Since
you say this, I shall sleep here for
contention's sake." They said,
"What contention do you mean,
you being a mere boy? Do you
say you have strength to fight?
you have nothing but mouth- and
word-strength; you may overcome
us with the mouth; strength itself. you have none, for you are
just born. Now we know that
you are a child indeed. Words
are your wisdom; that surpasses

bona kanye na obaba betu." Ba
tula ke. Wa tula ke naye. Wa
lala.

us, as well as our fathers." So
they were silent, and he too was
silent. He went to sleep.

Uthlakanyana eats the birds, and deceives his mother.

Ya kala inkuku. Wa vuka, wa
ti, "Se ku sile." Wa ti, "Ngi se
ngi hamba mina, ngokuba inyoni
zami amakwababa nabantu ba nga
zi koka." Wa puma, wa fika kwabo. Ka vulanga, wa pakamisa isi-
valo sendhlu yakwabo, wa ngena
ke, unina e sa lele. Wa zibukula
embizeni, wa dhla ke inyoni zake ;
ka zi dhlanga inhloko zazo izinyoni
zonke ; wa zi dhla izidumbu zazo,
wa zi kqeda zonke. Wa puma,
wa ola umkquba, wa ngena, wa u
tela ngapantsi embizeni, wa beka
izinhloko ngapezulu ; wa nameka.
Konke loku u sa lele unina. Wa
puma ngapantsi kwesivalo. W' e-
muka ingcozana, wa buya futi,
wa ti, " Mame, mame, ngi vulele,"
njengokuba e sa fika nje. Wa
ngena, wa ka 'manzi, wa geza ; wa
ti, " Ngi pe ke izinyoni." Wa be
te e ngena, wa ti, " Ni lala futi !
ku nga ze inyoni zi gukquke umkquba zonke, ngokuba ilanga li se
li pumile ; ngi y' azi zi ba njalo
inyoni, inxa ilanga li se li pumile,
njengokuba li se li pumile nje ; si
nge zi funyane ; si nga funyana
ngapantsi." Wa e se zubukula
ke ; wa ti, " Ku se ku njalo ; ku
umkquba wodwa ; ku se ku sele
inhloko zodwa." Wa ti unina,
" Kw enziwe ini na ?" Wa ti,
" U y' azi ini na ?" wa ti, " I
mina ow aziko. Wena u um-
ntwana omncinane nje. Wa ngi
zala ini ? Angiti kwa tsho mina,
nga ti, ' Ngi zale masinya ; iukomo zikababa zi ya pela esiba-

The cock crew. He awoke and
said, "It is now day. I am now
going, for my part ; for the crows
and men may take my birds out
of the traps." He left, and went
to his own house. He did not
open the door ; he raised it, and
so went in, his mother still sleeping.
He uncovered the pot, and eat his
birds ; he did not eat the heads
of them all ; he eat their bodies,
every one of them. He went out
and scraped up some cowdung, and
returned and put it in the bottom
of the pot, and placed the heads
on the top of it ; and luted it
down. He did all this, his mother
being still asleep. He went out
under the door. He departed a
little way, and came back again,
and said, "Mother, mother, open
the door for me," as though he had
only just come. He went in, and
took water, and washed. He then
said, "Just give me my birds."
He had said on his first going in,
"You sleep for ever ! The birds
may have all turned into dung, for
the sun is already up. I know
that birds do so turn when the sun
has risen, as it has risen now. We
may not find them, but something
instead of them at the bottom."
He uncovered the pot, and said,
"It is even so now ; there is nothing but dung ; the heads alone
are left." His mother said, " How
has it been done ?" He said, "Do
you know how ?" And then, " It
is I who know. You are but a
little child. Did you give birth to
me ? Did not I myself say, 'Give
birth to me at once ; the cattle of

yeni? Wa ka wa mu zwa umntwana e tsho njalo, e ti, ka zalwe na, e ng' umntwana e kohliwe 'zindaba na? Ngi mdala kakulu. A ngi si ye wako: nobaba lo o naye ka si ye ubaba, umuntu nje, umuntu wetu nje; ngokuba mina ngi lalile nje kuwe, wena u ng' umfazi wake. A si z' ukuhlala ndawo nye nani; ngi za 'kuzihambela nje ngedwa, ngi hamba nje, ngi ni shiye, ni zihlalele kona lapa ndawo nye. Mina ngi za 'uhamba umhlaba wonke nje." Z' opulwa. Wa ti unina, "Wo! Mntanami, u tshilo! wa ti, 'zi nga ze zi gukquke umkquba ngapantsi kwembiza?' Nembala se ku umkquba wodwa ngapantsi; ku se ku izinhloko zodwa ngapezulu." Wa ti umfana, "Ake ngi zi bone." Wa bona, wa zi dhla inhloko yena futi, wa zi kqeda: wa ti, "Loku inyoni zami u zi dhlile, a ngi se zi uku ku nika nenhloko lezi zazo, ngokuba wena u dhle inyama yazo." Wa zi kqeda inhloko ke.

my father are coming to an end in the kraal?' Did you ever hear a child say thus, 'Let me be born,' he being a child who could be worsted by anything? I am very old. I am not your child.[16] And that father whom you are with, he is not my father; he is a mere man, one of our people, and nothing more. As for me, I merely lay down in you, you being his wife. We will not live together. I shall set out on my own account by myself, just travelling about, and leave you, that you may live together here alone. For my part, I am going to travel over the whole world."[17] The contents of the pot were taken out. His mother said, "Alas, my child, you have spoken truly; you said that 'the birds might turn into dung at the bottom of the pot!' Truly there is now nothing but dung at the bottom, and the heads alone at the top." The boy said, "Just let me see them?" He looked, and eat up the heads also himself, every one of them: and said, "As you have eaten my birds, I will not now give you even these heads of them; for it is you who have eaten their flesh." So he finished the heads.

[16] "I am very old," says Uthlakanyana. "I am not your child." So in *Campbell's Highland Tales* there is an account of a "child not yet a year old, which had not spoken or attempted to speak, which suddenly addressed his mother," as they were passing near Glen Odhar, thus:

" 'Many a dun hummel cow,
With a calf below her,
Have I been milking
In that dun glen yonder,
Without dog, without man,
Without woman, without gillie,
But one man,
And he hoary.'

The good woman threw down her child, and ran home." Uthlakanyana's mother was much more cool on the exhibition of her child's marvellous power. (*Vol. I., p.* cvii.—See also *Grimm's Home Stories.* "The Fairy Folk. 'Third Tale.'")

[17] Uthlakanyana feigns a reason for quitting the home into which he has intruded himself, and where he is acceptable to no one but to her who considers herself his mother. Other demons are not so accommodating. It is necessary

Uhlakanyana goes to the traps, and gets trapped himself.

Wa tata intonga yake, wa puma, e teta, e ti, "Inyoni zami, hai, ukuba zi dⱨliwe, ngi ⱨleli ngi ti, ngi za 'kudⱨla inyoni zami, e be zi pekiwe. Kanti ku za 'kulalwa futi, zi ze zi gukꝗuke umkꝗuba zonke." Wa tula. Wa hamba nje. Wa fika ke ezitiyweni zezimu; wa koka ke inyoni. U te e sa koka, la fika izimu. Wa ti, "Musa uku ngi bulala," e bajisiwe umfana. Izimu li bonile ukuba inyoni zi ya kokwa umuntu. Loku inomfi la i beka ngezinti pambi kwezitiyo, wa banjwa ke i yo inomfi. Wa ti, "Musa uku ngi tshaya; ngi za 'ku ku tshela. Ngi koke, u ngi ⱨlanze inomfi; u buye nami. Ku nanyoko na?" La ti izimu, "U kona." Wa ti umfana, "Kepa u ng' onela ni na, u nga ngi koki, u ngi ⱨlanze inomfi, u buye nami? Ngi ya 'kubaba; a ngi yi 'kuba mnandi; inxʼ u ugi tshaya nje, a ngi yi 'kuba mnandi; ngi ya 'kubaba. Ngi ⱨlanze, u buye nami; u zʼ u

He took his walking-stick and went out, chiding thus, "It was not right that my birds should be eaten whilst I was imagining that I was going to eat my birds, which had been cooked: yet, forsooth, she was going to sleep for ever, until all the birds became dung." He was silent. He went on his journey, and came to the traps of a cannibal; so he took out the birds. As he was taking them out, the cannibal arrived. The boy, being caught, said, "Don't kill me." The cannibal had seen that the birds were taken out by someone. Therefore he put birdlime on sticks in front of the traps, and he was caught by the birdlime. He said, "Don't beat me, and I will tell you. Take me out, and cleanse me from the birdlime, and take me home with you. Have you not a mother?" The cannibal replied, "I have a mother." The boy said, "Why then do you spoil me, and not take me out, and cleanse me from the birdlime, and take me home with you? I shall be bitter; I shall not be nice; if you beat me in this way, I shall not be nice; I shall be bitter. Cleanse me, and take me home

to devise various plans for the purpose of getting rid of them. In the Danish Traditions we find an account of one whom "a shrewd female engaged to drive from the house," which she did as follows:—"One day, when he was out in the field, she killed a pig, and made a pudding of it, together with the skin and hair, which, on his return, she placed before him. As was his custom, he began slashing away at it, but as he ate he gradually became thoughtful, and at length sat quite still with the knife in his hand, and eyeing the pudding: he then exclaimed, 'Pudding with hide, and pudding with hair, pudding with eyes, and pudding with bones in it. I have now thrice seen a young wood spring up on Tiis lake, but never before did I see such a pudding! The fiend will stay here no longer!' Saying these words, he ran off, and never returned." (*Thorpe, Op. cit. Vol. II., p. 174.*) Luther suggested a more summary process; he recommended such a child, which is said to have "had no human parents," to be thrown into the Moldau; regarding it as a creation of the devil—"a mere mass of flesh and blood, without any soul." (*Michelet, Op. cit., p. 325. See also p. 326.*)

ngi beke kwenu, ngi ze ngi pekwe unyoko; u ngi beke ng' ome ubumanzi; u hambe wena, u ngi shiye nje ekaya; ngi nga pekwa u kona; ngi nga mubi; ngi nge be mnandi."

with you, that you may put me in your house, that I may be cooked by your mother. Set me there, that I may dry; and do you go away, and just leave me at your home. I cannot be cooked if you are there; I shall be bad; I cannot be nice."

Uthlakanyana is taken home by the cannibal, and delivered to the cannibal's mother.

La m tata ke, la buya naye kanye nazo izinyoni zalo. La fika ekaya kunina, la ti, "Mame, nantsi inyamazana e b' i dhla inyoni zami. Namhla ngi i funyene, ngi i bambile ngenomfi yami; i te, a ngi i koke, ngi i hlanze ubumanzi benomfi. Ya ti, a ngi nga i tshayi; ya ti, i ya 'kubaba, inxa ngi i tshayile. Nga vuma ke, nga i hlanza ke, nga i twala ke. Ya ti, a ngi namame na? Nga ti "U kona" kuyo inyamazana le. Ya ti, i ya 'upekwa u we, ngi nge ko mina. Ya ti, i nge be mnandi, inxa i pekiwe ngi kona. Ngi ya vuma ke. U z' u i peke kusasa. A i lale nje. Li nomfana wakwabo ba vumelana, ba ti, "A i lale."

So the cannibal took him, and went home with him; he took also his birds. On coming home to his mother, he said, "Mother, here is the animal which was eating my birds. I have found him to-day; I caught him with my birdlime. He told me to take him out, and cleanse him from the birdlime. He told me not to beat him. He said he should be bitter if I beat him. So I assented; I cleansed him, and brought him home. He asked if I had not a mother? I told him—I mean this animal here —that I had. He said he would be cooked by you, when I was absent. He said he should not be nice, if cooked in my presence. So I assent. Do you cook him in the morning. Just let him lie down to-night." The cannibal and a boy, his brother, both assented, saying, "Just let him lie down to-night."

Uthlakanyana avoids being boiled by boiling the cannibal's mother.

Kwa sa kusasa, la ti, "Mame, nantso ke inyamazana yami." Wa ti Uhlakanyana, "Ngi tabate, u ngi beke pezu kwendhlu, ng' ome, ngi hlatshwe ilanga;" e ti u kona e ya 'kubonisa izimu ngalapo li tshona ngakona. Wa bekwa ke pezulu endhlini. La hamba ke nomfana wakwabo; ba tshona

In the morning, the cannibal said, "Mother, take care of my game." Uthlakanyana said, "Take me, and put me on the top of the hut, that I may dry in the sun's rays"; thinking he should then be able to see in which direction the cannibal would disappear. So he was placed on the top of the hut. The cannibal and his brother

ngokalo. W' e*h*la U*h*lakanyana, wa ti, "Mame, u sa lele na?" Wa ti unina wezimu, "Yebo." Wa ti U*h*lakanyana, "Vuka, si pekane." Wa ti, "Nami u za 'u ngi peka ingcozana; ku za 'kupekwa ngenkulu imbiza, ngokuba ngi za 'kukukumala, ngi i gcwale imbiza. Nantsi imbiza enkulu, e nga peka mina." Wa ti unina wezimu, "Yebo ke, u k*q*inisile wena; ngokuba u ya zazi nokupekwa kwako." Wa ti, "Tata ke, u i beke eziko." Wa basa U*h*lakanyana, wa basa ingcozana; wa ti, "Muningi umlilo." Wa ti, "Ake si zwe amanzi ukuba a se tshisa ini?" Wa fak' isand*h*la; wa ti, "K*q*a. Ku fanele u ngi fake; a ku k*q*alwe ngami." Wa ti "Yebo ke" unina wezimu. Wa m tata, wa m faka, wa zibekela; wa tula pakati embizeni. Wa ti, "Ng' opule ke." Wa m opula. Wa ti, "Yiya! Ake ku nge ku ya baswa. Wa basa U*h*lakanyana; wa ti, "Ngi w' ezwile amanzi ukuba a ka fudumali. Ake ku baswe." Wa basa kakulu; wa lunguza, wa funyana e se bila. Wa ti, "Tukulula ke ingubo zako, ngokuba kaloku amanzi a se fanele ukuba u ngene, ngokuba nami ngi ngene e nje. Kodwa wena; a se fudumele ka*h*le manje." U*h*la-

departed, and disappeared over the ridge of the hill. Uthlakanyana got down, and said, "Mother, are you still lying down?" The cannibal's mother said, "Yes." Uthlakanyana said, "Get up, and let us play at boiling each other. You will boil me a little, and I you. Let the boiling be done in the great pot; for I shall swell out very much, and fill the pot. There is the great pot which is fit for boiling me in." The cannibal's mother said, "Yes, surely; you say the truth; for you know yourself, and about your being boiled." He said, "Take it, then, and put it on the fire." Uthlakanyana kindled the fire; he kindled it a little, and said, "The fire is abundant." He said, "Let us just feel the water, if it is already hot." He put in his hand, and said, "Just the thing! You must put me in. Let us begin with me." "Yes, surely," said the cannibal's mother. She took him, and put him in, and put the lid on. He was silent in the pot. At length he said, "Just take me out." She took him out. He said, "Out upon it! Let us just kindle the fire a little."[18] Uthlakanyana made up the fire, and said, "I have felt the water that it is not warm; let us make up the fire." He made a great fire, and looked in, and found it boiling. He said to the cannibal's mother, "Take off your clothes, for the water is now fit for you to go in; for I too went in when it was just so: now for you; it is now pleasantly warm." Uthlaka-

---

[18] *Ake ku nge ku ya baswa.*—The conjunctive mood of *ukunga* after *ake*, followed by the present tense of the indicative mood, as here, is used to express a wish that something may be done slightly, or for a little time. The following are examples:—*Ake u nge u ya vula,* "Do you open the door a little;" *Ake ngi nge ngi ya lima,* "Just let me dig a little;" *Ake a nge u ya li bamba,* "Just let him hold the horse for a little while."

kanyana wa kqala uku m tukulula. Wa ti, "Ngi yeke, ngi zitukulule mina; musa uku ngi kqinela. U ngi kqiuelela ni?" Wa ti U*hla*kanyana, "Ku nani na, in*x*a ngi ku tukululile, ngi inyamazana nje e za 'kud*h*liwa amadodana ako nawe? Ku nani na, ngi inyamazana nje, e za 'ud*h*liwa amadodana ako kanye nawe na?" Wa m faka, wa zibekela. Wa kala, wa ti, "Hlakanyana, ng' opule. Nga tsha!" Wa ti, "Kqabo! Ku ka tshi wena; ukuba u se u tshile, u nga u nga tsho ukuba so u tshile. Ngi y' ezwa, ngi indoda; in*x*a umuntu e ti, 'Ngi ya tsha,' ka ka tshi; in*x*a e se e tshile, ka tsho u ya tsha njalo, a tshe ku be ukupela." Wa ti, "Hlakanyana, ngi ya vutwa." Wa ti "Kqa" U*hla*kanyana; wa ti, "Ku ka vutwa. Nank' u sa tsho ukuti, u ya vutwa. Ngi y' azi in*x*a umuntu e se vutiwe, ka tsho ukuti, ngi se ngi vutiwe; u ya tula nje ukuba u se vutiwe." Wa vutwa ke, wa tula. Wa ti U*hla*kanyana, wa ti, "Manje ke ngi ya kolwa ukuba u vutiwe, ngokuba ku sa tsho manje; manje se u tule; u kona ngi ti u vutiwe ke; u za 'ud*h*liwa ke amadodana ako. Vutwa ke. U kona

nyana began to unfasten her clothes. She said, "Leave me alone, that I may undress myself; don't urge me. Why do you urge me?" Uthlakanyana said, "Of what consequence is it if I have undone your things, I who am mere game, which is about to be eaten by your sons and you? Of what consequence is it, I being mere game, which is about to be eaten by your sons and you?" He put her in, and put on the lid. She cried out, "Uthlakanyana! take me out! I am scalded to death!"[19] He said, "No, indeed. You are not yet scalded to death. If you were scalded to death, you could not say you were scalded to death. I am a man, and so understand that if a man says, he is scalding to death, he is not yet scalded; if he is scalded, he does not say he is scalding; he is scalded, and that is all." She said, "Uthlakanyana, I am being done." Uthlakanyana said, "No, you are not yet done. There, you are now saying that you are being done. I know, when a man has been thoroughly done, he does not say constantly, 'I am already done.' He just says nothing, when he is already done." So she was boiled, and said no more. Uthlakanyana said, "Now, then, I perceive that you are done, because you no longer say so now. Now you have become silent; that is the reason why I think you are thoroughly done. You will be eaten by your children. Do away, then! I see now you are

---

[19] One cannot give this idiom, *Nga tsha*, the full force in an English translation. It is the aorist tense, and is used interjectionally. Its meaning is either hyperbolical, to arrest the attention and fix it on some imminent danger, as *Wa fa!* "You are dead!" or it expresses a sudden, unexpected act, which has just been completed, as *Sa tsha!* "The gun fired." An instance of the use of this tense occurs in the first paragraph of this Tale: *Inkomo zikababa za pela.* Uthlakanyana exaggerates; he says, *are devoured:* the mother, in repeating his words, says, *zi ya pela,* "are coming to an end,"—are *being* devoured.

u vutiwe impela manje, ukuba u | boiled indeed, because you are now
se u tule." | silent."[20]

Uthlakanyana puts on the clothes of the cannibal's mother, and becomes
a witness of the cannibal's feast.

Wa tata ke izingubo, w' ambata zonke, wa mkulu ngezingubo lezo. Wa lala lapa ku be ku lele isalukazi, unina wezimu. Ba fika, ba ti, "Mame." Wa ti, "We," ngelincane ilizwi njengonina. Wa ti, "Ni ngi bizela ni na?" Wa ti, "Nantsi inyamazana yenu; i se i kukumele, i se inkulu, imnandi, njengoba i be i tsho. D*h*la nini[21] ke; a ngi zi 'kuvuka mina. Kade ngi i d*h*la." B' opula ke umkono; ba se be d*h*la. Wa ti umfana wezimu, "Lezi 'zand*h*la kungati ezikama." La ti izimu elikulu, "U kuluma njani na? u ya m *h*lolela uma." Wa ti, "Aike! a ngi sa tsho." Ba d*h*la njalo, ba kqeda umkono. B' opula umlenze, ba d*h*la. Wa pinda umfana wezimu, wa ti, "Lolu 'nyawo kungati olukama. Noko u te ezand*h*leni, ngi nge tsho ukuti kungati ezikama, ngi ya tsho. Futi ukuti lolu 'nyawo lungati olwake." La m tshaya. Wa pendula U*h*lakanyana, e lele; wa ti, "Mntanami, lo

Uthlakanyana then took the garments of the cannibal's mother, and put them all on, and was big by means of the garments: he then lay down where the old woman, the cannibal's mother, had lain. The cannibals came at length, and said, "Mother." Uthlakanyana answered, "Yes," with a little voice like the mother. "Why do you call me? There is your game: it is now swollen to a great size, and is nice, just as he said. Do you eat. I shall not get up. I have already eaten of it." They drew out an arm. They eat. The cannibal's boy said, "These hands are just like mother's." The elder cannibal said, "How are you speaking? You are prognosticating evil to mother." He replied, "No; I withdraw the saying." So they eat, and finished the arm. They drew out a leg, and eat. The cannibal's boy again said, "This foot is just like mother's. Although you said as regards the hands, I might not say they were just like mother's, I say it. I say again that this foot is just like hers." The cannibal beat him. Uthlakanyana spoke, still lying down, and said, "My child, that

[20] A somewhat similar trick is played with equal success by Maol a Chliobain, on the Giant's mother. She persuades her to open the sack in which she was suspended, to be killed on the Giant's return; she escapes, and transfers the old woman to her place in the sack, and she is killed by her own son. *(Campbell, Op. cit. Vol. I., p. 255.)* So Peggy succeeds in baking the cannibal-witch in her own oven, which she had heated for the purpose of baking Peggy. *(Grimm's Home Stories.* "Hans and Peggy."—See also "The Tale of the Shifty Lad," a Highland Uthlakanyana, how he managed to hang his master in roguery. *(Campbell, Op. cit. Vol. I., p. 328.)*

[21] D*h*la nini = yid*h*la ni.

umtakati a nga ngi dhla yena, ngokuba u ti, e dhla inyamazana, e be i biza ngami, e i fanisa nami. Tula nje, mntanami, dhlana[22] nje wena."

wizard would eat me, for his part; for when he is eating game, he calls it by my name, and thinks he sees a resemblance to me. Just be silent, my child, and go on eating."

Uthlakanyana thinks it is time to be off, and sets off accordingly.

Wa ti, "Ake ni lunge, ngi ke ngi pume, ngi ye 'kutunda; ngi za 'kubuya. Ni hlale, ni dhle njalo nina." La ti izimu, lapa e semnyango Uhlakanyana, la ti, "Yebo, lesi 'sitende kungati esake umame." Wa finyela Uhlakanyana; w' esaba kaloku; wa puma ngamandhla emnyango; wa hamba ngamandhla ukushiya indhlu ye-zimu. Wa kqala uku zi tukulula izingubo; wa zi vutulula zonke; wa gijima, wa kqiuisa kakulu. Wa bona ukuti, se ngi kude manje; a ba sa yi 'ku ngi funyana. Wa memeza, wa ti, "Ni dhla unyoko njalo, mazimu!" 'Ezwa amazimu a puma. Wa ti umfana wezimu, "Ngi te, kungati izandhla lezi ezikama, nonyawo lwake." Ba m kxotsha; wa funyana umfula u gcwele. Uhlakanyana wa pen-duka uhlakulo[23] pezu kwamanzi. A fika amazimu; a funyana unya-wo emhlabatini; a lu bona uhla-kulo; la lu tata, la ti, "U wele." La ponsa uhlakulo, la ti, "U te," la tsho li ponsa uhlakulo. Kanti

Uthlakanyana said, "Just get out of the way of the door; I am going out; I shall be back again presently. Do you go on eating." When Uthlakanyana reached the doorway, the elder cannibal said, "Surely this heel is like mother's." Uthlakanyana drew out his legs; he was afraid now; he went out as fast as he could, and hastened to get away from the cannibal's house. He began to undo the garments; he slipped them all off, and ran with all his might. He saw at length that he was far enough off that they could not catch him; so he shouted, "You are eating your mother, all along, ye cannibals!" The cannibals heard, and went out. The cannibal's boy said, "I said, these are like mother's hands and her foot." They ran after him. Uthlakanyana came to a swollen river, and changed himself into a weeding-stick on its banks. The cannibals came, and found his footprints on the ground; and saw too the weed-ing-stick. The cannibal took it up, and said, "He has got across." He threw the weeding-stick, say-ing "He did thus," throwing the stick as he spoke. However, it

---

[22] Dhlana = yidhla.

[23] *Uhlakulo.*—An old fashioned wooden pick, which is gradually giving place to iron. It is made of hard wood, carved to somewhat the shape of a hand, and hardened by placing the edge in hot ashes. It is now used by old people, or by those who are too weak to use the heavier iron tool. The natives use it stooping. It is about a foot and a half long. It is sometimes carved into the shape of a hand at each end.

u ye; u fike, wa penduka u*h*la-kulo. Wa tokoza ukuba 'eme ngapetsheya; wa ti, "Na ngi weza!" A ti, "Ah! kanti u ye u*h*lakulo, loku si ti lu*h*lakulo nje." A buya ke.

was Uthlakanyana; on coming to the river, he had turned into a stick. He was happy when he stood on the other side, and said, "You put me across!" They said, "Oh, it was he, forsooth, who was the stick, when we thought it was a mere stick." So they turned back.

Uthlakanyana circumvents a hare, and gets a dinner and a whistle.

Wa wela ke; wa hamba: wa fumana umvund*h*la; wa ti, "Mvu-nd*h*la, woza lapa, ngi ku tshele indaba." Wa t' umvund*h*la, "K*q*a! a ngi funi uku*h*langana nawe." Wa ti, "Ngi za 'ku ku tshela, U*h*lakanyana indaba e be si z' enza nozimu[24] ngapetsheya kwomfula." Wa k*x*waya njalo umvund*h*la. Wa sondela U*h*la-kanyana; wa u bamba umvu-nd*h*la; wa u *h*loma elutini; wa u *h*luta uboya; wa bas' umlilo; wa w osa; wa u d*h*la: wa baz' i-tambo; wa l' enz' ivenge. Wa hamba ke, wa hamba ke.

Thus he passed over the river, and went on his way: he fell in with a hare, and said, "Hare, come here, and I will tell you a tale." The hare said, "No. I do not wish to have anything to do with you." He replied, "I will tell you some tales about the business which I Uthlakanyana have had with Mr. Cannibal, on the other side the river." The hare still avoided him. At length he got nearer and nearer, and caught hold of the hare. He impaled him on a stick, and plucked off the hair,[25] and lighted a fire, and roasted and eat him. He carved one of the bones, and made a whistle. And went on his way.

Uthlakanyana is circumvented by an iguana, and loses his whistle.

Wa funyana uk*x*amu e semtini pezulu: wa ti, "Ah! sa ku bona, *h*lakanyana." Wa ti, "Yebo, ngi bona wena, k*x*amu." Wa ti uk*x*amu, "Ngi boleke ke ivenge lako; ngi ke ngi zwe ukuba li ya teta ini na?" Wa ti U*h*lakanyana,

He fell in with an iguana, high up in a tree: he said to him, "Good morning, Uthla-kanyana." He said, "I thank you; good morning to you, igua-na." The iguana said, "Lend me your whistle, that I may just hear if it will sound." Uthlakanyana

[24] *Nozimu.*—Uthlakanyana left the word *izimu,* "a cannibal," and used *Uzimu,* a proper name. Had he spoken of having had anything to do with a cannibal, the hare might have been afraid that he was a cannibal's agent: but when he spoke of *Uzimu,* the hare, supposing him to speak of a man so called, would be likely to listen willingly to his tale.

[25] The natives do not skin hares; they pluck them.

"Kqabo! a ngi naku ku bo-leka ivenge lami. A ngi tandi." Wa ti, "Ngi ya 'kubuya, ngi ku nike." Wa ti, "Puma ke esizi-beni;" (ngokuba umuti u m' esizi-beni;) "woza lapa elubala; ngi y' esaba esizibeni. Ngi ti, imbande yami u nga ze u ngene nayo esizi-beni, ngokuba u ng' umuntu o hlala esizibeni." Wa puma ke wa ya elubala. Wa m boleka ke; wa li tshaya ke ivenge. Wa ti, "Wo! li ya teta ivenge lako. A u ngi boleke, ngi ze ke ngi li tshaye na ngomso." Wa ti Uhla-kanyana, "Kqa! li lete. Ngi se ngi tanda ukuhamba manje." Wa ti, "Kqa! u so ngi bolekile." Wati, "Leti ngamandhla." Wa tukutela Uhlakanyana; wa m bamba ukxamu; wa ti, "Leti." Wa tshaywa ke Uhlakanyana ngomsila; wa tshaywa kakulu ngomsila; w' ezwa ubuhlungu ka-kulu; wa i shiya imbande yake; wa ngena esizibeni ukxamu nayo imbande kahlakanyana.

said, "No indeed! I cannot lend you my whistle. I don't like to." The iguana said, "I will give it back to you again." He said, "Come away then from the pool; ' (for the tree was standing over a pool of the river;) "and come here into the open country; I am afraid near a pool. I say, you might run into the pool with my flute, for you are a person that lives in deep water." So the iguana came away, and went to the open country. Uthlakanyana lent him the whistle. He played on it, and said, "My! your whistle sounds. Just lend it to me, that I may play it again to-morrow." Uthlakanyana said, "No! bring it to me. I now want to be off." The iguana said, "No! you have now lent it to me." He said, "Bring it directly." Uthlakanyana was angry; he laid hold of the iguana, and said, "Give it up." But the iguana smote Uthlakanyana with his tail; he hit him very hard, and he felt a great deal of pain, and let go his flute; and the iguana went away into the deep water with Uthla-kanyana's whistle.

Uthlakanyana steals some bread, and escapes without punishment.

Wa hamba ke Uhlakanyana, wa ya kwenye indawo. Wa fumana ku bekwe isinkwa sekxegu; wa si tata, wa baleka naso. La ti ikxe-gu, uba li m bone, "Beka isinkwa sami, hlakanyana." Wa e se gijima e ngena esiningweni. La fika ke ikxegu, la faka isandhla, la m bamba. Wa ti Uhlakanyana, "He, he! wa bamba impande." La m yeka, la bamba futi; la bamba impande. Wa e se ti ke Uhlakanyana, e kala, "Maye!

So Uthlakanyana went on his way to another place. He found some bread belonging to an old man hid away; he took it, and ran away with it. When the old man saw him, he said, "Put down my bread, Uthlakanyana." But he ran into a snake's hole. The old man came, and put in his hand, and caught hold of him. Uthla-kanyana said, "Ha, ha! you caught hold of a root." He left hold of him, and caught hold again; this time he caught hold of a root. Then Uthlakanyana said,

maye ! wa ngi bulala !"[26] La kqinisa kakulu, la za la katala, li bamba impande njalo : la za l' emuka. Wa si d*h*la ke isinkwa, wa si kqeda ; wa puma, wa hamba.

crying, "My ! my ! you have killed me !" The old man pulled with all his might, until he was tired ; he pulling the root all the time. At length he went away. Uthlakanyana eat all the bread, and then went on his way.

Uthlakanyana becomes the servant of a leopard.

Wa hamba ke U*h*lakanyana : wa funyana ingwe, i zalele ; i nge ko yona, abantwana be bodwa. Wa *h*lala kubo abantwana. Ya za ya fika ingwe, i pete impunzi. Ya kukumala ; ya tukutela ukuba i m bone ; ya tukutela kakulu ; ya i beka pantsi impunzi ; ya hamba ya ya kuye. U*h*lakanyana wa ti, "Nkosi yami, musa ukutukutela. U inkosi impela wena. Ngi za 'ku*h*lala nabantwana bako, u yozingela wena ; ngi ya 'ku ba londa, u hambile, u ye 'kuzingela. Ngi za 'kwaka ind*h*lu en*h*le, u nga lali lapa pantsi kwelitshe nabantwana bako. Ngi za 'ku y aka ka*h*le, ngi i fulele ind*h*lu yako." Ya ti, "Yebo ke ; ngi ya vuma, in*x*' u za 'kusala nabantwana bami, u ba londe, ngi hambile. Ngi se ngi ya vuma ke."

Uthlakanyana went on his way, and fell in with a leopard which had cubs ; she, however, was not at home, but only the children. He staid with the children. At length the leopard came, carrying a buck. She swelled herself out, and was angry when she saw him ; she was very angry ; she put down the buck, and went towards him. Uthlakanyana said, "My lord, dont be angry. You are a lord indeed, you. I am going to stay with your children ; you will go to hunt ; and I will take care of them when you have gone to hunt. I shall build a beautiful house, that you may not lie here at the foot of a rock with your children. I shall build your house well, and thatch it." The leopard said, "Very well then ; I agree if you will stay with the children, and take care of them when I have gone out. Now then I agree."

Uthlakanyana gives the leopard a lesson in suckling.

Wa ti U*h*lakanyana lapo ke, "Ngi za 'ku ku nikela abantwana, u ba ncelise ngabanye." Wa i nikela ke umntwana. Ya ti, "Leti nomunye umntwana wami. Musa ukuti 'K' anyise yedwa.' A b' anyise bobabili, omunye a nga kali."

Uthlakanyana then said, "I will give you the children, that you may suckle them one by one." So he gave her one child. She said, "Bring my other child also. Don't say, let one suck by itself. Let them both suck together, lest the other cry." Uthlakanyana

[26] *Wa bamba impande. Wa ngi bulala.*—Examples of the aorist used interjectionally. We cannot express them in an English translation. But somewhat of the meaning may be gained by comparing them with such expressions as "Caught !" when a policeman puts his hand suddenly on a prisoner. Or as when a sportsman has made a successful shot, and says, "Dead !" "Hit !" "Killed !"

Wa ti U*h*lakanyana, "K*q*abo! Ake w anyise lowo kuk*q*ala, and' uba ngi ku nike omunye, lowo e se e buycle kumi." Ya ti, "K*q*abo. A ng' enzi njalo mina uku ba ncelisa kwami. Musa uku ngi fundisa loko uku ba ncelisa abanta bami. Ba lete kanye nje bobabili." Wa ti U*h*lakanyana, "Woza, u lete lowo e ngi ku nike kuk*q*ala." Ya za ya m nika owokuk*q*ala; wa i nikela ke omunye. Ya ti, "Puma manje lapo, u ze lapa, u ze 'ku*h*linza impunzi yami, u peke inyama njengokutsho kwako, ngokuba u te, u za 'upeka." Wa suka ke, wa *h*linza, wa peka. Ya d*h*la ke ingwe nabantwana bayo. Kwa lalwa: kwa vukwa kusasa.

said, "Not at all! Just suckle that one first, and I will give you the other when that one has come back to me." She said, "By no means. I do not do in that way, for my part, when I nurse them. Don't teach me the suckling of my children. Just bring them both together." Uthlakanyana said, "Come, hand over that one which I gave you first." At length she gave him back the first; and then he gave her the other. She said, "Now come out from there, and come to me, and skin my buck, and cook its flesh, according to your word, for you said you would cook." So he went, and skinned the buck, and boiled it. The leopard eat, and her little ones. They went to sleep. They woke in the morning.

Uthlakanyana eats the leopard and her cubs.

Ya ti, "Sala ke, u londe. Nampo ke abantwana[27] bami; u ba g*c*ine ke." Wa y·aka ind*h*lu, wa i k*q*eda; wa y enza umnyango, wa mncinane kakulu; w' emba umgodi omude, wa ya, wa puma kude, intunja yawo umgodi; wa n*q*uma imikonto yake ya mine. Ya fika ingwe; ya fika nempunzi; ya ti, "Hlakanyana!" Wa ti, "Hi!"

The leopard said, "Stay here, and keep things safe. I trust my children to you; preserve them." Uthlakanyana built a house, and finished it: he made it with a very small doorway; and he dug a long burrow, which had a distant outlet, and cut off the hafts of four assagais. The leopard arrived; she brought a buck with her; she said, "Uthlakanyana!" He answered, "Ay, ay!" Uthlakanyana had

---

[27] *Nampo ke abantwana*, comp. *Mame, nantso ke inyamazana yami*, p. 17. —The demonstrative adverbs in *o* always point to something with which the person addressed has some concern. *Nampo abantwana*, "there are the children," is an answer to a question, and implies that they are near the enquirer, though he does not see them. *Nampo ke abantwana*, "there, then, are the children," implies that some understanding has been previously entered into with the person addressed, and that they are now entrusted to his care, that he may act towards them in accordance with the previous understanding. Thus a man pointing out to another a horse running away, if near at hand, he says, *Nanti li baleka*, "there it is running away." If it is at a considerable distance, he says, *Nantiya li baleka*. But if the owner asks, *Li pi ihashi lami na?* "where is my horse?" the answer would be, *Nanto li baleka*. And if he had been warned beforehand that it would run away, *Nanto ke li baleka*.

wa sabela. Umntwana wa be e
se m d*h*lile omunye; wa e se
munye umntwana. Ya ti, "Leti
ke abantwana bami." Wa i nika
ke ingwe; ya m anyisa. Ya ti,
"Leti omunye." Wa ti, "Leti
lowo ke." Ya ti, "Ai; leti bobabili." W' al' Uklakanyana, wa ti,
"Wo k' u lete lowo kuk*q*ala, and'
uba ngi ku nike lo." Ya m nikela
ingwe. Wa buya wa pindelisela
lowo; ngokuba umntwana u se
emunye. Ya ti, "Puma ke, u ze
'u*h*linza inyamazana." Wa puma
ke, wa i *h*linza, wa i peka. Ya
d*h*la ke ingwe nomntwana. Wa
ngena. Ya ti yona, "Nami ngi
za 'ungena manje." Wa ti U*h*lakanyana, "Ngena ke manje." Ya
ngena. Kwa k*q*ina ukungena;
ngokuba U*h*lakanyana umnyango
u w enzile ngobu*h*lakani bake,
ngokukumbula ukuba umntwana
'eza 'ku mu d*h*la, ingwe i tukutele
kakulu; wa ti, "U kona i ya 'ku-
minyana, i nga ngeni ka*h*le; u
kona i ya 'kuti i sa minyene, ngi
be ngi hamba ngapantsi emgodini
omude; u kona i ya 'kuti i fika,
ngi be se ngi kude nend*h*lu."
Wa ngena ke emgodini o ngapakati kwend*h*lu leyo: ya se i
ngena ingwe. Ya ngena ke, ya
funyana umntwana emunye. Ya
ti, "Wo! kanti U*h*lakanyana
lo,—kanti u nje! Umntanami
u pi? U mu d*h*lile." Ya ngena
emgodini ke, lapa e ngene kona,
i ti, i ya 'kupuma ngalapaya;
wa e se pume kuk*q*ala, e se
buya e ngena futi, w' embela
imikonto emnyango. Ya b' i fika
kona ngasemnyango, ya *h*latshwa
imikonto yomine; ya fa. Wa

now eaten one of the cubs; there
was but one left. She said, "Just
bring me my children." So he
gave it her, and she suckled
it. She said, "Bring me the
other." He replied, "Hand back
that one." She said, "No; bring
them both." Uthlakanyana refused, and said, "Just hand back
that one first, and then I will give
you this." The leopard gave it
him. He gave it back to her again.
For now there was but one
child. She said, "Come out now,
and skin the buck." So he went
out, and skinned it, and cooked it.
The leopard eat and her little one.
Uthlakanyana went into the house.
The leopard said, "I too shall go
in now." Uthlakanyana said,
"Come in then." She went in.
It was hard to go in; for Uthlakanyana had cunningly contrived
the doorway, remembering that he
intended to eat the cub, and the
leopard would be very angry; he
said, "She will be thus com-
pressed, and not easily enter;
thus, whilst she is squeezing in,
I shall go down into the long
hole; and thus, when she gets
in, I shall be far from the house."
So he went into the hole which was
in the house. And the leopard
entered. When she entered, she
found only one child. She said,
"Dear me! so then this Uthlakanyana,—so then he is a fellow
of this kind! Where is my child?
He has eaten it." She went into
the hole, into which he had gone,
intending to get out the other
end; Uthlakanyana had got out
first, and returned to the house,
and fixed his assagais in the earth
at the doorway. When she came
to the doorway, she was pierced
by the four assagais, and died.
Uthlakanyana came to her when

fika i s' i file; wa jabula; wa tata umntwana, wa m bulala wengwe. Wa hlala ke, wa dhla ingwe nomntwana wayo, wa kqeda; wa twala umlenze, wa hamba, w' emuka, ngokuba e be ng' umuntu o nga hlali ndawo nye.

she was dead; he was happy; he took and killed the leopard's child. So he staid and eat up the leopard and her child; he took, however, one leg, and went on his travels, for he was a man that did not stay in one place.

[In another version of the Tale, this story is told of a doe, which had "thirteen children." Uthlakanyana engages himself as nurse, and eats the kids one after another in thirteen days by a similar stratagem. The story continues thus :—

Wa e se baleka Uhlakanyana. Ya m kxotsha impunzi. Uhlakanyana wa fumanisa ugcwele umfula. Wa fika wa penduka imbokondo. Impunzi ya i tata imbokondo, ya i ponsa ngapetsheya kwomfula, ya ti, "Wo! uma ku be u yena lo, nga se ngi m bulala manje." Wa fika Uhlakanyana, wa ti, "Wa ngi ponsa mina, hlakanyana, Bogcololo, mina, mahlab'-indod'-i-s'-emi."

Then Uthlakanyana fled. The doe pursued. Uthlakanyana came to a full river. On his arrival he turned into an upper millstone.[28] The doe took it up, and threw it across the river,[29] sayiug, "Oh! if this were he, I would now kill him." When Uthlakanyana reached the other side, he said, "You threw me, Uthlakanyana, Bogcololo, me, 'Mathlab'-indod'-i-s'-emi."]

Uthlakanyana falls in with a cannibal, whom he gets into trouble, and leaves to die.

E sa hamba, wa hlangana nezimu. La ti izimu, la ti, "Nga ku bona, hlakanyana." Wa ti Uhlakanyana, "Ngi bona wena, malume wami." La ti izimu, "Nga ku bona, mfana kadade wetu." Wa ti, "Ngi bona wena, malume wami." Wa ti, "Woza lapa, ngi ku tshele indaba e be si z' enza nongwe ngemva lapa; woza lapa ngi ze 'ku ku tshela indaba e be si z' enza nongwe." La ti, "Yebo ke." Wa ti, "Ake u dhle; nantsi inyama." La bonga izimu,

On his journey he fell in with a cannibal. The cannibal said, "Good morning, Uthlakanyana." Uthlakanyana replied, "Good morning to you, my uncle." The cannibal said, "Good morning to you, child of my sister." Uthlakanyana replied, "Good morning to you, my uncle." He said, "Come here, and I will tell you a business I and Mrs. Leopard have had together behind here; come here, and I will tell you a business I and Mrs. Leopard have had together." The cannibal said, "Certainly." Uthlakanyana said, "Just eat; here is some

---

[28] The native women use two stones in grinding—the upper a hard pebble; the lower a large flat stone, which is soft, and somewhat hollowed. The upper is made to perform about a half revolution backwards and forwards in the hollow of the lower; and the meal is collected in front on a mat.

[29] This is related of Litaolane in the Basuto Legend of Kammapa. (*Casalis' Basutos, p.* 349.)

la ti, "Mfana kadade, u ngi sizile; ngi be se ngi lambile kakulu kakulu." La d*h*la ke izimu, naye e d*h*la. Kwa vela izinkomo 'zimbili—enye im*h*lope, enye imnyama. Za bonwa lizimu; la ti, "Nanziya inkomo zami." Wa ti U*h*lakanyana, "Yami emnyama." La ti izimu, "Yami em*h*lope, em*h*lope na ngapakati." Ba hamba ke, ba ya kuzo, ba z' ek*q*ela. Wa ti U*h*lakanyana, "Malume, a kw akiwe ind*h*lu." La ti izimu, "U k*q*inisile; ko*n*a si za 'u*h*lala ka*h*le, si d*h*le inkomo zetu." Ya pangiswa ke ind*h*lu, y' akiwa; kw' epiwa utshani. Wa ti U*h*lakanyana, "Ake ku *h*linzwe eyako, malume wami, em*h*lope kuk*q*ala, na ngapakati; si ke si bone ukuba i njalo ke na, njengokuba u tshilo; wa ti, im*h*lope na pakati." La vuma izimu; la ti, "Yebo." Ya bulawa ke inkomo; ya *h*linzwa ke; ba i fumana y ondile. Wa ti U*h*lakanyana, "A ngi i d*h*li mina e nje. Ake ku banjwe eyami." La vuma izimu. Ya bulawa; ya funyanwa i nonile kakulu. La ti izimu, "Mfana kadade, u *h*lakanipile impela; ngokuba u *h*le[31] wa i bona wena, ukuba i nonile eyako le." Wa ti U*h*lakanyana, "A ku fulelwe ind*h*lu ke manje; and' uba si d*h*le ukud*h*la kwetu. Izulu u ya li bona, ukuba si za 'uneta." La ti izimu, "U k*q*inisile, mfana kadade; u indoda impela, lok' u ti a si fulele ind*h*lu, ngokuba si za

meat." The cannibal thanked him, and said, "Child of my sister, you have helped me; I was very, very hungry." The cannibal eat, and Uthlakanyana eat with him. Two cows made their appearance.—one white, the other black. They were seen by the cannibal; he said, "There are my cows." Uthlakanyana said, "The black one is mine." The cannibal said, "The white one is mine, which is white[30] also inside." They went on to them, and turned them back. Uthlakanyana said, "Uncle, let a house be built." The cannibal said, "You say well; then we shall live comfortably, and eat our cattle." The house was hastily built, and the grass gathered. Uthlakanyana said, "Let your cow be killed first, my uncle, which is white outside and in, that we may just see if it is, as you said, white also inside." The cannibal assented. So the cow was killed, and skinned; they found it lean. Uthlakanyana said, "I don't eat, for my part, a thing like this. Let-mine be caught." The cannibal assented. It was killed, and found to be very fat. The cannibal said, "Child of my sister, you are wise indeed, for you saw at a glance that this cow of yours was fat." Uthlakanyana said, "Let the house be thatched now; then we can eat our meat. You see the sky, that we shall get wet." The cannibal said, "You are right, child of my sister; you are a man indeed, in saying let us thatch the house, for we shall get

---

[30] White, i.c., fat.

[31] *U hle.*—This verb is often used with no very definite meaning, at least, such as we can translate. And often it can be omitted without affecting the sense even to the apprehension of a native. It is here translated "at a glance," or forthwith, or at first. It implies that what the other saw and said, without any one else at the time seeing, has turned out to be correct. *U vele wa i bona* is also used, "You saw it at the first."

'uneta." Wa ti U*h*lakanyana, "Ak' w enze ke wena; mina ngi za 'kungena ngapakati, ngi ku *h*lomele end*h*lini." L' enyuka izimu. Inwele zalo za zinde kakulu kakulu. Wa ngena ngapakati; wa li *h*lomela ke. Inwele wa z' akela kona, e tekeleza, e k*q*inisa inwele zezimu kakulu; wa u loku e zi tekelezela njalo, e z' akela njalo, e zi kcapuna kakulu, e k*q*inisa ukuba ku ze ku k*q*ine kona end*h*lini. Wa bona ukuba ziningi inwele lezi, a li se nakwe*h*la pezulu, in*x*a ngi puma ngapakati kwend*h*lu. U*h*lakanyana, ukupuma kwake, wa y' eziko, lapa ku pekiwe kona ibele lenkomo. W' opula; wa beka esitebeni; wa tata umkonto; wa sika; wa funda. La ti izimu, "W enza ni, mnta kadade? Ake u ze, si k*q*ede ind*h*lu; and' uba si kw enze loko; si za 'ku kw enza nawe." Wa ti U*h*lakanyana, "Ye*h*la ke. A ngi se nako ukuza ngapakati kwend*h*lu. Ku pelile ukufulela." La ti izimu, "Yebo ke." La ti, li y' esuka, kwa k*q*ina ukusuka. La kala, la ti, "Mfana kadade, w enze njani na ukufulela kwako?" Wa ti U*h*lakanyana, "Bonisa wena. Mina ngi fulele ka*h*le; ngokuba umsindo a u zi 'kuba-ko kwimi; se ngi za 'kud*h*la ka*h*le; ngi nga sa bangi namuntu,

wet." Uthlakanyana said, "Do you do it then; I will go inside, and push the thatching-needle for you, in the house." The cannibal went up. His hair was very, very long. Uthlakanyana went inside, and pushed the needle for him. He thatched in the hair of the cannibal, tying it very tightly; he knotted it into the thatch constantly, taking it by separate locks and fastening it firmly, that it might be tightly fastened to the house.[32] He saw that the hair (thus fastened in) was enough, and that the cannibal could not get down, if he should go outside. When he was outside Uthlakanyana went to the fire, where the udder of the cow was boiled. He took it out, and placed it on an eating-mat; he took an assagai, and cut, and filled his mouth. The cannibal said, "What are you about, child of my sister? Let us just finish the house; afterwards we can do that; we will do it together." Uthlakanyana replied, "Come down then. I cannot go into the house any more. The thatching is finished." The cannibal assented. When he thought he was going to quit the house, he was unable to quit it. He cried out, saying, "Child of my sister, how have you managed your thatching?" Uthlakanyana said, "See to it yourself. I have thatched well, for I shall not have any dispute. Now I am about to eat in peace; I no longer dispute

---

[32] In the Basuto Legend of the Little Hare, the hare has entered into an alliance with the lion, but having been ill-treated by the latter, determines to be avenged. "My father," said he to the lion, "we are exposed to the rain and hail; let us build a hut." The lion, too lazy to work, left it to the hare to do, and the "wily runner" took the lion's tail, and interwove it so cleverly into the stakes and reeds of the hut that it remained there confined for ever, and the hare had the pleasure of seeing his rival die of hunger and thirst. (*Casalis' Basutos, p. 354.*)

ngokuba se ngi ngedwa enkomeni yami." Wa ti, "U b' uza 'ùti ni, loku eyako i zakcile, a i nonile nje. Ye*h*la ngamand*h*la ako o kwele ngawo. A ngi nako ukuza 'kusombulula." Wa sika enyameni em*h*lope. Wa ti, "Mina ke." La ti, "Wo lete[33] ke. Kwela ke, u lete lapa, mfana kadade. Ngi size; u ngi tukulule, ngi ze lapo kuwe. A ngi yi 'ku w enza umsindo. Ngi za 'kupiwa nguwe; ngokuba inkomo eyami ngi i bonile ukuba y ondile; inkomo e nonile eyako. Ubani na o wa ka wa nomsindo entweni yomuntu, ku nge yake?" La fika izulu namatshe, nemibane. Wa tuta U*h*lakanyana, wa tutela end*h*lini konke oku inyama, wa *h*lala end*h*lini. Wa basa. La fika izulu namatshe nemvula. La kala izimu pezu kwend*h*lu; la tshaywa ngamatshe; la fela kona pezulu. La sa izulu. Wa puma U*h*lakanyana, wa ti, "Malume, ye*h*la ke, u ze lapa. Li se li sile izulu. A li sa ni; nesik*q*oto a si se ko, nokubaneka a ku se ko. U tulele ni na?"

with anybody, for I am now alone with my cow." He continued, "What would you have said, since yours is thin, and has no fat at all? Come down by your own strength with which you went up. I cannot come and undo you." And he cut into the fat meat, and said, "Take this." The cannibal said, " Bring it at once then. Mount, and bring it to me, child of my sister. Help me; undo me, that I may come to you. I am not going to make a noise. You shall give me; for I have seen that my cow is lean; the fat one is yours. Whoever made a dispute about the property of another man, to which he had no right?" The sky came with hailstones and lightning. Uthlakanyana took all the meat into the house; he staid in the house, and lit a fire. It hailed and rained. The cannibal cried on the top of the house; he was struck with the hailstones, and died there on the house. It cleared. Uthlakanyana went out, and said, " Uncle, just come down, and come to me. It has become clear. It no longer rains, and there is no more hail, neither is there any more lightning. Why are you silent?"

Wa i d*h*la ke inkomo yedwa, wa ze wa i k*q*eda. Wa hamba ke.

So Uthlakanyana eat his cow alone, until he had finished it. He then went on his way.

Uthlakanyana meets a cannibal, who will not trust him.

Wa *h*langana nelinye izimu, li pete isigubu esikulu. Wa ti, "Malume." La ti, "Ngi umalume wako ngani na?" Wa ti, "Ku ng' azi na?" La ti, "A ngi kw azi mina." Wa ti, "K*q*abo!

He met another cannibal, carrying a large musical calabash. He said, "Uncle!" The cannibal said, "How am I your uncle!" He said, "Don't you know?" The cannibal replied, "I don't know, for my part." Uthlakanyana

[33] *Wo lete* is a paulo-post future imperative. It implies that a thing is required to be done at once. *Wo leta* is indefinite, applying to any future time.

U umalume impcla." La ti izimu, "A ngi bu tandi lobo 'bukqili. Ngi ya kw azi wena, ukuba u Uhlakanyana. A ngi kohliwa mina. Ngi indoda. Tula nje. A ngi yi 'kuza nga vuma[34] ukuba u ng' owodade wetu." Wa ti, "Kqa! Ngi boleke isigubu lesi." L' ala izimu, la ti, "Kqa! A ngi nakuhlangana nawe impela." Wa li dela.

said, "You don't mean it! You are my uncle indeed." The cannibal said, "I do not like that cunning of yours. I know you; you are Uthlakanyana. I am not deceived, for my part. I am a man. Just hold your tongue. I shall never admit that you are my sister's child." He said, "No? Lend me this calabash." The cannibal refused, saying, "No! I can have no communication with you whatever!" Uthlakanyana left him.

Uthlakanyana makes the cannibal who would not trust him the means of frightening another cannibal.

Wa hamba; wa fumana elinye izimu; wa fumana li sendhlini. Wa ngena. La ti, "U vela pi na?" Wa ti, "Ngi vela ngalapa. Be ngi nozimu, umalume wami; nawe u umalume wami." Kanti li ya landela lona lelo a hlangene nalo, l' ala nesigubu. La ti leli a li funyene endhlini, la ti, "A si shuke ingubo yami, mfana kadade." Ba i shuka ke. S' ezwakala isigubu; sa ti bu kakulu. Wa puma Uhlakanyana, wa ti, "U ya i zwa na le 'ndaba?" La ti, "I pi ke?" Wa ti, "Nantsi pandhle." La puma izimu, la lalela; la si zwa isigubu si teta kakulu. La ngena, la ti, "I shuke, si i shuke." La kqinisa; kwa kona umsindo wokuteta kwesikumba. Sa fundekela kakulu. Kwa ti umsindo wa fika u namapika ka-

He went on his way, and found another cannibal in a house. He went in. The cannibal said, "Whence come you?" He replied, "I came from yonder. I was with Mr. Cannibal, my uncle; and you, too, are my uncle." However, the cannibal he had met, who refused to lend him the calabash, was following. The one he found in the house said, "Let us bray my skin, child of my sister." So they brayed the skin. The calabash sounded "Boo" very loudly. Uthlakanyana ran out, and said, "Do you hear this?" The cannibal said, "Where?" He said, "Here outside." The cannibal went out, and listened; he heard the calabash sounding very loudly. He went in again, and said, "Bray the skin, and I will bray it too." He worked hard at it; there arose a great noise from braying the skin. The calabash resounded exceedingly; and now the sound came

34 *A ngi yi 'kuza nga vuma.*—The aorist after the future in the negative, is the strongest mode of expressing a negation. It may be rendered, as here, by "never," "I will *never* allow;" lit., "I will never come I allowed."

loku. Wa ti U*h*lakanyana, " A-
ngiti u te, a ku ko umsindo na
pand*h*le ? U s' u fika namapika
ngani ? " Sa tet' eduze manje.
Ba puma bobabili ; ba baleka bobabili. Wa vela umnikaziso isigubu. Kwa ti izimu, l' ema kwenye
intaba, U*h*lakanyana w' ema
kwenye intaba, la buza, la ti, " U
ng' ubani na, wena o s' etusako ? "
La ti eli pete isigubu, la ti, " Ngi
Umuyobolozeli. Nembuya ngi ya
i yobolozela ; umuntu ngi m gwinya nje. A ngi m d*h*lafuni ; ngi m
gwinya nje." La baleka ke ukuba
li zwe loko ukuti, umuntu ka d*h*la-
funywa.

with loud blowings. Uthlakanyana
said, " Did you not say there was
no noise outside ? Why is it now
approachiug with loud blowings ? "
It sounded at hand now. Both
went out ; both fled. The owner
of the calabash appeared. The
cannibal was now standing on one
hill, and Uthlakanyana on another ;
the cannibal asked, " Who are you
who are thus alarming us ? " The
cannibal who was carrying the
calabash said, " I am Mr. Guzzler.
I guzzle down wild spinach ; and
as for a man, I just bolt[35] him ; I
do not chew him ; I just bolt
him." The cannibal ran away
when he heard that a man was not
chewed.

Uthlakanyana comes back, and gains the cannibal's confidence.

Wa buya ke U*h*lakanyana,
w' eza kuleli lesigubu. Li se li
ngenisile end*h*lini. Wa fika U*h*lakanyana, wa ti, " Malume, mina
na lapa ngi be ngi *h*leli ngi umu-
ntwana nje : na kuwe ngi sa za
'kuba umntwana wako, ngokuba
na lapa ngi be ngi umntwana
nje. Ngi tanda uku*h*lala kuwe ;
ngokuba u umalume wami nawe."
La ti, " Kulungile ; ngokuba wena umnciuane kumi : *h*lala ke."
Ba *h*lala ke nezimu lesigubu. La
ti, " Sala ke lapa, u bheke umuzi
wami, umfokazi e ngi m k*æ*otshile
a nga ze 'kutshisa umuzi wami."
Wa ti U*h*lakanyaua, " Yebo ke ;
hamba ke, u ye u zingele." La
hamba ke. Wa *h*lala ke.

Uthlakanyana returned to him
of the calabash. He had already
taken possession of the house.
Uthlakanyana came, and said,
" Uncle, I was living here as a
child, as I have in all other places
where I have been ; and with you
too I will stay, and be your child ;
for I lived here as a mere child, as
well as in all other places. I wish
to live with you, for you too are
my uncle." The cannibal said,
" Very well, for you are smaller
than I. Stay." So he and the
cannibal of the calabash lived
together. The cannibal said, " Just
stay here, and watch my kraal,
that the vagabond I have driven
away may not come and burn my
kraal." Uthlakanyana said, " Certainly. Do you go and hunt."
So the cannibal departed ; and
Uthlakanyaua remained.

---

[35] Gargantua swallowed alive five pilgrims with a salad ! (*Rabelais. Book
I., ch. xxxviii.)*

Uthlakanyana brings a little army against the cannibal, which proves too much for him.

Wa tata iika, w' emuka Uhlakanyana. Wa hlangana nenyoka; wa i bamba, wa i faka eikeni. Wa hlangana nomnyovu; wa u faka eikeni. Wa hlangana nofezela; wa m bamba, wa m faka eikeni: zonke ezilumako, ezinobuhlungu kakulu, wa zi bamba, wa zi faka eikeni. La gcwala iika. Wa bopa, wa twala, wa buya, wa ngena endhlini. La fika izimu. Wa ti, "Malume, namhla nje ku fanele ukuba umnyango u ncitshiswe, u be muncinane: mubi umnyango omkulu." La ti izimu, "Kqa. A ngi u funi umnyango omncinane." Wa ti, "Yebo ke; ngi ya vuma. Ngi sa za 'kuhamba, ngi ye ekakomame;[36] ngi ye 'kufuna umzawami, ngi ze naye lapa; a z' a hlale lapa." Iika wa hamba nalo; wa li tukusa. Kwa hlwa ke, wa fika endhlini kona lapa izimu la li kona, wa fika nezintungo zokuncipisa umnyango wendhlu. Wa vula, wa ngena; wa pinda wa puma. Wa w aka ke umnyango, wa mncane, a kwa lingana nomntwana, ukuba a nga puma kona. Kwa sa, e se e hleli emnyango Uhlakanyana, wa ti, "Malume, malume!" La ti, "Ubani?" Wa ti, "U mi, malume." La ti, "U we, mfana kadade?" Wa ti, "Yebo. Ngi vulele; ngi zoku ku tshela indaba; ngi buye endhleleni; a ngi finyelelanga; indaba embi e ngi i zwile." La vuka izimu, la ti li ya vula ke, kwa kqina. La ti, "Mfana ka-

Uthlakanyana took a bag, and departed. He fell in with a snake; he caught it, and put it in his bag. He fell in with a wasp; he put it in his bag. He fell in with a scorpion; he caught it, and put it in his bag: all biting, and deadly poisonous, animals he caught and put in his bag. The bag was full. He tied it up, and carried it back again to the house. The cannibal came. Uthlakanyana said, "Uncle, it is proper that the doorway should this very day be contracted, that it may be small: a large doorway is bad." The cannibal said, "No. I do not like a narrow doorway." He said, "Very well; I agree. I am now going to my mother's kraal, to fetch my cousin, and return here with her, that she may live here." He took the bag with him, and hid it. When it was dark, Uthlakanyana came to the house where the cannibal was, with some rods for the purpose of contracting the doorway. He opened the door, and went in; and again went out. He built up the doorway, making it small: it was not large enough for a child to go out. In the morning Uthlakanyana, still stopping at the doorway, said, "Uncle! Uncle!" The cannibal said, "Who are you?" He said, "It is I, uncle." He said, "You, child of my sister?" He replied, "Yes; open the door for me; I come to tell you news; I come back from the road; I did not reach my mother: it is bad news which I have heard." The cannibal arose. When he tried to open the door, it was firm. He said, "Child of my sister, it is

---

[36] Ekakomame = ekaya kubo kamame, that is, the place where his mother was born.

dade, ku k*g*inile ukuvula." Iika li ngapakati ; u li ngenisile U*h*la-kanyana ebusuku, ukuncipisa kwake umnyango lowo. Wa ti, " Tukulula iika lelo, u li lete, u li veze lapa. Nami ngi mangele ngokuncipa kwomnyango. Tukulula, u li tintite ; u li veze kule intubana ; umnyango ngi za 'ku w andisa." La tukulula kaloku. Kwa puma inyoka ; ya lum' isand*h*la : kwa puma inyosi ; ya suzela esweni : kwa puma umnyovu ; wa suzela esi*h*latini. La ti izimu, " Mfana kadade, loku o kw enzile nam*h*la nje, a ngi bonanga ngi ze ngi ku bone, lo nga zalwa umfazi nendoda. Ngi size ; ngi ya d*h*liwa lapa end*h*lini yami ; a ngi sa boni." (Ufezela wa li suzela izimu.) Wa ti U*h*lakanyana, " Nami a ng' azi uba lezo 'zilwane zi ngene njani eikeni lami lapo." La ti izimu, " Vula ke, ngi pume." Za puma zonke izilwane, za li d*h*la ; la fa ngobu*h*lungu bezinyoka, nezinyosi, naofezela, neminyovu. La kala, la kala ke, la ze la fa. La fa ke izimu.

hard to open." The bag was inside ; Uthlakanyana had put it in in the night, when he contracted the doorway. He said, " Just undo that bag, and bring it, and put it here. I too wondered at the contraction of the doorway. Untie the bag, and shake it, and bring it to this little hole : as for the doorway, I will enlarge it." The cannibal now undid the bag The snake came out, and bit his hand. The bee came out, and stung him in the eye ; the wasp came out, and stung him on the cheek. The cannibal said, ." Child of my sister, this thing which you have done to-day, I never saw the like, since I was born of a woman and man ! Help me ; I am being eaten up here in my house. I can no longer see." (The scorpion too stung the cannibal.) Uthlakanyana said, " I too am ignorant how those animals got into my bag." The cannibal said, " Open, that I may get out." All the animals came out of the bag, and eat the cannibal, and he died of the poison of snakes, and of bees, and scorpions, and wasps. He cried and cried until he died. So the cannibal died.

Uthlakanyana mocks the dead cannibal, and instals himself as owner of the house.

Wa vula ke U*h*lakanyana, wa vula ke, e ti, " Malume, u se u tukutele na ? Kwa b' u se zwakala manje na, lo be ngi ti u ya kala na ? Malume wami, kuluma. U tulele ni na ? A u tshaye isigubu sako, ngi lalele, ngi zwe." Wa za wa ngena. Wa fika se li file. Wa li kipa end*h*lini. Wa ngenisa ; wa lala ; wa *h*lala manje.

Uthlakanyana opened the door, and said, " Are you still angry, my uncle ? Do you no longer cry out so as to be heard ; for I thought you were screaming ? My uncle, speak. Why are you silent ? Just play your calabash, that I may listen and hear. At length he entered ; when he came, the cannibal was dead. He took him out of the house, and took possession of it. He slept, and was happy now.

The original owner of the house comes back, and submits to Uthlakanyana.

La fika izimu, umninikaّzindّhlu. La ti, "Mfana kadade, ngi ku bonile ; ngi be ngi kona lapa, ngi bona, ukuvala kwako lapa emnyango, ukuba u indoda, loko u valela umuntu owa ngi kڑotsha emzini wami." Wa ti Uّhlakanyana, "Nawe manje ngi se ngi mkulu kunawe, ngokuba w' aّhluliwe umngane wako, mina ng' aّhlule yena. Ngi se ngi ya ku tola nawe namّhla." La ti izimu, "Kulungile, ngokuba ku bonakele ukuba ng' aّhluliwe mina." Ba ّhlala ke, ba ّhlala ke.

The cannibal, the owner of the house, came, and said, "Child of my sister, I have seen you. I was here at hand, and saw, when you closed up the doorway, that you are a man, since you shut in a man who drove me away from my kraal." Uthlakanyana said, "And you—now I am greater than you ; for you were surpassed by your friend, and I have surpassed him. I am now finding[87] you too to-day." The cannibal said, "It is right ; for it is evident that I am surpassed." So they remained for some time.

Uthlakanyana cannot forget the iguana, from whom he gets back his whistle.

Wa ti Uّhlakanyana, "Ngi y' e-muka nami. Imbande yami, ku se loko ng' amukwa ukڑamu." Wa hamba ke, wa vela, w' enyusa umfula. Ukڑamu wa b' e alukile, e yokudّhla ubulongwe a bu dّhlako ; nembande e i pete. Wa fika Uّhlakanyana, wa kwela pezulu emtini a tamelako kuwo ; wa memeza, wa ti, "Kڑamu ;" wa ti, "Kڑamu." Wa ti ukڑamu, "Ngi bizwa ubani na ? Loku mina ngi ze 'kuzifunela, lowo o ngi bizayo, k' eze lapa." Wa ti Uّhlakanyana, "U kڡinisile ke. Se ngi za ke, lapa u dّhla kona." W' eّhla Uّhla-

Uthlakanyana said, "I too am going away. My flute ! It is now a long time since it was taken away from me by the iguana." So he set out ; he came to the place, and went up the river. The iguana was out feeding, having gone to feed on the dung, which is its food, and carrying the flute with it. Uthlakanyana mounted on the tree, where the iguana sunned itself, and shouted, "Iguana ! iguana !" The iguana said, "Who calls me ? Since I have come here to find food for myself, let him who calls me come to me." Uthlakanyana said, "You are right. I am coming to the place where you are feeding." Uthla-kanyana descended, and came to

---

[87] To find, that is, to admit as a dependent into the family, and to provide for a person. The use of *find* in this sense is found in the old ballad of Adam Bell :—

> "There lay an old wife in that place,
> 　A little beside the fire,
> Whom William had *found* of charity
> 　More than seven year."

kanyana; wa fika, wa ti, "I pi imbande yami?" Wa ti, "Nantsi." Wa ti, "Ku njani ke nam*h*la nje? Si pi ke isiziba? Si kude!" Wa ti uk*x*amu, "U za 'u ng' enza ni? lo nantsi nje imbande yako, noka-nye ya shiwa u we nje; nga ti ngi ku bizela yona, wa u se u hambile." Kodwa ke U*h*lakanyana wa m tshaya; kwa tshaywa uk*x*amu; w' amukwa imbande. Wa m bulala, wa m shiya e se file.

the iguana, and said, "Where is my flute?" He replied, "Here it is." Uthlakanyana said, "How, then, is it now? Where, then, is the deep water? It is far away!" The iguana said, "What are you going to do to me, since there is your flute? And at the first it was left by you yourself; I called you to give it to you, but you had already gone." But Uthlakanyana beat him; the iguana was beaten, and had the flute taken away. He killed the iguana, and left him dead.

Uthlakanyana returns to the cannibal, but finds the house burnt, and determines to go back to his mother.

Wa hamba ke, wa buyela ezi-mwini. Wa fika, izimu li nga se ko, nend*h*lu i s' i tshile. Wa *h*lala nje obala, wa *h*lupeka nje. W' esuka lapo, ngokuba ind*h*lu a i se ko; wa hamba nje. Wa za wa ti, "A se ngi ya kumame, loku naku se ngi *h*lupeka."

Then Uthlakanyana set out, and returned to the cannibal. When he arrived, the cannibal was no longer there, and the house was burnt. So he lived in the open air, and was troubled. He left that place because there was no house, and became a wanderer. At length he said, "I will now go back to my mother; for behold I am now in trouble."

Uthlakanyana's arrival at home.

Wa buyela ke ekaya, wa fika kunina. Kwa ti ukuba unina a m bone, loku kwa se ku isikati 'a*h*lukana naye, wa tokoza noku-tokoza unina e bona umntanake e buyile. Wa ti unina, "Sa ku bona, mntanami; ngi ya tokoza ngokubuya kwako. Ku*h*le impela ukuba umntwana, noma 'a*h*lukene nonina isikati eside, a pinde a buyele kunina. Nga se ngi dabu-kile, ngi ti, u ya 'kufa, loku w' emuka u se muncinane; ngi ti, umakazi u ya 'kud*h*la ni na?" Wa ti yena, "O, se ngi buyile,

So he returned home, and came to his mother. When his mother saw him, since it was now a long time that he had separated from her, she greatly rejoiced on seeing her child returned. His mother said, "How are you, my child? I am delighted at your return. It is right indeed that a child, though he has separated from his mother a long time, should again return to her. I have been troubled, saying, you would die, since you departed from me whilst still young; saying, what would you possibly eat?" He replied, "O, now I am returned, my mother;

mame; ngi kumbule wena." Wa ku fiħla ukuħlupeka, ngokuba wa ti, "Uma ngi ti kumame, ngi buye ngokuħlupeka, ku ya 'kuti mħla ng' ona kuye, a ngi kxotshe; a ti, Muka lapa, u isoni esidala; na lapa w' emuka kona, w' emuswa i le 'mikuba." Ngaloko ke wa ku fiħla loko; wa kulisa ukuti, "Ngi buye ngokutanda wena, mame," 'enzela ukuze unina a m tande njalonjalo; ku nga ti ngamħla be pambene a m tuke. Ngokuba Uħlakanyana amakcala 'ke u be wa fiħla ngokwazi ukuba um' e wa veza, a nga patwa kabi.

for I remembered you." He concealed his trouble; for he said, "If I say to my mother, I am come back because of trouble, it will come to pass, when I am guilty of any fault towards her, she will drive me away, and say, Depart hence; you are an old reprobate: and from the place you left, you were sent away for habits of this kind." Therefore he concealed that, and made much of the saying, "I have returned for the love of thee, my mother;" acting thus that his mother might love him constantly, and that it might not be, when he crossed her, that she should curse him. For Uthlakanyana concealed his faults; knowing that if he recounted them, he might be treated badly.

On the following day Uthlakanyana goes to a wedding, and brings home some umdiandiane.

Kwa ti ngangomuso wa hamba, wa ya eketweni; wa fika wa buka iketo: ya sina intombi. Ba kǥeda ukusina, wa goduka. Wa fika entabeni, wa fumana umdiandiane; wa u mba; wa fika ekaya, wa u nika unina, wa ti, "Mame, ngi pekele umdiandiane wami. Ngi sa ya 'kusenga." Wa u peka unina. Wa vutwa, wa ti unina, "Ake ngi zwe uma kunjani." Wa dħla, w' ezwa kumnandi; wa u kǥeda.

On the morrow he went to a marriage-dance: on his arrival he looked at the dance: the damsel danced. When they left off dancing, he went home. He came to a hill, and found some umdiandiane;[38] he dug it up. On his arrival at home, he gave it to his mother, and said, "Mother, cook for me my umdiandiane. I am now going to milk." His mother cooked it; when it was done, his mother said, "Just let me taste what it is like." She eat, and found it nice, and eat the whole.

His mother, having eaten the umdiandiane, redeems her fault by a milk-pail.

Wa fika Ukcaijana, wa ti, "Mame, ngi pe umdiandiane wami." Wa ti unina, "Ngi u dħlile, mntanami." Wa ti, "Ngi pe

Ukcaijana came, and said, "Mother, give me my umdiandiane." His mother said, "I have eaten it, my child." He said,

[38] Also called *Intondo,* an edible tuber, of which the native children are fond. Grown up people rarely eat it, except during a famine. But a hunting party, when exhausted and hungry, is glad to find this plant, which is dug up, and eaten raw. It is preferred, however, when boiled.

umdiandiane wami ; ngokuba ngi u mbe esigqumagqumaneni ; be ngi y' emjadwini." Unina wa m nika umkqengqe.   Wa u tabata, wa hamba nawo.

" Give me my umdiandiane ; for I dug it up on a very little knoll ; I having been to a wedding." His mother gave him a milk-pail. He took it, and went away with it.

Uthlakanyana lends his milk-pail, for which when broken he gets an assagai.

Wa fumana abafana b' alusile izimvu, be sengela ezindengezini. Wa ti, " Mina ni, nanku umkqengqe wami ; sengela ni kuwona ; ni ze ni ngi puzise nami." Ba sengela kuwo. Kwa ti owoku-gcina wa u bulala. Wa ti Ukcai-jana, " Ngi nike ni 'mkqengqe[39] wami : 'mkqengqe wami ngi u nikwe 'mama ; mama e dhle 'mdi-andiane wami : 'mdiandiane wami ngi u mbe 'sigqumagqumaneni ; be ngi y' emjadwini." Ba m nika umkonto. Wa hamba ke.

He fell in with some boys, herding sheep, they milking into broken pieces of pottery. He said, " Take this, here is my milk-pail ; milk into it ; and give me also some to drink." They milked into it. But the last boy broke it. Ukcaijana said, " Give me my milk-pail : my milk-pail my mo-ther gave me ; my mother having eaten my umdiandiane : my um-diandiane I dug up on a very little knoll ; I having been to a wedding." They gave him an assagai. So he departed.

Uthlakanyana lends his assagai, for which when broken he gets an axe.

Wa funyana abanye abafana be dhla isibindi, be si benga ngezim-bengu. Wa ti, " Mina ni, nank' umkonto wami ; benga ni ngawo, ni ze ni ngi pe nami." Ba u ta-bata, ba benga, ba dhla. Kwa ti kwowokupela w' apuka umkonto. Wa ti, " Ngi nike ni 'mkonto wa-mi : 'mkonto wami ngi u nikwe 'bafana ; 'bafana be bulele 'mkqe-ngqe wami : 'mkqengqe wami ngi u piwe 'mama ; 'mama e dhle 'mdi-

He fell in with some other boys, eating liver, they cutting it into slices with the rind of sugar-cane. He said, " Take this, here is my assagai ; cut the slices with it ; and give me some also." They took it, and cut slices and eat. It came to pass that the assagai broke in the hands of the last. He said, " Give me my assagai : my assagai the boys gave me ; the boys having broken my milk pail : my milk-pail my mother gave me ; my mo-ther having eaten my umdiandiane:

[39] It will be observed that when Uthlakanyana offers to lend his property to others he speaks correctly ; but when it has been destroyed, and he demands it back again (that is, according to native custom, *something of greater value* than the thing injured), he speaks incorrectly, by dropping all the initial vowels of the nominal prefixes. By so doing he would excite their compassion by making himself a child, who does not know how to speak properly. But there is also a humour in it, by which foreigners are ridiculed, who frequently speak in this way. The humour is necessarily lost in the translation.

andiane wami : 'mdiandiane wami ngi u mbe 'sigꝗumagꝗumaneni, be ngi y' emjadwini." Ba m nika izembe. Wa hamba.

my umdiandiane I dug up on a very little knoll, I having been to a wedding." They gave him an axe. He departed.

Uthlakanyana lends his axe, for which when broken he gets a blanket.

Wa fumana abafazi be teza izinkuni ; wa ti, " Bomame, ni teza ngani na ?" Ba ti, " A si tezi ngaluto, baba." Wa ti, " Mina ni, nantsi imbazo yami. Teza ni ngayo. Uma se ni kꝗedile, i lete ni kumi." Kwa ti kwowoku- pela y' apuka. Wa ti, " Ngi nike ni 'mbazo yami : 'mbazo yami ngi i nikwe 'bafana ; 'bafana b' apule 'mkonto wami : 'mkonto wami ngi u piwe 'bafana ; 'bafana b' apule 'mkꝗengꝗe wami : 'mkꝗengꝗe wa- mi ngi u nikwe 'mama ; 'mama e dhle 'mdiandiane wami : 'mdiandi- ane wami ngi u mbe 'sigꝗumagꝗu- maneni, be ngi y' emjadwini." Abafazi ba m nika ingubo. Wa i tabata, wa hamba nayo.

He met with some women fetching firewood ; he said, " My mothers, with what are you cut- ting your firewood ? " They said, " We are not cutting it with any- thing, old fellow." He said, "Take this ; here is my axe. Cut with it. When you have finished, bring it to me." It came to pass that the axe broke in the hand of the last. He said, " Give me my axe : my axe the boys gave me ; the boys having broken my assagai : my assagai the boys gave me ; the boys having broken my milk-pail : my milk-pail my mother gave me ; my mother having eaten my um- diandiane : my umdiandiane I dug up on a very little knoll, I having been to a wedding." The women gave him a blanket. He took it, and went on his way with it.

Uthlakanyana lends his blanket, for which when torn he gets a shield.

Wa funyana izinsizwa 'zimbili, zi lele-ze. Wa ti, " Ah, bangane, ni lala-ze na ? A ni nangubo ini ?" Za ti, " Kꝗa." Wa ti, " Yembata ni yami le." Z' embata ke. Za zinge zi donsisana yona, ngokuba incane : ya za ya dabuka. Wa ti kusasa, " Ngi nike ni 'ngubo ya- mi : 'ngubo yami ngi i nikwe 'bafazi ; 'bafazi b' apule 'zembe lami : 'zembe lami ngi li nikwe 'bafana ; 'bafana b' apule 'mkonto wami : 'mkonto wami ngi u nikwe

He found two young men sleep- ing without clothing. He said, " Ah, friends. Do you sleep with- out clothing ? Have you no blan- ket ? " They said, " No." He said, " Put on this of mine." So they put it on. They continually dragged it one from the other, for it was small : at length it tore. He said in the morning, " Give me my blanket : my blanket the women gave me ; the women having broken my axe : my axe the boys gave me ; the boys having broken my assagai : my assagai

'bafana; 'bafana b' apule 'mkꝗengꝗe wami : 'mkꝗengꝗe wami ngi
u nikwe 'mama; 'mama e d*h*le
'mdiandiane wami : 'mdiandiane
wami ngi u mbe 'sigꝗumagꝗumaneni, be ngi y' emjadwini." Za m
nika ihau.   Wa hamba ke.

the boys gave me; the boys having
broken my milk-pail : my milk-pail
my mother gave me; my mother
having eaten my umdiandiane :
my umdiandiane I dug up on a
very little knoll, I having been to
a wedding." They gave him a
shield. So he departed.

*Uthlakanyana lends his shield, for which when broken he receives a
war-assagai.*

Wa fumana amadoda e lwa
nesilo, e nge namahau. Wa ti,
" A ni nahau na?"   A ti, "Kꝗa."
Wa ti, " Tata ni elami leli, ni lwe
ngalo."   Ba li tata ke ; ba si
bulala isilo.   Kwa dabuka um-
ghabelo wokupata.   Wa ti, " Ngi
nike ni 'hau lami : 'hau lami ngi
li nikwe 'zinsizwa ; 'zinsizwa zi
dabule 'ngubo yami : 'ngubo yami
ngi i nikwe 'bafazi ; 'bafazi b' apule
'zembe lami : 'zembe lami ngi li
nikwe 'bafana ; 'bafana b' apule
'mkonto wami : 'mkonto wami ngi
u nikwe 'bafana ; 'bafana b' apule
'mkꝗengꝗe wami : 'mkꝗengꝗe wami ngi u nikwe 'mama ; 'mama e
d*h*le 'mdiandiane wami : 'mdiandiane wami ngi u mbe 'sigꝗumagꝗumaneni, be ngi y' emjadwini."
Ba m nika isinkemba. Wa hamba ke.

He fell in with some men fighting with a leopard, who had no
shields. He said, " Have you no
shield ?"   They said, " No."   He
said, " Take this shield of mine,
and fight with it."   They took it ;
and killed the leopard. The hand-
loop of the shield broke. He said,
" Give me my shield : my shield
the young men gave me ; the
young men having torn my blanket : my blanket the women gave
me ; the women having broken
my axe : my axe the boys gave
me ; the boys having broken my
assagai : my assagai the boys gave
me ; the boys having broken my
milk-pail : my milk-pail my mother
gave me ; my mother having eaten
my umdiandiane : my umdiandiane
I dug up on a very little knoll, I
having been to a wedding." They
gave him a war-assagai. So he
went on his way.

Loko a kw enza ngaso kumbe
ngi nga ni tshela ngesinye 'sikati.

What he did with that, perhaps
I may tell you on another occasion.

USIKULUMI KAHLOKOHLOKO.[40]

The father of Usikulumi has his male children destroyed.

Ku tiwa kwa ku kona inkosi etile; ya zala amadodana amaningi. Kepa ya i nga ku tandi ukuzala amadodana; ngokuba ya i ti, ku ya 'kuti um' amadodana a kule, a i gibe ebukosini bayo. Kwa ku kona izalukazi ezi miselwe ukubulala amadodan' ayo leyo inkosi; ku ti umntwana wesilisa i nga m zala, a be se siwa ezalukazini, ukuba zi m bulale; zi be se zi m bulala. Z' enza njalo kubo bonke abesilisa aba zalwa i leyo inkosi.

It is said there was a certain king; he begat many sons. But he did not like to have sons; for he used to say it would come to pass, when his sons grew up, that they would depose him from his royal power.[41] There were old women appointed to kill the sons of that king; so when a male child was born, he was taken to the old women, that they might kill him; and so they killed him. They did so to all the male children the king had.

Usikulumi is born, and preserved by his mother's love.

Kwa ti ngesinye isikati ya zala indodana enye; unina wa i sa ezalukazini e i godhla. Wa zi nika izalukazi; wa zi ncenga kakulu

He happened on a time to beget another son; his mother took him to the old women, concealing him in her bosom. She made presents to the old women, and besought

---

[40] Usikulumi ka*h*loko*h*loko, "Usikulumi, the son of Uthlokothloko." Usikulumi, "an orator," or great speaker. I*h*loko*h*loko, "a finch." Uthlokothloko may be either his father's name, or an *isibongo* or surname given to himself intended to characterize his power as a great speaker.

[41] "In the Legends of Thebes, Athens, Argos, and other cities, we find the strange, yet common, dread of parents who look on their children as their future destroyers." (*Cox. Tales of Thebes and Argos, p. 9.*) Thus, because Hecuba dreams that she gives birth to a burning torch, which the seers interpret as intimating that the child to be born should bring ruin on the city and land of Troy, the infant Paris is regarded with "cold unloving eyes," and sent by Priam to be exposed on mount Ida. So because the Delphic oracle had warned Laïus that he should be slain by his own child, he commanded his son Œdipus to be left on the heights of Cithæron. In the same manner Acrisius, being warned that he should be slain by his daughter Danae's child, orders her and her son Perseus to be enclosed in an ark, and committed to the sea. But all escape from the death intended for them; all "grow up beautiful and brave and strong. Like Apollo, Bellerophon, and Heracles, they are all slayers of monsters." And "the fears of their parents are in all cases realised." (See Cox, Op. cit., and *Tales of the Gods and Heroes.*) The Legend of Usikulumi has very many curious points in common with these Grecian Myths. There is the father's dread; the child's escape at first by his mother's love; in his retreat, like Paris on the woody Ida, he becomes a herder of cattle, and manifests his kingly descent by his kingly bearing among his fellows; he is discovered by his father's officers, and is again exposed in a forest, in which lives a many-headed monster, which devours men; the monster, however, helps him, and he becomes a king, and returns, like one of the invulnerable heroes, to justify his father's dread, and to give the presentiment a fulfilment.

ukuba zi nga i bulali, zi i se kwoninalume, ngokuba kwa ku indodana a i tanda kakulu. Unina wa zi ncenga ke kakulu izalukazi, wa ti a zi y anyise. Za y anyisa, za i sa kwoninalume wendodana, za i beka lapo kwoninalume.

them earnestly not to kill him, but to take him to his maternal uncle, for it was a son she loved exceedingly. The mother, then, besought the old women very much, and told them to suckle the child. They suckled him, and took him to his uncle, and left him there with his uncle.

He goes with the herdboys, and acts the king.

Kwa ti ekukuleni kwayo ya ba insizwana, ya tanda ukwalusa kwoninalume ; ya landela abafana bakwoninalume ; ba y azisa, be i dumisa. Kwa ti ekwaluseni kwabo ya ti kubafana, "Keta ni amatshe amakulu, si wa tshise." Ba wa keta, ba w enza inkqwaba. Ya ti, "Keta ni itole eliɦle, si li ɦlabe." Ba li keta emɦlambini a ba w alusileyo. Ya t' a ba li ɦlinze ; ba li ɦlinza, b' osa inyama yalo, be jabula. Abafana ba ti, "W enza ni ngaloko na ?" Ya ti, "Ngi y' azi mina e ngi kw enzayo."

It came to pass when he had become a young man that he liked to herd the cattle at his uncle's, and followed the boys of his uncle's kraal ; they respected and honoured him. It came to pass, when they were herding, he said to the boys, "Collect large stones, and let us heat them."[42] They collected them, and made a heap. He said, "Choose also a fine calf, and let us kill it." They selected it from the herd they were watching. He told them to skin it ; they skinned it, and roasted its flesh joyfully. The boys said, "What do you mean by this ?" He said, "I know what I mean."

He is seen and recognised by his father's officers.

Kwa ti ngolunye usuku b' alusile, kwa hamba izinduna zikayise, zi tunywa ngu ye ; za ti, "U ng' ubani na ?" Ka ya ze ya zi tshela. Za i tata, zi nga balisi, zi ti, "Lo 'mntwana u fana nenkosi yetu." Za hamba nayo, zi i sa kuyise.

It happened one day when they were herding, the officers of his father were on a journey, being sent by him ; they said, "Who are you ?" He did not tell them. They took him, without doubting, saying, "This child is like our king." They went with him, and took him to his father.

[42] It is not at the present time the custom among the natives of these parts to bake meat by means of heated stones, which is so common among some other people, the Polynesians for instance. We should therefore conclude either that this Legend has been derived from other people, or that it arose among the Zulus when they had different customs from those now existing among them.

The officers make him known to his father for a reward.

Kwa ti ekufikeni kwazo kuyise, za ti kuyise, "Uma si ku tshela indaba en*h*le, u ya 'ku si nika ni na?" Wa ti uyise wayo indodana ezinduneni, "Ngi ya 'ku ni nika izinkomo ezi-nombala,[43] ezi-nombala o te wa ti, noma o te wa ti, noma o te wa ti." Z' ala izinduna, za ti, "K*q*a; a si zi tandi." Kwa ku kona ik*q*abi elimnyama lezinkabi e zi gud*h*le lona. Wa ti, "Ni tanda ni na?" Za ti izinduna, "Ik*q*abi elimnyama." Wa zi nikela. Za m tshela ke, za ti, "Ku te ekuhambeni kwetu sa bona umntwana o fana nowako." Nangu uyise wa i bona leyo 'ndodana ukuba eyake impela; wa ti, "Owa mu pi umfazi na?" Ba ti aba m aziyo ukuba wa m fi*h*la, ba ti, "Okabani, umfazi wako, nkosi."

When they came to his father, they said to him, "If we tell you good news, what will you give us?" His father said to the officers, "I will give you cattle of such a colour, or of such a colour, or of such a colour." The officers refused, saying, "No; we do not like these." There was a selected herd of black oxen, at which they hinted. He said, "What do you wish?" The officers said, "The herd of black oxen." He gave them. And so they told him, saying, "It happened in our journeying that we saw a child which is like one of yours." So then the father saw that it was indeed his son, and said, "Of which wife is he the child?" They who knew that she concealed the child said, "The daughter of So-and-so, your wife, your Majesty."

The king is angry, and commands him to be taken to the great forest, and left there.

Wa buta isizwe, e tukutele, wa ti, a ba i se kude. Sa butana isizwe; kwa suka unina futi nodade wabo. Wa ti, a ba i mukise, ba ye 'ku i beka kude ku*h*lati-kulu. Ngokuba kwa kwa ziwa ukuba ku kona isilwane esikulu kulelo '*h*lati, oku tiwa si d*h*la abantu, esi namakanda amaningi.

He assembled the nation, being very angry, and told them to take his son to a distance. The nation assembled; his mother and sister also came. The king told them to take away his son, and to go and put him in the great forest. For it was known there was in that forest a great many-headed monster which ate men.

His mother and sister accompany him to the great forest, and leave him there alone.

Ba hamba be ya lapo. Abaningi a ba finyelelanga; ba dinwa,

They set out for that place. Many did not reach it; they be-

---

[43] It was formerly, and is still, a custom among the Zulus to separate their oxen into herds according to the colour; and the different herds were named accordingly. Thus :—*Umdubu*, the dun-coloured; *intenjane*, dun with white spots; *umtoto*, red; *inkone*, with a white line along the spine; *impemvu*, black with white muzzle, or white along the belly, &c.

ba buyela emuva. Kwa hamba unina, nodade wabo, nendodana, bobatatu. Unina wa ti, "Ngi nge mu shiye elubala; ngo ya, ugi m beke kona lapo ku tiwe, ka ye kona." Ba ya ku*h*lati-kulu; ba fika, ba ngena e*h*latini. Ba ya 'ku m beka etsheni elikulu eli pakati kwe*h*lati. Wa *h*lala koua. Ba m shiya, ba buyela emva. Wa *h*lala e yedwa pezu kwetshe.

came tired, and turned back again. The mother and sister and the king's son went, those three. The mother said, "I cannot leave him in the open country; I will go and place him where he is ordered to go." They went to the great forest; they arrived, and entered the forest, and placed him on a great rock which was in the midst of the forest. He sat down on it. They left him, and went back. He remained alone on the top of the rock.

Usikulumi is aided by the many-headed monster, and becomes great.

Kwa ti ngesinye isikati sa fika isilwane esi-'makanda-'maningi, si vela emanzini. Lapo kuleso 'silwane ku pelele izinto zonke. Sa i tata leyo 'nsizwa; a si i bulala-nga; sa i tata, sa i pa ukud*h*la, ya za ya kulupala. Kwa ti i s' i kulupele, i nga sa dingi 'luto, i nesizwe esiningi, e ya piwa i so leso 'silwane esi-'makanda-'maningi (ngokuba kuleso 'silwane kwa ku pelele izinto zonke nokud*h*la na-bantu), ya tanda ukuhambela ku-yise. Ya hamba nesizwe esikulu, se ku inkosi.

It came to pass one day that the many-headed monster came, it coming out of the water. That monster possessed everything. It took the young man; it did not kill him; it took him, and gave him food, until he became great. It came to pass when he had become great, and no longer want-ed anything, having also a large natiou subject to him, which the many-headed monster had given him (for that monster possessed all things, and food and men), he wished to visit his father. He went with a great nation, he being now a king.

He visits his uncle, and is received with great joy.

Ya ya konalume; ya fika kona-lume; kodwa unalume a ka y aza-nga. Ya ngena end*h*lini; kodwa abantu bakonalume ba be nga y azi nabo. Ya ti induna yayo ya ya 'kukcela inkomo kunalume; ya ti induna, "U ti Usikulumi ka*h*loko*h*loko, mu pe inkomo en*h*le, a d*h*le." Uninalume wa li zwa lelo 'bizo ukuti Usikulumi ka*h*loko-*h*lolo, w' etuka, wa ti, "Ubani?"

He went to his uncle; but his uncle did not know him. He went into the house; but neither did his uncle's people know him. His officer went to ask a bullock of the uncle; he said, "Usiku-lumi, the son of Uthlokothloko, says, give him a fine bullock, that he may eat." When the uncle heard the name of Usikulumi, the son of Uthlokothloko, he started, and said, "Who?" The officer

Ya ti, "Inkosi." Uninalume wa puma ukuya 'ku m bona. Wa m bona ukuti ngu ye Usikulumi kaḥlokoḥloko. Wa jabula kakulu; wa ti, "Yi, yi, yi!" e ḥlab' umkosi ngokujabula, wa ti, "U fikile Usikulumi kaḥlokoḥloko!" Kwa butwa isizwe sonke sakonalume. Unalume wa m nika iḥlepu lezinkabi ngokujabula okukulu; wa ti, "Nazi izinkabi zako." Kw' enziwa ukudḥla okukulu; ba dḥla, ba jabula ngoku m bona, ngokuba ba be ng' azi ukuti ba ya 'kubuya ba m bone futi.

replied, "The king." The uncle went out to see him. He saw it was Usikulumi, the son of Uthlokothloko, indeed. He rejoiced greatly, and said; "Yi, yi, yi!" sounding an alarm for joy, and said, "Usikulumi, the son of Uthlokothloko, has come!" The whole tribe of his uncle was assembled. His uncle gave him a part of a herd of oxen for his great joy, and said, "There are your oxen." A great feast was made; they eat and rejoiced because they saw him, for they did not know that they should ever see him again.

He reaches his father's kingdom; his father is grieved at his arrival, and tries to kill him.

Wa dḥlula, wa ya kubo kuyise. Ba m bona ukuba ngu ye Usikulumi kaḥlokoḥloko. Ba m bikela uyise; ba ti, "Nantsi indodana yako, owa i laḥla kuḥlati-kulu." Wa dabuka nokudabuka okukulu. Wa buta isizwe sonke; wa ti, ka si ḥlome izikali zaso. Ba butana abantu bake bonke. Wa ti uyise, "Ka bulawe Usikulumi kaḥlokoḥloko." W' ezwa loko Usikulumi kaḥlokoḥloko, wa puma wa ya ngapaudḥle. Kwa butana isizwe sonke. Wa ti uyise, "Ka ḥlatshwe ngomkonto." W' ema obala, wa ti Usikulumi kaḥlokoḥloko, "Ngi kcibe ni, ni nga zisoli."[44] Wa tsho loko ngokutemba ukuba ka yi 'kufa; noma be m kciba kakulu,

He passed onward, and went to his father's. They saw that it was Usikulumi, the son of Uthlokothloko. They told his father, saying, "Behold your son, whom you cast away in the great forest." He was troubled exceedingly. He collected the whole nation, and told them to take their weapons. All his people assembled. The father said, "Let Usikulumi, the son of Uthlokothloko, be killed." Usikulumi heard it; and went outside. The whole nation assembled. His father commanded him to be stabbed with a spear. He stood in an open space, and said, "Hurl your spears at me to the utmost." He said this because he was confident he should not die; although they hurled their spears at him a long time, even till

[44] *Ni nga zisoli,* "without self-reproof."—This saying is used to give a person liberty to do exactly as he wishes; *e. g.*, if it is said, *Hamba u yo'zikelela umbila ensimini yami,* "Go and gather mealies for yourself in my garden," the person addressed will not consider himself at liberty to take to the utmost of his wishes, but will gather a few. But if the words *u nga zisoli* are added, he will understand that no limit is put by the owner to his wishes.

noma ku ze ku tshone ilanga, ka yi 'kufa. W' ema nje, kwa za kwa tshona ilanga. Ba m kɔiba be nge namandʰla oku m bulala. Ngokuba wa e namandʰla okuba a nga fi ; ngokuba leso 'silwane sa m kɕinisa, ngokuba sa s' azi ukuba u ya kubo ; s' azi ukuti uyise ka i fun' indodana ; s' azi ngokwaso ukuti ba ya 'ku m bulala Usikulumi kaʰlokoʰloko ; sa m kɕinisa.

the sun set, he should not die. He merely stood, until the sun set. They hurled their spears at him, without having power to kill him.[45] For he had the power of not dying ; for that monster strengthened him, for it knew that he was going to his people, and that his father did not want his son ; it knew, by its own wisdom, that they would kill Usikulumi, the son of Uthlokothloko, and gave him strength.

[45] There are two Legends in which we find the account of an invulnerable hero, against whom the assagais of armies are thrown in vain—this of Usikulumi kathlokothloko, and the other that of Ulangalasenzantsi. It is remarkable how wide spread Legends of this kind are. The invulnerability of the good Balder, the beloved of the gods, is ensured by his mother exacting an oath from all created things, not to injure her son. "When the gods had thus, as they imagined, rendered all safe, they were accustomed, by way of sport, to let Balder stand forth at their assembly for all the Æsir to shoot at him with the bow, or to strike or throw stones at him, as nothing caused him any harm." But the insignificant mistletoe was omitted. And the bright god is killed by the mistletoe, through the treachery of Loki. *(Thorpe's Northern Mythology. Vol. I., pp. 72, 74.)*

> "So on the floor lay Balder, dead ; and round
> Lay thickly strown, swords, axes, darts, and spears,
> Which all the gods in sport had idly thrown
> At Balder, whom no weapon pierced or clave ;
> But in his breast stood fixed the fatal bough
> Of mistletoe, which Lok, the accuser, gave
> To Hoder, and unwitting Hoder threw :
> 'Gainst that alone had Balder's life no charm."

(Max Müller. Comparative Mythology. Oxford Essays. 1856, p. 66.) Whether such a Legend arose spontaneously all over the world, or whether, having had an origin in some poetical imagining, it has travelled from a common centre, and become modified in its journeying in accordance with place and circumstances, it is not easy to determine. The possibility of a hero rendering himself invulnerable by medicinal applications, is not only quite within the compass of a Zulu's imagination, but appears to be something that would very naturally suggest itself to him. At the present time he has his *intelezi*, plants of various kinds, by which he can ensure correctness of aim : his assagai flies to the mark not because of his skill, but because his arm has been anointed. And the doctors medicate a troop before going to battle, to render it invulnerable to the weapons of the enemy. But together with the application of their medicines they give the soldiers certain rules of conduct ; and of course all that fall in battle are killed because they neglected the prescribed observances !—So also in the Polynesian Legends there are two instances of invulnerability produced by magic. Maui transforms himself into a pigeon, and visits his parents ; "the chiefs and common people alike catch up stones to pelt him, but to no purpose, for but by his own choice no one could hit him." *(Sir George Grey. Polynesian Mythology, p. 30.)* And Rupe in like manner transforms himself into a pigeon, and flies in search of his sister Hinauri to Tinirau's people, in the island of Motu-tapu. They try in vain both to kill it with spears and to noose it. *(Id., p. 86.)*

Usikulumi kills all his father's people, and departs with the spoil.

B' a*h*luleka uku m kciba. Wa ti, "N' a*h*lulekile na?" Ba ti, "Se s' a*h*lulekile." Wa tata umkonto, wa ba *h*laba bonke; ba. fa bonke. Wa d*h*la izinkomo. W' emuka nempi yake kulelo 'lizwe nezinkomo zonke. Nonina wa hamba naye, nodade wabo, e se inkosi.

They were unable to pierce him with their spears. He said, "Are you worsted?" They said, "We are now worsted." He took a spear, and stabbed them all, and they all died. He took possession of the cattle; and departed with his army from that country with all the cattle. His mother too went with him and his sister, he being now a king.

* * *

UZEMBENI; [46]

OR,

USIKULUMI'S COURTSHIP.

* * *

Uzembeni, having destroyed all other people, wishes to eat her own children, but finds the flesh bitter.

UZEMBENI umfazi omkulu. Wa zala intombi zambili; kepa wa d*h*la abantu kulelo 'zwe lapa a ye kona, wa za wa ba k*q*eda, e ba d*h*la nezinyamazane; a bulale umuntu kanye nenyamazane; a peke inyama yomuntu neyenyamazane 'ndawo nye. Ku te ukuba ba pele abantu ba ti nya, kwa sala yena nentombi zake ezimbili. Intombi zake za zi iduma ezizweni, zi dume ukuba 'n*h*le. Enye intombi yake (kwa ti ngokupela kwabantu, e ba k*q*edile), wa i bamba intombi yake, wa i kipa isi*h*lati sanganxanye; wa si peka, wa si d*h*la: sa baba; ka be sa tanda uku i k*q*edela, ngokuba inyama yayo ya m *h*lupa ngokubaba: wa mangala, ka k*q*o-

UZEMBENI was a great woman. She had two daughters; but she devoured the men of the country where she lived, until she had destroyed them all: she ate men and game; she killed man together with deer; and boiled the flesh of man and the flesh of deer together. It came to pass that, when men were utterly consumed, there were left herself and her two daughters. Her daughters were celebrities among the tribes, on account of their beauty. One of her daughters (it happened because there were no more men, she having destroyed them) she caught, and tore off her cheek on one side, and boiled it and ate it: it was bitter; she no longer wished to eat her up, because her flesh annoyed her by its bitterness: she won-

[46] Uzembeni, "Axe-bearer," or Uzwanide, "Long-toe."

ndanga uma ku ini loku, ukuba inyama i babe na? Ngaloko ke intombi zake za sinda kuye ngokubaba loko.

dered, and did not understand why the flesh was bitter. Therefore her daughters escaped from her through that bitterness.

Usikulumi comes to court Uzembeni's daughters.

Kwa fika insizwa, umntwana wenkosi. Igama laleyo 'nsizwa Usikulumi, 'eza 'uketa intombi enhle kulezo 'ntombi. Wa fika emini, Uzembeni e nge ko, e yozingela. Elinye igama lake ku tiwa Uzwanide; ngokuba izwani lake la li lide kakulu; i lona a be bonakala ngalo e sa vela, ku tunqa izintuli; ku be ku ti e nga ka veli, ku be se ku vela izintuli, z' enziwa uzwani lwake; ngokuba lu be lu fika kukqala, lapa e ya kona Uzwanide. Ku te ke ukuba a fike Usikulumi; nembala, wa zi fumana intombi lezo zombili; wa bona nembala ukuba zinhle. Wa zi tanda, naye za m tanda; ngokuba wa umntwana wenkosi, e bukeka. Kodwa za m kalela kakulu izinyembezi, zi ti, "A u fiki 'ndawo lapa. Si ya hlupeka; a s' azi uma si za 'u ku beka pi, loku umame u dhla 'bantu. Nati u si bona nje si ya hlupeka." Ya t' enye, "A u bheke isihlati sami. U yena nje umame! A s' azi una si za 'ku ku beka pi."

There came a young man, the child of a king. The name of the youth was Usikulumi; he came to select a pretty girl from those girls. He came by day, when Uzembeni was not there, she having gone to hunt. Another of her names is Long-toe; for her toe was very long; it was that by which she was recognised, as she was coming in sight, the dust being raised; and before she appeared, the dust appeared, being raised by her toe; for it came first to the place where Long-toe was going. So when Usikulumi arrived, he found indeed the two damsels. He saw that truly they were beautiful. He loved them, and they loved him also; for he was a king's son, and good-looking. But they wept many tears on his account, saying, "You have come nowhere[47] by coming here. We are troubled; we do not know where we can put you; for our mother eats men. And as for us you see us in nothing but trouble." One of them said, "Just look at my cheek. It is my very mother![48] We do not know where we shall put you."

[47] *A u fiki 'ndawo,* "You have come nowhere," lit., "You have not come to a place," that is, you have come to a place where you will find no good, and may find evil. It is said when there is famine, or illness, or danger in a place. So, *A ngi suki 'ndawo,* "I come from nowhere," that is, from a place where there was no pleasure nor profit; as when a man has left an inhospitable kraal, where he has not been provided with food. So, *A u yi 'ndawo,* "You are going nowhere."

[48] Telling Usikulumi that the injury of the cheek *is her mother,* that is, her mother's doing, as though she was ever present in the injury. So also of property or benefits; the natives point to the property or gifts, and say, *U yena lo, na lo, na lo,* "That is he, and he, and he," instead of his.

The girls dig a hole in the house, and conceal him in it.

Ku njalonjalo Usikulumi e fika lapo ezintombini, u fika yedwa. Ekaya wa puma e hamba nom-*h*lambi wake wezinja ; kodwa wa zi shiya em*h*langeni. Intombi z' enza ikcebo lokuti, "Uma si ti, ka hambe, Uzwanide u ya 'ku m landa ;" z' emba umgodi pakati kwend*h*lu, za m faka, za buya za fulela, za *h*lala pezu kwawo.

To return ;[49] Usikulumi came to the damsels alone. He left home with his pack of dogs ; but he left them in a bed of reeds. The girls devised a plan, saying, "If we tell him to depart, Long-toe will pursue him ;" they dug a pit in the house, and put him in, and again covered it up, and sat over it.

Uzembeni returns, and scents the game.

Lwa vela utuli ekumukeni kwe-langa. Za ti, "Nango ke e s' eza." Lwa fika uzwani kukqala, wa landela emva kwalo. U t' e sa fika wa *h*leka yedwa, wa *h*leka, wa bukuzeka, e ti, "Eh, eh ! end*h*lini yami lapa nam*h*la nje ku nuka zantungwana. Banta bami, n' enze njani na ? Leli 'punga li vela pi na ?" Wa ngena, wa *h*leka yedwa, e ba bansa, e ti, "Banta bami, ku kona ni lapa end*h*lini ?" Izintombi za ti, "Yiya ! musa uku si fundekela ; a s' azi uma uto si lu tata pi." Wa ti, "Ake ngi zifunele ke, banta bami." Za ti, "A s' azi no za 'ku ku funa uma

Towards sunset the dust appeared. They said, "Lo, she is now coming." The toe came first ; she came after it. As soon as she came, she laughed to herself ; she laughed, and rolled herself on the ground, saying, "Eh, eh ! in my house here to-day there is a delicious odour. My children, what have you done ? Whence comes this odour ?"[50] She entered the house ; she laughed to herself, patting them, and saying, "My children, what is there here in the house ?" The girls said, "Away ! don't bother us ; we do not know where we could get anything." She said, "Just let me look for myself, my children." They said, "We do not know even what you want to find ; for there is just

[40] *Ku njalonjalo.*—A mode of expression by which a subject interrupted is again taken up. *Revenons à nos moutons.* It is also used with the meaning, *Under these circumstances.*

[50] Although there are here no corresponding words, one cannot fail to be reminded of the "Fee fo fum, I smell the blood of an Englishman," &c. The gigantic ogress here, as in the Legends of other countries, scents out the prey, and longs to be tearing human flesh.—So when Maui wished to gain possession of the "jaw-bone of his great ancestress Muri-ranga-whenua, by which the great enchantments could be wrought," and had approached her for the purpose, she "sniffed the breeze" in all directions ; and when she perceived "the scent of a man," called aloud, "I know from the smell wafted here to me by the breeze that somebody is close to me." (*Grey's Polynesian Mythology, p.* 34.) And in the Legend of Tawhaki, the scout of the Ponaturi, a race who inhabited a country underneath the waters, on entering the house where Tawhaki and Karihi were concealed, "lifted up his nose and turned sniffing all round inside the house. (*Id., p.* 64. See also *Campbell, Op. cit. Vol. I., pp.* 9, 252.)

u za 'ufuna ni; ku nge ko 'luto njena." Wa ti, "Ake ni suke pela, ngi zifunele." Za ti, "A si yi 'kusuka. Si ng' azi 'luto tina. Yenza o ku tandayo nje. A s' azi uma u za 'kuti ni kitina, loku naku se wa s' ona, se si nje." Ya tsho i m kombisa isiẖlati sayo a si dẖlako. Wa dela, wa lala.

nothing here." She said, "Just move then, that I may seek for myself." They said, "We will not get up. We know of nothing, for our parts. Just do as you will. We do not know what you will do to us, since you have already injured us, and we are now as we are." She said this, pointing to her cheek, which she had eaten. She gave up, and went to sleep.

Usikulumi runs away with one of Uzembeni's daughters.

Kwa sa kusasa, wa puma, wa ya 'uzingela. U t' e sa puma za bona ukuba lwa pela utuli, u se tshonile. Za m kipa Usikulumi. Ya t' enye, "A si hambe." Enye ya ti, "O, mnta kababa, hamba wena. Mina ngi nge hambe nawe, ngi hambe ngi ku ẖleba kulo. U ngi bona uma se ngi nje; umame wa ng' ona. Sa u hamba wedwa. Mina se ngi ẖlalele ukuba Uzwanide a ze a ngi kꝗede."

In the morning she went out to hunt. As soon as she was gone,[51] they saw the dust cease, she having gone over the hill. They took out Usikulumi. One said, "Let us go." The other said, "O, child of my father, do you go. I cannot go with you to be a disgrace to you in his presence. You see how I am; my mother injured me. Do you go alone. I shall stay, that Long-toe may make an end of me."

They travel night and day, hoping to escape Uzembeni.

Ya hamba ke nosikulumi; la za la tshona be hamba. Wa ya ngasemẖlangeni, e landa izinja zake: wa zi tata; za hamba naye. Kwa za kwa ẖlwa. Kwa sa be hamba, be nꝗenile ukuti, "Uma si lala, u ze 'u si funyana. A si hambe imini nobusuku, ku ze ku se; kumbe si nga m shiya."

So she went with Usikulumi; they travelled till the sun set. He went by the way of the bed of reeds to fetch his dogs: he took them; and they went with him. At length it became dark. In the morning they were still journeying; they travelled in fear, saying, "If we sleep, she will come up with us. Let us go day and night, until the morning; perhaps we shall leave her behind."

[51] This is intended to intimate the rapidity of her motion. She went so rapidly that the dust raised by her progress ceased to be visible, as it were, whilst she was in the act of leaving the house; *e sa puma*, "as she was going out." She quitted the house, and *at once* disappeared over a distant hill.

Uzembeni pursues them, and they ascend a lofty tree.

Wa fika ekaya Uzwanide. Wa fumana intombi yake inye. Ka be sa buza wa se d*h*lula, ukuti, "Umntanami u ye nga pi?" Wa hamba kwa sa. Ku te emini ba lu bona utuli, Usikulumi nentombi. Ya 'tsho intombi kusikulumi, ya ti, "Nango ke Uzwanide, u yena lowa ke; u se fikile. Si za 'kuya nga pi ke?" Ba se be bona umkoba omude; ba gijima, ba kwela kuwo; izinja za sala ngapantsi.

Long-toe came home: she found one daughter only. Without hesitation she went forward, saying, "Where has my child gone?" She went until the morning. At noon Usikulumi and the damsel saw the dust. She said to Usikulumi, "Behold Long toe; that is she yonder; she has now come up with us. Where can we go?" And they saw a lofty yellow-wood tree; they ran, and climbed into it; the dogs remained at its foot.

Uzembeni attempts to hew down the tree, and is torn in pieces by the dogs.

Wa fika Uzembeni; umfazi o namand*h*la kakulu. Wa fika nembazo yake. Wa bheka pezulu, wa ba bona. Ka be sa buza ngembazo emtini; wa ba se u ya u gaula ngamand*h*la umuti, izinja za se zi m luma; wa u gaula ngamand*h*la. Ku te uma u zwakale ukuteta umuti, se w apuka, izinja za m bamba ngamand*h*la: enye ya m n*q*uma in*h*loko, nenye umkono; ezinye za m kipa izito zonke, zi ya 'ku m la*h*la lapaya kude; ezinye za donsa amatumbu.

Long-toe came. She was a very powerful woman. She came with her axe. She looked up, and saw them. Without hesitation she applied her axe to the tree; and when she was now hewing the tree with all her might, the dogs bit her: she cut it with might. And when the tree was heard to creak, it now breaking, the dogs seized her firmly: one tore off her head, another her arm; others tore off her limbs, and took them away to a distance; others dragged away her intestines.

The tree becomes sound, and Uzembeni comes to life again.

Wa *h*luma umuti masinyane, wa ba njengokuk*q*ala. Wa buya Uzembeni wa vuka; za *h*langana zonke izito zake; wa vuka, wa tata imbazo, wa gaula ngamand*h*la

The tree grew immediately, and resumed its original condition.[52] Uzembeni came to life again; all her limbs came together; she rose up and took her axe, and hewed

[52] A similar thing is related of a magical tree in the Legend of Itshe-likatunjambili, given below.—In the Legend of "The King of Lochlin's Three Daughters," the widow's eldest son, who chose "the big bannock with his mother's cursing in preference to a little bannock with her blessing," went into the forest to cut timber to build a ship. "A great Uruisg [or Urisk, a "lubberly supernatural"] came out of the water, and she asked a part of his bannock." He refused. "He began cutting wood, and every tree he cut would be on foot again; and so he was till the night came." *(Campbell's Highland Tales. Vol.*

umuti ; ku te uma u zwakale u teta, izinja za buya za m nquma in*h*loko nezito ; kwa ba i leyo ya gijima nesiuye, i ya emfuleni edwaleni, zonke z' enza njalo ; za tata izimbokondo, za gaya izito, z' enza impupu.

the tree with might ; and when the tree was heard to creak, the dogs again tore off her head and limbs, and each went with one to the river, to a rock : all did the same ; they took large pebbles, and ground her limbs to powder.

Uzwanide having been ground to powder, Usikulumi escapes.

Wa sala w' e*h*la Usikulumi nentombi emtini ; ba gijima, b' emuka, be ya kubokasikulumi. Za i tela emanzini inyama kazembeni, i se impupu. Za hamba ke, zi landela Usikulumi. Wa fa ke Uzembeni, wa pela. Wa fika ekaya Usikulumi kubo, kwa kalwa isililo. Kwa *h*latshwa izinkomo, kwa jabulwa kakulu, be ti, "Le 'ntombi en*h*le kangaka u i tata pi na ? Sa si nga sa tsho uma u se kona. Sa se si ti, u file."

Whereupon Usikulumi and the damsel descended from the tree, and ran away to Usikulumi's people. The dogs cast Uzembeni's flesh, when ground to powder, into the water; and then they followed Usikulumi. So Uzembeni died ; and Usikulumi came home to his people ; they made a funeral lamentation.[53] Then they killed oxen and rejoiced greatly, saying, "This so beautiful damsel, where did you get her ? We thought you were no longer in the land of the living. We thought you were dead."

I., pp. 236, 237.) So Rata "went into the forest, and having found a very tall tree, quite straight thoughout its entire length, he felled it, and cut off its noble branching top, intending to fashion the trunk into a canoe ; and all the insects which inhabit trees, and the spirits of the forest, were very angry at this, and as soon as Rata had returned to the village at evening, when his day's work was ended, they all came and took the tree, and raised it up again, and the innumerable multitude of insects, birds, and spirits, who are called 'The offspring of Hakuturi,' worked away at replacing each little chip and shaving in its proper place, and sang aloud their incantations as they worked ; this was what they sang with a confused noise of various voices :—

    'Fly together, chips and shavings,
    Stick ye fast together,
    Hold ye fast together ;
    Stand upright again, O tree ! ' "

This occurs again and again, until Rata watches, and catches one of them. They tell him he had no right to fell the forest god. He is silent. They tell him to go home, and promise to build the boat for him. *(Sir George Grey's Polynesian Mythology, p.* 111—114.)

[53] If a person who has disappeared for some time, and is supposed to be dead, unexpectedly returns to his people, it is the custom first to salute him by making a funeral lamentation. They then make a great feast.—A similar custom appears to prevail among the Polynesians. Thus Rehua is represented as making his lamentation on the approach of Rupe ; and Rupe appears to reply by a lamentation. *(Grey's Polynesian Mythology, p.* 84.) So "Ngatoro-i-rangi wept over his niece, and then they spread food before the travellers." *(Id., p.* 169.) On Hatupatu's return, who was supposed to have been slain by his brothers, "the old people began to weep with a loud voice ; and Hatupatu said, 'Nay, nay ; let us cry with a gentle voice, lest my brethren who slew me should hear.'" *(Id., p.* 189.) So all the people weep over Maru-tuahu on his arrival. *(Id., p.* 252.)

ANOTHER VERSION OF A PORTION OF THE TALE.

A swallow meets with Usikulumi, and gives him a charm.

Kwa ti Usikulumi e hamba e ya kwazembeni e ya 'ukǫoma intombi, e ng' azi 'luto ngozembeni, 'azi intombi lezo, e ku tiwa zin*h*le; wa hamba ke, wa *h*langana nenkwenjane; ya ti kuye inkwenjane, "Sikulumi, lapa u ya kona a u yi 'ndawo; ku yi 'ku*h*lala ka*h*le. U ya 'ulondolozwa ubani na? O, ngi *h*lin*h*le mina; isikumba sami u si tunge, u si fake ezindukwini zako lapa, ukuze ngi ku tshele uma Uzembeni e za 'ku ku d*h*la." Wa i bamba ke inkwenjane, wa i *h*lin*h*la, wa si tunga isikumba sayo, wa si faka ezindukwini.

It happened that as Usikulumi was on his way to Uzembeni to court her daughters, he knowing nothing of Uzembeni, knowing only about the damsels, which were said to be beautiful, he journeyed and met with a swallow. The swallow said to him, "Usikulumi, there is no place where you are going; you will not be prosperous there. Who will be your protector? O, skin me, and sow up my skin, and put it on your rods, that I may tell you when Uzembeni is coming to eat you." So he caught the swallow, and skinned it, and sewed its skin, and put it on his rods.

The swallow's skin warns Usikulumi of danger.

Wa fika kona kwazembeni. Ku ti ukuba a fike Uzembeni, isikumba leso sa m tshela Usikulumi, sa ti, "Nanku ke Uzembeni." Ku te ebusuku, lapa se ku lelwe end*h*lini kazembeni, Usikulumi e lele nganxanye kwend*h*lu; kwa ti ebusuku Uzembeni wa vuka, wa nyonyoba, e ya 'ubamba Usikulumi; isikumba sa m vusa Usikulumi, sa ti, "Vuka ke manje. Nanku Uzembeni e se fikile." Wa vuka ke Usikulumi. Uzembeni wa buyela emuva; ngokuba u tanda uku m zuma e lele.

He arrived at Uzembeni's. When Uzembeni came, the skin told Usikulumi, saying, "There is Uzembeni." And in the night, when they lay down in Uzembeni's house, Usikulumi sleeping on one side of the house, it came to pass that in the night Uzembeni awoke, and stole stealthily, she going to lay hold of Usikulumi; the skin awoke him, and said, "Awake now. Lo! Uzembeni is at hand." So Usikulumi awoke; and Uzembeni went back again; for she wished to take him by surprise.

The swallow's skin tells him to make his escape.

Kwa za kwa sa; and' uba isikumba si m tshele Usikulumi, si ti, "Muka ke manje; ngokuba Uzembeni u se mukile." Wa puma ke nentombi leyo. E se hamba ke, e baleka, e balekela Uzembeni, wa za wa fika endaweni e nomuti. Sa ti isikumba, "Kwela kulo 'muti, ngi ku londoloze kona.

At length it dawned, whereupon the skin said to Usikulumi, "Depart now; for Uzembeni has already set out." So he departed with the damsel. So he went and fled from Uzembeni, until he came to a place where there was a tree. The skin said, "Climb into this tree; I will preserve you there.

Izinja zi za 'kulwa naye Uzembeni, zi m bulale." Wa kwela ke em-tini. Wa fika ke Uzembeni, wa u gaula. Kwa ti lapa se u za 'ku-wa, izinja za m kcita. Wa buya wa vuka. Ngemuva za m kcita nya. Isikumba sa ti, " Ye*h*la manje. Uzembeni u se file. Ko-dwa u ya 'kubuy' a vuke. Ye*h*la, u hambe ngamand*h*la."

The dogs will fight with Uzembeni, and kill her." He climbed into the tree. Uzembeni came, and hewed the tree. When it was about to fall, the dogs tore her in pieces. She came to life again. After that they utterly tore her in pieces, and scattered the frag-ments. The skin said, "Descend now. Uzembeni is now dead; but she will come to life again. Descend, and go speedily."

Uzembeni comes to life again.

Nembala Uzembeni wa sala wa vuka, loku izinja zi be zi m gaye, za m enza impupu, za m tela ema-nzini. Wa sala wa *h*langana, wa vuka. Wa vuka be nga se ko. Wa funa ; ka be sa ba tola. Wa ḍela, wa goduka.

And truly Uzembeni afterwards came to life, although the dogs had ground her to powder, and thrown her into the water. She again joined piece to piece, and came to life again.[54] She came to life again, when they were no longer on the tree. She sought them, but did not find them any more. So she gave up, and went home.[55]

[54] So Heitsi Kabib, a very different character, however, from Uzwanide, "died several times, and came to life again." (*Bleek's Hottentot Fables and Tales, p.* 76.)

[55] In Basile's *Pentamerone* we find a tale which has some points of resem-blance with this. Petrosinella is a beautiful damsel in the power of an ogress, who confines her in a tower, to which access can be gained only by a little win-dow, through which she ascends and descends by means of Petrosinella's hair ! A young prince discovers her in her retreat, and reaches her in her tower by the same means as the ogress, the ogress having been sent to sleep by poppy-juice. But a neighbour discovers the lovers' interviews, and tells the ogress. She says in reply that Petrosinella cannot escape, "as she has laid a spell on her, so that unless she has in her hand the three gallnuts which are in a rafter in the kitchen, it would be labour lost to attempt to get away." Petrosinella overhears their conversation ; gets possession of the gallnuts ; escapes with the prince from the tower by means of a rope-ladder ; the neighbour alarms the ogress, who at once pursues them "faster than a horse let loose." Petrosinella throws a gallnut on the ground, and up springs a Corsican bulldog, which rushes on the ogress with open jaws. But she pacifies the dog with some bread ; and again pursues them. Another gallnut is thrown on the ground, and a fierce and huge lion arises, which is preparing to devour her, when she turns back, strips the skin off a jackass which is feeding in a meadow, and covers herself with it : the lion is frightened, and runs away. The ogress again pursues, still clothed with the ass's skin. "They hear the clatter of her heels, and see the cloud of dust that rises up to the sky, and conjecture that it is she that is coming again." Petrosinella throws down the third gallnut, when there starts up a wolf, "who, without giving the ogress time to play a new trick, gobbles her up just as she is, in the shape of a jackass." (*p.* 117.)

Tales in which ogres are represented as having beautiful daughters, which are courted and won by princes, are very common in the "Folk-lore" of different nations. (See Basile's "Dove," *Op. cit., p.* 180. Compare also "The Young King of Easaidh Ruadh;" and "The Battle of the Birds." *Campbell, Op. cit. Vol. I., pp.* 1, 25.)

UNTOMBINDE. [56]

Untombinde urges her father to allow her to go to the Ilulange.

INTOMBI yenkosi Usikulumi ka-*h*loko*h*loko, Umbokondo - i - gaya-abagayi, Ukqulungu-umlomo-wa-otetwa, ya ti, "Ba*b*a, ngi y' elulange. Mame, ngi y' elulange, ngomunye unyaka." Wa ti uyise, "A ku yi, lu buya ko: ku ya 'uyela futi." Ya vela futi ngomunye unyaka, ya ti, "Baba, ngi y' elulange. Mame, ngi y' elulange." Wa ti, "A ku yi, lu buya ko: ku ya 'uyela futi." Kwa vela unyaka, ya ti, "Baba, ngi y' elulange." Ya ti, "Mame, ngi y' elulange." Ba ti, "Elulange a ku yi, lu buya ko: ku ya 'uyela futi." Wa vuma uyise, wa vum' unina.

THE daughter of the king Usikulumi, the son of Uthlokothloko, Umbokondo-i-gaya-abagayi,[57] Ukqulungu - umlomo - waotetwa, [58] said, "Father, I am going to the Ilulange.[59] Mother, I am going to the Ilulange, next year." Her father said, "Nothing goes to that place and comes back again:[60] it goes there for ever." She came again the next year, and said, "Father, I am going to the Ilulange. Mother, I am going to the Ilulange." He said, "Nothing goes to that place and comes back again: it goes there for ever." Another year came round. She said, "Father, I am going to the Ilulange." She said, "Mother, I am going to the Ilulange." They said, "To the Ilulange nothing goes and returns again: it goes there for ever." The father and mother consented (at length).

She collects two companies of maidens, and sets out.

Ya buta intombi zi ikulu nge-n*x*enye kwo*h*langoti lwend*h*lela; ya buta intombi za likulu ngen*x*enye kwo*h*langoti lwend*h*lela. Za hamba ke. Za *h*langana nabahhwebu. Za fika z' ema amakcala

She collected a hundred virgins on one side of the road, and a hundred on the other. So they went on their way. They met some merchants. The girls came and stood on each side of the path,

---

[56] Untombinde, Tall-maiden.

[57] Umbokondo-i-gaya-abagayi, Upper millstone, which grinds the grinders.

[58] Ukqulungu-umlomo-waotetwa, Pouter of the Abatetwa.

[59] A river, not now known to the natives.

[60] So the king's daughter beseeches the fisherman's son, her husband, not to go to "a little castle beside the loch in a wood." "Go not, go not," said she; "there never went man to this castle that returned." (*Highland Tales. Vol. I., p. 82.)*

omabili end*h*lela, za pa*h*la ind*h*lela.
Za ti, "Bahhwebu, si tshele ni
u*h*langa olu*h*le lapa lwentombi; lo
si 'mitimba 'mibili." Ba t' abahhwebu, "U mu*h*le, tintakabazana;
u nge fike kuntombinde wenkosi,
o ng' uk*q*wek*q*wana lotshani; o
ng' amafuta okupekwa; o ng' in-
yongo yembuzi." Ba ba bulala
laba abahhwebu, be bulawa umtimba katintakabazana.

on this side and that. They said,
"Merchants, tell us which is the
prettiest girl here; for we are two
wedding companies." The merchants said, "You are beautiful,
Utintakabazana; but you are not
equal to Untombinde, the king's
child, who is like a spread-out surface of good green grass; who is
like fat for cooking; who is like a
goat's gall-bladder!"[61] The marriage company of Utintakabazana
killed these merchants.

*They arrive at the Ilulange, and bathe: the Isikqukqumadevu steals
their clothes.*

Ba fika ke emfuleni elulange.
Ba be pake ingxota; ba be pake
imbedu; ba be pake iminaka; ba
be bince imintsha yendondo. Ba
i kumula, ba i beka ngapezulu
kwesiziba solange. Ba ngena, ba
bukuda yomibili imitimba. Ba
bukuda, ba puma. Kwa puma
inye intombazana, ya fumanisa
iminaka i nga se ko yonke, nem-
bedu zonke, nengxota, nemintsha
yendondo. Ya ti, "Puma ni;
izinto ka zi se ko." Ba puma
bonke. Ya ti inkosazana Untombinde, "Kw enziwa njani na?"
Ya t' enye intombi, "A si bonge.
Izinto zi muke nesik*q*uk*q*umadevu." Ya t' enye intombazana,
"Sik*q*uk*q*umadevu, ngi nike izinto
zami, ngi muke. Ng' enziwe
Untombinde wenkosi, o te, 'Kwa

So they arrived at the river Ilulange. They had put on bracelets,
and ornaments for the breast, and
collars, and petticoats ornamented
with brass beads. They took them
off, and placed them on the banks
of the pool of the Ilulange. They
went in, and both marriage companies sported in the water. When
they had sported, they went out.
A little girl went out, and found
nothing there, neither the collars,
nor the ornaments for the breast,
nor the bracelets, nor the petticoats
ornamented with brass beads. She
said, "Come out; the things are
no longer here." All went out.
Untombinde, the princess, said,
"What can we do?" One of the
girls said, "Let us petition. The
things have been taken away by
the Isik*q*uk*q*umadevu."[62] Another
said, "Thou, Isik*q*uk*q*umadevu,
give me my things, that I may
depart. I have been brought into
this trouble by Untombinde, the
king's child, who said, 'Men bathe

---

[61] These are terms of flattering admiration. The gall-bladder of the goat,
inflated and dried, and stuck in the hair, is a sign of having been honourably
received at the place where a person has been sent as a messenger.

[62] Isik*q*uk*q*umadevu, A bloated, squatting, bearded monster.

Some natives suppose that the Tale of the Isik*q*uk*q*umadevu is a fabulous
account of the first large ship that appeared to their fathers, being probably a
slaver. Others think it is a corrupted tradition of Noah's ark. See appendix
at the end of this tale.

kcibi-kulu ku ya gezwa : kwa ku geza aobaba bamandulo.' U mina ngi ku bangela Intontela?" Sa m nikela umuntsha. Ya kqala enye intombi, ya si bonga, ya ti, "Si-kqukqumadevu, ngi nike izinto zami, ngi muke. Ng' enziwe Untombinde wenkosi ; wa ti, ' Ku-kcibi-kulu ku ya gezwa : kwa ku geza aobaba bamandulo.' U mina ngi ku bangele Intontela ?" Wa kqala umtimba wonke, wa za wa pela, w' enza njalo. Kwa salela yena Untombinde wenkosi.

in the great pool : our first fathers bathed there.' Is it I who bring down upon you Intontela ?"[63] The Isikqukqumadevu gave her the petticoat. Another girl began, and besought the Isikqukqumadevu : she said, "Thou, Isikqukqumadevu, just give me my things, that I may depart. I have been brought into this trouble by Untombinde, the king's child ; she said, 'At the great pool men bathe : our first fathers used to bathe there.' Is it I who have brought down upon you Intontela ?" The whole marriage company began, until every one of them had done the same. There remained Untombinde, the king's child, only.

Untombinde refuses to petition the Isikqukqumadevu, and the monster seizes her.

Wa t' umtimba, "Bonga, ntombinde, Usikqukqumadevu." W'ala, wa ti, "A ng' 'uze nga si bonga Isikqukqumadevu, ng' umnta wenkosi." Sa m tabata Isikqukqumadevu, sa m paka kona esizibeni.

The marriage party said, "Beseech Usikqukqumadevu,[64] Untombinde." She refused, and said, "I will never beseech the Isikqukqumadevu, I being the king's child." The Isikqukqumadevu seized her, and put her into the pool.

The other girls lament her, and return to tell the tale.

Intombi ezinye za kala, za kala, z' esuka, za hamba. Za fika ekaya enkosini ; za fika, za ti, "U tatwe Isikqukqumadevu Untombinde." Wa t' uyise, "Kade nga ngi m

The other girls cried, and cried, and then went home. When they arrived, they said, "Untombinde has been taken away by the Isikqukqumadevu." Her father said, "A long time ago I told Untom-

[63] *Intontela.*—The name of one of the military kraals of the Zulu king. The use of this word suggests either that the Tale is of recent origin, or has undergone modern corruption. It may, however, be an old name adopted by the Zulus. The question implies that armies were sent to contend with the monster.

[64] They here say, not Isikqukqumadevu, but Usikqukqumadevu ; thus flattering and magnifying the monster by giving it a personal name. It is something as though they said, "My Lady, Usikqukqumadevu."

tshela Untombinde ; ng' ala nga ti, ' Elulange a ku yi, lu buya ko : ku ya 'uyela futi.' Nanko ke u yela futi."

binde so ; I refused her, saying, ' To the Ilulange, nothing goes to that place and returns again : it goes there for ever.' Behold, she goes there for ever."

The king sends an army against the monster, the monster destroys it, and the whole country.

Ya t' inkosi ya kipa amabandhla ezinsizwa, ya ti, "Hamba ni, ni lande Isikqukqumadevu, esi bulele Untombinde." A fika emfuleni amabandhla, a hlangana naso se si pumile, se si hlezi ngapandhle. Si ngangentaba. Se si fika si i ginga yonke impi leyo ; se si hamba si ya kona emzini wenkosi ; si fika si ba ginga abantu bonke, nezinja ; sa ba ginga izwe lonke kanye nenkomo. Sa fika sa ginga abantwana kulelo 'zwe be babili ; be amapahla, izibakxa.

The king mustered the troops of young men, and said, "Go and fetch the Isikqukqumadevu, which has killed Untombinde." The troops came to the river, and fell in with it, it having already come out of the water, and being now on the bank. It was as big as a mountain. It came and swallowed all that army ; and then it went to the very village of the king ; it came, and swallowed up all men and dogs ; it swallowed them up the whole country, together with the cattle. It swallowed up two children in that country ; they were twins, beautiful children, and much beloved.

A father, who escaped, pursues the Isikqukqumadevu, and kills it.

Se ku sinda uyise kuleyo 'ndhlu ; se i hamba indoda i tata amawisa amabili, i ti, " Mina, ngi ya 'ubulala Isikqukqumadevu." Se i tata umdhludhlu wayo womkonto ; i se hamba. Se i hlangana nenyati, se i ti, " U ye ngapi Usikqukqumadevu ?. U muke nabantwana bami." Se zi ti izinyati, " U funa Unomabunge, O-gaul'-iminga." Se zi ti, " Pambili ! pambili ! Ma-

But the father escaped from that house ; and the man went, taking two clubs, saying, "It is I who will kill the Isikqukqumadevu." And he took his large assagai and went on his way. He met with some buffaloes, and said, "Whither has Usikqukqmadevu gone ? She has gone away with my children." The buffaloes said, " You are seeking Unomabunge, O-gaul'-iminga.[65] Forward ! forward ![66] Our mo-

---

[65] Unomabunge, Mother of beetles. This name shows that the monster was a female. O-gaul'-iminga, The feller of lofty thorn-trees.

[66] This reminds one of the man who pays a visit to his child's mysterious godfather : on reaching the house he finds inanimate things talking and acting ; and on enquiring where the godfather lived, receives for answer, from each in succession, "One flight of stairs higher." "Up another flight." "Up another flight." ("The Godfather." *Grimm. Op. cit., p.* 170.)

metu!" Se i *h*langana nezilo, se i ti, "Ngi funa Usik*q*uk*q*umadevu, o muke nabantwana bami." Se zi t' izilo, "U funa Unomabunge, O-gaul'-iminga, O-nsiba-zimak*q*embe. Pambili! pambili! Mametu!" Se i *h*langana nend*h*lovu, se i ti, "Ngi buza Usik*q*uk*q*umadevu, o muke nabantwana bami." Se i ti, "U bula Unomabunge, O-gaul'-iminga, O-nsiba-zimak*q*embe. Pambili! pambili! Mametu!" Se i fika kuyena Unomabunge: indoda i m fumana e k*q*uk*q*ubele, e ngangentaba. Se i ti, "Ngi funa Usik*q*uk*q*umadevu, o tata abantwana bami." Se si ti, "U funa Unomabunge; u funa O-gaul'-iminga, O-nsiba-zimak*q*e-

ther!"[67] He then met with some leopards, and said, "I am looking for Usik*q*uk*q*umadevu, who has gone off with my children." And the leopards said, "You are looking for Unomabunge, O-gaul'-iminga, O-nsiba-zimak*q*embe.[68] Forward! forward! Our mother!" Then he met with an elephant, and said, "I enquire for Usik*q*uk*q*umadevu, who has gone away with my children. It said, "You mean Unomabunge, O-gaul'-iminga, O-nsiba-zimak*q*embe. Forward! forward! Our mother!" Then he came to Unomabunge herself: the man found her crouched down, being as big as a mountain. And he said, "I am seeking Usik*q*uk*q*umadevu, who is taking away my children." And she said, "You are seeking Unomabunge; you are seeking O-gaul'-iminga, O-nsiba-

[67] "Mametu!" an oath. The essence of the Zulu oath consists, not so much in swearing by a person, as in calling upon him in an elliptical sentence, the meaning of which would be quite unsuspected by the uninitiated. "Mametu," my mother, means in the native mind, What I say is true, if not I could be guilty of incest with my mother. The Zulu swears thus by his nearest relatives, *e. g.*, "Mametu," my mother; "Dade wetu," my sister; or, "Nobani wetu," my So-and-So, mentioning his sister by name; "Mkwekazi," my mother-in-law; or "Bakwekazi," all the wives of my father-in-law. So the women swear in like manner: "Bane wetu," my brothers; "Bafana," boys of my kraal; "Omkulu waodade," father of my sisters-in-law; or "Mezala"; or "Ngi funga ubaba"; or "Ngi funga aban*h*loni," I swear by those who are reverenced, viz., fathers, brothers, &c., or simply "Ben*h*loni."

Another common oath is by the names of the chief, as "Tshaka"; "Dingan"; "Kukulela." But a man does not swear by his wife, child, or brother. He swears by his father when dead, "Ngi funga ubaba," which is equivalent to saying, I could disinter and eat my father, if it is not true; or, "Ngi nga ngi d*h*la ubaba," I might eat my father; or simply, "Matambo kababa," my father's bones; or "Baba," my father.

A chief or great man swears by Ikwantandane, that is, a place in Zululand where Usenzangakona and Utshaka are buried. They use this formula, "Ngi m pande ekwantandane," I could scratch him up at Ikwantandane; that is, I could disinter the chief buried there; or simply "Kwantandane." Thus Kwantandane is equivalent to swearing by the inviolability of the king's grave. Other oaths are of a similar character; "Ngi ngene enkosini," I could enter the king's presence; "Ngi ngene esigod*h*lweni," I could go into the king's palace; or simply, "Sigod*h*lo"; "Ngi ngene emapotweni," I could enter the harem; or simply, "Mapote."

Another oath is by the grave of a nameless king. "Ngi funga inkosi i kwadukuza," I swear by the king, he being at the kraal of Udukuza; or simply, "Dukuza."

[68] O-nsiba-zimak*q*embe, One whose feathers are long and broad.

mbe. Pambili! pambili! Mametu!" Se i fika, se i si gwaza isigakqa; se si fa Isikqukqumadevu.

zimakqembe. Forward! forward! Our mother!" Then the man came and stabbed the lump; and so the Isikqukqumadevu died.[69]

All that the Isikqukqumadevu had devoured come out of its dead body, and Untombinde among the rest.

So ku puma inkomo, so ku puma inja, so ku puma umuntu nabantu bonke; se ku puma yena Untombinde. Lowo ke e se fika Untombinde, e buyela kona enkosini uyise Usikulumi kahlokohloko; e se fika e tatwa Unhlatu, umunta wenkosi Usibilingwana.

And then there came out (of her) cattle, and dogs, and a man, and all the men; and then Untombinde herself came out. And when she had come out, she returned to her father, Usikulumi, the son of Uthlokothloko. When she arrived, she was taken by Unthlatu,[70] the son of Usibilingwana, to be his wife.

Untombinde goes to Unthlatu's people to be acknowledged, but finds no bridegroom.

Wa s' emuka Untombinde, e ya 'kuma. E fik' e ma ngasenhla. Se ku tiwa, "U ze 'kwendela kubani na?" Wa ti, "Kunhlatu." "Ku tiwa, "U pi na?" Wa ti, "Ng' ezwa ku tiwa inkosi Usibilingwana u zele inkosi." Kwa tiwa, "Amanga: ka ko. Kodwa

Untombinde went to take her stand in her bridegroom's kraal.[71] On her arrival she stood at the upper part of the kraal. They asked, "Whom have you come to marry?" She said, "Unthlatu." They said, "Where is he!" She said, "I heard said that king Usibilingwana has begotten a king." They said, "Not so: he is not

---

[69] Whakatau was more successful. When Hine-i-te-iwaiwa at length reaches him, and asks, "Can you tell me where I can find Whakatau?" he misleads her by replying, "You must have passed him as you came here." (*Grey. Op. cit., p.* 118.)

[70] Inhlatu, A boa-constrictor. Unhlatu, The boa-man. It is clear, notwithstanding the explanation of the name given in the Tale, viz., that when an infant he was wrapped in a boa's skin, that Unthlatu had a peculiar snake-like appearance. His skin was bright and slippery. Compare "The Serpent," in the *Pentamerone.* A prince is "laid under a spell by the magic of a wicked ogress to pass seven years in the form of a serpent." In which form he loves and woos a king's daughter.

[71] When a young woman is going to be married, she goes to the kraal of the bridegroom, to *stand* there. She stands without speaking. Her arrival may be expected or not by the bridegroom's people; but they understand the object of her visit. If they like her they "acknowledge" her by killing a goat, which is called the imvuma, and entertain her kindly. If they do not like her, they give her a burning piece of firewood, to intimate that there is no fire in that kraal for her to warm herself by; she must go and kindle a fire for herself.—It appears to be the custom among the Polynesians also for the young woman to "run away" to the bridegroom, as the first step towards marriage. (*Grey, Op. cit., p.* 238.)

wa ka wa zala; wa ti uma c umfana wa la*h*leka." Wa kala unina, nkuti, "Le intombi i b' i zwc ku tiwa ni na? Lo 'mutwana nga m zala wamunyc; wa la*h*leka, kwa ukupela na!" Ya *h*lala intombi. Uyise inkosi wa ti, "I *h*lalelc ui na?" Kwa tiwa, "Ka i mukc." Ya buya ya ti inkosi, "Ka i *h*lale; loku amadodana ami a kona, i ya 'uzckwa i wo." Y' akelwa ind*h*lu, ya *h*lala kona end*h*lini. Ba ti abautu, "A i *h*lale nonina." W' ala unina, wa ti, "Ka y akelwe ind*h*lu."

here. But he did beget a son; but when he was a boy he was lost." The mother wept, saying, "What did the damsel hear reported? I gave birth to one child; he was lost: there was no other!"[72] The girl remained. The father, the king, said, "Why has she remained?" The people said, "Let her depart." The king again said, "Let her stay, since there are sons of mine here; she shall become their wife." She had a house built for her, and she remained there in the house. The people said, "Let her stay with her mother." The mother refused, saying, "Let her have a house built for her."

Untombinde receives a nocturnal visitor, who eats and drinks, and departs.

Ku te uma y akiwe ind*h*lu, unina wa bek' amasi nenyama notshwala. Ya ti intombi, "U ku bekela ni loku na?" Wa ti, "Ngi be ngi ku beka, noma u nga ka fiki." Ya tula ke intombi, ya lala. Ku te ebusuku wa fika Un*h*latu, wa ka emasini, wa d*h*la inyama, wa puza utshwala. Wa *h*lala, wa *h*lala, wa puma.

It came to pass that, when the house was built, the mother put in it sour milk, and meat, and beer. The girl said, "Why do you put this here?" She said, "I used to place it even before you came." The girl was silent, and lay down. And in the night Unthlatu came; he took out from the sour milk,[73] he ate the meat, and drank the beer. He stayed a long time, and then went out.

Untombinde is troubled on finding the food gone.

Ku te kusasa Untombinde wa sibukula emasini; wa fumana ku kiwc: wa sibukula enyameni; wa bona i d*h*liwe: wa sibukula e-tshwaleni; wa fumana se bu d*h*liwe. Wa ti, "O, umame u beke loku 'kud*h*la. Ku za 'utiwa ku

In the morning Untombinde uncovered the sour milk; she found some had been taken out: she uncovered the meat; she saw that it had been eaten: she uncovered the beer; she found that it had been drunk. She said, "O, mother placed this food here. It will be

---

[72] *Na* is not here an interrogative, but a strong affirmative.
[73] That is, for the purpose of eating; and below, the milk had been taken out, that is, eaten.

ntshontshwe u miua." Wa ngena unina; wa sibukula, wa ti, "Ku dhliwa ini na?" Wa ti, "Ka ng' azi." Wa ti, "Nami ngi bone se ku dhliwe." Wa ti, "Ku m zwanga lo 'muntu na?" Wa ti, "Kqa."

said that I have stolen it." The mother came in; she uncovered the food, and said, "What has eaten it?" She said, "I do not know. I too saw that it had been eaten." She said, "Did you not hear the man?" She said, "No."

Untomblinde receives a second visit, and the person speaks to her.

La tshona ilanga. Ba ku dhla loko 'kudhla okutatu. Kwa hlatshwa intondolo. Kwa bekwa inyama, kwa bekwa amas', kwa bekwa utshwala. Kwa hlwa, kwa lalwa. Wa ngena Unhlatu; wa i pumputa intombi ebusweni. Ya vuka. Wa ti, "U zokwenza ni lapa na?" Ya ti intombi, "Ngi zokwenda." Wa ti, "Kubani na?" Ya ti intombi, "Kunhlatu." Wa ti, "U pi na?" Ya ti, "Wa lahleka." Wa ti, "Kepa wa lahleka njalo, u gaua kubani na?" Ya ti, "Kuyena." Wa ti, "Ni ya m azi ini ukuba u ya 'kuvela na?" Wa ti, "Loku amadodana enkosi e kona, a u gani kuwo na, uma ni hlalele umuntu owa lahlekayo na?" Wa ti, "Dhlana, si dhle inyama." Ya t' intombi, "A ngi ka i dhli inyama." Wa ti Unhlatu, "Amanga. Nami, umnyeni wako u ya ba nikela abami be nga ka i dhli, ba i dhle." Wa ti, "Puza, namp' utsbwala." Ya ti, "Utshwala a ngi ka bu dhli; ngoba ka ngi ka hlatshiswa."

The sun set. They[74] ate those three kinds of food. A wether was slaughtered. There was placed meat; there was placed sour milk; and there was placed beer, in the house. It became dark, and she lay down. Unthlatu came in; he felt the damsel's face. She awoke. He said, "What are you about to do here?" She said, "I come to be married." He said, "To whom?" The girl said, "To Unthlatu." He said, "Where is he?" She replied, "He was lost." He said, "But since he was thus lost, to whom do you marry?" She said. "To him only." He said, "Do you know that he will come?" He said, "Since there are the king's sons, why do you not marry them, rather than wait for a man that is lost?" He said, "Eat, let us eat meat." The girl said, "I do not yet eat meat."[75] Unthlatu said, "Not so. As regards me too, your bridegroom gives my people meat before the time of their eating it, and they eat." He said, "Drink, there is beer." She said, "I do not yet drink beer; for I have not yet had the imvuma slaughtered for me." He said, "Not so. Your

[74] Unthlatu's people, that is, those belonging to his mother's house in the royal kraal, ate what remained of the sour milk, meat, and beer.

[75] A damsel may not eat meat or amasi in her lover's kraal, until she is actually married.

Wa ti, "Amanga; nomyeni wako u ya ba nikela abami utshwala, be nga ka *h*latshiswa." Kwa sa, wa puma; u kuluma njalo, intombi a i m boni. Ama-suku onke lawo u y' ala entombini, i ti, i ya 'uvutela umlilo. Wa puma. Intombi y' esuka, e ya 'kupumputa esi*h*lakeni, i ti, "A ngi zwe, lo be ngi valile, uma u pume pi na?" Ya fumana ku sa valwe ngokuvala kwayo; ya ti, "Lo 'muntu u pume pi na?"

bridegroom too gives my people beer before they have had any thing killed for them." In the morning he went away; he speaking continually, the girl not seeing him. During all those days he would not allow the girl, when she said she would light a fire.[76] He went out. The girl arose, going to feel at the wicker door, saying, "Let me feel, since I closed it, where he went out?" She found that it was still closed with her own closing; and said, "Where did the man go out?"

Untombinde receives a third visit, and the visitor makes himself known.

Wa ngena unina kusasa, wa ti, "Mngane, u b' u kuluma nobani na?" Ya ti, "K*q*a; be ngi nga kulumi namuntu." Wa ti, "Ku be ku d*h*la ubani na lapa ekud*h*leni na?" Ya ti, "Ka ng' azi." Ba ku d*h*la loko 'kud*h*la. Kwa vezwa okwobutatu. Ba ku peka utshwala nenyama namasi. Kwa *h*lwa, wa fika Un*h*latu, wa m pumputa ebu-sweni, wa ti, "Vuka." Wa vuka Untombinde. Wa ti Un*h*latu, "Ngi k*q*alele elunyaweni, u ngi pumpute, u fike en*h*loko, u zwe uba ngi njani na." Ya m pumputa intombi; ya fumana umzimba o tshelclayo; w' ala ukubambela izand*h*la. Wa ti, "U ya tanda ini uma ngi ti vutcle na?" Ya ti intombi, "Yebo." Wa ti, "Ngi shiyelc uguai ke." Ya m shiyela. Wa ti, "A ngi ncikide kuwe kwe-sako isand*h*la." Wa ncikida, wa bema. Wa tshak' amate. Amate a

The mother came in the morn-ing, and said, "My friend, with whom were you speaking?" She said, "No; I was speaking with no one." She said, "Who was eating here of the food?" She said, "I do not know." They ate that food also. There was brought out food for the third time. They cooked beer and meat, and prepared sour milk. In the evening Unthlatu came, and felt her face, and said, "Awake." Untombinde awoke. Unthlatu said, "Begin at my foot, and feel me till you come to my head, that you may know what I am like." The girl felt him; she found that the body was slippery; it would not allow the hands to grasp it. He said, "Do you wish that I should tell you to light the fire?" She said, "Yes." He said, "Give me some snuff then." She gave him snuff. He said, "Let me take a pinch from your hand." He took a pinch, and sniffed it. He

---

[76] So Cupid visits Psyche unseen and unknown every night, leaving her at the dawn of day. In the Neapolitan tales, a fairy falls in love with a prince, and in like manner visits him every night, without making herself known, or allowing herself to be seen. *(Pentamerone.* "The Myrtle.")

ti, "Yeti, nkosi! wen' umnyama! wen' ungangezintaba!" Wa nci-kida, wa tshaka amate; a ti, "Yeti, nkosi! yeti, wen' ongange-zintaba!" Wa ti ke, "Vutela umlilo." Wa u vutela Untombi-nde, wa fumana umzimba okazi-mulayo. Y' esaba intombi, ya mangala, ya ti, "Nga za nga u bona umzimba onje." Wa ti, "U ya 'kuti kusasa u bon' ubani na?" Ya ti, "Ngi ya 'kuti, A ngi bona-nga 'muntu." Wa ti, "U ya 'kuti ni kulo 'nyoko owa zala Un*h*latu na, ngokuba u ya *h*lupeka na, ngokuba wa nyamalala na? U ti ni yena unyoko na?" Ya ti, "U ya kala, u ti, kazi ku d*h*liwe ubani na: ungaba ngi nga bona lo 'muntu o d*h*la loku 'kud*h*la." Wa ti, "Ngi y' emuka." Ya t' into-mbi, "Wena u *h*lala pi na, lo wa la*h*leka umncinane nje na?" Wa ti, "Ngi *h*lala pantsi." Ya ti, "W' emukela ni na?" Wa ti, "Ng' emukela abafo wetu: ba be ti b' eza 'u ngi faka igade empi-

spat. The spittle said,[77] "Hail, king! thou black one! thou who art as big as the mountains!" He took a pinch; he spat; the spittle said, "Hail, chief! hail, thou who art as big as the moun-tains!" He then said, "Light the fire." Untombinde lighted it, and saw a shining body. The girl was afraid, and wondered, and said, "I never saw such a body."[78] He said, "In the morning whom will you say you have seen?" She said, "I shall say that I have seen no one." He said, "What will you say to that your mother,[79] who gave birth to Unthlatu, because she is troubled at his disappearance? What does your mother say?" She replied, "She weeps and says, 'I wonder by whom it has been eaten. Would that I could see the man who eats this food.'" He said, "I am going away." The girl said, "And you, where do you live, since you were lost when a little child?" He said, "I live underground." She asked, "Why did you go away?" He said, "I went away on account of my brethren: they were saying that they would put a clod of earth into

---

[77] In one of the versions of "The Battle of the Birds," the Giant's Daugh-ter, before setting out with the king's son, "spat at the front of her own bed, and spat at the side of the giant's bed, and spat at the passage door." "The giant awoke, and shouted, "Rise, daughter, and bring me a drink of the blood of the king's son." "I will arise," said the spittle in front of his bed. When he shouted again the second and third time, the spittle at the side of her bed, and at the door, answered. (*Campbell. Op. cit. Vol. I.*)

[78] The Zulu very frequently expresses a strong affirmation by a negation, as:—*A li lihle leli 'hashi*, The horse is not beautiful; it is more, very beautiful indeed. *A ku si yo indhlala lapa, inkulu*, There is no famine here, it is great: that is, We have nothing whatever to eat. Here we have an affirmation to ex-press a strong negative, *Nga za nga u bona umzimba onje=A ngi bonanga ngi bona umzimba onje*. Lit., I came I saw such a body, I at length saw, &c. So below, *Sa za sa m bona umuntu onje, o 'mzimba u nga fani nowabantu*, We never saw such a man, whose body does not resemble the body of men. It is another instance of the interjectional aorist.

[79] The wife calls her husband's mother, Mother.

njeni; ngoba be hhauka, ngoba ku tiwa ngi inkos'. Ba ti, 'Ini uma inkosi i be ncinane; ku ti tina si bakulu si *h*lale na?'"

my windpipe;[80] for they were jealous, because it was said that I was king. They said, 'Why should the king be young, whilst we who are old remain subjects?'"[81]

Unthlatu tells Untombinde to call his mother.

Wa ti entombini, "Hamba ke, u ye 'kubiza unyoko lowo o *h*lupekayo." Wa ngenu unina, e fike nayo intombi. Wa fika wa kala unina, e kala kancinane isigungwana. Wa ti, "Nga ngi ti ni ke na? Nga ti, 'Umutanami owa la*h*lekayo owa e 'mzimba obutshelezi.'" Wa e se ti, "Wo ti ni kubaba?" "A ku gaywe utshwala izwe lonke."

He said to the girl, "Go and call that your mother who is afflicted." The mother came in with the girl. The mother wept, weeping a little in secret. She said, "What then did I say? I said, 'It is my child who was lost, who had the smooth body.'" He then said, "What will you say to my father?" She said, "I will say, Let the whole country brew beer."[82]

Unthlatu's mother tells his father of Unthlatu's return, and the nation is assembled.

Wa e se ti uyise, "Bu za 'kwenza ni na?" S' e ti unina, "Ngi za 'ubona abantu; ngoba nga ngi inkosikazi. Nga kitshwa ngoku-

The father said, "What is the beer to do?" The mother said, "I am going to see the people; for I used to be queen. I was de-

[80] It was formerly a custom, if a woman gave birth to twins, to kill one by placing a clod of earth in its mouth, so as to obstruct the respiration; for they supposed that if both were allowed to live, they would destroy the father's strength. Also in time of famine the father would sometimes kill a young infant in the same way, to preserve the mother's strength. So here Unthlatu's brothers purpose to kill him by a similar method.

[81] Here we have the tale so common among all people, where a younger brother is represented as an object of jealousy and enmity, or of contempt and neglect, is persecuted, and an attempt made on his life; but he escapes, and becomes a great man, superior to all. There is the beautiful, touching history of Joseph in the Holy Scriptures. In the Hawaiian traditions we have the legend of Waikelenuiaiku (*Hopkins, Hawaii*, p. 67). That of Hatupatu in the Polynesian Mythology, who on his return is as much admired for his noble looks as Unthlatu:—"Hatupatu now came out of the storehouse, and as his brothers gazed on him, they saw his looks were most noble; glared forth on them the eyes of the young man, and glittered forth the mother-of-pearl eyes of the carved face on the handle of his sword, and when the many thousands of their tribe who had gathered round saw the youth, they too were quite astonished at his nobleness; they had no strength left, they could do nothing but admire him: he was only a little boy when they had seen him before, and now, when they met him again, he was like a noble chief, and they now looked upon his brothers with very different eyes from those with which they looked at him." (*Grey, Op. cit., p.* 191.) See also "The Brown Bear of the Green Glen." *Campbell, Op. cit. Vol. I., p.* 164. "The Golden Bird," and "The Three Feathers." *Grimm, Op. cit., p.* 226, *and p.* 227.

[82] Equivalent to saying, "I will assemble the whole nation."

ngabi namntwana." Se bu gaywa ke utshwala; se be *h*leka abantu, be ti, " U tumela utshwala. U za 'weuza ni na, lo so kwa ba isaliwakazi nje na, sa puma ebukosini ?" Ba vutwa utshwala; ba butana abantu; ya ngena impi pakati kwesibaya, i *h*lome izi*h*langu, ya pelela yonke. Wa buka uyise, wa ti, " Ngi za 'ubona oku za 'wenziwa u lo 'mfazi."

posed because I had no child." So the beer was brewed; and the people laughed, saying, " She sends for beer. What is she going to do, since she was the rejected one, and was deposed ?" The beer was ready; the people came together; the soldiers went into the cattle enclosure; they had shields, and were all there. The father looked on and said, " I shall see presently what the woman is about to do."

Unthlatu makes himself known to his father and to the nation.

Wa puma ke Un*h*latu. Abantu ba kcitsheka ame*h*lo ngokukazimula kwomzimba wake. Ba mangala, ba ti, "Sa za sa m bona umuntu onje, o 'mzimba u nga fani nowabantu." Wa *h*lala ke. Kwa so ku maugala uyise. Se ku d*h*lalwa umkosi. Se ku tshaywa izing*q*ong*q*o zamahhau, o ngangamakosi onke. Untombinde e se nikelwa umsila wesilo; unina e se nikelwa umsila wensimba; se u d*h*lala ke umkosi; Un*h*latu e se bekwa ke e buyiselwa ebukosini. Se ukupela kwayo ke.

UMANGALI KANDHLOVU (LEAH).

Unthlatu came out. The eyes of the people were dazzled by the brightness of his body. They wondered, and said, " We never saw such a man, whose body does not resemble the body of men." He sat down. The father wondered. A great festival was kept.[83] Then resounded the shields of Unthlatu, who was as great as all kings. Untombinde was given a leopard's tail;[84] and the mother the tail of a wild cat;[85] and the festival was kept, Unthlatu being again restored to his position as king. So that is an end of the tale.

ANOTHER VERSION OF A PORTION OF THE TALE.

The pigeons foretell the birth of Unthlatu.

Ukuzalwa kukan*h*latu. Wa zalwa ngokubikwa amavukutu; a fika kunina emabili; la t' elinye, " Vukutu." Elinye, " U ti ' Vukutu' ni, loku e nga zali na ?" Elinye la ti, " Vukutu; u m azi

The birth of Unthlatu. He was born in accordance with the prophecy of pigeons; two came to the mother; one said, "Vukutu."[86] The other said, " Why do you say ' Vukutu,' since she has no children ?" The other said, " Vu-

---

[83] *Ukudhlala umkosi* will be explained in another place.

[84] The sign of being the queen or chief wife, the mother of the future sovereign.

[85] The sign that she is no longer queen, because a new king has taken the government, and his wife is therefore queen,—a sign of her being "queen dowager."

[86] *Vukutu*, the native mode of imitating the cooing of the pigeon.

ngani ukuba ka zali na ?" Wa tsho ke unina, ukuti, " U kqinisile; a ngi zali." La t' elinye, "Vukutu; u nga si nika ni, uma si ku tshela ukuba u ya 'kuzala na ?" Wa kipa izinto zake zonke; ka shiya nakunye ngokutanda umntwana. A nqaba ngokuti, " Konke loku a si ku funi. U nawo umpanda wezin*h*lakuva na ?" Wa ti, " U kona." A ti, " U lete." Wa u tata ke, wa puma nawo, wa u bulalela pand*h*le; za kc̣iteka izin*h*lakuva; a zi d*h*la ke, a kq̣eda. A ti, " Fulatela." A m *h*laba izin*h*langa zambili esinq̣eni, a ti, " Se u za 'uzala ke." 'Emuka ke; naye wa hamba, wa goduka. Wa si tata ke isisu. Kepa eku si tateni kwake isisu wa jabula kakulu; loku wa e kade e nga se 'mfazi waluto ngoku*h*letshwa ubunyumba; loku abanye abafazi ba be zala, be zala amakwababa; kepa lawo 'makwababa a *h*lupa kakulu kuleyo 'ndh*l*u yakwabo-n*h*latu ngokukc̣ita um*l*ota; ya za y' esuswa en*h*la nomuzi y' emiswa esangweni, ngokuba e nge 'mfazi waluto. En*h*la nomuzi w' emela ukuba e iukosikazi; futi e intombi yenkosi enkulu; kepa ngoku nga zali kwake igama lobukosikazi la ncipa; i ngaloko ke indh*l*u e ya suswa ngako.

kutu; how do you know that she has no children ?" So the mother said, " He is correct; I have no children." The other said, " Vukutu; what will you give us if we tell you that you shall have a child ?" She took out all she had; she did not leave a single thing, because she longed for a child. They refused, saying, " We do not like all this. Have you not a vessel full of castor-oil berries ?" She said, " There is a pot of berries." They said, " Bring it." So she took it, and went out with it, and broke it outside; the seeds were scattered; they ate all of them. They said, " Turn your back to us." They scarified her in two places on the loins, and said, " You will now have a child." So they departed; and she returned home. So she became pregnant. And when she became pregnant she greatly rejoiced; for she had been for a long time a wife no longer of any consequence through being reproached with barrenness; but the other wives gave birth, giving birth to crows; but those crows caused much trouble in Unthlatu's house by scattering the ashes;[87] at length it was taken away from the upper part of the kraal, and was placed near the entrance, because she was a wife of no consequence. She had her place at the upper part of the kraal because she was the queen; she was also the daughter of a great king; but through her not having children, the name of queenship was less and less spoken of; it was on this account that the house was removed.

---

[87] *Kwabo-nhlatu*, Unthlatu's house; that is, the house of his mother. The houses in a polygamic kraal are called after the wives.—"Scattering the ashes," that is, the children of the other women came into the hut of Unthlatu's mother, and played about the fire-place. This she would have borne from her own children, but not from those of other women.

Unthlatu when born is cradled in a boa's skin.

Kwa ti ngam*h*la e zala Un*h*latu wa mangala e bona umntwana omu*h*le kakulu. Kwa ku kona isikumba sen*h*latu esa tungwa, si vela kubo; wa m faka sona, wa m fi*h*la ukuze abafazi aba zekwe naye ba nga m bulali; ngokuba yena e zele umuntu, bona be zala izilwane. Wa m fi*h*la ngaloko ke: indaba a y' ezwakala ewake; ya za y' ezwakala kubo lap' e zalwa kona umfazi lo.

When she gave birth to Unthlatu, she wondered on seeing so very beautiful a child. There was there a boa's skin which was sewn up; it came from her people; she put it on him; she concealed him, that the wives who had the same husband as herself might not kill him; for she had given birth to a man; they gave birth to animals. She hid him on that account: the matter was not mentioned at the kraal into which she had married; but it was known at her native kraal.

Unthlatu leaves his mother, to avoid being killed by his brothers.

Wa fi*h*lakala ke kakulu ngako loko ukwesaba ukubulawa. Unina w' a*h*lukana naye, e nga m tshelanga ukuti, "Mame, ngi y' emuka, ngokuba ngi za 'ubulawa." Wa hamba ngapand*h*le kukanina. Unina wa funa wa funa, w' a*h*luleka; wa dela. Kepa ind*h*lu yona y' akiwa ngokuti, "A i be kona njalo ind*h*lu yake."

The child, therefore, was diligently concealed, for fear of his being killed. He separated from his mother, not having told her, "Mother, I am going away, for I shall be killed." He went independently of his mother. His mother sought and sought in vain; and gave up all hope. But his house was built; for it was said, "Let his house be there always."

The mother places food for her lost child.

Unina wa zinge e tata utshwala nenyama nokunye ukud*h*la, a ku beke kona elawini; ku se kusasa a yo'ubheka, a fike, ku d*h*liwe kancinane kouke. Kwa ti uma ku fike izintombi zi za 'ugana, za buzwa ukuti, "Ni za kubani na?" Za ti, "Kun*h*latu." Wa kala

The mother habitually took beer and meat and other food, and placed it there in the youth's house;[88] in the morning when she went to see, on her arrival, a little of all was eaten. When damsels came to marry, they were asked, "To whom do you come?" They said, "To Unthlatu." The

[88] *Ilau* is a term applied to the hut of a young man; and to the hut built for a young married woman, which it is the custom to build with great care; if this is not attended to the young bride is offended, and expresses her feelings by saying, *Ngi 'dikazi*, I am a widow who has come here to be married again, for whom no *ilau* is built. The hut of a chief is also called an *ilau*. He does not, as a common man, go to his several wives' huts, but calls them to live with him in succession.

unina ukuti, "U pi na? loku a ngi m azi mina." Uyise wa ti, "A zi yekwe; a zi nga kitshwa, ngokuba a kona amadodana a ya 'u zi zeka, uma e nge ko njalo Un*h*latu." Amadodana lawo amakwababa. Kwa za kwa fika Untombinde, naye e za 'ugana kun*h*latu. Unina wa ti, "U pi na?" Untombinde wa ti, "A ngi m azi. Si zwa ku tiwa u zelwe." Unina wa ti, "Wena, ya*h*lukana nezinye izintombi, u ye elawini lapaya, u *h*lale kona wedwa." Nembala ke Untombinde wa *h*lala kona, ngokuba wa e tandwa kakulu unina. I ngaloko ke Un*h*latu a za wa bonwa ngako; wa bonwa ngontombinde lowo, o yena a m veza obala. Ngokufika kukan*h*latu ebusuku wa fumana Untombinde; wa ti, ka nga m vezi; ekupeleni wa bonwa.

UMPENGULA MBANDA.

mother cried, saying, "Where is he, for I do not know?" The father said, "Let them be left alone; let them not be driven away, for there are sons who will marry them, although Unthlatu is not here at all." Those sons were crows. At length Untombinde came, she too coming to marry Unthlatu. The mother said, "Where is he?" Untombinde said, "I do not know. We hear it said that he has been born." The mother said, "Do you separate from the other damsels, and go into the youth's house yonder, and stay there alone." Surely then Untombinde remained there because she was much loved by the mother. It was then by these means that Unthlatu was seen at last; he was seen by means of Untombinde, who was the person who made him known. Through the arrival of Unthlatu by night he found Untombinde; he told her not to make him known; but at last he was seen.

APPENDIX.

MONSTERS.

"TALES of giants and monsters," says Tylor, "which stand in direct connexion with the finding of great fossil bones, are scattered broadcast over the mythology of the world." (*Op. cit., p.* 314.) A belief in the former existence of giants is implied, rather than clearly stated, in the Legends of the Zulus. Neither that, nor the belief in monsters, appears to have arisen among them from the observation of huge fossil remains. The Isik*q*uk*q*umadevu is the great monster of these Tales. It is a river monster, capable of living on the land. It answers to the Kammapa of the Basuto Legends. In the Tale of Usikulumi we read of a many-headed monster (*p.* 43), which was, like the Isik*q*uk*q*umadevu, destructive in its usual habits, but proved friendly to Usikulumi. We are at once reminded of the many-headed Hydra of antiquity, slain by Hercules; of the Minotaur, slain by Theseus; of the sea monster sent by Neptune to ravage Æthiopia to punish the vanity of Cassiope, which Perseus turned into a rock by the magic power of Medusa's head. Again, in the Neapolitan Tales, Minuccio is represented as killing, by means of an enchanted leaf, a monstrous dragon, who "tore with his claws, broke in pieces with his head, crushed with his tail, craunched with his teeth, poisoned with his eyes, and killed with his breath,"—a monster which, like the Isik*q*uk*q*umadevu, "made nothing of an army." ("The Dragon." *Pentamerone.*) In the Highland Tales we hear of a "three-headed monster of the loch," which was about to devour the king's daughter, but was killed by the fisherman's son. *("The Sea Maiden." Campbell, Op. cit. Vol. I., p. 76.)* In the German Folk-lore we find the Tale of a seven-headed dragon, which was killed by the young huntsman. *("The Two Brothers." Grimm's Home Stories, p. 253.)* In the Polynesian Mythology, Kupe in his wandering is attacked by a "monstrous cuttle-fish," which "raised its arms above the waters to catch and devour the canoe, men and all." But Kupe kills it with an axe. *(Grey, Op. cit., p. 208.)*

In the legendary lore of the American Indians we read of the monstrous Mishe-Nahma, the sturgeon, king of fishes, which

> "Opened its great jaws and swallowed
> Both canoe and Hiawatha."

In the mythology of the Hindus we hear of "Hari, the preserver of the universe," who, to save "the holy king Satyavrata," assumed the form of a small fish, and in that form addressed the king, asking for his protection. The fish by a succession of rapid growths at length attained a magnitude, which suggested to the king that he had to do with an incarnate deity. The god at length revealed himself to him, and promised him preservation in the approaching deluge, into the waters of which "the three worlds were about to be plunged." "On the appointed day the god, invoked by the king, appeared in the form of a fish, blazing like gold, extending a million of leagues with one stupendous horn, on which the king, as he had been commanded by Hari, tied the ship with a cable made of a vast serpent." *(Hardwick. Christ and other Masters. Vol. I., p. 312.)* In the traditions of the same people we find the myth of the world-supporting tortoise and elephant.

In the legends of the Mussulmans we read of a camel "one hundred cubits high," which came forth from the cleft mountain at the prayer of Salih. Besides other miraculous properties it could speak, and on being touched by Gabriel's flaming sword gave birth to a young camel resembling itself in every respect. It visited the dwellings of the people daily, calling them by name, and supplying them with milk. *(Weil's Legends of the Mussulmans, p. 42.)* The Ojibwa legend represents the dormouse as having been originally "the largest animal in the world ; when it stood up it looked like a mountain." It was reduced to its present size by the heat of the sun, whilst engaged in freeing it from the snare in which it had been entrapped. *(Tylor. Op. cit., p. 341.)*

In the northern mythology, again, we have the monster Jormungand, or Midgard's Serpent, which All-father "cast into the deep ocean which surrounds all lands ; but there it grew and became so great that it encircles the whole world, and bites its own tail." *(Thorpe. Op. cit. Vol. I., p. 50.)* And the wolf Fenrir, another offspring of Loki and Angurboda, is a monster of but little less dimensions than Midgard's Serpent. Having broken the chains Læding and Dromi, he was at length effectually bound by "the chain Gleipnir, which was composed of six materials, viz., the sound of a cat's footstep, a woman's beard, the roots of a mountain, a bear's sinews, a fish's breath, and a bird's spittle." "The foam which issues from his mouth forms the river called Von." *(Id., p. 49—52.)* The Greeks had their Nemæan Lion ; the American Indians their "great bear of the mountains."

We shall remember, too, the huge serpent which killed all the companions of Cadmus ; against which a rock was hurled without effect, though its force was sufficient to shake the walls of a city, and by the weight of which a lofty oak was bent. *(Ovid's Met. Book III., l. 53—95.)*

Then there is Sinbad's whale mistaken for an island ; and the Roc's egg, which was fifty paces round.

Do we need anything more to explain the world-wide traditions of monsters —chimæras, gorgons, sea-serpents, &c.,—than superstitious ignorance acting on a poetic or morbid imagination ? The untrained mind naturally looks outside itself for a power to aid or to destroy ; and sees in all striking natural phenomena, and in all unusual or unaccountable events, the presence of a personal agency ; and nothing is more natural than to proceed to a description of the imaginary agent,—to clothe the idea with a form more or less in correspondence with the characteristics of the visible phenomenon whether of terror or of health-giving ; and then to give it a "local habitation and a name." It has been said, "The philosophy of an early people is intimately mingled with mythology, and mythology, like nature, has an inexhaustible power of producing life." It has exerted this power all the world over to produce monsters. When once the imagination, excited by any cause, has given birth to the conception of a monster, the example will be rapidly followed, and their appears to be no limit to the number or variety of monsters which may spring up, or to the grotesqueness of the forms, possible and impossible, with which the human mind will clothe the offspring of the imagination.

The foregoing was already in type when my attention was directed by my friend Mr. Sanderson, of Durham, to an article on real and fabulous monsters, in *Household Words*, entitled, "A Set of Odd Fellows." After noticing many "bewildering shapes" assumed by real monsters of the deep, the writer proceeds :—

"Fantastic, however, as Nature herself has been in this part of her domain, Superstition has surpassed her. Poetry, also, has not forgotten her divine mission to create. Romance has been out upon the pathless waters, and brought back news of its inhabitants, mingling facts with fancies. And Investigation itself, in its early days, has babbled to the world of prodigies within the ocean depths as strange and appalling as any within the limits of acknowledged Fable.

"We have already quoted a passage from the Faery Queene, touching sea-monsters ; but the catalogue which the poet goes on to give us is so fearfully fine, and is such a condensed cyclopædia of fabulous marine zoology, that we cannot forbear appending it : —

> " ' Spring-headed hydres, and sea-shouldering whales ;
> Great whirlpools, which all fishes make to flee ;
> Bright scolopendraes, armd with silver scales ;
> Mighty monoceros, with immeasured tayles ;
>
> The dreadfull fish that hath deserved the name
> Of Death, and like him lookes in dreadfull hew ;
> The griesly wasserman, that makes his game
> The flying ships with swiftnes to pursew ;
> The horrible sea-satyre, that doth shew
> His fearefull face in time of greatest storme ;
> Huge ziffins, whom mariners eschew
> No lesse than rockes, as travellers informe ;
> And greedy rosmarines, with visages deforme.
>
> All these, and thousand thousands many more,
> And more deformed monsters thousand fold,
> With dreadfull noise and hollow rombling rore
> Came rushing, in the fomy waves enrold.'

Book ii. c. 12.

What a passionate earnestness, as though the writer had been really scared with his own imagination, is there in the above repetition of the word 'thousand !'

"Olaus Magnus, Archbishop of Upsal, in Sweden, who lived in the sixteenth century, is one of the chief authorities in support of the wild stories which were once in circulation respecting sea-monsters. He tells us of a species of fish seen on the coast of Norway, whose eyes, which are eight or ten cubits in circumference, appear, when glaring upward from the black chasmy water-depths, like red and fiery lamps ; of the 'whirlpool,' or prister, who is 'two hundred cubits long, and very cruel,'—who amuses himself by upsetting ships, which he securely fastens by entangling them in the windings of his long tail, and who is most readily put to flight by the sound of a trumpet of war, cannon balls being utterly ineffective ; of a sea-serpent (resembling that astounding phantom of the deep of which we have heard so much lately) who goes ashore on clear summer nights, to regale himself on calves, lambs, and hogs, and who 'puts up his head like a pillar, and catcheth away men' from off the decks of ships; and of other marvels too numerous to mention. But we are, even yet, so imperfectly acquainted with the multiform vitality of the ocean, that we must take care we are not treading unawares upon the remote twilight boundaries of fact. Are scientific enquirers yet sure that those strangely vanishing islands, which at times appear and disappear in the solitary northern seas, are not the prominent parts of some stupendous kraken?"

AMAVUKUTU.

THE following curious legend, claiming to speak of an event in the history of primitive man, is inserted here because of its correspondence with the tale of Unthlatu's birth, into which it was probably inserted from some older tradition. Of a similar character and equally curious is the resuscitation of a damsel which had been devoured by a lion, by placing her heart in milk. "Now the woman took the first milk of as many cows as calved, and put it into a calabash, where her daughter's heart was; the calabash increased in size, and in proportion to this the girl grew again inside." *(Bleek's Hottentot Fables, p. 55.)*

KWA ti amavukutu ekukqaleni, ekudabukeni kwokukqala eluhlangeni, a fika ekaya, a funyaua umfazi e hleli pandhle, a ngena, a tunqisa umlota endhlini yake. Wa kala. Wa b' e umfazi; wa b' e nga zali. Wa ti, "A ze 'ku ngi hleka, a bona ngi nge namntwana wokukcita umlota." A fika amavukutu ematandatu; la ti elinye, "Vukutu." La ti elinye, "U ti 'Vukutu' ni na?" La ti elinye, "Vukutu," la pinda. La ti elinye, "U ti 'Vukutu' ni na?" Ngapambili ke kwake lowo 'mfazi.

IT happened in the beginning, at the first breaking off from the source of being,[89] that some rock pigeons came to a house; they found a woman sitting outside; they went in and scattered the ashes in her house. She cried. She was a married woman; she had no child. She said, "They have come to laugh at me; they saw that I have no child to scatter the ashes." There came six pigeons; one said, "Vukutu." Another said, "Why do you say 'Vukutu?'" The first repeated, "Vukutu." The other said, "Why do you say 'Vukutu?'" This was done in the presence of that

---

[89] *Eluhlangeni* or *ohlangeni*, "from the *source of being*." This somewhat paraphrastic rendering of the word *uhlanga* is perhaps the nearest approach we can make to an intelligible English meaning. *Uhlanga* is a source—personal or local—of other things, which may resemble the *uhlanga* from which they sprung, or be quite distinct from it. There are, therefore, many kinds of *uhlanga*. The notion of *time*,—except so far as it is involved in that of precedence,—is never wrapped up in the word *ohlangeni*; it is not therefore, as has been erroneously supposed by some, a term convertible with *ekukqaleni*, "in the beginning." The personal *Uhlanga*, from which, according to the Zulus, all things out-came *(vela)* in the beginning, will be fully treated of when we come to their religious mythology.

Kepa la ti, "Tata upondo," la ti elinye, "u zilumeke." La ti elinye, "Vukutu," futi. La ti elinye, "Tata upondo, u zilumeke, u kupe i*h*lule, u tele embizeni, u nameke, u beke ngenyanga ezishiyangalombili, u nameke. Kwo ti ngenyanga yesishiyangalolunye, (la ti,) u ze u zibukule ngenyanga yesishiyangalolunye."

Wa zibukula ke, wa funyana umntwana; i*h*lule se li nomntwana pakati embizeni. La ti ivukutu, "Mu kipe ke namu*h*la, u mu fake em*h*lantini, u m pe ke uku-d*h*la." La fika elinye, la ti, "M ambese ngengubo zake, mu beke emsamo wend*h*lu; mu fi*h*le, ba nga m azi abafaz' abanye; mu pe ke kakulu, a kule masinya." Wa kula ke masinya.

Ya fika indoda yake kusi*h*lwa. Wa bas' umlilo kakulu umfazi. Indoda a i m azi umntwana lowo, umntwana we*h*lule nje. Wa m tata ke umfazi umntwana emsamo wend*h*lu, w' e*h*la naye, wa *h*lala, wa m beka ngapambili kwake; wa tata ukud*h*la kwake umntwana, wa ku beka ngapambili kwake umntwana, wa ti, "Yid*h*la ke; nanku ukud*h*la kwako, mutanami." Ya mangala indoda yake, ya kuluma, ya ti, "Lo u mu tata pi? Okabani lo 'mntwana?" Wa t' umfazi, "Owami, owe*h*lule lami, owamavukutu, a ngi tshelako ubu-*h*lakani: a ti, a ngi gcabe, ngi zilumeke, ngi kupe i*h*lule, ngi li tele embizeni, li ya 'kuba ng' umntwana. La umntwana ke."

Kepa i ya jabula, ya m bonga, ya ti, "Ngi ya tokoza, ngi ya jabula namu*h*la. Se u nomntwana wako. Ku*h*le kakulu." Yebo, ya tsho njalo lapo ke. Wa kula njalo umntwana ke we*h*lule.

Umpondo kambule (Aaron).

woman. And the other answered, "Take a horn and cup yourself." The other said again, "Vukutu." The other said, "Take a horn and cup yourself, and draw out a clot, and place it in a pot, and lute it down, and set it aside for eight months; lute it down, and in the ninth month, (the pigeon said,) uncover it."

She uncovered it, and found a child; the clot had now a child inside it, in the pot. The pigeon said, "Take him out now, and put him in a bag, and give him food." Another came and said, "Wrap him in his blankets, and put him at the back of the house; hide him, that the other women may not know; give him a great deal of food, that he may grow immediately." So the child grew immediately.

Her husband came in the evening. The woman lit a very great fire. The husband did not know of the child, the child of the clot only. The wife took the child from the back of the house, and came forward with him, and sat down, and placed him before her; she took the child's food, and put it before him, and said, "Just eat; see thy food, my child." The husband wondered, and spoke, and said, "This child, where did you get him? Whose is this child?" The woman said, "It is my child, the child of a clot of my blood, the child of the pigeons, which taught me wisdom: they told me to scarify and cup myself, and take a clot, and put it in a pot, and it would become a child. So it became a child."

And the husband rejoiced and gave her thanks, and said, "I am happy and rejoice this day. You have now a child. It is very good." Yes surely the husband said so. So the child of the clot grew up.

USITUNGUSOBENHLE.[90]

Usitungusobenthle and her sister go out to gather ubenthle.

Kwa ti Usitungusoben*h*le, ba be 'zintombi. Omunye e ng' udade wabo intombi yend*h*lu 'nkulu. Be hamba namabuto abo[91] ezintombi, be ya 'kuka uben*h*le, ba hamba be bu ka, be bu shiya end*h*lcloni. Ba ya ba finyelela cmikaulweni lapa be za 'ubuya kona. Wa ti ke udade wabo wend*h*lu enkulu, wa ti, a ka tandwa uyise; u tanda wend*h*lu enciuane. Ba buya ba guk*q*uka. Ba ti ba hamba, ba bu buta; kepa wa bu shiya o tandwa uyise, wa ko*h*lwa. Ku ti be senkangala se be buya, wa bu kumbula uben*h*le bake.

As regards Usitungusobenthle; there were two damsels; the one who was her sister was a child of the great house. As they were going with their female attendants to gather ubenthle,[92] they walked along plucking it, leaving it by the way-side. They reached the point where they would turn back. Her sister, the child of the great house, said she was not beloved by her father; he loved the child of the inferior house. They turned back. They walked and collected the ubenthle; but she who was loved by her father forgot, and left hers. When they were on the high land, on their way back, she remembered her ubenthle.

The female attendants refuse to return with Usitungusobenthle: she returns alone, and falls in with a cannibal.

Wa ba nga ti[93] kwezake intombi cz'amabuto ake, "Ngi pelekezcle ni, ngi lande uben*h*le bami." Z' ala zonke nczake nezodade wabo: zi yaliwe udade wabo. Wa buya ke yedwa. Wa hambahamba, wa fumana izimu, li *h*lezi end*h*lini lapa bu kona uben*h*le bake. Wa ti e sa u fika, wa fu-

She vainly asked her female attendants one after another, saying, "Do you accompany me, that I may fetch my ubenthle." All refused, both her own and her sister's: they had been enjoined by her sister (to refuse). So she returned alone. She went and went, and fell in with a cannibal sitting in a house, where her ubenthle was. When she arrived, she found him

---

[90] Bundle-of-ubenthle.

[91] Amabuto abo, pronounced amabutw abo; the o becoming w before the vowel. It does not appear desirable to note by spelling such peculiarities.

[92] A fibrous plant, with which ornaments, &c., are made.

[93] *Wa ba nga ti.*—The meaning of this form is, She addressed first one and then another in vain. As below, *Wa ba nga lunywa,* He was bitten in vain, that is, without shrinking or manifesting pain.

mana li tola izibungu, li zi d*h*la. Li m biza, la ti, "Ngena, u ze 'ku ngi tolisa." Wa ngena, wa fika wa tola, wa zinge e li nika izibungu, li d*h*la.

hunting for maggots[94] and eating them. He called her, saying, "Come in, and help me to find." She entered and went and found, and gave him maggots continually, and he ate.

Usitungusobenthle's sister and the attendants make a false report.

Ekaya ba fike ba ti, "I tombile leyo 'ntombazana, Usitunguso-ben*h*le." Ku *h*latshwe inkomo; isizwe sonke si pelele ngoku*h*laba, uba ku tombe inkosazana.

The others arrived at their home; they said, "The little maid, Usitungusobenthle, has become a woman." An ox is slaughtered, and the whole tribe comes together at the slaughter, because the princess has come to maturity.[95]

The cannibal puts Usitungusobenthle into his bag, and walks off with her.

La ti izimu la m faka em*h*lanti-ni ; wa ti ke wa puma nalo izimu, li y'ekaya kubo kasitungusoben*h*le. Ba fumana abafana be babili ba-kwabo, be sematoleni, abanye be sezinkomeni, be d*h*l' inyama. La ti, "Ngi sikele ni inyama." Ba li sikela izimu. La ti, "Ngi za 'ku ni tshela um*h*lanti womuntu om-kulu."

The cannibal put Usitunguso-benthle into his bag, and she went with the cannibal, and he went to Usitungusobenthle's home. They fell in with two of her brothers, who were with the calves ; and others were with the cattle, eating meat. The cannibal said, "Cut off some meat for me." They cut off some for him. He said, "I will tell you something about the bag of a great person."[96]

Usitungusobenthle speaks in the bag, and her brothers recognise her voice.

Ba li pa, la d*h*la. Ba ti, "U bete um*h*lanti, u te u zo 'u si tshela." La u beta ke. Ya ti ke intombazana, Usitungusoben*h*le, i

They gave him meat, and he ate. They said, "Beat the bag[97] you said you would tell us of." So he beat it. The little girl, Usi-tungusobenthle, who was in the

[94] In a native hut which is not properly attended to, maggots come up from the floor. The cannibal is represented as eating them. The badly cared for house and the food are both intended to disparage the cannibal, by intimating that his habits are different from those of other men.

[95] The ceremonies performed on such occasions will be given in another place.

[96] The brothers of Usitungusobenthle understand by this that there is something mysterious which probably concerns themselves, being children of the king, in the cannibal's bag.

[97] That is, "Out with this tale about the bag."

ngapakati em*h*lantini, ya ti, "Ngi ya 'kukuluma, ngi ti ni? Ngi shiyiwe nje abakababa; b' alile uku ngi pelekezela, ngi ye 'kutabata uben*h*le bwami." B' ezwa abafana bakwabo, b' ezwa ngelizwi; ba ti, "Mu pelekezele ni, a ye kubaba, a ye 'kud*h*la inyama e kcebileyo kubaba ekaya." Ba mu pelekezela ke, ba mu sa end*h*lini yakwabo Usitungusoben*h*le.

bag, said, "What shall I say? I have been left by my father's children, who refused to accompany me to fetch my ubenthle." The boys, her brothers, heard; they understood by her voice; they said, "Do you accompany him to our father's, that he may eat fat meat at our father's house." So they accompanied him, and brought him to Usitungusobenthle's home.

Usitungusobenthle's brothers take the cannibal to their father.

La fika ke kwabo. Wa li sikela unina kasitungusoben*h*le; la d*h*la. Ba ti, "U bete ke um*h*lanti womuntu omkulu." La u beta ke izimu. Wa ti umntwana, "Ngi ya 'ukuluma ngi ti ni? Ngi shiyiwe ngabakababa." Wa ti unina, "A ku yokubizwa inkosi uyise." Wa fika ke, wa ti, "A ke a bete um*h*lanti;" 'ezwe i kuluma, ya ti, "Ngi ya 'kuti ni? Ngi shiyiwe ngabakababa."

So the cannibal came to her people. Her mother cut him some meat, and he ate. They said to him, "Just beat the bag of the great person." So the cannibal beat it, and the child said, "What shall I say? I have been forsaken by my father's children." The mother told them to call the king, her father. So he came, and said, "Just let him beat the bag." And he heard her say, "What shall I say? I have been forsaken by my father's children."

The father sends the cannibal to fetch water in a leaky calabash, and takes Usitungusobenthle out of the bag.

Wa ti ke uyise, "Li nike iselwa, li ye 'kuka amanzi." Wa li kcamusa iselwa ngesilanda. La hamba ke izimu, li ya 'kuka 'manzi. La libala ukuka 'manzi, iselwa li vuza. Ba be tola na ofezela nenyoka neziuja, ku fakwa em*h*lantini; wa kitshwa umntwana, intombi, Usitungusoben*h*le ng' uyise.

So her father told them to give the cannibal a calabash, that he might go and fetch water. The father made a hole in it with a spear.[98] So the cannibal went to fetch water. The cannibal was detained fetching water, for the calabash leaked. They procured scorpions, and snakes, and dogs, and put them in the bag; and the little girl, Usitungusobenthle, was taken out by her father.[99] They

[98] In like manner the woman gives Moorachug a sieve to fetch water in. *(Campbell. Op. cit. Vol. I., p. 160.)* The Danaides are punished by being compelled to the infinite, unceasing labour of filling a vessel full of holes with water.

[99] A tale similar to this in many respects, and containing some incidents from other legends, is related of Tselane, among the Bechuanas. *(Abbousset's South Africa, p. 98.)* See also above, p. 33. "U*h*lakanyana."

Kwa fakwa izilo zonke, ezi lumayo zonke, emhlantini wezimu. La fika izimu, la ti, "Ini ukuba ni ngi nike iselwa elivuzayo?" Ya ti inkosi ya li bulala, ya ti, "U nikwe inkosikazi. Ku nani i nga ku funeli iselwa eli nga fanga, eli kqinileyo na?"

put all kinds of biting animals into the cannibal's bag. The cannibal came, and said, "Why did you give me a leaky calabash?" The king had made a hole in it, but he said, "The queen gave it to you. How was it she did not find for you an unbroken, strong calabash?"

The cannibal departs with his bag full of venomous animals.

La ti ke izimu, "Umhlanti wami u sa hlezi ini ke na?" Ba ti, "U se hlezi ngaloko 'kuhlala kwawo, u be u u beka ngako." La twala ke izimu; la piwa nenyama, la goduka, li ya ekaya emzini walo. La fika, la u beka pandhle umhlanti walo; la ti, "A ku baswe umlilo, ku pekwe imbiza."

The cannibal said, "Is my bag still there?" They said, "It is still in the same place and condition as you put it." The cannibal took it up; he was given meat, and went home to his kraal. When he arrived he put his bag down outside, and told them to make a fire and boil the pot.

The cannibal's death.

I b' i tsha. La tumela umntwana walo, la ti, ka tabate umhlanti. Wa lunywa umntwana; wa u lahla. La tuma omunye futi; wa hamba wa ti, u ya u tabata; wa lunywa naye; wa u lahla. Izilwane ezi pakati emhlantini za luma abantwana bezimu. La ti, "Ni nga be ni sa ngena endhlini lapa," kubantwana balo. La ti, a u tatshatwe inkosikazi. Ya lunywa. Ya ti, "Bahle; ba tsho abantwana ukuba u ya luma lo 'mhlanti wako." La ti ke, "Ngi valele ni ngapakati, ni vimbe nentunjaua." Ba vala ke, ba puma. La u tabata ngokwalo. La ba nga lunywa, la kqinisela. La u kupa, la u nikina. Za kumbula kulo zonke ezi fakiwe ngapakati. La

The pot was boiling. He sent one of his children to fetch the bag. The child was bitten, and left it. He sent another; he went, and when he was taking hold of it, he too was bitten; and left it. The animals which were in the bag bit the cannibal's children. He told them not to come into the house any more. He told his chief wife to fetch it. She was bitten, and said, "The children are right; they said truly this bag of yours bites." So he said, "Shut me up inside the house, and close up even the little holes."[1] They shut him up, and went out. He took the bag by himself. He was bitten again and again without shrinking. He emptied the bag, and shook it. All the animals which were inside rushed upon him. He screamed.

---

[1] Thus giving them to understand that as they had spoken evil of the food he had in his bag, they should not only not have any of it, but should not even see what it was.

kala. La kala ngapakati, li ko-
*h*lwe lapa li nga puma ngakona.
Kwa ti ku 'sikati, ba vula; se li
k*q*ediwe; se ku sele amatambo
odwa. La puma li gijima, la ya
odakeni; la fika, la *h*laba ngen-
*h*loko. Kwa ngena izinyosi ematanjeni alo, se li umuti !

He screamed inside, being unable to get out anywhere. After
some time they opened the door,
when he was already made an end
of, and nothing was left but bones.[2]
He ran out, and went to a mud-
hole; when he arrived, he fell in
head foremost. And bees entered
into his bones, he being now a
tree !

Usitungusobenthle's father kills the girls who had forsaken her.

Kwa ti ekaya inkosi ya biza
Usitungusoben*h*le, ya ti, ka pume.
Z' ala ke intombi. Ya fika ya
fika ya ya end*h*lini, lapa ku
tonjiswe kona. Ya fumana be
y ambeso enye intombi ngomuti,
ku tiwa, ng' Usitungusoben*h*le.
Ya zi biza zonke; za puma ke, za
pelela. Ya tola ukuni, ya tabata
isitshetshe, ya zi n*q*amula zonke
intombi.

UFUSI MBELE (DEBORAH).

At home the king called for
Usitungusobenthle, and told her
to come out. But the girls refused.
He went to the hut, where the
ceremonies of puberty were being
performed. He found that they
had decorated another girl with
branches of trees, and it was said
she was Usitungusobenthle. He
called them all; they came out
every one of them. He got a
block,[3] and took a sword, and cut
off the heads of all the girls.

USITUNGUSOBENHLE NAMAJUBATENTE.[4]

Usitungusobenthle is carried off by Pigeons.

KU tiwa, kwa ku kona intombi i
tombile, Usitungusoben*h*le ibizo
layo. Kwa ti abantu bomuzi wabo bonke ba hamba ba ya 'kulima
kude nomuzi wabo, nezintombi za
hamba futi nazo, za ya 'kuka

IT is said there was a girl, who
had come to womanhood, whose
name was Usitungusobenthle. All
the people of her kraal went to
dig at a distance from the kraal:
the girls also had gone to pluck

---

[2] An exaggeration of course.
[3] This mode of punishing criminals is no longer practised among the
Zulus; neither do they know when it was. They say merely that it was common to execute in this way in the time of long ago.
[4] *Amajubatente.*—Pigeons. Although the idea of birds is practically kept
up at first, it is soon left, and the Amajubatente are evidently a people, probably a people riding on horses.

incapa ; wa sala yedwa Usitungu-soben*h*le. Kwa ti kwa fika Ama-jubatente ; a fika Amajubatente, a mu tabata Usitungusoben*h*le, a hamba naye e ndiza pezulu ; a dabula ngalapa ku kona onina, lapa be lima kona, a m lengalengisa pezu kukanina. Usitungusoben*h*le wa kala e bona unina, wa ti, "Mame, mame, ng' emuka nama-jubatente." A m lengisa. Unina wa linga uku m bamba ; e m da-bukisa nje kodwa unina, a hamba naye Usitungusoben*h*le ; nonina futi wa landela, e hamb' e kala. Kwa za kwa *h*lwa, a fika emtini, a kwela pezulu, a *h*lala kona pezulu. Unina wa lala ngapantsi kwomuti. Kwa ti ngapakati kwobusuku a m tata Amajubatente Usitunguso-ben*h*le, a hamba naye, a ya kubo.

incapa ;[5] and Usitungusobenthle was left alone. Some Amajuba-tente came and took away Usi-tungusobenthle ; they carried her flying through the air ; they passed near the place where her mothers[6] were digging, and moved her backwards and forwards in the air over her mother's head. Usi-tungusobenthle shouted when she saw her mother, "Mother, mother, I am going away with the Amaju-batente." They suspended her in the air. Her mother tried to lay hold of her. But they were merely distressing her mother, and went away with Usitungusoben-thle : her mother also followed, going and weeping. When it was evening they came to a tree and perched on the top, and stopped there on the top. The mother lay down at the foot of the tree. In the night the Amajubatente took Usitungusobenthle, and went away with her to their own country.

Usitungusobenthle becomes the queen of the Pigeons.

Kwa sa unina ka b' e sa wa bona pezu kwomuti Amajubatente. Wa se u ya buya, wa pindel' emu-va. Amajubatente a fika ekaya kubo, nositungusoben*h*le futi. A ti Amajubatente, "A ka be inko-sikazi." Wa e se ba inkosikazi. Wa zala umntwana. (Indoda yake ya Ijubatente nayo.) Wa pinda wa zala omunye futi ; wa pinda wa zala omunye futi : abatatu 'kupela.

In the morning the mother could no longer see the Amajuba-tente on the tree ; so she went back again. And the Amajuba-tente went to their home with Usitungusobenthle. The Amaju-batente said, "Let her be queen." So she became queen accord-ingly. She gave birth to a child. (Her husband was an Ijubatente also.)[7] Again she gave birth to a second child ; again she gave birth to a third child : three altogether.

---

[5] *Incapa.*—A soft kind of grass.

[6] *Mothers.*—The children of the polygamist call all the wives Mother, as well as their mother properly so called.

[7] The notion of the marriage between human beings and animals is very common ; and like another very common notion with which it is associated,— the possibility of holding intercourse with and understanding the language of beasts, birds, and fishes,—may perhaps be regarded as an indication of that

The men go to hunt, leaving Usitungusobenthle alone with an old woman.

Kwa ti kwa menywa inkqina; ya ya ukuzingela kude; ya hamba nendoda futi kasitungusoben*h*le; nabantwana bake; bonko abantu be ya 'kuzingela nabo. Wa sala nesalukazi ekaya Usitungusobe-n*h*le; bobabili ba sala ekaya. Wa se kcebe ikcebo kubantwana bake, wa ti, " A no zigulisa."

It happened that a hunting party was called out; it went to hunt at a distance; Usitunguso-benthle's husband went also and her children; and all the people went to hunt. Usitungusobenthle remained at home with an old woman; they two remained at home. Usitungusobenthle devised a plan with her children; she told them to feign sickness.

Usitungusobenthle's children feign sickness, and return to their mother.

Ya puma inkqina kusasa. Ba ti be sa puma ekaya, wa ti omkui-wana[8] umntwana wake wa ziwisa

The hunting party went out in the morning. As they were leaving home, the bigger boy of Usi-

sympathy with all living things, which was characteristic of early man, as it is now the characteristic of childhood. The emotional mind naturally yearns towards the lower world of living things, and asks whether there may not be some closer relationship between them and man than is commonly supposed to exist; loves to watch their habits, and longs to comprehend their language. And the philosopher appears more and more disposed to seek for and to acknowledge the existence of relationships, which a few years ago would have been scornfully rejected as derogatory to human dignity. (See an interesting and excellent paper on the subject by Mr. Charles S. Wake. *Anthropological Journal. No. III., p.* 365.)

Be this as it may, the notion is very common in the tales of all people. Here the husband is a Pigeon; in the Highland tales it is a Hoodie, or Royston Crow; or a Dog; or a Frog. In the German a Horse; or a Rabbit. In the Neapolitan a Serpent. In the Hottentot an Elephant. And we have our own tale of Beauty and the Beast. But in the progress of the tale the characteristics of the animal are lost; there is nothing but the name; all its actions, thoughts, and language are human. And it generally turns out that it is a "prince under spells."

So here the progress of the tale shows that men and not pigeons are meant. They are unable to fly across a river. The introduction of animals instead of men into a tale is easily explained as regards Zulu. *Ijubatente*, a pigeon, becomes a proper name by changing the initial *i* into *u;* thus, *Ujubatente*, The Pigeon-man. Such names are common, as, *Undhlovu*, The Elephant-man; *Unyoni*, The Bird-man; *Unhlatu*, The Boa-man, &c. In the Kafir legends there is never, so far as I know, any allusion to *horses*. The Zulus are not a nation of horsemen; and horses have only recently been introduced amongst them. This tale may originally have been a narrative of an inroad of horsemen, who carried off a native girl. Nothing would be more natural than for them to say on such an occasion, "It was not men, but pigeons, that took her away." The name of a bird would be given them to intimate their velocity. It is not uncommon at the present time to hear an old man speak of riding on horseback as *flying*. If a person complain of fatigue from riding, he would ask, "How can you be tired, since you have merely *flown*, and not gone on your feet?" If this be a correct surmise, it will throw some light on the origin of the tale, both as regards locality and time.

[8] *Omkuiwana*, dim. of *kulu*, lit., biggish, somewhat big, that is, the one who was big as compared with the other two, the bigger.

pantsi, wa ti, " Maye, nga puka."
Wa ti uyise, " Ka buye a ye
'kaya." Ya d*h*lulela ngapambili
futi. Wa ti omunye umntwana
ow elama omkuiwana, wa ti, " Maye, nga fa isisu." Wa ti uyise, "Ka
buye futi naye." Ya d*h*lulela ngapambili futi. Wa ti omuncinyane,
" Ngi pela ikanda." Wa ti uyise,
" Ka buye futi naye." B' enza
ngamabomu, be ko*h*lisa uyise, be
ti, i kona be za 'umuka. Ba pelela bobotatu ekaya kunina.

tungusobenthle fell down design-
edly, and cried out, " O dear, I am
hurt." His father told him to go
home. The hunting party again
went on. Another child, the next
to the eldest, said, " O dear, I have
a sudden pain in my stomach !"
His father told him too to go back.
The hunting party again went on.
The little one said, " My head is
in pain all over." His father told
him to go back also. They did
this wilfully, deceiving their father,
thinking by this means to get
away. All three were now at
home with their mother.

Usitungusobenthle escapes with her children. An alarm is given.

Unina wa bopa impa*h*la yake,
wa tata abantwana bake, wa
hamba nabo. Si te si k*q*abuka
isalukazi, wa e nga se ko Usitungusoben*h*le, e se hambile ; sa
memeza, sa ti, " Yi, yi, yi," (si
*h*laba umkosi,) " inkosikazi i mukile nabantwana benkosi." W' e-
zwa omunye kwabazingelayo, wa
ti, " Tula ni ! U ti ni lowo na ?
Ku nga ti, u ti, ' Inkosikazi i mukile nabantwana benkosi.' " Ba
ti ba m bamba, ba ti, " U *h*lolela
abantwana benkosi." Ba m bulala. Sa pinda sa memeza futi, sa
ti, " Yi, yi, yi ; inkosikazi i mukile
nabantwana benkosi." Wa ti
omunye futi, " Ni m bulele kodwa
ubani. U kona umuntu o memezayo. Ku nga ti u ti, ' Inkosikazi
i mukile nabantwana benkosi.' "
Ba m bamba lowo futi, ba m
bulala, be ti, " U *h*lolela abantwana benkosi." Sa pinda futi, sa

The mother tied up her luggage,
and took her children, and went
away with them. When the old
woman first observed their departure, Usitungusobenthle was no
longer there, she having already
set out. She shouted, saying,
" Yi, yi, yi," (giving an alarm,)
" the queen has gone away with
the king's children." One of the
hunters heard, and said, " Keep
still ! What does that person
say ? It is as if she said, ' The
queen has gone away with the
king's children.' " They laid hold
of him, and said, " You are devising ill luck[9] for the king's
children." So they killed him.
Again the old woman shouted and
said, " Yi, yi, yi ; the queen has
gone away with the king's children." Again another said, " You
have indeed killed So-and-so.
There is someone shouting. It is
as if she said, ' The queen has
gone away with the king's children.' " They caught hold of him
too, and killed him, saying, " You
are devising bad luck for the king's
children." Again the old woman

---

[9] Or prophesying evil.

memeza, sa ti, "Yi, yi, yi; inkosikazi i mukile nabantwana benkosi." W' ezwa futi omunye, wa ti, "Kǫabo. Ni ba bulele kodwa abantu. U kona umuntu o memezayo, u ti, 'Inkosikazi i mukile nabantwana benkosi." Ba m bamba futi; ba m bulala naye futi; ba ti, "U hlolela abantwana benkosi, ukuba b' emuke." Sa pinda isalukazi okwesine, sa memeza, sa ti, "Yi, yi, yi; inkosikazi i mukile nabantwana benkosi." Wa pinda owesine futi, wa ti, "Tula ni, si zwe. Ni ba bulele kodwa. U kona umuntu o memezayo. Ku nga ti u ti, 'Inkosikazi i mukile nabantwana benkosi.' A ke ni ngi yeke; ni nga ngi bulali mina. Si ke si buye si yokuzwa ekaya, ngasekaya, ukuba a ku ko 'muntu o memezayo na?" Ya ti inkosi ya m yeka lowo 'muntu. Ba hamba, ba ya ekaya. Ba fika ekaya. Sa ti isalukazi, "Inkosikazi i mukile nabantwana benkosi." Wa ti umuntu, "Ngi te ni ke na? Ngi ni tshele, nga ti, u kona umuntu o memezayo."

cried, saying, "Yi, yi, yi; the queen has gone away with the king's children." Again another heard, and said, "No then. You have killed indeed those men; but there is a person shouting, and saying, 'The queen has gone away with the king's children.'" They caught hold of him too, and killed him also; they said, "You are devising bad luck for the king's children, that they may go away." Again the old woman cried for the fourth time, saying, "Yi, yi, yi; the queen has gone away with the king's children." Again a fourth said, "Be still, and let us listen. You have indeed killed those men; but there is someone shouting; it is as if she said, 'The queen has gone away with the king's children.' Just leave me alone; do not kill me too. Let us just go back to hear at home, I mean near home, if there is not someone shouting." The king let that man be. They returned home. The old woman said, "The queen has gone away with the king's children." The man said, "What did I say then? I told you there was someone shouting."

The king sets out in pursuit with a large army.

Ba butana bonke abantu benkosi yamajubatente. Ya ti, a ba m lande Usitungusobenhle. Ba hamba, impi eningi kakulu e 'zinkulungwane, nayo inkosi yamajubatente futi.

All the people of the king of the Amajubatente assembled. The king told them to fetch Usitungusobenthle. They set out a great army many thousands strong, and the king of the Amajubatente went with them.

The sea divides at Usitungusobenthle's word, and she and her children pass through.

Usitungusobenhle wa fika elwandhle; wa ti, "Lwandhle, lwandhle, lwandhle, wo ti dam'! ngi Usitungusobenhle." Ulwandhle

Usitungusobenthle came to the sea; she said, "Sea, sea, sea, divide! I am Usitungusobenthle." The sea at once divided; and she

lwa se lu ti dam'. Wa se wela nabantwana bake, wa *h*lala ngapetsheya. Ya fika impi yamajubatente elwand*h*le, ya m bona Usitungusobenhle e *h*lezi ngapetsheya kwolwand*h*le. Ya fika ya mangala i m bona ngapetsheya kwolwand*h*le.

and her children went through,[10] and sat down on the other side. The army of the Amajubaténte arrived at the sea, and saw Usitungusobenthle sitting on the other side of it. They wondered when they saw her on the other side of the sea.

The army is persuaded to follow, and is drowned.

Wa ti Usitungusoben*h*le w' aluka intambo ende kakulu, wa i ponsa ngapetsheya, wa ti, "Woza ni, ngi ni weze." E ba bin*q*a, e ba bin*q*a nje. Wa e se tole itshe elibukali. Usitungusoben*h*le wa ti, "Bambela ni, ni be baningi entanjeni." Ba i bamba intambo, ba baningi. Wa i donsa intambo Usitungusoben*h*le. Ba ti lapo be pakati, wa i n*q*uma intambo, b' emuka nolwand*h*le. Wa ti, "Maye! B' emuka abantu benkosi;" e zenzisa, e n*q*ume ngamabomu. Wa ti kwabanye futi, "I bambe ni intambo futi." Ba se be i bamba, se be baningi. Wa ba donsa. Kwa ti lapo be pakati kwolwand*h*le, wa i n*q*uma futi intambo. Wa ti, "Maye! B' emuka abantu benkosi." Wa sel' e i ponsa futi, e ti, i m punyukile. Wa e se ti, "Bambela ni, ni be

Usitungusobenthle plaited a very long rope, and threw it across, and said, "Come along, I will cross you over."[11] But she was merely chaffing them. She had found also a sharp stone. Usitungusobenthle said, "A great many of you lay hold of the rope." A great many of them laid hold of it; Usitungusobenthle drew it. And when they were in the middle she cut the rope, and they were carried away by the sea. She said, "Woe is me! The people of the king are carried away." But she was dissembling, for she had purposely cut the rope. Then she said to the others also, "Lay hold of the rope again." Many laid hold of it. She drew them across. And when they were in the midst of the sea, she cut the rope again; and said, "Woe is me! The people of the king are carried away." Again she threw the rope, saying it had slipped from her hand. And then she said, "A

[10] A somewhat similar tale is told of the Heitsi Eibip of the Hottentots; or, according to Knudsen, of some other person. (*Bleek's Hottentot Fables*, p. 75, *and Note*.) When pursued, on arriving at some water he said, "My grandfather's father, open thyself, that I may pass through, and close thyself afterwards."

[11] In the legend of Maol a Chliobain, it is said that when she had successfully plundered a giant, and again and again eluded his pursuit by leaping a stream he could not pass, she at length killed the giant by a stratagem similar to that by which Usitungusobenthle killed the pursuing army. "So Maol a Chliobain stood on the bridge (made of a hair), and she reached out a stick to him, and he went down into the river, and she let go the stick, and he was drowned. (*Campbell. Op. cit. Vol. I., p.* 260.) In this Highland legend, and in that above, as well as in that of Ulangalasenthla and Ulangalasenzantsi, given below, the pursuers and pursued hold a conversation across the river, and the pursuers are foolish enough to believe that the pursued will help their enemies to catch them, and so perish for their misplaced confidence.

baningi futi." Ba se be i bamba intambo. Kwa ti lapo be pakati labo futi, wa i nquma iutambo, b' emuka namanzi olwand*h*le. Kwa za kwa sala a ba ba bangaki ngapetsheya, se be bancinyane kambe. Wa ti omunye walabo abaseleyo, "Ba za ba pela. abantu benkosi." Ba se be buyela emuva.

great many of you hold on again." And they held on to the rope. And when they too were in the midst of the sea, she cut the rope, and they were carried away by the water of the sea. At length there remained a very few on the other side, they being now few indeed. And one of those who remained said, "At last the people of the king are come to an end." So they turned back.

Usitungusobenthle returns to her home, and finds it desolate.

Wa sel' e hamba ke Usitungusoben*h*le, e sel' e fika ezweni lakubo. Wa fika abantu be nga se ko; se ba d*h*liwa Isik*q*uk*q*umadevu. Wa bona intaba eya i nge ko ku-k*q*ala : wa ti, "I pi le 'ntaba na?" Wa hamba, wa sondela kuyo, ngalapa kwa ku kona umuzi wakubo : wa fumana into enkulu, ukuti Isik*q*uk*q*umadevu, o kad' e ti intaba.

Then Usitungusobenthle set out, and arrived at the country of her people. When she came, there were no people left; they had been eaten by the Isik*q*uk*q*umadevu. She saw a mountain which used not to be there formerly : she said, "What is this mountain?" She went on and approached it, near the place where the village of her people formerly stood : she found a great thing, to wit, the Isik*q*u-k*q*umadevu, which she at first thought was a mountain.

Usitungusobenthle rips open the Isikqukqumadevu, and animals and men come out of it, and all things are renewed.

Wa sondela eduze naso, wa hamba ngapantsi kwaso, e pete umkonto ; wa si dabula ngapantsi

She approached close to it, and went under it, carrying a knife in her hand, and cut open its belly.[12]

---

[12] In a former tale, the Isik*q*uk*q*umadevu swallows Untombinde, and is killed by a man who had been bereaved of his children by the monster. Here the monster is killed by a woman. In the Basuto legend "Litaolane took a knife, and, deaf to his mother's entreaties, went to attack the devourer of the world. Kammapa opened his frightful jaws, and swallowed him up." But Litaolane cuts his way out, killing the monster, and making way for the natives of the earth to escape from the living grave. In the American Indian legends, there is an account of a monstrous sturgeon of the Big-sea-water, Lake Superior, which swallowed Hiawatha and his canoe. Hiawatha

> " Groped about in helpless wonder,
> Till he felt a great heart beating,
> Throbbing in that utter darkness.
> And he smote it in his anger
> With his fist the heart of Nahma."

The monster dies, and Hiawatha is delivered from his prison by the birds of prey. (*Longfellow's Hiawatha.*)

esiswini. Kwa puma kukqala inkuku; ya ti, "Kukuluku! Nga li bon' izwe!" Ngokuba kad' i nga sa li boni. Ngemva kwenkuku kwa puma umuntu; wa ti, "Hau! Nga za nga li bon' izwe!" Ngasemuva kwake kwa puma inkomo; ya ti, "Uuum! Nga li bon' izwe!" Ngemva kwayo kwa puma inja; ya ti, "Hau, hau, hau! Nga li bon' izwe!" Ngemva kwayo ya puma imbuzi; ya ti, "Me, me! Nga li bon' izwe!" Ngemva kwayo kwa puma imvu; ya ti, "Be, be! Nga li bon' izwe!" Ngemva kwayo kwa puma izinto zonke. Kwa buywa, kw' akiwa, kwa buswa futi; kwa ba njengaloko kade kunjalo.

Kwa sokuba ukupela ke.

Ulutuli·Dhladhla (Usetemba).

There came out first a fowl; it said, "Kukuluku![13] I see the world!" For for a long time it had been without seeing it. After the fowl there came out a man; he said, "Hau! I at length see the world!" After him there came out a bullock; and said, "Uuum! I see the world!" After the bullock there came out a dog; it said, "How, how, how! I see the world!" After the dog there came out a goat; it said, "Mey, mey! I see the world!" After the goat there came out a sheep; and said, "Bey, bey! I see the world!" After the sheep there came out all other things. And men again built houses, and were again happy; and all things returned to their former condition. And that was the end of it.

ULUHLAZASE.

Two princesses with their attendant maidens go to bathe.

Kw' esukela,[14] intombi za ya 'ugeza, zi hamba namakosazan' emabili: encane i tandwa uyise kakulu; eukulu e nga i tandi. Enkulu kwa ku Ubu*h*laluse; encane ku Ulu*h*lazase. Za fika ke esizibeni. Za bukuda.

Once on a time some damsels went to bathe, accompanying two princesses: the younger was much beloved by her father, but he did not love the elder. The elder was named Ubuthlaluse, and the younger Uluthlazase.[15] They came to the pool, and sported in the water.

[13] The sounds used by the natives to imitate those of the various animals are here given.

[14] A narrative which is supposed to be a mere fiction is opened by *Kw' esukela.* It is thus known that fiction and not fact is about to be related. They sometimes open it by, *Insimu y' esuka, i sukela pezulu.*

[15] *Ubuhlaluse* and *Uluhlazase* are proper names of women. Feminine proper names are formed in two ways, by prefixing *Uno,* or suffixing *se;* as, Uno-mali, or, U-mali-se. So U-bu*h*lalu-se, The bead-woman. It may be a name invented to commemorate the introduction of *beads* among the natives.— U-lu*h*laza-se may mean, The green-woman, a similar compliment being intended by it as by Ukqwekqwana lotshani, given to Untombinde, p. 56. Or, as *luhlaza* also means jet-black, it may mean, The jet-black woman.

The Isikqukqumadevu takes away their garments.

Zi te lapo zi ti zi za 'upuma, za si bona ke Isikqukqumadevu. Sa tata izigheghe zazo. Za puma izintombi, za ti, "Sikqukqumadevu, si nike izigheghe zetu." Sa zi nika. Zi buye zi suke futi ezinye zi tsho njalo, zi ti, "Sikqukqumadevu, si nike izigheghe zetu." Za pela intombi.

When they were about to go out, they saw the Isikqukqumadevu. It took their garments.[16] The damsels quitted the water, and said, "Isikqukqumadevu, give us our garments." It gave them. Again others said the same, crying, "Isikqukqumadevu, give us our garments." Every one of the damsels did so.

Uluthlazase refuses to ask for her garments, and is left by the others.

Y' ala inkosazana ukutsho esikqukqumadevwini, ukuti, a si i nike isigheghe sayo, Uluhlazase inkosazana. Enkulu sa i nika Isikqukqumadevu. Encinane a i nikwanga, ngokuba ya i zikqenya. Za i ncenga ezinye intombi, za ti, "Yitsho ke, nkosazana, esikqukqumadevwini." A ya ze ya vuma ukutsho. Za ti ezinye 'zintombi, "Se si za 'ku ku shiya." Za i shiya ke.

But the princess Uluthlazase refused to ask the Isikqukqumadevu to give her her garment. The Isikqukqumadevu had given the elder princess hers. It did not give the younger one, because she was proud. The other damsels besought her, saying, "O princess, just ask the Isikqukqumadevu." But she would on no account agree to ask. The others said, "We will now leave you." So they went away.

The princess fights with the Isikqukqumadevu.

Ya bona ukuti ya shiywa ezinye 'zintombi, ya si bamba Isikqukqumadevu, i ti, i s' amuka isigheghe sayo. Ya lwa nesikqukqumadevu. Isikqukqumadevu sa i hhudula intombi, sa tshona nayo esizibeni. Kwa lwa futi nayo esizibeni intombi. Y' ahlulek' intombi; s' ahluleka nesikqukqumadevu. Sa hlala naso manje esizibeni, ngokuba se si katele. Ya hlala nentombi, ngokuba nayo se i katele. Sa lala kona Isikqukqumadevu nentombi.

When she saw that she was forsaken by the other damsels, she laid hold of the Isikqukqumadevu, thinking she would take away from it her garment. She fought with the Isikqukqumadevu. It dragged her along on the ground, and sank with her in the pool. She continued to contend with it also in the pool. The damsel was unable to conquer, and so was the Isikqukqumadevu. It now rested in the pool, because it was tired; and the girl rested also, because she was tired. The Isikqukqumadevu slept there, and so did the girl.

---

[16] *Isigheghe* is that portion of the female dress which answers to the *isinene* of the male, which may be translated the *kilt*.

*The Isikqukqumadevu goes to fetch assistance, and Uluthlazase
escapes.*

Kwa sa kusasa, Isikqukquma-devu sa hamba, se si funa ukuya 'ubiza ezinye Izikqukqumadevu, ngokuba se s' a*h*lulekile, intombi i namand*h*la. Kwa vela esinye isilwanyana, sa tshela intombi, sa ti, "Hamba, ngokuba Isikqukqu-madevu si yobiza ezinye Izikqu-kqumadevu." Ya si tata ke leyo 'ntombi isigheghe sayo; ya kupuka ke emanzini; ya hamba ke, ya y' ekaya.

In the morning the Isikqukqu-madevu departed, wishing to call other Izikqukqumadevu, for it was unable to conquer, for the damsel was strong. There came another animal, and said to her, "Go away, for the Isikqukqumadevu has gone to call others." So she took her garment, and went up out of the water, and returned home.

The other girls deceive Uluthlazase's parents, and are killed.

Ya fika ekaya, intombi zi ti, "I tombile." Ya ngena end*h*lini kwabo. Wa kala unina, wa ti, "U vela pi? loku izintombi zi ti, u tombile." Ya ti, "Za ngi shiya esikqukqumadevwini." Unina wa tshela uyise, ukuti, "Umntwana, naugu wa e sesikqukqumadevwini." Uyise wa tata umkonto wake, wa u lola, wa zi vimbezela izintombi, wa ti, "Veza ni umntanami, ngi m bone." Za m *h*leka intombi. Za ti, "Uku m tanda kwako ku ya bonakala; ngokuba u t' a u m bone e tombile." Wa t' uyise, "Pela, ngi ti, ngi vezele ni yena, ngi m bone." Z' enqaba intombi, za ti, "U tombile; a si yi 'ku ku vezela yena." Wa tukutela uyise, wa ngena end*h*lini: za m bamba intombi; wa wa kqabula amakuko,

When she reached her home, the other girls were reporting that she had come to puberty. She went into her mother's house. Her mother wept, saying, "Whence comest thou? For the other girls say that the signs of puberty have come upon thee." She replied, "They left me with the Isikqukqumadevu." The mo-ther told her father, saying, "Our child, behold she was with the Isikqukqumadevu." The father took his assagai, and sharpened it, and barred the way against the other girls, and said, "Produce my child, that I may see her." The girls laughed at him. They said, "Your love for her is evideut, for you would see her whon she has the signs of puberty upon her." The father said, "Notwithstand-ing, I say, bring her out to me, that I may see her." The girls refused, saying, "She has the signs of puberty; we will not bring her out." The father was angry; he went into the hut: the girls caught hold of him; he pulled aside the mats; he saw that his

wa bona ukuba umntanake ka ko. Wa zi bamba ke izintombi, wa pumela nazo pand*h*le, wa zi bulala zonke. Wa i bulala ke nenkosazana yake Ubu*h*laluse, wa zi bulala zonke intombi. Ba buz' abantu ukuti, "Nkosi, abantwana u ba bulalele ni na?" Wa ti, "Ba m bulele Ulu*h*lazase. Ba m shiya esikqukqumadevwini." Wa m veza ke Ulu*h*lazase. Ba mangala ke abantu bonke ngokuba za fike za ti, u tombile.

child was not there. So he seized the girls, and dragged them outside, and killed them all. He killed also his princess Ubuthlaluse; he killed all the girls. The men asked, "Sir, why have you killed the children?" He replied, "They killed Uluthlazase. They left her with the Isikqukqumadevu." He brought her forth. So all the people wondered, for the girls had said, "She has the signs of puberty."

The father summons the nation, and goes in quest of the Isikqukqumadevu.

Wa si mema ke isizwe uyise kalu*h*lazase, wa ti, "A ko funwa Isikqukqumadevu." Kwa hanjwa ke nenkosazan'. Ya ba tshengisa ke isiziba. A ngena ke amadoda esizibeni. Sa tukutela Isikqukqumadevu, sa puma; ba si bulala.

Then Uluthlazase's father summoned the nation, and commanded the men to go in quest of the Isikqukqumadevu. The princess went also, and showed them the pool. The men entered the water; the Isikqukqumadevu was in a rage, and came out, and they killed it.

The damsels which the Isikqukqumadevu had devoured are recovered, and their fathers rejoice.

Za puma ke intombi zonke zelizwe lonke; ngokuba be si hambe si *h*lala esizibeni sentombi, si d*h*la intombi zi nga file. Kwa buywa nazo ke, kwa yiwa ekaya. Kw' ezwakala koyise bentombi ukuti, "Abantwana benu ba velile." B' eza nenkomo zokuza 'utata abantababo. Ba zi nika Usikulumi. Ba hamba nazo ke intombi zabo.

Then there came out all the damsels of the whole country; for it was accustomed to go and remain in the pool where the damsels bathed, and devour them alive. They went home with them. The damsels' fathers heard it reported that their children had come forth; and they came with cattle with which to take back their children.[17] They gave them to Usikulumi. And went away with their children.

[17] It is a custom among the Zulus if a child has been lost, and found by another man, for the parent to reclaim it by the offering of a bullock. The fathers are here represented as not merely fetching their children which the Isikqukqumadevu had devoured, but bringing cattle, as it were to redeem them.

Uluthlazase becomes queen.

Ya busa inkosazan' Uluhlazase; wa busa nezincane ke intombi. Uyise ke wa hlaba inkomo zokujabulisa umntanake, uba wa e dhliwe Isikqukqumadevu. Ba m bonga kakulu abantu, oyise bentombi, owa koka abantababo esikqukqumadevwini, ngokuba wa si bulala.

Then Uluthlazase the princess governed; she governed with the young girls, [who were not grown up when the others forsook her.] Then her father slaughtered cattle to make his child glad, because she had been carried away by the Isikqukqumadevu. And the men, the fathers of the damsels, thanked him exceedingly, who had taken their children out of the Isikqukqumadevu, because he killed it.

What the Isikqukqumadevu was like.

Ku tiwa Isikqukqumadevu a si naboya, sa si isilwane eside, si sikulu. Intombi lezo sa si zi ginya, si nga zi dhli.

UNYAOSE KCIYA,
(SOPHIA, UMKAJOSEFA.)

It is said that the Isikqukqumadevu was hairless; it was a long and large animal. It used to swallow the young girls without eating them.[18]

ULANGALASENHLA NOLANGALASENZANTSI.[19]

(ULANGALASENTHLA AND ULANGALASENZANTSI.)

KWA ku te ekukqaleni, kwa zalwa Ulangalasenhla, kwa zalwa Ulangalasenzantsi. Yebo.

IT used to be said long ago that Ulangalasenthla was born, and then Ulangalasenzantsi. That was it.

[18] This legend is very inferior in its general style to many of the others, and is devoid of life and incident. It was related by a young Ibakca woman. But it is worth retaining, as it appears to be made up of many others. Thus we have the two princesses, going with their attendants to bathe, as in the tale of Untombinde; but here the name is Uluthlazase; she is, however, the daughter of Usikulumi. Then the girls do not deceive in that tale, but go home weeping and report that she has been taken away by the Isikqukqumadevu. There is no fight there, as here, between the damsel and the monster, but she is swallowed up by it like others; and the army sent against it by Usikulumi is also destroyed; and it is ultimately killed by a man who has lost "twin children which were much beloved." Some of the other incidents are related in the tale of Usitungusobenthle; but there a cannibal takes the place of the Isikqukqumadevu. Then in a third tale Usitungusobenthle is carried off at the age of puberty by pigeons, and, after her escape from captivity, kills the Isikqukqumadevu, which had swallowed all her people, &c.

[19] Ulangalasenhla, Sun-of-the-West. Ulangalasenzantsi, Sun-of-the-East.—

Ulangalasenzantsi goes to fetch his children: his way is obstructed by ten swollen rivers, which divide, and he passes onward.

Wa ti Ulangalasenzantsi, "Ngi za 'kulanda abantwana bami, ngi bute izinkabi ezi lishumi." Wa tata ingubo embi, e 'sidwaba nje; wa hamba ke, e landa 'bantwana kulangalasen*h*la. Wa funyana umfula u g*c*wele; wa ponsa enye inkabi·; wa damuka umfula; wa wela. Wa hamba ke kaloku ke. Wa funyana omunye u g*c*wele; wa ponsa enye futi; wa vuleka umfula; wa wela; wa hamba ke. Wa funyana omunye u g*c*wele; wa ponsa enye yobutatu; wa vuleka umfula; wa hamba ke. Wa funyana omunye u g*c*wele; wa ponsa enye; wa vuleka umfula; wa hamba ke. Wa hamba kwowesi*h*lanu umfula; wa funyana u g*c*wele; wa ponsa enye; wa vuleka; wa hamba ke; wa wela. Kwa za kwa ba kwoweshumi; wa hamba ke, e se wele oweshumi umfula. Wa hamba ke, wa hamba ke, e se hamba yedwa, inkabi se zi pelile ezi lishumi.

Ulangalasenzantsi said, "I am going to fetch my children, when I have collected ten oxen." He took a good-for-nothing old, ragged garment, and so went to fetch his children, which were with Ulangalasenthla. He came to a swollen river; he threw in one ox;[20] the river divided, and he passed through. So now he went on his way. He came to another swollen river; again he threw in an ox; the river opened, and he passed through. So he went on his way. He came to another swollen river; he cast in a third ox; the river opened; and so he went on his way. He came to another swollen river; he cast in another ox; the river opened; and so he went on his way. He went to the fifth river, and found it full; he cast in another ox; the river opened; and he went on his way and passed through. So he went on his way, he having at length crossed the tenth river. So he went and went, going now alone; the ten oxen being now all disposed of.

These words, used as the names of the two kings, show that the legend had its rise among people dwelling on the *Eastern shore*, —that is, where the course of the rivers is towards the east. The sea is *below*, the mountains *above;* and so the Eastern sun, rising from the sea, is the Lower sun; and the Western, setting over the mountains, is the Upper sun.

[20] It is a custom among native tribes of South Africa to pay respect to rivers, which would appear to intimate that formerly they were worshipped, or rather that individual rivers were supposed to be the dwelling-place of a spirit. Thus when a river has been safely crossed, it is the custom in some parts to throw a stone into its waters, and to praise the *itongo*. Thompson, in his *Travels in Southern Africa*, speaking of the religion and superstitions of the Amak*x*osa, says :—"Sometimes they sacrifice to the rivers in time of drought, by killing an ox and throwing a part of it into the channel." *(Vol. II., p.* 352.) When Dingan's army was going against Umzilikazi, on reaching the banks of the Ubulinganto, they saluted it, saying, "*Sa ku bona, bulinganto,*" and having strewed animal charcoal *(umsizi)* on the water, the soldiers were made to drink it. The object of this was to deprecate some evil power destructive to life. which was supposed to be possessed by the river. It is a custom which cannot fail to recall what is recorded of Moses under somewhat different circumstances. (Exod. xxxii. 20.) There can be little doubt that Ulangalasenzantsi threw the oxen into the rivers as a sacrifice to the *amatongo*, or more probably to river-gods.

He comes to a spring, and falls in with his daughter's child.

Wa fika ke emtonjeni lapa·ku kiwa koná amanzi omuzi kalangalasen*h*la. Wa funyana abantwana abancinane be baningi kakulu. Wa fanisa umntwana, wa ti, "Lo 'mntwana okabani na?" Ba ti, "Okalangalasen*h*la." Wa ti, "U-nina ubani na?" Ba ti, "Umalangalasenzantsi." Wa ti, "A!" Wa ti, "Woza lapa." Wa tata um*h*langa. (Ngokuba be be ye 'kuka um*h*langa bonke abantwana.) Wa u kcoboza um*h*langa walowo 'mntwana wakwandodakazi yake, wa ti, "Hamba ke, u ye kunyoko, u ti, k' eze 'eze 'kukelela wena; u ti, 'Um*h*langa wami, mame, u file; hamba wena, u ye 'ku ngi kelela um*h*langa wami.'" Wa hamba ke unina, wa fika em*h*langeni.

So at length he came to a spring, where the water of the village of Ulangalasenthla was fetched. He found there very many little children. He thought he saw a resemblance in one of the children, and said, "Whose child is this?" They said, "Ulangalasenthla's." He said, "What is his mother's name?" They said, "Umalangalasenzantsi." [21] He said, "Ah!" He said, "Come here." He took a reed. (For all the children had gone to gather reeds.) He crushed the reed of that child, the child of his daughter; and said, "Just go to your mother, and tell her to come and pluck a reed for you; say, 'Mother, my reed is broken; do you go, and pluck a reed for me.'" So his mother went, and came to the bed of reeds.

Ulangalasenzantsi makes himself known to his daughter.

Wa t' e sa fika, wa puma Ulangalasenzantsi, wa ti, "Woza lapa, mntanami." Y' etuka inkosikazi, ya kala, ya ti, "Baba, u vela pi? loku Ulangalasen*h*la u ti, a nge ku bone ngame*h*lo ake; a nga ku bulala, ngokuba e *h*leli nabantwana bako, u za 'kwenza njani na?" Wa ti Ulangalasenzantsi, wa ti, "U za 'kuti, ngi zitolele uwhahiwhahi lwami olu ng' Ubombi. U nga tsho ukuba ngi u ye Ulangalasenzantsi. U ngi fi*h*le kuye Ulangalasen*h*la. U ti ngi umfokazi nje." Wa ti, "U babele ni na lapa, loku u ya songelwa; ku

When she came, Ulangalasenzantsi went out, and said, "Come hither, my child." The queen started and cried and said, "My father, whence do you come? Since Ulangalasenthla says, he cannot set eyes upon you; he could kill you, because he has possession of your children, what will you do?" Ulangalasenzantsi said, "You shall say, 'I have taken under my protection, for my own service, my tall man, whose name is Ubombi.' [22] Do not say I am Ulangalasenzantsi. Conceal me from Ulangalasenthla. Say I am merely a foreigner." She said, "What is your business here, seeing that you are threatened, and

---

[21] *Umalangalasenzantsi,*—that is, the daughter of Ulangalasenzantsi.
[22] *Ubombi.*—A ragged, shabby fellow.

tiwa u nge ze wa vela lapa?"
Wa ti, "U za 'udhla ni na? loku
kini ni dhla izinkwa zodwa, lo lapa
ku dhliwa utshwala bodwa; ukudhla kwamadoda." Wa ti, "U za
'u ngi gayela umbakqanga; u ngi
beke endhlini yakwasalukazi sa-
kwako. A ngi yi 'kuvela, a nga
ngi bona Ulangalasenhla. Ngi ya
'kuvela, ngi se ngi pumule. Ngi
za 'uke ngi pumule, and' uba ngi
ba bute abantwana bonke besizwe
sakiti. Ngi lande bona bonke
nawe. Ngi za 'ku m bulala umyeni wako."

it is said you are not to make your
appearance here?" She also said,
"What will you eat; since at
home you eat bread only, whilst
here beer only is drunk; that is
the men's food?" He said, "You
shall grind for me, and make me
stiff porridge; and put me in the
house of the old woman of your
family. I will not appear openly,
Ulangalasenthla may see me. I
will appear openly when I have
rested. I will just rest, and then
collect all the children of our
nation. I fetch them all and you.
I am about to kill your husband."

Ulangalasenzantsi appears openly to Ulangalasenthla.

Kwa sa ngelobutatu ilanga, wa
puma endhlini Ulangalasenzantsi.
Wa puma Ulangalasenhla, wa
kuluma, wa ti, "Lo u vela pi na?
Ubani lo na? O nga ti Ulangalasenzantsi na?" Wa ti, "I mina.
Ngi lande abantwana bami bonke
besizwe sakwiti." (Ba be tunjwe
impi kalangalasenhla.) Wa ti,
'Wo! Laba 'bantwana u nge ze
wa ba landa: abami. Ku za wa
b' ezwa."

On the morning of the third
day Ulangalasenzantsi went out of
the house. And Ulangalasenthla
went out and said, "Whence
comes this fellow? Who is he?
Is he not like Ulangalasenzantsi?"
He said, "It is I. I am come to
fetch all the children of our nation." (They had been taken captive by Ulangalasenthla's army.)
He said, "Wo! You shall never
take away the children: they
are mine. You shall never gain
possession of them."[23]

Ulangalasenthla summons his soldiers, and orders them to kill Ulanga-
lasenzantsi.

Wa biza umfana, wa ti, "Memeza impi yami, i ze 'kuzwa.
Nantsi indaba i fikile." Ya fika
impi yake. Wa ti, "Mu bulale
ni Ulangalasenzantsi. Ngi y' ala

He called a boy, and said,
"Summon my soldiers, that they
may come and hear. There has
arisen a matter of great importance." His soldiers came. He
said, "Kill Ulangalasenzantsi. I

[23] *Ku za wa b' ezwa,* i.e., *a ku sa yi 'kuze wa b' ezwa,* "You shall never feel
them,"—that is, lay hand on them, so as to possess them. This is said when a
dispute has arisen about children, and implies either a threat to kill the person
to whom it is addressed; or merely an assurance that he will lose his case.
If he gains the case, as he is walking off with the children, he may say in deri-
sion to his opponent, "I ba pi o te a ngi 'uze nga b' ezwa na? A si bo labo
na?" Where are those whom you said I should never lay hand on? Are they
not these?

nabantwana." Ba m pousa bonke ngemikonto. Ya t' imikonto a ya fika kuyo; ya ,hlaba nje kodwa. Wa i buta youke; wa ba nikela yona. Ba pinda ba ponsa. A i fikanga; 'emi nje yena; a ya fika futi imikonto yabo. Wa ti, " Ngi n' ahlulile ke kaloku. Leti ni ke abantwana bonke." Wa vuma Ulangalasenhla. Wa ti, " Yebo, u s' ahlulile." Wa ba buta bonke, wa ti, " Mu nike ni abantwana bakubo." Ba butana ke bonke. Wa ti, " Nampa ke abantwana bakini. Hamba ke." Wa hamba ke.

refuse to give up the children." All hurled their spears at him. The spears did not reach him; they merely fell on the ground. He collected them all, and gave them to the soldiers. Again they hurled their spears. They did not reach him; he remained standing; their spears did not reach him the second time. He said, "So I have conquered you now. Bring me then all my children." Ulangalasenthla agreed. He said, " Yes, you have now conquered us." He collected them all, and said, " Give him all the children of his people." So they all came together. He said, " Behold the children of your people. So go in peace." So he went on his way.

Ulangalasenthla sends his army after Ulangalasenzantsi.

Kwa ti emuva Ulangalasenhla wa landelisa impi yake yonke. Wa ti, " Hamba ni ke. Ku lungile. Ni m kqedel' enhle kanye nabantwana bake; ni buye ke nina, bauta bami." Ya hamba ke impi. Ya hamba ke, a ya fika; kwa u loku i hamba nje i nga fiki.

It came to pass afterwards that Ulangalasenthla made all his army pursue him. He said, " Go. You can kill them now.[24] Put an end to him in the wilderness, together with his children; and then do you come back, my people." So the army set out. It did not come up with him; though it went diligently, it did not come up with him.

They come to a flooded river, which divides, and allows them to pass.

Ba za ba ya ba fika emfuleni o 'manzi abomvu; omkulu kakulu; be u funyana u gcwele kakulu. Ulangalasenzantsi wa pakamisa intonga yake yobukosi; wa i pakamisa, umfula wa nqamuka, ba wela bonke. Ba hlala ke, ba y' etula imitwalo yabo, ba jabula, ba dhla, ba peka nokupeka.

Ulangalasenzantsi and his children at length came to a river whose waters were red; it was very great: they found it very much flooded. Ulangalasenzantsi raised his royal rod; he raised it, and the river was stayed, and they all passed over. Then they sat down, and took off their loads, and rejoiced and ate; they cooked a large quantity of food.

[24] *Ku lungile.*—It is right,—that is, we can readily kill them. If a man is has placed himself in such a position, as cipice, he shouts, *Wa lunga!* "You are they have got into such a position that pursuing another, and he sees that he by running towards an impassable precipice, he shouts, *Wa lunga!* "You are all right!"

The soldiers arrive at the river ; it divides : they enter ; it closes, and overwhelms them.

Ya fika impi pezu kwomfula. Ya memeza, ya ti, "Ni wele pi na ?" Ba ti, "Si wele kona lapo. Wela ni, ni ze 'ku si bulala." Ba ti bona, "K*q*abo ! A ni welanga lapa. Si t*sh*ele ni ?" Wa tata intonga yake Ulangalasenzantsi ; wa i pakamisa ; umfula wa n*q*a-muka. Wa ti, "Wela ni ke manje." Ba ngena bonke. Um-fula ubanzi. Ba te be pelele em-fuleni, wa i beka intonga yake ; umfula wa ba zibekela bonke.

The army reached the bank of the river. They shouted and said, "Where did you cross over ?" They said, "In this very place. Do you cross over, and come and kill us." They said, "No indeed ! You did not cross here. Tell us." Ulangalasenzantsi took his rod, and raised it, and the river was stayed. He said, "Cross over now then." They all entered. The river was wide. When they were all in the river, he dropped his rod, and the river overwhelmed them all.

Ulangalasenzantsi and his children rejoice.

Ba tokoza ; ba d*h*lala abantwana bake Ulangalasenzantsi ; ba jabula kakulu. Wa ti yena, "A ni boni ke na ? Ba pelile abe be za 'ku si bulala." Wa ti, "Twala ni ke, ni hambe, ni ye kwiti." Ba twala ke, ba hamba ke.

They rejoiced ; the children of Ulangalasenzantsi played ; they rejoiced exceedingly. He said, "Do you not see then ? They are come to an end, who were coming to kill us." He said, "Take up your loads, and let us go to our people." So they took up their burdens, and set out.

Ulangalasenzantsi and many others die in the way ; a few reach their home.

Wa fa end*h*leleni Ulangala-senzantsi. Ba hamba bodwa ke kaloku. Kwa vela umfo wabo owa be e kona kubo abantwana ; wa hamba nabo. Kwa vela ukufa, kwa ba bulala abadala ; ba sala abancane, ba sala nendoda yanye. Ba hamba ke njalo, ba za ba ya ba fika ezweni lakubo. Kwa kalwa kakulu. Kwa tiwa, "U pi umfo wenu ?" Wa ti, "U fele ezin-d*h*leleni." Kwa tiwa, "U fele pi

Ulangalasenzantsi died in the way. The people now went by themselves. His brother, who had been with the children, came, and went with them. Death came, and killed the old men. The young remained ; they remained with only one man. And so they journeyed, and at length came to the country of their people. There was a great lamentation. They said, "Where is your brother ?" He replied, "He died in the way." They said, "Where did he die ?"

na?" Wa ti, "Nami a ngi bonanga lap' e fele kona. Nomunye nomunye umfo wetu a ngi m bonanga, a ngi ba laħlanga nje; ba fa, ngi nga ba boni. Sa hamba kabi; sa hamba pakati kwezita. A ng' azi nokuba ba bulawa izita ini na."

Ba ħlala ke; b' aka ke; ba jabula ke; ba za ba buya b' anda.

Le 'nsumansumane indaba endala pakati kwakiti. Ku tiwa insumansumane, ngokuba labo aba be i kuluma kade ba dħlula kakulu; a ku s' aziwa uma i vela pi. Kepa ku tiwa insumansumane endala, ku nga ka fiki nabamħlope kulo 'mħlaba.

Umpondo kambule (Aaron).

He replied, "Neither did I see where he died. And another and another of our brethren, I did not see them, I did not bury them; they died without my seeing them. We journeyed with difficulty through the midst of enemies. I do not know even that they were killed by the enemy."

So they remained, and built houses, and rejoiced, and at length again became a great people.

This legend is an old tale amongst our people. It is called a myth, because they who used to tell it passed away a very long time ago; and it is no longer known whence it was derived. But it is said that it was an old legend, even before the white men came to this country.[25]

[25] Whatever may have been the origin of this tale, there are few who will not at once refer it to the history of Moses and Pharaoh. Vasco de Gama discovered Natal in 1497. In 1600 the Dutch trading vessels began to touch at the Cape, and in 1650 they formed a settlement there. A crew of a wrecked English ship passed through Natal to Capetown in 1683. (*Holden's History of Natal, p.* 36.) Kolben says:—"The *Caffres* traffick with the Rovers of the *Red* Sea, who bring 'em Manufactures of Silk for Elephants' Teeth. These Manufactures the *Caffres* exchange, as Ships from *Europe* touch at *de Natal*, for *European* commodoties; often for Tar, Anchors, and Cordage; which they exchange again with the Rovers of the *Red* Sea. The Silk they put not off to the Europeans, they dispose of to the Monomotapos. The *Portugueze* of *Mozambique* trade not a little with 'em." (*Kolben. Op. cit. Vol. I., p.* 82.) It is certain, therefore, that for many years the natives of Natal have had abundant opportunities of receiving from others the substance of this tale, which they may have worked up into a tale of their own. For whencesoever derived, it is now essentially Zulu in its character and accessories. At the same time, we cannot deny that it may be a tradition of the sojourn of the Israelites in Egypt and their deliverance from bondage, handed down from generation to generation, gradually becoming more and more corrupted, until the natives scarcely recognise of themselves any resemblance between it and the Scripture narrative, which they now have an opportunity of hearing from the missionaries, or reading for themselves. In another tale the sea divides at the word of Usitungusobenthle, when she is flying from the country by whose people she had been taken captive. And in the Hottentot fables, in like manner, Heitsi Eibip when pursued by an enemy prays, and the water divides, and he and his people pass through; and the enemy, attempting to follow, are destroyed. These facts show the wide-spread existence of such a tradition, and would appear to suggest some common origin. Dr. Bleek has shown that the Hottentot language belongs to the class of languages spoken in North Africa; and it may be regarded as an established fact that the Hottentots came from the north, having been separated from the northern tribes by the intrusion of another people, speaking a language of another class—the alliterative or Kafir language. (*Bleek's Comparative*

UBABUZE. [26]

Ubabuze obtains his father's permission to visit a maiden.

Kw' esukela, inkosi igama layo Ubabuze; kepa ya i tsandza ukuya entombini. Uyise wa y alela, abatali bayo; wa tsi, "Musa ni 'kuya kuleyo 'ntombi, ngobane a ku yi, lu buya ko." Kepa inkosi Ubabuze wa tsi, "Ndi ya tsandza ukuya lapo." Kepa uyise wa m vumela manje, wa m nika itinkomo etiningi; wa tsi, a k' a kambe ke. Wa m nika abantu[27] futs' bokukamba naye.

It happened that there was a king, whose name was Ubabuze; and he was wishing to visit a damsel. His father and mother objected; the father said, "Do not go to see that damsel, for no one goes there and comes back again." But the king Ubabuze said, "I wish to go there." Then the father assented, and gave him many cattle, and bid him good bye. He gave him also men to accompany him.

Ubabuze sets out with his people : he goes by the wrong road.

Wa kamba ke; abantu wa ba butsa bonke, wa kamba ke. Wa m tshena k' uyise ukutsi, "Mntwanami, u nga kambi ngaleyo 'ndhlela ey enyuka entsabeni; a u bo kamba ngendhlela yentsambeka." Wa kamba ke. Kepa kwa tsi ekwahlukaneni kwendhlela tombini, wa i yeka Ubabuze lowo leyo 'ndhlela uyise a b' e tsi, a t' a kambe ngayo; wa kamba ngaleyo 'ndhlela uyise a b' e tsi, a t' a nga kambi ngayo.

So he set out; he assembled his men, and set out. His father told him, saying, "My child, do not go by that road which goes up the mountain; but go by the road which runs round it." So he set out. But it came to pass that, at the separation of the two roads, Ubabuze left the road by which his father had told him to go; and went by that road by which his father told him not to go.

Grammar, p. viii.—*Prof. Max Müller's Lectures. Second Series, p.* 11.) It may not, therefore, be unreasonably surmised that they brought this tradition with them from their former home; and have imparted it to the Kafirs. It is worth noticing that in one of the Scotch legends, the daughter of a magician helps a lad, with whom she has fallen in love, to perform the difficult tasks appointed him by her father, and among other things "she strikes the sea with a rod, and makes a way to the island, where the nest was," which he had been commanded to fetch. *(Campbell. Op. cit. Vol. I., p.* 51.) So in "The Three Musicians," the dwarf is possessed of a magical rod, with which he struck the waters, "and immediately they divided, and left a passage, across which they passed with dry feet." *(Bechstein's Old Story-Teller, p.* 136.)

[26] This tale was told by a woman of the Amabakca, and it is printed in their dialect.

[27] *Abantu.*—I have not attempted to represent by orthography the sound the Amabakca give to *t* in this and in many other words, when followed by certain vowels. It is difficult to say whether the *t* is followed by a slender *f, v, u,* or *w* sound.

Ubabuze gets into trouble, and loses all his cattle and men.

Kwa tsi pambili wa fukana iti-lwanyana etiningi ; ta m bona e sa vela, ta m memeta e se kudze, ta tsi, " Babuze, babuze bankosi ! " Wa tsi ke Ubabuze, " Ubawo u be ngi tshena, e tsi, te ndi nga kambi ngale 'ndhlela ; wa tsi indhlel' imbi, i namadzhamtela." Ngaloku 'kutsho kwawo wa wa nika inkomo taningi. A buya a pindzha futs', a tsi, " Babuze ban-kosi ! " Wa w engeta futs', wa wa nika inkomo, ukudhla kwamadzhamtela. A ti kqedza ke, in-komo ta pela manje. A buya a kcela futs', a ts', " Babuze ban-kosi ! " Wa wa pa abantu manje. A buya a pindzha futs', a ts', " Babuze bankosi ! " Wa ba. kqe-dza manje abantu. A kcela futs' amadzhamtela. Wa kohlwa ma-nje, ngobane abantu se be pelile. Wa kamba e se yedvwa manje.

It came to pass that, on going forward, he fell in with many wild beasts ; they saw him as soon as he appeared, and shouted to him when he was still at a distance, and said, " Ubabuze, Ubabuze, son of the king ! " Ubabuze said, " My father told me not to go by this road ; he said it was a bad road, and infested by hyenas." At the saying of the hyenas he gave them many cattle. They said again, " Ubabuze, son of the king ! " He again gave some more cattle in addition to the first, the food for the hyenas. At length the cattle were all gone. The hyenas again asked, and said, " Ubabuze, son of the king ! " Now he gave them men. Again they said, " Ubabuze, son of the king ! " He now gave them all his people. The byenas again asked. He did not know what to do, for the men were all gone. He went on his journey alone now.

Ubabuze is helped by a mouse.

A buya a kcela futs', a ts', " Babuze bankosi ! " Wa gijima, wa fukana imbiba pambili. Ya ts' imbiba, " Ng' obule, u patse isikumba sami." Wa y obula kamsinya, ngokubane nanka amad-zhamtela e se ta 'kudhla, e se kedute. Wa si tata isikumba ke, sa m fukula manje ke, e se fika e funa uku mu dhla ; sa m paka-misela etulu emafwini ; a kamba pansi ke amadzhamtela. A buyela emva amadzhamtela.

The hyenas again asked, saying, " Ubabuze, son of the king ! " He ran, and fell in with a striped mouse in front. The mouse said, " Skin me, and carry my skin in your hand." He skinned it imme-diately, for there were the hyenas coming to eat him, they being now near at hand. So he took the skin, and it now bore him aloft when the hyenas came, wishing to eat him ; it lifted him on high to the clouds ; the hyenas went on the ground. The hyenas turned back again.

Ubabuze is conveyed through the air to his destination.

Sa m kambisa ke isikumba emafwini ; sa m bcka ekcaleni kwomuti, lapo ku kona intombi a i tsandzako. Wa ngena ke ekaya, e se e kamba pansi manje. U kamba naso ke isikumb' esi, e si bopelc etintongeni take. Ba *h*laba umkosi ke ekaya ngokujabula okukulu, ngokutsi, " Wa fika umyeni wenkosatana."

The skin bore him in the clouds, and put him down at the side of the kraal where was the damsel which he loved. He went into the house, he now walking on the ground. He took with him the skin, having bound it to his rods. They celebrated a festival at the kraal with great joy, saying, " A husband has come for the princess."

Ubabuze remains there a year, and then sets out with the wedding party.

Wa *h*latshiswa inkomo. Wa *h*lala ke. Wa ta wa pela lo 'nyaka a ye ngawo, e sa *h*leli kona. Uyise wentombi kwa ts' uba ku pele unyaka wa mema umtsimba omkulu wokuba u yotshatisa intombi yake. Ba ba ningi abantu abakambako.

They killed cattle for him, and he staid there. At the end of the year in which he went, he was still staying there. The damsel's father, when the year was ended, assembled a large marriage party, that it might go to the wedding of his daughter. Very many people of that place went.

Ubabuze takes many cattle with him.

Wa tsi, " Ngi nike ni futsi inkomo etiningi, ngobane ku kona amadzhamtela end*h*leleni; ngobane nami lapa nda ndi te nesive esiningi, nda ndi si nikwe ubawo, sa d*h*liwa amadzhamtela end*h*leleni." Wa m nika ke inkomo etiningi. Wa kamba ke nayo intombi ke nenkomo nabantu.

Ubabuze said; " Give me also many cattle, for there are hyenas in the way ; for I, when I was coming with many men, which my father gave me, the hyenas ate the whole of them in the way." So he gavc him many cattle. And he set out with the damsel, and the cattle, and the people.

Ubabuze restores to the mouse its skin, and kills an ox for it.

Wa fika ke lapo amadzhamtela a m beka kona ; wa fukana inyama yembiba, wa si beka kc isikumba enyameni yembiba ; wa i *h*labela ke imbiba inkabi, wa i shiya ke yonke leyo 'nyama, ya sa i d*h*liwa imbiba.

He came to the place where the hyenas left him ; he found the flesh of the striped mouse, and put its skin on it ; and then killed an ox for it, and left the whole of its flesh, and the mouse ate it.

Ubabuze's party exterminate the hyenas.

Wa fika emadzhamteleni; a buya a kcela futs', a ts', "Babuze bankos'!" A ka wa nikanga 'luto. Umne wabo intombi wa li gwaza elinye idzhamtela, eli inkosi yawo; a f' onke amadzhamtela.

He came to the hyenas; they begged again, saying, "Ubabuze, child of the king!" He did not give them anything. The brother of the damsel killed one of the hyenas, which was their chief; and all the hyenas died.

Ubabuze reaches home with his bride, and there is great rejoicing.

Ba kamba kaḿle ke manje. Ba vela ke ekaya kubo, kwa kalwa, ubane ku bonwe inkosi i sa buya, lo kwa ku tsiwa, I ya 'kufa. Ya fika ke ekaya ke; kwa ḿlatshwa inkomo ke etiningi; kwa ḿlatshiswa umtsimba nayo inkosi indodzana yabo. Ba tshata ke. Wa inkosikati ke. Abane wabo a ba be be sa buyela ekaya. Wonke umtsimba w' aka kona.

And so they now travelled prosperously. They came to their home. They made a funeral lamentation when they saw the king return, for they thought he would die. So he came to his home; and many oxen were killed; they killed for the marriage party, and for the king, their child. They were married, and she became the queen. Her brothers never went home again. The whole marriage party lived there.

UNYAOSE KCIYA,
(SOPHIA, UMKAJOSEFA.)

UMUNTU NENYONI.

(THE MAN AND THE BIRD.)

A woman goes to labour in the field: her labour is rendered useless by a wagtail.

Ba ti kambe, ab' az' insumansumane, kwa ku kona kukqala indḿlala enkulu, ku nge ko izinkomo futi. Kwa ti umfazi wa ya 'kulima ensimini; kwa ti kwa fika inyoni, ibizo layo umvemve. Umfazi wa lima, wa buya, wa y' ekaya. Kwa ti kusasa wa buya wa ya futi ukuya 'kulima. Kwa ti indima e be i lime izolo, ka bi

THEY say who are acquainted with old wives' tales, that there was formerly a great famine, and, besides, there were not any cattle. A woman went to dig in the garden; and there came a bird, which is called umvemve.[28] The woman dug, and went home again. In the morning she went again to dig. The new ground, which she

---

[28] The wagtail.

sa i bona; wa fika, se ku njengo-tshani nje. Wa ti, "Indima e ngi i lime izolo i pi na?" e kulu-ma yedwa. Wa pinda wa lima futi, e se pinda okobubili. Kwa ti e sa lima, kw' eza inyoni, ya *h*lala pezu kwomuti ebusweni bake, ya ti, "Tshiyo, tshiyo, tshiyo! Um*h*laba kababa lo, e ngi ti ng' a-la nawo. U b' u ngi pikelele. Zidinjana, mbembe! Bewana, sa-kasaka! Mpinyana, pok*g*opok*g*o! Gejana, ntshi!"

had dug yesterday, she could no longer see; she arrived at the place, and it was just like the grass. She said, "The ground I dug yesterday, where is it?" speaking to herself. She dug again the second time. As she was dig-ging there came the bird, and sat on a tree in front of her, and said, "Tshiyo, tshiyo, tshiyo! That is the land of my father, which I have always refused to allow to be cultivated. You have acted in opposition to me. Little clods, turn back again! Little seeds, be scattered in all directions! Little pick-handle, snap to pieces! Little pick, fly off!" [29]

The woman again tries, but the wagtail, as before, renders her labour vain.

Kwa ti wa ya 'kulima futi; umfazi wa fika; indima e be i lime izolo, futi e nga sa i boni; so ku njengaloku be ku njalo: ngo-kuba izidinjana za ti mbembe; nembeu ya ti sakasaka; nompini wa puka; negejo la ti ntshi. Wa pinda wa lima futi. Ya fika inyoni, ya ti, "Tshiyo, tshiyo, tshiyo! Um*h*laba kababa lo, e ngi ti ng' ala nawo. U b' u ngi pikelele. Zidinjana, mbembe! Be-wana, sakasaka! Mpinyana, po-k*g*opok*g*o! Gejana, ntshi!" Kwa se ku ba njengokutsho kwayo. Izidinjana za ti mbembe; nembeu ya ti sakasaka; nompini wa puka; negejo la ti ntshi.

The woman went to dig again; she came; a second time she could no longer see the ground she had dug on the day before; it was now as it used to be: for the little clods had turned back; the seed was scattered; and the handle was broken; and the pick was off. Again she dug. The bird came, and said, "Tshiyo, tshiyo, tshiyo! That is my father's land, which I have always refused to have culti-vated. You have acted in oppo-sition to me. Little clods, turn back again! Little seeds, be scattered! Little pick-handle, snap to pieces! Little pick, fly off!" And so it was in accordance with its saying. The little clods turned back; and the seed was scattered; and the handle was broken; and the pick flew off.

---

[29] These diminutives are to be understood as spoken in contempt, and not to refer to size.

She goes home and tells her husband of the wonderful bird.

Wa buya futi umfazi ukuya ekaya, wa ya 'kutshela indoda yake; wa ti kuyo, "I kona inyoni e ngi ti lapa ngi limayo, i fike, i ti kwimi, 'Umhlaba kababa lo, e ngi ti ng' ala nawo. U b' u ngi pikelele. Zidinjana, mbembe! Bewana, sakasaka! Mpinyana, pokqopokqo! Gejana, ntshi!' Se ku njengokutsho kwayo."

The woman went home again to tell her husband; she said to him, "When I am digging, there is a bird which comes and says to me, 'That is my father's land, which I have always refused to have cultivated. You have acted in opposition to me. Little clods, turn back! Little seed, be scattered! Little handle, snap to pieces! Little pick, fly off!' And it is as it says."

The husband catches the bird, and obtains a feast, which he eats alone.

Kwa ti kusasa kwa puma umfazi kukqala, wa ya 'kulima, se be kcebe ikcebo lokuti, "Uma se ngi lima, wo fika, wena ndoda, u ze 'kubona oku tshiwoyo inyoni." Ya landela indoda, ya hlala eduze nomfazi, ya kcatsha. Kwa ti umfazi e lima, ya fika inyoni futi, ya pinda ya tsho njalo. Indoda ya se i zwa, ya vumbuluka pantsi, ya pakama, ya i bona inyoni e kulumayo : ya i sukela, ya i kqotsha; ya baleka inyoni, nendoda nayo futi. Inyoni ya tshona ngalukalo, indoda ya tshona ngalukalo futi; ya i kqotsha njalo; ya za ya dinwa inyoni; ya i bamba. Ya ti inyoni, "A k' u ngi yeke; ngi za 'ku kw enzela umlazana." Indoda ya ti, "Ake w enze ke, ngi bone." Y' enza, ya kam' umlaza, ya ti khla. Ya puza indoda. Ya ti futi, "Ake w enz' isangqondwane." Ya ti puhlu, puhlu, puhlu.

In the morning the woman went out to dig first, they having devised a plan, to wit, "When I am digging, you shall come, husband, to see what the bird says." The husband followed, and sat near the woman, in concealment. As the woman was digging, the bird came again, and said the same as before. The husband heard it, and came up from under the bush on the ground, and raised himself, and saw the speaking bird : he sprang at it, and drove it away ; the bird fled, and the man also ran after it. The bird passed over the hill, the man passed over also ; he drove it without ceasing ; at length the bird was tired, and the man caught it. The bird said, "Leave me alone, and I will make you some whey." The man said, "Just make it then, that I may see." The bird made it, and strained the whey ; it gurgled.[30] The man drank. He said also, "Just make curds too." It made a flopping noise.[30] The man ate, and was

---

[30] *Khla, Puhlu.*—These are onomatopoetic words, and are intended to imitate the sound occasioned respectively by taking out the stopper of the calabash for the purpose of pouring out whey, and that occasioned by pouring out the thick curds.

Ya d*h*la indoda, y' esuta, loku kad' i lambile; i jabula, ya ti, i tole inkomo. Ya hamba nayo, ya fika end*h*lini kwayo, ya i faka embizeni, ya i nameka, ukuba abantwana nomfazi wayo ba nga i boni, ku be isisulu sayo yodwa; ngokuba ya ku zuza yodwa.

satisfied, for he had been a long time hungry; and said, rejoicing, that he had found a cow.[31] He went home with it, and put it in a pot in his hut, and luted it down, that his wife and children might not see it; that it might be his own private titbit; for he got it by himself.

The husband again feasts alone, by night, when the rest are asleep.

Kwa ti umfazi wa ya 'kulima, nendoda ya ya 'kulima; ba buya bobabili futi; indoda ya fika, kwa *h*lwa; ba lala bouke; yona kodwa a ya ze ya lala: ya ya embizeni, ya zibukula. Wa fika, inyoni i s' i te kcoka pezulu: wa i bamba ngesand*h*la; wa ka amasi, wa kela esitsheni sake; wa buya, wa i faka embizeni, wa i nameka. Wa d*h*la amasi yedwa, se be lele bonke abantwana nonina.

The wife went to dig, and the husband went to dig; both came back again; the husband returned when it was dark; they all lay down to sleep; but the man did not sleep: he went to the pot, and uncovered it. The bird was sitting on the top: he held it in his hand; he poured out the amasi[32] into his vessel; and again put the bird into the pot, and luted it down. He ate the amasi alone, all the children and their mother being asleep.

One of the children, having seen the father feasting, reveals the discovery to the other.

Kwa ti kusasa indoda y' emuka, ya ya 'kugaula izibonda; umfazi wayo wa ya 'kulima; kwa sala abautwana bodwa. Kanti omunye umntwana u m bonile uyise e d*h*la amasi yedwa, wa ba tshela abanye kusasa, wa ti, "Ngi m bonile ubaba; ku kona e be ku d*h*la kusi*h*lwa, se si lele sonke; u zibukule embizeni; nga bona e ka amasi kona; nga tula nje, nga ti, i kona e ya 'kuti a nga hamba a

In the morning the man went to cut poles, and his wife went to dig; and the children remained alone. But one of the children had seen his father eating the amasi alone, and said to the other children, "I saw father; there was something which he was eating in the night, when we were all asleep; he took the cover off the pot; I saw him pour out amasi from it; I was silent, and said, there is something which will take him to a distance; and then

---

[31] This wonderful bird was only a little inferior to Mick Purcell's Bottle, which he purchased of one of the "Good People" with his last cow, from which proceeded at suitable times "two tiny little fellows," who spread his table with the best of food, on gold and silver dishes, which they left behind; very considerately remembering that Mick and his family required other things besides food! (*Croker's Fairy Tales.* "Legend of Bottle Hill," p. 33.)

[32] *Amasi.*—Sour milk, but properly prepared, not what we should understand by sour milk. The native name is therefore retained.

ye kude, si sale, si wa d*h*le amasi, loku e si ncitshayo." Ba sala, ba ya 'kuzibukula embizeni ; ba i fumana inyoni i s' i te kcoka pezulu kwamasi ; ba i bamba ; ba d*h*la, ba d*h*la, ba d*h*la, ba d*h*la, ba za b' esuta. Ba sibekela futi. Wa ti uyise, "Banta bami, ni d*h*le ni na, ni suti kangaka nje na ?" Ba ti, "A si suti 'luto," be m ko*h*lisa.

we will eat amasi, for he begrudges us." Then they went to uncover the pot ; they found the bird sitting on the top of the amasi ; they held it ; they ate, they ate, they ate, they ate, until they were satisfied. They covered it up again. The father said, " My children, what have you been eating, to be so stuffed out ?" They said, " We are not stuffed out with anything," deceiving him.

All the children watch their father at his solitary nocturnal feast.

Kwa *h*lwa indoda y' enza njalo futi, se be lele bonke futi. Kanti omunye u ba tshelile ikcebo, ukuba ba ze ba nga lali, ba ke ba bheke ukuba uyise wabo u ya 'kwenza njani na. Lapa se be lele bonke, y' enza njalo ke indoda ; ya zibukula, ya d*h*la, ya d*h*la ; ya buya, ya sibekela. Kanti se be m bonile abantwana bake, ukuba u ya ba ncitsha ukud*h*la. Ba ti, " Ku ya 'kusa kusasa, si ya 'kubona ukuba ka yi 'kumuka ini na."

In the night the husband did the same again, when they were all again lying down. But one of them told them a plan, that they should not sleep, but just see what their father would do. When they had all lain down, the man did as before ; he opened the pot, and ate, and ate ; and then covered it up again. But his children had seen him, and knew that he begrudged them food. They said, " The morning will come, and we shall see if he will not go out."

During the feast of the children, the bird escapes.

Kwa ti kusasa y' emuka indoda. Ba ya ba zibukula ; ba fika, inyoni i s' i te kcoka pezulu ; ba i susa ; ba d*h*la, ba d*h*la. Wa ti o i peteyo ya m punyuka, ya baleka, ya ti dri ; ya *h*lala emnyango. Omunye umntwana, Udemazane ibizo lake, wa ti, " Demane, nansi inyoni kababa i muka bo !" Udemane wa ti, " Ake w enze ka*h*le, mnta kababa, ngi sa funda 'mtanyana." Y' esuka inyoni emnyango, ya ti dri ; ya *h*lala pand*h*le ebaleni. Wa

In the morning the man departed. The children went and uncovered the pot ; when they came, the bird was sitting on the top ; they took it out, and ate, and ate. The bird slipped from him who held it, and flew away with a whir, and stopped at the doorway. One of the boys, Udemazane by name, said, " Udemane, see father's bird is going away then !" Udemane said, " Wait a bit, child of my father, I am in the act of filling my mouth." The bird quitted the doorway with a whir, and stopped outside in the open space.

ti Udemazane futi, "Demane, nansi inyoni kababa i muka bo!" Wa ti Udemane, "Ake w enze ka*h*le, mnta kababa, ngi sa funda 'mtanyana." Y' esuka inyoni ebaleni, ya ti dri; ya *h*lala pezu kwotango. Wa pinda wa tsho njalo Udemazane. Inyoni ya ze ya ndiza, ya hamba, y' emuka. Kwa ku pela.

Udemazane said again, "Udemane, see father's bird is going away then!" Udemane said, "Just wait a bit, child of my father, I am in the act of filling my mouth." The bird quitted the open space with a whir, and pitched on the fence. Udemazane said the same words again. The bird at length flew away and departed. That was the end.

The father, finding the bird gone, mourns in vain for his titbit.

Wa buya uyise. Kwa ti kusi*h*lwa, e ti u se za 'kutola isisulu sake, ka be sa i bona inyoni, amasi futi e nga se nga nani. Wa mangala, wa biza abantwana bake, wa ti, "Ku pi o be ku lapa embizeni na?" Ba ti abantwana, "A si kw azi." Omunye wa ti, "K*q*abo! Ba ya ku ko*h*lisa, baba. Inyoni yako ba i yekile; y' emuka; namasi futi si wa d*h*lile." Wa ba tshaya kakulu, e mangalele isisulu sake, e ti u se za 'kufa ind*h*lala. Kwa so ku ba 'kupela ke.

The father returned. At night, when he thought he was going to get his titbit, he no longer saw the bird, and there was no longer much amasi left.[33] He wondered, and called his children, and asked, "What has been here at the pot?" The children said, "We don't know." But one said, "No, then! They are deceiving you, father. They have let go your bird, and it has gone away; and we have eaten the amasi also." He beat them very much, punishing them for the loss of his titbit,[34] thinking he should now die of famine. So that was the end.[35]

ULUTULI DHLADHLA (USETEMBA.)

---

[33] Lit., Was no longer as big as anything.

[34] Lit., charging them with having taken away his titbit.

[35] The reader will find the power of rendering labour vain, ascribed to a bird in the above tale, ascribed to all beasts, in a legend of Central America:—
"When the two princes Hunahpu and Xbalanque set themselves one day to till the ground, the axe cut down the trees and the mattock cleared away the underwood, while the masters amused themselves with shooting. But the next day when they came back, they found the trees and creepers and brambles back in their places. So they cleared the ground again, and hid themselves to watch, and at midnight all the beasts came, small and great, saying in their language, 'Trees, arise; creepers, arise!' and the trees returned to their places." (*Tylor's Early History of Mankind, p.* 356.) Compare also Note 52, p. 51.

UKCOMBEKCANTSINI.

The wives of a certain king give birth to crows. His queen has no child.

.Kwa ku kona inkosi etile ku-leso 'sizwe ; ya i zala abantwana aba amagwababa, i nga m zali umntwana o umuntu ; kuzo zonke izind*h*lu i zala amagwababa. Kepa

THERE was a certain king of a certain country ; he used to have children who were crows,[36] he had not one child that was a human being ; in all his houses[37] his children were crows. But his queen

[36] There are among the natives legends of women giving birth to crows, and to beings resembling horses and elephants. Such legends probably had their origin in monstrous births, which bore a real or fancied resemblance to such animals. This notion of human females giving birth to animals is common among other people. In the Prose Edda we read of the woman Gefjon, who had four sons by a giant, who were oxen. (*Mallet. Northern Antiquities, p.* 398.) And of the hag, Járnvid, who was the mother of gigantic sons, who were shaped like wolves. (*Id., p.* 408.) Loki gave birth to the eight-legged horse, Sleipnir. (*Id., p.* 434.) In the *Pentamerone* we read of a woman who brought forth a myrtle, which turned out to be a fairy, who ultimately married a prince. ("The Myrtle.") Pasiphae gave birth to the monstrous Minotaur ; and Leda to two eggs, from each of which sprang twins. And in a recent number of *All the Year Round* we read of a Mary Loft, living during the last century, who succeeded in persuading many men of science, that she had become the mother of sixteen rabbits !

But this giving birth to animals is almost always, in these tales, spoken of as a disgrace to the human being, and is felt to be a reproach. In some tales a charge of giving birth to animals is made against a queen by malice for the purpose of taking away the king's affection. And the term *Igwababa* (crow) is an epithet of contempt ; it is not clear in some of the tales whether we are to understand it in this way or literally. It is evident, however, in the tale of Ukcombekcantsini, that we are to understand the word literally. All the children of the king were crows. It is amusing to see how the people appear to think that giving birth to such animals is better than sterility. We alluded above to the notion of marriage with animals as possibly intimating a sympathy with the lower world of animal life. But clearly it is not such a sympathy as would allow, or scarcely even suggest, the possibility of overleaping the natural antipathy which exists between the human and all other animal species. This is evident from the repugnance which is frequently expressed for the bridegroom whilst under the animal form ; and which is overcome only, when under that form he manifests the dispositions of man ; the sympathy is with the human spirit even when manifesting itself under the form of a lower animal ; the love is for the human being which the animal form conceals ; and whilst that form is ascribed to the wicked influence of magic, love often becomes the immediate means of delivering the spell-bound being from his degradation. Such tales, therefore, really become parables in which the power of love over brute nature, to exalt and elevate it, receives illustration. The invariably much greater repugnance expressed for giving birth to animals, on the other hand, may be a kind of protest against degeneration. Many such legends were originally, no doubt, metaphorical, or alluded to some real fact misunderstood and misexplained.

. [37] Each wife of a polygamist has her own dwelling and establishment ; each such separate establishment is called a house.

inkosikazi yayo ya i nge namntwa-na, kwa ku tiwa inyumba; ya *h*lala isikati eside i nga zali. Be i *h*leka bonke nabesifazana labo bona aba zala amagwababa, be ti, "Ka-nti tina si ya zala namagwababa odwa lawa, kepa wena a u zali 'luto. Kepa u ti u umuntu wo-kwenza ni na?" A kale, a ti, "Kepa nga zenza ini na? loku nani ni ya zala ngokuba kwa tiwa, Zala ni."

had no child; it was said she was barren; she remained a long time without having any child. All used to jeer her, and even the very women who gave birth to crows, saying, "We indeed do give birth only to crows; but you give birth to nothing. Of what use then do you say you are?" She cried, saying, "But did I make myself? For even you are mothers, because it was said, 'Be ye mothers.'"[38]

The childless queen receives assistance from some pigeons.

Wa ze w' emuka wa ya 'ulima; ngesikati sokulima, kwa ti lapa insimu e se za 'u i kqeda, kwa fika amavukutu emabili; a fika kuyena e *h*lezi pansi, e kala. La ti elinye kwelinye, la ti, "Vukutu." La ti elinye, "U ti 'Vukutu' ni na, u nga buzi uma u kalela ni na?" Wa ti, "Ngi ya kala ngokuba ngi nga zali. Abanye abafazi benkosi ba ya zala amagwababa, kepa mina a ngi zali 'luto." La ti elinye, "Vukutu." La ti elinye, "U ti 'Vukutu' ni, u nga buzi ukuti uma si m zalisa a nga si nika ni?" Wa ti, "Ngi nga ni nika konke e ngi uako." La ti, "Vukutu." La ti elinye, "U ti 'Vukutu' ni, u nga buzi ukuti ukud*h*la kuni a nga si nika kona na?" Wa ti, "Ngi nga ni nika amabel' ami." La ti, "Vukutu." La ti elinye, "U ti 'Vukutu' ni, loku si nga wa d*h*li amabele?" Wa ti, "Ngi ya 'u ni nika amadumbi." La ti, "Vukutu." La ti elinye, "U ti

At length she went to dig; when she was digging, and the garden was now nearly finished, two pigeons came to her as she was sitting on the ground and weeping. One said to the other, "Vukutu." The other said, "Why do you say 'Vukutu,' and not ask why she is crying?" She said, "I am crying because I have no child. The other wives of the king give birth to crows; but I give birth to nothing." One said, "Vukutu." The other said, "Why do you say 'Vukutu,' and not ask her what she will give us, if we give her power to have a child?" She replied, "I could give all I pos-sess." One said, "Vukutu." The other said, "Why do you say 'Vukutu,' and not ask what food she will give us?" She said, "I would give you my amabele."[39] One said, "Vukutu." The other said, "Why do you say 'Vukutu,' since we do not eat amabele?" She said, "I will give you ama-dumbi."[40] One said, "Vukutu." The other said, "Why do you say

---

[38] *Kwa tiwa, Zala ni.*—This saying is worthy of note. It is common among the natives. They say it is a reference to the word which Unkulunkulu, when he broke off all things from Uthlanga in the beginning, uttered, deter-mining by an ordinance all future events.

[39] *Amabele*, Native corn.

[40] *Amadumbi*, a kind of arum, the tubers of which are used as food.

'Vukutu' ni, u nga ti, a si wa tandi amadumbi." Wa bala konke ukud*h*la a nako. A kw ala. Wa ze wa ti, "'Kupela kokud*h*la e ngi nako." La ti, "Vukutu : u nawo amabele ; kepa tina si funa in*h*lakuva." Wa ti, "O, ngi nazo in*h*lakuva, makosi ami." La ti elinye, "Vukutu." La ti elinye, "U ti 'Vukutu' ni, u nga ti a ka tshetshe masinya, a ye ekaya a yo'utata in*h*lakuva ?"

'Vukutu,' and not tell her we do not like amadumbi ?" She mentioned all the kinds of food she had. They refused it all. At length she said, "That is all the food I have." The pigeon said, "Vukutu : you have amabele ; but for our part we like castor-oil seeds." She said, "O, I have castor-oil seeds, sir." One said, "Vukutu." The other said, "Why do you say 'Vukutu,' and not tell her to make haste home at once, and fetch the castor-oil seeds ?"[41]

The queen fetches castor-oil seeds for the pigeons.

W' esuka masinyane umfazi, wa gijima, wa ya ekaya ; wa fika wa zi tata in*h*lakuva, zi sempandeni, wa zi tululela ek*q*omeni ; wa zi twala, wa ya nazo ensimini. Wa fika, la ti elinye, "Vukutu." La ti elinye, "U ti 'Vukutu' ni, u nga ti, a ka tele pansi ?" Wa zi tela pansi in*h*lakuva. A kcotsha amavukutu, a k*q*eda.

The woman ran home at once ; on her arrival she took the castor-oil seeds which were in a pot,[42] and poured them into a basket, placed them on her head, and went with them to the garden. On her arrival one said. "Vukutu." The other said, ●Why do you say 'Vukutu,' and not tell her to pour the seeds on the ground ?" She poured the castor-oil seeds on the ground. The pigeons picked them all up.

The pigeons draw blood from her, and tell her what to do with the clot.

A ti e se k*q*edile, la ti elinye, "Vukutu." La ti elinye, "U ti 'Vukutu' ni, u nga buzi uma u ze nalo upondo nen*h*langa na ?" Wa ti, "K*q*a." La ti elinye, "Vukutu." La ti elinye, "U ti 'Vu-

When they had eaten them all, one said, "Vukutu." The other said, "Why do you say 'Vukutu,' and not ask her if she has brought a horn and a lancet ?"[43] She said, "No." One said, "Vukutu." The other said, "Why do you say

---

[41] Compare the conversation between the Ravens in the tale of "The Faithful Johan." (*Grimm. Op. cit., p.* 29.) And that between the gold and the silver pigeons in "The Battle of the Birds." (*Campbell. Op. cit. Vol.* I., p. 37.)

[42] *Umpanda* is an earthen pot which is cracked, and no longer of any use but for holding seed, &c.

[43] *Inhlanga* is a term applied both to the small knife with which the natives scarify, and to the scarifications.

kutu' ni na, u nga ti, ka hambe a lande upondo nen*h*langa?" Wa gijima, wa fika ekaya, wa tata upondo nen*h*langa, wa buya masinyane. Wa fika, la ti elinye, "Vukutu." La ti elinye, "U ti 'Vukutu' ni, u nga ti, ka fulatele?" Wa fulatela. La ti elinye, "Vukutu." La ti elinye, "U ti 'Vukutu' ni, u nga m gcabi esin*q*eni na?" La m gcaba. Kepa uma se li k*q*edile uku m gcaba, la tata upondo, la tela kona i*h*lule. La ti elinye, "Vukutu." La ti elinye, "U ti 'Vukutu' ni, u nga ti uma e se fikile ekaya, a ka ze a fune isitsha esikulu, a tele pakati kwaso, ku ze ku fe inyanga ezimbili, k' and' uma a zibukule esitsheni?" Wa buya, wa fika, w' enza njalo.

'Vukutu,' and not tell her to go and fetch a horn and a lancet?" She ran home, and fetched a horn and a lancet, and came back immediately. On her arrival one said, "Vukutu." The other said, "Why do you say 'Vukutu,' and not tell her to turn her back to us?" She turned her back to them. One said, "Vukutu." The other said, "Why do you say 'Vukutu,' and not scarify her on the loins?" The pigeon cupped her; but when he had finished cupping her, he took the horn, and poured the clotted blood into it. One said, "Vukutu." The other said, "Why do you say 'Vukutu,' and not tell her on reaching home to find a large vessel, and pour the clotted blood into it, until two moons die; and then uncover the vessel?" She went home and did so.

She finds two children in the clot at the end of four months.

Wa *h*lala inyanga za za za ba mbili. Kwa ti uma so ku twasa eyesitatu inyanga, wa funyanisa abantwana be babili. Wa ba kipa kuleso 'sitsha. Wa buya wa ba

She remained two months: when the third new moon appeared, she found two children;[44] she took them out of the vessel; and placed them again in another

[44] In Stephens' *Incidents of Travel in Central America* there is a curious legend, which may be compared with this. An old woman mourned that she was childless. She took an egg, covered it with cloth, and laid it in a safe place. She examined it daily, and at length was gladdened by finding it hatched, and a baby born. The baby thus obtained had many characteristics in common with Uthlakanyana. In the Polynesian mythology, Maui is represented as having been prematurely born as his mother was walking on the sea shore; she wrapped the abortion up in a tuft of her hair, and threw it into the foam of the surf; it became enfolded in sea-weed, and the soft jelly-fish rolled themselves around it to protect it. His great ancestor, Tama-nui-ki-te-Rangi, attracted by the flies, "stripped off the encircling jelly-fish, and behold within there lay a human being." And Maui became the Great Hero. In the same legends the origin of Whakatau, the great magician, is still more remarkable :—"One day Apakura went down upon the sea-coast, and took off a little apron which she wore in front as a covering, and threw it into the ocean, and a god named Rongotakawiu took it and shaped it, and gave it form and being, and Whakatau sprang into life, and his ancestor Rongotakawiu taught him magic and the use of enchantments of every kind." (*Grey. Op. cit., pp.* 18, 19, *and p.* 116.)— Compare also the Highland legend of the birth of Gili-doir Maghrevollich, or The Black Child, Son to the Bones. (*Scott's Lady of the Lake.* Note on the

faka kwenye imbiza. Wa *h*lala kwa ba izinyanga ezintatu e nga bheki kona. Wa ti·lapa e se bheka ngeyesine inyanga, wa funyana se be bakulu, se' be *h*leka; rewa, jabula kakulu.

large pot. She remained three moons[45] without looking into it. When she looked on the fourth moon, she found them now large, and laughing. She greatly rejoiced.

She conceals the children, and feeds them by night.

Wa puma e ya 'ulima. Wa fika en*h*le, wa *h*lala pansi, la ze la tshona, e ti, "Umakazi ba nga sinda ini abanta bami? loku ngi *h*lekwa abanye abafazi; ingani nabo a ba zali 'bantu, ba zala amagwababa." Kwa ze kwa ti ntambama wa buya wa fika ekaya. Kwa ti kusi*h*lwa, lapa e se za 'ulala, a vale emnyango ngesivalo na ngesi*h*land*h*la, e ti, kona ku ya 'kuti noma·umuntu e d*h*lula emnyango a nga boni 'luto. Wa *h*lala. Kwa ti lapa e se bona ukuti abantu a ba sa nyakazi pakati kwomuzi, w' esuka, wa ba

She went to dig. When she reached the garden, she sat down till the sun went down, saying, "Can it be that my children can live? For I am jeered by the other women; and even they, forsooth, do not give birth to human beings; they give birth to crows." In the afternoon she would return home. When it was evening, and she was about to lie down, she shut up the doorway with the wicker door, and with a mat, saying, "Then, although any one pass by the door, he will see nothing." She waited, and when she saw that the people no longer went up and down in the village, she took her

line, "Of Brian's birth strange tales were told.") But the production of a "fetcher," as recorded in the Icelandic legends, is still more remarkable. A woman steals a dead man's rib, over which she performs certain incantations, and lays it on her breast; three times she goes to Communion, but uses the wine to inject into the extremities of the bone; on the third time the "fetcher has acquired his full life and strength." When she can no longer bear him on her breast, she makes a wound in her thigh and places him to it, and he draws from thence his nourishment for the rest of his existence. The "fetcher" becomes a kind of familiar to his mother, who employs him for the purpose of sucking the cows of other people, the milk of which he brings home, and disgorges into his mother's churn.—To the same class of eccentric thought may be referred the origin of the good old Raymond's steed,

> "Which, Aquilino for his swiftness hight,"

was bred by the Tagus. His dam

> " When first on trees bourgeon the blossoms soft,
>   Prick'd forward with the sting of fertile kind,
> Against the air casts up her head aloft,
>   And gathereth seed so from the fruitful wind;
> And thus conceiving of the gentle blast,
> (A wonder strange and rare), she foals at last!

> " And had you seen the beast you would have said
>   The light and subtle wind his father was;
> For if his course upon the sands he made,
>   No sign was left what way the beast did pass."

—*Tasso's Jerusalem Recovered. Fairfax.* B. vii., LXXV—LXXVII.

[45] That is, three months from the time of putting the clot into the first vessel; one from the time she placed it in the second.

tata abantwana, wa ba beka okcansini, wa tata ubisi, wa ba nika;
omunye o umfana wa lu puza, intombazana ya lw ala. Kwa ti lapa
e se kade e *h*lezi nabo, wa buye
wa ba buyisela endaweni yabo;
wa lala.

children, and placed them on a
mat, and took milk and gave
them; the· boy drank it, but the
little girl refused it. When she
had remained with them a long
time, she put them back again into
their place; and slept.

The crows trouble the queen.

Kwa ti ukukula kwabo, ba kula
masinyane bobabili; ba ze ba kasa
be nga bonwa 'muntu; ba ze ba
hamba, unina e ba fi*h*la kubantu.
Ba *h*lala, be nga pumeli pand*h*le,
unina 'ala, e ti, uma be pumile ba
ya pand*h*le, ba ya 'ubonwa amagwababa, a ba bulale, ngokuba a e
m *h*lupa na send*h*lini. Ku ti uma
e vukile kusasa wa ya 'kuka amanzi, wa hamba wa ya 'ulima, ku ti
e se buya ntambama a funyanise
amanzi e se kcitiwe ind*h*lu yonke
nomlota so u kitshiwe eziko, so ku
m*h*lope end*h*lini. A ti, "Loku ku
ng' enza ngokuba ngi nga zali namagwababa odwa lawa; ngokuba
nami uma ngi ya zala, nga ku nga
ng' enzi loku 'kwenza; ngokuba se
nga *h*lupeka kangaka, na sendodeni
eya ngi zekayo i nga sa ng' enzi
'muntu ngokuba ngi nga zali."

As regards their growth, both
grew very fast; at length they
crawled on the ground, not having
been seen by any one; at length
they walked, their mother concealing them from the people. They
remained in the house, not going
out, their mother not allowing
them, saying, if they went out
they would be seen by the crows,
and they would kill them; for
they used to vex her in her very
house. For it was so that when she
had risen in the morning, and
fetched water and then went out
to dig, when she returned in the
afternoon, she found the water
spilt over the whole house, and
the ashes taken out of the fire-
place, and the whole house white
with the ashes. She said, "This
is done to me because I do not
give birth even to these crows; for
if I too gave birth, I should not
be treated thus; for I have now
been afflicted for a long time in
this way; and even with my husband who married me it is the
same; he no longer regards me as
a human being, because I have no
child."

The queen gives the girl a name.

Ba kula ke abantwana bobabili,
ba ze ba ba bakulu. Ya ti intombazana ya ze ya ba ikqikiza;
nomfana wa ba insizwa. Wa ti

Both grew until they were great
children; the little girl was at
length a grown-up maiden, and the
boy a young man. The mother

unina, "Loku se ni ngaka noba-bili, banta bami, kepa a ni nawo amabizo,—" wa ti kowentomba-zana, "Wena, igama lako Ukco-mbekcantsini." Wa ti umfana, "Mina, u nga ngi ti igama, ngo-kuba nami igama lobudoda ngi ya 'u li tiwa ubaba, se ngi kulile ; a ngi tandi ukutiwa igama manje." Wa vuma ke unina.

said to them, "Since you are now so big, my children, but have no name,—" she said to the girl, "As for you, your name is Ukco-mbekcantsini."[46] The boy said, "For my part, do not give me a name ; for I too will receive my name of manhood, when I have grown up, from my father ; I do not wish to have a name now." So the mother agreed.

The boy and girl go out when their mother is absent, and make some acquaintances.

Kwa ti emini unina e nge ko, wa ti owentombazana, "A si ha-mbe si ye 'kuka amanzi, loku ama-gwababa e wa kcitile amanzi kama." Wa ti umfana, "Angiti umame wa s' alela ukuba si hambe pand/le na ?" Wa ti owentomba-zana, "Si za 'ube si bonwa ubani na, loku abantu bonke ba yo'ulima na ?" Wa vuma ke umfana. Ya tata imbiza yamanzi intombazana, ya hamba ya ya emfuleni, be hamba bobabili. Kepa lona um-fana insimbi yake wa e m/lope ; kepa intombazana ya i kazimula kakulu. Ba hamba ke, ba fika emfuleni, ba ka amanzi. A ti uma e se gcwele embizeni, ya ti kowo-mfana, "Ngi twese." Wa ti lapa e se za 'u m twesa, ba bona udwe-ndwe lwabantu abaningi b' eza emfuleni. Ba fika ba ti, "Si pu-zise." Wa wa ka amanzi ngen-debe, wa nika o pambili. Kwa pinda kwa tsho omunye futi, wa ti, "Ngi puzise." Wa wa ka, wa m puzisa. Ba tsho bonke, wa ze wa ba kqeda e ba puzisa.

It happened at noon when the mother was not there, the girl said, "Let us go and fetch water, since the crows have spilt the water of our mother." The boy said, "Did not mother forbid us to go outside ?" The girl said, "By whom shall we be seen, since all the people have gone to dig ?" The boy agreed. The girl took a water-vessel ; she went to the river, both going together. But as for the boy, his peculiarity was that he was white ; but the girl was very shining. So they went, and reached the river, and dipped water. When she had filled the vessel, she said to the boy, "Put it on my head." When he was just about to put it on her head, they saw a line of many people coming to them. When they came to the river, they said, "Give us to drink." He dipped water with a cup, and gave the first. The second asked also, saying, "Give me to drink." He gave him to drink. All asked in like manner, until he had given them all to drink.

[46] *Ukcombekcantsini,* The-mat-marker.

They tell their new acquaintances something about themselves, and learn something about their acquaintances.

Ba ti, " N' aba kumu p' umuzi na ?" Ba ti, "S' aba kulo o ngapezulu." Ba ti, "Ku kona 'muntu kona na ?" Ba ti, "Kqa; a ku ko 'muntu." Ba ti, " N' aba kui p' indhlu na ?" Ba ti, "S' aba kule e gcine esangweni." Ba ti, "Inkosikazi i i pi na ?" Ba ti, "Inkosikazi kwa ku yena uma; kepa kwa ti ngokuba e nga zali ya kitshwa indhlu yakwake, ya bekwa esangweni." Ba buza ba ti, "Po, nina n' aba kusi pi isizwe na ?" Ba ti, " Tina si vela le, si hamba si funa intombi enhle kakulu, ngokuba ku za 'uzeka inkosi yakwiti." Ba ti, " U kona i za 'ukqala ukuzeka ini na ?" Ba vuma. Ba ti, " Ni uhlobo lu ni na ?" Ba ti, " Tina s' Abahhwebu." Ya ti intombi, " Nenkosi yakwini Umhhwebu na ?" Ba ti, " Kqa; umuntu nje; i tina sodwa es' Abahhwebu. Nati a si baningi; si ibuto linye nje." Ba hamba ke Abahhwebu.

They said, "To what village do you belong ?" They replied, "To that one on the hill." They said, " Is there any one at home ?" They said, "No; there is no one." They said, " To which house do you belong ?" They said, "To that which is last near the main entrance." They said, "Which is the queen ?" They replied, " The queen was our own mother; but it happened that, because she had no child, her house was removed, and placed near the entrance." The children enquired of them, " And you, to what nation do you belong ?" They replied, " We came from yonder. We are looking for a very beautiful damsel; for the king of our nation is going to be married." They said, " Is he then about to take his first wife ?" They assented. They asked, " Of what nation are you ?" They said, " We are Abahhwebu." The girl said, " And the king of your nation, is he an Umhhwebu ?" They replied, " No; he is not of the same race as ourselves; we only are Abahhwebu. And we are not many; we are but one troop." So the Abahhwebu departed.

The queen is displeased.

Wa y etwesa ke imbiza yamanzi, ba kupuka ba fika ekaya, ba hlala. Kwa ti ntambama wa fika unina, e vela 'ulima; wa ti, "Amanzi a kiwe ubani na ?' Ba ti, " A kiwe i tina." Wa ti, "Angiti ng' ala ukuba ni pumele pandhle ? Kepa ni tshelwe ubani ukuti, Hamba ni

The boy put the water-vessel on her head. They went up the hill to their home, and sat down. In the afternoon when the mother returned from digging, she asked, " By whom was this water fetched ?" They said, " By us." She said, " Did I not forbid you to go outside ? By whom, then, were

ni yokuka 'manzi na ? " Wa ti umfana, " Be ng' ala mina, kepa wa ti Ukcombekcantsini, ' A si hambe si yokuka 'manzi.' " Wa ti unina, " A ni bonwanga 'muntu ini na ?" Ba ti, " Si boniwe Abahhwebu, be udwendwe olukulu. Ba ti, ' N' abakabani na ? ' Sa ti, ' S' aba kona kulo 'muzi.' " Ba binda ke. Ba hlala izinsuku eziningi. Kodwa kubo ba be ng' aziwa namunye umuntu; ba b' aziwa Abahhwebu bodwa.

you told to go and fetch water ?" The boy said, " I refused for my part, but Ukcombekcantsini said, ' Let us go and fetch water.' " The mother said, " Did no man see you ? " They replied, " We were seen by some Abahhwebu, who formed a very long line. They asked us whose children we were; we said we belonged to this village." They were then silent. They remained for many days. But they were unknown to any one of their own village; they were known by the Abahhwebu only.

A large company come to the rogal kraal, with cattle, to ask the king's daughter in marriage.

Kwa ti ngesikati esinye kwa fika izinkomo eziningi ntambama, zi hamba nabantu abaningi. Ba ti bonke abantu lapo ekaya, " Impi ; i vela 'ku zi dhla pi lezi 'nkomo ezingaka na ? " Ba bona abantu abaningi b' eza ekaya ; ba zi shiya ngapandhle kwomuzi ezinye inkomo, b' eza nezinye ekaya. Ba fika, ba zi ngenisa esibayeni ; b' enyuka ba ya ngasenhla ; ba fika b' ema ; ba kuleka ngokukcela intombi kuyise. Kwa tula nje bonke abantu ekaya, be tula ngokumangala, be ti, " U kona ini umuntu o ng' eza 'kukgoma amagwababa na ? Loku a i ko intombi e umuntu lapa ekaya." Kepa ba kuleka ngokungati ba ya y azi intombi. Ba ze ba ti abesifazana, " Uma ku zo'ukgonywa, i pi intombi kulezi zetu na ? U ya 'ujabula umfazi intombi yake e ya 'ukgonywa ngalezi 'nkomo eziningi kangaka."

It came to pass on another occasion there came very many cattle in the afternoon with very many people. All the people of the village said, " It is an army ; into what place has it made a forray, and taken so many cattle as these ? " They saw many men coming to their village ; they left many of the cattle outside ; they entered with others into the very village. On their arrival they drove them into the cattle-pen, and went to the upper part, and stood there and respectfully asked his daughter from the father. All the people of the village were silent, being silent from wonder, saying, " Is there a man who could come and select from among crows one to be his bride ? For there is not a girl who is a human being in this village." But the men asked as though they knew the damsel. At length the women said, " If you are come to select a bride, which is the damsel among all these of ours ? That mother will be glad whose daughter shall be selected with so many cattle as these."

The mothers of the crows jeer the queen.

Ba puma ke bonke ekaya besifazana, b' ema pand*l*e; abanye ba gijima be ya esangweni, be ti, " Ye, ye! u ya dela umfazi o nga zalanga uma abakabani laba abayeni na ?" be tsho ngokubin*g*a lona o nge naye umntwana, ngokuba ba be ng' azi ukuba u yena o nentombi impela; ngokuba bona ba be zala amagwababa nje. A puma ngokutukutcla amadoda noyise wamagwababa, e ba futa abesifazana, e ti, " Suka ni; suka ni! ni *l*laba 'mikosi ngazi pi intombi zenu na, loku ni zele amagwababa nje na ? U kona umuntu o nga kcita inkomo zake ezingaka e lobola igwababa na ?" Ba ti, " Tshetsha *n*i, ni 'ngene ezind*l*lini, ni yeke lowo 'msindo."

All the women went out of the houses and stood outside; some ran to the entrance, saying, " Ye, ye! is the woman who has no child satisfied as to whose are these bridegroom's men ?" saying thus for the purpose of jeering the childless one, for they did not know that it was she who really had a girl; for they had given birth to crows only. The men went out in anger together with the father of the crows, he being in a rage with the women, and saying, " Away with you; away with you! For which girls of yours do you make this huzzahing ? since you have given birth only to crows. Who would cast away so many cattle as these for a crow's dowry ?" The men said, " Make haste into your houses, and cease this noise."

The king tells them he has no daughter; but they persist in asking his daughter in marriage.

Wa ya kubayeni umnikazimuzi, e ti, " Mina a ngi nantombi. Nga zala amagwababa odwa nje. Tata ni inkomo zenu, ni goduke, ni ye kwini." Ba ti, " Si ya ku ncenga, si ti, musa uku s' ala; ngokuba si y' azi ukuba i kona intombi lapa ekaya, e umuntu." W' efunga nokufunga umnikazimuzi, e ti, " A i ko intombi lapa ekaya." Ba ze ba bhekana abayeni, be funa, be funa ukubuza kulabo Abahhwebu bona ba be zile kuk*g*ala; ba ti, " Imbala na i bona intombi lapa

The owner of the village went to the bridegroom's men, and said, " As for me, I have no girl. I am the father of mere crows, and of nothing else. Take your cattle, and go home with them to your people." They replied, " We beseech thee not to refuse us; for we know that there is a damsel at this place which is a human being." The head of the village swore solemnly that there was no damsel at his home. At length the bridegroom's people looked at each other, being desirous of enquiring of the Abahhwcbu who had come there at first; they asked them, " Did you in truth see a damsel at

ekaya na?" Ba ti Abahhwebu, "Sa i bona lapa ekaya: si nga i komba ind*h*lu e ya ngena kuyona." Ba ti, "I i pi na?" Ba ti, "I leya e landela e sekugcineni." Ba ti, "Tina, munumuzana, si ya y azi impela intombi yako; si nga i komba nend*h*lu e kuyoua." Wa ti umnikazimuzi, e tsho ngokutukutela, wa ti, "Imbala laba 'bantu ba *h*lakanipile nje na! Loku ngi ya ni tshela mina 'yisewabautwana, ngi ti, a i ko intombi e umuntu lapa ekaya. Kepa ni ngi pikela inkani ngokuba ni ze 'ku ngi *h*leka ngokuba ngi nga zalanga 'muntu. Leya ind*h*lu e ni i kombayo, umnikaziyo a ka zalanga negwababa lodwa lelî."

this place?" The Abahhwebu replied, "We did see one at this place: we can point out the house into which she entered." They enquired which it was. They said, "It is that which is the last but one." They said, "O chief of this village, we are indeed acquainted with your daughter; we can even point out the house in which she is." The chief of the village replied, speaking in anger, "Are these men then truly so very wise? For I the father of the children tell you, there is not a girl in this place that is a human being. But you dispute the matter with me, because you have come to laugh at me, because I am not a father of human beings. That house to which you point, the occupier of it has not given birth to so much as a crow."

The queen salutes the strangers.

Wa ti owesifazana waleyo 'nd*h*lu ngokuzwa izwi lendoda li tsho njalo, wa puma end*h*lini e ti, "Nampa abayeni bakadade! Ngena ni end*h*lini, ni *h*latshiswe, bakwenyana bami. Ngokuba mina noma ngi nga zalanga, kepa nina ni ngi bonile uma nga zala."

The woman of that house, when she heard her husband saying thus, left her house, saying, "Behold the bridegroom's people of our princess![47] Come into the house, and have cattle killed for you, my sons-in-law. For though I have had no child, yet you have seen that I have a child."

She presents her children to the king.

Y' esuka indoda yake, ya ya kona end*h*lini; ya fika, ya ti, "Loku ngi be ngi ti wena a u namntwana. Kepa uma u pume u *h*labe umkosi, u nayo ini umntwana na?" Wa ti, "Loku ngi nga zali umntwana, ngi m tate pi na?"

Her husband went to the house and said, "I thought you had no child; but, since you have come out and shouted, have you a child?" She replied, "Since I do not have children, where could I get a child?" He said, "I ask

47 *Dade* is equivalent to *Nkosazana*, "Princess." But *Dade wetu* would mean "Our sister." The bride calls the Imbulu by this name, *Dade*, "Princess," as a mark of deference.

Wa ti, "Ngi ya buza, mntanami, ngi tshele uma umkosi u u *h*labele ku pi na?" Wa ti, "Ng' u *h*labele abantwana bami oku nge si bo abendoda, abami nje." Ya ti indoda, "Ba pi na?" Wa ti, "Puma ni, a ni bone." Ba puma umfana nentombazana. Wa ti ngoku ba bona kwake uyise, wa wela pezu kwomfana, wa m bamba e kala, e ti, "Hau! hau! Kanti abafazi ba nesibindi esingaka na? Ku ngani ukuba u fi*h*le abantwana ba ze ba be ngaka, be ng' aziwa 'muntu na?" Wa ti, "Wa ba tata pi laba 'bantwana na?" Wa ti, "Nga ba nikwa amavukutu, a ngi gcaba esin*g*eni. Kwa puma i*h*lule, la telwa esitsheni, kwa ze kwa ba abantu, ngi b' ond*h*la; nga ngi nga tandi uku ni tshela, ngokuba amagwababa a e nga ba bulala."

thee, my child, tell me for what have you shouted?" She replied, "I have shouted for my children, who are not the children of a man, but mine only." Her husband said, "Where are they?" She said, "Come out, that he may see you." The boy and girl came out. When the father saw them, he fell on the boy, and embraced him, crying and saying, "Hau! hau! Have women indeed so great courage? How is it that you have hidden the children till they are so big as this, they being unknown to any one?" He said, "Where did you get these children?" She replied, "The pigeons gave them to me. They scarified me on the loins; there came out a clot; it was placed in a vessel; at length it became human beings; I nourished them; I did not like to tell you, for the crows might have killed them."

They order an ox to be slaughtered for the strangers.

Wa vuma ke uyise, wa ti, "Ba za 'u*h*latshiswa 'nkomo ni na, loku izimbuzi ba ng' eze ba *h*latshiswa yona; ku fanele ukuba ba *h*labe itole lenkabi." Wa vuma ke unina. Wa ya wa puma end*h*lini, wa fika kubayeni e se *h*leka, e jabula, e ti, "Puma ni, ngi ni kombise inkomo yenu." Wa puma umyeni, wa ba munye; wa m kombisa itole lenkabi. La *h*latshwa, la d*h*liwa.

The father agreed and said, "Which bullock shall be slaughtered for them? For as for the goats, they must not have a mere goat killed; it is proper that they kill a young ox." So the mother agreed. She went out of the house, and came to the bridegroom, now laughing and happy, and saying, "Come out, that I may point out to you your bullock." The bridegroom went out alone; she pointed out to him the young ox. It was killed and eaten.

The bridegroom is accepted.

Kwa ti ngangomso wa ti uyise, "Ku fanele ukuba a *h*latshiswe umntwana naye kanye nenkomo e

On the morrow the father said, "It is proper that the girl too have a bullock killed for her toge-

za 'ukela abayeni bake." Wa vuma ke unina. Ya *hlatshwa* inkomo. Wa puma uyise, wa ti, "Ku fanele ukuba i *kqedwe* yonke imikuba yalo 'mntwana, ngokuba ngi ya tanda ukuba abayeni bake b' emuke naye um*hlana* b' emukayo, ngokuba amagwababa a nga m bulala." Kw' enziwa yonke imikuba yake neyoku*hlatshiswa* izimbuzi, ngokuba um*hlana* e tombayo a ka *hlatshiswanga*, ngokuba wa e ng' aziwa 'muntu. Wa kela abayeni, kwa *hlatshwa* inkomo, kwa d*hliwa* inyama.

ther with that with which she is about to dance[48] before her bridegroom's people." So the mother agreed. The father arose and said, "It is proper that all the customs of this child be fully carried out, for it is my wish that her bridegroom's party take her with them on the day of their departure, for the crows may kill her." So all her customs were completed by having goats killed for her, for when she came to puberty she had nothing killed for her, because no one knew of her. She danced f(r the bridegroom's party; the cattle were killed, and the flesh eaten.

The king advises them to set out on the morrow.

Wa ti uyise, "Esinye isito a no si beka, banta bami, ni ze ni hambe ni d*hla* end*hleleni* nomfazi wenu." Ba ti abayeni, "Yebo, baba; nati se si tanda ukuhamba kusasa." Ba vumelana ka*hle*.

The father said, "Do you set aside a leg, my children, that you and your wife may have food on your journey." They replied, "Yes, father; and we are desirous of going in the morning." They were entirely of one heart.

The queen forewarns them.

Wa ti unina kubayeni, "Uma se ni hambile, no bona inyamazane elu*hlaza* eud*hleleni*; i ya 'uvela enkangala; ni nga i k*xotshi*; a no i yeka nje, kona ku ya 'ulunga ukwenda komntanami."

The mother said to the bridegroom's party, "When you have set out on your journey, you will see a green animal in the path; it will make its appearance on the high land; do not pursue it, just leave it alone; then the marriage of my child will be fortunate."[49]

---

[48] This ceremony is for the purpose of openly acknowledging the bridegroom by the bride. A mat is placed on the ground in the middle of the cattle-pen; the bridegroom and his party sit at the upper end of the enclosure; the bride and her maids pass, dancing, from the entrance to where they are sitting; one then takes the bridegroom by the hand, and leads him down to the mat, and leaves him standing on it. The mat is not afterwards touched by the bride's party, because the bridegroom's feet have stood on it; it is hlonipa'd, that is, respected by them; but it is taken away by someone belonging to him.

[49] *Insimango*, a large kind of baboon, is possibly here meant. It is said to be green; its skin is valuable, being used only for the ornaments of chiefs and great men. Its colour is grey with a greenish tint.

The bridal party sets out together; but are separated in the way.

Kwa sa ké kusasa ba hamba. Kepa umyeni nomakoti wake ba be ketelwe izinkabi ezimbili ezinkulu, be kwelc pezu kwazo bobabili, amabuto e hamba pambili onke, kepa bona be hamba emuva bodwa nezintombi eziningi eza zi menyiwe esizweni sikayise, zi hamba nabo emuva. Ba ze ba fika enkangala; ba i bona ke leyo 'nyamazane unina a ba yala ngayo, wa ti, a ba ze ba nga i buɦali. Amabuto a gijima onke, a i kxotsha inyamazane. Wa ti umakoti, "B' alele, ba nga i kxotshi inyamazane. Angiti uma u ni tshelile, wa ti, 'Ni nga i kxotahi inyamazane' na?" Wa ti, "O, u ti ku za 'uba nani, wena, na? A ba i kxotshe nje; a i nakcala." B' ema isikati eside lapo umakoti nomyeni nezintombi zakubo kamakoti. Wa ze wa ti umyeni, "O, se si katele ukuma elangeni; ake ngi hambe masinyane, ngi yoku ba buyisa, si hambe. So ku semini." Wa hamba ke.

On the following morning they set out. But two large oxen were selected for the bridegroom and his bride, and they were placed upon them, their soldiers going before them, and they following alone with many damsels which had been summoned from her father's tribe. At length they reached the high land; and then they saw that animal respecting which the mother had warned them, telling them not to kill it. All the soldiers ran and pursued the animal. The bride said, "Forbid them to pursue the animal. Did not my mother tell you not to pursue it?" The bridegroom answered, "O, of what consequence do you say it will be? Just let them pursue it; it is no matter." The bride and bridegroom, and the bride's damsels, remained there a long time. At length the bridegroom said, "O, we are now tired with standing here in the sun. Let me go at once and bring back the men, that we may go on our way. It is now noon." So he departed.

An Imbulu accosts the bride, and deceives her.

Ba sale, ba ɦlala isikati eside, be nga m boni umyeni; wa ze wa ti umakoti kwezinye intombi, "Se ngi katele ukuma, se ng' omile na amanzi." Kwa ti e sa kuluma loko, kwa fika kubona Imbulu, ya ti, "Sa ni bona, makosazana amaɦle." Ba vuma. Ya ti Imbulu,

After that they remained a long time, without seeing the bridegroom; at length the bride said to the other damsels, "I am now tired with waiting; and I am longing for water." As she was speaking these words, an Imbulu[50] came to them, and said, "Good day, beautiful princesses." They acknowledged the salutation. The

[50] The Imbulu is a large land lizard, living mostly in forests. It is a stupid harmless animal. The natives say it is very fond of milk, and that it sucks the cows when they are in the open country. It is not uncommon for boys who have robbed their fathers of the milk of the cows whilst herding them, to lay the blame on the Imbulu.

"Ake w eḣlike, ngi bone uma si nga ngi fanela ini isikaka sako na?" Wa ti, "A ngi tandi ukweḣlika." Ya ti Imbulu, "Hau! Ake w eḣlike; u zo'ubuye u kwelele." Wa ze w' eḣlika umakoti. Ya tata'isikaka, ya binca Imbulu, ya ti, "Kwa ngi fanafanela!" Ya ti, "A u lete nolembu lwako lolo, ke ngi bone uma nalo lu nga ngi fanela ini na?" W' ala, wa ti, "Ngi ya l' esaba ilanga mina, dade." Ya ti, "Ngi tsheleke, ngi za 'u ku nika masinyane." Wa i nika. Ya lu faka ulembu, ya ti, "Ake ngi kwele enkabini yako lapa, ngi bone uma nami ku nga ngi fanela ini na?" Wa ti, "Kwela, u buye w eḣlike masinyane." Ya kwela ke Imbulu, ya ti, "Ncinci! Kwa ngi fanafanela!" Wa ti, "Sa w eḣlika ke." Ya ti, "A ngi tandi; a ngi ze ng' eḣlika." Wa ti, "Yeḣlika, ngi kwele." Ya ti Imbulu, "U ke wa vumelane ukuba ngi kwele; a ngi sa yi 'kweḣlika mina."

Imbulu said, "Just come down, that I may see if your dress is suitable for me." She replied, "I do not wish to come down." The Imbulu said, "Hau! Just come down; you will get up again at once." At length the bride descended. The Imbulu took her dress, and girded it on, and said, "O! how well it fits me!" The Imbulu said, "Bring me your veil,[51] that I may see if it too would become me." The bride refused, saying, "I am afraid of the sun, princess." The Imbulu said, "Lend it to me; I will return it to you immediately." She gave her the veil. The Imbulu put on the veil, and said, "Just let me get on your ox, that I may see if that too would become me." She said, "Get up, but come down again immediately." So the Imbulu mounted, and said, "Ncinci! How admirably it suits me!" She said, "Come down now then." The Imbulu said, "I do not wish to come down; I shall never come down." The bride said, "Get down, that I may mount." The Imbulu replied, "You gave me permission to get up; I shall never come down again, for my part."

The bride and her maids are turned into birds.

Z' esuka ke izintombi zonke kanye nomakoti; za gukquka intaka. Wa ti umakoti yena wa ba uluve. Ba ya eḣlatini, ba ḣlala kona, se be inyoni.

Then the bridesmaids and the bride departed; they turned into finches, and the bride turned into an uluve.[52] They went to the forest, and remained there, being now birds.

---

51 *Ulembu.*—The veil is now no longer used among the natives; it is known only in nursery tales. It is said to have been an ancient custom for the bride to veil her face. She now partially conceals it with a prepared skin.

52 *Uluve*, a bird, a kind of finch.

The bridegroom is uneasy.

Ba fika abayeni nesikumba sen-yamazane, se be i *ɦ*linzile. Ba hamba pambili. Ba ti be se kude nentombi, wa ti umyeni, "Hau! hau! Band*ɦ*la! ni ya bona umakoti u se njani nje na, ukuba a be mncane kangaka, a fipale? w enziwa ini na? nentombi zi pi na?" Ba ti, "O, nkosi, kumbe intombi zi diniwe uku*ɦ*lala elangeni, za ze za buyela ekaya kubo; si ya bona o kw enze umakoti ilanga, ngokuba u be nga *ɦ*lali elangeni." Wa ti, "Noma ku njalo, nga ku bonakala okwelanga; umzimba wami se u jambile, kungati a ku se yena umakoti wami lo." Ba fika pambi kwake, ba ti, "Zi pi intombi na?" Wa kuluma umakoti ngokungati ulimi lwake lu botshiwe, e tshwatshwaza, e ti, "Zi buyile za ya ekaya."

The bridegroom's men arrive with the skin of the animal which they had skinned. They went in front. When they were still at a distance from the damsels,, the bridegroom said, "Hau! hau! My men! do you see the bride, how small she is become, and that she no longer shines? what has happened to her? and where are the bridesmaids?" They replied, "O, sir, perhaps the girls were tired with sitting in the sun, until they went back to their own homes; we see what the sun has done to the bride, for she was not accustomed to sit in the sun." He replied, "And if it is so, that which is done by the sun would be evident. My body is weak;[53] it seems to me that this is not my bride." They came in front of her, and said, "Where are the damsels?" The bride answered as though her tongue was tied, speaking rapidly and thickly, saying, "They have gone home."[54]

[53] If a man feels his body weak and languid without being able to account for it, he considers it an omen of approaching evil. When the Troll had put her own daughter in the place of the young queen, the queen's "little dog, Locke, was never cheerful afterwards; the little infant wept uninterruptedly, and *a weight lay on the king's mind.*" (*Thorpe's Yule-tide Stories.* "The Princess that came out of the water," *p.* 61.)

[54] Roland leaves his bride to go home to prepare the marriage festival, but falls into the toils of new enchantments, and forgets his betrothed and his faith. When his marriage with another is about to be celebrated she joins the bridal party, and when it comes to her turn to sing, her voice is recognised by Roland. Between the time of being forsaken and again recognised, like Ukcombekcansini and her damsels, she occupies herself in secretly doing all the work in a shepherd's cottage, who had plucked her in the form of a flower into which she had transformed herself, and taken her to his home. She assumed the human form during the absence of the shepherd. (*Grimm.* "Roland and his Bride," *p.* 222.) One of the fisherman's "golden children," through pursuing a fine stag, is led into enchantments, by which he is lost to his bride, till released by his brother. (*Id.* "The Golden Children," *p.* 326.) The king's son leaves the giant's daughter, who had helped him to perform the laborious tasks imposed on him by her father, and finally to escape from him; and through allowing himself to be kissed by a dog, loses all recollection of her, till reminded of her, when he was about to be married to another, by a conversation between two pigeons. (*Campbell. Op. cit. Vol. I., p.* 251.) See also several such tales in *Thorpe's Yule-tide Stories, pp.* 202, 216, 447.

The birds jeer Ukakaka.

Ba hamba ke, amabuto e hamba pambili ; naye umyeni wa hamba pambili namabuto ake ; wa sala emuva umakoti, e hamba nenkabi yedwa. Kwa ti nina se be kude naleyo 'ndawo, ba bona inyoni eziningi zi *hlala* ngapambili kwabo, esikqungweni, zi ti, " Ukakaka wenkosi wa hamba nesilwane ! " Za ti, " Yiya, u gada nembulu ! " Wa ti, " Hau ! bandhla ! ni y' ezwa oku kulunywa i lezi 'nyoni ; zi ti ni na? Na ke na zi zwa inyoni zi kuluma na?" Ba ti, " O, nkosi, ukuma kwazo inyoni ze*hla*nze ; zi ya kuluma." Wa binda ke. Ba hamba.

Kwa ti ngapambili futi za ya ngapambili kwabo, za ti, " Ukakaka, Ukakaka wenkosi wa hamba nesilo ! Yiya, u gada nembulu ! " Kepa loko Ukakaka kwa ku m *hlupa* kakulu en*hl*iziyweni yake. Kwa ti lapa se be ya ngasekaya, za buyela emuva izinyoni, za *hlala* e*hl*atini ; ba ngena ekaya, be hamba pambili bonke, umakoti be m shiya yedwa emuva.

So they went forward, the soldiers going in front, and the bridegroom himself went in front with his soldiers ; the bride[55] remained behind, going alone with the ox. When they were at some distance from that place, they saw many birds pitched on the grass in front of them, saying, " Ukakaka the king's child gone off with an animal ! " They said, " Out upon him, he is running off with an Imbulu ! " He said, " Hau ! my men ! You hear what these birds say : what do they say ? Did you ever hear birds speak ? " They said, " O, sir, the manner of birds of the thorn country ; they speak."[56] So he was silent. They went forward.

In front also the birds went before them, and said, " Ukakaka, Ukakaka, the king's child gone off with an animal ! Out upon him, he runs off with an Imbulu." But that troubled the heart of Ukakaka very much. When they were near home, the birds turned back and remained in the forest. They entered their home, all the men going in front, leaving the bride alone behind them.

The king is dissatisfied with the bride.

Esibayeni kwa ku kona amadoda amaningi e *hl*ezi nenkosi, uyise kakakaka. Wa ngena umakoti e

In the cattle-pen there were many men sitting with the king, Ukakaka's father. The bride en-

---

[55] That is, the Imbulu, the false bride.

[56] In one of the versions of "The Little Gold Shoe," a bird exposes the deceit which they are practising on the prince, by crying

" Chop heel and clip toe !
In the oven is she whom fits the gold shoe."

"What was that?" inquired the prince, wondering. "Oh," answered the queen, "it was nothing ; it was only the song of a bird." (*Thorpe's Yule-tide Stories, p.* 125.) See Appendix at the end of this tale.

hamba yedwa ; w' enyuka wa ya ngasen*h*la. Ba ti abantu bonke aba sesibayeni, "Ini yona le e fika nomntwana wenkosi na ?" Ya tsho inkosi ngokutukutela i m biza i ti, "Mina lapa, wena mfana." Wa ya Ukakaka ngokwesaba, ngokuba wa e bona ukuba uyise u tukutelc kakulu. Wa fika, wa ti, "Ini lena o fika nayo na ? Intombi a ba ti Abahhwebu in*h*le i yona lena na ?" Wa ti, "Tshetsha u ba bize bonke, b' eze lapa kumina ; Abahhwebu ba za 'ubulawa bonke, loku be k*q*amba amanga, ba ti ba i bonile intombi en*h*le." Wa ti Ukakaka, "K*q*a, nkosi baba, nami nga i bona intombi ; ya in*h*le kakulu ; Abahhwebu ba be k*q*inisile, ngokuba nami nga i bona, uma in*h*le kakulu." Wa ti uyise, "Kepa se i nani po na ?" Wa ti, "A ng' azi. Kwa ku tiwe ekaya kubo, a si ze si nga i bulali inyamazane. Kepa tina sa i bulala ; si te se si fika si vela 'ubulala inyamazane, sa fika intombi se i nje. Zi nga se ko zakubo intombi. Si ya hamba, nami ngi ya bona ukuba a ku se yona intombi e ngi pume nayo ekaya."

tered, going alone ; she went up to the upper part of the enclosure. All the men who were in the enclosure said, "What is that which has come with the prince ? " The king spoke in anger, calling his son, saying, "Come here, you boy." Ukakaka went in fear, because he saw that his father was very angry. On coming to him he said, "What is that with which you have come ? Is that thing the damsel which the Abahhwebu said was beautiful ?" He said, "Make haste, and call them all to come here to me ; all the Abahhwebu shall be killed ; for they have lied in saying they had seen a beautiful damsel." Ukakaka said, " No, king, my father ; I too saw the damsel ; she was very beautiful ; the Abahhwebu spoke the truth, for I too saw her, when she was very beautiful." The father replied, " What then is the matter with her now ? " He said, " I do not know. We were told at her home on no account to kill a certain animal. But we killed it, and when we returned from killing it, on our arrival the damsel was as she is. And the damsels of her people were no longer there. As we went along I too saw that it is not the damsel with whom I left her home."

Ukakaka is also dissatisfied.

Wa binda ko uyise. Ba *h*lala kwa ba izinsukwana. Kepa Ukakaka wa e nga vumi ukuba ku tiwe umakoti wake, e ti, ka ka zeki. U kona e ya 'uzeka intombi en*h*le. Kepa abantu bonke be mangala ngaleyo 'ntombi, be ti, "Kungati a ku si 'muntu lo."

So the father was silent. They tarried a few days. But Ukakaka would not allow her to be called his wife, saying, he had not a wife yet. The time would come when he should marry a beautiful girl. And all the people wondered at the girl, and said she was not like a human being.

The bride and her maids assume their own forms, and visit the bride-groom's kraal.

Kepa kwa ku kona isalukazi ekaya kulowo 'muzi, sa si ngenazo izito, sa si nemikono yodwa, si ḥlala nje ekaya, igama laso kwa ku tiwa Uḥlese; ku tshiwo ngokuba ukuhamba kwaso sa si gingcika ngomzimba nje. Ku mukwe ku yiwe ekulimeni, zi sale zi fike izintombi se zi gukqukile abantu, zi fike ekaya, zi ye kuyena Uḥlese, zi ti, "Konje u ya 'kutsho u ti, u ke wa bona izintombi lapa ekaya na?" A ti Uḥlese, "O, kqa, banta bami, ngi ya 'kuti ngi be ngi ba bona pi abantu lapa na, loku ngi Uḥlese nje na?" Za puma; za tata izimbiza zonke zomuzi zoḥlangoti lwawo umuzi, za ye za ka amanzi. Za fika nawo, za kqazula utshwala umuzi wonke, za kelela amanzi, za fudumezela amanzi; za ka amanzi, za sinda ezindḥlini zomuzi wonke; za hamba za ye za teza za beka izinkuni umuzi wonke. Za ya kuḥlese, za

But there was an old woman who lived at that village; she had no legs, but only arms; she remained at home doing nothing; her name was Uthlese;[57] she was so called because iu walking she rolled along with her body only. The people had gone to dig; when they were gone, the damsels again turned into human beings,[58] and came to that place; they went to Uthlese, and said, "Will you then say that you have seen any girls here at home?" Uthlese replied, "O, no, my children. I will say, how could I see people here since I am but Uthlese?" They went out, and took all the vessels from one side of the village, and went to fetch water. They came with the water: they crushed mealies for making beer for the whole village; they fetched water again and again, and boiled it for the beer; they fetched water, and smeared[59] the floors of the houses of the whole village; they went and fetched firewood, and placed it in the whole kraal. They went to Uthlese, and said,

---

[57] *Uhlese.—Ukuti* hlese, to shuffle along in walking. *Uhlese,* Shuffler.

[58] Twelve brothers were changed into twelve ravens because their sister plucked the white lilies, in which her brothers' destiny was in someway wrapped up. (*Grimm.* "The Twelve Brothers," *p.* 44.) In the tale of the Hoodie, the bridegroom is a man by day and a hoodie by night. (*Campbell. Op. cit. Vol. I.,* p. 63.) The six princes who were changed into swans by their stepmother's enchantments, resumed their human form for a quarter of an hour every evening. (*Grimm.* "The Six Swans," *p.* 190.) In Hans Christian Andersen's beautiful tale of the Wild Swans, the princes were swans as long as the sun was above the horizon, and resumed their human form from sunset to sunrise. In the tale of "The Beautiful Palace," we read of "three fair damsels" who could put off and resume the plumage of doves at pleasure. (*Thorpe. Yule-tide Stories, p.* 159.) And the white bear threw off his beast shape at night. (*Dasent. Popular Tales from the Norse, p.* 27.) In Snend's Exploits we read of a Troll who "in the daytime transformed himself into a dragon, and his twelve sons flew about as crows; but every night they became men again." (*Thorpe's Yule-tide Stories, p.* 340.)

[59] The natives smear the floors of their houses with cow-dung or goat-dung, to keep them free from insects and dust.

ti, " Hlese, u ya 'kuti kw enziwe ubani konke loku na?" Wa ti, " Ngi ya 'kuti, kw enziwe u mina." Za hamba ke, za ya endhle; za fike za penduka inyoni futi.

" Uthlese, who will you say has done all this?" She said, "I will say I did it." They went to the open country, and on their arrival again became birds.

The women wonder at the work done by unknown hands.

Kwa ti ntambama ba fika abantu, bá ti bonke ekaya besifazana, " Hau! be ku sinda 'bani ekaya lapa na? no ke amanzi? no teze izinkuni na? no kqazulile utshwala? wa fudumezela na?" Ba ya bonke kuhlese, be buza, be ti, " Kw enziwe ubani loku na?" Wa ti, " U mina. Ngi te, nga hlese, nga hlese, nga ye nga ka amanzi; nga hlese, nga hlese, nga ye, nga teza; nga hlese, nga hlese, nga ye, nga kqazula; nga hlese, nga hlese, nga fudumezela." Ba ti, " Hau! kw enziwe u we konke loku, hlese, na?" Wa ti, " Ehe." Ba hleka, be jabula, be ti, " Wa si siza Uthlese ukwenzela utshwala umuzi wonke." Ba lala.

In the afternoon when the people returned, all the women of the village said, "Hau! Who has been smearing the floors here at home? And who has fetched water? and firewood? and crushed mealies for beer? and heated the water?" All went to Uthlese, and asked her by whom it was done. She said, "It was done by me. I shuffled and shuffled along, and went and fetched water; I shuffled and shuffled along, and went and fetched firewood; I shuffled and shuffled along, and crushed the mealies; I shuffled and shuffled along, and heated the water." They said, "Hau! was all this done by you, Uthlese?" She said, "Yes." They laughed and were glad, saying, "Uthlese has helped us by making beer for the whole village." They retired to rest.

The bride and her maids pay a second visit.

Kwa sa kusasa, b' emuka ba ya 'ulima. Za fika izintombi zonke, zi twele izinkuni. Wa ti Uhlese, " Ye, ye, ye! nampa omalokazana bakababa. Kuhle umtimba u ngena ekaya." Ba zi beka izinkuni umuzi wonke; ba gaya, be bukeza utshwala; ba peka umuzi wonke; ba ye ba ka amanzi; ba gaya imi-

On the following morning they went to dig. All the damsels came, carrying firewood. Uthlese said, "Ye, ye, ye! behold the daughters-in-law of my father. It is well that the wedding party should come home." They placed firewood for the whole kraal; they ground the mealies which they crushed the day before for the beer; they made beer in every house in the kraal; they fetched water; they ground malt, being

tombo, b' eza 'kwenza umlumiso; ba vubela. Ba ya kuẖlese, ba ti, "Sala kaẖle, salukazi setu." Wa ti, "Yebo, mtimba kanomama." Ba hamba ke. Kwa ti ntambama ba fika abesifazana bonke ekaya, ba buye ba ya kuẖlese, be ti, "Ku bukeze 'bani na? kwa peka 'bani na?" Wa ti Uẖlese, "Ngi te, nga ẖlese, nga ẖlese, nga ye nga teza; nga ẖlese, nga ẖlese, nga gaya; nga ẖlese, nga peka; nga ẖlese, nga ya 'kuka amanzi; nga ẖlese, nga ẖlese, nga gaya imi-tombo; nga ẖlese, nga vubela; nga ẖlese, nga ti ng' eza lapa endẖlini, nga ẖlala." Ba ẖleka be ti, "Manje si zuze isalukazi soku si sebenzela." Ba ẖlala; ba lala.

about to make umlumiso; [60] they mixed the malt with the mealie-mash. They went to Uthlese, and said, "Good bye, our grand-mother." She replied, "Yes, bridal party of my mother's mother." So they departed. In the afternoon all the women came home, and again went to Uthlese, and said, "Who has ground the mash? who has cooked?" Uthlese said, "I shuffled and shuffled, and went and fetched wood; I shuffled and shuffled, and ground the mash; I shuffled, and boiled water; I shuffled, and fetched water; I shuffled and shuffled, and ground malt; I shuffled, and mixed it with the mealie-mash; I shuffled, and came back here to the house, and sat down." They laughed, saying, "Now we have got an old woman who will work for us." They sat down; they retired to rest.

They pay a third visit.

Kwa sa kusasa za fika izintombi, be nga se ko abantu bonke; kepa Uẖlese wa e ẖlezi pandẖle. Za ya kuyena, za ti, "U muẖle wena, ẖlese, ngokuba u nga tsheli 'mu-ntu." Za ngena ezindẖlini, za gaya imitombo, za vubela isijingi, za veva utshwala e be zi bu lumisile izolo, za tela amahhabulo esiji-ngini e be zi si vubela, z' enzela ukuze bu tshetshe ukubila. Za butela ezingcazini lobo e be zi bu vova; za tata enye ingcazi, za ya nabo kuẖlese obu ngengcazi. Za

On the following day the dam-sels arrived, when no one was there; but Uthlese was sitting outside. They went to her, and said, "You are a good creature, Uthlese, because you do not tell any one." They went into the houses, they ground malt, they mixed the mash, they strained the beer they had set to ferment rapidly on the day before, they poured the grains[61] into the mash they had mixed, that it might quickly ferment. They collected into large earthen vessels that which they had strained; they took another vessel, and went with the beer that was in the vessel to Uthlese. On coming to her they

[60] *Umlumiso*, beer, generally a small quantity, the fermentation of which is pressed onward, that it may be soon ready for drinking.

[61] *Amahhabulo* differ from *izinsipo*. The *amahhabulo* are the sediments of beer whilst actively fermenting, and which are used to excite fermentation in new beer. The *izinsipo* are the refuse sediment, when the beer is fit for use.

fika za puza, zi pa U*h*lese e *h*leka e jabula, e ti, "A ngi 'uze nga ni tsho nina ; no ze n' enze njengoku-bona kwenu."

drank, and gave also to Uthlese ; she laughed, and was joyful, and said, "I will never tell, for my part ; you shall do just as you like."

The women look out for something wonderful.

Ba buya b' emuka ba ya 'ku-*h*lala end*h*le, se be penduka inyoni. Kwa ti ntambama ba fika abafazi bonke ba bona ukuba sonke isi-jingi si vutshelwe. Ba ti, "O, u se katele U*h*lese i tina si m buza si ti, ' Kw enziwe ubani?.' A si binde nje. Ku kona um*h*lola o ya 'uze, u vele lapa ekaya."

Again they departed and went into the open country, again turn-ing into birds. In the afternoon all the women came and saw that all the mash was mixed. They said, "O, Uthlese is wearied with us for asking her by whom it was done. Let us just say nothing. There is something wonderful which is about to happen here at home."

Ukakaka learns the secret from Uthlese.

Kepa kwa ti kusi*h*lwa Ukakaka wa ya ku*h*lese, wa m ncenga wa m ncenga, e ti, "Hau ! kulu, ngi tshele uma loku kw enziwa ini na?" E se ti U*h*lese, "U mina, mntanemntanami." E se ti, "Hau ! kulu. A u kw azi ukwenza loku. Ngi tshele uma kw enziwe ubani na ?" E se ti, "Emini ni muka ni ti nya, ku sale ku fike intombi eziningi ; kepa pakati kwazo ku kona intombi en*h*le kakulu ; um-zimba wayo u ya kazimula ; i zona ke ez' enza utshwala lapa ekaya." Wa ti Ukakaka, "Wo ! kulu. A zi tshongo ini ukuti zi ya 'kuza ngomso na ?" Wa ti U*h*lese, "O, zi ya 'kuza." Wa ti Ukakaka, " Ngi ya 'kuza nami emini kakulu, ngi ze ngi zi bone lezo 'ntombi." Wa ti, "Kodwa u nga zi tsheli, kulu." Wa ti, "K*q*a ; a ngi yi 'ku zi tshela." Ba lala ke.

But in the evening Ukakaka went to Uthlese and earnestly be-sought her, saying, "Hau ! grand-mother, tell me by what means this is done?" Uthlese replied, "By me, child of my child." He said, "Hau ! grandmother. You could not do it. Tell me by whom it has been done?" She said, "At noon, when every one of you are gone, there come many dam-sels ; but among them there is one most beautiful ; her body is glistening ; it is they who make beer here at home." Ukakaka said, "Oh ! grandmother. Did they not say they would come to-morrow?" Uthlese replied, "O, they will come." Ukakaka said, "I too will come at noon, and see the damsels." He said, "But do not tell them, grandmother." She replied, "No, I will not tell them." So they retired to rest.

The bride and her maids pay a fourth visit.

Kwa sa kusasa, b' emuka abantu bonke, be ya 'kulima. Za sale za fika izintombi ; za ngena ezindhlini, za vova utshwala umuzi wonke. Za ti uma se zi kqedile ukuvova, za bu gcwalisa ngezimbiza umuzi wonke ; za tata ingcazi enkulu kakulu, za bu tela ngayo, zi bu hlanganisela bomuzi wonke ngenkamba. Ya gcwala leyo 'ngcazi. Za puma nayo, za ya kuhlese ; za fike za bu beka ; za tata ubulongwe, za sinda umuzi wonke ; za tshayela wonke umuzi ; za teza izinkuni, za beka emabaleni omuzi wonke ; za ngena endhlini lapa ku kona Uhlese ; za tata izinkamba, za puza utshwala.

On the following day all the people departed, going to dig. Then the girls came ; they went into the houses ; they strained the beer in the whole kraal. When they had strained it all, they poured it into vessels in the whole kraal ; they took a very large earthen vessel, and poured into it, collecting the beer of the whole kraal with a vessel. They filled the earthen vessel. They went out with it, and went to Uthlese ; on their arrival they set it on the ground ; they took cowdung, and smeared the floors of the whole kraal ; they swept the whole kraal ; they fetched firewood, and put it in the courts of the whole kraal ; they went into the house in which was Uthlese ; they took vessels and drank beer.

Ukakaka surprises them.

Ku te lapa se zi puzile kakulu utshwala, wa ngena Ukakaka ; za m bona, z' esuka za ya emnyango, zi ti zi ya puma, kona zi za 'kubaleka, a ze a nga zi boni. Wa vimba emnyango, e ti, "Hau ! mnta kababa, kcombekcansini ; ng' enze ni kuwe na kangaka na, loku u ngi hlupe kangaka na ?" Wa hleka Ukcombekcansini, e ti, "Eh, eh. Yeka ni Ukakaka ! Angiti u wena owa ngi kipa emzini kababa ; wa fike wa ngi shiya enkangala ; wa hamba nembulu

When they had drank a great deal of beer, Ukakaka entered the kraal ; when they saw him, they went to the doorway, thinking to go out, and then escape without his seeing them. But he blocked up the doorway, saying, "Hau ! child of my father, Ukcombekcansini, what great evil have I done you, that you have troubled me to this degree ?" Ukcombekcansini laughed, saying, "Eh, eh. Out upon Ukakaka ! Was it not you who took me from my father's kraal, and left me on the high lands, and went away with an Imbulu ?"[62] He replied, "I saw it

[62] The king's son is brought to the recollection of Messeria, by the little dove chiding her mate by saying,

 "Out upon thee !
 Thou hast served me
 As the king's son served Messeria."

(*Thorpe's Yule-tide Stories, p. 293.*)

na?" Wa ti, "Nga ngi bona ukuba a ku si we. Kepa ngokuba ngi nga sa ku boni, nga ko*h*lwa uma w enze njani na?" Ba *h*lala ke, Ukakaka e jabula nokujabula e ti, "Nga ngi ti, 'Ngi ya 'kuze ngi fe,' ngi nga sa ku bonanga."

was not you. And because I no longer saw you, I did not know what you had done." So they remained, Ukakaka rejoicing greatly and saying, "I said, 'I shall soon die,' when I no longer saw you."

Ukakaka tells the king that the true bride has come.

Kwa ti lapa se ku ntambama ba fika abantu. Wa puma Ukakaka wa ya kuyise e mamwateka ngokujabula, e ti, "Nam*h*la nje ke, baba, i fikile intombi eya ngi la*h*lekela enkaugala." Wa tsho e *h*leka uyise ngokujabula, e ti, "I pi na?" Wa ti, "Nausiya en*dh*lini."

When it was afternoon the people came. Ukakaka went out to his father, smiling with joy, and saying, "To-day then, my father, the damsel has come, who was lost to me on the high lands." His father asked, laughing for joy, "Where is she?" He said, "Yonder in the house."

They prepare a punishment for the false bride.

Wa ti uyise, "Tshela abantu bonke lapa ekaya, u ti, a ku suke amadoda 'embe umgodi masinya lapa esibayeni; u ti kwabesifazana a ba peke amanzi ngamakanzi onke." Wa ba tshela ke. Kwa ti so kw enziwe konke loko kwa tiwa, a ku pume abafazi bonke, b' eze 'kwek*q*a lowo 'mgodi o mbiwe esibayeni; kwa se ku bekiwe ubisi pakati emgodini; wa bizwa nomakoti lowo; kwa tiwa, "Woza nawe, u ye esibayeni; ku ya'kwek*q*iwa umgodi abantu bonke besifazana." Loko kwa kw enziwa ngokuba ku tiwa uma imbulu i bona ubisi i ya 'uziponsa, i ye 'ku*dh*la ubisi. Kwa yiwa ke esibayeni. Wa ti umakoti, "Ngi y' esaba ukuya esibayeni sasemizini." Ba ti, "Hamba; a ku nakcala." Wa hamba ke; wa fika esibayeni. B' ek*q*a abanye besifazana. Kwa tiwa naye a k' ek*q*e. Wa ti lapa

His father said, "Tell all the people here at home, that all the men are to dig a pit immediately here in the cattle enclosure; and tell the women to boil water in all the pots." So he told them. When all that was done, all the women were ordered to come and leap over the pit which had been dug in the cattle enclosure; some milk had been put in the pit; and the bride[63] too was called; it was said, "Do you too go to the cattle enclosure; all the women are going to jump over the pit." This was done because it was said, when the Imbulu sees the milk, it will throw itself in and go to eat the milk. They went to the kraal. The bride said, "I am afraid to go into the cattle-pen of strangers." They said, "Go; it is no matter." So she went, and came to the cattle-pen. The other women leapt. She was told to leap too. When she was about to leap, she

---

63 That is, the false bride.

e ti u y' ek*q*a, wa e se bona ubisi, umsila wa se u sombuluka, wa ziponsa pakati emgodini, e bona ubisi. Kwa se ku suka abantu bonke be gijima, be tata amanzi a bilayo ngamakanzi, b' eza nawo, be wa tela emgodini. Ya fa imbulu.

saw the milk,[64] her tail unfolded, and she threw herself into the pit, on seeing the milk. Then all the people ran and took the boiling water, and came with it and poured it into the hole. The Imbulu died.[65]

The nation is called to the royal wedding.

Kwa se ku tshelwa abantu bonke, be ti, "Namu*h*la u fikile umakoti." Kwa jabulwa; kwa tunywa abantu, kwa tiwa a ba hambe isizwe sonke, be tshela abantu, be ti, a ku butane iketo, inkosi i ganiwe. Kwa sa kusasa. Kwa butana amadoda nezinsizwa nezintombi nabafazi; ku ketwa; umakoti naye e se sina, nentombi zakubo; kwa *h*latshwa inkomo eziningi, kwa se ku d*h*liwa kwa ti ngensukwana.

All the people were told that the true bride had come. They rejoiced; and men were sent and told to go to the whole nation and tell the people to assemble for a dance, for the prince had been accepted by a damsel. On the following day men and youths, and maidens and women, assembled; they danced; and the bride and her maidens also danced; many cattle were killed; and they ate meat for several days.

[64] The cat which fell in love with a young man, and was by Venus changed into a beautiful girl and became his bride, retained the cat's disposition under the human form, and quitted her husband's side to catch a mouse which was playing in their chamber. "What is bred in the bone will never out of the flesh."

[65] Basile's *Pentamerone* is a series of tales related to gratify the fancy of a slave who for a time had succeeded in snatching her reward from Zoza. A prince named Taddio was confined by enchantments in a tomb, from which he could be liberated only if a woman would fill a pitcher suspended near the tomb with her tears; by this means she would bring the prince to life, and have him for her husband. Zoza had nearly filled the pitcher when she fell asleep. A black slave had been watching her, and whilst she was asleep, filled the pitcher with her own tears. The prince awoke, and took the slave to his home. Zoza after much suffering, and only by the aid of magic, at length convinced the prince of the deceit, and became his bride. The slave was punished by being buried in a hole up to her neck, that she might die a more lingering death.—In the tale of "The Three Citrons," a black slave takes the place of a prince's beautiful bride; the bride is transformed into a dove; and the prince, like Ukakaka, on his return, is surprised at finding a black woman instead of the fair damsel he had left; the slave tells him it is the result of magic. The prince by magic detects the deception. The slave is punished by being cast on a pile of burning wood.—In Grimm's *Home Stories* we find a tale still more similar to the above. An aged queen sent her daughter to be married to the prince of a far distant country, accompanied by one female attendant. The condition of her prosperity was that she should preserve a white handkerchief on which the mother had dropped three drops of her own blood. In the journey the handkerchief was lost; and the servant at once obtained a power over her mistress. Like the Imbulu, she succeeded in getting the clothes and horse of the princess in exchange for her own, and assumed her name. She was received as the princess at the king's palace, and the princess is sent to herd the geese. The deception is at length detected; and the servant killed by being placed in a barrel full of spikes. The young prince marries the true bride, and, like Ukakaka and Ukcombekcansini, "both reigned over the kingdom in peace and happiness till the end of their days." ("The Goose-herd.")

Ukcombekcansini reigns with Ukakaka.

Ya ti inkosi, "A ku gaulwe umuzi kakakaka." Wa gaulwa, w' akiwa masinyane ; kwa ba umuzi omkulu kakulu ; wa e se bekwa umakoti, ku tiwa u yena e inkosikazi. Z' epa utshani izintombi, za fulela umuzi wonke lowo wakumakoti ; z' emuka ke, za pindela kubo. Wa sale wa busa yena nendoda yake.

LYDIA, UMKASETEMBA.

The king ordered Ukakaka's kraal to be built. The wattles were cut, and the kraal built at once ; it was a very large kraal ; and the bride was appointed, it being said, it is she who is queen. The damsels plucked grass, and thatched the whole village of the bride ; they then departed and went back to their people. And she then reigned together with her husband.

APPENDIX.

THE "LITTLE BIRDS."

IN the legend-producing period, birds appear to have struck in a peculiar manner the fancy of man. Some were birds of evil omen, as the crow and raven ; and auguries were derived from their flight, &c. The same superstitions exist at the present time among the natives of this country. Thus a large bird called *ingqungqulu* or *inhlazinyoni*, if it cross the country in rapid flight, is supposed to be an omen of war in the direction in which it is flying. And if the *utekwane*, a bird to which the natives ascribe many peculiar powers, pass through a village, crying, it is considered as an omen of an approaching marriage, or of great fecundity in the herd.

But it is "the little birds" which are messengers, and who come with their tale of warning or instruction. "The belief," says Dasent, "that some persons had the gift of understanding what the birds said, is primæval. We pay homage to it in our proverbial expression, 'a little bird told me.' Popular traditions and rhymes protect their nests, as in the case of the wren, the robin, and the swallow."

This power of understanding the speech of birds not only exists in the legends of the Zulus, as we have seen from several of the tales already given, but even in recent times there have been those who pretended to comprehend their language, and to whom they have been prophets of the future. Umpengula, my native teacher, has given me several interesting accounts of the peculiar character of his brother Undayeni. He was a remarkable man, one of those who possess that high-strung, sensitive nervous system, which appears to place them *en rapport* with the spirit-world, and to give them capacities of sympathy which are not possessed by common men. He was the subject of dreams, which were realised, and of visions ; and often saved himself and family from impending danger by his prophetic insight into the future. It may be worth remarking that this peculiar power was not natural, that is, he was not born with it, but it manifested itself after a contest with a leopard which lasted the greater part of a day, and which nearly proved fatal to him. When he began to manifest these peculiar powers, his friends expected that he had been elected by the spirits to be a diviner ; and ascribed the fact of his not attaining to that eminence to a dispute between the spirits of his own house and those of his maternal uncle ; the latter wishing to give him the power and the former objecting, and thus he was only a wise man and interpreter of dreams, "half-way between divining and not divining." Together with these powers he also comprehended the language of birds. The following is the account given by his brother :—

ENYE indaba eya ngi mangalisayo kandayeni, wa ba ikumushi le-nyoni. W' ezwa inyoni e ku tiwa umvemve u kuluma esibayeni, u ti, " Lima ni kakulu nonyaka nje. Ni za 'kutenga izinkomo." Kepa leyo 'ndaba wa i tshela abantu, wa ti, " Ngi zwile umvemve, u ti, a si lime kakulu, si za 'kutenga izinkomo. Nami ngi ya vuma ukuti u kqinisile."

Kepa kubantu loko 'kutsho ku-kandayeni kwa ba insumansumane, ukuti, " U ti, ndayeni, u zwe inyoni i tsho njalo na ? " Kepa wa ti yena, " Ngi ti, i za 'kubuye i tsho okunye futi." Nembala nge-zinsukwana si ᶊlezi esibayeni um-vemve wa kwitiza, si ng' ezwa uma u ti ni ua. Kepa yena wa ti, " Lalela ni ! Nans' indaba." Sa tula. Wa kuluma umvemve ngako ukukwitiza. Wa buza Undayeni, wa ti, " Ni zwile ke ?" Sa ti, " A si zwanga. Si zwe umvemve u kwitiza nje okuningi." Kepa yena wa ti, " U ti, ' Ngalo 'nyaka o ya 'kuza li za 'kubalela.' "

Kepa loko kwa si ᶊlekisa. Umvemve lowo wa kuluma izin-daba eziningi Undayeni a zi zwa-yo ; kepa a si tshele, sa m ᶊleka sonke, sa ti, " U ya pupa ! Ubani o ng' ezwa ukukuluma kwenyoni, o nge si yo inyoni na ? " Nembala ngalowo 'nyaka kwa fika Ungoza. O ! sa tenga izinko-mo eziningi kwabakangoza. Nge-muva kwalowo 'nyaka sa ba

ANOTHER thing which astonished me in Undayeni was that he was an interpreter of the language of birds. He heard the bird which is called the wagtail speaking in the cattle-pen, and saying, " Dig extensively this year. You will buy many cattle [with the corn]." And he told the matter to the people, saying, " I have heard the wagtail telling us to dig exten-sively, and we shall buy many cattle. And I agree with it, that it has spoken truly."

But that saying was like a fable to the people, and they asked, " Do you say, Undayeni, that you heard the bird say this ?" And he replied, " I say it will pre-sently return, and say something else." And indeed after a few days, as we were sitting in the cattle-pen, the wagtail jabbered, we not understanding what it said. But he said, " Listen ! There is news." We were silent. The wagtail spoke by jabbering. Un-dayeni enquired of us, saying, " Have you understood then ? " We replied, " We did not under-stand. We heard the wagtail jabbering very much, and nothing more." But he said, " It says that next year it will be a dry season."

But that made us all laugh. That wagtail spoke many things which Undayeni heard ; and when he told us we all laughed and said, " You are dreaming ! Who can understand the language of birds, who is not himself a bird ? "

But truly, that year Ungoza came. O ! we bought many cattle with our corn of the people of Ungoza. The year after we had a

nendhlala enkulu, sa ya 'kutenga emahlatini. Sa ku bona loko okwa tshiwo Undayeni. Kepa ngalowo 'mvemve wa si tshela njalo oku tshiwo i wo, e ti, " Uma ekukulu-meni kwawo ni beka indhlebe kahle, ni ya 'kuzwa u kuluma in-daba." Kodwa loko sa mangala ngako, ngokuba a ku banga ko 'muntu namunye pakati kwetu owa ku kqondayo. Ngi tsho na namhla nje umvemve uma ngi zwa u kuluma, ngi beke indhlebe, ngi ti, " Kumbe ngi za 'kuzwa li linye izwi." Kepa, kqa, ukuzwa! Ngi sa mangala ngaloko 'kutsho kuka-ndayeni ; indhlala nga i bona, nenala nga i bona.

great famine, and went to buy corn in the forest-land. And so we saw that which Undayeni had said. And as regards the wagtail he told us continually what was said by it, saying, "If when it speaks you give an attentive ear, you will hear it speaking something of im-portance." And we wondered at that, for there was not one amongst us who understood the bird's speech. But I say that even to this very day when I hear a wag-tail speaking, I listen attentively, thinking, "It may be I shall hear one word." But, no, so as to un-derstand! And I still wonder at the saying of Undayeni ; the famine I saw, and the abundance I saw.

Umpengula also relates the following anecdote :—

INDABA yekwababa ela biza Um-peza kamzenya, li m biza ehlatini, ku balekiwe, ku punyiwe emakaya, ku balekelwa Amazulu. Kepa abantu ba hlangana ngokuzwa ukuba Amazulu a lwa namabunu, 'eza 'kwahluleka ; ba tanda uku-tumba izinkomo ; loku Amazulu a libele impi, a w azi ukubheka izin-komo, a kandanisekile kakulu impi yamabunu ; a w azi 'kubheka izin-datshana.

THE account of a crow, which called Umpeza, the son of Umze-nya, it calling him in the forest, where the people had fled from their homes, running away from the Zulus. But the people assem-bled on hearing that the Zulus were fighting with the Dutch, and were about to be conquered ; and they wished to take the cattle, for the Zulus were detained by the army, and were unable to look after the cattle ; and being much pressed by the Dutch force, they could not attend to little matters.

Ngaloko ke ba puma abantu ukuya kuleyo 'nzuzo yezinkomo. Ku te be sa puma nje, ikwababa la memeza ; abantu ba bhek' in-dhlebe, be zwa umsindo, be ng' e-zwa 'zwi eli tshiwoyo. Kepa ikwababa la fundekela ngokubiza, li ti, " We, mpeza ! we, mpeza ! u nga yi kuleyo 'ndhlela yako ; u ya 'kufa ; a ku yi 'kubuya 'muntu kule 'mpi ; abantu ba ya 'kupela. Buyela ekaya."

The men, then, went out to that spoil of cattle. It happened as they were going from home, a crow cried out ; the men listened, hear-ing a noise, but not hearing a word that was said. But the crow was very urgent, crying and say-ing, "I say, Umpeza! I say, Um-peza! do not go by the way you are going ; you will die ; there will not return one man from the army ; the people will all die. Go home again."

Kwa ti uma li zwakale ka/le lelo 'zwi kwabanye, ba li kumusha ngokuti, "Ikwababa li y' ala, li ti, 'A ku yi 'kubuya 'muntu.'" Kepa abanye a b' czwanga lelo 'zwi lokuti, "A ku yi 'kubuya 'muntu," nelokuti, "We, mpeza!" Ba pika, a ba kolwanga, ngokuba inyoni i ng' azanga i kuluma nabantu. Ba kangwa inzuzo a ba ya 'ku i zuza; ngaloko ke ba hamba.

Kepa Umpeza w' enyela umzimba ngokuyolelwa ukufa. Wa buyela ekaya, nabanye ba kolwa izwi lokufa. Iningi la hamba; kepa kubo bonke labo a ku buyanga noyedwa, ukupela Usihhile yedwa owa sindayo. Ba bulawa bonke Amazulu. Ekufikeni kwake ekaya wa ti, "Ni bona mina nje 'kupela; a ni sa yi 'kubona mumbe." Ngaloko ke ba kolwa abaseleyo ezwini lekwababa e li ba tshelile. Kwa tshiwo ke ukuti, "Kanti izinyoni lezi zi ya kuluma, kodwa a zi k/ondwa 'muntu." Kwa /laliwa ke, kwa pela loko 'ku/lupeka. Ngemva kwesikati iminyango cminingi ya buba kakulu ngaleyo 'mpi. Umpeza wa /lala isikati eside; u s' and' ukufa kona manje, se ku indoda endala kakulu.

When some heard thoroughly that saying, they interpreted it, saying, "The crow forbids us to go; it says, 'Not a single man will return.'" But others did not hear the word, "Not a single man will return," nor that, "I say, Umpeza!" They disputed, and did not believe, for birds were never known to speak with men. They were fascinated by the spoil they expected to gain; and so they went.

But the body of Umpeza became weak and languid through being told beforehand of death. He returned home, and others who believed the word about death. The greater number went; but from among the whole not one returned, but Usichile alone, who escaped. They were all killed by the Zulus. When he came home he said, "You see me alone; you will never see any of the rest." Those therefore who remained believed in the word which the crow had spoken. And so it was said, "Forsooth these birds speak, and no one understands them." So they lived, and that trouble came to an end. After a time many households were destroyed through that Zulu army. Umpeza lived a long while; he has only just died at the present time, being a very old man.

The possession of this power of comprehending the language of birds is in old legends frequently associated with the influence of serpents. Thus, the young serpent which Melampus had brought up, played around him whilst he slept, and softly touched his ears. On awaking he found himself able to comprehend the chirping of birds. Iamus, the son of Evadne, was fed with honey by two serpents, sent to take charge of him by Apollo; and when he had grown up, he besought Apollo to open his ears that he might reveal to the sons of men the hidden things of nature and of futurity. "Apollo touched his ears, and straightway the voices of the birds spake to him clearly of the things which were to come, and he heard their words, as a man listens to the speech of his friend." (Cox. *Tales of Thebes and Argos*, p. 175.) Whilst in the legends of the North we read of Sigurd, who, incited by Regin, slew the serpent; whilst roasting the heart he accidentally touched it with his finger, and conveyed a portion of the blood to his tongue, when he immediately understood the language of birds, and heard them conversing with each other of Regin's duplicity, and of the benefits Sigurd might obtain by eating the whole of the heart which he was roasting for Regin. (*Thorpe. Northern Mythology. Vol. I., p.* 97.) This legend has found its way into the tales of the people in Germany in "The White Snake," (*Grimm, p.* 75,) and in the Highlands in "Fearachur Leigh." (*Campbell. Op. cit. Vol. II., p.* 361.) The faithful Johan, through well understanding the language of birds, learns from them how to save his master from destruction. (*Grimm, p.* 29.) And the prince, when the little bird sang on the tree, understood its language, and detects the deceit of the pretended bride. (*Dasent. Op. cit., p.* 427.)

Among the North-American Indians the same power of conversing with birds and beasts is ascribed to Hiawatha in beautiful connection with the simplicity with which childhood looks on created things, and the readiness with which it sympathises with the lower world of animal life, and claims for itself a brotherhood with all living creatures.

It is a raven which instructed Adam and Eve what to do with their dead. (*Weil. Biblical Legends of the Mussulmans, p.* 24.) In these legends the reader will find numerous instances of man holding intercourse with animals, &c. (see pp. 38, 40, 44, 104, 152.) It appears to be supposed that originally man had a language in common with animals. All nature is represented as weeping in sympathy with Adam, when he was expelled from Paradise, "and the birds, and the beasts and insects," until "the whole universe grew loud with lamentation" (p. 16); and that "the brute creation lost the power of speech" only when the ox had reproached Adam with his transgression (p. 25). Compare also "the frightful shriek which all nature uttered" when Kadbar, assisted by the priests, slew the wonderful camel, which, at the prayer of Salih, God had caused to come out of the rocky mountains (pp. 42, 45).

It is the guinea-fowl which warns the brothers of the approach of their sister for the purpose of killing them, and when the murder has been accomplished reports the fact to their parents. (*Bleek's Hottentot Tales.* "A Bad Sister," *p.* 65.) It is a bird that pursues Macilo, and constantly reminds him that he has killed his brother, and at length "finds the sister of the victim and says to her, 'I am the heart of Maciloniane; Macilo has murdered me; my corpse is near the fountain in the desert.'" (*Casalis' Basutos, p.* 339.) And that tells the parents that the younger of their two boys had been cast into the water by his elder brother. (*Zulu Legend to be given below.*)

When Kasimbaba had climbed to heaven to seek Utahagi, a little bird shows him Utahagi's house. (*Tylor. Op. cit., p.* 347.) The little birds tell the kind child how to perform the various difficult tasks imposed on her by the old witch who lived underground. (*Dasent. Op. cit.* "The Two Stepsisters," *p.* 132.—Compare "The Two Caskets." *Thorpe. Yule-tide Stories, p.* 102.) And it is three sparrows, or in the corresponding tale three doves, which pronounce three blessings on the generous princess, and three curses on her churlish step-sister. (*Thorpe. Idem.* "The Beautiful Herd-girl," *p.* 35 and 42.)

It strikes one as singular and interesting that there should be so universally spread about among widely differing people this curious notion. In addition to those already mentioned, I will point out a few more instances from the folk-lore of other people. We saw above that the swallow talks with Usikulumi, and by means of its skin protects him from danger and saves him from destruction (p. 53). It is Mama, the woodpecker, that comes to the despairing Hiawatha, and tells him of the place in the body of Megissogwon where alone he can be wounded. (*Longfellow's Hiawatha.*) A fairy in the form of a bird dropped a root on the arm of the king when he was about to kill Porziella, and he was seized with such a trembling that the weapon fell from his hand. (*Pentamerone.*) It was a bird that told Kurangaituku of the destruction of her home by Hatupatu. (*Grey. Op. cit., p.* 187.) And it was the untimely laughter of the little Tiwakawaka that caused the death of Maui and the failure of his enterprise. *(Id., p. 57.)* It is a little bird which warns the damsel that had been enchanted by her foster-mother, saying,

> "Look not at the billows blue,
> For then thou wilt turn gray."

(Thorpe. Yule-tide Stories, p. 64.) That gives warning to the betrayed bride by the words :—

> " Return, return, unhappy bride,
> Within this den the murderers hide."

(Grimm. "The Robber Bridegroom," *p.* 166.*)* It is the little bird that exposes the deception of the false bride. *(Campbell. Op. cit. Vol. II., p.* 288. —*Thorpe. Yule-tide Stories, p.* 125.*)* And that restores the forgotten bride to the recollection of the prince. *(Thorpe. Id.,* "The Mermaid," *p.* 203 ; "Singorra," *p.* 220 ; "Goldmaria and Goldfeather," *p.* 451.—*Dasent. Popular Tales from the Norse,* "Katie Woodencloak, *p.* 427.*)*

I here insert an account of the peculiar habits, almost amounting to intelligence, of the honey-bird. It was given me by a native, but has been substantially corroborated by whitemen who have themselves been led by it to deposits of honey. It is quite possible that many of the superstitions relating to birds had their origin in such or similar manifestations as are here described. The childlike mind has no theory to support ; it makes no arbitrary distinctions between intelligence as manifested by man, and intelligence as manifested by brutes ; where it sees actions implying intelligence, there it believes intelligence exists. Such a thought is probably at the bottom of the theory of transmigration, and of the possibility of there being an intercommunication between man and the lower animals.

INHLAMVU.

(THE HONEY-BIRD.)

INHLAMVU inyoni e bizelayo izinyosi. Pakati kwabantu abamnyama ku tiwa i inkosi. Uma umuntu e i ponsa ngetshe lapo e nga i landelanga, ku tiwa ka 'muntu waluto. Ngokuba noma umuntu e nga zi boni izinyosi, ka tsho ukuti, "A ngi i tshaye, i kqamb' amanga." A ku njalo. Zona zi kona ; noma ku nge zona, okunye. Uma e nga ku boni, ka nga i twesi ikcala ; ngokuba i tshaywa i y' esaba ukubizela abantu izinyosi.

Ku ti ngesikati lapo umuntu e hamba e ng' azi 'luto, noma u se e lambe okubi, ka namand*h*la okuhamba ngamand*h*la, u se zitwele ; ku fike inyoni, In*h*lamvu ibizo

THE Inthlamvu is a bird which by its cry calls men to places where there are honey-bees. Among black men it is said to be a chief. If a man throws a stone at it when he does not follow it, he is regarded as a man of nought. For if a man does not find bees, he should not say, "Let me throw a stone at it, it is a liar." It is not so. The bees are there ; or if they are not there, there is something else. If he does not see it, he must not blame the bird ; for if it is struck it is afraid to call men to the place where there are honeybees.

It happens when a man is walking, unconscious of anything, or perhaps he is very hungry, and is unable to walk fast, being a burden to himself ; then may come a bird,

layo. A ti e hamba, kumbe i vele ngapambili, 'ezwe se i tseketse kakulu, a kqale uku wa zuza amandhla ngokukolwa ukuti, "Se ngi suti, ngokuba ngi bizelwa isiminya." Kepa a tsho. ke, uku i vumela kwake, ukuti, "Eh!" noma, "Tseketse!" U ya i bonga kukqala, e ti, "Hlamv' e bizela amanina ekulimeni! Ehe! Yitsho, ngi zwe u ti ni." Lapo ke i se i kala ngokukala okukulu; i se i bangalase pakati kwesikqa; naye u se e jabula kakulu; i hambe pambili, ngokuba pela yona i umhholi. Umuntu ka buzi ukuti, "Ngi za 'kuya ngapi?" U landela yona njalo; i hambe, i m linde; ngokuba i ya ndiza, yena u ya nofoza; uma i suka i ya kude, i buye i m hlangabeze. Lapa e nga s' ezwa nakukala, se ku te nya, a bo sa te,[66] "U ye ngapi na?" Ku ti nya, a kqale ukumemeza kakulu ngokuti, "O-o-o-yi!" e ti, ka i zwe, ukuba u ya i funa. Lapo ke e se mi eduze lapa i m shiye kona; ngokuba noma se i buya, i buya i ye lapa i m shiye kona; a i zwe, i s' eza i bangalisile; 'enanele kakulu, ukuti, "E-ha!" I ze i fike kuye. Uma i nga m̂ boni, i hlale emtini, a ze a vele obala, a i bone, nayo i m bone; i muke ke, i hlale ngapambili; i ze i fike lapa se zi seduze, li kqale ukuncipa izwi; a

its name is Inthlamvu. As he is walking along, perhaps it appears in front of him, and he hears it loudly chirping, and he begins to gain strength through faith, saying, "My hunger is already appeased, because I am called for a reality." So he says in answer, "Eh!" or "Chirp!" He first praises it, saying, "Thou honcy-bird, who calls the women when they are digging! Yes! yes! Speak, that I may hear what you say." Then it cries with a very great crying, and makes a great noise in the bushes; and the man too is very glad; the bird goes in front, for in fact it is a guide. The man does not ask where he is going. He follows it continually; it goes and waits for him; for it flies, but he passes with difficulty through the underwood. If it goes a great distance in front, it returns and meets him. When he does not hear even its cry, and it is quite silent, he says again and again, "Where are you gone?" If there is no sound, he begins to shout very loud, saying, "O-o-o-yi!" telling it to understand that he is looking for it. And then he still stands near the place where the bird left him; for when it comes back, it comes back to the place where it left him; and he hears it coming and making a great noise, and he cheers it very much, shouting, "E-ha!" At length it comes to him. If it does not see him and stops on a tree, he at length stands forth, and sees it, and it sees him, and so it departs and pitches in front: at length it comes near the place where the bees are, and begins to

---

[66] This is a common mode of expression, the exact grammatical structure of which is not clear: *bo* occurs with or without *sa* or *ya*, as above, or in the following sentences:—*Wa bo sa te*, or *Wa bo ya te*, or *Wa bo te*; *Ngi bo ya te*, or *Ngi bo sa te*; *Nga bo ku ya ti*, or *Nga bo ku sa ti*. It is used to express the rapid, fruitless repetition of a similar act from haste, alarm, restlessness, &c.

ze a ti, "A ngi hambe nga-mand*h*la, se i bekile," 'ezwa i nk*q*wininize kancinyane; kanti a i ka beki; u za 'uti uma 'fike kona, i ti i sa m bona, i suke i k*q*ale ukuhambela pansi'; 'azi nga-loko ukuti, k*q*a, se zi seduze. Ku ti uma indawo i sobala, i y' esuka, i ya *h*lala ngapambili; i se i tsho, i tula; a bo ku i vumele, i twiki-twikize, i tule, i kombe; a ti uma i bona, a bone se i hamba, a k*q*ale ukusinga; a bo sa te, "Ah! Na-ziya, zi ngena pansi kwomuti." Lapo ke se zi ngena ubutaputapu, a sondele; i *h*lale; a ti uma e se fika impela, i suke i *h*lale njeya eduze, i buke, naye a i bone i tule nya; a zi mbe, a zi tape; a i bekele amak*q*afazi; ikekana a li *h*lome otini, ukuze i d*h*le; kona ugomso i ya 'ku m biza futi.

Kepa lelo 'kekana a i li d*h*li, i d*h*la izimpukane ezindizayo. A hambe ke, ngokuba pela ku tiwa uma umuntu e i bekela uju, i tsha izwi. Ku ti kumbe uma ku izwe eli vame izinyosi, a ti, e sa zi twele, e ti, u ya 'kufuna indawo yokuba a zi d*h*lela kona; i be se i fika, 'ezwe, se i tsho. Kepa u se i vumela ngokujabula; kodwa ngokuba i m kcebisile, ka sa yi 'ku i landela, ngokuba se kw anele kuye. A hambe ke, a goduke.

Futi ema*h*lanzeni zi tolwa ngayo. Umfazi u ya i landa; uma i fika e lima, a bize omunye, ba i lande,

cry less loudly. And he says, "Let me make haste, for it has now pitched," when he hears it gently crying; but it has not yet settled; but when he approaches, it begins to go towards the ground; and he thereby knows that the bees are near at hand. If the place is ex-posed, it goes and settles in front; it chirps and is silent; he again and again responds to it, it chirps and is silent, and points in the direction of the bees. When it sees him it flies off, and he catches sight of it, and begins to mark down the bees; again and again he says, "Ah! There they are entering at the foot of the tree." And when he sees them going in in crowds he draws near; and the bird is still: when he reaches the very place, the bird comes and waits over against him and looks on; and he sees that it is quiet; he digs out the bees and takes out the honey; he places the young bees for the bird, and sticks a piece of comb on a stick, that it may eat; and then it will call him again on another day.

But it does not eat the comb, it eats the young bees which can fly. So the man sets out; for it is said if a man places honey for it, it will lose its voice. Perhaps if it is a country which abounds in honey, as he is carrying it off looking for a place where he can eat it, it comes again, and he hears it cry-ing, and he responds to it gladly; but since it has given him abun-dance he will not follow it again; for he has enough, so he goes home.

And in the thorn-country bees are found by it. A woman follows it; if it comes to her when she is digging, she calls another woman, and they follow it, and the hus-

indoda i bone umfazi e fika nezinyosi. Ku ti uma ku kona inyoka
emgodini, s' azi ukuba abantu ba
lunywa futifuti lapa e ti u tapa
izinyosi; ngokuba a si tandi ukuba
umgodi si u kǫede; futi ukumba
kwomuntu ohlakanipileyo ka w o-
ni umlomo e zi ngena ngawo; u
hlaba ekcaleni, 'enze umlomo, o ya
'ku puma amakeke; ka si u kǫedi
lowo 'mgodi ngokumba; ngokuba
uma si u kǫeda, leso 'siganga zi
nge buye zi s' ake; si ya lingani-
sela, ukuze si buye si fune itshe, si
vimbe kahle.

Uma ku kona inyoka, ku ti lapa
umuntu e tapa, kumbe a bone ku
puma amakeke e nezimbobo; kumbe a ti ku kona impande; kepa
uma ku kona impande a ya dabuka; ku ti kwelokupela lapa
inyoka y enǫike ngalo, a ti lapa e
ti u bamba ikeke lokupela, amehlo
ka wa boni pakati, u funisela ngesandhla nje, 'ezwe se i m hlaba; a
pume ngokubaleka, a bone isandhla
se s' opa; u dhliwe. Uma ku
imamba, u. ya 'kufela kona lapo;
uma ku inyoka enye, kumbe a hla-
nguleke. Manje se si ti, si nga
ka zi mbi, si kǫale ngokuba si
beke induku emlonyeni womgodi,
ukuze si bone noma zi nenyoka,
noma i nge ko. Uma i kona, kwo
ti umuntu e sa i beka nje induku
zi ḅe se zi hamba pezu kwayo; a
ti, "O, zi nenyoka!" Lowo 'm-
godi u ya 'ku u shiya, uma ku
umuntu owesabayo. Uma ku o
nesibindi, a u hlikize wonke, ukuze
a zi tape e bona. Ku njalo ke.

band sees his wife returning with
honey. When there is a snake in
the hole, we know that people are
frequently bitten when they are
taking out honey; for we do not
like to destroy the hole; and a
wise man when he digs does not
injure the hole by which the bees
enter; he digs at the side, and
makes a hole by which he can
take out the comb; we do not destroy the hole by digging; for if
we destroy it, that swarm of bees
will not repair it; we measure the
hole we have made, that we may
find a stone and close it up nicely.

If there is a snake in the hole,
when the man takes out the honey,
perhaps he sees that there are
holes in the comb; perhaps he says
it is roots which have occasioned
the holes; but if it is roots, the
combs are broken. At the last
where the snake is coiled up, when
he thinks to grasp the last comb,
(the eyes cannot see inside, he is
searching about with his hand
only,) he feels himself wounded;
he draws his hand out rapidly, and
sees it bleeding; he has been
bitten. If it is an imamba, he
will die there and then. If it is
another snake, perhaps he may
live to have remedies applied.
Now, before we dig, we begin by
putting a stick into the mouth of
the hole, that we may see if there
is a snake with the bees or not.
If there is, as soon as the man
puts the stick in, the bees will
walk on it. So he says, "There
is a snake," and will leave that
hole if he is a timid man; but if
he is brave, he will break down
the whole, that he may see what
he is about when he is taking out
the honey. That is how it is.

Ku ti uma i bizela isilo i zwakala ngokugubaza, i tshaya amapiko; lapo umuntu u se e ya 'kubuya. Kodwa kukqala a ku banga njalo; kwa ku ng' aziwa ukuba y' enza ni, kwa za kwa bonwa loko lapa i kona, ukuti, "O, kanti i ngi bizela isilo." Noma imbuzi i file, noma inkomo i d*h*liwe isilwane, noma inyoka i zisongile, inyoka enkulu.

Njengaloku kwa ti si s' ake embava. Ubaba e bulele inyati, sa vuka kusasa, si ya 'utwala inyama; ku te uma ilanga se li fudumele, kwa fika In*h*lamvu, ya si biza masinyane; si baningi, sa ketana ukuze si i lande; abanye ba kqonda lapa ku yiwa kona; sa i landela ke. Lokupela u sebusika izwe li tshile, a ku fi*h*leke 'luto; ku te uma i fike enziweni, ya *h*lala, ya beka obala; sa hamba ka*h*le, si ti, "Eh! izinyosi ezi lapa obala ezani na?" Si te si sa fika, y' esuka, ya *h*lala njeya eduze, ya tula. Sa funa, sa funa; s' a*h*luleka. S' emuka si hamba si teta. Kepa ya fika futi, ya si buyisela kona. Sa funa, sa funa, ngokuba tina si funa izinyosi; kanti a i si bizeli zona, i si bizela okunye. Ku te pakati kwokufuna nga bona uto lu zisongile pansi kwomuti, lu nesango lu dumbile. Nga ti,

When it calls a person to a place where there is a leopard, it is heard striking its sides with its wings; and then a man will turn back. But at first it was not so; it was not understood what it was doing, until the place was seen where the leopard was; and he said, "O, it calls me to where there is. a leopard forsooth." Or it may call to a place where there is a dead goat, or a bullock devoured by wild beasts, or a great snake coiled up.

As it happened to us when we were living on the Imbava. Our father having killed a buffalo, we awoke early in the morning to go and fetch the flesh; when the sun was now hot, there came a honey-bird, and called us urgently; as we were many, we chose some of us to follow it; some set out for the place where we were going; I and others followed it. As it was winter the whole country had been burnt, and nothing was concealed by long grass; when it arrived at the site of an old village, it stopped and pitched in the open space; we proceeded gently, saying, "Why, what kind of bees are those which are in an open situation?" When we came up, it flew away, and pitched again near at hand over against us, and was silent. We looked and looked, but found nothing. We went away, going along and talking. But it came again, and took us back to the same place. We searched and searched, for we were looking for honey; but it, forsooth, was not calling us for honey; it was calling us for something else. As we were searching, I saw something bent on itself under a tree; it had an opening, and was large. I

"Nans' insimbi yami." Sa gijima sonke si pangelana kona. Nga i tabata; ya sinda. Nga ti, "U 'nsimbi ni le?" Abanye ba ti, "Insimbi impela." Kepa sa piki-sana. Sa funa amatshe, sa i tshaya etsheni, sa ti, "Ah! kanti, ubedu lwensimbi yetusi elibomvu." Sa hamba ke; ya tula. Kwa ku pela.

UMPENGULA MBANDA.

shouted, "Behold my piece of metal." We all ran hurrying together to the place. I took it up; it was heavy. I said, "What metal is this?" The others said, "It is really metal." But we disagreed. We found a stone and struck it, and said, "Ah! so it is a collar of red brass." So we walked away; it was silent; and that was the end of it.

The natives also affect to hear in the cry of certain birds sounds resembling human speech; thus, they say the female of the *insingizi* cries, *Ngi y' emuka, ngi y' emuka, ngi ya kwabetu*, "I am going away, I am going away to my people." To which the male replies, *Hamba, hamba, kad' u tsho*, "Go, go, you have said so before:"—an amusing illustration of what frequently passes between a native and his wife. The *utekwane* is represented as saying, *Nga ngi ba ngi muhle; ng' oniwa i loku na loku*, "I should be beautiful, but I am spoiled by this and by this;" that is, it points to certain parts of its form which it represents as ugly. And one of our schoolgirls lately gave an articulate meaning to the cry of the ringdove, saying it called her brother Ungadenzima to eat the wild medlars, *Gu-gu, ngadenzima, a vutiwe amatulwa, ngadenzima. Gu-gu,* "Coo-coo, 'Ngadenzima; the wild medlars are ripe, 'Ngadenzima. Coo-coo."

ITSHE LIKANTUNJAMBILI.

(THE ROCK OF TWO-HOLES; OR, THE CANNIBAL'S CAVE.)

THE following fragment, a portion doubtless of some extensive legend, the details of which however I have as yet failed to trace out, is here inserted as an introduction to the tale of "The Girl and the Cannibals," in which allusion is made to the Rock of Two-holes.

ITSHE likantunjambili indhlu lapa kwa hlala kona Amazimu; kepa li vulwa ngokuhlakanipa kwomni-nilo; a li vulwa ngezandhla, li vulwa ngomlomo; ukuba umuntu a fike, a memeze ngasendaweni yomnyango; kepa lowo 'mnyango a u naluto lokuba umuntu a lu bambe ngesandhla, a u vule. Nga-loko ke ukuvulwa kwalo ukume-meza igama lendhlu leyo lokuti, "Litshe likantunjambili, ngi vu-lcle, ngi ngene." Kepa li noku-

THE Rock of Two-holes, a house where cannibals lived; but it was opened by the cunning of the owner; it was not opened by hands, it was opened by the mouth; that is, when a man came, he shouted near the doorway; but that doorway had nothing which a man could take hold of with his hand, and open it. Therefore it was opened by shouting the name of the house, and saying, "Rock of Untunjambili,[67] open for me, that I may enter." But it could

[67] A personal name, meaning Two-holes.

pendula, uma li nga tandi ukuvuleka kulowo 'muntu, o t' a li m
vulele ; li ti, uku m pendula,
"A li vulwa abantwana ; li vulwa
izinkwenjane zona zi hamba pezulu." 'Ezwe ukuba "A li vumi
ukuvuleka kumi, li valiwe." Nanto ke ilizwi e ngi l' aziyo ngetshe
likantunjambili. Nam*h*la se si ti,
"Itshe lelo kanti ku tshiwo izin-
d*h*lu lezi zabelungu." Kepa ku
sale izwi li be linye lokuti, "Leyo 'nd*h*lu i vulwa izinkwenjane : "
li nga tsho ukuba i vulwa abantu :
kepa lezi zi vulwa abantu. A si
k*g*ondi uma leyo 'nd*h*lu e vulwa
izinyoni ezi hamba pezulu i njani-
na. Ku ya bonakala ; kepa a ku
bonakalisi ukuba i lezi e si zi bonayo impela, noma a si zo. Ku
imfumfu loko kitina.

UMANJANJE MBANDA.

answer if it did not wish to open
to that man, who asked it to open
for him ; it said in answer, "The
Rock is not opened by children ; it
is opened by the swallows which
fly in the air." And he perceived
that it would not open to him,
but remained closed. That, then,
is what I have heard of the
Rock of Untunjambili. Now we
say, "So then that Rock means
these houses of the whitemen."
But there is still left one word, to
wit, "That house is opened by the
swallows :" it does not say it is
opened by men ; but these are
opened by men. We do not understand what kind of a house that
is which is opened by birds which
fly in the air. It is evident ; yet
it is not very evident, whether it
is these houses which we really
see, or whether it is not they. It
is not clear to us.[68]

[68] The Rock of Two-holes has a considerable resemblance to the cave mentioned in the Forty Thieves, and which was opened and shut by a word. It is
curious that the Sesamum should figure in both stories ; there as the word—
"Open Sesame"—by which the rock was opened ; here as the means employed
by the girl in making her escape from the Amazimu. That was the abode of
robbers ; this of cannibal thieves. The power of opening solid bodies by a word
or charm is mentioned in many tales of different countries. The Nama woman
and her brothers, when pursued by the elephant, address a rock with these
words, "Stone of my ancestors ! divide for us." The rock divides, and they
pass through. The elephant addresses it in like manner ; the rock divides, and
closes upon him again and kills him. (*Bleek's Hottentot Fables*, *p.* 64.)—The
"Manito of the Mountain"

"Opened wide his rocky doorways,
Giving Pau-Puk-Keewis shelter,"

when he was pursued by Hiawatha. But though Hiawatha

"Cried in tones of thunder,
' Open ! I am Hiawatha ! ' "

he

"Found the doorways closed against him,"

(*Longfellow's Hiawatha.*)—So Hatupatu, when he was nearly overtaken by
Kurangaituku, "repeated his charm, 'O rock, open for me, open.' The rock
opened, and he hid himself in it." (*Grey. Op. cit., p.* 188.)
Ogilby informs us that there was a hollow sycamore tree at El Mattharia
(Materea, Heliopolis) respecting which the Turks related the following legend :
—"This tree by a miracle was split in two parts, between which the Virgin
Mary, with her child Jesus and Joseph, put themselves to disappoint the perse-
cuting pursuers, whereinto they were no sooner entered, but it immediately by

INTOMBI NAMAZIMU.

(THE GIRL AND THE CANNIBALS.)

Some cannibals steal a sheep.

Kwa ti Amazimu 'emuka a ya 'kuzingela; a ya kude. A fumana abafana b' alusile izinkomo nezimvu nezimbuzi. Ku kona inkungu, a i tata inqama yemvu ekulupeleyo, a hamba nayo. Abafana ka ba ze ba wa bona. A hamba nayo end*h*lini yawo, a fika end*h*lini yawo.

It happened that some cannibals went to hunt; they went a great distance. They found some boys herding cattle and sheep and goats. There was a fog, and they took a fat ram of the sheep, and went away with it. The boys did not see them. They took it to their house.

The cannibals leave a captive maiden, warning her not to roast the sheep during their absence.

Ku kona intombi a e tumbile kukqala emzini otile. Ya i nabane wabo. Kwa ti Amazimu 'emuka e i yalile, a ti, "U nga y osi inyama yemvu emini." Ngokuba a e saba amanye Amazimu; ngokuba a ya 'kuza uma 'ezwa ipunga lenyama, a i tabate intombi, e nge ko a ng' abanikaziyo. A ya kude.

There was a girl, whom they had before taken captive at a certain village. She had some brothers. When the cannibals went away, they had exhorted her, saying, "Do not roast the flesh of the sheep by day." For they were afraid of other cannibals; for they would come if they smelt the odour of the meat, and take the girl when her owners were absent. They went to a distance.

Other cannibals, attracted by the scent of the roasted meat, discover the maiden's retreat.

Kwa ti emini enkulu, intombi ya lamba, ya y osa inyama, ya i d*h*la. Amanye Amazimu a li zwa ipunga lenyama, a ti, "Um, um!

At noon the girl was hungry; she roasted some meat and ate it. Some other cannibals smelt the odour of the meat, and said, "Um,

like miracle closed again, till the Herodian child-slaughterers passed by, and then suddenly reopened to deliver its charge, so as at this day it is to be seen." (*Ogilby's Africa, p.* 73.)

In the tale "Dummburg," there is the account of a door leading to concealed treasures, which was opened and closed by the words, "Little door, open!" and "Little door, shut!" (*Thorpe. Yule-tide Stories, p.* 482.)

Ku nuka ngapi leli 'punga elimnandi na ?" A sezela, 'ezwa
ipunga elimnandi. A fika lapo
ku kona intombi.

um! Whence comes this delicious
smell?" They snuffed up the air,
perceiving the delicious scent.
They came to the place where the
damsel was.

The Rock of Two-holes.

Kwa ku kona itshe elikulu lapa
ya i *h*lala kona ; ibizo lalelo 'litshe
kwa ku tiwa Itshe-likantunjambili ; ngokuba la li ind*h*lu pakati
kwalo ; ku tiwe futi lelo 'litshe
kambe la li vulwa ngokutsho
kwomninilo ; la li valwa futi umninilo, a ti, "Vuleka," li vuleke ;
a ti, "Valeka," li valeke. Ngokuba la li bizwa u ye yedwa.

There was a great rock where
she was staying ; the name of the
rock was, Itshe-likantunjambili ;
for it was a house inside ; it is also
said that that rock was opened by
the word of its owner ; it was also
closed by its owner, who said, "Be
opened," and it opened, or he said,
"Be closed," and it closed. For it
was summoned by him alone.

The cannibals summon the damsel to open to them.

Kwa ti e sele e yokuzingela
umninilo, intombi i pakati. Wa
i valela kona ngapakati, ngokuba
kwa ku inyamazane yake. Wa i
yala, wa ti, i nga y osi inyama
emini, ngokuba wa e saba amanye
amazimu. Kwa ti se i lambile, ya
y osa inyama, ya d*h*la. Kwa t'u-
ba amanye amazimu 'ezwe ipunga
layo, a ti, "Um, um! Ku vela
ngapi leli 'punga elimnandi na ?"
A sezela ngalapo ku vela kona
ipunga—usi ; a ya ngakona, a fika
etsheni likantunjambili, igama lalo.
Elinye kuwo la ti, "Litshe likantunjambili, ngi vulele, ngi ngene."
Wa ti o pakati, ukuti intombi ya
ti, i zwa ukuba amanye amazimu,
a si ye umninilo, ya ti, "Yiya! a
li muke izimu eli-si*h*lutu. A si
ye lowo umninile 'ndawo."

When the cannibal, the owner
of the rock, went out to hunt,
the damsel remained inside. He
shut her up inside because she
was his game. He exhorted her
not to roast meat at noon, for he
was afraid of the other cannibals.
But when she was hungry, she
roasted the flesh, and ate. When
some other cannibals smelt the
odour of the meat, they said, "Um,
um! Whence comes this delicious
odour ?" They snuffed up the air
in the direction whence the odour
—the nice odour—came ; and
went in that direction, and came
to the rock of Untunjambili.
That was its name. One of them
said, "Rock of Untunjambili,
open to me, that I may enter."
She who was inside, that is, the
girl, on hearing that it was other
cannibals, and not the owner of
the rock, said, "Away! let the
long-haired cannibal depart. It is
not the owner of this place."

*A cannibal feigns the voice of the owner of the Rock of Two-holes,
and is admitted.*

L' emuka, la ya, la tshisa izwi lalo ngegeja. La buya, la ya futi etsheni likantunjambili; la fika, la tsho ngezwi elinçinyane, eli lingene izwi lomninileyo 'ndawo; la ti, "Litshe likantunjambili, ngi vulele, ngi ngene." Ya vula; la ngena; la d*h*la inyama ě be i tshiwo. Intombi ya ti ukuba i li bone, ya pel' amand*h*la. La ti izimu, "Hamba si hambe, ngi nga ku d*h*li." Intombi ya tutumela, y' esaba kakulu. Ya li nika inyama, la d*h*la, l' esuta. La ti kuleyo 'ntombi, "Hlala lapa ngi ze ngi buye; ngi sa ya 'kuzingela." La ti la puma, la hamba.

The cannibal departed, and made his voice hoarse with a hoe; and returned to the rock of Untunjambili; he came and said, with a little voice,[69] which resembled the voice of the owner of the place, "Rock of Untunjambili, open to me, that I may enter." She opened; the cannibal entered, and ate the meat which has been mentioned. When the girl saw him, she lost all power. He said, "Let us go together, that I may not eat you." The girl trembled, and was greatly afraid. She gave him meat; he ate and was satisfied. He said to the girl, "Stay here till I come back. I am now going to hunt." He went out, and went on his way.

The maiden escapes, and is pursued.

Intombi y' azi ukuba li za 'ku i d*h*la; ya puma. Ya tela udon*q*a esigujini, ya hamba. La fika izimu, la ti, "Litshe likantunjambili, ngi vulele, ngi ngene." Kwa ti tu; ngokuba intombi i mukile. La pinda futi, la tsho njalo. Kwa ti nya. L' azi ukuba intombi i pumile. La mema amaningi, a i landa intombi. A fika end*h*leleni, a bona udon*q*a; (ngokuba amazimu a e lu tanda udon*q*a;) a kcotsha.

The girl knew that he would return and eat her; she went out; she poured sesamum into a calabash, and went away. The cannibal came and said, "Rock of Untunjambili, open for me, that I may enter." There was silence; for the girl had departed. Again he said the same words. There was perfect silence. So he knew that the girl had departed. He called many cannibals, and they pursued the girl. They came to a path, and saw sesamum scattered on the ground; (for cannibals are fond of sesamum;) they gathered

---

[69] In "The Wolf and the Seven Young Kids," the wolf having demanded admission, feigning to be their mother, they replied, "No, no; we shall not open the door; you are not our mother; she has a gentle loving voice, but yours is harsh; for you are a wolf." The wolf went away, and "swallowed a great lump of chalk to make his voice more delicate." (*Grimm's Home Stories, p. 22.*)

I kw enzile intombi loko kambe, ukuba a z' a ti amazimu, uma e fumanisa udonqa, a libale ukukcotsha, i ze i wa bone ; ngokuba y' azi intombi ukuti a za 'ku i landa. A i landa amazimu. A fumana udonqa, a tola. Ya wa bona ngotuli, ya ti, "I wo lawaya." Ya tela udonqa kakulu pansi ; ya hamba, ya hamba ngamand*h*la. A fika lapo i tele kona udonqa, a kcotsha, a libala ; ya hamba kakulu ngamand*h*la. Ya bona futi ukuba a kqub' utuli ; y' enza njalo futi ; ya tel' udonqa, ya hamba ngamand*h*la. Ya bona ukuba a se seduze ; ya tela futi okokupela esigujini, ya hamba.

it up.[70] The girl had done this, that the cannibals, when they found the sesamum, might stop to pick it up, that she might see them ; for the girl knew they would follow her. The cannibals followed her. They found the sesamum, and picked it up. She saw them coming by the dust, and said, "There they are yonder." She poured a large quantity of sesamum on the ground, and went on quickly. They came where she had poured the sesamum, they picked it up, and loitered ; and she went with very great speed. Again she saw them raising the dust, and she did the same again ; she poured sesamum on the ground, and went on quickly. She saw that they were now near ; again she poured all that was in the calabash, and went on.

She, being tired, ascends a high tree ; the cannibals come up to it, and sit at its foot.

A katala amazimu, a *h*lala pansi. Ya hamba ; ya dinwa futi nayo. Ya bona umuti omude kakulu, umkulu. Ya hamba kuwo, ya kwela kuwo, ya *h*lala kwelenyoni. 'Esuka amazimu, a hamba ; i s' i kude kakulu. A fika emtini, e se diniwe futi, a *h*lala pansi kwawo, e pumula, e ti, a za 'kubuya a i lande futi, uma e se pumulile.

The cannibals were tired, and sat down. She went on ; but she was tired too. She saw a very high tree ; it was a great tree. She went to it, and climbed into it, and sat on a bird's twig.[71] The cannibals arose and pursued their journey, she being now a great way off. They came to the tree ; they being now again tired, they sat down at the foot of the tree, resting and saying they would presently pursue her again, when they had rested.

[70] The reader will remember numerous instances in the tales of other people, in which the pursued is represented as throwing something behind him to delay the pursuer. But in those tales the thing thrown down has some magical power, and becomes a lake, a forest, or a mountain of rock, to be overcome only by great physical strength. In this the appeal is made to a mere childish appetite. (*The Pentamerone.* "Petrosinella," and "The Flea."— *Thorpe. Yule-tide Stories,* p. 223. "Singorra."—*Dasent. Op. cit.,* p. 91. "The Mastermaid."—*Campbell. Op. cit.* Vol. I., p. 33. "The Battle of the Birds.")

[71] *Kwelenyoni,* viz., *igaba,* twig or branch. That is, she sat on the topmost twig.

They discover her, and try to cut down the tree.

Kanti intombi ya i pete isitsha samanzi esi vuzayo; sa vuzela pezu kwawo; 'ezwa ku ti kco, kco. 'Etuka, a ti, " Ku ini loko na?" A bheka pezulu, a i bona intombi i *h*lezi kwelenyoni. E. jabula, a u gaula umuti ngezimbazo, ngokuba a e zi pete izimbazo: a u gaula, amanye a *h*lala ngalapaya kwomuti, amanye a *h*lala nganeno. Wa ti umuti lapo u s' u za 'kuwa, wa buya wa tengatenga, wa ti nya, wa ti g*xh*li pansi, wa ba njengaloko kad' u njalo. A pinda a gaula futi, amanye 'ema ngalapaya, amanye 'ema nganeno, amanye 'ema emakcaleni omabili. A u gaula; wa ti lapo u s' u za 'kuwa, w' enza njalo futi, wa buya wa ti g*xh*li pansi, wa ba njengaloko kad' u njalo futi. A pinda a gaula futi; kwa ti lapo u s' u za 'kuwa, wa buya wa ti g*xh*li pansi, wa ba njengaloko kad' u njalo futi.

The girl was carrying a vessel of water, which leaked;[72] it leaked upon the cannibals; they heard a sound, "Kho! kho!" They were frightened, and said, "What is that?"[73] They looked up, and saw the girl sitting on the very top, on a mere bird's twig. They were glad, and began to cut down the tree with their axes, for they had axes in their hands: they hewed the tree, some standing on one side, and some on the other. When the tree was now about to fall, it worked backwards and forwards, became still, and then sank down and became firm, and was just as it was at first. Again they hewed, some before and some behind, some on each side. They hewed it; and when it was about to fall, it did the same again; it settled down and became firm, and was again just as it was at first. Again they hewed; and when it was about to fall, again it settled down and became firm, and was again just as it was at first.

The maiden's brother has a dream, and goes to seek his sister.

Umne wabo intombi wa e pupile kusi*h*lwa intombazana, udade wabo, i d*h*liwa amazimu ngasendaweni etile, a y aziyo. Kwa ti kusasa wa puma nezinja zake ezinkulu kakulu, wa ya 'kuzingela ngalapo e be pupile ngakona. Wa

The brother of the girl had dreamed in the night that the little girl, his sister, was being eaten by cannibals, near a certain place, which he knew. In the morning he went out, taking with him his very great dogs; he went to hunt in the direction of the place of which he had dreamed.

---

[72] I have ventured to make a slight alteration in this place. The original is, "Kwa ti intombi ya piswa umtondo, ya tunda pezu kwawo." Which, though not at all offensive to native notions of delicacy, I do not translate for English readers.

[73] Compare this with the tale of Fritz and Catherine, who had ascended a tree for safety. During the night some thieves came and sat at the foot of the tree. Catherine was carrying a bag of nuts, a bottle of vinegar, and a door. These were dropped one after another. The vinegar sprinkled them, and the door frightened them away. (*Grimm. Op. cit.*)

ti e zingela wa bona isik*x*uku sa-mazimu, si pansi kwomuti, si gaula umuti. Wa ya kona nezinja zake ezinkulu; wa fika kona, wa ti, "Ni gaula ni lapa, bangane bami, na?" Ba ti, "Woza, u si gau-lise,[74] mfo wetu. Nansiya inya-mazane yetu, i pezulu." Wa bheka pezulu, wa bona ukuba udade wabo. Wa pel' amand*h*la. Wa ba ziba, wa ba gaulisa umuti. Wa linga kancinyane ukugaula, wa ti, "Ake si bem' uguai, bangane bami." Ba *h*lala pansi. Wa so-ndeza izinja zake eduze kwake. Wa k*x*ataz' uguai, wa ba nika. Wa ti, lapo be bemayo, wa ba nika izinja zake, za ba bamba, za ba k*x*otsha, zi hamba zi ba bulala. Ba fa bonke. Kwa ku pela ke.

As he was hunting he saw a crowd of cannibals under a tree, hewing the tree. He went to them with his great dogs; he came to them, and said, "What are you hewing here, my friends?" They said, "Come and help us hew, our brother. There is our game on the top of the tree." He looked up, and saw that it was his sister. His heart sunk. He turned away their attention from his agitation, and helped them hew the tree. He tried very little to hew; and then said, "Just let us take some snuff, my friends." They sat down. He made his dogs come to his side. He poured out some snuff, and gave them; and when they were taking it, he set his dogs on them; they laid hold of them, and drove them, the dogs running and killing them. They all died. So there is an end.

He delivers his sister, and they return home together.

Wa tsho kudade wabo, wa ti, "Ye*h*la, mnta kababa." W' e*h*la, wa hamba nomne wabo, wa fika ekaya kunina. Unina wa m enzela ukud*h*la okukulu, e jabula. Wa *h*laba izinkabi eziningi; ba d*h*la bonke nayo indodakazi yake. Kwa sokuba ukupela ke.
ULUTULI DHLADHLA (USETEMBA).

He said to his sister, "Come down, child of my father." She came down, and went with her brother, and came home to her mother. Her mother made her a great feast, with rejoicing. She slaughtered many oxen; and all ate together with her daughter. So there is the end.

ADDITION TO THE FOREGOING TALE BY ANOTHER NATIVE.

The brother goes up the tree with his sister, and they find a beautiful country.

Ku tiwa wa kwela nomfo wabo pezulu; wa bona ilizwe eli*h*le kakulu. Ba funyanisa ku kona ind*h*lu en*h*le kakulu; leyo 'nd*h*lu

It is said, her brother also ascend-ed the tree, and saw a very beau-tiful country.[75] They found a very beautiful house there; that house

---

[74] *Gaulisa*, help us to hew; *gaulela*, hew for us. By the former they ask for co-operation in the labour; by the latter they ask to have the work done for them.

[75] See Appendix at the end of this tale.

ya i lu*h*laza, pansi kungati i gu-d*h*liwe, nelizwe lakona pezulu la li li*h*le kakulu, be hamba kulona ngezikati zonke, be li buka, ngokuba be li k*q*abuka. Kepa pansi ba be buka ku kude kakulu, be nga se namand*h*la okweuka ukuya kona, ngokuba ba b' esaba amazimu, be ti, ba ya wa bona e hamba pansi e funa ukud*h*la.

was green, and the floor was burnished; and the country of the upper region was very beautiful; they walked about there continually, and looked at it, for they saw it for the first time. But the earth they saw was at a great distance below them; they were no longer able to go down to it, for they feared the cannibals, thinking they saw them going about on the earth, seeking for food.

They find an ox, which they kill and roast; but are detected by the cannibals.

Ba hamba ba ya ezweni eli pambili. Ba fika ba tola inkomo, inkabi enkulu; ba i k*q*uba, ba ya nayo end*h*lini bobabili; ba fika ba i *h*laba leyo 'nkomo, ba *h*linza isikumba, ba s' eneka elangeni; sa ti si nga k' omi ba basa end*h*lini. Amazimu 'ezwa ulusi lwenyama ukunuka kwayo, a k*q*alaza, a bheka pezulu, a i bona ind*h*lu. Wa ti umfama, "Kungati leli 'zimu i lona ela si k*x*otsha em*h*labeni."

They set out, and went to the country in front of them. They at length found a bullock—a large ox; they drove it, and went both of them to the house with it; when they arrived they killed that bullock, and flayed it, and spread the skin in the sun; before it was dry they lit a fire in the house. The cannibals smelt the odour of the meat; they looked hither and thither, they looked up, they saw the house. The youth said, "That cannibal is like the one who pursued us on the earth."

They make a rope of the hide.

Wa ti udade wabo, "A si li kupule li ze lapa kutina; loku u nomkonto nje, li ya 'kwesaba uku si d*h*la; ngokuba amazimu a ya w esaba umkonto." Wa ti umne wabo, "Si ya 'ku li kupula ngani na?" Wa ti udade wabo, "A ng' azi kuwena." Wa ti umue wabo, "A si benge isikumba, loku si se manzi nje, si li kupule ngawo umkcilo wesikumba." Wa e se puma end*h*lini nomkonto, wa benga isikumba sa ze sa ba siniugi kakulu, sa pela isikumba.

The sister said, "Let us draw him up here to us; since you have a spear he will be afraid to eat us; for cannibals are afraid of a spear." Her brother said, "With what can we draw him up?" The sister said, "I do not know so well as you." The brother said, "Let us cut the skin into strips, since it is still moist, and draw him up by a rope of hide." He then went out of the house with his assagai, and cut the skin into strips, until it was very long, and the whole skin was cut up.

They devise a plan for drawing up a cannibal.

Ba u tata umkcilo, ba u ponsa ubuningi bawo pansi, ba ti ezimwini, " Bamba umkcilo lowo, u kwele ngawo." La ti izimu, "Hau! we mamo! Ngi za 'kuwa uma ngi kwela ngomkcilo, ngokuba umncane ; u za 'ugqushuka." Ba ti, "Kqa; a u z' 'ukqabuka ; si y' azi ukuba u lukuni. Kwela ke." Izimu la u bamba umkcilo, la kwela. Kepa lapa se li pakati emkatini na pezulu, ba ti be kuluma bobabili, e ti umfana, "A si li yeke, li we pansi." I ti intombazana, "A si li kwelise, li ze lapa kutina, si li ḥlupe, ngokuba nati a si ḥlupe." Wa ti, "Si za 'ubuye si li kwelise futi." Wa vuma ke udade wabo. Wa li yeka umne wabo izimu ; la wa pansi, la ti, "Maye! Baba! Nga fa! Na ti, ni za 'u ngi bamba ngomkcilo ; se ni ngi yekile ; se ngi limele isinqe, nga wa ngaso." Wa ti umne wabo, "Kqa, zimu, a si ku yekanga ngamabomu ; ku punyukile umkcilo ; manje si za 'uponsa okqinile kakulu umkcilo ; u bambe u kqinise."

They took the rope, and threw down the greater portion of it to the earth, and said to the cannibal, "Lay hold of the rope, and climb up by it." He said, "Hau! we mamo! I shall fall if I climb by the rope, for it is small, and will break." They said, "No! it will not break ; we know that it is strong. So climb." The cannibal seized the rope, and climbed. But when he was midway, halfway between above and below, they spoke each to the other, the youth saying, "Let us leave go of him, that he may fall down." The girl said, "Let us raise him, that he may come here to us, that we may harass him, for us too the cannibals have harassed." He replied, "We will raise him again." His sister agreed. The brother let go the cannibal ; he fell down, and cried, "Woe is me! Father! Dead! You said, you would hold me by the rope ; now you have let me go ; and my loins are now injured ; I fell on my loins." The brother said, "No, cannibal, we did not let you go on purpose ; the rope slipped ; now we are about to throw you a very strong rope ; catch hold of it firmly."[76]

They tantalise the cannibal by eating in his presence.

Nembala ke la u bamba izimu umkcilo, la kwela, ba li fikisa kubona pezulu, ba li beka endḥlini,

Surely then the cannibal caught hold of the rope, and climbed ; they raised him up to where they were, they placed him in the

[76] In Bleek's *Hottentot Fables*, the jackal plays the lion a similar trick. The jackal having built a tower for himself and family, and placed his food upon it to be out of the power of the lion, when the lion comes, he cries out, "Uncle, whilst you were away we have built a tower, in order to be better able to see game." "All right," says the lion ; "but let me come up to you." "Certainly, dear uncle, but how will you manage to get up? We must let down a thong for you." The lion ties himself to the thong, and is drawn up ; and when he is nearly at the top the thong is cut by the jackal, who exclaims, "Oh, how heavy you are, uncle! Go, wife, and fetch me a new thong." This is repeated several times. *(Op. cit., p.* 7.)

ba ngena; ba *h*lala b' osa inyama, imibengo ya mitatu. Wa ti umne wabo, "Se i vutiwe inyama; a si *dh*le manje." Ba i tata ke inyama, ba i *dh*la. Izimu la ba bheka, la kconsa amate. Wa ti umne wabo, "Musa ukukconsa amate. Ngi za 'u ku gwaza, loku u kconsa amate." Ba *h*lala ke, ba i k*q*eda inyama.

house, and went in; they sat and roasted flesh, three strips.[77] The brother said, "The flesh is now ready; let us eat it now." So they took the meat, and ate it. The cannibal looked at them; his mouth watered. The brother said, "Do not allow your mouth to water. I will stab you, since your mouth waters." They sat and ate all the roasted meat.

The cannibal is prevented from appeasing his hunger.

Kwa ze kwa *h*lwa ba lala. Izimu la lala ngaseziko, inyama ya i bekiwe cduze nomnyango; bona be lele ngasen*h*la. Kwa ti ebusuku izimu la vuka la nyonyoba, la ya la u tata umswani, la u k*q*apuna ngesand*h*la. Wa e se vuka udade wabo, e ti kumne wabo, "Vuka, vuka! Nangu e se k*q*apuna umswani." Wa ti umne wabo, "U k*q*atshunywa ubani na?" Wa ti udade wabo, "U k*q*atshunywa izimu." Wa e se vuka ke umne wabo ngamand*h*la, e ti, "Beka, beka umswani wenkomo yami. U u nikwe ubani na?" La ti, "Ai, tina, nkos'; be ngi ti, a ku si wo owako; be ngi ti, u za 'u u kcita." Wa ti, "U beke masinya. Ngi nga ku gwaza." La u beka ke izimu umswani. Ba lala.

When it was dark they lay down. The cannibal lay near the fireplace; the flesh had been placed near the doorway, and they lay at the upper part of the house. In the night the cannibal awoke, and went stealthily, and took a handful of the contents of the ox's stomach. The sister awoke, saying to her brother, "Awake, awake! There is some one taking handfuls of the contents of the ox's stomach." The brother said, "By whom is it being taken?" The sister said, "By the cannibal." The brother then awoke at once, saying, "Put down, put down the contents of the stomach of my bullock. Who gave it to you?" He said, "No, indeed, my lord; I thought it was not yours; I thought you were going to throw it away." He said, "Put it down at once. I could stab you." The cannibal put it down. They slept.

The cannibal dies.

Kwa sa. Ba *h*lala insuku cziniugi, be i *dh*la inyama. Izimu be nga li niki 'luto. Amatambo be wa ponsa ngapansi; be li lindile izimu ukuba li nga kcotshi 'luto

The day dawned. They tarried many days, eating the meat. As for the cannibal, they gave him nothing. The bones they cast down to the earth; they watched the cannibal, lest he should pick

[77] The natives cut their meat into long strips, and griddle them on the fire.

pansi. La *h*lala ke izimu li fa ind*h*lala. Kwa ti ebusuku la fa. Ba lala be nga li boni. Kwa ti kusasa ba vuka ba bona ukúba se li file. Ba li la*h*la ngapansi.

up something from the ground. So the cannibal remained dying of famine. It happened during the night that he died. They were asleep, and did not see him die. In the morning when they awoke they saw that he was already dead. They cast him to the earth.

The sister proposes that they shall go down from the tree and seek their sister.

Wa ti udade wabo, "A si hambe si fune udade wetu, loku uma wa e si tshela e ti, u kóna udade wetu omunye owendileyo. A si m fune ke, si ze si m tole; si *h*lale kuyena, loku se ba fa obaba noma, se si sobabili nje." Wa ti umne wabo, "Uma s' e*h*le—Ai! a si 'ku wa bona ini amazimu na?" Wa ti udade wabo, "Loku se sa *h*lala lapa isikati eside kangaka, u ti a se kona amazimu na?" Wa ti umne wabo, "A si hambe ke s' e-*h*like, si ye 'ku m funa."

The sister said, "Let us go and look for our sister, for our mother used to tell us that there is another sister of ours who is married. Let us seek her until we find her, and live with her, since our fathers and mothers are dead, and there are now we two only." Her brother said, "When we have gone down—No! shall we not see the cannibals?" The sister replied, "Since we have now staid here so long a time, do you think the cannibals are still there?" The brother said, "Let us set out then, and descend, and go and seek her."

They find their sister, and live with her in peace.

Ba tata umkcilo owa u sele kuleyo a ba be kwelisa ngayo izimu; ba u kcwilisa emanzini, wa tamba. Ba ti emini ba funa ukuni olukulu, ba lu mbela pansi, lwa tsho'na kakulu, ba tekelezela umkcilo lona ugongolo; ba se b' euka ngawo umkcilo ba ze ba fika pansi. Ba u shiya ke umkcilo u lenga ogongolweni. Ba hamba ba d*h*lula ematanjeni alelo 'zimu ela fayo. Ba d*h*lula ba hamba ba funa udade wabo; ba hamba inyanga ya ze ya

They took the rope which was left with which they raised the cannibal; they soaked it in water until it was softened. And during the day they sought a large log, and fixed it in the ground; it went in very deep; they fastened the rope to the log, and descended by the rope until they reached the ground. So they left the rope hanging from the log. They set out, and passed the bones of the cannibal which had died. They went on and sought their sister; they travelled until that moon

fa be nga m boni. Kwa ti lapa se
ku twasa enye inyanga ba m tola.
Ba fika ba m bona udade wabo,
kodwa ba be nga m azi igama lake
uma ubani." Wa ba bona yena,
wa ba biza ngamagama abo, wa ti,
"Songati abantwana bakwetu laba." Wa vuma. Wa ti, "Ni
vela ngapi na?" Ba ti, "Kade
s' a*h*lukana naobaba noma. Kepa
sa si *h*lutshwa amazimu. Si vela
ezweni eli*h*le pezulu e sa si *h*lezi
kulona, si nga *h*lutshwa 'luto. Sa
ze sa li kwelisa elinye izimu, sa li
*h*lupa nati; sa ze sa li ncitsha
uku*h*la, la fa, sa li la*h*la; s' e*h*lika
ke nkuyo'ufuna wena. Si ya ja-
bula se si ku tolile."

Ba *h*lala ka*h*le bobatatu kuleyo
'ndawo.

USKEBE NGUBANE,
(LYDIA, UMKASETEMBA.)

died, without finding her. But
when another new moon came
they found her. When they arrived they saw their sister, but
they did not know her name. She
saw them, and called them by
their names, saying, "These are
like our children." They assented.
She said, "Whence come you?"
They replied, "Long ago we separated from our fathers and mothers. But we were troubled
much by the cannibals. We are
now come from a beautiful country
above, where we tarried without
any trouble. We raised a cannibal,
and we too harassed him; we refused to give him food; he died;
and we cast him out: then we
descended to go and seek you.
We are happy now we have found
you."

All three lived in peace at that
place.

APPENDIX.

THE HEAVEN-COUNTRY.

UBANI *o nga pot' igode lokukupuka a ye ezulwini?* "Who can plait a rope
for ascending that he may go to heaven?"—It is remarkable that with this native saying to express an utter impossibility, there should also be found the
legend of an ascent to heaven by a tree, so common in various parts of the
world. Like other unadvanced people the Zulus think that the heaven is at no
great distance above the earth. Utshaka claimed to be king of heaven as well
as of earth; and ordered the rain-doctors to be killed because, in assuming
power to control the weather, they were interfering with his royal prerogative.
These doctors have medicines and other means by which they imagine or pre-
tend that they are able to influence the heaven, bring rain, repel a storm, send
the lightning-stroke to kill an enemy, or circle a kraal with an influence which
shall protect it from its fatal power.

In the Polynesian Mythology we read of a tree whose tendrils reached the
earth, and by which it was possible to ascend to heaven. By these tendrils
Tawhaki ascended to heaven to seek Tango-tango. *(Grey. Op. cit., p. 71.)*
Rupe too ascends to the tenth heaven, it is not clear by what means, breaking
through heaven after heaven, as though they were solid roofs overlaying each
other. *(Id., p. 83.)* In the Zulu legend the floor of the heavenly house is
burnished. Tylor, in his interesting work, *Researches into the Early History of
Mankind,* has collected from different sources various legends of this kind.
There is Chakabech, who ascended with his sister by a tree to heaven, and
found a beautiful country *(p. 342.)* And Chapewee, who "stuck a piece of
wood into the earth, which became a fir-tree, and grew with amazing rapidity,

until its top reached the sky." By this tree he reached the stars, and found a firm plain and a beaten road by which the sun pursued his daily journey (*p. 343*). These legends are from America. In the Malay Island of Celebes there is found the legend of Utahagi, who, like Tawhaki, had married a daughter of heaven and been forsaken by her, and ascended to heaven in search of her, by rattans (*p. 347*). We have in our own Nursery Tales "Jack and the Bean-stalk." In connection with these myths we may remember too those of the American Indians. Nokomis was swinging in a swing of grape-vines in the moon; her companions severed the vine, and she fell to the earth, where she gave birth to Hiawatha's mother. And Osseo, who descended from the evening star,

> " Once, in days no more remembered,
> Ages nearer the beginning,
> When the heavens were closer to us,"

was together with several others, by the power of magic, again raised to the evening star, to descend again to earth when the spell was broken.

In a Dayak tale Si Jura ascends by a large fruit tree, the root of which was in the sky, and its branches, hanging down, touched the waters, and reaches the country of the Pleiades. He there obtains the seed of three kinds of rice, with which he returns to be a blessing to mankind. But in the beautiful myth of Mondamin—the Spirits' grain, Mondamin descends from heaven in the form of a beautiful youth to fight with Hiawatha, and to be overcome by him; that from his body, when buried, there might spring up the magic-plant.

In other legends we have the account of an ascent from regions under the earth to its surface. In that of the Mandans this was effected by a grape-vine. In the Zulu legend, to be given hereafter, the ascent is mentioned, but not the means.

Then in the mythology of the North we have "Yggdrasil, the largest and best of trees; its branches spread themselves over the whole world, and tower up above the heavens." (*Thorpe. Northern Mythology. Vol. I., p. 13.*) And should "the mythic Yggdrasil have been to the men of remote ages the symbol of ever-enduring time," (*Mallet's Northern Antiquities, p. 493,*) and of a strictly spiritual significance, it yet might be that which suggested the various legends, which have become mere senseless children's tales in different parts of the world. Or all may have had a common origin in some older tradition now lost for ever.

But, as Tylor says, "it must be remembered in discussing such tales, that the idea of climbing, for instance, from earth to heaven by a tree, fantastic as it may seem to a civilized man of modern times, is in a different grade of culture quite a simple and natural idea, and too much stress must not be laid on bare coincidences to this effect in proving a common origin for the stories which contain them, unless closer evidence is forthcoming. Such tales belong to a rude and primitive state of knowledge of the earth's surface, and what lies above and below it. The earth is a flat plain surrounded by the sea, and the sky forms a roof on which the sun, moon, and stars travel. The Polynesians, who thought, like so many other peoples, ancient and modern, that the sky descended at the horizon and enclosed the earth, still call foreigners *papalangi*, or 'heaven-bursters,' as having broken in from another world outside. The sky is to most savages what it is called in a South American language, *mumeseke*, that is, the 'earth on high.' There are holes or windows through this roof or firmament, where the rain comes through, and if you climb high enough you can get through and visit the dwellers above, who look, and talk, and live very much in the same way as the people upon earth. As above the flat earth, so below it, there are regions inhabited by men or man-like creatures, who sometimes come up to the surface, and sometimes are visited by the inhabitants of the upper earth. We live as it were upon the ground floor of a great house, with upper storeys rising one over another above us, and cellars down below." (*Op. cit., p. 349.*)

The Arabs believe that there "are Seven Heavens, one above another, and Seven Earths, one beneath another; the earth which we inhabit being the highest of the latter and next below the lowest heaven." (*Lane's Arabian Nights. Vol. I., p. 18.*)

UMBADHLANYANA AND THE CANNIBAL.

Kwa ku kona umfana igama lake Umbad*h*lanyana kamak*q*ubata; wa ti e se mucane wa tanda ukuzingela izinyamazane. Kwa ti ngesinye isikati Umbad*h*lanyana wa hamba wa ya 'uzingela, wa bulala uk*c*ilo; wa ti lapa e sa hamba e m pete uk*c*ilo, wa bona ku vela amazimu amaningi: a m hhak*q*a pakati, a ti, "Sa 'u bona, mbad*h*lanyana kamak*q*ubata." Wa vuma. Kwa ti 'emi pakati kwawo amazimu, l' esuka elinye izimu, la tata uk*c*ilo, la mu d*h*la. Kwa ti lapa se li mu d*h*lile uk*c*ilo izimu, Umbad*h*lanyana wa finyela, wa ba mfutshane, wa ziponsa emakaleni ezimu. La ti izimu, "Thi, mbad*h*lanyana, puma; uk*c*ilo owako." Wa ti Umbad*h*lanyana, e kuluma pakati emakaleni ezimu, wa ti, "Be kw enzelwa ni ukuba ku d*h*liwe uk*c*ilo wami, ku buye ku antiwe ku za 'ud*h*liwa nami? Nanto[83] elinye, fik*c*i." La pinda izimu la timula ngamand*h*la, la ti, "Thi, mbad*h*lanyana, puma; uk*c*ilo

There was a boy whose name was Umbadhlanyana,[78] the son of Umak*q*ubata;[79] when he was a child he liked to hunt game. On one occasion Umbadhlanyana went to hunt, and killed an uk*c*ilo;[80] as he was going along carrying the uk*c*ilo, he saw many cannibals make their appearance: they enclosed him in the midst of them, and said, "Good day, Umbadhlanyana Kamak*q*ubata."[81] He saluted in return. As he was standing in the midst of the cannibals, one of them took away the uk*c*ilo, and ate it. When the cannibal had eaten the uk*c*ilo, Umbadhlanyana contracted himself and became short, and threw himself into the nostrils[82] of the cannibal. The cannibal sneezed, and said, "Come out, Umbadhlanyana; the uk*c*ilo is yours." Umbadhlanyana answered, speaking in the nostrils of the cannibal, "Why did you eat my uk*c*ilo, and then say you would eat me too? There is another morsel, which will quite fill you." The cannibal sneezed again violently, and said, "Come out, Umbadhla-

---

[78] *Umbadhlanyana.*—The meaning of this word is not clear; but it implies a small person, a dwarf. It reminds us of the term *imbatshelana* applied to Uthlakanyana (p. 3).

[79] *Umakqubata.*—*Ukuti kqu-kqu-kqu* is applied to the mode in which a short person, incapable of making strides, runs, viz., by a succession of short rapid steps. *Umakqubata* is a man who runs in this way.

[80] *Ukcilo* is a very small bird. There are three very small birds, the incete, the intiyane, and the ukcilo; this last is the smallest, about the size of the humble bee.

[81] Ka-makqubata, the son of Umakqubata; the *ka* is equivalent to Mac, or O', as in MacGregor, O'Connor.

[82] In the tales from the Norse Thumbikin hides himself from his mother in the horse's nostril. (*Dasent, p.* 430.)

[83] *Nanto*, not nanti; that is, Umbad*h*lanyana speaks as though he was a great way off from the cannibal. Elinye, that is, ik*q*ata, a slice of meat. *Ukuti fikci*, to fill up entirely.

owako." Wa ti, "Be kw enzelwa ni uma ku d*h*liwe ukcilo wami; ku buye ku tiwe ku za 'ud*h*liwa nami? Nanto elinye, fikci."

Lapo amazimu onke, lapa e se bona Umbad*h*lanyana e se ngene emakaleni ezimu, a baleka onke; wa sale wa puma Umbad*h*lanyana emakaleni ezimu; la fa.

Umbad*h*lanyana kamakqubata. Umakqubatshana. Uma-'sila-'kugijima-u-gijimisa-'kufana. Inqataba-kazana-owa-bukca-amatulwa-wa-nika-umnguni. Inyatikazi-e-netole. Usomzinza-ngotwane-ubakazi-yena-umfo-a-nga-i-zinza-na?

LYDIA, (UMKASETEMBA.)

nyana; the ukcilo is yours." He replied, "Why did you eat my ukcilo, and then say you would eat me? There is another morsel, which will quite fill you."

Then all the cannibals, when they saw that Umbadhlanyana had gone into the nostrils of the cannibal, fled; and then Umbadhlanyana came out of his nostrils, and the cannibal died.

Umbadhlanyana kamakqubata. Umakqubatshana.[84] Uma-'sila-'kugijima-u-gijimisa-'kufana. I-nqataba-kazana-owa-bukca-amatulwa-wa-nika-umnguni. Inyatikazi-e-netole. Usomzinza-ngotwane-ubakazi-yena-umfo-a-nga-i-zinza-na?[85]

A M A Z I M U.

(CANNIBALS.)

NG' azi kodwa ukuba ku tiwa, Amazimu a *h*lubuka abanye abantu, a ye 'ku*h*lala entabeni. Ngo'kuba kukqala Amazimu a e ng' abantu. Kwa kcitek' izwe; kwa kona ind*h*lala enkulu; ba tanda ukud*h*la abanye abantu ngobunzima bend*h*lala. Kwa ti ind*h*lala inkulu, abantu be dinga, ku nge ko indawo a ba nga tola ukud*h*la

ALL I know is, that it is said that the Amazimu deserted other men and went to live in the mountains. For at first the Amazimu were men. The country was desolate; there was a great famine; and they wished to eat men because of the severity of the famine. When the famine was great, and men were in want and there was no place where they could obtain food,

[84] *Umakqubatshana.*—As Umakqubata means the small, rapid stepper, so Umakqubatshana is a diminutive of this word, meaning a very small, rapid stepper,—the Little Umakqubata. *Uma-'sila-'kugijima-u-gijimisa-'kufana,* "When-he-escapes-by-running-he-runs-as-though-he-would-die." *Inqataba-kazana-owa-bukca-amatulwa-wa-nika-umnguni,* "Little-strong-one-the-son-of-the-little-one-who-mixed-together-wild-medlars-and-gave-umnguni." *Inyatikazi-e-netole,* "Buffalo-cow-with-a-calf." *Usomzinza-ngotwane-ubakazi-yena-umfo-a-nga-i-zinza-na?* "Chief-of-dancers-with-a-rod-(viz., at an *ijadu*) can-any-stranger-handle-the-dancing-rod-like-him? *Umnguni* is a name applied to the Zulus; it is also given to the Amakxosa.

[85] We may judge from this string of epithets (*izibongo,* praise-giving names) that we have here but a small fragment of the life and adventures of Umbadhlanyana. If we knew them all, he would be found probably to rival or even surpass our old friend Uthlakanyana.

kuyo, ba kqala ukubamba abanye abantu, ba ba d*h*la ke. Kwa so ku tiwa ukubizwa kwabo, kwa tiwa Amazimu ; ngokuba leli 'zwi lamazimu, ukukumusha kwalo, ku ukuhhula, ukuminza. A *h*lubuka ke abantu, a tanda ukud*h*la aba-ntu. Uku*h*lubuka kwawo kambe a shiya abantu, a d*h*la abantu ; a kxotshwa abantu. A hamba ezin-daweni zonke, a hamba e funa abantu ; kwa so ku tiwa isizwe esinye, ngokuba abantu ba ba izinyamazane kuwo. Ka wa b' e sa lima ; ka wa b' e sa ba nanko-mo, ka wa b' e sa ba nazind*h*lu, ka wa b' e sa ba nazimvu, ka wa b' e sa ba nazinto zonke a e nazo e se ng' abantu. A hamba e *h*lala emhumeni. A ti a nga fumana umhume, be se ku ba ind*h*lu yawo leyo, e se ya 'kuzingela abantu. A ti a nga tola umuntu, e be se ya emhumeni ; a buya a u shiye futi lowo 'mhume, a hamba e funisisa abantu. A nga bi nandawo. Uma e nga ba toli abantu, a hambe njalo, e be suka a funa abantu.

A ti a nga m bona umuntu e hamba yedwa, e be se ya kuye, a m yenge, a zitshaye o nomsa, a m pate ka*h*le, a kulume ka*h*le naye ; ku nga ti ka z' ukwenza 'luto. A ti umuntu lapo e se libele e ng' azi 'luto, e ti abantu abamnene nje, a b' e se m bamba : a ti ingabe wo-namand*h*la, a lwe nawo, um*h*la-umbe a wa kxotshe ; m*h*laumbe a m a*h*lule, a m tate, a b' e se a ya 'ku mu d*h*la. A buy' a zingele njalo ; ngezikati zonke ku i wona umsebenzi wawo ukuzingela.

they began to lay hold of men, and to eat them. And so they were called Amazimu ; for the word Amazimu when interpreted means to gormandise,—to be glut-tonous. So they rebelled against men ; they forsook them, and liked to eat them ; and men drove them away. They went everywhere seeking men for food, and so they were regarded as a distinct nation, for with them men became game. They no longer cultivated the soil ; they no longer had cattle or houses or sheep, nor any of those things which they had had whilst they were men. They went and lived in dens. When they found a cave, it became their dwelling place, whilst they went to hunt men. If they caught a man, they went to the cave ; again they left it, to go and hunt men. They had no fixed habitation. If they did not catch a man, they were constantly on the move, going about hunting for men.

If they saw a man going alone, they went to him ; they decoyed him, and made themselves out merciful people ; they treated him kindly, and spoke gently with him ; and appeared incapable of doing any evil. When the man was thus beguiled and entirely unsuspicious, regarding them as pleasant people only, they would then lay hold of him :[86] if he was a powerful man, he might fight with them, and perhaps drive them off ; or they might overcome him, and carry him away to eat him. Again they hunted ; at all times their occupation was to hunt.

---

[86] How exactly this description corresponds with that given of the way in which the Thugs decoy their victims.

Ku ti uma e ba bona abantu, noma baningi, um*h*laumbe ba ya w' azi; ba ti ba nga bona Amazimu e za kubo, ba k*q*ale uku-lungisa izikali zabo: Amazimu ingabe maningi, a ti *h*le; abantu nabo be se ti *h*le, b' enza u*h*la. Be se be sondelana, Amazimu e se sondela nawo; kodwa abantu be sondela ngezibindi ezikulu, ngokuba ba y' azi ukuba Amazimu abantu aba namand*h*la kakulu, ba lwe. Ingabe ba lwe, um*h*laumbe ba nga lwi; ba baleke abantu ngokubuka nje kodwa, ngokuba Amazimu a e sabeka. Abanye aba nezibindi ba lwe nawo, um*h*laumbe ba wa k*x*otshe Amazimu, a baleke, a ba shiye, ngokuba Amazimu abantu aba namajubane kakulu, ba nga lw enzi 'luto, ba wa yeke.

A buye a zingele njalo, a *h*la-ngane nabanye: a ti a nga *h*la-ngana nabanye, ba ti ba nga bona ukuba Amazimu, ba baleke, a ba k*x*otshe wona, a z' a ba fumane; a ti a nga ba fumana, a ba bambe. Abanye ba kcatshe, a nga ba boni. A ti a m bonileyo, uma e nga kca-tshanga, ku be kudekude naye, a m k*x*otsha njalo, a z' a katale. Ngokuba uma umuntu e nga kca-tshanga, e pika ngokugijima nje, a m k*x*otshe a z' a m fumane, ngo-kuba wona a y' epuza ukukatala. A b' e se m *t*wala, a hambe naye, e funa indawo esiteleyo kubantu e*h*lane; e be se fika, a m peke, a mu d*h*le.

When they saw many men, per-haps the men recognised them, and when they saw the Amazimu coming to them they began to pre-pare their weapons: if the Ama-zimu were numerous they threw themselves into line; and the men too threw themselves into line, forming a row. Then they drew near to each other, the Amazimu too drawing near; but the men drew near with great courage,[87] for they knew that the Amazimu were very powerful men and fought. Perhaps they fight, perhaps they do not fight; but the men run away on casting one glance at them, for the Amazimu were terrible. Some who are brave may fight with them, and perhaps beat them; they then run away, and leave the men behind, for the Amazimu were very swift; and the men can do nothing, and give over the pursuit.

Again the Amazimu hunt and fall in with other men: when they fall in with them, perhaps they see that they are Amazimu, and run away, and the Amazimu pursue them, until they overtake them; when they overtake them they lay hold of them. Others hide them-selves, and they do not see them. If they have caught sight of a man who has not hid himself, he must run a great distance, they pursuing him till he is tired. For if a man does not hide himself, but contends with them by running only, they pursue him till they overtake him, for they do not readily tire. Then they carry him away with them, seeking a place concealed from men in the wilderness; when they come to such a place, they boil and eat him.

[87] That is, it required very great courage to think of fighting them.

<table>
<tr><td>I loko ke e ngi kw aziyo e ngi ku zwile ngab' azi 'nsumansumane.</td><td>This then is what I know by hearsay from those who are acquainted with legends.</td></tr>
</table>

ULUTULI DHLADHLA (USETEMBA).

APPENDIX.

CANNIBALISM.

IT is a common opinion among the natives of these parts, that cannibalism was introduced at a comparatively recent period, having arisen in times of famine. Arbousset found this notion prevalent among tribes in immediate contact with the Marimo or Bechuana cannibals. *(South Africa, p. 88.)* He speaks of cannibalism as having been formerly "one of the most active causes of depopulation" *(p. 91);* but adds that now (1852) "it is only in secret that they indulge their taste for human flesh." We do not know on what kind of evidence such statements are founded. The Marimo, like the cannibals of the Zulu legends and those who are said once to have infested Natal, speak of men as "game."

There are various forms in which cannibalism is said to be practised by the savages of Africa. Some eat their own dead, as the Amanganja on the Shire. In allusion to some such custom Purchas remarks :—"The Grecians burned their dead Parents, the Indians intombed them in their owne bowels." Others sell their dead to neighbouring tribes as an article of food, and purchase their dead in return. In times of famine they are said to adopt the system of buying the people of other tribes with their own wives and children, to gratify their craving for human flesh. Some eat·"witches condemned to death"; others object to such food on the ground of its "being unwholesome." Others devour only prisoners of war, as an indication of savage triumph ; this probably is the most common form of cannibalism. Besides these there are said to be others who may be regarded as professional cannibals, who look upon men generally as their game, and hunt them as they would any other game. *(Savage Africa. Winwood Read, p. 156, &c.—Explorations and Adventures in Equatorial Africa. Du Chaillu, pp. 84, 88.)*

Herodotus alludes to another form of cannibalism :—"Eastward of these Indians are another tribe, called Padæans, who are wanderers, and live on raw flesh. This tribe is said to have the following customs :—If one of their number be ill, man or woman, they take the sick person, and if he be a man, the men of his acquaintance proceed to put him to death, because, they say, his flesh would be spoilt for them if he pined and wasted away with sickness. The man protests he is not ill in the least ; but his friends will not accept his denial —in spite of all he can say, they kill him, and feast themselves on his body. So also if a woman be sick, the women, who are her friends, take her and do with her exactly the same as the men. If one of them reaches to old age, about which there is seldom any question, as commonly before that time they have had some disease or other, and so have been put to death—but if a man, notwithstanding, comes to be old, then they offer him in sacrifice to their gods, and afterwards eat his flesh." *(Rawlinson's Herodotus. Vol. II., p. 407.)*

Winwood Read suggests that cannibalism might be "a partial extension of the sacrificial ceremony." *(Op. cit., p. 158.)* And it seems by no means improbable that it had, in some instances, its origin in human sacrifices. It is worth noting that the Zulu-Kafir considers it as unnatural, and that those who practise it have ceased to be men. They distinguish, too, between the man who has eaten human flesh from necessity in time of famine, and the cannibal proper.

One cannot, however, avoid the belief that there is, and always has been, very much exaggeration in the accounts of cannibalism. It is perfectly clear that the cannibals of the Zulu legends are not common men ; they are magnified into giants and magicians ; they are remarkably swift and enduring ; fierce and terrible warriors. They are also called "long-haired." This would make it appear probable that the cannibals which once infested Southern Africa were not natives of these parts, but people of some other country. The Fans, the mountain cannibals of Western Africa, are said to have longer and thicker hair than the coast tribes. Their hair is said by Burton to hang down to their shoulders; but it is still woolly. *(Winwood Read, p. 144.—Du Chaillu, p. 69. —Captain Burton. Anthropological Review, p. 237.)* The hair of the Fulahs or Fellatahs is said to be "more or less straight, and often very fine." *(Types of Mankind. Nott and Gleddon, p. 188.)* Again Barth mentions seeing at Erarar-n-sakan, near Agades, a long-haired race, which he thus describes:—

"They were very tall men with broad, coarse features, very different from any I have seen before, and with long hair hanging down upon their shoulders, and over their faces, in a way that is an abomination to the Tawarek; but upon enquiry I learnt that they belonged to the tribe of Ighdalen or Egbedal, a very curious mixed tribe of Berbe and Soughay blood, and speaking the Soughay language." *(Travels in Central Africa. Vol. I., p. 404.)*

But none of these can be considered as answering to the description of long-haired as given in the Zulu legends of cannibals; neither could they possibly have formed their historical basis. Indeed, at the present time we occasionally meet with natives with long hair reaching to the shoulders, or standing out from six to nine inches, like a fan, from the head. It may be worth while to compare with the Zulu legends those of the Scotch Highlands, where we have accounts of Gruagachs, that is "long-haired," gigantic magicians and cannibals, who play a somewhat similar part to the long-haired Amazimu of South Africa. *(Campbell. Op. cit. Vol. I., p. 1. Vol. II., pp. 186, 188.)*

It is probable that the native accounts of cannibals are, for the most part, the traditional record of incursions of foreign slave-hunters. The whites are supposed to be cannibals by the Western Africans, because they hunt and buy slaves. *(Winwood Read, p. 160.)* And even though the object for which slaves are purchased by the whiteman may be well understood, yet the use of "*eat*" every where among Africans for the purpose of expressing to *waste utterly,* and which across the Atlantic, in the elegant slang of the backwoods, is translated by "chaw up," would very naturally give rise to the notion of men-eaters. Read relates that a slave just brought from the interior, after gazing on him intently for some time, asked, "And are these the men that eat us?" Which he supposes to intimate a belief that white men are cannibals; but the native might have meant nothing more than that they were a wasting and destroying people. It is when different tribes come into contact, and the superior is continually driving further and further back, and straitening more and more the feebler one, that legends of this kind spring up. A few years ago in Natal the children were frightened by being told that the whitemen would eat them; and no doubt they are still used to the present time, in retired places, as nursery bogies. And should the whiteman cease to be an occupant of Natal, there would be legends of men-eating, long-haired, gigantic, flying whitemen, magicians, and wizards told around the hut-fires of the next generation. To the savage the arts and habits of the whiteman appear to be magical; and his adroitness and skill are supposed to be the result of spells.

But it is not only the savage who imagines that the superior which is opposing him is a cannibal; but the superior has his mind filled with a similar dread of the savage neighbour whom he is oppressing, and who is destined to disappear before his steadily advancing progress. The Ancients had their Anthropophagi. And European travellers have so generally ascribed cannibalism to savages, that a cannibal and a savage are all but convertible terms in the minds of many.

We may refer, for instance, to a passage in the *Arabian Nights,* in "The Story of Ghanim, the Son of Eiyoob." The black slave says to another, "How small is your sense! Know ye not that the owners of the gardens go forth from Baghdad and repair hither, and, evening overtaking them, repair to this place, and shut the door upon themselves, through fear, lest the blacks, like ourselves,

should take them and roast them and eat them?"   Upon which Lane remarks
in the note :—"I am not sure that this is to be understood as a jest; for I have
been assured by a slave-dealer, and other persons in Cairo, that sometimes
slaves brought to that city are found to be cannibals; and that a proof lately
occurred there, an infant having been eaten by a black nurse.   I was also told
that the cannibals are generally distinguished by an elongation of the os coccy-
gis; or, in other words, that they have tails!"

We find from *Willis' Pencillings by the Way* that Turkish children are
taught to believe that the Franks are cannibals.   He relates the following anecdote :—"'Hush, my rose!' said the Assyrian slave, who was leading a Turkish
child, 'these are good Franks; these are not the Franks that eat children.
Hush!'"   A relic this possibly of traditions of the times when European warriors, under the banners of the Cross, strove to wrest the Holy Sepulchre from
the possession of the Saracens.   Accompanying the army of the Crusaders, led
by Cœur de Lion, there was a body of unarmed fanatics, who were known by
the name of Thafurs.   The Saracens, being possessed with the idea that they
fed on the dead bodies of their enemies, which the Thafurs took care to encou-
rage, regarded them with the greatest horror, and dreaded them even more than
they did the armed knights.   Hence probably arose the tradition of the cannibalism of Richard himself, which is preserved in *Ellis's Specimens of Early
English Metrical Romances*.   The Rhymster tells us that a deputation was sent
by Saladin to offer immense treasure for the ransom of prisoners.   Richard told
the ambassadors that he needed not their treasures, and added,

> "But for my love I you bid
> To meat with me that ye dwell;
> And afterward I shall you tell."

The first course consisted of *boiled Saracens' heads*, which were served up having
affixed to them the names of the prisoners who had been slain for the horrible
feast.   Richard, "without the slightest change of countenance, swallowed the
morsels as fast as they could be supplied by the knight who carved them."

> "Every man then poked other;
> They said, 'This is the devil's brother,
> That slays our men, and thus hem eats!'"

Richard apologised for the first course on the score of "his ignorance of their
tastes."   And then told them that it was useless for Saladin to keep back sup-
plies in the hope of driving away the Christian army by starvation; for,
said he,

> "Of us none shall die with hunger,
> While we may wenden to fight,
> And slay the Saracens downright,
> Wash the flesh, and roast the head,
> With oo Saracen I may well feed
> Well a nine or a ten
> Of my good Christian men.
> King Richard shall warrant,
> There is no flesh so nourissant
> Unto an English man,
> Partridge, plover, heron, ne swan,
> Cow ne ox, sheep ne swine,
> As the head of a Sarazyn.
> There he is fat, and thereto tender,
> And my men be lean and slender.
> While any Saracen quick be,
> Livand now in this Syrie,
> For meat will we nothing care.
> Abouten fast we shall fare,
> And every day we shall eat
> All so many as we may get.
> To England will we nought gon,
> Till they be eaten every one."

(Quoted by Sir Walter Scott.)

In connection with the above the following account relating to real facts in Zulu life will be interesting :—

INDABA ngokud*h*liwa kwomuntu e d*h*liwa inkosi e b' i banga naye.

Inkosi e d*h*liwayo eyezizwe, uma ku kona ukuzondana ngokweisana. Ku ti uma impi yenye inkosi i puma i ya kwenye, i i tete nge-ziuyembezi ngokuti, "Ngo ka ngi zwe ke, band*h*la lakwetu! Uma ni b' a*h*lulile nje, ngi nga boni ubani lapa, a ngi yi 'kukolwa. Ku ya 'kuba ku*h*le ni i bambe inkosi yakona, ni nga i shiyi, i ze lap', ngi y ekɋe, ukuze izizwe zi ng' azi."

Nembala ke i pume ngokutuku-tela okukulu kwenkosi, i tukutelele leyo e zondana nayo. I *h*langane, kumbe i *h*langana njalo, izin*h*loli zakona se zi banjiwe, ukuze zi tsho lapa inkosi yakona i kɋatshe kona. Nembala zi tsho uma z' esaba uku-bulawa. Impi y a*h*luka kabili, i ye lapo, lapa inkosi i kona ; i kɋa-buke se i banjwa ngokuzumeka. Uma ku tiwe, a ba nga i bulali, ba nga i bulali ngokuti, "Si ya 'kwapuka ukutwala umuntu ; ku-*h*le a zihambele, a zitwale yena."

THE account of a man being eaten by the chief with whom he had contended.

The chief that is eaten is one of a foreign nation, when there is mutual hatred through mutual contempt between two chiefs. It happens when the army of one chief goes to attack another, the chief addresses the soldiers with tears, saying, "I shall soon hear then of your doings, soldiers of my father ! If you merely conquer them, and I do not see So-and-so[88] here, I shall not be satisfied. It will be well for you to catch their chief, and not leave him behind, but let him come here, that I may leap[89] over him, that the nations may know me."

So then the army is levied through the great rage with which the chief rages against the chief which is at enmity with him. When the armies meet, perhaps, at the very time of meeting, the spies of the place are seized that they may tell where their chief is concealed. And indeed they tell, if they are afraid of being killed. The army is distributed into two divisions, and one goes to the place where the chief is ; he first becomes aware of its presence when he is suddenly seized. If they have been told not to kill him, they do not kill him, thinking, they should be burdened excessively by carrying a dead man ; and that it would be well for him to walk for himself, and carry himself.

[88] *So-and-so*, mentioning the chief who is about to be attacked by name.

[89] *Ngi y ekɋe.*—As the weasel leaps over a snake which it has killed (see p. 4), so a native chief leaps over the captive chief of another tribe which is brought before him ; or over his dead body. He also leaps over a lion, which his people have killed and brought home. This is done as an indication of perfect triumph. But sometimes a chief fears to leap over another chief of great reputation, lest he should be killed by the medicines with which he has been "charmed" by his doctors.

Nembala ke ba i bambe. I ya kqabuka impi yayo e libele uku-lwa nenye, i bone se ku kqutshwa inkosi yayo, i pel' amand/la, ngo-kuti, "O, a si s' azi ukuba si sa lwela 'bani, loku nanku se be m bambile nje." I kciteke nje, ku be ukupela, ku d/liwe izinkomo.

Ku fikwe nayo ekaya. I nga ka fiki, ku hambe izigijimi pambili zokuya 'kuti, "Nkosi, si m bambile ubani namu/la." I be i zilungisa ke leyo 'nkosi e bikelwayo, i ku-mbula ukuti, "Konje uma ngi nga zilungisi, ngi nga fa, ngokuba a ngi kw azi ukugeza kwale 'nkosi uma i b' i geza ngani. Ku ya 'kuba kubi uma ngi ti ngi ya kuyo, ngi ye ngi nge nasibindi, loku uma ngi tshaywa uvalo se ngi ya 'kufa, ngokuba isitunzi sake a ngi s' .azi; kumbe si nga ng' a-pula."

I bize inyanga yoku i kqinisa, ukuze i ye ngesibindi. Nembala ke i ya ya se i ya i kqalabile, i nga s' esabi 'luto. Loku leyo e banji-weyo i se i /lezi pansi, se i umfo-kazana nje, se i zibonela ukuti, "Nam/la nje se ngi sekufeni." I fike le e za 'ku i bulala, i y ekqe kaningi, ekupeleni i i bulale. Lapa se i file i /lalc pezu kwayo; i y' e-suka se i i kcwiya umzimba wonke, ku nga shiywa nendawana

So then they seize him. And his soldiers which have been de-tained fighting with the enemy are first aware of it when they see their chief driven before the hos-tile army; their courage fails, and they say, "O, we' can no longer fight for So-and-so, since behold there he is already a pri-soner." So the army is scattered, there is an end of opposition, and the cattle are captured.

The victors take him to their own country. But before the arrival of the captive chief, mes-sengers go forward to tell their chief, saying, "Chief, we have made So-and-so prisoner this time." Whereupon the chief who receives the information prepares himself, and remembers, saying, "So then, if I do not prepare myself, I may die, for I do not know with what medicines he has washed himself. It will be bad if I go to him with-out courage, for if I am struck with dread, I shall die at once, for I do not know how terrible his in-fluence[90] may be; perhaps it will break me."

And he calls a doctor to strengthen him that he may go to the captive chief boldly. So in-deed he goes having confidence, and fearing nothing. Since the chief who has been taken prisoner is now sitting on the ground, and is now a man of nought, already seeing that he is now about to die. So the chief comes who is about to kill him, he leaps over him again and again, and at last kills him. When he is dead he sits upon him; he then cuts off small por-tions from every part of the body, without leaving a single place of

---

[90] *Isitunzi* is used to express what we mean by *presence*. It is applied either to a reverential presence, which however in the native mind is not separated from fear; or to a terrible presence. It means also *prestige*. And what is called "fascination" would be ascribed to *isitunzi*.

yomzimba ; kumbe i i nǥume in-ɦloko, i londolozwe endaweni yen-kosi, ukuze leyo 'nɦloko i be inɦloko e ku bulawa ngayo amanye amakosi ngokutata isibindi kuyo ngoku i bheka.

Leyo 'nyama yonke i bekwe odengezini, i ɦlanganiswe nemiti yobukosi, i tshiswe i ze i be um-sizi ; inkosi i ncinde ngayo, i y e-nza izembe. Ku tshiwo ke lapa se i wezwa ngamazibuko, ukuti, "Bani kabani owa dɦla ubani, a kwa ba 'ndaba zaluto." Ku tshi-wo ngokuba a mu dɦla umzimba e nga mu dɦlanga 'zinkomo ; ku tshiwo amakǥiniso.

Ku ti lapa ku za 'upuma impi, lelo 'kanda li tatwe li bekwe eduze nemiti yenkosi e za 'kwelatshwa ngayo, ukuze i m' isibindi, ngo-kuti, "Na lo ngi ya 'ku m enza njenga lo. U za 'kuza lap', ku tatwe izinto zakona, ukuze ba ba tome, zi letwe kuleli 'kanda lomu-ntu owa nǥotshwa." Kw enziwe umlingo wokuba nabo ba ze ba nǥotshwe njenga lo owa nǥo-tshwayo.

consequence in the whole body ;[91] perhaps he cuts off his head, that it may be kept in the chief's house, that the head may be a means of killing other chiefs, by giving him courage when he looks on it.

All the flesh which is cut off is placed on a sherd, and mixed with king-medicine,[92] and burnt until it is charcoal ; the king eats it with the tips of his fingers, making it an izembe.[93] And so it is said, when his praises are recorded, "So-and-so, the son of So-and-so who ate So-and-so, without any harm resulting." It is said thus because he ate his body and did not eat his cattle only ; it is said truly.

When an army is about to be levied, the head is placed near the king-medicine with which the chief is about to be treated, that he may have courage, saying, "And this fellow, I shall treat him as I did this. He shall shortly come here, and his things be taken, (that my people may be successful when fight-ing with his people,) and be brought to this head of the man that was conquered." The head, is made a charm with which they too may be conquered as he was.

[91] The parts selected are the skin from the centre of the forehead and the eyebrow ; this is supposed, when eaten, to impart the power of looking stead-fastly at an enemy ; the nose, the right ear and hand, the heel, the prepuce and glans penis.

[92] *King-medicine*, that is, medicines which are supposed to have the power of producing kingly power and feelings in a man. Just as they say head-medi-cine, or eye-medicine, &c.

[93] *Izembe* is a mixture of various substances used either for medical or ma-gical purposes. It is thus prepared. The medicines are placed in a sherd over the fire and charred : when the sherd is red hot, the contents of the stomach of a bullock, goat, or sheep, or the dregs of beer, are squeezed over it, in such a way that the fluid drops into the sherd, and is stirred into the charred medi-cines. The fingers are then dipped into the hot preparation, which is rapidly conveyed to the mouth and eaten. When it is done with a magical object, the person whilst eating spits in different directions, especially in the direction of those he hates, or who are at enmity with him, and whom he thus, as it were, defies, fully believing that he is surrounding himself with a preserving influence against their machinations and power, and at the same time exerting an influ-ence injurious to them. In the minds of savages, medicine, magic, and witch-craft are closely allied. These and kindred superstitions will be fully discussed hereafter.

I njalo ke indaba yokud*h*liwa kwomuntu kwabamnyama. Ka d*h*liwa njengenyama yenkomo; u d*h*liwa ngokutshiswa nemiti emikulu, ku ncindwe ngaye. Ku njalo ukud*h*liwa kwenkosi.

Ukukcwiywa kwenkosi e bulewe enye. ku ukudumaza okukulu kuleso 'sizwe, ngokuba ku tiwa, " Nina, kade sa ni d*h*la ; se ni lapa esiswini : a ni se 'luto kitina."

UMPENGULA MBANDA.

Such, then, is the account of a man being eaten among black men. He is not eaten like the flesh of cattle; he is eaten when he has been charred with great medicines, and the chief eats it with the tips of his fingers. Such is the mode of eating a chief.

For a chief to have been killed by another chief and to have had portions cut from his body, is a great humiliation of his tribe, for it is said, "As for you, we ate you long ago; you are now here in our stomachs : as regards us you are nothing at all."

UGUNGQU-KUBANTWANA.

An old woman lives at her son-in-law's kraal.

KWA ku kona isalukazi esitile kukqala ; sa si *h*lezi kandodakazi ; sa si umkwekazi. Umkwenyana wa si nika amasi, wa' ti, a si wa d*h*le ; ngokuba kwa ku nge ko 'kud*h*la okuningi, kwa ku ind*h*lala. Sa w' ala amasi. Wa si nik' inkomo, e t' a si wa d*h*le ; s' ala, sa ti, si nge d*h*le amasi kamkwenyana.

THERE was in times of long ago a certain old woman ; she was living with her daughter ; she was the mother-in-law.[94] Her son-in-law offered her amasi, telling her to eat ; for there was not much food, it was a famine. She refused the amasi. He offered her a cow, telling her to eat the milk : she refused, saying, she could not eat the milk of her son-in-law.[95]

---

[94] Viz., in that household.

[95] The father-in-law and mother-in-law may not eat their son-in-law's milk. The bride elect cannot eat milk at the lover's kraal, until she is actually married. Neither can a suitor, either before or after marriage, eat it at the bride's kraal. If a lover eat milk at the bride's kraal, or the young woman eat it at the suitor's kraal, it is equivalent to breaking off the engagement. Those of the same house only eat each other's milk, that is, brothers and sisters and cousins. But the chief's milk can be eaten by any of his people, for he is as it were the father of them all ; they are one house,—all brethren in him. The milk of other people is termed *ikwababa*, "a crow,"—that is, carrion.

She steals her children's milk.

Ngesikati sokulima sa si lamba kakulu; si buye emini, si fike si vule end*h*lini kamkwenyana, si tulule amasi, si wa d*h*le. Kepa lapa se li tshonile ilanga, a ti umkwenyana, "Buya," (e tsho kumkake,) "u yo'upeka izinkobe, si vube amasi, ngokuba igula se li gcwele." Ba fike, a zi peke izinkobe, a gaye umkcaba; i suke indoda i tate igula, i finyanise igula, lize, so ku kona umlaza. Ba kale nabantwana be lambile, nomkwekazi a ti, "Ba za 'kufa abantwana bomntanami, ngokuba isela li d*h*la igula ngend*h*lala enga-ka." Isalukazi s' enzé njalo zonke izikati. Kodwa be ng' azi indoda nomkayo uma li d*h*liwa unina wabo.

In the digging-season she was very hungry; she was iu the habit of returning home at noon, and on her arrival to open her son-in-law's house, and pour out the amasi and eat it. But when the sun had set, her son-in-law said, speaking to his wife, "Go home and boil some maize, that we may mix it with the amasi, for the calabash is now full."[96] On their arrival she boiled maize, and made a soft mass; the husband went and took the calabash; he found it empty; there was now nothing but whey in it.[97] They and their children cried, being hungry; and the mother-in-law said, "My child's children will die, for a thief is eating their milk, through this great famine." The old woman did thus at all times. But the husband and wife did not know that the milk was eaten by their mother.

The son-in-law detects her; and sets her an impossible task.

Indoda ya lalela, ya m bamba unina; kodwa unina wa kala, wa ti, "Ngi ya kqala nam*h*la nje." Wa ti umkwenyana, wa ti, "Hanba, u yo'u ngi tatela amanzi lapa sele li nga kali; kona ngi nga yi ku ku veza kubantu."

The husband lay in wait, and caught their mother; but their mother cried, saying, "I did it for the first time this very day." Her son-in-law said, "Go and fetch for me water at a place where no frog cries; and I will not expose you to the people."

She sets out to fetch water from a pool where no frog cries.

Wa m nika isigubu. Wa hanba, wa hamba, kwa za kwa ba sikati eside, e d*h*lula imifula emi+ingi; wa fika emifuleni a nga ' azi; wa buza wa ti, "Ku kona

He gave her a water-vessel. She went on and on for a long time, passing many rivers; she came to rivers which she did not know; she asked, "Is there any

---

[96] The daily milk is poured into a large calabash; the whey is drawn off, nd fresh milk poured in, till it is quite full; the amasi thus obtained is then aten.

[97] This implies that she had drawn off the whey into another vessel, and eturned it to the calabash when she had eaten the curds.

'sele nje lapa na?" La ti, "K*hh*we, ngi kona." Wa d*h*lula; wa ya wa fika kweny' indawo; wa si bona isiziba, wa ya wa fika kona, wa k' amanzi; la ti isele, "K*hh*we, ngi kona." Wa tulula, wa hamba 'enza njalo, amasele nawo e kona kuzo zonke iziziba. Wa fika kwesinye isiziba, wa ti, "Ku kona 'sele nje lapa na?" La tula. Wa *h*lala pansi, wa ka amanzi. Kwa ti, lapa e se gcwala, ngokuba isigubu sa si sikulu, la ti, "K*hh*we, ngi kona." Wa buya wa wa tulula amanzi, e se kala e ti, "Maye, mamo! nga ke nga zenza ukud*h*la amasi akamkweuyana." Wa d*h*lula.

frog here?" A frog answered, "K*hh*we,[98] I am here." She passed on, and came to another place; she saw a pool; she went to it and dipped water; a frog said, "K*hh*we, I am here." She poured it out. She travelled acting thus, and the frogs answering in like manner, for there were frogs in every pool. She came to another pool and said, "Is there any frog here?" No frog answered. She sat down and dipped water. But when the vessel was nearly full (for it was a large one), a frog said, "K*hh*we, I am here." She poured out the water again, now crying and saying, "Woe is me, mamo! I merely took of my own accord the amasi of my son-in-law for food." She passed on.

She reaches a pool of delicious water.

Wa fika esizibeni esikulu kakulu; wa bona izind*h*lela eziningi ezi ya kona esizibeni; w' esaba. Kwa ku kona imitunzi eminingi ngapezulu kwesiziba. Sa fika isalukazi esizibeni, sa *h*lala pansi, sa ti, "Ku kona 'sele nje lapa na?" Kwa tula. Sa pinda. Kwa tula. Sa kelela amanzi esigujini, s' egcwala isigubu. Sa ti uma se si gcwele, sa puza kakulu, sa ze sa pela isigubu: sa buye sa ka s' egcwala; sa puza, a sa be si sa si k*q*eda, so kubu*h*lungu isisu, ngokuba kwa kw ala ukuba a yeke ukupuza, kumnandi.

She came to a very great pool; she saw many paths which went to the pool. She was afraid. There were many shady trees on the banks of the pool. She went to the pool and sat down; she said, "Is there any frog here?" There was no answer. She repeated her question. There was no answer. She dipped water into the vessel; the vessel was full. When it was full, she drank very much, until the vessel was empty. She dipped again till it was full; she drank; she was no longer able to drink the whole, she had a pain in the stomach, for she was unable to leave off drinking, it was so nice.

The animals warn her of the arrival of Ugungqu-kubantwana.

Kepa lapa se si tanda ukusuka si hambe, kw' ala ukuba si suke;

But when she wished to arise and depart, she was unable to

____
[98] As pronounced by the native, this is an exact imitation of the croaking of a frog.

sa si donsa isigubu, sa ya pansi kwomtunzi, sa ħlala kona, ngokuba kwa ku nga vumi ukuba si hambe. Kwa ze kwa ba ntambama; kwa fika imbila, ya ti, "Ubani o ħlezi emtunzini wenkosi?" Sa ti, "U mina, baba. Ngi te ngi y' esuka, kwa ti keħle keħle." Ya ti imbila, "U zo'u m bona Ugungqu-kubantwana." Sa ya, sa puza esizibeni, sa ya sa ħlala pansi kwomtunzi. Kwa buya, kwa fika impunzi, ya ti, "Ubani o ħlezi emtunzini wenkosi?" Sa ti, "U mina, baba. Ngi te ngi y' esuka, kwa ti keħle keħle." Ya ti impunzi, "U zo'u m bona Ugungqu - kubantwana." Kwa fika isilo, sa ti, "Ubani o ħlezi emtunzini wenkosi?" Sa ti, "U mina, baba. Ngi te ngi y' esuka, kwa ti keħle keħle." Sa ti isilo, "U zo'u m bona Ugungqu-kubantwana." Za fika zonke, zi tsho njalo. Kepa kwa za kwa nga li nga tshona zi fika ziningi kakulu nezinkulu; zonke izilo zi tsho njalo.

arise; she dragged the water-vessel, and went into the shade, and sat down there, for she was unable to walk. At length it was noon; there came a rock-rabbit,[99] and said, "Who is this sitting in the shade of the king?"[1] She said, "It is I, father. I was about to depart; but my limbs failed me." The rock-rabbit said, "You will soon see Ugungqu-kubantwana."[2] She went and drank at the pool, and returned to the shade. A duiker[3] came and said, "Who is this sitting in the shade of the king?" She said, "It is I, father. I was about to depart, but my limbs failed me." The duiker said, "You will soon see Ugungqu-kubantwana." A leopard came and said, "Who is this sitting in the shade of the king?" She said, "It is I, father. I was about to depart, but my limbs failed me." The leopard said, "You will soon see Ugungqu-kubantwana." All animals came saying the same. And when at length it was about sunset, there came very many and great animals; all the animals said the same.

A huge animal arrives, and the old woman is alarmed.

Kwa ti lapa ilanga se li tshona, w' ezwa umsindo omkulu ku ti gungqu, gungqu. W' esaba e tutumela. Kwa ze kwa vela okukulu pezu kwezilo zonke a zi bonileyo. Kwa ti lapa se ku velile, za ti kanye kanye, za ti, "U ye lowo ke Ugungqu-kubantwana." Wa fike wa ti e se kude, wa ti,

When the sun was now setting, she heard a great noise,—gungqu, gungqu. She was afraid and trembled. At length there appeared something greater than all the animals she had seen. When it appeared they all said with one accord, "That is Ugungqu-kubantwana." When she came in sight, whilst still at some distance, she

---

[99] Rock-rabbit, improperly so called. The Daman or Hyrax Capensis has been improperly placed among the Rodentia; it belongs to the Pachydermata. "They are," says Cuvier, "Rhinoceroses in miniature."

[1] All through this tale the mother of beasts is called king or chief.

[2] See Appendix A at the end of the tale.

[3] The Cephalopus Mergens.

"Ubani, ubani o hlezi emtunzini kagungqu-kubantwana ? " Lapo isalukazi sa si nga se namandhla okukuluma; kwa se ku nga ti so ku fikile ukufa kusona. Wa pinda wa buza futi Ugungqu-kubantwana. Sa pendula isalukazi, sa ti, " U mina, nkosi. Ngi be nga ti ngi y' esuka, kwa ti kehle kehle." Wa ti, " U zo'u m' bona Ugungqu-kubantwana."

said, "Who, who art thou sitting in the shade of Ugungqu-kubantwana ? " Then the old woman had no more any power to speak; it was now as though death had already come to her. Ugungqu-kubantwana asked a second time. The old woman replied, "It is I, my lord. I was thinking of departing, but my limbs failed me." She said, " You will soon see Ugungqu-kubantwana."

Ugungqu orders the old woman to be eaten.

Wa ya emfuleni; wa fika, wa gukqa ngamadolo, wa puza isiziba; loku sa si sikulu kakulu, wa puza kwa ze kwa vela udaka olupansi esizibeni. Wa buya wa hlala pansi. Kepa amaula a e kona e izinduna kagungqu-kubantwana; ku kona nezimpisi. Wa ti Ugungqu, " A ka dhliwe." Za vuma izimpisi. Kepa amaula a ti, " U ya 'udhliwa e se kulupele, nkosi." Wa pinda wa ti, " A ka dhliwe." A ti amaula, "So ku hlwile; u ya 'udhliwa kusasa, nkosi."

She went to the river; when she reached it, she knelt on her knees, and drank the pool; although it was very great, she drank until the mud at the bottom of the pool appeared.[4] She then sat down. And there were oribes[5] there, who were the officers of Ugungqu-kubantwana; there were also hyenas. Ugungqu-kubantwana said, "Let her be eaten." The hyenas agreed. But the oribes said, "She shall be eaten when she is fat, O chief." Again she said, "Let her be eaten." The oribes said, "It is now dark; she shall be eaten in the morning, O chief."

She is delivered by four oribes.

Kwa hlwa; ba lala, nezilwane zonke za lala. Kepa izilwane ezinye z' epuza ukulala ngokuba zi tanda ukuba a dhliwe. Kwa ti lapa se ku busuku kakulu za se zi lele zonke. Kepa amaula amane a e nga ka lali wona, a vuka, a tata isalukazi, a si pakamisa, a si beka emhlana kuwona omatatu. La ti lesine iula l' etwala isigubu.

It was dark; they slept, and all the animals slept. But some animals put off sleeping because they wished that she should be eaten. At length it was midnight and all were asleep. But four oribes had not gone to sleep; they arose and took the old woman, and raised her and placed her on the back of three of them; the fourth oribe took the water-vessel. They ran

---

[4] Compare what is said of Behemoth, Job. xiv. 22, 23.
[5] Redunca Scoparia.

A gijima ngobusuku; a ye, a m beka ekcaleni kwomuzi ngapandʰle; a buya ngamajubane, e ti, u kona e ya 'ufika ku nga ka si. Nembala ke a fika masinyane.

during the night, and went and placed her on the border of her village on the outside. They returned with speed, saying, then they should arrive before morning. And truly they soon arrived.

The oribes contrive to throw suspicion on the hyenas.

La ti elinye kwamanye, "Si ya 'kwenze njani na? A si veze ikcebo ukuze ku nga bonwa ukuba i tina esi si balekisile." A ti amanye, "Loku izilwane ezi tanda ukudʰla abantu isilo nebubesi, nezinye izilo nezimpisi—" La ti elinye, "A si ze si bekce udaka ezimpisini, ngokuba i zona ezi tanda ukudʰla abantu; i ya 'kuvuma inkosi, i ti, 'Zi i tatile, za ye, za i dʰlela kude inyamazane yenkosi;' ngokuba uma si bekca esilweni, si ya 'kuzwa, ngokuba into e nolunya kakulu, si vuke, ku vuke abantu bonke, inkosi i ti, i tina esi tatile inyamazane yayo, sa ya 'u i dʰla." A vuma ke onke amaula. A fika, udaka a lw esulela ezitweni zempisi, a e se zesula amaula, a lala endaweni lapa e be lele kona.

One said to the other, "What shall we do? Let us devise a plan, that it may not appear that it is we who have enabled her to flee." The others said, "Since the animals which like to eat men are the leopard, the lion, other wild beasts, and hyenas—" Then one said, "Let us smear mud on the hyenas, for it is they who like to eat men; and the chief will agree and say, 'They have taken the game of the chief, and gone and eaten it at a distance;' for if we smear the leopard it will feel, (for it is a very wrathful creature,) and awake, and all the people will awake, and the chief say, it is we who have taken away the game, and gone to eat it." So all the other oribes agreed. They went and smeared the mud on the legs of the hyenas; and when they had cleansed themselves they went and lay down where they had lain.

Ugungqu devours the hyenas.

Kwa sa kusasa za vuka izilo zonke, 'za ti, "I pi inyamazane yenkosi? Inkosi i za 'ubulala amaula, wona 'alile ukuba i dʰliwe." A e se vuka masinyane, e ti amaula, "Inkosi i za 'ubona izinyawo zabantu bonke. Uma be nga hambanga, zi ya 'kuba zinʰle. Kepa uma be hambile, ku

In the morning all the animals arose and said, "Where is the game of the chief? She will kill the oribes, it was they who objected to its being eaten." The oribes at once awoke, saying, "The chief will look at the feet of all the people. If they have not gone any where, they will be clean. But if they have

ya 'ubonakala udaka ezinyaweni na sezitweni zabo." Ya vuma inkosi, ya ti emauleni, "Tshetsha ni masinya, ni bheke izito ezi nodaka, ba banjwe, ba letwe labo kumina. Kwa se ku suka zonke izilwane, zi bhekana; kwa funyanwa ezimpisini udaka. A ti amaula, "Izimpisi ezi m tatile, za ye za mu d*h*la, ngokuba ku izinto ezi tanda ukud*h*la." Za tatwa izimpisi, za yiswa enkosini. Ya fika inkosi ya zi tata, ya zi d*h*la zontatu izimpisi.

gone, there will be seen mud on their feet and on their legs."[6] The chief agreed, and said to the oribes, "Make haste at once, and look for the muddy legs, and let them be seized and brought to me." All the animals stood forth, and looked at each other; there was found mud on the hyenas. The oribes said, "It is the hyenas who have taken and eaten her, for they are animals which like to eat men." The hyenas were seized and taken to the chief. She seized the three hyenas, and ate them.

The old woman is received by her son-in-law.

Sa *h*lala isalukazi ekceleni kwomuzi, sa ze sa bona umuntu wasekaya; wa tshela umkwenyana waso; wa ya wa si tata kanye nesigubu. Umkwenyana wa *h*lala e puza lawo 'manzi a fike nomkwekazi.

The old woman remained at the border of the kraal; at length she saw some one belonging to her home; he told her son-in-law; he went and fetched her and the water-vessel. The son-in-law continually drank the water which his mother-in-law had brought.

She sets her son a dangerous and difficult task.

Kwa ti um*h*lana e pelayo sa ti isalukazi, "Loko nami nga ya nga ka amanzi, nawe hamba u yo'u ngi tatela isibindi sengogo." Kwa gaywa izinkwa eziningi, a ya 'uhamba e zi d*h*la end*h*leleni, ngokuba kwa ku kude kakulu. Kwa

It came to pass on the day the water was finished the old woman said,[7] "Since I went and fetched water, do you go and fetch for me the liver of an ingogo."[8] Many loaves were made for him to eat on his journey, for it was a great way

---

[6] In the Basuto legend of the Little Hare, the hare "rose in the night and drank the water of the king, and then took some mud and besmeared the lips and the knees of the jerboa that was sleeping at his side." The mud is witness, and with one voice all the animals condemn the jerboa to death. (*Casalis. Op. cit., p.* 352.) And in the Hottentot fable, the jackal smeared the hyena's tail with fat, and then ate all the rest that was in the house. When accused in the morning of having stolen it, he pointed to the hyena's tail, as a proof that he was the thief. (*Bleek. Op. cit., p.* 18.) Comp. "The fox cheats the bear out of his Christmas fare." (*Thorpe. Yule-tide Stories, p.* 280.)

[7] The son-in-law had spell-bound the old woman to do what was apparently an impossibility. Having accomplished it and returned, she avenged herself by binding him to enter on a dangerous adventure. Compare the tale of Mac Iain Direach, where the step-mother and son bind each other by spells. (*Campbell. Op. cit. Vol. II., p.* 328.)

[8] See Appendix B.

sa kusasa e zi twala izinkwa, wa hamba ę lala end*h*le; wa za wa fika lapa i twasayo inyanga, wa zi funyanisa izingogo ziningi kakulu, z' ek*q*a 'odongeni, zi d*h*lala. Wa fika naye e se gijima, e hamba ngezand*h*la na ngenyawo. Za ti ezinkulu, " Nansi ingogo yetu." Za ti ezincane, " Ingogo njani le na, e-nwele ngamuntu; e-me*h*lwana ngamuntu; e-nd*h*letshana ngamuntu; e-makalana ngamuntu ?" Za ti ezinkulu, " Ingogo, ingani ingogo nje; ingani ingogo nje." Za binda ke ezincane. Kepa uma zi *h*lezi zodwa, zi *h*leka, zi ti, " A ku si yo ingogo le, si ya bona tina." Za ze za buya za ya ekaya.

off. In the morning, carrying the loaves, he set out on his journey, sleeping in the open air; at length he arrived at the new moon, and found very many izingogo, leaping on the bank of a river, at play. He approached them, he too now running and going on his hands and feet. The old izingogo said, " There is our ingogo."[9] The young ones said, " What kind of an ingogo is that, which has hair like a man; and little eyes like a man; and little ears like a man; and little nostrils like a man ?" The old ones said, " It is an ingogo: by such and such things we see it is nought but an ingogo; by such and such things we see it is nought but an ingogo." So the little ones were silent. But when they were by themselves they laughed, saying, " That is not an ingogo; we see, for our parts." At length they returned to their homes.

The man is suspected and watched by the young izingogo.

Wa fika wa bona ukuba kanti ku kona 'unina-kulu, o se mdala. Kwa sa kusasa za ti, " Hamba, wetu; si yo'uzingela." Wa ti, " Ngi katele; a ngi z' ukuya nam*h*la nje." Za hamba ke zonke ezinkulu; za ti ezincane, " Tina a si zi 'kuya 'ndawo." Za ti ezinkulu, " A si ze si fike se ni tezile izinkuni zokupeka." Za ti ezincane, " A si tandi ukushiya ukulu yedwa nomuntu o fikileyo." Za hamba ke za ya 'uzingela; za ze za buya, za fika ezincane zi *h*lezi; za tukutela ezinkulu, za ti,

On his arrival he saw that there was at the kraal a grandmother, who was now old. In the morning they said, " Go, our fellow, we are going to hunt." He said, " I am tired; I shall not go to-day." All the old ones went; the young ones said, " As for us, we shall not go any where." The old ones said, " Let us come home by and bye, and find that you have already fetched firewood for cooking." The little ones said, " We do not like to leave grandmother alone with the person who has come." So they went to hunt. At length they returned; on their arrival the little ones were sitting still; the old ones were angry, and

9 That is, they claim him as one of themselves, whom, having come to them, they would use as a dependent.

"Tina se si vela 'uzingela; kepa nina a ni yanga 'kuteza." Za binda ezincane. Kwa pekwa izinyamazane. Za dhla, za lala.

said, "We are already come from hunting; but you have not been to fetch firewood." The little ones were silent. The game was cooked. They ate, and lay down.

He hunts with the izingogo.

Kwa sa kusasa za ti, "Hamba, si ye 'uzingela." Wa hamba nazo. Za ya za zingela, za buya ntambama; za funyanisa ezincane nazo se zi vela 'kuteza. Za fika, za peka izinyamazane zazo. Ya ti lena ingogo e s' and' ukufika, ya ti, lapa izinyamazane se zi vutiwe, ya ti, "A no ngi bekela umlenze, ngokuba isisu sibuhlungu. A ngi 'uze nga i dhla inyama." Za vuma ke, za u beka umlenze. Za lala.

In the morning they said, "Let us go and hunt." He went with them. They went and hunted, and returned in the afternoon; they found the little ones too now returning from fetching wood. They cooked their game. The newly arrived ingogo[10] said, when the game was dressed, "Just put aside a leg for me, for I have a pain in my stomach. I cannot just now eat meat." They assented, and put him aside a leg. They lay down.

He kills their grandmother, and runs off with her liver.

Kwa ti kusasa za buza za ti, "Isisu si njani na?" Ya ti, "Si se buhlungu." Za ti, "A si hambe tina, si yo'uzingela." Za hamba ke; ya sala yona nezincane. Kwa ti zi s' and' ukumuka, ya ti, "Hamba ni, ni yo'u ngi kelela amanzi emfuleni, ngi ze ngi puze." Za tata isigubu, za hamba naso. Kepa sa se si vuza isigubu si nembobo ngapansi. Za fika emfuleni, za kelela amanzi, sa vuza isigubu. Z' epuza kakulu ukubuya emfuleni, kwa za kwa ba semini kakulu. Kanti ku te zi sa puma ya se i suka ingogo, i tata umkonto, ya gwaza unina-kulu walezi izingogo ezi nge ko; ya i dabula isifuba nesisu, kwa vela isibindi, ya

In the morning they asked him how his stomach was. He said, "It is still painful." They said, "Let us go and hunt." So they went, and he remained alone with the little ones. As soon as they were gone, he said, "Do you go and fetch me some water from the river, that I may drink." They took a water-vessel and went with it. But the vessel leaked, having a hole in the bottom. They arrived at the river, and dipped water; the vessel leaked. They took a long time in returning from the river, until it was midday. But as soon as they went out, the ingogo[11] arose and took a spear, and killed the grandmother of the izingogo which were absent; he cut open the chest and bowels; the liver appeared; he took it out; he

---

[10] That is, the man who had just arrived pretending to be an ingogo.
[11] That is, the man.

si kipa, ya kqalaza, ya bheka pe-zulu, ya bona uvati, ya lw etula, ya baleka.

looked on every side; he looked upwards and saw an uvati;[12] he took it down and fled.

The young izingogo give the alarm.

Kwa ti lapa se li tshona ilanga za buya izingogo ezincane, za ti zi se senzansi kwomuzi, za bona igazi eliningi li gijime ngendhlela, se l' omile ngokuba wa e i gwazile ekuseni. Za ya se zi gijima ekaya, za fika za ngena endhlini; kepa indhlu ya inde kakulu, 'ku nga kanyi kakulu pakati kwayo. Za fika, za m bona unina-kulu e se file. Za puma zi gijima ngama-ndhla, zi kala, zi bheka ngalapa ku yiwe 'uzingela ngakona. Za zi bona ezinkulu izingogo; za ti ezi-ncane, zi tsho zi tsho zi tsho zi ti, "Ingogo njani le e-mehlo nga-muntu lena na?" Za ti ezinkulu, "Kw enze njani na?" Za ti ezi-ncane, "U m bulele ukulu." Za gijima, za lahla izinyamazane, za pata imikonto, za ti, "U bheke ngapi lowo 'muntu e be si ti in-gogo?" Za ti ezincinane, "A si m bonanga; be si ye 'kuka amanzi; sa m funyana ukulu e se file, si nga sa m boni yena."

When the sun was setting the little izingogo returned; when they were in the lower part of the village, they saw much blood which had run on the path, now dry, for he had stab-bed the old ingogo in the morn-ing. They at once ran home; on their arrival they entered the house; but the house was very long, and not very light inside; they found their grandmother dead.[13] They went out running with all their might, crying, and looking in the direction whither they had gone to hunt. When they saw the old ones, the little ones cried out again and again, saying, "What kind of an ingogo is that who has eyes like a man?" The old ones said, "What has happened?" The little ones re-plied, "He has killed grand-mother." They ran, they threw down their game; they carried their spears in their hands. They asked, "In what direction has the man gone who we thought was an ingogo?" The little ones said, "We saw him not; we had gone to fetch water; on our return we found grandmother dead; but saw no more of him."

[12] *The Uvati*, or fire-producing apparatus of the natives, consists of two sticks cut from an *umuti womlilo*, "fire-tree," that is, a tree which will readily yield fire by friction. The *usando* is preferred. The sticks are called male and female; the male is small, a foot or two long and pointed; the female is some-what larger and longer, as it is more rapidly worn out; it is notched in the middle with three notches; the one which is uppermost is called the mouth; it is larger than the others, and in this the point of the male-stick works; from the mouth on each side are two smaller notches, which are called eyes. The male-stick is rotated between the hands, its point working in the mouth of the female-stick, lying on the ground; by rubbing, dust is formed, which collects in the eyes, and falls from them on dry grass, which is placed underneath; when enough is collected, the male-stick is rotated with greater rapidity, the dust is ignited, and fire is produced.

[13] See Appendix C.

They pursue the murderer.

Za landela ngegazi lapa be ku hambe ku kconsa igazi kona. Za gijima, kwa ku lapa se ku *h*lwile za lala end*h*le. Kwa sa kusasa za vuka za gijima ngamand*h*la kakulu. Kwa ti lapa se ku semini, wa bheka umuntu o pete isibindi, wa bona utuli oluningi ngasemuva kwake. Wa gijima kakulu. Kepa zona izingogo za zi nejubane kunaye, ngokuba yena wa e umuntu, zona zi izilwane. Kwa ti emini kakulu za m bona. Kwa nga ti zi ya ndiza ngoku m bona kwazo. Wa bona ukuba zi zo'u m funyanisa. Wa ya w' enyuka ngomango omude kakulu ;. wa ti e dundubala, za zi fika nazo ngapansi kwomango. W' e*h*la, wa funyanisa isik*q*ungwa si siningi kakulu, kw enile ; wa tata uvati, wa *h*lala pansi, wa lu pe*h*la, wa vuta umlilo, wa tshisa isikota, wa zungeza leyo 'ntaba e nomango ; za baleka izingogo ngokuba za zi w esaba umlilo. Za buyela ngalapaya kwentaba ; wa e se gijima e k*q*onda pambili, kwa ze kwa *h*lwa e nga zi boni.

They followed his track by the blood where it had gone dropping in the path. They ran ; when it was dark they slept in the open country. In the morning they awoke and ran with all their might. When it was noon, the man who was carrying the liver looked and saw much dust behind him. He ran very fast. But the real izingogo were more swift than he ; for he was a man ; they were animals. At midday they saw him. It was as though they flew through catching sight of him. He saw that they would soon catch him. He ascended a very long steep place ; when he was at the top, they were reaching the bottom ; he descended ; he found very much long and thick grass ; he took the uvati, and sat down, and churned[14] it, and kindled a fire, and set the grass on fire ; it surrounded the steep hill ; the izingogo fled, for they feared the fire ; they went back from the mountain by the way they came. And he ran forward until it was dark without seeing them.

He escapes.

Wa lala. Kwa sa wa vuka wa baleka wa ye wa lala kwomunye umuzi u senkangala. Kwa sa kusasa e vuka e gijima. Kwa ti emini wa bheka ngasemuva, wa zi bona zi za zi gijim' izingogo. Ku ti e be zi sele emuva, se zi katele, zi nga m bona zi gijime kakulu, ku buye ku nga titi se ku pelile ukukatala kuzona. Wa bona futi ukuba zi za 'u m bamba. Wa pe*h*la uvati, wa vuta umlilo, wa

He slept. In the morning he awoke and fled ; he went and slept at another village on the high land. In the morning he awoke and ran. At noon he looked behind him, and saw the izingogo coming to him running. And those who had lagged behind being now tired, when they saw him, ran rapidly ; it was again as if their fatigue was at an end. Again he saw they were about to catch him. He churned the uvati, and kindled

---

[14] Other people also apply the term *churn* to the mode of producing fire by friction.

tshisa isikota; za bona umlilo u vuta, z' ema. Wa gijima, a ka be e sa zi bona; wa ze wa lala kwa ba kabili end*h*leleni e nga zi boni. Kwa ti ngolwesitatu, um*h*la e za 'ufika kubo, wa zi bona emini, za m kœotsha; wa tshetsha wa sondela œduze nemizi, za se zi buyela emuva.

fire, and burnt the grass: when they saw the fire burning, they halted. He ran and saw them no more; until he had slept twice in the way he did not see them. On the third day, the day he would reach his own people, he saw them at noon; they pursued him; he hasted and approached near the villages, and then they turned back.

The izingogo boil and eat their grandmother.

Za fika ekaya. Za fika, za m tata uniua-kulu, za m peka ngembiza enkulu. Wa lala é pekiwe eziko. Kwa za kwa sa zi i kwezela; kwa ti na kusasa za kwezela kwa ze kwa ba semini. Kwa ti ntambama za m epula, za m beka ezitebeni; wa *h*lala, wa za wa pola. Za ti ezinkulu kwezincane, "A si d*h*le ukulu, kona si nga yi 'kufa." Za mu d*h*la ke, za m kqeda.

They reached their own home. On their arrival they took the grandmother, and boiled her in a large pot. They took a whole day cooking her.[15] Until it was morning they kept up the fire, and during the morning they kept up the fire. At noon they took her out of the pot, and placed her on the feeding-mats; she remained there till she was cold. The old ones said to the little ones, "Let us eat your grandmother, then we shall not die."[16] So they ate her up.

The son-in-law reaches home.

Wa e se fika ekaya umkwenyana waleso 'salukazi; wa fika wa si nika isibindi. Sa ti, "W enzile, mntanami."

The son-in-law of the old woman reached his home; on his arrival he gave her the liver. She said, "You have done well, my child."

LYDIA, (UMKASETEMBA.)

[15] The natives reckon their days' journey by the times they sleep. *Nga lala katatu*, "I slept three times,"—that is, I took three days. *U ya 'kulala kahlanu*, "You will sleep five times,"—that is, you will take five days. Here it is said, the dead grandmother slept or lay down when cooked,—that is, they were not satisfied with the ordinary time, but left her one day in the pot over the fire.

[16] This is in allusion to a strange medical theory or superstition. When a serious disease invades a kraal, a doctor is summoned not merely to treat the disease, but to give "courage-medicines." He selects, among other things, the bone of a very old dog which has died a natural death, from mere old age, or of an old cow, bull, or other very old animal, and administers it to the healthy as well as to the sick people, that they may have life prolonged to the same extent as the old animal of whose remains they have partaken. This is the native "Life-pill." The izingogo eat the old woman that they may not die.

APPENDIX (A).

UGUNGQU-KUBANTWANA.

UGUNGQU-KUBANTWANA, kwa ku tshiwo ngokuba e unina wezilo zonke, ngokuba a e inkosi yazo; nesiziba leso za zi fika kukqala izilwane zi puze, zi m shiyele, ngokuba wa e nge ze a puza kukqala, ngokuba a e nga pela onke amanzi, zi nga ka puzi, uma e puzile kukqala; kepa umzimba wake ngenxenye kwohlangoti wa e milile ilizwe, ngenxenye ku kona imifula namahlati amakulu; kepa leyo 'mifula eya i kuyena za zi nga tandi uku i puza, ngokuba ya i fana namanzi; isiziba leso e za zi puza kusona kwa ku nga ti ubisi; ngaloko ke zi nga puzi kweminye imifula, zi puze kona esizibeni. U tiwa Ugungqu ngokuba wa e zwakala e se kude, ukuti u y' eza, ngokuba uma e hamba be ku zwakala umsindo omkulu, b' ezwa ukuba so ku fika yena ngokuti gungqu, gungqu.

LYDIA.

UGUNGQU-KUBANTWANA was so called because she was the mother of all animals, for she was their chief; and as regards the pool, the animals used to go to it first and drink, and leave water for her; for she could not drink first, for all the water would have been exhausted before the animals had drunk if she had drunk first; and as to her body, on one side there was a country, on the other rivers and great forests; but the rivers which were in her the animals did not like to drink, for they were like common water; that pool at which they drank was, at it were, milk; therefore they did not drink at other rivers, they drank at the pool. She was called Ugungqu because when she was still at a distance she was heard coming, for when she was moving there was heard a great noise, and they heard that she was coming by the gungqu, gungqu.[17]

In other legends of South Africa the elephant is represented as the king of beasts. The Basuto tale of the Little Hare has so many things in common with this of Ugungqu-kubantwana, that one cannot doubt that they have a common origin. There a woman longs for the liver of a fabulous animal, the niamatsane; her husband goes to hunt one to gratify her; he finds a large herd, but as they could "leap three sleeps at a bound,"—that is, a distance equal to three days' journey,—and "their backs and legs were like a live coal," he has some difficulty in catching one, and succeeds at last only by means of magic; he kills one, and gets possession of the longed-for liver; his wife devours it with avidity, but it is as a burning fire within her, and she rushes to the great lake and drinks it dry; and remains, overpowered by the excessive draught, stretched on the ground, unable to move. The king of beasts, when informed, tells several animals to go and punish the woman, but one after another makes an excuse. The ostrich at length goes to her, and gives her such a violent kick that the water spouts up into the air, and rushes in torrents into the lake. The animals do not dare to drink the water; but the hare goes stealthily by night, and drinks, and then smears the lips and knees of the jerboa with mud, that the charge may fall on it. (*Casalis. Op. cit., p.* 350.) Compare also "The Elephant and the Tortoise." *Bleek. Op. cit., p.* 27.

---

[17] *Gungqu, gungqu.*—This word is intended as an imitation of the noise produced by the animal, which is said to resemble that made by a heavily laden wagon passing over a bad road. The English reader will not be able to pronounce the click; but he will succeed in producing a sound sufficiently similar by uttering *gunghu,* nasalising and aspirating strongly the *g.*—Another native adds, she was so called because she swallowed every thing that came in her way, so that when she moved the contents of her stomach rattled.

APPENDIX (B).

THE IZINGOGO.

THE Izingogo are fabulous animals,—*degenerated men*, who by living continually apart from the habitations of men have become a kind of baboon. They go on all fours, and have tails, but talk as men; they eat human flesh, even that of their own dead.

IZINGOGO, kwa ku nga ti za zi abantu; kepa kwa ti ngokutanda kwazo za ʍlala endʍle, kwa za kwa tiwa izilwane, ngokuba za zi ʍlala endʍle, ngaloko ke umuntu za mu dʍla. Kepa úma ku fika umuntu o vela kubantu 'enza imikuba e njengeyazo, zi jabule zi ti, "Naye u ingogo," ngokuba 'enza njengazo. Kepa abantwana a se be ʍlakanipile, ukuʍlakanipa kwabo kwa ku dʍlula okwezinkulu, ngokuba ba be m kɣwaya, be ti, "A ku si yo ingogo;" noma ezinkulu zi tukutela zi ba tshaye abantwana, ba pike noma zi ba tshaya. Kwa ku ti uma zi hambile zi yo'udʍlala odongeni, zi fike zi pikisane ngokwekɣa, zi ti o nga kw azi ukwekɣa a ka si yo ingogo; nezincane z' ekɣe; kepa uma ku fika umuntu e ti u ingogo, be zi ya naye odongeni, zi ti a k' ekɣe njengazo; ngokuba ku tiwa ukwekɣa za zi lula ngokuba za zi dʍla ibomvu; ku ti uma se zi kɣedile ukwekɣa, zi me odongeni olukulu, zi fulatele enzansi zonke, zi ti, "A si tsheke sonke, si 'ye 'kubheka inʍle yake uma i njengeyetu na?" Uma i njalo, zi ti u ingogo; uma i nge njalo, zi mu dʍle; ku ti uma lowo 'muntu o fikile kuzona, uma e nga tsheki njengazo, zi mu dʍle. Be ku ti uma umuntu e ya kona a bunjelwe izinkwa zebomvu, a ʍlale ekaya e dʍla zona, ku ze ku fe inyanga, e nga sa ku dʍli ukudʍla, e se dʍla ibomvu lodwa; a hambe nalo eli pete izigakɣa eziningi, kona e ya 'kuti uma e se fikile kuzona izingogo naye a tshekis' okwazo, zi be se zi ti naye ingogo.

THE Izingogo were apparently men; but it came to pass by their own choice they lived in the open country, until they were called animals; for they lived in the open country, and therefore they ate man. But when there arrived a man who came from other men who practised the same habits as themselves, they rejoiced, saying, he too was an ingogo, because he did as they did. But the discernment of the children, who were now sharp, was greater than that of the older ones, for they were on their guard against him, saying, "It is not an ingogo;" and even though the old ones were angry and beat them, they denied notwithstanding they were beaten. They used to go and play on the bank of a river; on their arrival they contended by leaping, saying, that he who could not leap was not an ingogo; the little ones leaped too; and if there came a man feigning to be an ingogo, they would go with him to the bank, and tell him to leap like them; for it is said, when they leapt they were light, because they ate red earth.

*   *   *   *   *

*   *   *   *   *

*   *   *   *   *

Izingogo za zi hamba ngezinyawo ezine; za zi nemisila; kodwa za zi kulumisa kwabantu.

The Izingogo used to go on all fours; they had tails; but they talked like men.

LYDIA.

It may be well to compare this account of the Izingogo with Gulliver's account of the Yahoos. The native imagination has quite equalled Swift in describing degenerate man.

This will be the proper place to introduce the native legend on the origin of baboons. According to this theory, man is not an elevated ape, but the ape is a degenerated man.

UKUVELA KWEZIMFENE.

(THE ORIGIN OF BABOONS.)

EMAFENENI isizwe esa penduka izimfene. Abantu ba kona ba vama ukuvilapa, be nqena ukulima; ba tanda ukud*h*la kwabanye abantu, ngokuti, "Si ya 'kupila, noma si nga limi, uma si d*h*la ukud*h*la kwabalimayo." Inkosi yakona, kwatusi, isibongo sakona, ya buta isizwe sakona, ya ti, "A ku fuuwe ukud*h*la ku be umpako ukuze ku d*h*liwe, loku ku za 'upunywa emakaya ku yiw' end*h*le." Nembala ke kwa ba njalo. Kwa butwa ukud*h*la konke nezinkwa, kwa pekwa; kwa tatwa imipini yamagejo okulima: ya patwa ukuze ba zipisele ngayo ngemuva. U lapo ke a ba penduka ngako izimfene. A si zwa 'ndab' enkulu a ba y enza ukuze ba penduke izimfene, ukupela ukupisela impini njalo; ya mila ya ba umsila; kwa vela noboya; ba puka ubuso, ba ba izimfene ke. Ba hamba emaweni; imizi yabo ya ba amawa. Na nam*h*la nje ku sa tshiwo njalo uma i bulewe imfene, ku tiwa, "Umuntu wakwatusi. Emafeneni lapa ku dabuka kona izimfene."

UMAMADUNJINI, UMKATUTA.

AMONG the Amafene was the tribe which became baboons. The people of that tribe were habitually idle, and did not like to dig; they wished to eat at other people's houses, saying, "We shall live, although we do not dig, if we eat the food of those who cultivate the soil." The chief of that place, of the house of Tusi, the surname of that tribe, assembled the tribe, and said, "Let food be prepared, that it may be food for a journey, for we are going to leave our homes and go into the wilderness." And they did so. All kind of food was collected, and bread made; and they took the handles of digging-picks: they took these that they might fasten them on behind. It was then that they turned into baboons. We do not know any long account of what they did that they might turn into baboons, but only that they thus fastened on the pick-handles; they grew and became tails; hair made its appearance on their bodies; their foreheads became overhanging, and so they became baboons. They went to the precipices; their dwellings were the rocks. And even to this day it is still said, when a baboon is killed, "It is one of Tusi's men. The Amafene is the nation from which the baboons sprang."

ANOTHER VERSION.

Ku tiwa, imfene kwa ku umuntu, uhlobo lwabantu bakwatusi. I y' aziwa uhlobo lwayo lapa ya vela kona. Na manje ku sa tiwa emafeneni, isizwe sakona. Ku tiwa, umuntu wakona wa ba ivila elikulu; w' engena ukusebenza imisebenzi yonke; wa tanda ukudhla oku setshenzwe abanye abantu; kepa wa hlupeka kakulu, abantu be m sola, be m hleka, be m dumaza ngobuvila bake : wa za wa tata umpini wegejo lake, wa u faka ngemva, ukuze a be inyamazane, a dhle ngokweba loko 'kudhla a ba m sola ngako. Wa lal' endhle, wa ba imfene.

Wa fika ngolunye usuku e se imfene, umuntu e lindile; kepa w' ahluleka ukulinda, wa lala. Imfene leyo ya ngena ensimini, ya dhla ya dhla, y' ezwa ukuba se y esuti; ya hamba ya ya lapa lo 'muntu e lele kona, y' apula ugonoti lwebele, ya hamba nalo uku lw enza uswazi lwokuba i ze i m vuse ngalo; ya kwela ekxibeni e lele ubutongo, ya m tshaya ngalo kakulu; wa vuka ngokwetuka, wa kuza; ya ba se y ehla ke, se i puma ensimini : wa kqalaza ukuti, " Hau! Umuntu o ngi tshayileko u ye ngapi na!" Wa bona i se y enyuka i ya eweni; wa ti, " Konje nga ba ngi tshaywa i yo le 'mfene." W' ehla wa bona izinyawo zayo pansi kwekxiba. Wa hlola insimu, wa fumana se i dhliwe.

It is said, the baboon was a man of the nation of men who are called Amatusi. The nation from which it sprang is known. And to this day the Amafene say, the baboons descended from them. It is said, a man of that nation was a very great idler; he was disinclined to do any kind of work; he liked to eat what others had worked for; but he was greatly troubled when men scolded him, and laughed at him, and ridiculed him for his idleness : at length he took the handle of his hoe, and fastened it on behind, that he might become an animal, and eat by stealing the food, for which they scolded him. He slept in the open country, and became a baboon.

He came one day, when he was now a baboon, where a man was watching; but he got tired of watching, and went to sleep. The baboon entered the garden; he ate and ate, until he felt satisfied; he went to the place where the man was sleeping; he broke off a reed of corn; he took it with him that he might use it as a switch for the purpose of arousing him; he climbed into the watchhouse, he being asleep, and hit him hard with the reed; he woke with a start, and cried out with surprise; the baboon at once descended from the watchhouse, and went out of the garden : he looked on this side and that, saying, " Hau ! Where has the man gone that struck me ?" He saw the baboon now ascending the precipice, and said, " So then I was struck by that baboon." He descended, and saw the footprints below the watchhouse. He examined the garden, and found it already wasted.

Ku njalo ke ngemfene. Ku tiwa umuntu wakwatusi. Labo 'bantu bakwatusi na namhla nje ba se kona, abona ba penduka izimfene. Ku tshiwo njalonjalo, ku ti, uma izimfene zi kala eweni, z' enza umsindo, ku tiwe kubo 'ngokulaula, "Nampo abantu ba-kwini eweni, be kuluma." Noma zi dhla amasimu, ngoku ba laulela, ku tiwe, "Bani, tshela ni abantu bakwini laba, ba yeke ukudhla kwetu; si yä zilimela; nabo a ba lime njengati."

I loko ke e ngi kw aziyo ngem-fene.

UMPENGULA MBANDA.

Such, then, is the history of the baboon. It is said to be one of the Amatusi. The Amatusi still exist to the present time, the very people who became baboons. And when the baboons are crying on the precipice, and making a noise, it is continually said to them in jest, "Behold your people on the precipice, talking." Or if they have devoured the gardens, it is said in sport, "You So-and-so, tell those people of yours to leave alone our food; we dig for ourselves; and let them too dig for themselves, as we do."

This, then, is what I know about the baboon.

It is quite noteworthy that among the Mussulmans there is a similar legend of the descent of apes from man :—

"On one of Solomon's progresses from Jerusalem to Mareb, he passed through a valley inhabited by apes, which, however, dressed and lived like men, and had more comfortable dwellings than other apes, and even bore all kinds of weapons. He descended from his flying carpet, and marched into the valley with a few of his troops. The apes hurried together to drive him back, but one of their elders stepped forward and said, 'Let us rather seek safety in submission, for our foe is a holy prophet.' Three apes were immediately chosen as ambassadors to negotiate with Solomon. He received them kindly, and inquired to which class of apes they belonged, and how it came to pass that they were so skilled in all human arts? The ambassadors replied, 'Be not astonished at us, for we are descended from men, and are the remnant of a Jewish community, which, notwithstanding all admonition, continued to desecrate the Sabbath, until Allah cursed them, and turned them into apes.'" (*Weil's Biblical Legends of the Mussulmans, p. 205.*)

APPENDIX (C).

IZIMU ELA TOLWA UMASENDENI.

(THE CANNIBAL WHOM UMASENDENI RECEIVED INTO HIS HOUSE.)

THE following tale, told as an historical fact of comparatively modern times, bears so much resemblance to that of the slaughter of the grandmother of the izingogo, that it is inserted here :—

UMFO wetu, Umasendeni ibizo lake, wa tola umfokazi; wa ti, "Ngi ku tolile; hlala lapa; izwe li indhlala, ku nge ko amabele."

My brother, whose name is Uma-sendeni, received a stranger into his house; he said to him, "I have received you into my house; stay here; there is famine in the land; there is no corn." So the

Wa *hl*ala ke umfokazi, wa *hl*ala insukwana nje. Wa ti ngelinye ilanga, "Ngi ya fa nam*hl*a. A ngi zi 'kupuma ngomzi lo." Wa e be e fa ebu*hl*ungu unina kamasendeni. Kwa ti ukuba b' emuke abantu ekaya, wa nu bamba umfokazi, wa m bulala, wa m peka ke, wa mu d*hl*a ke. Wa m beka izitsha zonke, wa twala, wa hamba, w' emuka. Ya buya ke indodana, ya fika, ya funyana se ku kubi end*hl*ini; ya fumana se kw ande inyama end*hl*ini. Ya kala ke, ya ti, "Woza ni, bantu! ni ze 'ku ngi buka; loku nank' um*hl*ola; umame u d*hl*iwe umfokazi, e be ngi m tolile." Ba butana ke ekaya. Ba ti, "Ku boni ke? Si be si nga tshongo na, ukuti, 'Lizimu leli?' Wa ti wena, umuntu wako. Wa ti, 'Ka 'zimu.' Sa ti, 'Lizimu,' tina." Wa m twala ke unina ngazo izitsha zonke, e ya 'u m la*hl*a ngezitsha.

UMPONDO KAMBULE (AARON).

stranger staid; but he staid only a few days. He said one day, "I am ill to-day. I shall not go out from this kraal." Umasendeni's mother had been suffering from pain. When the people had left home, the stranger laid hold of her and killed her, and boiled her and ate her. He filled all the vessels with her, and loaded himself, and went on his way. Her son came back again, and found the house befouled; he found that there was much flesh in the house. So he cried, saying, "Come ye, people! come and look upon me; for here is a prodigy; my mother has been eaten by the stranger whom I took into my house." So they assembled in his house; and said, "Do you not see then? Did we not say this man was a cannibal? You said for your part, he was your dependent; you denied that he was a cannibal. We said, on our part, that he was a cannibal." So he carried out his mother in all those vessels, and went and buried her in them.

UMKXAKAZA-WAKOGINGQWAYO.

The birth of Umkxakaza.

KWA ku kona inkosi etile; ya zala umntwana; w' etiwa igama, kwa tiwa Umkxakaza-wakogingqwayo. Loko kwa ku tshiwo ngokuba kwa ku puma impi i kxakaza izikali, w' etiwa ukuti Umkxakaza; nokuti o wakogingqwayo, kwa ku tshiwo ngokuba impi

THERE was a certain king: he had a child; her name was Umkxakaza-wakogingqwayo.[18] That name was given because an army went out to battle rattling weapons, and so she was named Umkxakaza; and further the name Wakogingqwayo was given because

---

18 *Umkxakaza-wakogingqwayo.*—The·rattler·of·weapons·of·the·place·of·the·rolling·of·the·slain.

ya gwaza kakulu abantu, kwa tiwa se be ginggika nje ; kwa tshiwo ke ukuti wakoginggwayo. Kwa buye kwa zalwa onıunye umntwana ; w' etiwa igama, kwa tiwa Ubalatusi, ngokuba wa e nga ti u fana netusi.

the army killed very many men, and when they were rolled altogether on the ground, she was named Wakoginggwayo. Again he had another child ; she was named Ubalatusi,[19] because she resembled brass.

Her father's rash promise.

Wa ti Umkxakaza lapa e se kula, wa ti uyise, "Bheka, wena, umhlana u tombayo ku ya 'ubutwa izinkomo eziningi zokuza uku ku buyisa ; ngokuba ezako izinkomo zi ya 'udhliwa ngemikonto, ku hlaselwe ezizweni ezi kude, zi fike zi kcime ilanga."

When Umkxakaza was growing up, her father said, "Look you, on the day when you are of age there shall be collected many cattle for the purpose of bringing you home ;[20] for the cattle which shall be brought to you shall be taken at the point of the spear, and forays be made into distant nations, and when they come they will darken the sun."

Umkxakaza's maturity.

Wa za wa kula Umkxakaza. Wa ti e nabanye bodwa endhle wa ba tshela ukuti, "Ngi tombile." Za jabula izintombi, za gijima, za ya emizini yonke, zi mema ezinye intombi ; za fika, za hlala kuyena ; za buye z' esuka, za m shiya, za ya ekaya, za ya 'upanga umuzi wonke.

At length she came to maturity. When she was with others in the open country she said to them, "I am of age." The damsels rejoiced, and ran to all the villages, calling other damsels ; they came and remained with her ; again they left her and went home, going to plunder the whole village.[21]

The size of the town in which she dwelt.

Kepa umuzi wa umkulu ngokungenakulinganiswa, ngokuba izindhlu zawo za zi nga balwa ; ngokuba umuntu, uma e memeza, e

But the town was immeasurably large ; for the rows of its houses could not be counted, for if a man standing in the middle of the

---

[19] *Ubalatusi.*—Composed of um-*balu*, "a colour ;" and i-*tusi*, "brass." The brass-coloured one.

[20] *Ukubuyisa.*—When a princess royal comes of age, she quits her father's home, and goes out into the wilds, from which she is brought back by having a bullock slaughtered on her account. Other girls tell her parents where she is ; and all law and order are at an end ; and each man, woman, and child lays hold on any article of property which may be at hand, assagais, shields, mats, pots, &c. The king says nothing, it being a day of such general rejoicing, that it is regarded as improper to find fault with any one. If during this reign of misrule, any thing is taken which the chief really values, he can obtain it again only by paying a fine.

[21] See preceding note.

pakati esibayeni, ngalapa kwo*h*langoti be be ng' ezwa uma u kona
umuntu o memeza esibayeni ; ngokuba umuntu uma e vela okalweni
u be ti imizi eminingi, kanti umuzi
munye.

cattle-enclosure shouted, people
standing on one side could not
hear that there was any one shouting in the cattle-enclosure; for a
man standing on the top of a hill
would say it was many villages,
when in reality it was but one.

Umkxakaza despises her father's offering.

Za buya izintombi, za ya. kuyena Umk*x*akaza. B' etuka aba
sekaya ngokubona izintombi zi zo-
'panga ; ba ti, "U tombile umntwana wenkosi." Uyise wa kipa
amashumi amabili okuya 'ku m
buyisa end*h*le. Wa fike Umk*x*a-
kaza, wa ti, "A ngi boni 'luto."
Kwa pindelwa ekaya ; wa fike
uyise, wa kipa amashumi amane ;
ba ya nawo kumk*x*akaza ; wa ti
Umk*x*akaza, "A ngi boni 'luto."
Ba pindela ekaya. Wa fika uyise,
wa kipa ikulu. Wa ti, "Hamba
ni nalo." Ba hamba, ba fika kum-
k*x*akaza. Wa ti Umk*x*akaza,
"Nansi in*h*lamvu yelanga." Ba
pindela ekaya.

The damsels returned to Um-
k*x*akaza. The people at home
wondered when they saw the damsels coming to plunder ; they
shouted, "The king's child is of
age." The king selected twenty
head of cattle to go and bring her
back from the open country. But
Umk*x*akaza said, "I do not see
anything." They were taken home
again. Then the father selected
forty; they went with them to
Umk*x*akaza ; Umk*x*akaza said, "I
do not see anything." They went
home again. Her father selected
a hundred, and said, "Go with
them." They went with them to
Umk*x*akaza. Umk*x*akaza said,
"There is the globe of the sun."
They returned home.

A larger offering is made, but still despised.

Kepa abantu bonke pakati kwesizwe sikayise ba be gijima nenkomo, bonke be ti, "U tombile
Umk*x*akaza-wakogingqwayo." Ku
te uma ba fike labo aba be yisile
izinkomo kumk*x*akaza, ba fika ba
nikwa amakulu amabili ; ba ya
nawo. Wa fike wa ti Umk*x*akaza,
"Ngi sa li bona ilanga. Kwo ze
ku kcitshwe ilanga njengokutsho
kukababa." Ba buya ba ya enkosini. Kwa fike kwa gijinyiswa

But all the men belonging to
her father's tribe were running
with cattle, shouting, "Umk*x*a-
kaza-wakogingqwayo is of age."
When those who had taken the
cattle to Umk*x*akaza returned,
they were given two hundred ;
they went with them ; Umk*x*a-
kaza said, "I still see the sun.
Until the sun is darkened according to my father's saying [I will
not return."][22] They returned to
the king. Men ran to the whole

[22] It is necessary to add these words to complete the sense. Such elliptical
modes of expression are common in Zulu.

abantu ezweni lonke, be tata izinkomo kubantu bakayise, nezikayise za *h*langaniswa, za yiswa 'ndawo nye zonke. Wa ti Umkxakaza, " Ngi sa li bona ilanga." Ba buya ba ya ekaya.

nation, taking the cattle from her father's people, and the cattle of her father were collected and all brought to one place. Umkxakaza said, "I still see the sun." They returned home.

Again she despises a still larger offering.

Kwa fike kwa kitshwa impi; ya ya 'ku zi *dh*la ezizweni; ya buya nazo. Za yiswa. Wa fike wa ti Umkxakaza, "Ngi ya li bona ilanga." Kwa buye kwa kitshwa impi; ya buya nenkulungwane eziningi. Wa fike wa ti Umkxakaza, u ya li bona ilanga.

An army was levied; it went to spoil foreign nations of their cattle, and came back with them. They were brought to Umkxakaza. She said, "I still see the sun." Another army was levied, and returned with many thousand. But Umkxakaza said, she still saw the sun.

The army sent to obtain cattle fall in with Usilosimapundu.

Kwa puma impi futi. Ba hamba, ba ya, ba fika ba zi bona izinkomo zi *dh*la esigodini esikulu kakulu. A ba zi balanga uma za zi 'makulu 'mangaki na. Kepa kwa ku kona nezim*h*lope nezimtoto nezinsundu nezimnyama nezibomvu; ezinye impondo zi bheke pansi; ezinye impondo zi pume za kxega; kwenye lu pume lu be lunye; zi nemibala eminingi. Kepa kwa ku kona isilwanyazane esikulu si *h*lezi ngapezulu kwaso leso 'sigodi esa si nezinkomo; igama laso kwa ku Usilosimapundu. Kwa ku tshiwo ngokuba kwa ku kona izintaba namapunzu ezintatshana ezincane; kwa tshiwo ukuti Usilosimapundu. Kepa kwa ku kona ngenxenye kwaso imifula emikulu; ngenxenye kwa ama*h*lati amakulu; ngenxenye kwa amawa amakulu; ngenxenye kwa ku senkangala njc.

Again an army was levied. They set out, and at length saw some cattle feeding in a very large valley. They did not count how many hundred they were. But there were both white and dun, and brown, and black, and red; the horns of some were directed downwards;[23] the horns of others were moveable;[24] others had only one horn. They were of various colours. And there was a very huge beast sitting on the hills overhanging that valley, where were the cattle. The name of the beast was Usilosimapundu.[25] It was so called because there were hills, and elevations of little hills (upon it); and so it was named Usilosimapundu. And there was on one side of it many rivers; and on another side great forests; and on another side great precipices; and on another side it was open high land.

---

[23] Cattle whose horns hang down are called *imidhlovu.*
[24] These are called *amahlawe.*
[25] *Usilosimapundu.*—A beast covered with small elevations. The rugose, nodulated, beast.

Usilosimapundu's officers.

Kepa pakati kwemiti yonke eya i kona kuleso 'silwane, kwa ku kona imiti emibili, ya i mide kakulu pezu kwemiti yonke; amagama ayo kwa ku Imidoni yombili. Kwa ku i yona ku izinduna zikasilosimapundu.	And amidst all the trees which were on the beast, there were two trees; they were very much higher than all the rest; they were both named Imidoni.[26] It was they who were the officers of Usilosimapundu.

The soldiers contemn Usilosimapundu, and are threatened.

Wa ti Usilosimapundu lapa e i bona impi i kquba izinkomo, wa ti, "Lezo—lezo 'nkomo e ni zi kqubayo ezikabani na?" Ba ti, "Yiya; a si suke lesi 'silosimapundu." Wa ti, "Eh, eh! Hamba ni nazo ke."	When Usilosimapundu saw the army driving away the cattle, he said, "Those—those cattle which you are driving away, to whom do they belong?" They replied, "Out on you; let the rugose beast get out of the way." He replied, "Eh, eh! Go off with them then."[27]

Description of Usilosimapundu.

Kepa kuyena kwa ku bonakala umlomo wodwa namehlo; ubuso bake ba bu idwala. Kepa umlomo umkulu, ubanzi kakulu, kepa ubomvu; kwamanye amazwe a semzimbeni kuyena kwa ku sebusika; kwamanye ku sekwinhla. Kepa kowokwake konke loko.	But as regards the beast there appeared only a mouth and eyes; his face was a rock; and his mouth was very large and broad, but it was red; in some countries which were on his body it was winter; and in others it was early harvest. But all these countries were in him.[28]

[26] Water-boom.

[27] "Eh, eh! go off with them then."—These words are to be regarded as a threat. They mean, Very well, I let you take them now, but see to it, you will suffer for it by and bye.

[28] We are forcibly reminded of Milton's description of Leviathan, which,

> "Hugest of living things, on the deep
> Stretched like a promontory, sleeps or swims,
> And *seems a moving land.*"

This fabulous animal of the Zulus "seems a moving land." It may possibly have some connection with the notion found among other people that the world is an animal. A similar one appears now and then, but not in a definite form, to crop out in the thoughts of the natives of this country. Some parts of this account would lead us to suppose that the basis of the legend is a traditional recollection of a landslip, or some extensive convulsion of the earth.

We may compare this beast overgrown with trees, &c., with Es-sindibad's great fish. The captain says:—"This apparent island, upon which you are, is not really an island, but it is a great fish that hath become stationary in the midst of the sea, and the sand hath accumulated upon it; so that it hath be-

The cattle at length darken the sun, and Umkxakaza is satisfied.

Ba zi kǫuba ke izinkomo zikasilosimapundu. Ba ti be ya nazo ngasekaya, kwa ku nga ti li za 'kuna, ngokuba ilanga nezulu kwa ku nga bonakali; ku site utuli lwazo. Ba ze ba ti, "Hau! loku izulu be li sile, le 'nkungu i vela pi e si nga sa boni i yona na?" Ba buya ba bona uma kw' enza utuli; ba vela ngasekaya. Kepa ba bona kumnyama, a ba be be sa zi bona inkomo; ba ye ba zi sa kumkxakaza. Wa fike wa ti, "Nazi ke ezi kcima ilanga."

They drove off the cattle of Usilosimapundu. As they were going with them near home, it was as if it was going to rain, for neither sun nor heaven appeared; they were concealed by the dust raised by the cattle. At length they said, "Hau! since the sky was clear, whence comes this mist through which we are no longer able to see?" Again they saw that it was occasioned by the dust; they came near home; and they saw it was dark, they could no longer see the cattle; they took them to Umkxakaza. She said, "Behold then the cattle which darken the sun."

Umkxakaza returns home.

Ba buya ke ba ya ekaya. Wa fika umgonqo se w akiwe, wa pela, nencapa se y endhlelwe. Wa fika, ba ngena nentombi, ba hlala emgonqweni.

So they went home again. On her arrival the umgonqo[29] was already completed, and the incapa spread on the ground. She entered the umgonqo with the damsels, and remained there.

There is universal rejoicing.

Kepa bonke abantu aba be pumile impi, a ku ko namunye pakati kwabo owa e nga i hlabile inkomo; bonke kulowo e hlabe eyake inkomo. Kepa eziningi izinkomo a zi hlinzwanga ngobuningi bazo. La ti igwababa la

And as for all the men who had gone out with the army, there was not one among them who had not killed a bullock; every one in the town killed his own bullock. But many of the cattle were not skinned because they were so many. The crow skinned for itself; the

come like an island, and trees have grown upon it since times of old." And with the huge tortoise, "upon whose back earth collected in the length of time, so that it became like land, and produced plants." (*Lane's Arabian Nights.* Vol. III., p. 6 and p. 79.) Compare also the monster Ugungqu-kubantwana (p. 176); and "the Unkulunkulu of beneath," who has a forest growing on one side, given below.

[29] *Umgonqo* is a small hut or chamber erected within a house, in which a girl when of age is placed. She is kept there for one, two, or three months, and fed for the purpose of making her fat; but if there should be a scarcity of food, she may be allowed to go out at the end of a few weeks. Umkxakaza is represented as remaining in the umgonqo for several years.

ziḥlinzela ; namankqe a ziḥlinzela ; nezinja za ziḥlinzela. Kwa nuka inyama yodwa pakati kwesizwe. Kodwa ku nga ḥlatshwa kuzona ezikasilosimapundu ; ku ḥlatshwa kulezi zikayise.

vultures skinned for themselves ; and the dogs skinned for themselves. There was no other smell but that of meat throughout the whole nation. But the cattle of Usilosimapundu were not slaughtered, but those belonging to her father.

All the people go to dig in the royal garden, leaving Umkxakaza and her sister alone.

Wa ḥlala iminyaka e nga balwa emgonqweui. Abantu a ba be be sa m azi ; w' aziwa intombi zodwa, ngokuba za z' ala uma abantu b' eze emgonqweni ; ba ti aba ngenile endḥlini, ba ḥlale nje, be nga m boni e ḥlezi pakati emgonqweni. Ku te ngesikati eside ba ti bonke abantu, "A ku ze 'kuti e nga ka pumi Umkxakaza, ku hanjwe ku yiwe embutisweni wenkosi." Ba vuma bonke abantu, ngokuba ba be ti, "Ku ya 'kuba 'buḥlungu uma be vuna e se pumile, ngokuba ku ya 'kwenziwa utshwala esizweni sonke." Kwa ti e s' eza 'upuma, kwa vukwa ekuseni kakulu abantu bonke ; kepa ekaya lapa kubo, kwa ku kona utshwala umuzi wonke ; enxenye bu voviwe, enxenye bu vutshelwa, enxenye bu isijingi. Kwa sa ba hamba ke bonke abantu ; kwa sala yena nodade wabo ekaya. Kepa umbutiso wenkosi wa u kude kakulu ; be vuka be ti u kona be ya 'ubuya masinya kusiḥlwa.

She remained uncounted years in the umgonqo. The people no longer knew her ; she was known only by the damsels, for they would not allow people to enter the umgonqo ; and those who entered the house merely sat down without seeing her, she remaining inside the umgonqo. It happened after a long time all the people said, "Before Umkxakaza come out, let all the people go to the royal garden."[30] All the people agreed, for they had said, "It will be painful to harvest after she has come out, for beer will be made throughout the whole tribe." It happened when she was about to go out, all the people rose very early in the morning ; but at her father's there was beer in the whole village ; in one place it was strained ; in another it was mixed with malt ; in another it was soaking. In the morning all the people set out ; there remained herself and her sister only at home. But the royal garden was very far off ; when they arose they thought that by arising early they could return early in the evening.

There is thunder and an earthquake.

Kwa ti so ku isikati be mukile, b' ezwa ku duma izulu, kwa zama-

Some time after their departure Umkxakaza and her sister heard

[30] *Umbutiso,* the royal garden, in which all the tribe assembles to dig and sow for the king.

zama um*h*labati na send*h*lini lapa be *h*lezi kona. Wa ti Umkxakaza, "Ak' u pume u bone, balatusi, uma ini leyo na, izulu ukuduma be li balele kangaka." Wa puma Ubalatusi, wa bona ku. mi i*h*lati esangweni ; a ka be e sa bona uma isango li ma pi na. Wa ngena end*h*lini, wa ti, "U za 'ubona, mntanenkosi, ku kulu ku sesangweni ; utango nganxanye lw apukile, so lu lele pansi nje."

the heaven thundering, and the earth moved even in the very house where they were sitting. Umkxakaza said, "Just go out and see, Ubalatusi, what this is, the heaven to thunder when it was so bright ?" Ubalatusi went out, and saw a forest standing at the entrance of the village, and she could no longer see where the entrance was. She came into the house, and said, "You will see, child of the king, there is something huge at the gateway ; the fence is broken down on one side, and is now just lying on the ground."

They are visited by strange guests.

Kwa ti be sa kuluma, kwa se kw apuka amakqabunga amabili

As they were speaking, two leaves[31] broke off from the Imi-

[31] *Speaking Trees* are heard of in the legends of other people ; but I know of none in which any such personal action is ascribed to them as here. In the Amanzi stories, collected among the negroes of the West Indies, we read of a Doukana Tree which was covered with fruit ; a lazy man went daily to this tree alone and ate the fruit, but never took any home to his wife and children. When one only was left, it is represented as assuming the power of volition, and effectually eluding all his efforts to catch it. (*Dasent. Popular Tales from the Norse, p.* 503.) In the same stories, the trees cry out "Shame" when the lion is about to devour the woman who had set him free (*p.* 490).

Shakspeare makes Macbeth say,

> " Stones have been known to move and trees to speak
> Augurs."

Comp. "Prince Hatt, or the Three Singing Leaves." *Thorpe's Yule-tide Stories, p.* 17. Also "The Two Caskets," *p.* 99 ; and "Temptations," *p.* 369. —"The Two Step-sisters." *Dasent., p.* 134.

Comp. also Hiawatha's appeal to the different forest-trees to give him the materials for building a canoe, and their answers. (*Longfellow.*) And the address " of the green reed, the nurse of sweet music, divinely inspired by a gentle breeze of air," to Psyche. (*Apuleius, p.* 117.)

We close this note on speaking trees by the following extract from the tale of "Lilla Rosa" :—"One day, while wandering on the sea-shore, she found the head and leg of a fawn that had been killed by the wild beasts. As the flesh was still fresh, she took the leg and set it on a pole, that the little birds might see it the better, and come and feed upon it. She then lay down on the earth, and slept for a short time, when she was wakened by a sweet song, more beautiful than anything that can be imagined. Lilla Rosa listened to the delightful notes, and thought she was dreaming ; for nothing so exquisite had she ever heard before. On looking around her, she saw that the leg which she had placed as food for the little fowls of heaven was changed to a verdant linden, and the fawn's head to a little nightingale sitting on the linden's summit. But every single small leaf of the tree gave forth a sweet sound, so that their tones together composed a wondrous harmony ; and the little nightingale sat among them and sang his lay so beautifully, that all who might hear it would certainly have imagined themselves in heaven." (*Thorpe's Yule-tide Stories, p.* 43.)

emidonini, a fika end*h*lini lapa be *h*lezi kona. A fike a ti, "Tata isigubu, balatusi, u ye 'kuka 'manzi emfuleni." Wa tata isigubu, wa ya emfuleni. A *h*lala e m bhekile Ubalatusi. Kepa emfuleni wa kelela isigubu, s' egcwala, kw' ala uma 'esuke. A ze a ti amak*q*abunga, "Puma, mkxakaza, u hambe u fune amanzi ekaya lapa." Wa ti, "Ngi tombile; a ngi pumi emgon*q*weni." A ti, "Si ze s' azi ukuba u tombile; kepa si ti, Puma, u ye 'kuka amanzi." Wa puma wa ye, wa wa ka amanzi kwenye ind*h*lu, wa buya nawo. A ti amak*q*abunga a ti, "Pemba." Wa ti, "A ngi kw azi ukupemba." A ti amak*q*abunga, "Si ze s' azi uma a u kw azi ukupemba; kepa

doni, and entered the house where they were sitting. On their arrival they said, "Take a water-vessel, Ubalatusi, and go and fetch water from the river." She took the water-vessel and went to the river. They sat waiting for Ubalatusi. But at the river she dipped water into the water-vessel; when it was full she was unable to leave the place.[32] At length the leaves said, "Go out, Umkxakaza, and look for water here at home." She said, "I am of age, and I do not yet quit the umgon*q*o."[33] They replied, "We already knew that you were of age; but we say, Go and fetch water." She went and fetched water from another house, and came back with it. The leaves said, "Light a fire." She replied, "I cannot light a fire." They said, "We already knew that you could not light a fire;

[32] This inability to move from being spell-bound is common in the nursery tales of all countries. In the tales of the North is a story of a bride who had been separated from the bridegroom; whilst waiting for him she is annoyed by the importunity of other lovers. She gives them permission to come one at a time by night, but before retiring to her chamber, sends them to do something for her, to lock the door, to fasten the gate, or to tie up the calf; and by a spell fastens them to the object till morning. (See *Thorpe. Yule-tide Stories.* "The King's Son and the Princess Singorra," *p.* 218.—"Goldmaria and Goldfeather," *p.* 449.—*Campbell. Op. cit.* "The Battle of the Birds." *Vol. I., p.* 36.) The girl who attempts to steal a few feathers from Dummling's golden goose, has her hand and fingers instantly fixed to it; and all who approach and touch her are in like manner fixed, and are compelled to follow Dummling in a long line wherever he wishes to go. (*Grimm. Op. cit., p.* 282. "The Golden Goose.") Marama-kiko-hura by her enchantments fixed a boat so firmly to the earth that no human strength could move it. (*Sir George Grey. Op. cit., p.* 145.)

The master smith's three wishes all refer to this power of binding others by a spell. "Well," said the smith, "first and foremost, I wish that any one whom I ask to climb up into the pear-tree that stands outside by the wall of my forge, may stay sitting there till I ask him to come down again. The second which I wish is, that any one whom I ask to sit down in my easy chair which stands inside the workshop yonder, may stay sitting there till I ask him to get up. Last of all, I wish that any one whom I ask to creep into the steel purse which I have in my pocket, may stay in it till I give him leave to creep out again." (*Dasent. Popular Tales from the Norse, p.* 123. Compare "The Mastermaid," *p.* 96.)

[33] Compare this treatment of Umkxakaza with the method adopted by Hacon Grizzlebeard to subdue "the proud and pert princess for whom no suitor was good enough." (*Dasent. Popular Tales from the Norse, p.* 50.)

si ti, Pemba." Wa pemba. A ti amakqabunga, "Tata ikanzi, u li beke eziko." Wa ti Umkxakaza, "A ngi kw azi ukupeka." A ti amakqabunga, "Si ze s' azi uma a u kw azi ukupeka; kepa si . ti, Peka." Wa li beka eziko, wa tela amanzi. A ti amakqabunga, "Hamba, u yo'kcapuna amabele esilulwini kweuu, u zo'utela lapa eziko." Wa ye wa wa kcapuna amabele, wa tela eziko. A hlala; za vutwa izinkobe. A ti, "Zibukula ilitshe, u gaye izinkobe." Wa ti, "A ngi kw azi ukugaya, ng' umntwana wenkosi. Bheka ni,"—e ba tshengisa izandhla, ngokuba inzipo zake za zinde kakulu. La tata umkonto, la ti, "Leti izandhla lapa kumina." La zi nquma inzipo ngomkonto, la ti, "Gaya ke." Wa ti Umkxakaza, "A ngi kw azi, ng' umntwana wenkosi." A ti amakqabunga, "Si ze s' azi uma a u kw azi ukugaya, nokuba u umntwana wenkosi." L' esuka elinye ikqabunga, la zibukula ilitshe, la tata imbokondo, la tata inkobe, la gaya, la ti, "Bheka, ku tiwa ukugaya." L' esuka, la ti, "Gaya." Wa gaya umkcaba, wa muningi kakulu. A ti, "Tata isikamba sakwenu samasi, u beke lapa." Wa si tata. A ti, "Tata ukamba olukulu, u beke lapa." Wa lu tata. A ti amakqabunga, "Lu geze." Wa lu geza. A ti amakqabunga, "Hamba u kete igula elikulu emaguleni akwenu, u lete

but we say, Light a fire." She lighted a fire. The leaves said, "Take a cooking-pot and place it on the hearth." Umkxakaza said, "I cannot cook." The leaves replied, "We already knew that you could not cook; but we say, Cook." She put the pot on the fire, and poured water into it. The leaves said, "Go and bring some corn from your corn-basket, and come and pour it into the pot." She went and fetched some corn, and put it on the fire. They sat; the corn was boiled. They said, "Turn up the millstone, and grind the boiled corn." She replied, "I cannot grind, I am the king's child. Look here," — showing them her hands, for her nails were very long.[34] One of the leaves took a knife and said, "Hand hither your hand to me." It cut off the nails with the knife, and said, "Now grind." Umkxakaza said, "I cannot grind; I am the king's child." The leaves said, "We already knew that you could not grind, and that you were the king's child." One of the leaves arose and turned up the millstone, and took the upper stone, and put the boiled corn on it and ground it, and said, "See, that is called grinding." It quitted the stone, and said, "Grind." She ground a large mass of corn. They said, "Take your pot of amasi, and put it here." She took it. They said, "Take a large pot and place it here." She took it. The leaves said, "Wash it." She washed it. The leaves said, "Go and pick out the milk calabash from your calabashes, and bring it here." Um-

---

[34] Chiefs and great men allow their nails to grow long; such long nails are regarded as honourable. But women are not allowed to have long nails, as they would interfere with their work. Umkxakaza being the chief's child, has allowed her nails to grow. Cutting the nails is a reproof for her idleness and uselessness.

lapa." Wa ti Umkxakaza, "Igula lakwetu likulu ; ngi nge ze nga li tata ngedwa. Li tatwa abantu abatatu." A ti amakqabunga, "Hamba, si hambe nawe." Ba puma ba hamba, ba fika ba li tata igula, b' eza nalo. A ti, "Li tulule." Wa sondeza isikamba, ba li tululela kona, na kulolo ukamba ba tululela kulona. Ba tata imbenge, ba tela umkcaba ; ba tata enye imbenge, ba zibekela umkcaba. Ba buya ba tata enye imbenge, ba zibekela amasi a sokambeni. La tata ukezo, la lw eleka ngapezulu kwembenge ; la tata ukamba namasi, li yisa kusilosimapundu.

kxakaza said, "Our milk-calabash is large ; I cannot carry it alone. It is carried by three men." The leaves said, "Go, and we will go with you." They went and fetched the calabash, and came back with it. The leaves said, "Empty it." She brought the pot near, and they poured the amasi into it ; they also poured it into the large pot. They took a basket, and placed in it some of the ground corn ; they took another basket and placed it on the top of the ground corn. Again they took another basket, and covered the amasi which was in the pot. One of the leaves took a spoon, and put it on the top of the basket ; and took the pot and the amasi to Usilosimapundu.

Usilosimapundu's eating.

La fika kuyena, wa tata umkcaba kanye nembenge kanye nembenge e zibekela umkcaba ; wa kamisa, wa ku faka esiswini, lezo 'mbenge zombili nomkcaba. Wa buye wa tata amasi e zitshekelwe ngembenge, wa faka esiswini kanye konke nokezo.

When the leaf came to him, he took the ground corn together with the basket, and together with the basket which covered the ground corn ; he opened his mouth, and put it in his stomach, both the two baskets and the ground corn. Again he took the amasi which was covered with the basket, and put it all at once into his stomach, together with the spoon.

The leaves force Umkxakaza to eat amasi.

L' enyuka la ya la ngena endhlini, la ti, "Yetula inkezo ezintatu." La ti, "Mina, nant' ukezo ; yidhla, si dhle." Wa ti Umkxakaza, "A ngi wa dhli mina amasi,

The leaf went up again and entered the house. It said, "Take down three spoons." It said, "Look here, here is a spoon ; eat, and we will eat with you." Umkxakaza said, "For my part, I do not eat amasi, for I am still under the

ngokuba ngi tombile." A ti ama-kqabunga, "Si ze s' azi ukuba u tombile, a u wa dhli amasi ; kepa si ti, Yidhla." Wa kala Umkxa-kaza-wakogingqwayo, e ti, " Hau ! We mame ! ubani o za 'kudhla amasi e tombile na ?" E tsho ngokuba kwa ku ya 'kuti, umhlana e wa dhlayo, ku hlatshwe izinkabi eziningi, ngokuba e wa nikwa uyise kahle. A ti amakqabunga, " Yidhla masinya." Wa tata ukezo ; ba dhla, ba kqeda.

obligations of puberty."[35] The leaves said, "We already knew that you were of age, and that you did not yet eat amasi ; but we say, Eat." Umkxakaza-wakogingqwayo cried, saying, "Hau ! O ! my mother ! who would eat amasi before the ceremonies of puberty are completed ?" She said this because when she should eat amasi many oxen would be slaughtered, because it would be given her properly by her father. The leaves said, "Eat immediately." She took a spoon ; they ate all the amasi.

They spoil the village, and Usilosimapundu devours everything in it.

'Euka a ya endhlini e sesangwe-ni. A fike a kipa izimbiza ezi notshwala, ezinye zi nesijingi, na-makcansi, nezitebe ; konke oku sendhlini a yisa esangweni. Loku umuzi wa umkulu, a kipa umuzi wonke izinto, e nga shiyi nalunye uluto endhlini. Ku te lapa e se ya 'kukipa kabo-mkxakaza, wa ti Umkxakaza, " Ni ze ni ngi shiyele umpanjana, u semsamo, u vune-kiwe ; no'ubona mncane." A ya a kipa ; a shiya izimbiza ezinkulu kakulu zi notshwala obu voviwe ; a shiya wona ke umpanjana. 'Euka a ya esangweni. Konke

The leaves went down to the house which was near the gate-way. As soon as they arrived, they took out the pots containing beer, and pots which contained the boiled meal, and mats and vessels ; everything that was in the house they took to the gateway. And though the village was large, they took out the things from the whole village, and did not leave anything in a single house. When they were about to take the things from the house of Umkxakaza's mother, Umkxakaza said, "Just leave for me the little pot,[36] it is in the upper part of the house, it is luted down with cowdung ; you will see it, it is little." They went and took out the things ; but they left the very large pots which contain-ed beer which was strained ;[37] they left too the little pot. They went down to the gateway.

[35] That is, she had not quitted the umgonqo, and was still bound by the customs which are observed on coming to puberty, one of which is, that the young woman is not to eat amasi until she is called by her father to quit the umgonqo. When she comes out, they slaughter for her a bullock (*inkomo yo-kwemula*), the caul of which is placed over her shoulders and breasts ; the head is shaved, and the whole body bathed ; she dances, and then she can eat amasi.

[36] The natives, not having boxes or cupboards, keep their ornaments, &c., in pots, or in sacks made of skins.

[37] "Beer which was strained,"—that is, already fit for use.

loko okwa kitshwa kulowo 'muzi wa ku dhla, wa ku kqeda Usilosimapundu. Kodwa wa e nga hlafuni, wa e ġwinya nje.

Everything that was taken out of the village Usilosimapundu entirely ate up. But he did not chew it, he merely swallowed it.

The leaves drink.

Kwa ze kwa pela izinto ezi kitshwe kulowo 'muzi, e nġ' esutanga Usilosimapundu. 'Enyuka amakqabunga, a fika, a ngena endhlini lapa e shiye kona izimbiza ezimbili ezi notshwala; l' esuka elinye ikqabunga, la ponseka kwenye imbiza, nelinye la ponseka kwenye. Kepa ekupumeni kwawo ezimbizeni amakqabunga, izimbiza zombili za zize. A zi tata, a zi yisa esangweni kusilosimapundu. Wa fika wa zi tata zombili, wa zi faka emlonyeni, wa gwinya.

At length all the things which were in that village were taken out, but Usilosimapundu was not satisfied. The leaves went up and entered the houses where they had left two pots of beer; one of the leaves threw itself into one of the pots, and the other cast itself into the other; and when the two leaves came out of the pots, both pots were empty. They took them and carried thèm to the gateway to Usilosimapundu. He took them both, and put them in his mouth, and swallowed them.

Umkxakaza goes to Usilosimapundu.

Wa ti umlomo kasilosimapundu wa zamazama ngamandhla; wa ti, "Yeuka ke,' mkxakaza-wakogingqwayo." Umkxakaza wa ngena endhlini, wa tata umpanjana, wa u sibukula, wa kipa itusi lomzimba wake, wa li faka emzimbeni; wa kipa isikcamelo sake setusi; wa kipa ingubo yake yetusi; wa kipa ukcansi lwake lwetusi; wa kipa induku yake yetusi; wa kipa umuntsha wake wezindondo, wa binca, wa pumela pandhle; w' e ma e bambe ingubo yake nesikcamelo sake, 'emi ngokcansi lwake na ngenduku yake. Wa ti Usilosimapundu, "A u fulatele ke,

The mouth of Usilosimapundu moved with rapidity; he said, "Come down now then, Umkxakaza-wakogingqwayo." Umkxakaza went into the house, and took the little pot, and uncovered it; she took out the brazen ornaments for her body, and put them on; she took out her brazen pillow;[38] she took out her garment ornamented with brass; and her sleeping mat ornamented with brass; she took her walking stick of brass; she took out her petticoat ornamented with brass beads; she dressed herself and went outside; she stood holding her garment and pillow, resting on her sleeping mat, and rod. Usilosimapundu said, "Just turn your back to me,

---

[38] The native pillow is generally made of some tree; a fantastic piece is often chosen, with three or four branches, which, when cut, resembles a little stool; sometimes it is a mere block of wood. The princess is represented as having a brazen pillow.

mkxakaza-wakogingqwayo." Wa fulatela. Wa ti, "A u penduke ke, mkxakaza - wakogingqwayo." Wa penduka. Wa ti Usilosimapundu, "A u *h*leke ke, mkxakaza-wakogingqwayo." Kepa Umkxakaza a ka tandanga uku*h*leka, ngokuba wa e *h*lupeka e shiya uyise non*i*na nokubusa kwake. Wa ti Usilosimapundu, "Yeuka ke, mkxakaza - wakogingqwayo." W' euka wa fika kusilosimapundu.

Umkxakaza-wakogingqwayo." She turned her back to him. He said, "Now turn again, Umkxakaza-wakogingqwayo." She turned. Usilosimapundu said, "Just laugh now, Umkxakaza-wakogingqwayo." But Umkxakaza did not wish to laugh, for she was in trouble, because she was leaving her father and mother and her princely position. Usilosimapundu said, "Come down now, Umkxakaza-wakogingqwayo." She went down to Usilosimapundu.

Her sister and mother have a presentiment of evil, and hasten home.

Kepa ngokweuka kwake kwa ku nga ti intombazana yakwabo ya i zwile emfuleni ; ya sukuma ngamand*h*la nesigubu, ya kupuka. Nonina kwa ku nga ti u zwile, ngokuba wa shiya abantu bonke emuva aba be hamba naye.

But by her going down it was as if her little sister at the river felt her departure ;[39] she started up suddenly with her water-vessel, and went up to the village. And it was as if her mother felt it, for she left all the people behind which were walking with her.[40]

Usilosimapundu runs off with Umkxakaza.

Wa kwela Umkxakaza-wakogingqwayo. U te e s' and' ukukwela, w' esuka masinyane Usilosimapundu, wa gijima ngamand*h*la. Ku te lapa e ti site ngentaba intombazana ya ku bona oku sitelayo, kepa a ya kw azi uma ku ini na. Kanti nonina ku te ku sitela wa e ku bona ; kepa a k' azanga uma ku ini na.

Umkxakaza wakogingqwayo mounted on Usilosimapundu. As soon as she had mounted, Usilosimapundu speedily ran off. When he was just becoming hidden behind a hill, the sister saw something which was disappearing, but did not know what it was. And the mother too, when it was becoming concealed, saw it ; but did not know what it was.

[39] "Felt her departure,"—was sensible of her departure. There is an allusion here to what is called sympathy or presentiment, by which a person is impressed with a feeling that he must go to a certain place, or that something is about to happen to a certain person which requires his immediate presence, &c.

[40] The sympathetic impression of the mother has its correspondence not only in the legends of other people as the relic of an old and effete faith, but to the present day the reality of such impressions forms a part of the creed not only of the natives of South Africa, but of a large number of educated people in all parts of the world. We cannot enter into the consideration of such a question here, further than to remark that it rarely happens that a wide-spread belief is without any foundation In facts, badly observed, it may be, and worse interpreted, but still facts, which it is always worth while to examine, to discuss, and to classify.

The sister and mother reach the town together.

Ba fika kanyekanye ekaya iutombi nonina. Unina wa bona utango ekceleni lw apukile; wa ti, "Ku ini o be ku lapa na?" Wa ti Ubalatusi, "Ngi ti isilwanyazane okwa d*h*liwa inkomo zaso." Wa ti unina, "U b' u ye ngapi wena na?" Wa ti, "Ngi tunywe amakqabunga ukuka 'manzi ngesigubu emfuleni. Kwa fike kw' ala ukuba ngi suke." Unina wa ti, "Maye! Kepa ni ti u se kona umntanami lapa ekaya na? Ini e ngi te, ngi vela lapaya, ya i ti site lapaya na?" Wa gijima unina, wa ye wa ngena emgonqweni; wa fika e nge ko. Wa puma, wa ngena kwenye ind*h*lu; wa funyana e nge ko. Wa ngena kwenye; wa funyana e nge ko. Wa gijima ngejubane, wa pindela emuva emadodeni, wa ti, "Tshetsha ni; umntanami u mukile nesilwanyazane o kwa tatwa inkomo zaso." Ba ti, "U si bonile ini na?" Wa ti, "Ku kona oku sitele ngentaba lapa ngi vela ngasekaya. Futi umntanami a ka se ko ekaya."

They arrived home both together, the girl and her mother. The mother saw the fence broken down on one side; she said, "What has been here?" Ubalatusi said, "I say it was the beast whose cattle were taken away." The mother said, "Where had you gone?" She said, "I had been sent by the leaves to fetch water with a vessel from the river. On my arrival I was unable to get away again." Her mother said, "Alas! but do you say that my child is still here at home? What was that which became hidden yonder, as I reached that place yonder?" The mother ran, and entered the umgonqo; on her arrival she was not there. She went into another house; she did not find her there. She went into another; she did not find her there. She ran swiftly back again to the men, and said, "Make haste; my child is taken away by the beast who was plundered of his cattle." They said, "Have you seen him?" She replied, "There is something which disappeared behind the hill as I came near home. And my child is no longer there."

The king and his army arm, and pursue the beast.

Ba hamba ba fika ekaya, ba *h*loma bonke. Ba' ya ba hamba ngomkondo waso; ba si bona, ba ya kusona, si mi, si ba lindile. Ba fika kusona, sa *h*leka, sa ti, "Yenza ni ke bo; yenza ni masinya, ngi hambe; li tshonile." Ba ponsa, ba ponsa. Omunye umkonto wa ponseka esizibeni; omunye wa ponseka etsheni; omunye wa wela esikoteni; omunye wa

They went home, and all armed. They set out on the tracks of the beast; they saw it, they went to it, it having stood still and waited for them. They came to it; it laughed and said, "Do what you are going to do; do it quickly, that I may go; the sun has set." They hurled and hurled their spears. One spear was thrown into a pool; another on a rock; another fell in the grass; another

wela e*h*latini; yonke ya pela i nga gwazanga 'luto. Ba pelelwa imikonto. Sa ti isilwane, "Hamba ni, ni yo'*h*loma futi." Ba buyela ekaya, ba yo'u*h*loma. Ba buya ba ponsa; kw enze njalo futi; a ba gwazanga 'luto. Ba ti, "Se s' a-*h*lulekile." Wa ti Usilosimapundu, "Sala ni ku*h*le."

fell in the forest; all were used, without stabbing anything. They had not a single spear left. The beast said, "Go and arm again." They went home to arm. Again they hurled their spears; it happened again as before; they did not stab any thing. They said, "At length we are worsted." Usilosimapundu said, "Good by."

The army tries in vain to rescue Umkxakaza.

Ba kala abantu bonke, be ti, "A ku m e*h*lise." Wa vuma ke, w' e*h*la, e ti, "Ye*h*lika ke." Ba m anga, be kala, naye e kala. Ya m faka pakati impi yonke yakubo Umk*x*akaza. Kepa sa ti ukubona isilo, sa ti, "Kanti ba ya funa ukumuka naye." Sa penduka, sa ba dabula pakati; kwa ku nga ti ku kona oku m ponsa pezulu Umk*x*akaza; sa penduka naye, sa hamba naye.

All the people cried, saying, "Let her come down." He assented, and she came down, on his saying, "Descend then." They kissed her, weeping, and she too weeping. The whole army of her people put Umk*x*akaza in the middle. But when the beast saw it, he said, "Forsooth they want to go off with her." He turned round, and passed through the midst of them; it was as though something threw Umk*x*akaza into the air; he turned back with her, and went away with her.

Umkxakaza's father and mother, and brother and sister, follow the beast.

Kw' esuka unina nodade wabo noyise nomne wabo, be si landela. Ba hamba, ku ti lapa si lele kona, nabo ba lale. Ku se si vuka, nabo ba hambe naso. Unina e hamba e kala. Kepa uyise nomne wabo nodade wabo ba katala, ba buyela emuva. Unina wa hamba naso. Ba ye ba lala. Wa ti Usilosimapundu wa ka imfe nombila, wa pa unina kamk*x*akaza. Wa d*h*la.

Her mother and sister, and father and brother, followed the beast. They went on, and where the beast rested, there they too rested. In the morning when he awoke, they too went with him. The mother went weeping. But the father and brother and sister were tired and turned back. Her mother accompanied the beast. They went some distance, and rested. Usilosimapundu plucked sugarcane and maize, and gave it to the mother of Umk*x*akaza. She ate.

The mother also, being tired, turns back.

Kwa sa Usilosimapundu e hamba naye, unina kamkxakaza wa hamba. Wa ze wa katala, wa ti, a si m eꞵlise Umkxakaza, a m bone. Sa ti, "Yeꞵlika ke, mkxakaza-wakogingqwayo ; yeꞵlika, a ku bone unyoko." W' eꞵlika. Ba kala bobabili nonina. Wa m anga unina, e ti, "Hamba kuꞵle ke, mntanami."

In the morning, when Usilosimapundu set out, the mother of Umkxakaza set out. At length she was tired, and asked the beast to allow Umkxakaza to come down that she might see her. He replied, "Get down then, Umkxakaza-wakogingqwayo ; get down, that your mother may see you." She got down. They both wept, both she and her mother. Her mother kissed her, saying, "Go in peace, my child."

The beast takes Umkxakaza to a beautiful cave, and leaves her there.

Wa ti Usilosimapundu, "Kwela, mkxakaza." Wa kwela. Sa hamba naye, sa ya, sa m beka kude, lapa e nga s' azi uma ku pi kubo na. Sa fika enxiweni ; ku kona isiguai esikulu pakati kwenxiwa ; ekceleni kwesiguai kwa ku kona umgodi omuꞵle, u gudꞵliwe ngonwali, u kazimula kakulu pakati kwawo ; ku kona ingubo nokcansi nesikcamelo nesigubu samanzi.

Usilosimapundu said, "Get up, Umkxakaza." She got up. He went away with her, and put her afar off, where she did not know in what direction the country of her people was. He came to the site of an old village ; there was a large tobacco garden in the midst of it ; on the border of the garden there was a beautiful cave ; its floor was smeared with fat, it was very bright inside ; and there was a blanket and sleeping mat there, a pillow, and a vessel of water.

The beast's parting address.

Wa ti Usilosimapundu, "Hlala lapa ke, mkxakaza-wakogingqwayo. Ngi ti uyiꞵlo ngi mu dꞵlile kakulu, ngokuba uma w ende be ya 'uzuza izinkomo eziningi ngawe. Kepa ngi mu dꞵlile, ngokuba a u sa yi 'ku m bona ; naye a ka sa yi 'ku ku bona. Sala lapa ke. Uyiꞵlo wa ngi dꞵla inkomo zami eziningi ; nami ke ngi mu dꞵlile."

Usilosimapundu said, "Stay here, Umkxakaza-wakogingqwayo. I say, I have spoiled your father excessively ; for when you married, he would have got many cattle for you. And I have spoiled him, for you will never see him again, and he will never see you. Stay here then. Your father spoiled me by taking away my many cattle ; and now I have spoiled him."

Umkxakaza sleeps alone in the cave.

Wa hamba ke Usilosimapundu, w' emuka. Wa sala wa *h*lala yedwa lapa, e *h*lezi nemfe imbili nezikwebu zombila ezine a zi piwe Usilosimapundu. Wa *h*lala, wa ze wa lala kona emgodini. Kwa ti kusasa wa vuka w' etamela ilanga. Wa tata imfe, wa y apula, wa i la*h*la ; wa y apula, wa i la*h*la ; wa shiya ilungu la ba linye ; wa li *h*luba, wa li d*h*la. Wa tata umbila, wa w osa, wa w apula wa w apula, wa d*h*la isinqamu esi pakati, wa u la*h*la wonke kanye nemfe.

So Usilosimapundu departed. And she remained there alone, with two sugarcanes and four ears of maize which Usilosimapundu had given her. She sat until she lay down to sleep there in the cave. In the morning she awoke and sat in the sun. She took a sugarcane, and broke off a joint, and threw it away. She broke off another, and threw it away ; she left one joint only, she peeled it, and ate it. She took the ears of maize, and roasted them ; she rubbed off the grain, she rubbed off the grain, and ate the portion which was in the middle, and threw the rest with the sugarcane.[41]

Umkxakaza is frightened by the approach of a strange being.

Kwa ti emini, se li balele, wa bona uluto lu za kude ; ngokuba kwa ku senkangala ; ku kona umuti umunye, umuti nje. Kwa ye, kwa *h*lala pansi kwawo lowo 'muti. Wa buye wa ku bona, ku za ku k*x*uma. Wa ya wa ngena emgodini Umk*x*akaza. Kwa ngena esiguaini ; kwa hamba, ku ka uguai. Ku ti lapa ku bona inyawo, kw esabe ; ku bheke, ku buye ku ke futi uguai, kwa ye kwa m beka ngapand*h*le kwesiguai. Kwa ya emgodini. Wa ku bona Umk*x*akaza-wakoging*q*wayo ; wa sukuma, wa veza isand*h*la ; kwa bona isand*h*la, kwa baleka, kwa shiya uguai. Kwa hamba, kwa ye kwa tshona. Wa sale wa *h*lala kwa ze kwa *h*lwa.

At noon, the sun being now bright, she saw something coming in the distance ; for it was on the high land ; there was there one tree, one tree only. The thing went and sat under the tree. Again she saw it approaching by leaps. Umk*x*akaza went into the cave. The thing entered the tobacco garden ; it went plucking the tobacco. When it saw footprints, it was frightened ; it looked, and again plucked the tobacco, and went and put it outside the garden. It entered the cave. When Umk*x*akaza-wakoging*q*wayo saw it, she arose and thrust out her hand ; it saw the hand, and fled, and left the tobacco. It went and disappeared over a hill. She remained till it was dark.

---

[41] Great people and men select the joints of the sugarcane which are in the middle, rejecting both the upper and lower joints. In like manner chiefs and great men reject the grains of maize which are at the ends of the ear, selecting those only which are in the middle.

Two of these strange beings visit the cave.

Kwa sa kusasa wa puma, wa *h*lala pand*h*le Umk*x*akaza ; wa bona futi ku za ku kubili, ku hamba kŭ k*x*uma ; kwa ye kwa *h*lala emtunzini. Kwa buye kw' esuka kwa ya esiguaini. Wa ngena emgodini Umk*x*akaza. Kwa ngena, kwa ka uguai ; kwa ti loku a ku bonile izolo, kwa ka kw etuka, kw esaba ; ku ti, "Hau, nyawo, nyawo, ti vela pi na ?" Ku ti okunye, "U ti bona pi na ?" Ku ti, "Nati."[42] Kwa ye kwa m beka uguai ngapand*h*le. Kwa buye kw' ez' emgodini. Wa sukuma Umk*x*akaza, wa veza izand*h*la ezimbili. (Wa bona ukuba Amad*h*lungund*h*lebe.) A bona

In the morning Umk*x*akaza went and sat outside ; again she saw two things coming, proceeding by leaps ; they went and sat in the shade of the tree. Again they arose and went to the tobacco garden. Umk*x*akaza went into the cave. On entering the garden they plucked the tobacco ; the one which she saw the day before plucked starting and afraid ; it said, "O, footprints, footprints, whence did they come ?" The other said, "Where did you see them ?" It replied, "There." They went and put the tobacco outside. Again they entered the cave. Umk*x*akaza arose and thrust out both hands. (She perceived that they were Amadhlungundhlebe.[43]) When they saw the hands,

[42] These creatures are represented as talking a strange dialect ; it resembles that of the Amaswazi ; and is introduced to make them appear ridiculous.

[43] Keightley has remarked in his Fairy Mythology, p. 28 :—"An extensive survey of the regions of fancy and their productions will incline us rather to consider the mental powers of man as having a uniform operation under every sky, and under every form of political existence, and to acknowledge that identity of invention is not more to be wondered at than identity of action." However comprehensive we may be disposed to make this sentiment, there will still be left many tales in the folk-lore of different peoples so similar not only in their general characteristics, but also in their details ; and also some things so strange, that one feels compelled to refer them to a common origin. This of Half-men belongs to this class. It is so strange, wild, and eccentric, that it is not easy to conceive that it could arise spontaneously in two minds. Yet we find allusions to "One-legged men" in various authors.

Pliny mentions a nation of Monosceli. The Marquis of Hastings states that during his sojourn in India he found the germ of fact from which many of the most incredible tales of ancient history has grown. "A Grecian author mentions a people who had only one leg. An embassy from the interior was conducted into the presence of the viceroy, and he could by no persuasion prevail upon the obsequious minister to use more than one of his legs, though he stood during the whole of the protracted audience."

It is quite possible that such a custom as that of standing on one leg as a ceremony of etiquette should become the starting point of the legends, in which we meet with the account of half-men. "The Shikk," says Lane in his notes to the Introduction to the *Arabian Nights, p.* 33, "is another demoniacal creature, having the form of half a human being, (like a man divided longitudinally ;) and it is believed that the Nesnas is the offspring of a Shikk and a human being.

"The Nesnas is described as resembling half a human being, having half a head, half a body, one arm and one leg, with which it hops with much agility." It is said to be found in several places. "It resembled a man in form, excepting that it has but half a face, which is in its breast, and a tail like that of a sheep." A kind of Nesnas is also said to inhabit "the island of Raig in the sea of Es-Seen or China, and to have wings like those of a bat."

izand*h*la, a baleka a ye a tshona.
A fike, a bika enkosini yawo, e ti,
" Ku kona oku semgodini wen-
kosi."   Ya ti inkosi yamad*h*lungu-
nd*h*lebe, " Ku njani na ? "   A ti,
" Kubili."

they fled, and disappeared behind
a hill. On reaching their chief,
they told him, saying, "There is
something in the chief's cave."
The chief of the Amadhlungundhlebe said, "What is it like?"
They said, "There are two."

Many come to the cave, and Umkxakaza expects to be killed.

Kwa menywa amanye Ama-
d*h*lungund*h*lebe. Kwa sa kusasa
kwa hanjwa kwa yiwa kona emgodini wenkosi. Wa bona Um-
k*xx*akaza e vela e maningi kakulu,
wa ti, " Namu*h*la lu fikile usuku
e ngi za 'ubulawa ngalo."   A fika,
a *h*lala pansi kwomtun*z*i, lapo emtunzini a e *h*lala kona, e bema
uguai ; ngezikati zonke uma e ya
'kuka uguai, a y' a *h*lala kona emtunzini. 'Esuka a ya a ngena esiguaini, a ka uguai, a m beka ngapand*h*le ; ngokuba inkosi yakona
emad*h*lungund*h*lebeni ya i misele
ukuba umgodi wayo u tshanclwe
ngezikati zonke ; kepa i misele
bonke abantu aba ya 'kutshanela
lowo 'mgodi ba k*q*ale ngokuka
uguai, b' amuke uguai, ba m beke
ngapand*h*le. Kwa buz*w*a kulawo
amabili Amad*h*lungund*h*lebe, kwa
tiwa, " Ni ku bone pi na ? "   A
ti, " Be ku vele emgodiui."   Kwa
tiwa, " Hamba ni, ni ye, ni
lunguze emnyango ; ni bone uma
ku kona na ?"   A ya, e nyonyoba,
'esaba, a lunguza, 'a*h*luleka uku-
bonisisa, ngokuba umzimba wake
wa u kazimula. A buyela emuva,
a *t*i, " Kunyc, ku ya kazimula ; a
si ku bonisisi."   Ya ti inkosi
yamad*h*lungund*h*lebe, " A si tsho
kanyckanye, si ti, ' Umuntu, isilo
ini na ?"   A tsho ke onke, a ti,
" U umuntu u 'silo u ini na ?"
Wa ti Umk*xx*akaza, " Ngi umu-

Other Amadhlungundhlebe were
summoned ; and in the morning
they went to the chief's cave.
Umk*xx*akaza saw very many coming, and said, "The day has now
arrived in which I shall be killed."
When they reached the tree they
sat in the shade, there in the shade
where they sat and took snuff ;
always when they went to pluck
tobacco, they sat there in the
shade. They arose and went into
the tobacco garden, and plucked
tobacco, and put it outside ; for
the chief of the country of the
Amadhlungundhlebe had ordered
that his cave should be regularly
swept ; and he had ordered that
all people who went to sweep the
cave should begin with plucking
tobacco, and take and put it outside the garden. They enquired
of the two Amadhlungundhlebe
where they had seen it ? They
replied, "It appeared in the cave."
They were told to go and look into
the doorway, and see if it was
there. They went stealthily, being
afraid, and looked in ; they were
unable to see clearly, for her body
glistened. They came back, and
said, "It is one, it glistens ; we
cannot see it clearly." The chief
of the Amadhlungundhlebe said,
" Let us say all together, ' Is it a
man or a beast?' " So all shouted,
saying, "Are you a man or a
beast?" Umk*xx*akaza replied, " I

ntu." A ti, " Puma, si ku bone."
Wa ti Umkxakaza, " A ngi tandi
ukupuma, ngokuba ng' umntwana
wenkosi." Kwa tunywa amanye
Amad*h*lungund*h*lebe, kwa tiwa, a
wa gijime ngamand*h*la a yo'utata
inkomo, inkabi enkulu, a gijime, a
buye nayo. Ya fika inkabi, ya
*h*latshwa. Wa puma ke Umkxakaza-wakogingqwayo, e pete ingubo
yake nokcansi lwake nesikcamelo
sake nenduku yake, e bincile umuntsha wezindoudo. Wa beka pansi emnyango ingubo nesikcamelo,
w' ema ngenduku, nokcansi w' e-
ma ngalo. Ya ti inkosi yama-
d*h*lungund*h*lebe, " Penduka." Wa
penduka Umkxakaza. A ti Ama-
d*h*lungund*h*lebe, " Yeka! Uluto
lu lu*h*le! Kepa yeka, imilentelente!" A pind' a tsho e ti,
" Nga e ba mu*h*le uma ka si yo
imilentelente." A ti, a ka ngene
end*h*lini. 'Emuka onke, a pindela
emuva.

am a human being." They said,
" Come out, that we may see you."
Umkxakaza said, " I do not like
to come out, for I am a chief's
child." The chief sent some Amadhlungundhlebe, telling them to
run swiftly and fetch a bullock—a
large ox—and run back with it.
When the ox came it was slaughtered. Then Umkxakaza-wakogingqwayo came out, carrying her
blanket and her sleeping mat, and
pillow and rod, being girded with
her petticoat which was ornamented with brass beads. She
put down at the doorway the
blanket and pillow, and rested on
her rod, and on her sleeping mat
she rested too. The chief of the
Amadhlungundhlebe said, " Turn
your back towards us." Umkxakaza turned her back to them.
The chief of the Amadhlungundhlebe said, " Turn round."
Umkxakaza turned. The Amadhlungundhlebe said, " Oh! The
thing is pretty! But oh the two
legs!" Again they said, " It
would be pretty but for the two
legs." They told her to go into
the cave; and they all went away.

The Amadhlungundhlebe take away Umkxakaza.

Kwa fika kwa menywa Ama-
d*h*lungund*h*lebe amaningi. Kwa
sa kusasa, kwa yiwa kuyena Umkxakaza, ku petwe ulembu olubo-
nakalisa umzimba uma umuntu
e lw embete. A fika, a *h*lala emtunzini, e bema uguai. Wa ti
uma a wa bone Umkxakaza, wa
ti, " So ku ziwa 'kubulala mina."
A fika esiguaini, a ka uguai, a m
beka ngapand*h*le. A ngena, a ya
emgodini, a ti, a ka pume. Wa
puma; wa nikwa ulembu, wa

Many Amadhlungundhlebe were
called together. In the morning
they went to Umkxakaza; they
carried a veil through which, if
any one put it on, the body could
be seen. They came and sat in
the shade and took snuff. When
Umkxakaza saw them, she said,
" They are now coming to kill
me." They came to the tobacco
garden, they plucked tobacco, and
put it outside the garden. They
entered the cave, and told her to
come out. She went out; they
gave her the veil; she put it on,

binca lona, e m buka e ti, "Yeka! uluto nga lu lu*h*le,—kepa yeka imilentelente!" E tsho ngokuba we e nemilenze emibili nezand*h*la ezimbili; ngokuba wona a e fana —uma ku *h*linzwa inkomo yabelungu e datshulwe u*h*langoti nolunye u*h*langoti, wona Amad*h*lungund*h*lebe a e u*h*langoti lwa-nganxanye, lu nge ko olunye u*h*langoti. Wa sinelwa Umkxakaza a wona Amad*h*lungund*h*lebe. A sina a kqeda, a m tata, a ya naye ekaya.

they looking at her and saying, "Oh, it would be a pretty thing, —but, oh, the two legs!" They said thus because she had two legs and two hands; for they are like, —if an ox of the white man is skinned and divided into two halves, the Amadhlungundhlebe were like one side, there not being another side. The Amadhlungundhlebe danced for Umkxakaza. When they had finished dancing, they went home with her.

Umkxakaza is beloved by the chief, and called his child.

Wa bona umuzi wenkosi yamad*h*lungund*h*lebe, wa ti, "We! yeka lo 'muzi; umkulu njengokababa." Ngokuba wa mkulu kakulu. Wa ya wa bekwa end*h*lini e ngasen*h*la; kwa *h*latshwa izinkomo eziningi, e d*h*la inyama. Ku tiwa u umntwana wenkosi, ngokuba inkosi yamad*h*lungund*h*lebe ya i m tanda kakulu, i ti, umntwana wayo. E *h*lala esigod*h*lweni Umkxakaza esimnyama; ku kona ngenzansi esim*h*lope.

When she saw the village of the chief of the Amadhlungundhlebe, she said, "Alas! oh this village; it is large like that of my father." For it was very great. She was placed in a house at the top of the village; many cattle were killed, and she ate meat. She was called the chief's child, for the chief of the Amadhlungundhlebe loved her very much, and called her his child. Umkxakaza lived in the dark palace; there was a white palace at the lower part of the village.[44]

Umkxakaza becomes very fat, and the Amadhlungundhlebe wish to kill her.

Wa ze wa kulupala kakulu, w' a*h*luleka ukuhamba Umkxakaza. A ti uma e pumela pand*h*le esigod*h*lweni, a ti lapa e hamba e pakati emkatini wesim*h*lope nesimnyama a katale, a buyele end*h*lini. Ku ti uma e suka pansi ku sale isikcibi samafuta. Inkosi yamad*h*lungund*h*lebe i si puze isi-

At length Umkxakaza was very fat, and unable to walk. When she left the palace, ou getting halfway between the white and the dark palace, she was tired, and returned to the house. When she rose up there remained a pool of fat. The chief of the Amadhlungundhlebe used to drink the pool

[44] *Isigodhlo* is the dwelling, consisting of several huts, which belong to the chief—the royal buildings. "The dark isigodhlo" is that part where no visitors are allowed to enter; "the white isigodhlo" is entered by those who are called by the chief.

kcibi samafuta a puma kumkxakaza, ngokuba isizwe samadhlungundhlebe sa si dhla abantu. Ba ti abantu, "Nkos', a ka dhliwe, a kqonkqwe amafuta, loku amafuta e se pelela pansi nje." Kepa inkosi yamadhlungundhlebe ya i m tanda kakulu Umkxakaza-wakogingqwayo; i ti inkosi yamadhlungundhlebe, "U ya 'udhliwa ngi pi mina na?" A ti Amadhlungundhlebe, "O, nkos', loku ku isilima nje na? Into e nga sa kw azi ukuhamba i za 'kwenza ni i kcita amafuta enkosi?"

of fat which came from Umkxakaza, for the nation of the Amadhlungundhlebe used to eat men. The people said, "O chief, let her be eaten, and the fat melted down, for the fat is being wasted on the ground." But the chief of the Amadhlungundhlebe loved Umkxakaza wakogingqwayo very much, and said, "When she is eaten, where shall I be?"[45] The Amadhlungundhlebe said, "O chief, since she is a mere deformity? Of what use is a thing which can no longer walk, which is wasting the fat of the chief?"

Preparations are made for melting down Umkxakaza.

Ya ze ya vuma inkosi, inyanga se zintatu be i ncenga, be ti, "A ku kqonkqwe amafuta enkosi." Ya vuma ke. Kwa menywa abantu abaningi bamadhlungundhlebe, ba ya ba teza izinkuni eziningi; kw' embiwa umgodi omkulu; kwa baswa umlilo omkulu; kwa tatwa udingezi olukulu, lwa bekwa pezu kwezinkuni ezi basiwe.

At length the king assented, they having continued to beseech him for three months, saying, "Let the fat of the chief be melted down." So he assented. Many people of the Amadhlungundhlebe were summoned; they went and fetched much firewood; a great hole was dug; a large fire was kindled; a large sherd was taken and put on the fire which was kindled.

Umkxakaza, by her incantations, raises a tempest, which destroys many of her enemies.

La li balele kakulu, ku nge ko 'lifu nalinye. Lwa ze lwa ba bomvu udingezi. Kwa ti uma so lu bomvu kakulu, wa ya wa bizwa Umkxakaza; wa ya, be hamba naye. Kwa ti uma e sesangweni wa bheka, wa bona abantu be baningi kakulu; wa hlabela, wa ti,

"We, zulu le. Wo, mayoya, we.

It was very bright; there was not a single cloud. At length the sherd was red. When it was very red, Umkxakaza was called; she went with them. When she was at the gateway, she looked; she saw that there were very many people; she sang, saying,

"Listen,[46] yon heaven. Attend; mayoya, listen.

[45] That is, "So long as I live you will not touch her."

[46] *We!* is an interjection by which the attention of a person is arrested. *Wo!* is an interjection in which a kind of threat is implied if the requisite attention is not given. *Mayoya* is a kind of chorus. The whole song is addressed by Umkxakaza to the sky, as though she was its lord; it is a complaint that it is merely acting in an ordinary way, and not in the way she wishes, viz., so as to destroy her enemies. *Emabilweni,* lit, in the throat.

We, zulu. Li nga dumi noku- duma.	Listen, heaven. It does not thunder with loud thunder.
Li dumel' emabilweni. L' enza ni ?	It thunders in an undertone. What is it doing ?
Li dumela ukuna nokupendula."	It thunders to produce rain and change of season."[47]

[47] The belief in the power possessed by human beings of controlling the elements by incantations and other means, is as wide spread probably as the human race. At a future time we shall speak of the superstitious faith of the natives in weather-doctors, which will probably throw some light on the belief as it exists among civilized nations as a relic of the past, in novels or old legends. We would just allude to the curious fact that a modern philosophic thinker of no ordinary power, Professor Mansel, has thrown out the idea that it is not out of the bounds of possibility that man's scientific knowledge may one day be such as to enable him to do that which our forefathers were disposed to relegate to the domain of sorcery and witchcraft. He says :—"It is even conceivable that the progress of science may disturb the regularity of occurrence of natural phenomena. If men were to acquire vast power of producing atmospheric phenomena, the periodical recurrence of such phenomena would become more irregular, being producible at the will of this or that man. There is a remarkable note in Darwin's *Botanic Garden (Canto* iv., *l.* 320), in which the author conjectures that changes of wind may depend on some minute chemical cause, which, if it were discovered, might probably, like other chemical causes, be governed by human agency."

Thus the wisdom of the nineteenth century is leading men back again to the dreams of the childhood of our race.

We shall refer the reader to a few instances of the superstitious belief in power to control the elements.

We are told on the authority of a Bishop, Olaus Magnus, that Eric, King of Sweden, "was in his time held second to none in the magical art ; and he was so familiar with the evil spirits whom he worshipped, that what way soever he turned his cap, the wind would presently blow that way. For this he was called Windy-cap." *(Sir Walter Scott.* "The Pirate," Note 9.*)*

It is probable that this old legend of Eric, "Windy-cap," has come down to us in the saying, a "capful of wind." When the old heathen superstitions had been displaced by the preaching of Christianity, they disappeared rather in external form than in reality, and still held their place in the hearts of the people ; and the powers formerly ascribed to gods, or deified kings, or sorcerers, came to be referred to saints. Thus Langfellow,

> " Only a little hour ago
> I was whistling to Saint Antonio
> For a capful of wind to fill our sail,
> And instead of a breeze he has sent a gale."

Sir W. Scott, who appears to have no doubt that those who professed to raise and lay storms, really believed in their own powers, and therefore concludes that they were frenzied, remarks :—"It is well known that the Laplanders drive a profitable trade in selling winds." And he tells us of a Bessie Millie, at the village of Stromness, living in 1814, who helped out her subsistence by selling favourable winds to mariners ; just as in this country rain-doctors obtain large herds by selling rain.

In the Manx Legends we read of "the feats of Mannan," who,

> " From New-year-tide round to the ides of Yule,
> Nature submitted to his wizard rule :
> Her secret force he could with charms compel
> To brew a storm, or raging tempest quell."

(Elizabeth Cookson's Legends of Manx Land, p. 23.*)*

The reader is referred to the incantation of the "Reim-kennar" in Sir Walter Scott's "Pirate"; and to the mode in which she obtained

Ouke Amad*h*lungund*h*lebe a bona ilifu li lukuzela ngamand*h*la. Wa pinda Umkxakaza, wa *h*labela, wa ti,

"We, zulu le. Wo, mayoya, we.

We, zulu. Li nga dumi noku-
    duma.
Li dumel' emabilweni. L' enza
    ni ?
Li dumela ukuna nokupendula."

Izulu la *h*langanisa ngamafu ; la duma ngamand*h*la ; la na imvula enkulu. La k*c*ima udengezi ; la tata udengezi, la lu ponsa pezulu,

All the Amadhlungundhlebe saw a cloud gathering tumultuously. Umkxakaza again sang,

"Listen, yon heaven. Attend ; mayoya, listen.
Listen, heaven. It does not thunder with loud thunder.
It thunders in an undertone. What is it doing ?
It thunders to produce rain and change of season."

The whole heaven became covered with clouds ; it thundered ter- ribly ; it rained a great rain. It quenched the red hot sherd, and took it and tost it in the air ; it

"The power she did covet
    O'er tempest and wave."

Allusions to this power will be found in many of our poets. Thus in Shakspeare's "Tempest," Mira says :—

"If by thy art, my dearest father, you have
Put the wild waters in this roar, allay them :
The sky it seems would pour down stinking pitch,
But that the sea, mounting to the welkin's cheek,
Dashes the fire out."

So in H. K. White's "Gondoline," one of the witches boasts that

"She'd been to sea in a leaky sieve,
And a jovial storm had brewed."

See also *Thorpe's Yule-tide Stories*, p. 63. And for a fine description of the exertion of this power by Ngatoro, *Grey's Polynesian Mythology*, p. 140, and again *p.* 179. "Then the ancient priest Ngatoro, who was sitting at the upper end of the house, rises up, unloosens and throws off his garments and repeats his incantations, and calls upon the winds, and upon the storms, and upon the thunder and lightning, that they may all arise and destroy the host of Manaia." The storm arises in its might, and the hosts of Manaia perish.

So the elements obey the call of Hiawatha, when Pau-Puk-Keewis had found shelter from his wrath in the caverns dark and dreary of the Manito of the Mountains :—

"Then he raised his hands to heaven,
Called imploring on the tempest,
Called Waywassimo, the lightning,
And the thunder, Annemeekee ;
And they came with night and darkness,
Sweeping down the Big-Sea-Water,
From the distant Thunder Mountains."

(Longfellow's Hiawatha.)

In the legends of New Zealand we find a universal deluge ascribed to the prayer of Tawaki, "who called aloud to the gods, and they let the floods of heaven descend, and the earth was overwhelmed by the waters, and all human beings perished." (*Grey. Op. cit., p.* 61.) Compare with this the legend of St. Scolastica, who two days before her death, being unable to persuade her brother St. Benedict to remain with her a little longer, "bending her head over her clasped hands, prayed that heaven would interfere and render it impossible for her brother to leave her. Immediately there came such a furious tempest of rain, thunder, and lightning, that Benedict was obliged to delay his departure for some time." (*Mrs. Jameson's Legends of the Monastic Orders, p.* 12.)

lwa fa. Kwa ti Amad*h*lungun-
d*h*lebe a be hamba naye Umk*x*a-
kaza la wa bulala izulu, la m shiya
Umk*x*akaza ; la bulala nabanye
abantu ; ba sala abaningi nenkosi
yabo.

was broken to pieces ; the heaven[48]
killed the Amadhlungundhlebe
who were walking with Umk*x*a-
kaza, but left her uninjured ; it
killed some others also ; but many
remained with their chief.

Her enemies try again, and are destroyed.

La buya la balela nje. A ti
Amad*h*lungund*h*lebe, "A ku baswe masinyane, lu tshe masinya
udengezi ; a tatwe Umk*x*akaza a
pakanyiswe, a bekwe odengezini ;
kona e nga yi '*uh*labela." La
tshiswa udengezi ; lwa za lwa ba
bomvu. Ba ya 'ku m tata ; ba m
pakamisa. Kwa ti, lapa e sesangweni, wa bheka pezulu, wa ti,

Again the heaven became clear
and bright. The Amadhlungundhlebe said, "Let a fire be kindled immediately, that the sherd
may get hot at once ; and let Um-
k*x*akaza be taken, and raised and
placed on the sherd ; then she will
not be able to sing." The sherd
was made hot ; at length it was
red. They went to fetch her ; they
lifted her up ; when she was at the
gateway, she looked up and said,

"We, zulu le. Wo, mayoya, we.

  We, zulu. Li nga dumi noku-
    duma.
  Li dumel' emabilweni. L' enza
    ni ?
  Li dumela ukuna nokupendula."

"Listen, yon heaven. Attend ;
    mayoya, listen.
  Listen, heaven. It does not
    thunder with loud thunder.
  It thunders in an undertone.
    What is it doing ?
  It thunders to produce rain and
    change of season."

Kwa vela futi amafu. Wa pinda
Umk*x*akaza, wa ti,

"We, zulu le. Wo, mayoya, we.

  We, zulu. Li nga dumi noku-
    duma.
  Li dumel' emabilweni. L' enza
    ni ?
  Li dumela ukuna nokupendula."

Again the clouds made their appearance. Again Umk*x*akaza said,

"Listen, yon heaven. Attend ;
    mayoya, listen.
  Listen, heaven. It does not
    thunder with loud thunder.
  It thunders in an undertone.
    What is it doing ?
  It thunders to produce rain and
    change of seasou."

La na, la duma ngamand*h*la. La
i bulala inkosi yamad*h*lungund*h*lebe namanye Amad*h*lungund*h*lebe
amaningi, a fa. Kwa sala ingcozana nje. 'Esaba lawo a ingcozana

It rained and thundered terribly.
It killed the chief of the Amadhlungundhlebe, and many other
Amadhlungundhlebe ; they died ;
there remained a small number
only. The small remnant that
remained were afraid, and said,

---

[48] The heaven, that is, the lightning. But the natives speak of the heaven
as a person, and ascribe to it the power of exercising a will. They also speak
of a lord of heaven, whose wrath they deprecate during a thunder storm.

a seleyo, a ti, " A si nga be si sa m tinta ; kodwa a si 'm ncitshe ukudhla, a ze a zakce a fe."

"Let us not touch her again and again ; but let us grudge her food, until she gets thin and dies."

Umkxakaza escapes from the Amadhlungundhlebe.

Wa jabula Umkxakaza ngokuba e se m ncitsha ukudhla. Wa hlala wa ze wa zakca ; kodwa e nga zakcile, so ku pelile amafuta amaningi. Wa tata ikqoma, wa faka izingubo zake a e zi piwa inkosi yamadhlungundhlebe ; wa hamba e ku badhlile ekqomeni ; w' etwala, wa hamba e sindwa, ngokuba ezinye izingubo za z' enzwa ngendondo ; e hamba e lala endhle, ngokuba wa e saba Amadhlungundhlebe. Wa hamba isikati eside e nga dhli 'luto, wa ze wa ngena esizweni sabantu. Wa hamba e lala kusona ; enxenye komunye umuzi ba mu pa ukudhla ; enxenye kwomunye umuzi ba m ncitsha. Wa hamba wa ze wa zakca kakulu.

Umkxakaza rejoiced because they now gave her but little food. She remained until she was thin ; but she was not excessively thin, only much fat had disappeared. She took a basket, and placed in it the things which the king of the Amadhlungundhlebe had given her ; she set out when she had put them in the basket ; she carried it on her head, and went on her way burdened, for some of the garments were ornamented with brass beads. She journeyed sleeping in the open country, because she feared the Amadhlungundhlebe. She went a long time without eating, until she came among a nation of men. She travelled sleeping among them ; sometimes at one village they gave her food ; sometimes at another they refused her. She travelled until she was very thin.

She reaches her home.

Kwa ti ngolunye usuku wa vela okalweni, wa bona umuzi omkulu kakulu, wa ti, " We ! Yeka lo 'muzi ; u fana nomuzi wamadhlungundhlebe e ngi vela kuwona ; wona wa u fana nokababa." W' ehla e hona ezindhlini ezi ngasenhla ku tunqa umlilo ; wa fika esangweni, wa bona indoda i hlezi pansi kwomtunzi. Kepa inwele zayo za zi ngangezezimu. Wa dhlula nje, kodwa yena e fanisa e ti, " Songati ubaba lo."

It came to pass on a certain day she reached the top of a hill ; she saw a very large town ; she said, " Alas ! O that town ; it resembles the town of the Amadhlungundhlebe from which I come ; and that was like my father's." She went down, seeing in the houses at the top of the town the smoke of fire ; when she came to the gateway, she saw a man sitting in the shade ; but his hair was as long as a cannibal's. She merely passed on ; but she compared him, saying, " That man resembles my father."

She makes herself known to her mother.

Wa ya ngasen*h*la, e bona uma umuzi kayise. Wa fika unina e peka utshwala. Wa *h*lala pansi kwotango, wa ti, "Eh! nkosikazi! Emhhik*q*weni wako." Ba ti, "Sa u bona." Wa ti, "Yebo." Wa bona nonina e nga lungisile ekanda. Wa ti, "Kepa kulo 'muzi kw enze njani na? I naui leyo 'ndoda e sesangweni na?" Wa pendula unina, wa ti, "Wena, u vela ngapi na?" Wa ti, "Ngi vela le." Wa ti, "O, po, lapa, dade, kwa fiwa. Kw' emuka inkosazana yakwami. Uyise lowa o m bone esangweni. A u ngi boni nami ngi nje na?" Wa ti, "Y' emuka ya ya ngapi na?" Wa ti, "Ya hamba nesilwanyazane." Wa ti, "Sa si m tata pi?" Wa ti, "Wa e tombile; kwa tatwa inkomo zaso, ngokuba uyise wa e te, e nga ka tombi umntwana, wa ti, uma e se tombile, ku ya 'utatwa inkomo, a buyiswe ngazo end*h*le, zi k*c*ime ilanga. Kepa uyise a ka ze a ba nazo lezo 'nkomo; kwa ye kwa tatwa ezesilwanyazane." Ya ti intombi, "O, kepa, kanti ni kalela

She went to the upper end of the town, seeing that it was her father's. On her arrival her mother was making beer. She sat down under the wall, and said, ... "Eh! chieftainess! Give me of your umhhik*q*o."[49] They said, "Good day." She saluted in return. She saw that her mother's head was disarranged, and asked, "But what is the matter at this kraal? And what is the matter with that man at the gateway?" The mother answered, saying, "You, whence do you come?" She replied, "I come from yonder." The mother said, "O, indeed, here, princess, death entered.[50] The princess royal of my house went away. That is her father whom you saw at the gateway. Do you not see, too, in what condition I am?" She replied, "When she went away, whither did she go?" She said, "She went with the beast." She answered, "Where did he take her?" The mother said, "She was of age; the cattle of the beast were taken away; for her father had said, before she was of age, when she is of age, cattle should be taken with which to bring her home, which should darken the sun. But her father did not possess so many cattle; they went and took those of the beast." The girl said, "O, but, why do you cry

---

[49] *Umhhikqo* is beer in an early state of preparation; it is called *isijingi sobutshwala,* that is, beer-porridge. It consists of the ground mealies steeped in water till it is sour. When mealies have been ground and mixed with water and boiled, it is called *umpunga.* When crushed mealies are steeped in hot water till it is sour, it is *igwele.* When the mealies have been taken from the *igwele,* and ground, and boiled in the sour water of the *igwele,* it is *umhhikqo. Umpunga, igwele,* and *umhhikqo* are all thin porridge, somewhat of the consistence of gruel. Ground malt is added to the *umhhikqo,* and when fermentation has taken place, it is *utshwala* or beer.

[50] *Kwa fiwa,* lit., it was died.

ni, loku umntwana wenu w' enziwa i nina nje na? Na ni tatela ni inkomo zesilwanyazane? Kanti na m bulala ngamabomu." Wa ti lo 'mfazi, "Wo, yeka le 'ntwana! i bona ngoba ngi i pile umhhik*q*o wami. Se i ngi *h*leka ngomntanami e nga se ko. U kona umuntu o nga tanda uk*u*nika isilwanyazane na? Angiti u loku w' emuka umntanami lapa esizweni sikayise a ku sa buswa, se ku *h*lalwa nje na?" Wa ti, "Ngi lapa ke mina, mk*xa*kaza-wakogingq*wa*yo; noma na ngi la*h*la, ngi buyile futi mina."

then, since your child was treated badly by yourselves alone? Why did you take away the cattle of the beast? Forsooth, you killed her on purpose." The mother replied, "O, out upon the contemptible thing! it sees because I have given it my umhhik*q*o. It now laughs at me as regards my child which is dead. Does there exist a person who would be willing to give anything to the beast? From the day my child departed from the midst of her father's nation, has there been any longer any joy? do we not now just live?" She replied, "Here I am, I Umk*xa*kaza - wakogingq*wa*yo ; although you left me, here I am again."

The father summons the nation to rejoice at the return of his daughter.

Wa kala un*i*na, nabanye aba be *h*lezi emnyango. W' eza uyise e gijima, e ti, "Ni kalela ni na?" Ba ti, "Nang' Umk*xa*kaza e fikile!" Wa ti uyise, "Po, e fikile njalo ku kalelwa ni?" Wa tuma abantu uyise, wa ti, "A ba hambe isizwe sonke, be mema be t*sh*ela abantu, be ti, ' A ku gaywe utshwala ilizwe lonke, u fikile Umk*xa*kaza-wakogingq*wa*yo.' "

Her mother cried, and the others who were sitting by the door. The father came running, and saying, "Why are you crying?" They said, "Here is Umk*xa*kaza come!" Her father said, "Well, since she has thus come, why do you cry?" Her father sent men, telling them to go to the whole nation, summoning the people and telling them to make beer throughout the land, for Umk*xa*kaza-wakogingq*wa*yo had arrived.

The whole nation holds a great festival.

Kwa gaywa utshwala ilizwe lonke; kwa butwa abantu, b' eza nezinkomo, be bonga ngokuba inkosazana i fikile. Kwa *h*latshwa inkomo; kwa d*h*lalwa umkosi uyise nonina; uyise wa geka isi

Beer was made throughout the land; the people collected, bringing cattle, and rejoicing because the princess had arrived. Cattle were killed, and her father and mother had a great festival; her father cut his hair, and put on a

ɦlito, wa beka isikcokco; unina wa geka, wa beka inkeɦli. Kwa jabulwa ilizwe lonke.

head-ring ;[51] her mother cut her hair, and put on a top-knot.[51] There was rejoicing throughout the land.

Many kings come to woo Umkxakaza.

Kepa kwa ku dumile ezizweni zonke uknba i kona inkosazana i fikile, inɦle kakulu. Kwa ya inkosi, i vela kwelinye ilizwe, y' eza 'ku m kcela Umkxakaza. Uyise w' ala naye, wa ti, "U ya fika; wa e mukile nesilwanyazane; ngaloko ke a ngi tandi ukuba 'emuke; ngi ya tanda ukuɦlala ngi buse naye nje." Kw' eza amakosi amaningi; kepa uyise a fike a tsho ilizwi li be linye nje, A ze 'emuka amakosi e nga m zekanga Umkxakaza.

And it was rumoured among all the nations that the princess had returned to her home, and that she was very beautiful. A chief came from another country to ask Umkxakaza of her father. He refused, saying, "She is just come home; she was carried off by the beast; therefore I do not wish that she should go away; I wish to live and be glad with her." Many chiefs came; but her father gave them all but one answer. At length the chiefs went away, without getting Umkxakaza for a wife.

A distant king hears of her beauty, and sends an old man to fetch her.

Kepa kwa ku kona enye inkosi e kude; ya i zwe ukuba ku kona leyo 'ntombi. Ya tuma ikxeku; ya ti, "A ku ye lona." La hamba

But there was another chief of a distant country; he had heard that there was that damsel. He sent an old man; he said, "Let him go." The old man went.

[51] *The head-ring* is made by rolling together the midribs of the leaves of the vegetable ivory plant (*ingqondo zelala*) to about the size of the little finger; this is bound carefully and regularly with a small cord, and bent into a ring, which varies in size with different tribes; in this state it is called the *ukqondo*. This is sewn to the hair, and covered with the exudation of a species of coccus, called *ungiana*, or *ingiane*. The exudation is collected, and when the insect has been carefully separated, boiled to give it firmness; it is then placed on the *ukqondo*; it is black, and admits of a good polish.

I have never met with a native who could give me any account of the origin of the head-ring or *isikcokco*. It is a sign of manhood; and no one is permitted to assume it, until he has received the chief's command. It is regarded as the chief's mark, and must be treated with respect. If during a quarrel a man pluck off another's head-ring, it is regarded as a mark of contempt for the chief, and the man is heavily fined. The head-ring is kept in good order, except during affliction, when it is dull, being no longer burnished. It is thereby known that the man is in trouble. If a man quits his tribe, he sometimes takes off his head-ring, and is then called *igundela*, that is, one who is shorn.

The top-knot of the woman is formed of red clay. It is of a bright colour, and is placed on the top of the head. At certain periods the chief directs young men and women to sew on the head-ring, and to fix the head-knot or *inkeɦli*. Much attention is paid to the head-ring and head-knot, and the hair is kept shaven both inside and outside the ring, and all around the knot. When they are in trouble this is neglected, and it can be seen at once by the head that there is some cause of affliction.

ikxeku. La fika esangweni, la
gukquka isele elihle, li kazimula.
La ngena isele li kxokxoma, la
hlala empundwini. Umkxakaza e
dhlala nabanye ngasesangweni, ba
li bona isele lelo. Wa ti Umkxakaza, "Puma ni, ni zo'ubona loku
okuhle." Ba puma abantu bonke
be li buka, be ti, "La lihle isele!"

When he came to the entrance of
the town, he turned into a beautiful and glistening frog. The frog
entered leaping, and settled on the
gatepost. Umkxakaza was playing with others near the gateway.
They saw the frog. Umkxakaza
said, "Come out and see this beautiful thing." All the people came
out, looking at it, and saying,
"What a beautiful frog!"

Umkxakaza and her people follow the frog.

La kxokxoma, la puma ngesango. Ku te uma se li puma,
wa ti Umkxakaza, "Ngi pe ni
izinto zami, ni zi fake ekqomeni
zonke, ni hambe nazo." Kwa
kalwa, kwa tiwa, "Hau, u fika
kona manje, so u ya ngapi futi
na?" Wa ti, "Ngi za 'u li landela, ngi ze ngi bone lapa li ya
kona." Uyise wa kipa abantu
aba 'mashumi 'mabili, be twala
ukudhla nezinto zake. Ba hamba,
be li landela isele li kxokxoma, ba
ze ba katala.

It leapt out of the gateway.
When it had gone out Umkxakaza
said, "O, give me my things;
place them all in a basket, and set
out with them." They cried and
said, "O, you are just arrived;
and where now are you going
again?" She replied, "I am
going to follow the frog, to see
where it is going." The father
selected twenty men, to carry food
and her things. They set out,
following the frog as it leapt,
until they were tired.

The frog becomes an old man again, and proves treacherous.

Wa hamba nalo yedwa Umkxakaza. Ba ti uma se be bodwa
isele la penduka umuntu. Ku te
lapa se li penduke umuntu,
wa mangala Umkxakaza, wa ti,
"W enziwe ini uma u be isele
na!" Wa ti, "Ngi pendukile
nje." Wa ti, "U ngi yisa ngapi
na?" Wa ti, "Ngi ku yisa ekaya
enkosini yakwiti." Ba hamba
naye ba ze ba ba kwesinye isizwe.
Ku te lapa se be kude kakulu, wa
bona ihlati elikulu lapa indhlela i
dhlula kona. Ba ya ba fika ehlatini; kepa ikxeku lona la l' azi
uma so ku seduze ekaya. La ti,
"Hamba kakulu; ku kude lapa si

Umkxakaza travelled alone with
it; and when they were alone, the
frog turned into a man. When it
turned into a man, Umkxakaza
wondered and said, "What was
done to you, that you became a
frog?" He said, "I just became
a frog." She asked, "Where are
you taking me?" He replied,
"I am taking you home to our
chief." They went together till
they came to another nation.
When they had gone a great distance, she saw a large forest,
through which the path went.
They reached the forest; but the
old man knew that they were now
near home. He said, "Make
haste; the place to which we are

ya kona." Wa hamba wa fika e*h*latini. La m tata, la i d*h*lula ind*h*lela, la ya pakati kwe*h*lati. La ti, "Wo! Ulut' olu nje ngi te ngi yo' lu tatela om*u*nye *u*muntu nje?" L' ema naye esigcaweni. Kepa Umk*x*akaza wa mangala ukubona e*h*latini ukubona indawo en*h*le, ku nga ti ku *h*lala abantu. La ti ik*x*eku, "A ku ze konke oku zizelayo." W' ezwa Umk*x*akaza ku bila i*h*lati lonke, ku k*x*ak*q*aza ; w' esaba. L' *c*suka ik*x*eku, l' enyukela ngasen*h*la, la memeza, li *h*laba umlozi, li ti, "Fiyo, fiyo ! a ku ze oku zizelayo."

going is afar off." She reached the forest. The old man took her, and quitted the path, and went into the midst of the forest. He said, "Nay! Shall I take so beautiful a thing as this just for another man?" He stood still with her in an open place. But Umk*x*akaza wondered to see a beautiful place in the forest, as if men dwelt there. The old man said, "Let all beasts come, which come of their own accord." Umk*x*akaza heard the whole forest in a ferment, and crashing ; she was afraid. The old man departed, and went up the forest, and shouted, whistling, and saying, "Fiyo, fiyo !⁵² let all beasts come which come of their own accord."

Umkxakaza ascends a tree for safety, after transforming herself.

Umk*x*akaza w' ema, wa ti, "Dabuka, kanda lami, ngi fake izinto-zami." La dabuka ikanda lake, wa faka zonke izinto zake. La buya la *h*langana, kwa ku nga ti a ku si lo eli dabukile. Kepa la li likulu ngokwesabekayo, ngokuba uma umunt*u* e li bona la li sabeka. Wa kwela emtini ; wa ti e se pezulu, kwa buye kwa *h*langana imiti ; ngokuba wa e kwele imiti y enabile i *h*langanisile ; wa i penya, wa kwela, ya buye ya *h*langana.

Umk*x*akaza stood still and said, "Open, my head, that I may place my things inside." Her head opened, and she put in all her things. Her head again closed, and it was as though it had not opened. But it was fearfully large ; for when a man looked at it, it was fearful. She mounted a tree ; when she was on the top, the branches again came together ; for she had mounted where the trees were thick and united ; she turned aside the branches, and went up ; they again closed behind her.

All the beasts of the forest assemble at the call of the old man.

Wa bona Umk*x*akaza umuzi ngapambili kwalelo '*h*lati. Wa *h*lala pezulu emtini. Za fika izilo, zi funa ; zi li bamba ik*x*eku, li ti, "Ai, musa ni ukud*h*la mina ; ka

Umk*x*akaza saw a village in front of the forest. She remained on the tree. Wild beasts came, seeking for prey ; they caught hold of the old man ; he said, "No ; do not eat me ; she is no longer here

---

⁵² *Fiyo, fiyo,* intended to imitate the sound made by whistling.

se ko e be ngi ni bizela yena; a ngi sa m boni." Za li *hh*weba. La zi kuza, la ti, "Ngi yeke ni, banta bami; ngi ya 'u ni pa ngomso." Za muka ke. Ik*xx*eku la sala, nalo la hamba la ya ekaya.

for whom I called you; I no longer see her." They tore him. He scolded them and said, "Leave me alone, my children; I will give you something to-morrow." So they departed. The old man was left, and he set out and went home.[53]

Umkxakaza again joins the old man, who wonders at the size of her head.

Wa li bona Umk*xx*akaza se li pumele ngapand*h*le kwe*h*lati, w' e-*h*lika ngamand*h*la, wa gijima, wa puma e*h*latini. Wa ti lapa se li seduze nomuzi ik*xx*eku, wa li bona, wa ti, "Ngi linde, loku si hamba nawe : u ngi shiyela ni na ?" L'ema. Kepa la mangala li bona ikanda li likulu, ngokuba la li lincane ikanda likamk*xx*akaza. Kepa ik*xx*eku la l' esaba ukubuza ukuti, "W enziwe ini ?" ngokuba la m bizela izilwane.

When Umk*xx*akaza saw that he had gone outside the forest, she descended quickly, and ran out of the forest. When the old man was near the village, she saw him, and said, "Wait for me, for we travel together: why do you leave me ?" He halted. But he wondered when he saw that her head was large, for Umk*xx*akaza's head used to be small. But the old man was afraid to ask, "What has done this to you ?" for he had called the beasts to her.

The people wish to drive her away because of her deformity.

Ba ngena ke ekaya; w' ema emnyango ; la ti ik*xx*eku la kuleka enkosini yalo, li ti, "Ngi m tolile

They entered the village ; she stood at the doorway ; the old man made obeisance to his chief, saying,

[53] We find in one of the Northern tales something very like this. A damsel was passing through a forest guided by a white bear, who had given her strict directions not to touch anything as they were passing through. But the foliage glittered so beautifully around her that she could not resist the temptation, but put forth her hand and plucked a little silver leaf. "At the same moment the whole forest was filled with a terrific roaring, and from all sides there streamed forth an innumerable multitude of wild beasts, lions, tigers, and every other kind ; and they all went in pursuit of the bear, and strove to tear him in pieces." (*Thorpe's Yule-tide Stories*, p. 129.) Comp. "The Beautiful Palace east of the Sun and north of the Earth." At the word of the "very, very old woman" who ruled over the beasts of the field, there "came running out of the forest all kinds of beasts, bears, wolves, and foxes, inquiring what their queen's pleasure might be." In like manner all kinds of fishes assembled at the voice of their queen ; and all kinds of birds at the voice of theirs. (*Id.*, pp. 163, 164, 165.) So all the birds of the air, and all the beasts of the forest, were sent out to prevent the youth from obtaining the match of the wonderful horse, Grimsbork. (*Id.*, p. 258.) In "The Three Princesses of Whiteland," the lords of beasts, birds, and fish are old men. (*Dasent. Popular Tales from the Norse*, p. 212.)

umfazi wako. Kepa ikanda lake eli nga lungile." Ba ngeua end/hlini, ba /hlala. Abautu bonke ba mangala, ba ti, "Yeka e mu/hle; kepa ikanda, ungati isilwane." Ba ti, "A ka kꞵotshwe." Kepa kwa ku kona udade wabo wenkosi, 'ala e ti, "Mu yeke ni: uma e isilima u nani na?"

"I have found a wife for you. But it is her head that is not right." They entered the house, and sat down. All the people wondered, saying, "O, she is beautiful; but the head is like that of an animal." They said, "Let her be sent away." But the chief's sister was there; she objected, saying, "Leave her alone: if she is deformed, what of that?"

The king's sister asks Umkꞵakaza to go to a dance.

Kepa umyeni wa e nga m tandi e ti, "Loku ngi kꞵala ukuzeka, ngi inkosi, ngi kꞵale ngesilima na?" A ti udade wabo, "A ku nani. Mu yeke, a /hlale, noma u nga m zekile." Wa /hlala ke, be m biza ngokuti, Ukandakulu. Kwa vela iketo; ya m ncenga intombi i ti, "Hamba, si yo'buka iketo." Kepa a ti Ukandakulu, "Loku mina ngi isilima, ngi za 'u/hlekwa abantu, uma se be ngi kꞵotsha be ti ngi za 'kona iketo labo; loku uma ngi vela, intombi zi ya 'uyeka ukusina, zi baleke, zi bona mina." Ya ti, "Kꞵa, si ya 'u/hlala kude, uma be /hleka." Wa ti Ukandakulu, "A u z' usina ini wena na?" Ya ti, "Kꞵa, a ngi tandi, ngokuba ngi ya tanda uku/hlala nawe." Ngokuba leyo 'ntombi ya i m tanda kakulu, be tandana naye; ngako ke ya i nga tandi ukuya 'usina, i m shiya yedwa.

But the bridegroom did not love her, and said, "Since I am taking my first wife, and I a king, should I begin with a deformed person?" His sister said, "It is no matter. Let her alone, that she may stay, even though you do not marry her." So she staid, and the people called her Ukandakulu.[54] There was a gathering of the people to a dance: the damsel[55] asked her to go with her to look at the dance. But Ukandakulu said, "Since I am a deformed person, the people will laugh at me, when they drive me away, saying I came to spoil their dance; for if I make my appearance, the damsels will leave off dancing, and run away when they see me." She said, "No, we will sit down at a distance if they laugh." Ukandakulu said, "Will not you yourself dance?" She replied, "No, I do not wish to dance, for I wish to remain with you." For the damsel loved her very much, and she loved her in return; therefore she did not like to go to dance, and leave her alone.

The dance is broken up on the appearance of Umkꞵakaza.

Ba /hloba; be be hamba bobabili, be ya eketweni. Ba ti aba

They put on their ornaments, and went both to the dance. Those

<hr>

54 *Ukandakulu,* Big-head.
55 That is, the chief's sister.

ba bonayo ba baleka, ba ti, " Si kona isilima esi hamba nentombazana." Ba ti, "Si njani ?" Ba ti, " Hau, ikanda li y' esabeka kakulu." Kwa ti, be sa vela, kwa baleka abantu bonke ; ba ye ba kuzwa, kwa tiwa, " Musa ni ukuza lapa." B' esuka ba ye ba *h*lala egangeni, kwa za kwa pela ukusina ; ba buya ba *h*lala ekaya. Ku batshazwa isizwe sonke, si ti, " Ni nga ku bona oku zekwe inkosi."

who saw them fled, saying, "There is a deformed thing walking with the princess." They asked, "What is it like ?" They said, "O, the head is very fearful." And immediately on their arrival at the dancing-place, all the people fled ; and some warned them off, saying, "Don't come here." They went away, and sat on a hill, until the dance was ended ; then they returned and sat down at home. The whole nation exclaimed in wonder, "You should see the thing which the chief has married."

Umkxakaza assumes her original beauty, and makes herself known to the king's sister.

Kwa ba izinsuku eziningi, be *h*lezi ekaya. Kwa ti ngolunye usuku ba hamba ba ya 'ugeza. Ba fika ba geza, ba puma emanzini, b' ema pezu kwezidindi zotshani, b' enzela ukuze k' ome imizimba nezinyawo, ngokuba ba be kcopile izinyawo zabo. Ya kuluma intombi, i ti, " Hau, w' enziwa ini, kandakulu, ukuba nje na ?" Wa ti, " Ukuvela kwami nje." Ya ti intombi, " Hau, nga u ba umu*h*le, mnta kwetu, kandakulu ; w oniwe ikanda." Wa *h*leka Ukandakulu, wa e se ti, " Dabuka, kanda lami, ku pume izinto zami." La dabuka masinyane ikanda, kwa puma izinto zake, wa zi beka pansi. La *h*langana ikanda, la ba lincane. Ya ti intombi ngokubona loko, ya ziponsa kuyena, i m bamba ; ba *h*leka kakulu ngokungenakulinganiswa, i ti intombi, " Konje ku nga ba u yena e si ti Ukandakulu ?" Ba ging*q*ana odakeni, be *h*leka, b' a*h*luleka ukuvuka. Ba

They remained at home many days. On a certain occasion they went to bathe. They bathed, they went out of the water, and stood on the sods of grass, that their body and feet might dry, for they had scraped their feet.[56] The damsel spoke, saying, "O, what caused you, Ukandakulu, to be as you are ?" She replied, "It is natural to me merely." The damsel said, "O, you would be beautiful, child of my parents, Ukandakulu ; you are spoilt by your head." Ukandakulu laughed and said, "Open, my head, that my things may come out." Her head opened immediately, her things came out, and she placed them on the ground. Her head closed and was small again. The damsel, on seeing this, threw herself on her, laying hold of her ; they laughed immoderately, the damsel saying, "Truly can it be she whom we call Ukandakulu ?" They rolled each other in the mud, laughing, and unable to get

---

[56] " They had scraped their feet."—The natives when they wash rub their feet with a soft sandstone, to remove the cracks and inequalities.

ze ba vuka, ba geza futi. B' ema, i ti, "Wa w enze njani na ?" Wa ti, "Nga ngi fake izinto zami." Wa ku landa konke okw' euziwa ikxeku. Ya mangala intombi. Wa ti, "Nako ke okwa ng' enza uma ikanda lami li be likulu." Wa i nika enye ingubo kwezake yena Umkxakaza; wa binca yake yezindondo; wa i tshela, wa ti, "Ngi Umkxakaza-wakogingqwayo, igama lami."

up. At length they got up and bathed again. As they were standing, the damsel said, "What had you done?" She replied, "I had placed my things in my head." She then related all that was done by the old man. The damsel wondered; and Umkxakaza said, "That, then, was it that made me have a large head." Umkxakaza gave her one of her garments. She put on her own garment which was ornamented with brass beads, and told her, saying, "I am Um-kxakaza-wakogingqwayo; that is my name."

The people admire her, and the king loves her.

Ba buya ba ya ekaya; ba fika b' ema emnyango. Kwa puma abantu, ba ti, "Nansi intombi e zo'gana." Ba ti abanye, "Eyaka-bani?" Ba ti aba i bonileyo, "A si y azi uma i vela ngapi." Ba ti; "Inye?" Ba ti, "Zimbili. Kepa si ti enye i pelezela enye." Ba puma abantu bonke, ba buka be buza be ti, "I i pi e zo'gana ku-nina nobabili na?" Ngokuba be nga ba bonisisi, ngokuba ba be folile, be bheka pansi. Ya lulama intombi yakona ekaya, ya ti, "Ukandakulu lo." Ba mangala abantu bonke; ba gijima, ba tshela inkosi, ba ti, "U nga m bona Ukandakulu, lapa ikanda lake li njalo." Ya puma inkosi, ya m bona. Kwa bizwa inkomo, kwa hlatshwa inyama eningi. Kwa menywa isizwe sonke; ku tiwa, "A ku butane abantu, ku za 'uke-telwa inkosikazi." Ba mangala bonke aba m bona Ukandakulu.

They returned home; on their arrival they stood at the doorway. The people went out and said, "There is a damsel come to point out her husband." Others said, "Whose daughter is she?" Those who saw her said, "We do not know whence she comes." They asked, "Is she alone?" They replied, "There are two. But we say one accompanies the other." All the people went out and look-ed, asking, "Which of you two is come to point out a husband?" For they did not see them dis-tinctly, for they had bent down their heads, looking on the ground. The damsel of the village raised her head, and said, "This is Uka-ndakulu." All the people won-dered, and ran and told the chief, "You should see Ukandakulu when her head is as it is." The chief went out and saw her. He called for many cattle, and many were slaughtered. The whole na-tion was summoned; it was said, "Let the people assemble; they are going to dance for the queen." All wondered who saw Ukanda-

Kwa gaywa utshwala, kwa ketwa inkosi; ya m tanda kakulu. I ti intombi, "Ku njani ke manje, loku na ni ti, a ka kxotshwe na?"

kulu. Beer was made; the king danced; he loved Umkxakaza very much. His sister said, "How then is it now, since you gave directions that she should be sent away?"

The old man is killed; and Umkxakaza marries the king, and lives happily ever after.

La bulawa ikxeku ngokuba l' enze leyo 'mikuba. Wa ze wa buyela kubo nezinkomo zokwenda abayeni. Ba fika kubo; kwa tiwa, "U fikile Umkxakaza-wakogingqwayo." Kwa hlatshiswa abayeni izinkomo eziningi; ba m lobola masinyane, w' enda. Inkosi ya m tanda kakulu; wa ba umfazi wayo. Wa busa kahle nendoda yake.

LYDIA.

The old man was killed because he was guilty of such practices. At length she returned to her father's with the cattle by which the bridegroom's people declared her his chosen bride. They arrived at her father's; they said, "Umkxakaza-wakogingqwayo is come." The bridegroom's people had many cattle killed for them; they paid her dowry immediately. She was married. The king loved her very much; she became his wife. She reigned prosperously with her husband.

IZELAMANI.

(THE TWO BROTHERS.)

Two brothers go out to hunt, and fall in with an old woman.

KWA ti ukusuka, abanta bamntu munye ba ya 'uzingela; b' elamana. Ba fukanisa impanda, iminingi, y' enz' uluhla olude. Wa fika w' esaba omkulu impanda; wa i zibukula omncinane. Wa i zibukula yonke; kwa ti kwowokugcina kwa puma isalukazana.

IT happened in times long ago, that the children of a certain man went out to hunt; one was older than the other. They fell in with a large number of pots, forming a long row. When the elder brother came to them, he was afraid of the pots; the younger turned them up. He turned all of them up, and a little old woman came out of the last.[57]

[57] Compare the Basuto legend, "The Murder of Maciloniane." (*Casalis*, p. 339.) The differences and similarities are remarkable. In the Basuto legend the brothers had separated, and the younger finds the pots alone; "a monstrous

The old woman shows them something to their advantage.

Sa ti komkulu, "Ngi pelekezele." W' ala. Sa ti komncane, "Ngi pelekezele." Wa vuma omncane. Wa landela omkulu. Ba kamba, ba kamba, ba ya ba fika ezweni eli nomuti o nezinkomo; be pet' imbazo. Sa ti isalukazi kumncane, "Gaula lo 'muti." Wa gaula, kwa puma inkomo; wa gaula, kwa puma inkomo, zaningi; kwa ti ngemva kwa pum' imvu; kwa ti ngemva kwa pum' imbuzi; kwa ti ngemva kwa puma inkabi em*h*lope.

She said to the elder, "Come with me." He refused. She said to the younger, "Come with me." The younger one went with her, and the elder followed. They went on and on. At length they came to a country where there was a tree which had cattle. They carried axes in their hands. The old woman said to the younger boy, "Hew the tree." He hewed it; there came out a bullock; he hewed it, there came out a large number of cattle; and after that there came out a sheep, and after that a goat, and after that a white ox.[58]

As they return home, the elder forsakes the younger.

Sa sala lapo isalukazana. Ba kamba be k*q*ub' inkomo bobabili, be kamba nenja zabo a ba zingela ngazo. Ba kamba ke, izwe l' omisile, li nge namanzi. Ba ya ba vela pezu kwewa; wa t' omkulu, "Ngi kunge ngomkcilo, ngi yo'upuza amanzi lapa eweni, ku nge ko 'ndawo yokwe*h*la." Wa m kunga ke. Wa m e*h*lisa ke. Wa wa m beka;[60] wa puza, wa puza;

The little old woman remained there. They departed, both of them driving the cattle, with their dogs, with which they hunted. So they went on their way; the country was scorched[59] up, there being no water. At length they came to the top of a precipice; the elder said, "Tie a rope round me, that I may go and drink at the bottom of the precipice; for there is no way of going down." So he tied a rope round him, and let him down; at length he let him down to the bottom; he drank

man," with a very big leg, and one of the ordinary size, comes out of the pot; the man is killed by Maciloniane's dogs; and on cutting up the large leg an immense herd of beautiful cattle come out. Maciloniane is killed by his brother for the sake of a white cow; and a bird follows the murderer, and upbraids him, and proclaims the murder among the people of his village. *The bird was the heart of Maciloniane.*

[58] The enchanted princess gave Strong Frank a sword, saying, "When thou strikest on a tree, soldiers shall march out in multitudes, as many as thou requirest." (*Thorpe's Yule-tide Stories, p. 429.*)

[59] *Izwe l' omisile.*—Lit., the country scorched, or dried up, viz., grass, trees, and rivers; that is, there being no rain, the earth became hot, and dried up herbage, &c.

[60] Wa wa m beka *for* Wa ya wa m beka.

wa kolwa ke; wa m kupula. Wa t' omncane, "Nami ke ngi kunge, ngi yo'puza." Wa m kunga ke. Wa wa m beka, wa m yeka. Wa zi kquba inkomo omkulu. Wa ya wa fika ekaya kuyise nonina. Kwa tiw' omunye, "U m shiye pi na?" Wa ti, "Wa buya kukqala, mina ng' emuka nesalukazi, sa ya 'u ngi pa inkomo." Kwa lalwa ke.

and was satisfied; and he drew him up again. The younger said, "Tie a rope round me too, that I may go and drink." He tied a rope round him, and let him down to the bottom and left him. The elder one drove off the cattle. At length he came home to his father and mother. One asked, "Where have you left your brother?" He replied, "He returned before me; for my part, I went with an old woman; she gave me these cattle." They retired to rest.

The bird-messenger.

Kwa ti ku sa kusasa ya fik' inyoni, ya ti, "Tshiyo, tshiyo, tshiyo; umntanako u pakw' emanzini." Ba t' abantu, "Ni y' ezwa nje lc 'nyoni i ti ni na?" Ba t' abantu, "A i landelwe, lo i kalisa kwenhlamvu nje, e bizela abantu inyosi." Wa i landela unina noyise. Ya kamba njalo, i ti, "Tshiyo, tshiyo, tshiyo; umntanako u pakw' emanzini." Ya fika, ya tshona kona la be b' ehla kona, be puz' amanzi. Ya kal' i ngapansi. Wa lunguz' uyise kon' eweni, wa ti, "O, u bekwe ini lapo na?" Wa ti, "Ngi shiywe umfo wetu, be si puz' amanzi; ngi kqale ngayo, nga m ehlisa, nga m kupula. Wa ng' ehlisa ke, wa ngi yeka ke. Ngob' alile ukuzibukula umpanda: kwa puma isalukazana ke. Sa naxusa yena, sa ti, ka si pelekezele, a si yise ezweni. W' ala. Wa t' ub' ale ke, sa t' a ku kambe mina. Nga vuma ke mina.

Early in the morning a bird came, saying, "Tshiyo, tshiyo, tshiyo; your child has been put into the water." The men said, "Do you hear what this bird says?" The people said, "Let us follow it, since it cries like the honey-bird, when it is calling men to where there is honey." The father and mother followed it. It went on constantly saying, "Tshiyo, tshiyo, tshiyo; your child is put into the water." At length it descended to the place where they had gone down to drink. It still cried when it was at the bottom. The father looked over the precipice, and asked, "O, what placed you there?" He replied, "I have been left here by my brother when we were drinking water; I first let him down, and drew him up again. Then he let me down, and left me. For he refused to turn up the pots; and a little old woman came out. She besought him to accompany her, and take her to a certain country. He refused. When he refused she asked me to go. So I went.[61] She did

---

[61] How common is this kind of tale among other people, where a younger brother, or sister, or step-sister, gains great advantages by performing readily some act of kindness; whilst the elder suffers for his churlishness.

A sa bi sa tsho kuye ukuti, ka gaul' umuti; sa t' a ngi u gaule mina. Nga u gaula ke umuti; kwa puma inkomo nezimvu nembuzi, nenkabi em*h*lope. Sa ti ke inkomo ezami ke, mina ngi mncane. K,wa ku pela ke. Sa zi k*q*uba ke inkomo. U ngi yek' emanzini nje, w' esab' uku ngi gwaza."

not tell him after that to hew the tree; but she told me to hew it. So I hewed the tree, and there came out cattle, and sheep and goats, and a white ox. She said the cattle were mine, who am the younger. That was the end of it. So we drove the cattle. He left me in the water, for he was afraid to stab me."

The younger is rescued, and the elder disappears.

Wa e se ti uyise, "O! Kepa si za 'u kw enza njani, lo nanku u lapo nje pansi eweni?" Wa ti, "Landa ni umk*c*ilo ekaya, ni u ponse lapa, ngi zikunge, ngi u tekelezele kulo omunye a ngi yeke nawo." A buye ke uyise, ku *h*la-l' unina.

U m ponsel' umpako, a be be u d*h*la. Uyise a kamb' a kambe, a fik' ekaya, lapa a nga za i zeka kuyo indodana indaba le. A tshel' omunye 'muntu ukuya 'u m kupulisa. Ba ye ba fike ke, ba u ponse umk*c*ilo kuye, a u tekelezele, a ti, "Ngi kupule ni ke." Ba m kupula ke. Unina ke a be se kala ke. La e se m zekele indaba yabo yokukamba, ba buya, se be y' ekaya.

Ba te be fika ya se i balekile ke indodana enkulu; a y aziwa la i ye ngakona.

The father said, "O! What shall we do, since there you are at the foot of the precipice?" He said, "Fetch another rope from home, and throw it down to me here, that I may tie it round me, and fasten it to the one which he left with me." The father returned home, and the mother staid with him.

She threw him down the food they had taken for the journey. The father went, and reached his home; he did not tell the elder son. He told another person to go and draw him up. They went and threw him a rope; he fastened it, and told them to draw him up. So they drew him up. And his mother wept. When he had given them the account of their journey, they returned home.

When they arrived the elder son had already fled, and it was not known whither he had gone.

U*k*ofana Dhladhla.[62]

[62] There are peculiarities in the style of this tale which the Zulu student will at once note. The man is of the Amakuza tribe.

UBONGOPA-KAMAGADHLELA.

The king's child and Ubongopa-kamagadhlela.

Kw' esukela, inkosi ya tata abafazi abaningi. Wa mita omunye. Kwa zalwa inkomo. Ya ti, "Umzolwana ku zala Unobani, umntwana u ya 'kubekwa kule 'nkomo." Ibizo layo Ubongopa-kamagadhlela. Kwa zalwa umntwana, wa bekwa pezu kwenkomo; wa hlala pezu kwayo, wa lala kona; ka y embata ingubo; ukudhla kwa yiswa kona kumntwana. Kwa hlwa kwa valwa esangweni, abantu ba lala ezindhlini; umntwana wa lala pezu kwenkabi.

Kwa sa kusasa wa ti umntwana,

" Bongopa-kamagadhlela,
Bongopa-kamagadhlela,
U bo vuka;[64] ku ya vukwa;

U bo vuka; ku ya vukwa."

'Eme ke Ubongopa. Wa ti,

" Bongopa-kamagadhlela,
Bongopa-kamagadhlela,
U bo hamba; ku ya hanjwa;

U bo hamba; ku ya hanjwa."

Wa hamba wa ya 'kudhla; za fika edhlelweni lazo, za dhla. Wa ti,

" Bongopa-kamagadhlela,
Bongopa-kamagadhlela,
U bo buya; ku ya buywa;

U bo buya; ku ya buywa."

In the times of long ago, a king took many wives. When one was with child, an ox was born. The king said, "When So-and-So gives birth, the child shall be placed on this ox." The name of the ox was Ubongopa-kamagadhlela.[63] The child was born and put on the ox; he remained on it, and slept on it; he did not put on any blanket; food was taken there to him. When it was dark the gate of the village was closed, and the people went to sleep in the houses; the child slept on the ox.

In the morning the child said,

" Ubongopa-kamagadhlela,
Ubongopa-kamagadhlela,
Awake now; it is time to awake;
Awake now; it is time to awake."

Ubongopa stood up. He said,

" Ubongopa-kamagadhlela,
Ubongopa-kamagadhlela,
Set out now; it is time to set out;
Set out now; it is time to set out."

He went to graze; the cattle arrived at their pasture, and grazed. He said,

" Ubongopa-kamagadhlela,
Ubongopa-kamagadhlela,
Return now; it is time to return;
Return now; it is time to return."

---

[63] The meaning of *Ubongopa* is not known. *Uma-'gadhlela* is the name of Ubongopa's father. It is compounded of *Uma* and *gadhlela*, to strike against with the head, as rams in fighting. The full form would be *Uma-e-gadhlela;* it is a name implying, When he strikes with the head, *he conquers.*

[64] *U bo vuka* is a mode of speech common to the Amangwane, Amahlubi, &c. It is equivalent to the Zulu, *Sa u vuka.*

A buye ke; za buya, za fika ekaya. Wa ti,

"Bongopa-kamagad*h*lela,
Bongopa-kamagad*h*lela,
U bo ngena; ku ya ngenwa;

U bo ngena; ku ya ngenwa."

A ngene ke; za ngena zonke. Kwa fika ukud*h*la kwake; wa d*h*la kona pezulu enkabeni yake.

Wa za wa kula, umlilo e nga w azi, ingubo e nga y embati; e lala kona pezulu, a nga u nyateli um*h*labati; wa za wa ba insizwana.

So he returned; the cattle went home again. He said,

"Ubongopa-kamagadhlela,
Ubongopa-kamagadhlela,
Enter the pen; it is time to enter;
Enter the pen; it is time to enter."

So he entered, and all the cattle entered. His food was brought; he ate it on the top of his ox.

He lived thus until he grew up, being unacquainted with fire, not having worn any garment, and not having trodden on the ground. At length he was a young man.

Thieves come to steal the king's cattle.

Kwa fika amasela ezizwe, a ze 'kuba izinkomo. A vula esangwe-ni, a ngena, e pete izinduku. Be lele abantu, a b' ezwa. A zi tshaya izinkomo, a za vuka pansi. Z' a-puka izinduku zawo a wa zi pete-yo; 'emuka ebusuku.

Kwa sa kusasa wa ti, "Vuka, bongopa-kamagad*h*lela." Wa vu-ka. Wa ti, "Hamba u ye 'ku-d*h*la." Wa hamba; za hamba zonke izinkomo. Wa ti, a zi d*h*le; za d*h*la zonke. Za buya emini. Kwa fika ukud*h*la, wa d*h*la kona pezulu enkabeni. Wa ti, a zi hambe; za hamba. Wa ti, a zi d*h*le; za d*h*la. Wa ti, a zi buye; za buya.

Kwa *h*lwa, kwa valwa esangwe-ni; ba vala abantu ezind*h*lini, ba lala ubutongo. A fika amasela, a vela esangweni, e gone izinduku; a zi tshaya izinkomo; a za vuka; z' apuka izinduku. 'Emuka ebu-

There came some thieves from another tribe to steal the cattle. They opened the gate and went in, carrying sticks in their hands. The people, being asleep, heard nothing. They beat the cattle; they did not arise; the sticks which they carried were broken; and they went away again by night.

In the morning he said, "A-wake, Ubongopa-kamagadhlela." He awoke. He said, "Go to graze." He went; and all the cattle went. He told them to graze; and all grazed; they went home again at noon. His food was brought, and he ate it on the ox. He told them to go, and they went; he told them to eat, and they ate; he told them to return, and they returned.

In the evening the gateway was closed; the people shut themselves up in their houses, and slept. The thieves came and opened the gate-way, carrying sticks in their arms; they beat the cattle; they did not get up; the sticks broke. They

suku. A kuluma e hamba, a ti, "Lezi 'zinkomo zi nani, uba zi nga vuki?" A ti, "A si gaule izinduku kakulu."

Kwa sa ngolwesitatu, (a wa m boni umuntu o pezulu enkabeni,) wa ti, a zi vuke, zi hambe, zi ye 'kud*h*la. Wa hamba Ubongopa-kamagad*h*lela. Za d*h*la. Wa ti, a zi buye; za buya ngolwesitatu. Kw' eza ukud*h*la kwake, wa d*h*la kona pezulu enkabini, kubongopa. Wa ti, a zi hambe, zi ye 'kud*h*la; za ya. Wa ti, a zi buye; za buya. Kwa *h*lwa, a fika amasela ebusuku, a zi tshaya izinkomo; a za vuka; z' apuka izinduku; a za vuka iziukomo. A z' apula imisila, a za vuka. 'Emuka ebusuku. A teta, a ti, "A si gaule izinyanda ngambili, kona ku ya 'kuba kw apuka lezo, si tate ezinye." A ti, "A 'bonanga si ku bona loku."

Kwa *h*lwa ngolwesine, a pelekezela, a beka ekcaleni komuzi. Kwa valwa esangweni, ba lala abantu. A fika ebusuku, a vula, a ngena, a zi tshaya izinkomo, z' apuka izinduku, za pela izinyanda; a puma, a tata ezinye izinyanda, a ngena nazo esibayeni, a zi tshaya izinkomo, z' apuka izinduku; 'emuka.

Kwa sa kusasa wa ti, a zi hambe zi ye 'kud*h*la ngolwesi*h*lanu. Abantu ka ba tsheli ukuba ku fika

went away again by night. They conversed as they were going, saying, "What is the matter with these cattle, that they do not get up?" They said, "Let us cut a great many sticks."

On the morning of the third day, (they did not see a person on the ox,) he told them to get up and go to graze. Ubongopa-kamagadhlela went; the cattle grazed. He told them to return on the third day. His food was brought; he ate it on the top of the ox, on Ubongopa. He told them to go and graze; they went: he told them to return home; they returned. It was dark; the thieves came by night; they beat the cattle; they did not awake; the sticks broke; the cattle did not get up. They wrenched their tails; they did not get up. They went away in the night. They spoke passionately, saying, "Let us each cut two bundles of sticks, that when one bundle is broken, we may take the other." They said, "We never saw such a thing as this."

On the night of the fourth day, they brought the bundles by going and returning twice, and placed them outside the village. The gateway was shut, and the people slept. The thieves came by night; they opened the gate and went in; they beat the cattle; their sticks broke; the first bundles were used; they went and took the others, and went with them into the kraal; they beat the cattle; the sticks broke; and the thieves went away.

In the morning he told the cattle to go and graze on the fifth day. He did not tell the people

amasela ebusuku, a ze 'kuba izinkomo, ku be indaba yake a zazele.
Za hamba; wa ti, a zi d*h*le, za
d*h*la. Wa ti, a zi buye, za buya,
za fika ekaya. Kw' eza ukud*h*la,
wa d*h*la. Ba kuluma, uyise wa
ti, " Mntanami, u tukutele, izinkomo u ya zi tshaya kakulu imi-
vimbo." Ba bona ukuba zi vuvu-
kile,. zi tshaywe ngamasela ebusuku ; ba ti zi tshaywe u yena.

that thieves came by night to
steal the cattle; it was a matter
known only to himself. They
went; he told them to graze, and
they grazed; he told them to return, and they returned home.
His food was brought, and he ate.
The people talked; his father said,
" My child, you are passionate;
you have beaten the cattle with
many stripes." They saw that
they were swollen, having been
beaten by the thieves by night;
and thought he had beaten them.

They detect the king's son.

Kwa *h*lwa a fika ebusuku, a
vula esangweni, a ngena, a zi
tshaya izinkomo, a za vuka; z' a-
puka izinduku, za sala ngazinye.
Wa m bona omunye emaseleni, wa
ti, " Nang' umuntu ow' en*q*aba
nezinkomo." Ba ti, " Kuluma."
Wa kuluma, wa ti,

The next night the thieves came
again; they opened the gateway
and went in; they beat the cattle,
they did not awake; their sticks
broke, each man had but one left.
One of the thieves saw him, and
said, " There is the fellow who refuses to allow the cattle to move."
They said to him, " Speak." He
spoke and said,

" Bongopa-kamagad*h*lela,
Bongopa-kamagad*h*lela,
U bo vuka; ku ya vukwa;

U bo vuka; ku ya vukwa;

Ku boni uba si ya bulawa
Amasela awezizwe ? "

" Ubongopa-kamagadhlela,
Ubongopa-kamagadhlela,
Awake now; it is time to
awake;
Awake now; it is time to
awake;
Do you not see we are killed
By thieves of another tribe ? "

Wa vuka Ubongopa-kamagad*h*lela,
w' ema. Wa ti,

Ubongopa - kamagadhlela awoke
and stood up. He said,

" Bongopa-kamagad*h*lela,
Bongopa-kamagad*h*lela,
U bo hamba; ku ya hanjwa;
U bo hamba; ku ya hanjwa;
Ku boni uba si ya bulawa
Amasela awezizwe ? "

" Ubongopa-kamagadhlela,
Ubongopa-kamagadhlela,
Go now; it is time to go;
Go now; it is time to go;
Do you not see we are killed
By thieves of another tribe ? "

Wa hamba, za hamba. Kwa puma amankonyana ezind*h*lini, a
zikulula ezisingeni ; a vula em-

Ubongopa went, and all the cattle.
The calves came out of the house;
they freed themselves from the
cords by which they were tied;
they opened the door, and followed

nyango, a landela aonina. Ba lele abantu. Z' ema esangweni. Ba ti, "Kuluma, mfana. Sa ku gwaza." Wa ti, "Ni nge ngi gwaze." Wa ti,

" Bongopa-kamagadhlela,
Bongopa-kamagadhlela,
U bo hamba ; ku ya hanjwa ;
U bo hamba ; ku ya hanjwa ;
Ku boni uba si ya bulawa
Amasela awezizwe ? "

Wa hamba Ubongopa-kamagadhlela.

their mothers. The people were asleep. They stood still at the gateway. The thieves said, "Speak, boy. You are stabbed."[65] He replied, "You cannot stab me," and said,

" Ubongopa-kamagadhlela,
Ubongopa-kamagadhlela,
Go now ; it is time to go ;
Go now ; it is time to go ;
Do you not see we are killed
By thieves of another tribe ? "

Ubongopa-kamagadhlela went.

The king and people are alarmed at his absence.

Wa puma umuntu kulowo 'muzi lapa izinkomo zi puma kuwo, wa ti, "Inkosi i tombile, izinkomo i zi vuse ebusuku." Wa memeza uyise, wa ti, "A ku pekwe ukudhla, inkosi i tombile, uyise kabongopa." Kwa pekwa ukudhla isizwe sonke sikayise. L' emuka ilanga, la tshona, kwa hlwa. Kwa funwa, kwa kalwa, kwa tiwa, "Umntwana u dhliwe ini ebusuku na? Wa hamba nezinkomo namankonyana ezindhlini."

A man of the village from which the cattle had been driven went out of the house ; he said, "The king is of age,[66] for he has aroused the cattle by night." He called his father ; he said, "Let food be cooked ; the king, the father of Ubongopa,[67] is of age." The whole tribe of his father made beer. The sun declined, it set, it became dark. The people looked for him, and cried, saying, "What has devoured the child during the night? He set out with the cattle and the calves from the houses."

The boy tries the thieves' patience.

Ekuhambeni kwabo wa ti umfana,

" Bongopa-kamagadhlela,
Bongopa-kamagadhlela,
U bo ma ; ku y' emiwa ;

U bo ma ; ku y' emiwa ;

As they went the boy said,

" Ubongopa-kamagadhlela,
Ubongopa-kamagadhlela,
Stand still now ; it is time to stand still ;

Stand still now ; it is time to stand still ;

---

[65] *Sa ku gwaza.*—Aorist used interjectionally. "We stabbed you !" that is, you are as good as stabbed ; you are a dead man.

[66] "The king is of age."—When a youth comes to maturity, he drives the cattle out of the pen to a distance from his home, and does not return till noon. Here, as in some other tales, the prince royal is called *king*. But it is not now the custom to do so among the Zulus.

[67] He is called the father of Ubongopa, probably because he was in an especial manner his owner.

Ku boni uba si ya bulawa
Amasela awezizwe?"

Z' ema. A ti, "Kuluma. Sa ku gwaza." Wa ti, "Ni nge ngi gwaze." A ti, "U ini?" Wa ti, "A ngi si 'luto." A ti, "U gabe ngani? U tsho ngokuba w' enqaba nezinkomo zenkosi, sa za sa felwa inyanga ngawe?" Wa ti,

" Bongopa-kamagadhlela,
Bongopa-kamagadhlela,
U bo hamba; ku ya hanjwa;
U bo hamba; ku ya hanjwa;
Ku boni uba si ya bulawa
Amasela awezizwe?"

Za hamba ke.

Do you not see we are killed
By thieves of another tribe?"

They stood still. They said, "Speak. You are stabbed." He said, "You cannot stab me." They said, "What are you?"[68] He replied, "I am nothing." They said, "What do you boast of? Do you so speak because you would not let us take the chief's cattle, until we lost a whole month through you?" He said,

" Ubongopa-kamagadhlela,
Ubongopa-kamagadhlela,
Go now; it is time to go;
Go now; it is time to go;
Do you not see we are killed
By thieves of another tribe?"

So they went.

They reach the king, who boasts of what he will do.

Kwa tunywa elinye isela; la fika enkosini, la ti, "Si zi dhlile izinkomo, zi nomlingo, zi lala umuntu[69] pezulu kwenkabi, kubongopa-kamagadhlela." Kwa tiwa, "Buyela, u ti, A zi tshetshe, zi fike kimina." Za hamba ngamandhla, za vela okalweni. La ti, "Nanzo; zi nomfana pezulu enkabeni emhlope; u nomlingo, u ti, a zi me, zi me." Ya ti inkosi, "U ya 'kufika nazo, i hlatshwe inkomo leyo, a gabe ngayo. Loku ka lali pansi, u ya 'ulala." Za fika engudhleni, z' ema. Ya ti inkosi, "A zi hambe." Ba ti, "Z' ala nomfana, zi

One thief was sent forward. When he came to the chief, he said, "We have lifted some cattle, they are under magical power; there is a man that lies on an ox, on Ubongopa-kamagadhlela." The chief told him to return and tell them to hasten with the cattle to him. They travelled rapidly; they appeared on a ridge; the thief said, "There they are; there is a boy on a white ox; he has magical power; he tells them to halt, and they halt." The chief said, "When he comes, the ox, by which he practises his magic, shall be killed. And although he does not rest on the ground, he shall be made to rest on it." They came to the open space in front of the village, and halted. The chief told them to go on. The men replied, "The boy will not permit them; they

---

[68] " What are you ?"—An enquiry expressive of contempt. They have yet to learn what his power really is. The dry irony of conscious power in the reply, " I am nothing," is striking.

[69] This idiom is worth noting; it is the same as, " Izwe la fa indhlala," The country was destroyed by famine. Or below, "Indhlu i kanya izinkanyezi," The house is light by the stars, that is, starlight enters by holes in the roof.

vuma okwake." Ya ti, "Ka ku-lume." Wa ti,

" Bongopa-kamagad*h*lela,
Bongopa-kamagad*h*lela,
U bo hamba ; ku ya hanjwa ;
U bo hamba ; ku ya hanjwa ;
Ku boni uba si ya bulawa
Amasela awezizwe ? "

Wa hamba ke, za hamba.   Wa ti,

" Bongopa-kamagad*h*lela,
Bongopa-kamagad*h*lela,
U bo ngena ; ku ya ngenwa ;

U bo ngena ; ku ya ngenwa ;

Ku boni uba si ya bulawa
Amasela awezizwe ? "

Wa ngena ke esibayeni.

move at his word."   He com-manded him to speak.   He said,

" Ubongopa-kamagadhlela,
Ubongopa-kamagadhlela,
Go now ; it is time to go ;
Go now ; it is time to go ;
Do you not see we are killed
By thieves of another tribe ? "

Ubongopa went on, and the cattle too went on.   He said,

" Ubongopa-kamagadhlela,
Ubongopa-kamagadhlela,
Go into the pen now ; it is time for going in ;
Go into the pen now ; it is time for going in ;
Do you not see we are killed
By thieves of another tribe ? "

So he went into the pen.

The boy descends, and enters a hut.

Ba ti, " Ye*h*lika, mfana."   Wa ti, " Ka ng' e*h*li, a ngi nyateli pansi, ngi lala enkomeni. Lo nga zalwa a ngi w azi um*h*labati." Ya ti inkosi, " Ye*h*lika."   Wa ti, " A ng' azi."   Ya ti, " Kuluma, mfana."   Wa ti,

" Bongopa-kamagad*h*lela,
Bongopa-kamagad*h*lela,
A ng' e*h*le ; ku y' e*h*lwa ;

A ng' e*h*le ; ku y' e*h*lwa ;

Ku boni uba si ya bulawa
Amasela awezizwe ? "

W' e*h*la pansi. Ba ti, " Hamba, u ye end*h*lini." Wa ti, " A ng' a-zi end*h*lini." Ba ti, " Hamba, u ye end*h*lini." Wa ti, " A ngi yi." Ba ti, " U nani ? " Ba mu sa end*h*lini yomuntu ofileyo, e se ya

They said, " Come down, boy." He replied, " I do not get off; I do not walk on the ground; I remain on the ox; from the time of my birth I have never felt the ground." The chief said, " Come down." He said, " I cannot." He said, " Speak, boy."   He said,

" Ubongopa-kamagadhlela,
Ubongopa-kamagadhlela,
Let me get down ; it is time for getting down ;
Let me get down ; it is time for getting down ;
Do you not see we are killed
By thieves of another tribe ? "

He got down. They told him to go into the house. He said, " I cannot live in a house." They said, " Go into the house." He said, " I do not go." They said, " What is the matter with you ? " They took him to the house of a man who was dead, which was

gid*h*lika, e s' i kanya izinkanyezi. Ba ti, " Ngena." Wa ngena end*h*lini. Wa piwa ukud*h*la. Wa ti, "A ngi kw azi ukud*h*la kwapansi." Ba ti, " U ini ?" Kw' emuka ukud*h*la.

already falling into ruins, and the stars could be seen through its roof. They told him to go in. He went into the house. They gave him food. He said, "I do not understand food which is eaten on the ground." They said, " What are you ?" The food was taken away.

He raises a storm, which affects every one but himself.

Wa pimisa amate ; a bila, a ti, " Nkosi, wena wapakati, wen' umnyama, o ngangezintaba." A gcwala ind*h*lu. La duma izulu, la na kakulu ; kwa neta izind*h*lu zonke nezi nga neti. Ba memeza abantu, ba ti, " Inkosi i ya neta." Ya ti inkosi, " Umfana u se file, loku ku nje kimina, lo ngi nga w azi amatonsi." Ya ti, " Umfana, loku e *h*lezi pand*h*le, ka se ko ; u se file." La sa izulu. Kwa tunywa abantu, kwa tiwa, " A ba ye 'kubheka kuye." Ba fika, kw omile. Ba ti, " Ku ngani ukuba kw ome kumfana ? Ng' umfana o nemilingo. Sa vela, sa bona. Inkomo a i *h*latshwe yake, si bone ukuba ku ya 'kwenzeka lena imikuba e si i bonayo namu*h*la."

He spat ; the spittle boiled up and said, " Chief, thou child of the greatest,[70] thou mysterious[71] one who art as big as the mountains." It filled the house. It thundered and rained exceedingly ; all the houses leaked, even those which had never leaked before. The people shouted, saying, " The chief is wet." The chief said, " The boy is already dead, since I am in this state, for I never saw a drop enter my house before." He said, " Since the boy was sitting outside, he no longer lives ; he is dead." The heaven cleared. Some men were sent to go and see after him. When they arrived at his house, it was dry. They said, " How is it that it is dry in the boy's house ? He is a boy possessed of magical powers. We saw that at the first. Let his ox be killed, that we may see if these tricks will then be done which we now witness."[72]

They kill Ubongopa, but injure themselves.

Kwa bizwa abantu bonke, kwa tatwa umkonto, kwa ngena nawo esibayeni ; kwa bizwa umfana, ba ti, " Inkomo a i *h*latshwe." Wa ti, " Ngi ya 'kufa nxa ku file lena

All the people were summoned. A man took an assagai and entered the cattle-pen. The boy was called ; they said to him, " Let the ox be killed." He replied, " I shall die if that ox dies." They said,

[70] *Wena wapakati*, lit., child or man of the centre or innermost circle.

[71] *Umnyama*, Dark one, that is, one on whom we cannot look, fearful one, mysterious one.

[72] Compare this Ox with the Dun Bull in "Katie Woodencloak." (*Dasent. Popular Tales from the Norse, p.* 411.) And with the Horse Dapplegrim (*Dasent, p.* 313), or the Horse Grimsbork. (*Thorpe's Yule-tide Stories, p.* 253.)

inkomo." Ba ti, "U ini?" · La nikwa elinye isela umkonto, la i *h*laba ngomkonto, wa ngena eseleni. Ba ti, "Kuluma, mfana, inkomo i fe." Wa ti,

"Bongopa-kamagad*h*lela,
Bongopa-kamagad*h*lela,
U bo fana; ku ya fiwa;
U bo fana; ku ya fiwa;
Ku boni uba si ya bulawa
Amasela awezizwe?"

Wa ngena umkonto kubongopa. Wa wa pansi. Kwa tatwa izi-n*q*indi zoku m *h*linza. Wa y ata umuntu; wa zi*h*laba yena. Ba ti, "Kuluma, mfana. Sa ku gwaza." Wa kuluma, wa ti,

"Bongopa-kamagad*h*lela,
Bongopa-kamagad*h*lela,
U bo *h*linzwa; ku ya *h*linzwa;

U bo *h*linzwa; ku ya *h*linzwa;

Ku boni uba si ya bulawa
Amasela awezizwe?"

Ba i *h*linza; ya pela.

"What are you?" They gave one of the thieves the assagai; he stabbed at the ox with the assagai; but it pierced the thief. They said, "Speak, boy, that the ox may die." He said,

"Ubongopa-kamagadhlela,
Ubongopa-kamagadhlela,
Die now; it is time to die;
Die now; it is time to die;
Do you not see we are killed
By thieves of another tribe?"

The assagai pierced Ubongopa; he fell down. They took knives to skin him. A man divided the skin; he cut himself. They said, "Speak, boy. You are as good as stabbed." He said,

"Ubongopa-kamagadhlela,
Ubongopa-kamagadhlela,
Be skinned now; it is time to
be skinned;
Be skinned now; it is time to
be skinned;
Do you not see we are killed
By thieves of another tribe?"

They accomplished the skinning.

They go to bathe, to wash away the evil influence of Ubongopa.

A ti amadoda, "Basa ni umlilo kakulu." A ti amasela, "Ak' i yekwe ukwosiwa. Ke ku gezwe imizimba, ku kutshwe um*h*lola. Lena inkomo i nemilingo; zonke izenzo ezi kuyona ezinye." Kwa pela, ba i n*q*uma itshoba; wa zi-n*q*uma umuntu. Ba ti, "Kuluma, mfana. Sa ku gwaza." Wa ti,

"Bongopa-kamagad*h*lela,
Bongopa-kamagad*h*lela,
U bo n*q*unywa; ku ya n*q*u-
nywa;
U bo n*q*unywa; ku ya n*q*u-
nywa;

The men said, "Light a large fire." The thieves said, "Let us just omit for a time to roast the ox; let us first wash our bodies to get rid of the bad omen. This bullock had magical properties; all matters connected with it differ from those of other cattle. At last they cut off the end of the tail; a man cut himself. They said, "Speak, boy. You are as good as stabbed." He said,

"Ubongopa-kamagadhlela,
Ubongopa-kamagadhlela,
Let your tail be cut off; it is
time to have it cut off;
Let your tail be cut off; it is
time to have it cut off;

Ku boni uba si ya bulawa
Amasela awezizwe ? ”

Ba tabata izimbiza zobubende,
ba kelela, ba tela ezimbizeni ; ya
*h*lakazwa izito ; ya panyekwa esibayeni ; ba sika abafana, ba zibekela cyabo. Inkosi ya biz' abantu,
ya ti, “ Hamba ni, ni ye 'kugeza,
ande ni buye, ni i *dh*le.” Ba
hamba abantu bonke.

Do you not see we are killed
By thieves of another tribe ? ”

They took the vessels for the
blood, they dipped out from the
carcase, and poured it into the
vessels ; they cut off the limbs,
and hung up the bullock in the
cattle kraal ; the boys cut off
slices, and went and set them aside
for themselves. The chief called
the people, and said, “ Go and
bathe, and eat it after you come
back.” All the people went.

The boy brings Ubongopa to life again, and leaves the village.

Wa sala umfana, wa tabata isikumba, wa s' end*h*lala, wa beka
in*h*loko ; wa tabata izimbambo, wa
zi beka ; wa tabata olunye u*h*langoti, wa lu beka ; wa tabata umkono, wa u beka endaweni yawo ;
wa tabata umlenze, wa u beka
endaweni yawo ; wa tabata amatumbu, wa wa beka endaweni
yawo ; wa tabata isibindi, wa si
beka endaweni yaso ; wa tabata
ipapu, wa li beka endaweni yalo ;
wa beka ulusu, wa wola umswani,
wa u tela eluswini ; wa tabata
itshoba, wa li beka endaweni yalo ;
wa tabata ububende, wa bu tela
endaweni yabo ; w' embesa ngesi-
kumba, wa ti,

When they were gone, the boy
took the skin, and spread it on the
ground ; he placed the head on it,
he took the ribs and put them in
their place ; he took one side, and
placed it in its place ; he took a
shoulder, and put it in its place ;
he took a leg, and put it in its
place ; he took the intestines, and
put them in their place ; he took
the liver, and put it in its place ;
he took the lungs, and put them in
their place ; he placed the paunch
in its place ; he took the contents
of the paunch, and returned them
to their place ; he took the tail,
and put it in its place ; he took
the blood, and poured it into its
place ; he wrapped all up with the
skin, and said,

“ Bongopa-kamagad*h*lela,
Bongopa-kamagad*h*lela,
U bo vuka ; ku ya vukwa ;
U bo vuka ; ku ya vukwa ;
Ku boni uba si ya bulawa
Amasela awezizwe ? ”

“ Ubongopa-kamagadhlela,
Ubongopa-kamagadhlela,
Arise now ; it is time to arise ;
Arise now ; it is time to arise ;
Do you not see we are killed
By thieves of another tribe ? ”

Wa buya umpefumulo wayo, wa
ngena kuyona, ya bheka. Wa ti,

His breath came back again and
entered into him ; he looked up.
The boy said,

“ Bongopa-kamagad*h*lela,
Bongopa-kamagad*h*lela,
U bo ma ; ku y' emiwa ;

“ Ubongopa-kamagadhlela,
Ubongopa-kamagadhlela,
Stand up now ; it is time to stand ;

U bo ma ; ku y' emiwa ;

Ku boni uba si ya bulawa
Amasela awezizwe ? "

W' ema ke.   Wa ti,

" Bongopa-kamagadhlela,
Bongopa-kamagadhlela,
A ngi kwele ; ku ya kwelwa ;

A ngi kwele ; ku ya kwelwa ;

Ku boni uba si ya bulawa
Amasela awezizwe ? "

Wa kwela pezu kwayo.   Wa ti,

" Bongopa-kamagadhlela,
Bongopa-kamagadhlela,
U bo hamba ; ku ya hanjwa ;
U bo hamba ; ku ya hanjwa ;
Ku boni uba si ya bulawa
Amasela awezizwe ? "

Wa hamba Ubongopa.   Za hamba izindhlu, namasimu, nesibaya, zonke izinto zalowo 'muzi !

Stand up now ; it is time to stand ;

Do you not see we are killed
By thieves of another tribe ? "

So he stood up.[73]   The boy said,

" Ubongopa-kamagadhlela,
Ubongopa-kamagadhlela,
Let me mount ; it is time to mount ;

Let me mount ; it is time to mount ;

Do you not see we are killed
By thieves of another tribe ? "

He mounted the ox, and said,

" Ubongopa-kamagadhlela,
Ubongopa-kamagadhlela,
Go now ; it is time to go ;
Go now ; it is time to go ;
Do you not see we are killed
By thieves of another tribe ? "

Ubongopa set out.   And the houses and gardens, and cattle pen, and all the things of that village, followed him !

They pursue him.

Ba kupuka abantu emfuleni, wa ti omunye, " Bantu, bona ni umhlola.   Izwe li ya hamba lonke."

The men went up from the river.   One exclaimed, " See, ye men, a prodigy !   The whole country is going ! "   The chief

[73] Thor in one of his journeys, accompanied by Loki, rode in a car drawn by two he-goats.   At night they put up at a peasant's cottage ; Thor killed his goats, flayed them, and boiled the flesh for the evening repast of himself and the peasant's family.   The bones were all placed in the spread-out skins.   At dawn of day Thor " took his mallet Mjölnir, and, lifting it up, consecrated the goats' skins, which he had no sooner done, than the two goats re-assumed their wonted form." (*Mallet. Op. cit., p.* 436.)   " In the palace of Odin " the heroes feed on the flesh of the boar Sæhrimnir, " which is served up every day at table, and every day it is renewed again entire." (*Id., p.* 105.)   See also " The Sharp Grey Sheep," which, when it was about to be killed for its kindness to the princess, said to her, " They are going to kill me, but steal thou my skin, and gather my bones and roll them in my skin, and I will come alive again, and I will come to you again." (*Campbell. Op. cit. Vol. II., p.* 287.) —Comp. also " Katie Woodencloak." (*Dasent. Op. cit., p.* 420.)

We may also compare the story of Ananzi, who having eaten a baboon, " the bits joined themselves together in his stomach, and began to pull him about so much that he had no rest, and was obliged to go to a doctor." The doctor tempted the baboon to quit his victim by holding a banana to Ananzi's mouth. (*Dasent. Popular Tales from the Norse, p.* 502.)   Compare the howling of the dog in the belly of Toi. (*Grey. Op. cit., p.* 124.)

Ya mema inkosi isizwe sonke, ya ti, "Mu landele ni umfana, a bulawe." Wa hamba kakulu; wa b' ezwa ukuba se be seduze, wa ti,

" Bongopa-kamagad*h*lela,
Bongopa-kamagad*h*lela,
A u me; ku y' emiwa;

A u me; ku y' emiwa;

Ku boni uba si ya bulawa
Amasela awezizwe?"

Z' ema inkomo. Ba m memeza, ba ti, "Mana kona lapo, si ku bulale. Kade w' enza imikuba." Ba ti, "Yc*h*la, si ku bulale." W' e*h*lela pansi. Ba ti, "Suka enkomeni, imikonto i nga zi *h*labi." Ba i ponsa imikonto, a ya ze ya ya kuye, ya *h*laba pansi. Wa ba *h*leka, e ti, "Ini, ni 'madoda, ni baniugi, imikonto i nga ze ya tika kumi, i *h*labe pansi na?" La ba *h*leka elinye ibuto, la ti, "Ini ukuba n' a*h*lulwe umfana, ni lo ui *h*labe pansi, imikonto i nga ze ya fika kuye̒na na?" Ba tela abanye. Wa ti, "Ngi pe nini nami umkonto, ngi gwaze kini." B' ala, ba ti, "A si k' a*h*luleki." Ba m ponsa ngemikonto; ya *h*laba pansi. Ba i kcotsha, ba i ponsa kuye; a ya *h*laba kuye. Ba ti, "S' a*h*lulekile: a kw enzc nawe."

summoned the whole tribe, and said, "Follow the boy, and let him be killed." He went rapidly; but when he heard that they were near him, he said,

" Ubongopa-kamagadhlela,
Ubongopa-kamagadhlcla,
Stand still now; it is the time for standing still;
Stand still now; it is the time for standing still;
Do you not see we are killed
By thieves of another tribe?"

The cattle stood still. They shouted to him, saying, "Stand still in that very place, that we may kill you. For a long time you have practised magic." They said, "Come down, that we may kill you." He descended to the ground. They told him to stand apart from the cattle, that the assagais might not pierce them. They hurled their assagais; they did not reach him, but struck the ground.[74] He jeered them, saying, "Why what is this, you being men and so many too, the assagais do not reach me, but strike the ground?" One of the soldiers, laughing at them, said, "Why are you worsted by a boy, for the assagais strike the ground, and do not reach him?" Some gave in. He said, "Give me too an assagai, that I may make a stab at you." They refused, and said, "We are not yet worsted." They hurled their assagais at him; they struck the ground. They picked them up, and hurled them at him; they did not strike him. They said, "We are worsted: do you try also."

[74] Compare this with the contest of Ulysses with the suitors of Penelope.:
" Then all at once their mingled lances threw
And thirsty all of one man's blood they flew;
In vain! Minerva turned them with her breath,
And scatter'd short, or wide, the points of death!
With deaden'd sound one on the threshold falls,
One strikes the gate, one rings against the walls:
The storm pass'd innocent." (*Pope's Odyssey*, B. xxii. *l.* 280.)

The boy kills the chief, and all his people die.

Ba m nika imikonto, eminingi; wa y ala, wa kcela omunye. Ba m nika wa ba munye. Wa ti, "Ngi kcibe kinina?" Ba *h*leka. Wa pimisela amate pansi, a bila, a ti, "Nkosi, bayeti, wena o ngangezintaba." Wa ti, "Ngi *h*labe mina kinina?" Ba *h*leka, ba ti, "Yenza, si bone." Wa u ponsa enkosini yakona. Ba fa bonke.

They offered him many assagais; he refused them, and asked for one only. They gave him one. He said, "May I fling at you?" They laughed. He spat on the ground; the spittle fizzed, it said, "Chief, all hail, thou who art as big as the mountains." He said, "May I stab you?" They laughed and said, "Do so, that we may see." He hurled the assagai at their chief. They all fell down dead.

He restores them to life again.

Wa tabata uti lwomkonto, wa tshaya enkosini yakona; ya vuka, ba vuka bonke. Ba m memeza, ba ti, "Mana kona lapo, si ku gwaze." Wa ba *h*leka, wa ti, "Kade ni pi?" Ba ti, "Si ya fika." Wa ti, "Be ni file." Ba pika, ba ti, "Li gcine ilanga." Ba i ponsa imikonto eminingi kuye; ya *h*laba pansi. Ba ponsa abanye imikonto eminingi; ya *h*laba pansi. Ba i kcotsha, ba i ponsa eminingi; ya *h*laba pansi. A ba *h*leka amadoda, a ti, "Nika ni tina, si m bulale." A i ponsa imikonto eminingi; ya *h*laba pansi. A i kcotsha amadoda.

He took the haft of the assagai and smote their chief; he arose, and they all arose with him. They shouted to him, saying, "Stand where you are, that we may stab you." He laughed at them, and said, "Where have you already been?" They said, "We are just come." He said, "You were all dead." They said, "Bid the sun farewell."[75] Others hurled many assagais at him; they struck the ground. They picked them up, and again hurled many of them at him; they struck the ground. The men laughed at them, and said, "Give us the assagais, that we may kill him." They hurled many assagais; they struck the ground. The men picked them up.

The chief tries in vain to kill the boy.

Ya ti inkosi, "Gwed*h*lela ni mina, ngi m gwaze." Ya u ponsa inkosi umkonto; w' ema pansi. Ya ti, "Ng' a*h*lulekile, mfana. Ake w enze, si bone." Wa ti, "Ngi pe ni umkonto, ngi *h*labe nami." Ba m nika imikonto emi-

The chief said, "Get out of the way for me, that I may stab him." The chief hurled an assagai; it stuck in the ground. He said, "I am conquered, boy. Do you just try, that we may see." He said, "Give me an assagai, that I too may hurl it." They offered him

---

[75] Lit., End the sun,—that is, take a last view of the sun,—this is the last day you have to live.

ningi. Wa y ala, wa ti, "Ngi tanda munye." Ba m nika. Wa pimisela amate pansi ; a ti, "Nkosi, bayeti, wen' umnyama, wena wapakati." Wa ti, "Ngi *h*labe kinina?" Ba m *h*leka, ba ti, "Yenza, si bone." Wa u ponsa umkonto, wa *h*laba enkosini yakona. Ya fa, nabo bonke abantu.

many assagais. He refused them, and said, "I wish for one." They gave him one. He spat on the ground ; the spittle said, "Chief, all hail ! thou mysterious one, thou child of the greatest." He said, "May I stab you ?" They laughed and said, "Do it, that we may see." He hurled the assagai ; he struck their chief. He died, together with all his people.

He brings the people to life again, and leaves the chief dead.

Wa tabata umkonto, wa tshaya kubantu. Ba vuka abantu, ya sala inkosi. Ba ti, "Se si ng' abako. Se si za 'uhamba nawe."

He took an assagai and smote the people. The people arose, the chief remained still dead. They said, "We are now your people. We will now go with you."[76]

They are attacked on their journey by another tribe.

Ba d*h*lula kwesiny' isizwe. Ba *h*laba umkosi, ba ti, "Bulala ni. Nanku 'muntu 'emuka nabantu." Ya ba biza inkosi, ya ti, "A ba bulawe." Ba ya kubo, ba ti, "Ye*h*lika." Wa ti, "A ngi nyateli pansi." A ba tshela amasela,

They passed through another tribe. The people gave an alarm, and shouted, "Go and kill. There is a man going away with people." The chief called them, and ordered them to be killed. They went to them. They told him to come down from the ox. He replied, "I do not walk on the ground." The thieves told them, saying,

[76] We would refer the reader to the following similar instances :—

In Campbell's *Highland Tales* we read the account of the Red Knight, who meets his foster brethren, who were "holding battle against MacDorcha MacDoilleir, and a hundred of his people ; and every one they killed on one day was alive again on the morrow." This was effected by a "great toothy carlin," who had "a tooth that was larger than a staff on her fist." "She put her finger in their mouths, and brought them to life." (*Vol. II.*, p. 446—448.) In the tale of "The Widow and her Daughters," when the two eldest had been beheaded, the youngest "drew over them the magic club," and they "became lively and whole as they were before." (*Id. Vol. II.*, p. 269.)

See Grimm's *Home Stories*, "The Three Magical Leaves," p. 73.—"The Widow's Son" Jain is killed three times and brought to life again. (*Campbell. Op. cit. Vol. II.*, p. 295.)

Rata by repeating a "potent incantation" restores sixty of his warriors which had been slain to life again. (*Grey. Op. cit.*, p. 116.)

A spirit in the form of a flag found the place where Hatupatu was buried, and raised him to life again by enchantments. (*Id.*, p. 185.)

When the prince who had been transformed into a cat was disenchanted by having his head cut off, a large heap of bones also received life, and became a large body of courtiers, knights, and pages. (*Thorpe's Yule-tide Stories*, p. 75.)

The youth raises the father of the princess and her other relations by touching each of them with the hilt of the magical sword. (*Id.*, p. 167.)

a ti, "Wa si bulala nati." Ba ti, "Tina, ka z' 'u s' aḥlula." Ba m ponsa imikonto; ya ḥlaba pansi. Ba i wola, ba i ponsa; ya ḥlaba pansi. La ba ḥleka elinye ibuto, la ti, "Gwedḥlela ni tina, si ḥlabe." Ba i ponsa imikonto; ya ḥlaba pansi. Ba i wola. Ya ti inkosi, "Ngi nike ni mina, ngi m bulale." Ba ti abantu, "Si ya 'u ku babaza u m bulele." Ya ti, "Mina ngi namandḥla kakulu." Ya ponsa, y' aḥluleka.

"He killed us." They said, "But us he will not conquer." They hurled assagais at him; they struck the ground. One of the soldiers laughed at them, and said, "Make way for us, that we may stab him." They hurled their assagais; they struck the ground. They collected them. The chief said, "Hand them to me, that I may kill him." The people said, "We will praise you when you have killed him." He said, "I am very strong." He hurled the assagais; he was unable to kill him.

They try in vain to kill the boy; he kills the chief, and leads off the people.

Ya ti, "Yenza, mfana, ngi bone." Wa ti, "Ngi pe ni umkonto." Wa pimisa amate; a ḥlala pansi, a bila, a ti, "Bayeti, nkosi, wena wapakati." Ba m nika imikonto; wa y ala; wa tata wa ba munye; wa ti, "Ngi ḥlabe kinina?" Wa u ponsa enkosini yakona. Ba fa bonke. Wa u tata umkonto, wa tshaya enkosini yakona; ya vuka; ba vuka bonke.

Wa ti, "Ni sa buyela ini kimina?" Ba ti, "Tina, si sa pinda kuwe." Ba i ponsa imikonto, ya ḥlaba pansi. Ba i wola, ba i ponsa, imikonto ya ḥlaba pansi. Wa kcela umkonto, wa ti, "N' aḥlulekile?" Ba ti, "Yebo." Ba m nika umkonto wa ba munye. Wa ḥlaba enkosini, ba fa bonke. Wa tabata umkonto, wa tshaya kumuntu munye; ba vuka bonke; ya sala inkosi i file. Ba ti, "Se si ng' abako."

He said, "Do you try, boy, that I may see." He said, "Give me an assagai." He spat; the spittle remained on the ground and fizzed, and said, "Hail, chief, thou child of the greatest." They gave him assagais; he refused them, and took but one; he said, "May I hurl at you?" He threw the assagai at their chief. They all died. He took the assagai, and smote their chief; he arose, and all rose with him.

He said, "Will you yet again attack me?" They said, "For our part, we will still make another trial on you." They hurled the assagais; they struck the ground. They collected them, and threw them; they struck the ground. He asked for an assagai, and said, "Are you conquered?" They said, "We are." They gave him an assagai: he stabbed the chief; they all died. He took the assagai and struck one man; they all arose; the chief remained dead. They said, "We are now your people."

He sends messengers to his father.

Wa tuma abantu, wa ti, A ba ye kuyise, ba ti, "Ku y' eza Ubongopa-kamagad*h*lela." Wa kala uyise, wa ti, "Ni m bone pi na?" Ba ti, "U ba k*q*edile abantu." Ba ti, "U k*q*uba izinkomo eziningi." Wa tuma uyise abantu, wa ti, a ba buyele emuva. Ba fika, ba m tshela, ba ti, "Uyi*h*lo u pikile." Kwa kcatshunywa izinkomo, za bekwa inkomo e nombala; wa ti, kona uyise e ya 'ku m bona ngayo yakona lapo ekaya.

He sent some men to his father to tell him that Ubongopa-kamagadhlela was coming. His father cried, saying, "Where did you see him?" They said, "He has killed many people, and is coming with many cattle." His father told the men to go back again. On their arrival they told him his father refused to believe them. A few cattle were selected, and one bullock of a peculiar colour was placed among them. For he said his father would see that he was still living by that bullock which belonged to his village.

The nation prepares to receive him with joy.

Uyise wa memezela isizwe, wa ti, "A ku gaywe ukud*h*la." Wa ti, "Inkosi i ya buya." Ba fika abantu, ba ti, "Ng' amanga." Wa ti, "Hamba ni, ni ze 'ku i bona inkomo yalapa ekaya." Ba i bona abantu, ba ti, "Amak*q*iniso." Ba ti, "A ku funwe intombi, a fike se i *h*lezi." Kwa funwa intombi kabungani[77] kamakulukulu.

His father summoned the nation, and commanded them to make beer. He said, "The chief is coming back." The people said it could not be true. He said, "Go and look at the bullock belonging to our village, which has come back." The people saw it, and said, "It is the truth." They said, "Let a damsel be found, that on his arrival he may find her already here." They sought for a daughter of Ubungani, the son of Umakulukulu.

He returns to his home, and refuses to change his mode of life.

Ba hamba, ba vela okalweni, ba ti, "Uyi*h*lo u ti, 'Tshetsha.'" Ba hamba abantu nezinkomo kakulu. Ba vela okalweni ngasekaya. Ba m beka pambili Ubongopa-kamagad*h*lela. Za hamba kakulu, za fika osangweni. Ba puma abantu, ba buka. Wa jabula uyise nonina. Wa ti,

Those who were sent by his father reached the top of a hill, and said, "Your father tells you to make haste." The men and the cattle went rapidly. They appeared on a hill near their home. They placed Ubongopa-kamagadhlela in front: the cattle went rapidly, and reached the gateway. The people went out to see. His father and mother rejoiced. He said,

---

[77] *Ubungi*, the grandfather of Ulangalibalele.

" Bongopa-kamaga*dh*lela,
  Bongopa-kamaga*dh*lela,
  U bo ngena ; ku ya ngenwa ;
  U bo ngena ; ku ya ngenwa."

Za ngena esibayeni.

  Kwa gaulwa omunyo umuzi.
Wa ti, " Intombi a ngi i tandi,
ngokuba i hamba pansi." Y' e-
muka intombi. Wa ti, " Ngo za
ngi fe ngi *h*lezi pezulu." Kwa
tiwa ke, " Hlala kona lapo pezulu."

 W' alusa izinkomo zakubo.
W' enza leyo 'mikuba a e y enza
ekukqaleni.

  UMATSHOTSHA, (UMKAMAFUTA.)

" Ubongopa-kamagadhlela,
  Ubongopa-kamagadhlela,
  Go in now ; it is time to go in ;
  Go in now ; it is time to go in."

The cattle entered the enclosure.

  Another village was built. He
said, " I do not love the damsel,
because she goes on the ground."
The damsel departed. He said,
" I will live on the back of Ubongopa-kamagadhlela till my death."
So they said, " Stay then there on
his back."

  He herded the cattle of his
people. And continued to practise
the enchantments which he practised from his childhood.

UMDHLUBU[78] NESELESELE.

(UMDHLUBU AND THE FROG.)

The queen is hated by the other wives of the king.

Kw' esukela, inkosi ya zeka intombi yenye inkosi ; ya i tanda
kakulu ; abafazi bayo ba dabuka
ngoku i tanda kwayo. Y' emita,
ya zala umntwana wentombi ;
uyise wa m tanda kakulu. Wa
kula ; wa ti uma e isibak*x*a, abafazi b' enza ikcebo, ba ti, " Lok' u-
yise e nge ko, a si hambe si yokusika imizi." Ba tshela abantwana

ONCE on a time, a king married
the daughter of another king ; he
loved her very much ; his wives
were troubled on account of his
love for her. She became pregnant, and gave birth to a girl : the
father loved her exceedingly. The
child grew, and when she was a
fine handsome child, the other
wives formed a plot against her ;
they said, " Since her father is not
at home, let us go and cut fibre."[79]
They told the children not to agree

---

[78] *Umdhlubu*, Garden-of-ground-nuts.

[79] The fibre which is called *imizi* is derived from a kind of rush *(umhlahle)*.
It is used for binding up bundles, and for making the eating-mat. The natives
obtain fibre *(uzi)* of a longer kind from the bark of several trees ; *usando* and
umtombe, the barks of which are red ; *ubazi* and *umsasane*, the barks of which
are white. These barks are moistened and beaten, and so used ; or they are
twisted into cord.

ukuti, "Ni nga vumi uku m tabata umntwana." Unina wa biza
intombazana e sala naye. Y' ala
uku m tabata umntwana. Wa m
beleta unina, wa hamba naye.

to carry the child. The mother
called the little girl which nursed
her child. She refused to carry
her. The mother put her on her
back, and went with her.

The queen forgets her child.

Ba sika imizi, ba hamba njalo.
Kwa ti kwesiuye isi*h*lambo ba
*h*lala pansi, ba bema ugwai. Unina
wa bopa isitungu semizi, wa nika
umntwana, wa d*h*lala ngaso. B' e-
suka, ba sika imizi. Ba hamba
njalo. Wa ko*h*lwa umntanake
unina. Ba hamba njalo be sika ;
ba bopa, ba twala, ba goduka.

They cut fibre, and went on
continually. It came to pass in
one of the valleys[80] they sat down
and took snuff. The mother made
a bundle of fibre, and gave it to
the child : the child played with
it. They set out again and cut
fibre. They went on continually.
The mother forgot the child. They
went on continually cutting fibre ;
they tied it up into bundles, and
carried it home.

She seeks in vain for the lost child.

Ba fika ekaya, ba biza abaza-
nyana babantwana ; ba fika bonke.
Kodwa owake wa fika-ze. Wa
buza, wa ti, "U pi owami umntwana ?" Ba ti, "U hambe
naye." Wa dabuka ; wa kala, wa
gijima, wa ya 'kufuna. Ka m
tola ; wa buya.

When they came home, they
called the children's nurses : they
all came. But her's came without
the child. She asked, "Where is
my child ?" They said, "You
took her with you." She was
troubled, and cried, and ran to
find her. She did not find her,
and came back.

The polygamic wives rejoice.

Kwa kalwa kakulu. Sa tsho
isitembu, sa ti, "Ku njani ke
manje na ? Si l' apulile igugu
likayise. Intandokazi i jambisi-
siwe."

There was a great lamentation.
The polygamic wives said, "How
is it now then ? We have destroyed the father's darling. The pet
wife is utterly confounded."

A message is despatched to the king.

Kwa ya 'kubikelwa uyise ; kwa
tiwa, "Nkosi, umntanako u la*h*lekile, si yokusika imizi." Wa *h*lupeka kakulu uyise.

A messenger was sent to tell
the father ; it was said, "King,
your child has been lost, whilst we
were cutting fibre." The father
was greatly troubled.

[80] *Isihlambo*, here translated valley, is a depression between two hills,
where water runs in wet weather, or during storms.

The child is found by another queen.

Kwa ti kusasa isalukazi sasend*h*lu-nkulu sesiny' isizwe sa ya 'kuka amanzi; s' ezwa umntwana e d*h*lala; s' ezwa ku ti, "Ta, ta, ta." Sa mangala, sa ti, "Hau! ku ini loku na?" Sa nyonyoba, sa m funyanisa umntwana e *h*lezi e d*h*lala. Sa goduka, sa m shiya kanye nembiza yamanzi, kokubili. Sa biza inkosikazi yenkosi, sa ti, "Woza lapa." Ya puma inkosikazi end*h*lini. Sa ti, "Hamba, si hambe. I kona into emfuleni; u ya 'ku i bona." Ya hamba naso. Ba fika. Sa ti, "Nanku umntwana." Ya ti inkosikazi, "M tabate." Ya tsho ngokujabula. Sa m tabata. Ba fika emfuleni. Ya ti, "M geze." Sa m geza. Ya m tabata inkosikazi, ya m beleta, ya goduka.

In the morning an old woman of the royal household of another nation, went to fetch water: she heard the child playing; she heard something saying, "Ta, ta, ta." She wondered, and said, "Ah! what is this?" She went stealthily along, and found the child, sitting and playing. She went home, and left both her and the water-pot. She called the king's chief wife, and said, "Come here." The queen went out of the house. She said, "Let us go; there is something by the river which you will see." She went with the old woman. They arrived. She said, "Behold a child." The queen said, "Take her." She said so with joy. The old woman took her. They came to the river. The queen said, "Wash her." She washed her. The queen took her, and placed her on her back, and went home.

She is brought up with the queen's son.

Ya m ncelisa; ngokuba yona ya i zele umntwana womfana; ya m kulisa. Wa kula. Ba hamba bobabili nowake. Wa kula, wa intombi enkulu. Wa bekwa inkosi yezintombi; kw' enziwa ukudhla okukulu. Kwa *h*latshwa izinkomo eziningi. Ba jabula abantu bonke.

She suckled her, for she had given birth to a boy; she brought her up.[81] She grew. Both she and the queen's own child walked. She grew and became a great girl. She was appointed chief of the girls,[82] when a great feast was made. Many cattle were slaughtered, and all the people rejoiced.

The officers tell the queen's son to marry the foundling.

Ngemva kwaloko za ti izinduna kumfana, za ti, "I zeke le 'ntombi." Umfana wa mangala, wa ti, "Hau! ku njani loku na? Ant' udade wetu na? Sa ncela

After that the chief men said to the boy, "Marry this girl." The boy wondered, and said, "O! what is the meaning of this? Is she not my sister? Did we not suck together at my mother's

[81] Lit., She caused her to grow, that is, the queen nourished her.
[82] See Appendix (A).

kanye kumame na?" Za ti, "Kqa; wa tolwa esihlanjeni." W' ala, wa ti, "Kqa, udade wetu lo." Kwa sa futi, za ti, "Ku fanele u m tabate, a be umfazi wako." W' ala, wa hlupeka kakulu.

breast?"[83] They said, "No, she was found in a valley." He denied, and said, "No, she is my sister." The next morning they said, "It is proper you should take her to be your wife." He refused, and was greatly troubled.

An old woman imparts to the foundling the secret of her origin.

Kwa ti ngolunye usuku isalukazi sa tshena intombi, sa ti, "U y' azi na?" Ya pendula ya ti, "Ini na?" Sa ti, "U za 'kuzekwa." Ya buza ya ti, "Ubani na?" Sa ti, "Insizwa yakwenu." Ya ti, "Hau! kanjani na? Anti umne wetu lowo na?" Sa ti isalukazi, "Kqa; wa tabatwa esihlanjeni, wa kuliswa inkosikazi." Ya kala, i dabukile.

On another occasion an old woman said to the girl, "Do you know?" She answered, "What?" She said, "You are going to be married." She enquired, "To whom?" She said, "The young man of your own house?"[84] She said, "O! what is the meaning of this? Is he not my brother?" The old woman said, "No, you were taken from a valley, and brought up by the queen." She cried, being much troubled.

The foundling's grief.

Ya tabata imbiza yamanzi, ya hamba, ya fika emfuleni, ya hlala pansi, ya kala. Ya ka 'manzi, ya goduka. Ya hlal' ekaya. Wa i pa ukudhla unina: a ya ku vuma, y' ala. Wa pendula unina, wa ti, "Ini na?" Ya ti, "Kqa. Ku 'buhlungu ikanda lami." Kwa hlwa ke, ya ya 'kulala.

She took a water-pot, and went to the river, and sat down and wept. She filled her water-pot, and went home. She sat down in the house. Her mother gave her food; she did not like it, and refused. The mother asked, "What is it?" She said, "Nothing." There is a pain in my head." So it was evening, and she went to lie down.

She meets with a friend.

Kwa ti kusasa ya vuka, ya tabata imbiza yamanzi, ya fika emfuleni; ya hlala pansi, ya kala. Ya t' i sa kala, kwa puma iselesele

In the morning she awoke and took the water-pot, and went to the river; she sat down and wept. As she was crying, there came out

[83] It is not in accordance with native custom for a young man to marry his foster-sister.

[84] That is, the house in which you are living,—the house in which she had been brought up, and to which she supposed she belonged.

elikulu, la ti, "U kalela ni na?"
Ya ti, "Ngi ya *hlupeka.*" La ti
iselesele, "U *hlutshwa* ini na?"
Ya ti, "Ku tiwa, a ngi zekwe
umne wetu." La ti iselesele,
"Hamba, u tabate izinto zako
ezin*hle* o zi tandayo, u zi lete
lapa."

a great frog, and said, "Why are
you crying?"[85] She said, "I am
in trouble." The frog said, "What
is troubling you?" She replied,
"It is said that I am to become
the wife of my brother." The
frog said, "Go and take your
beautiful things, which you love,
and bring them here."

She quits her adopted home, and sets out in search of her own people.

Y' esuka, ya twala imbiza yamanzi, ya fik' ekaya ; ya tata enye
imbiza, ya tabata izinto zayo, ya zi
faka embizeni ; intonga yetusi, no-
muntsha kaben*hle,* neg*q*ila li k*q*o-
ndelwe ngezindondo zetusi, nek*q*e-
le, netusi, nobu*hlalu* bayo.   Ya
tabata lezo 'zinto, ya hamba, ya
fika emfuleni, ya zi kipela pansi.

She arose and took the water-
pot, and went home. She took
another pot, and fetched her things,
and put them in the pot ; she took
her brass rod, and her ubenthle
kilt, and a petticoat with a border
of brass balls ; and her fillet, and
her brass, and her beads. She
took these things, and went to the
river, and threw them out on the
ground.

La buza iselesele, la ti, "U ya
tanda na ngi ku yise kini na?"
Wa ti umntwana, "Yebo." La
tabata izinto, la zi ginga ; la m tabata umntwana, la m ginga, la
hamba naye.

The frog enquired, saying, "Do
you wish me to take you to your
own people?"   The child said,
"Yes." The frog took her things
and swallowed them ; he took her
and swallowed her ; and set out
with her.

The frog meets with a string of young men, who threaten to kill him.

La hamba la *hlangana* nodwendwe lwezinsizwa ; za li bona iselesele. Ya ti e pambili, "Ake ni
zokubona ; nanti iselesele elikulu
kakulu." Ba ti abanye, "A si li
bulale, si li ponse ngamatshe." La
ti iselesele,

In the way he met with a string
of young men ;[86] they saw the
frog. The one in front said, "Just
come and see : here is a very great
frog." The others said, "Let us
kill him, and throw stones at him."
The frog said,

[85] In Grimm's story of the Frog King, the princess is represented as having
dropped her golden ball into a well, and whilst standing by its side inconsolable
for the loss, and weeping bitterly, she hears a voice, which said, "What trou-
bles thee, royal maiden? thy complaints would move a stone to pity." This
voice she found to proceed from a frog, "which raised his thick ugly head out
of the water." The frog in this tale was an enchanted prince ; the princess is
the means of removing the enchantment, and becomes his wife.—When Cinder-
lass is weeping at the well, an exceedingly large pike rises to the surface, and
gives her assistance. (*Thorpe's Yule-tide Stories, p.* 114.)

[86] The natives walk in single file.

"Ngi iselesele nje; a ngi yi 'ku-
bulawa.
   Ngi yis' Umd*h*lubu kwelakubo
   izwe."[88]

Ba li yeka. Ba ti, "Hau! ku
ngani iselesele li kulume, l' enza
um*h*lola? A si li shiye." Ba
d*h*lula ke, ba hamba ke.

"I am but a frog; I will not be
killed.[87]
   I am taking Umdhlubu to her
   own country."

They left him. They said, "Hau!
how is it that the frog spoke,
making a prodigy? Let us leave
him." They passed on, and went
their way.

And a string of men.

La hamba ke neselesele. La
buya la *h*langana nodwendwe lwa-
madoda. Ya t' e pambili indoda,
"O, woza ni, ni zokubona iselesele
elikulu." Ba ti, "A si li bulale."
La ti iselesele,

"Ngi iselesele nje; a ngi yi 'ku-
bulawa.
   Ngi yis' Umd*h*lubu kwelakubo
   izwe."

Ba d*h*lula. La hamba iselesele.

And so the frog too went on
his way. Again he met with a
string of men. The one in front
said, "O, come and see a huge
frog." They said, "Let us kill it."
The frog replied,

"I am but a frog; I will not be
killed.
   I am taking Umdhlubu to her
   own country."

They passed on, and the frog went
on his way.

And some boys belonging to her father.

La funyanisa abafana b' alusile;
ba li bona; la bonwa okayise umfana. Wa ti, "Wau! Md*h*lubu
wenkosi! woza ni, si li bulale iselesele elikulu. Gijima ni, ni gaule
izinkandi, si li *h*labe ngazo." La
ti iselesele,

He fell in with some boys herding cattle: they saw him: he was
seen by a boy of the damsel's
father."[89] He said, "Wau! By
Umdhlubu the king's child! come
and kill a great frog. Run and
cut sharp sticks, that we may
pierce him with them." The frog
said,

---

[87] "I will not be killed."—A mode of deprecating death on the ground of
having some work in hand, the importance of which will be admitted to be too
great to allow of the messenger being put to death. When a person sentenced
to death, or threatened with it, says, "I will not be killed," he is at once understood, and asked, "What is it?" He explains, and if the reason is satisfac-
tory, they answer, "*Nembala*," (truly,) and the sentence is remitted.—Comp.
Jeremiah xli. 8, where Ishmael is represented as sparing ten out of the eighty
men he had ordered to be slain, because they had "treasures in the field" as
yet not harvested.

[88] *Kwelakubo izwe*, pronounced kwelakubw izwe.

[89] A boy of the damsel's father,—her half-brother.

"Ngi iselesele nje; a ngi yi 'ku-bulawa.
Ngi yis' Umd*h*lubu kwelakubo izwe."

"I am but a frog; I will not be killed.
I am taking Umdhlubu to her own country."

Wa mangala, wa ti, "O, madoda, a si nga li bulali. Li banga umu-nyu. Li dedele ni, li d*h*lule." Ba li dedela.

The boy wondered, and said, "O, sirs, do not let us kill him. He calls up painful emotions. Leave him alone, that we may pass on." They left him.

And her own brother.

La hamba, la fika kwabanye, la bouwa umne wabo; wa ti, "Md*h*lubu wenkosi! nanti iselesele elikulu kakulu. A si li kande ngamatshe, si li bulale." La ti iselesele,

The frog went on his way and came to others. He was seen by the girl's own brother: he said, "By Umdhlubu the king's child! There is a very great frog. Let us beat it with stones and kill it." The frog said,

"Ngi iselesele nje; a ngi yi 'ku-bulawa.
Ngi yis' Umd*h*lubu kwelakubo izwe."

"I am but a frog; I will not be killed.
I am taking Umdhlubu to her own country."

Wa ti, "O, li dedele ni. Li ku-luma okwesabekayo."

He said, "O, leave him alone. He speaks a fearful thing."

He arrives at her mother's village.

La d*h*lula, la fika ngasekaya, la ngena esi*h*la*h*leni ngenzansi kwo-muzi; la m kipa nezinto zake. La m lungisa, la m pak*q*ula ngom-pak*q*ulo wodou*q*a, la m gcoba, la m vunulisa.

He went on and came near her home: he entered a bush below the kraal: he placed her on the ground with her things. He put her in order: he cleansed her with udon*q*a:[90] he anointed her, and put on her ornaments.

She makes herself known to her mother.

Wa hamba ke. Wa tata into-nga yake yetusi, wa hamba, wa ngena ngesango, wa dabula pakati kwesibaya; wa hamba .pakati kwaso; wa fika entubeni, wa pu-

So she set out. She took her brass rod, and went and entered at the gateway, and she passed across the cattle enclosure: she, went in the middle of it: she came to the opening, she went out, and entered

[90] *Udon*q*a* is a small bush which bears white berries; when ripe they are gathered and bruised and formed into a paste; the body is first anointed with fat, and then rubbed over with the paste of the *udon*q*a*. This is one mode of cleansing, which is supposed more effectual than water. The natives use the *idumbe* in the same way.

ma, wa ngena end*h*lini yakwabo. Wa fika unina, wa ngena end*h*lini, wa ti, "U vela ngapi, ntombi, na?" Wa ti, "Ngi ya hamba nje." Wa t' unina, "Ngi tshele." Wa ti, "K*q*a, ngi hamba nje." Wa t' unina, "Ba ya dela abafazi aba nabantwana abangaka. Mina ngi ya *h*lupeka; umntwana wami wa la*h*leka; nga m shiya esi*h*lanjeni: wa fela kona." Wa pendula umntwana, wa ti, "Wa m la*h*lela ni na? W' enza ngoku nga m tandi?" Wa ti, "K*q*a; nga ko*h*liswa amakosikazi; 'ala ukuba umzanyana a m tabate." Wa m pendula, wa ti, "K*q*a. A ku ko umfazi o nga ko*h*lwa umntanake." Wa ti, "K*q*a; kw' enza ngoku nga jwayeli kwami ukupata umntwana; ngokuba wa e sala nomzanyana." Wa ti, "E-he; w' enza ngoku nga ngi tandi." Wa k*q*ala uku m bhekisisa; wa bona, "Umntanami lo."

the house of her mother. Her mother followed her into the house, and said, "Whence comest thou, damsel?" She said, "I am merely on a journey." The mother said, "Tell me." She said, "There is nothing, I am merely on a journey." The mother said, "Women are satisfied who have such fine children as you. For my part, I am in trouble: my child was lost: I left her in the valley: she died there." The child answered, saying, "Why did you leave her? Did you do it because you did not love her?" She said, "No; the queens made me forget her;[91] they would not allow the nurse to carry her." She said in answer, "No. There is no woman who can forget her own child." She said, "No; it happened through my not being accustomed to carry a child; for she used to remain with the nurse." She said, "Yes; you did it because you did not love me." She began to look very earnestly at her; she saw that it was her child.

Her mother rejoices.

Wa ti ukuba a m bone wa jabula. Wa bonga ngezibongo zake umntwana. Wa tata ingubo yake

When she saw her she rejoiced. She lauded with the laud-giving names of her child.[92] The mother

[91] "The queens made me forget her."—The reply of the child shows this to be the meaning of *kohliswa* in this place. The queens had so managed by giving her an unusual duty, and by beguiling her, to take away her attention from the child, that she was made to forget her.

[92] As braves receive laud-giving names from their chiefs, which express their noble actions, so a child which is much beloved by its parents, or which is remarkable for its actions and character, has praise-giving names invented for it. There is a youth in this neighbourhood named Untiye, a child of Umuka, who received the following praise-giving names from his grandfather—*Unganunameva*, "The-thorny-unganu." The *unganu* is a valuable tree in the native estimation, being a fruit-bearing tree, and used for carving vessels. But it has no thorns. The name therefore implies that he has qualities great and good like the *unganu*; but besides those he has other qualities which resemble thorns, and which occasion trouble. Another name, *Ihhoboshi-eli-vimbe-esangweni-kwapungula;—umakazi-abantwana-ba-ya-'kupuma-ngapi-na?* "Adder-which-obstructs-the-doorway-in-the-village-of-Upungula;—by-what-way-then-shall-the-children-go-out?" Both these laud-giving names have been strangely verified in the history and conduct of the young man. Thus in the tale, though Umdhlubu is lost, she is not forgotten; but her brothers swear by her name, and her mother's love invents laud-giving names for her.

unina, wa binca; wa tabata um-nqwazi, wa u faka ekanda; wa tabata isikaka sake sokwembata, w' embata; wa tabata umgqogqozo, wa puma, w' ekqa ngokujabula, wa halalisa; wa ngena esibayeni, wa dhlala e ngqabashiya. Ba mangala abantu, ba ti, "Ku ini kuntombinde namhla nje na? U jabulele ni kangaka na? Loku se i loku kwa fa umntanake wamazibulo, ka sa jabuli; i loku wa hlupekayo."

took her robe, and girded herself; she took her head-ornament, and put it on her head; she took her petticoat, and put it on; she took her staff, and went out; she leaped for joy, and balalaed;[93] she went into the cattle-pen; she played leaping about with joy. The people wondered and said, "What has happened to Untombinde to-day? Why does she rejoice so much? Since from the time her first-born died, she has never rejoiced, but has constantly been sorrowful."

Another woman joins in the rejoicings.

Kwa puma omunye ohlangoti lwangakwake, wa ti, "Ake ngi yo'ubona uma ku kona ni endhlini na? Ini ukuba ngi zwe inkosikazi i bonga ngezibongo zomntwana owa fayo na?" Wa hamba ke, wa ngena endhlini, wa m bona; wa puma, wa hlaba umkosi omkulu, wa bonga.

One from her side[94] went out, and said, "Just let me go and see what is in the house? Why do I hear the queen lauding with the laud-giving names of her dead child?" So she went, and entered the house, and saw her; she went out, and shouted aloud, and gave thanks.

The other women are confounded.

Ba puma bonke abantu. Ba gijima ba ya endhlini ngokupangelana. Ba kcindezelana emnyango. Ba m bona umntwana. Ba jabula abohlangoti lwangakwabo. Ba hlupeka abanye bonke, namakosikazi olunye uhlangoti a ti, "Hau! ku ngani na? Loku sa si ti, se si m bulele lo 'mntwana. U vukile futi. Si za 'ujambiswa kanye nabantabetu. Bu za 'upela ubukosi kwabetu abantwana."

All the people went out. They ran to the house, hurrying to get there first. They crowded each other together at the doorway. They saw the child. All the people on her side rejoiced. All the others were troubled, and the queens[95] of the other side said, "Ah! What does it mean? For we thought we had already killed this child. She has come to life again. We shall be confounded together with our children. The supremacy of our children is coming to an end."

---

[93] *Halala*, to shout halala, a shout of joy, like our huzzah.

[94] See Appendix (B).

[95] Every wife of a chief is queen, or chieftainess. So in other kraals each wife is chieftainess in her own house *(endhlini yakwabo)*, and all may be addressed by way of politeness as *amakosikazi*, "chief-wives," if the chief wife is not present; when she is, she alone is called *inkosikazi*.

The king is informed of her arrival.

Kw' esuka isigijimi, sa ya kuyise, sa hamba, sa fika, sa ti, "Nkosi, u vukile umntwana owa e file." Ya ti inkosi, "Hau! u ya *h*lanya na? U mu pi lowo 'mntwana na?" Sa ti isigijimi, "Umd*h*lubu." Wa ti uyise, "U vela pi na?" Sa ti, "A ng' azi, nkosi." Wa ti uyise, "Uma ku nge si ye, ngi ya 'ku ku bulala. Uma ku u ye, gijima, u *h*lab' umkosi kuzo zonke izindawo, ba bute izinkabi zonke ezinkulu, b' eze nazo."

A messenger set out and went to her father; he arrived and said, "O king, your child that was dead has come to life again." The king said, "Hau! Art thou mad? Which is that child?" The messenger said, "Umdhlubu." The father said, "Whence comes she?" He said, "I do not know, O king." The father said, "If it be not she, I will kill thee. If it be she, run, raise a cry in all places, that the people may bring together all the large oxen, and come with them."

The news is published, and the people rejoice.

Sa hamba, sa u *h*laba umkosi. Sa ti, "Inkosazana i fikile. Tshetsha ni nezinkabi." Ba buza abantu, ba ti, "I ipi inkosazana na?" Sa ti, "Umd*h*lubu wenkosi, owa e file."

Ba jabula; ba *h*loma izi*h*langu zabo; ba tabata izinkabi, ba zi k*q*uba, nezipo zabo zokujabulisa inkosazana; ngokuba i vuke ekufeni; ba i tola, be nga s' azi. Ba fika, ba *h*laba izinkabi eziningi na sezind*h*leleni, ukuze ku d*h*le amak*x*eku nezalukazi nabagulayo, aba nge namand*h*la okufika ekaya, lapo inkosazana i kona.

He went and raised a cry, and said, "The princess has come. Make haste with the oxen." The men asked, "Which princess?" He replied, "Umdhlubu the child of the king, who was dead."

They rejoiced; they took their shields; they took the oxen, and drove them; they took also their presents to gladden the princess; for she had risen from death; they found her when they no longer expected it. They came; they slaughtered many cattle, even in the ways, in order that the old men, and the old women, and the sick might eat, who were not able to reach the home where the princess was.

The king visits the princess.

Wa fika uyise, wa ti, "Puma, mntanami, ngi ku bone." Ka pendulanga. Wa *h*laba izinkabi ezi 'mashumi 'mabili. Wa vela emnyango, w' ema. Wa *h*laba amashumi amatatu. Wa puma. Wa ti uyise, "Hamba, u ye esiba-

The father came and said, "Come out, my child, that I may see you." She did not answer. He slaughtered twenty oxen. She made her appearance at the doorway, and stood still. He slaughtered thirty;[96] she came out. The father said, "Go into the cattle-

---

[96] Not thirty other cattle, but ten, making thirty altogether.

yeni, si ye 'ku ku ketela ngokujabula okukulu; ngokuba nga ngi
ti, u s' u file, kanti u se kona."
W' ema. Wa buya wa *h*laba amashumi amane. Wa hamba ke, wa
ngena esibayeni.

kraal; let us go to dance for you,
for our great joy; for I used to
say, you are already dead, but in
fact you are still alive." She
stood still. Again he slaughtered
forty oxen. Then she went, and
entered into the kraal.[97]

They dance for her.

Ba m ketela kakulu. Kodwa
olunye u*h*langoti lwomuzi a lu ja-
bulanga, a lu ketanga kanye nabantwana babo namakosikazi. Ba
k*q*eda ukuketa.

They danced for her very much.
But the other side of the kraal did
not rejoice; it did not dance together with the children and queens
of that side. They left off dancing.

The king sits with his child, and orders a fat ox to be killed for her.

Uyise wa ya naye endh*lini, wa
*h*lala naye, wa ti, "A ku tabatwe
inkabi entsha enonileyo, i *h*latshwe, ku pekelwe umntwana,
ukuze si d*h*le si jabule; ngokuba
u b' e file, u vukile ekufeni."

The father went with her into
the house, and sat down with her.
He said, "Let a fat young ox be
taken, and killed, and cooked for
the child, that we may eat and
rejoice, for she was dead, and has
risen from death."

The king and queen and her children rejoice together.

Ba jabula ke bonke abantu.
Umntwana wa buyela esikund*h*leni sake sobukosi bake. Uyise wa
husa kakulu, wa buyela kwokwo-
kukqala, wa *h*lala kulo 'muzi wake,
ngokuba wa e nga sa *h*lali kona
kakulu, ngokuba wa e kumbula
umntwana wake, owa e file. Ba
jabula kanye nonina nabantwana
bakwabo.

So all the people rejoiced. The
child returned to her royal position. Her father did right royally;
he returned to his former habits,
and lived at that kraal, for he had
ceased to be there much, because
he remembered his child which
had died. Her mother and the
children of her house rejoiced
together.

The frog is called by the king and rewarded.

Wa buza uyise, wa ti, "U ze
kanjani lapa na?" Wa ti umntwana, "Ngi twaliwe iselesele."
Wa ti uyise, "Li pi na?" Wa ti
umntwana, "Li lapaya esi*h*la*h*le-

Her father asked her, "How
did you come here?" The child
said, "I was brought by a frog."
The father said, "Where is he?"
The child replied, "He is yonder

[97] This custom of slaughtering cattle to induce a person to quit a house, to
move forward, &c., is called *ukunyatelisa*, to make to take steps.

ni." Wa t' uyise, "A ku tabatwe izinkabi; li yokuketelwa, li kupuke, li ze ekaya." Ba hamba ke, ba li ketela.

B' eza nalo ekaya. La ngeniswa end*h*lini, la piwa inyama, la d*h*la. Ya buza inkosi, ya ti, "U funa ni na, ngi ku kokele na?" La ti, "Ngi funa izinkomo ezimnyama ezinsizwa." Ya tabata izinkomo eziningi, nabantu, ya ti, "Hamba ni nalo." Ba hamba ke, ba fika ezweni lalo.

in the bush." The father said, "Let oxen be taken, that he may be danced for, and come up to our home." So they went and danced for him.

They brought him home. They brought him into the house and gave him meat, and he ate. The king enquired, "What do you wish that I should give you as a reward?" He said, "I wish some black hornless cattle." He took many cattle and people, and said, "Go with him." So they went and came to his country.

The frog becomes a great chief.

L' ak' umuzi omkulu, la ba inkosi enkulu. La *h*laba ngezikati zonke inyama; ku ze abantu ba ze 'kukcela inyama. Ba buze ba ti, "Ipi inkosi ye*h*u na, ey' ake lo 'muzi na?" Ba ti, "Uselesele." Ba ti, "Wa u tata pi na umuzi na ongaka na?" Ba ti, "Wa u tola ngokuba wa leta inkosazana yakiti enkosini; ya m nika izinkomo nabantu." Ba pendula ba ti, "Ni ng' abakaselesele na?" Ba ti, "Yebo. Ni nga m bizi kabi; u ya 'ku ni bulala, ngokuba u inkosi enkulu."

Wa tola Uselesele abantu abaningi. Ba *h*lubuka amakosi abo ngokubona uku*h*la okuningi kukaselesele. Wa busa ke Uselesele, wa ba inkosi.

The frog built a great town, and became a great chief. He slaughtered cattle continually; and men came to ask for meat. They enquired, "What is your chief who built this town?" They said, "Uselesele."[98] They enquired, "Whence did he obtain so large a town as this?" They said, "He got it because he brought our princess to the king; so he gave him cattle and men." They answered, saying, "Are you then the people of Uselesele?" They said, "Yes. Do not speak disrespectfully of him; he will kill you, for he is a great chief."

Uselesele took many people under his protection. They revolted from their chiefs through seeing the abundance of food at Uselesele's. So Uselesele reigned and became a king.

Umdhlubu's beauty is celebrated, and Unkosi-yasenthla sends his people to see her.

W' ezwa Unkosi-yasen*h*la ukuti, "I kona intomb' en*h*le kankosi-

Unkosi-yasenthla heard it said, "Unkosi-yasenzansi[99] has a beau-

<hr>

[98] *Uselesele*, a proper name, The-frog-man.
[99] Comp. p. 89, Note. Or we may render these words, King of the Uplands or Highlands; and King of the Lowlands.

yasenzansi, igama layo Umdhlubu."
Wa ti kubantu bake, "Hamba ni,
ni ye 'ku i bona, ukuba intombi e
njani na." Ba hamba ke, ba fika
kunkosi-yasenzansi, ba ti, "Nkosi,
si tunyiwe Unkosi-yasenhla ukuba
si kete intomb' enhle pakati kwabantwana bako."

tiful daughter, named Umdhlubu."
He said to his people, "Go and
see what kind of a damsel it is."
They went, and came to Unkosi-
yasenzansi, and said, "King, we
have been sent by Unkosi-yasenthla, that we might select a beautiful damsel from among your
children."

*The king's daughters are summoned, and Umdhlubu is chosen for her
surpassing beauty.*

Wa ba biza ke, b' eza, ba fika.
Ba za ba bona intombi yanye kuzo zonke, eyona y' ahlula ezinye
ngobuhle. Ngokukumbula, ukuba
uma inkosi i tume abantu ukuya
'uketa intombi enhle, ku fanele ba
bhekisise kakulu; ngokuba labo
'bantu ba amehlo enkosi ngoku ba
temba, b' enzela ukuze ba nga
solwa, lapa se i fike 'kaya. Ba i
bona imbi, i nga fani neutombi e
ketelwe inkosi, ba sole kakulu,
ngokuti, "Ku ngani ukuba inkosi
ni i hlebe, ni i ketele iuto embi
na?" Udumo lwalabo 'bantu lu
pele; ba suswe na sesikundhleni
esihle ngokuti a ba tembeki.
Ngaloko ke Umdhlubu ba m keta
ngalobo 'buhle ngokuti, "U yeua
lo yedwa o fanele ukuba inkosikazi
yenkosi kunazo zonke lezi."

He summoned them, and they
came. At length they saw one
only damsel which excelled all the
others in beauty. For they remembered, that if a king has sent
people to go and choose a beautiful
damsel, it is proper that they
should look very earnestly; for
those people are the king's eyes,
because he trusts them. They
look earnestly, that they may
not be reproved when the damsel is brought home. When
they see she is ugly, not like
a damsel which has been chosen for a king, they find great
fault, saying, "Why have you dis-
graced the king by choosing an
ugly thing for him?" The honour
of those men is ended; they are
removed from their honourable
office, because they are not trustworthy. Therefore they chose
Umdhlubu for her beauty-sake,
saying, "It is she only who is fit
to be the king's queen above all
the others."

The others are ashamed, and hate her.

I ngalo ke eza shiywako za
jamba, naonina ba jamba, nabane
wabo ba jamba. Kwabo-mdhlu-
bu kwa jabulwa. Ukujabula kwa

Therefore those who were left
were ashamed; and their mothers
were ashamed; and their brothers
were ashamed.[1] There was rejoicing in the house of Umdhlubu.

[1] That is, those belonging to the other side of the village.

kqala kumd*h*lubu, o bonakaliswe pakati kweziningi na seme*h*lweni abo bonke, ngokuti, "Nangu omu-*h*le impela!" Unina wa tsho en*h*liziyweni yake ukuti, "Nga m zala ka*h*le umntanami!" Naba-kwabo ba kuliswa, noma unina wabo a e kuliswe kade inkosi ngo-kutandwa. Nanto ke uzondo oloua lw' anda kuleyo 'nd*h*lu ya-kwabo-md*h*lubu; a lwa ba lu sa pela, ngokuba inkosi yezizwe ya pinda ya tanda Umd*h*lubu, loku nonina wake wa e tandwa futi ka-kulu uyise kamd*h*lubu. Ukuzo-ndeka kwa ba kukulu kwamanye amakosikazi ngobu*h*le bukamd*h*lu-bu, obwa tandwa inkosi yezizwe pezu kwabantwana bawo bonke. Ba jamba njalo. .

The joy began with Umdhlubu, who was conspicuous for beauty among many other damsels and in the eyes of them all, for it was said, "There is a beautiful woman indeed!" Her mother rejoiced in her heart, saying, "I did well when I gave birth to my child!" And the children of her house were exalted, although their mother had been long ago exalted [2] by the king, through being loved. There, then, was the hatred which increased towards that house of Umdhlubu; it never ceased, for a king of another nation loved Umdhlubu, as her mother also was loved very much by the father of Umdhlubu. There was a very great hatred in the hearts of the other queens, on account of the beauty of Umdhlubu, which was admired by the king of another people above all their own children. They were ashamed for ever.

Unkosi-yasenthla goes with a thousand head of cattle to take Um-dhlubu as his bride.

Ba bheka ke, ba keta Umd*h*lu-bu. B' emuka, ba ya 'kutshela inkosi. Ba fika ekaya, ba ti, "Nkosi, si i bonile intombi en*h*le, igama layo Umd*h*lubu." Ya ti inkosi, "Ehe; ku*h*le ke. Ku fanele ukuba si hambe, si ye kona, si tabate izinkomo ezi inkuluugwa-ne." Ba hamba ke.

So they looked, and chose Um-dhlubu. They departed to tell the king. They arrived home, and said, "King, we have seen the beautiful damsel; her name is Um-dhlubu." The king said, "Aye; it is well. We must set out and go thither, and take a thousand head of cattle." So they set out.

He arrives at the king's, and asks for Umdhlubu in marriage.

Wa ti Unkosi-yasenzansi e *h*lezi emtunzini pakati kwesibaya na-

Unkosi-yasenzansi, as he was sitting in the shade within the

[2] *Noma, &c.*—This mode of expression is used to imply that the exaltation is nothing new, but something super-added to a dignity already possessed. If any one addressed a great man by saying, *Si ya ku kulisa kule 'ndawo,* "We honour you in regard to that matter," he would reply, *Okwesinga'ki ukukuliswa na?* "Whence does that honour spring?" The man would at once understand that he claimed a previous honour, and would ask, *Umkulu ngapambili na?* "Has he a greatness before now?" They would say to a great man, *Bani, si ya ku kulisa kule 'ndawo, noma umkulu kade,*" "So-and-so, we honour you in that matter, though you are already great."

bantu bake, wa ti, "Ku ini lokuya na? Ku kona utuli olukulu olu *h*langene nezulu." B' esaba. Wa ti emabutweni ake, "Zilungiseleni, ngokuba a si kw azi oku zayo." Ngemva kwaloko kwa vela izinkomo, zi hamba uenkosi nabantu bayo. Ba ba *h*langabeza.

cattle-pen with his people, said, "What is that yonder? There is a great dust which rises to the heaven." They were afraid. He said to his soldiers, "Get ready to fight, for we do not know what is coming." After that the cattle appeared going with the king and his people. They went to meet them.

Wa ti, "Ngi ng' Unkosi-yasen*h*la, ngi ze kumd*h*lubu." Ba hamba naye, ba y' ekaya. Ba fika, ba kuleka. Uyise wa jabula um' ezwe loko.

He said, "I am Unkosi-yasenthla; I come to see Umdhlubu." They went with him home. When they arrived, they asked to have Umdhlubu given them. Her father rejoiced when he heard that.

The king assents.

Ba *h*labiswa. Ba kuluma noyise. Wa ti Unkosi-yasen*h*la, "Ngi ze kuwe, nkosi-yasenzansi, ngi funa ukutabata intombi yako; uma u vuma, ku lungile. Ngi ze nezinkomo ezi inkulungwane." Wa vuma uyise, wa ti, "Ku lungile."

They had cattle slaughtered for them. They spoke with the father. Unkosi-yasenthla said, "I come to you, Unkosi-yasenzansi, I being desirous of taking your daughter; if you assent, it is well. I come with a thousand cattle." The father assented, saying, "It is well."

Umdhlubu is given to Unkosi-yasenthla.

Wa buta izintombi zonke nabesilisa, amake*h*la nezinsizwa; wa kipa abantu boku m sebenzela Umd*h*lubu. Wa kipa itusi loku m endisa nobu*h*lalu, nezinkabi ezi 'makulu 'ma*h*lanu, wa ti, "Ku lungile ke. Hamba naye. Nansi induna yoku m endisa."

He assembled all the girls, and all the men, the young men with head-rings,[3] and the youth; he set apart men for the purpose of working for Umdhlubu. He took out brass and beads for her marriage, and five hundred oxen, and said, "Now it is right. Set out with her. There is an officer for the purpose of conducting the wedding ceremonies."

They are received with rejoicing by Unkosi-yasenthla's people.

Ba hamba naye, ba fika ekaya. Ba ti, be sa vela, kwa *h*latshwa umkosi omkulu, abantu ba vela

They went with him, and reached his home. As they were coming into sight, a great cry was raised,

[3] Head-ring.—See p. 210.

indawana zonke, ba ti, "I fikile inkosikazi kankosi-yasen*h*la." Ba jabula.

Kwa lalwa. Kwa ti kusasa, uma li pume ilanga, kwa fudumala, za puma izintombi namake*h*la nezinsizwa, za ya esi*h*la*h*leni, za *h*lala kona. Kwa fika isikati seketo, ba keta; ba i tabata esi*h*la*h*leni intombi; ya goduka, ya ya 'kusina.

and the people appeared in all directions, shouting, "The queen of Unkosi-yasenthla has come." They rejoiced.

They retired to rest. In the morning, when the sun had risen, and it was hot, the damsels went out with the young men and youth, and went into the bush; they sat down there. When the time for dancing arrived, they danced; they fetched the damsel from the bush; she went to the kraal to dance.

They complete the marriage ceremonies.

Ba sina ke, ba k*q*eda. Ya tata itusi, ya li beka pambili kukayise, ya kuleka, ya ti, "Nkosi, u ze u ngi londoloze, ngokuba manje se ngi pakati kwesand*h*la sako, u ngi gcine."

Ba *h*lala pansi wonk' umtimba. Ba ba ketela. Ba k*q*eda ukuketa. Kwa ti kusasa ya *h*laba intombi izinkomo ezi ishumi; ba d*h*la, ba jabula.

So they ended the dance. She took brass, and placed it before her father,[4] and prayed, saying, "Sire, take care of me for ever, for now I am in thy hand, preserve me."

The whole marriage party sat down. They danced for them. They ended the dance. In the morning the damsel killed ten bullocks; they ate and rejoiced.

The officer returns with a present for Umdhlubu's mother.

Ya tsho induna, ya ti, "Nkosi, se si funa ukuhamba, si goduke, ngokuba umsebenzi u pelile."

Ya tabata izinkomo ezi 'makulu 'ma*h*lanu, ya ti, ezikanina. Ba goduka.

The officer said, "Sire, we now wish to set out to return home, for the work is done."

The king took five hundred head of cattle, and sent them as a present to his mother.[5] They went home.

They build Umdhlubu's town.

Kwa sala izintombi. Wa e te uyise, a zi nga goduki, zi *h*lale naye, zi m sebenzele; nabantu abaningi, isilisa nesifazana sokwaka umuzi wake, ba *h*lala kona.

Ya ti inkosi, "Gaula ni manje umuzi wenkosikazi, i *h*lale nabantu bayo."

The damsels remained. Umdhlubu's father had said that they were not to return, but stay with her, and work for her; and much people, both male and female, remained there to build her town.

The king said, "Now build the town of the queen, where she may live with her people."

---

[4] That is, her husband's father.

[5] That is, his wife's mother.

Unkosi-yasenthla takes up his abode there.

W' akiwa ke umuzi, wa kqedwa. Ya ya kona; kwa *h*latshwa izinkabi eziningi, ukuze amabuto a d*h*le, a vutise umuzi wenkosikazi. Ya hamba nenkosi, ya ya 'ku*h*lala kona emzini omutsha. Ya m tabata ke Umd*h*lubu.

So the town was built and completed. The king visited it; many cattle were killed, that the soldiers might eat, and complete the queen's town. The king also went to live there at the new town. Thus he took Umdhlubu to be his wife.

The people return in safety to Unkosi-yasenzansi.

Ba fika abantu bakayise kamd*h*lubu ekaya, ba ti, "Nkosi, si sebenzile ka*h*le kakulu. Nazi izinkomo zikanina kamd*h*lubu; u zi piwe indodana yake. U te, a si ze si m konzele na kuyise na kunina."

Bonke ke ba pila ka*h*le 'ndawo nye.

MARY (UMKAMPENGULA).

The people of Umdhlubu's father reached their home, and said, "O king, we have done all things very well. There are cattle for Umdhlubu's mother; they are given to her by her son. He told us to give his respects to both his father and mother."

So all lived together in peace.

APPENDIX (A).

INDABA YENKOSI YENTOMBI.

(THE ACCOUNT OF A GIRL-KING.)

Ku ti lapa ku kona izintombi eziningi, kulowo 'mfula ow akiweyo izintombi zi *h*langane, zi beke inkosi yokuba i buse izintombi, ku nga bi ko intombi e zenzela ngokwayo. Nembala ke zi *h*langane zi buzane ngokuti, "Intombi e nga ba inkosi, i buse ka*h*le, i nga ba i pi na?" Zi fune, zi fune, zi beke, zi kipe, zi ze zi vumelane kuyo i be nye, zi ti, "Yebo, Unobani u ya 'kubusa."

Njalo ke noma ku ya fika amasoka azo, a ya bikwa kuyo; uma i nga tandi ukuba zi ye kuwo, zi nga yi; zi botshwe ngomteto wentombi leyo e inkosi. Uma ku

WHEN there are many young women, they assemble on the river where they live, and appoint a chief over the young women, that no young woman may assume to act for herself. Well, then, they assemble and ask each other, "Which among the damsels is fit to be chief and to reign well?" They make many enquiries; one after another is nominated, and rejected, until at length they agree together to appoint one, saying, "Yes, So-and-so shall reign."

So then when sweethearts come, they are reported to her; if she does not wish the damsels to go to them, they do not go; they are bound by the word of the damsel which is their chief. If

kona ey' onayo, i *hlauliswe* isi*hla*-
ulo esitile ezintweni zayo; lokupela a zi nankomo, a zi fuye 'luto,
i zona zi fuyiwe aoyise; imfuyo
yazo ubu*hlalu* netusi nokunye
kwezintwana; i loko ke oku imfuyo e zi *hlaula* ngako, uma enye
y euze ikcala. Ku ya buswa kakulu inkosi yazo.

Kepa abanye abantu ba ya pika,
ba ti, "A ku lungile ukuba ku be
kona iukosi yezintombi." A ba
tsho ngokuti, kubi; ba tsho ngokuba ku tiwa, iukosi e busa izintombi a i pati 'mntwana, i ya
bujelwa; ku njalo ke uyise wayo
'ale ukuba i buse. Kepa a kw a-
zeki ukuba ku isiminya impela,
ngokuba noma zi felwa, ezinye zi
ya ba pata.

Ku njalo ke ku ti ngesikati
sokuba ku ngena ulibo, ukuti
ukwin*hla*, amasoka a tandwa izintombi a wa d*h*li ukwin*hla* kuk*q*ala,
e nga ka biki ezintombini; futi
intombi i nge d*h*le ukwin*hla* i nga
ka biki enkosini yayo; futi na se-
sokeni i nge li bikele, uma i nga
n*q*omanga kuk*q*ala enkosini yazo.
A ku bikwa ugomlomo nje; ku
bikwa ngento, ku tiwe, "Nansi
into yokubika ukwin*hla*. U ng' e-
tuki; se ngi ya d*h*la." Uma ya
d*h*la i nga bikanga, i nekcala enkosini yezintombi; i ya 'ku*hlauli*-
swa, i pute kuko konke loko e be
i ya 'kuvunyelwa uma i lindile.
Ku ngokuba i nga lindanga i ya
hlupeka ngokuvinjelwa kuko konke.

any is guilty of an offence, she is
fined by a fine taken from something belonging to her; for in fact
they have no cattle nor any live
stock; their fathers possess such
things; their property consists of
beads and brass, and other such
little matters; this, then, is the
property with which they pay
their fines, if any do wrong. The
chief of the damsels exercises.
great authority.

But some will not permit their
daughter to be elected chief, for
they say, it is not proper that
there should be a chief of the
damsels. They do not say so because it is wrong, but because it is
said, a girl-king never nurses a
child, they all die; it is on this
account that her father will not
allow her to be king. But it is
not known that this is really true;
for although the children of some
die, the children of others grow up.

So then, at the time of the approach of the feast of firstfruits,
that is, when they are about to eat
new food, those young men who
are loved by the damsels do not
eat new food before they have
given notice to them; and a damsel cannot eat new food until she
has given notice to her chief; and
she cannot tell her sweetheart before she has first told the girl-king.
They do not give notice with the
mouth only, but with some present, saying, "Here is my present
by which I give notice that I am
about to eat new food. Do not
wonder; I am now eating it." If
she eat without having given notice, she has committed an offence
against the girl-king; she is fined,
and is refused all things which she
would have been allowed if she
had waited. Because she did not
wait she is vexed by being obstructed in all her wishes.

Amasoka uma e fika emgonqweni, lapa ku tombe intombi kona,—
ngokuba uma intombi i tombile u
lapo kw enziwa isidala sokuba
abatsha bonke ba *h*langane ukuba
ba ye emgonqweni lapo ku tonjiswe kona ; isidala ukuba ku y' aziwa ukuba leyo 'nd*h*lu lapa ku
tombele intombi kona, se ku in-
d*h*lu yamasoka nezintombi, lapa
ku ya 'kubizwa konke okubi, uku-
*h*lonipa ngalolu 'suku ku ya pela,
ku bizwa konke okwesabekayo,
njengokungati ukutomba kwen-
tombi ku kulula abantu eku*h*lupe-
keni konke ngoku*h*lonipa izinto
ezi nge bizwe obala, umuntu e ku
nga tiwa, uma e zi biza ngamagama
azo, u *h*lanya. Lapo ke emgonqweni abantu ba penduka izin-
*h*lanya bonke ; ngokuba ku nga bi
ko omkulu o nga ti, "Musa ni
ukupata loku." Hai, ku y' aziwa
ukuba lusuku lwesidala, ukuba
kw enziwe konke njengokutanda
kwezin*h*liziyo zaba semgonqweni.
Ngaloko ke ngesiuye isikati nga-
langa linye ku fika amasoka a vela
ezindaweni eziningi, nend*h*lu i be
ncinane ; a vinjelwe ukuba a ngene,
a ze a koke. Uma ku kona inkosi
yazo, ku boniswe yona leyo 'nto e
vula umnyango ; uma incinane
y ale, ku vezwe enkulu njalo.
Umfazi o lala emgonqweni 'ale
ukupuma, a vimbele amasoka, a
ko*h*lwe nezintombi, a ze a m kipe
ngento, a pume ke ; ba sale ke, ba

When young men come to the
umgonqo, where the ceremonies of
puberty are being performed,—for
when a damsel is of age, it is then
that the filthy custom is practised
of all the young people assembling
to go to the umgonqo where the
ceremonies of puberty are performed ; the filthiness is this, that it is
known that the house where a
damsel is subjected to the ceremonies of puberty is now a house of
sweethearts and damsels, where all
kind of evil will be spoken ;
modesty is at an end at that time,
and all fearful things are mentioned, as if the puberty of a young
woman set all free from all trouble
of behaving modestly in reference
to things which ought not to be
openly mentioned, and which if a
man mentioned them by name, he
would be regarded as mad. There,
then, at the umgonqo all people
become mad, for there is no one of
authority there who can say, "Do
not mention such things." No, it
is known that it is a day of filthiness, in which every thing may be
done according to the heart's de-
sire of those who gather around
the umgonqo. So, then, at one
time of the same day there come
young men from all quarters, and
the house is too small to admit
them ; they are prevented from
entering until they have made a
present ; if there is a girl-king,
she determines what shall open the
door ; if the present is small, she
refuses ; and so a larger offering is
made. The woman who sleeps in
the umgonqo[6] refuses to go out,
and obstructs the young men ; and
they are prevented from entering
also by the other damsels, until
they induce her to go out by a
present ; so she goes out, and the

---

[6] This word is not only applied to the umgonqo proper, but to the hut in
which it is built.

zid*h*lalele ngako konke. U njalo
ke umgon*q*o ukuhamba kwawo.

Umkosi wentombi, ukuba kw e-
nziwe utshwala obukulu, ku butane abantu abaningi, ba puze.
Kepa lowo 'mkosi a u d*h*laleli
ekaya njengomkosi wenkosi impela ; ai, u d*h*lalela emfuleni. Ku
ze 'kubuka aba tandayo. Abanye
ba nga zikatazi, ngokuba b' azi
ukuba ku umfanekiso nje. " Isifazana si kw azi ngani ukud*h*lalisa
kwenkosi impela na ? " U ba
mkulu lowo 'mkosi ngokuba kw e-
nziwe utshwala nje bokupuza.

Ku njalo ke ukubusa kwen-
tombi.

UMPENGULA MBANDA.

young people remain alone, and
sport after their own fancies in
every respect. Such, then, is the
conduct of the umgon*q*o.

The festival of a girl-king is
this,—much beer is made, many
people are assembled and drink.
But the festival is not kept at
home, as is that of one who is a
chief indeed. No, it is kept near
the river. Those who wish come
to look on ; some will not trouble
themselves to go, for they know it
is a mere play, and ask, " How
should woman know how to act
the king indeed ? " The festival
is great because there is much beer
to drink.

Such, then, is the government
of a girl.

APPENDIX (B.)

THE HERITAGE IN POLYGAMIC HOUSEHOLDS.

INDABA yo*h*langoti lwesitembu e
ku tiwa u*h*langoti lwakwabo umfana o inkosana kayise.

Abafazi aba zekwa ngezinkomo
zakwabo-mkulu ku se ifa lake
omkulu ; labo bonke naba zekwa

THE account of the side of a polygamic house which is called the
side of the house of the boy who
is the little chief[7] of his father.

The women who are taken to
wife by the cattle of the eldest
son's house,[8] become the heritage
of the eldest son ; all of them are

[7] The little chief of his father, that is, the heir-at-law,—the next chief or
head after the father. He is also called *inkosi*, "chief." To avoid confusion I
generally translate such terms by heir, or eldest son.

[8] It is important for the understanding of this matter to note the distinction made between *kwabo-mkulu*, which I have translated "the eldest son's
house," and *kwabo impela*, (or as expressed lower down *kwabo-mfana*,) which I
have translated "the eldest son's house in particular." The eldest son born to
the chief wife or *inkosikazi*, has two inheritances,—the one hereditary derived
from his father, and father's father backwards. This is the inheritance *kwabo-
mkulu*, and must descend from him, as it came to him by the law of inheritance,
that is, of primogeniture. The other is derived from his mother,—a cow or
more given her by her father, or by a friend, or obtained by labour, becomes a
new source of property, and is kept distinct in its appropriation from the pater-
nal heritage. The difference is similar to that between entailed and personal
property. But the entailed property of the native is invested in wives, girls,
and cattle, and is necessarily as fluctuating as any other moveable property.
The property of the eldest son's house *(ifa lakwabo-mkulu)* is the hereditary
estate. Note too the expression, *Abafazi bakwabo-leyo 'nkomo*, "The wives of
the house of that cow."

ngezinkomo zakwabo impela, ezi zalwa inkomo eya nikwa unina, e nikwa uyise noma uyise-mkulu; lezo 'nkomo zi ya 'uzeka abafazi bakwabo-leyo 'nkomo lapa ya vela kona, kwabo-mfana. Noma umuzi u ze u be mkulu ngabafazi balezo 'nkomo lowo 'muzi owake wonke lo 'mfana. Uma be pela bonke abantwana balezo 'nd/llu ifa lonke labo li butwa u yena; a ku ko namunye o nga banga nayo ukuti u/llangoti lwakwetu, u tsho ngokuba labo 'bafazi be zekwa ngenkomo zakwabo. A ba kude naye, ba se pansi kwake.

Kodwa umfazi o zekwa uyise ngenkomo e nge si yo yelifa, i inkomo yake nje, e nge bhekwe

his heritage, together with those who are taken to wife by cattle of his house in particular, which are the offspring of a cow, which his mother gave him, which her father or grandfather gave her;[9] women taken to wife by these cattle belong to the house whence that cow came, the son's house.[10] And even if the village at length become great through the wives of those cows,[11] the whole village is that boy's. If all the children of the several houses die, he is the heir of all their property; there is no one who can set up against him a claim, on the ground of its belonging to his side of the village, that is, on the ground that the women were taken to wife by cattle belonging to his house. They are not persons of another family;[12] they are subject to him.

But as to a woman whom his father takes to wife by a cow which does not belong to the hereditary estate, but is his own personal property, which is not re-

---

[9] A new estate is commenced by gifts to the mother,—by her labour,—by girls whom she may have after giving one over to the chief house,—or by gifts to the eldest son, or by his labour and by the labour of other children till they are married. If any such property is taken by the father to pay the dowry of a new wife, that wife belongs to the house to which the property belonged.

Some such custom as regards marriage as this here represented as in force among the natives, must have existed among the people of Asia in the time of Jacob; and the account here given is calculated to throw much light on the history of his life and that of his children. By recalling that familiar history and looking at it from a new point of view, we shall also be helped to understand better the state of the native law in such matters. It would appear that Leah was the inkosikazi or chief wife; and Rachel the second chief wife or hill; Rachel gives Jacob her maid Bilhah that *she might have children by her*, that is, the house of Bilhah is a secondary house under Rachel, who is the chieftainess of the secondary great house, and the children born to Jacob in that house are Rachel's. Then Leah follows Rachel's example, and gives Jacob Zilpah, and Zilpah's house is a secondary house under Leah, whose is the indhlu-nkulu or chief house. Reuben is the "little chief of his father;" and Joseph the "iponsakubusa." His position not only as the favourite of his father, but as the chief of the secondary great house, explains his dreams of superiority, and the jealousy of his half-brothers of the house of Leah.

[10] That is, the house of the eldest son,—the house of which his mother is the chief.

[11] That is, the wives who have been paid for by those cows.

[12] Lit., They are not at a distance from him, but are so near to him that if the heir die, he becomes heir.

inkosikazi, e nge i bauge futi; indoda i ya tsho enkosikazini ukuti, " Le inkomo, mabani, a i si yo inkomo yakwako ; ngokuba a ngi tatanga 'luto lwend*h*lu yako, neyakwetu futi ; inkomo yami e nge bangwe 'muntu ; ngi ya 'kuzeka ngayo umfazi wami, o nge si ye nowakwako, e owami ngedwa nje, umuzi wami ; ngokuba weua u umfazi kababa."

Leyo 'nkomo uku i tola kwake i loku, ukuba indoda i lime insimu yayo, amabele ayo a nga *h*langaniswa nawend*h*lu-nkulu, a be wodwa, i tenge inkomo ke.   Nako ke ukwa*h*luka kwaleyo 'nkomo.   Kumbe i liine uguai ; i nga tsho ukuba leso 'siguai esikamabani, i ti isiguai sami nje, nensimu leyo i nga i bizi ngend*h*lu yayo, ngokuba umfazi o inkosikazi u nga banga uma iuto i bizwa ngaye, a pind' amukwe.   Kw enzelwa loko ukuze a nga i bangi into enjalo.

Leyo 'nkomo ke, lapa se y andile, ya zeka umfazi, ku y' aziwa ukuti lowo 'mfazi ka si ye umfazi wakwa-nkosikazi, nowakwabo kandoda, ngokuba kulezo 'nd*h*lu zombili a ku pumanga 'luto.   Uma

garded by the chief wife [as belonging to her], and which she cannot claim. [When the husband comes home with such a cow,] he says to the chief wife, " This cow, daughter of So-and-so, is not a cow of your house, for I took nothing from your house, nor from the hereditary estate ; it is my cow on which no one can have a claim ; I shall marry with it my wife, who will not be a wife belonging to your house, but is my wife only, —my village ; for you are a wife whom I took by my father's cattle.

The husband gains such a cow in this way,—he cultivates a garden by himself, and the resulting produce is not mixed with the produce of the chief house, but is kept by itself, and he buys a cow with it.   Such, then, is the distinction between that cow [and the cattle of the hereditary estate].   Or he may cultivate tobacco ; he does not say the tobacco-field is the chief wife's, but he says, " It is my field," and he does not call the field by the chief wife's house, for a chief wife can put in a claim if a thing is called hers, when it has been taken away again.   The husband acts thus that no claim may be made to such a thing.

When that cow, then, has increased, and he has taken another wife by it, it is known that that wife does not belong to the chief wife's house, nor to the hereditary estate of the husband ;[13] for nothing has been derived from either for the purchase of the cow.   If

---

[13] The reader must bear in mind that in a large household there may be distinguished the following houses which have especial claims :—

1. *Indhlu yakwabo-mkulu*, or *yakwabo-kandoda*.   The hereditary estate.

2. *Indhlu yakwabo-ndodana enkulu*.   The house of the chief wife.   The eldest son is heir of the property derived from both these.   And the father cannot marry a wife by cattle belonging to either of these without placing the new wife under the chief wife, and whose house, viz., heir, has a claim upon the house of

izinkomo lezo zaleyo 'nkomo za zeka umfazi a za pela, ku se izinkomo zakwake lowo 'mfazi; ku tiwa u intaba.

Futi, ku tiwa indodana yake iponsakubusa, ukuti ka 'nkosi, kodwa emzini wakwabo uma se w andile u ya busa ngokwake kulowo 'muzi; ka pazamiswa 'luto.

Uma lezo 'nkomo zi sele ekuloboleni, uyise a nike inkosikazi yake inkomo yakwayo uma e nga tandi ukuba ezi seleyo zi be ezakwa-nkosikazi leyo e intaba. Uma e tanda a z' etule kona, a ti, " Nazi inkomo zakwako." I nga zi banga uma indoda i zek' umfazi o nge si ye ow elamana nenkosikazi, i nga banga kakulu ngokuti, " Ku ngani ukuba ngi d*h*liwe umuzi wami na?" I tsho ngokuba indoda se i ti, umfazi e ngi za 'u m zeka ka si ye wakwako. Umfazi wami nje.

the offspring of that cow are not all taken for the dowry of the wife, those which remain are the property of her house, and she is called a hill.[14]

Further, her son is called iponsakubusa,[15] that is, he is not chief; but in the village of his mother's house when it has become great, he is the only head there, and is in no way interfered with.

When cattle remain after paying the dowry, the father may give his chief wife a cow that it may be the property of her house, if he does not wish that they should belong to the house of that chief wife which is a hill. If he wish, he can give the cattle to her, saying, " Here are the cattle of your house." She can make a claim on them if the husband marry a wife and does not place her under herself; she can make a great claim, saying, " Why is my village devoured?" She says thus because the husband says, " The wife I am now about to take does not belong to your house; she is my wife the secondary wife; which claim is settled by the first born female child becoming the property of the chief house.

3. *Indhlu yakwabo*, the house of a secondary or tertiary, &c., wife.

4. The husband has his private or personal property, with which he can do as he pleases. This is the heritage of the eldest son, if unappropriated at the father's death.

5. *Indhlu yakwabo-ponsakubusa*. The secondary great house (*indhlu-nkulu yobubili*), which is constituted by the husband taking a secondary chief wife by his own private property. This house has no right to inherit the property of the great house but as the result of death carrying off all the heirs of the great house. Neither can the heir of the great house put in any claim to the heritage of this house, so long as any male child belonging to it survives.

[14] An *Intaba*, or hill, not a *ridge* to which we give the name of hill, but a hill which stands out alone, without any connection with other hills. She is so called because she stands out alone,—the commencement of a new house, owing nothing to the forefathers of the husband (*indhlu yakwabo-mkulu*), nor to the house of the chief wife.

[15] *Iponsa-'kubusa*, The-almost-a-chief. For he is not chief as regards his father's house; the eldest son of the chief wife is chief and heir of that; but he is chief and heir in the secondary great house. The place of the chief, in a kraal or in a hut, is on the right hand side of the doorway. If the eldest son of the great house and the *iponsakubusa* are both at the same time in the hut, the eldest son sits near the doorway on the right,—that is, the chief place,—the *iponsakubusa* on the left of the doorway. But if neither the eldest son nor the father is there, the *iponsakubusa* sits in the chief place above all the other children both of the great house and of his own. The *iponsakubusa* also sends the *insonyama* to the chief house.

Y' etuke ke inkosikazi, ngokuti, "Uma nga u zeka umfazi wako njalo o ngeni nami, kepa inkomo lezi zabantaʻ bami zi ya ngapi na? Tata ngezako, ukuze ku ku fanele loku o kw enzayo." Ukubanga ku vela ngendawo enjalo.

Futi, uma izinkomo ezi zeka umfazi o ku tiwa u intaba zincane, indoda ya silalelwa, a ya k*q*eda ngenkomo lezo, ya pinda ya tata kweza-send*h*lu-nkulu, ya k*q*eda nguzo, owa send*h*lu-nkulu u ya 'kubanga, ka yi 'kuvuma kumntwana o ku tiwa iponsakubusa; u ya 'kutsho, a ti, "K*q*a, naye u ind*h*lu yakwetu, ngokuba neza-kwetu izinkomo zi kona ezinko-meni eza zeka unina." Uyise uma e tanda ukuba lowo 'mntwana wake o iponsakubusa a nga buyeli end*h*lu-nkulu, a nga zi koka lezo 'nkomo a zi kipe ngezinye, ukuze ukumisa kukayise walo 'mntwana ku k*q*ine, ku nga kciteki.

Naye ke u no*h*langoti lwakwabo lwenkomo zakwabo; noma ku nge si zo zakwabo, uyise uma e nezin-komo zake nje, ezi nge bangwe 'ndawo, a nga w andisa lowo 'muzi ngokuzinge e tata umfazi e ti owa-kona njalo, u ze u be umuzi; labo 'bafazi bonke ba ifa lakona.

only." So that chief wife[16] starts saying, "If you thus take your wife who has no connection with me, what will become of my children's cattle? Take of your own cattle, that what you are doing may be right." The disputed right arises in such circumstances as these.

Further, if the cattle with which the wife who is a hill is taken are few, and the husband comes short, and does not make up the requisite number with the cattle which belong to himself, but takes some from those of the chief house, the heir of the chief house will put in a claim, and will not agree with the son who is called the iponsakubusa, but will say, "No, he too is a part of my house, for there are the cattle of my house too among the cattle by which his mother was taken to wife." If the father wishes that that child which is the iponsakubusa should not return to the great house, he may pay back the cattle which he took by others, that the appointment of the father of that child may not be futile and come to an end.

And that child also has his side of the village, which has been de-rived from the cattle of that house; and if there are no cattle of that house, if the father has cattle of his own, upon which no claim whatever can be made, he can enlarge that village by con-tinually taking a wife, and de-claring her to belong to that side, until it becomes a village; all those wives are the heritage of that side.

---

[16] That is, the chief wife of the other side,—the hill. She has the same right over cattle formally given to her by her husband as the chief wife has.

Uma iponsakubusa li pila, indhlu-nkulu i fe i pele, kepa ku sale noma umfanyana wendhlu yokugcina encinane, iponsakubusa a li naku li dhla ifa lendhlu-nkulu, i se kona indodana yohlangoti lwasendhlu-nkulu. Kodwa uma ku nga se ko namunye umfana, iponsakubusa li ya 'ku li dhla louke, li nga be li saba iponsakubusa, se li ba inkosi kanyekanye, loku inkosi i nga se ko.

Ku njalo ke ukuma kwesitembu. Ku njalo ukuma kwendoda endhlini yayo.

Kepa izinkomo zikayise wendoda nezendodana z' ahlukene; indodana i ti, izinkomo zikayise ezayo, uma uyise e nga se ko; kepa nayo i nazo zayo yodwa ez' ahlukene nezikayise, eya zi piwa uyise e se kona. Ngokuba kunjalo amadodana a zinge e piwa izinkomo oyise, ai eziningi, i ba nye; kepa y aude, lapa se y andile i nga zeka abafazi ababili ngasikati sinye, omunye i zekelwa uyise, uma e se kona, omunye owenkomo zayo. Nauso ke inhlangoti ezimbili.

Labo 'bantwana aba zalwa alabo 'bafazi ababili, a ba nakubusa kanyekanye pakati kwalo 'muzi. Owezinkomo zendoda u ya banga ubukulu ngokuti, "Namni kwetu ngi mkulu, ngokuba umame ka tatwanga ngenkomo zakwetu-mkulu." Kepa indodana e unina e zekwe ngenkomo zakwabo-mkulu, i yona e busayo pakati kwomuzi kayise-mkulu, uma ku nga zalwa uyise-mkulu omunye o inkosi; uma inkosi kayise-mkulu ku uyise

If the iponsakubusa live, and the chief house come to an end, yet if there remain but one little boy of the last little house, the iponsakubusa cannot inherit the property of the chief house, whilst there still remains a son of the side belonging to the chief house. But if there does not survive even one boy, the iponsakubusa inherits the whole, and has no fear, but is a chief in every respect, since the real chief is dead.

Such, then, is the condition of polygamy. And such is the position of a husband in his house.

And the cattle of a man's father and his own cattle are distinct; the son says his father's cattle are his own when the father is dead; but he too has his own which are distinct from those of his father, which his father gave him whilst living. For it is the custom for fathers continually to give cattle to their sons; not many, but one; but that one increases. When it has increased the son may marry two wives at the same time; one he takes to wife by the cattle of his father, if he is still living; the other is the wife of his own cattle. There, then, are the two sides.

The children which are born from those two wives have not power throughout the whole village. The child of the father's cattle[17] claims superiority, saying, "I too in our village am a great man, for mother was not taken with the cattle of our common grandfather." But the son, whose mother was taken with the cattle of the hereditary estate, is the one that has authority in the village of the grandfather, if the grandfather has not another son who is chief; if the chief of the grandfather is

[17] That is, the *iponsakubusa*.

wale 'ndodana, i yona i busayo umuzi wonke.

Kepa le e unina a zekwa ngenkomo zikayise nje, a i hlali pakati kwomuzi wakwabo-mkulu; i ya puma, i be nomuzi wayo yodwa. Kepa noko i pansi kwale eya zekwa ngenkomo zasendhlu-nkulu, i ze i fe, anduba le yenkomo zikayise i bu tate 'bukosi uma ku nga salanga 'luto lwendhlu-nkulu.

Uma indhlu-nkulu i kipa izinkomo zokuzeka umfazi ow elamana nayo, ku ti ngamhla lowo 'mfazi e zala umntwana wentombi, ka tsho ukuti owakwake, u y' azi ukuba owasendhlu-nkulu, ku buye izinkomo a letsholwa ngazo. Kepa mhla intombi le y endako, indodana yasendhlu-nkulu i nga zeka ngazo umfazi wayo, noma i m fuka endhlini yakwabo-ntombi, ngokutanda kwayo, i ng' enzi ngokuba i y' esaba ikcala, y enza ngokuba ku umuzi wayo. Njengaloku Uzita wa zeka unina kababazeleni; wa ba inkosikazi; wa zala Ubabazeleni, inkosi yake; ngemva kwaloku izinkomo zakwabo-babazeleni za zeka unina kansukuzonke, wa ba umnawe kababazeleni Unsukuzonke, ukuze uma Ubabazeleni e nga se ko, nenzalo yake i nga se ko, ku nga bangwa abantwana bakazita, kw aziwe ukuba u kona Uusukuzonke o nga dhla lelo 'fa, ku nga kulumi 'muntu, a be u li dhla ngakona li lunge naye. Uni-

the father of that son it is he who is head of the whole village.

But he whose mother was taken by the cattle of the father, does not remain in the village of the hereditary estate; he leaves, and has his own village by himself. And although he is inferior to him whose mother was taken by the cattle of the chief house, until he dies, yet then he takes the chief place, if there is no one remaining belonging to the chief house.

If the chief house takes a wife with cattle belonging to it which comes next in order after itself; when that wife has a female child, she does not say the child belongs to her house; she knows it belongs to the chief house, and the cattle with which her dowry was paid is thus restored. And when she is married, the son of the chief house can take a wife with the cattle which have come as her dowry; and if he places her in the kraal as though she had been purchased by the cattle of the house of the girl by whose dowry she has been taken to wife, according to his own pleasure, he does not thus because he is afraid of a lawsuit, but because the village is his own. For example, Uzita married the mother of Ubabazeleni; she was the chief wife; she gave birth to Ubabazeleni, Uzita's chief son; after that cattle belonging to Ubabazeleni's house took to wife the mother of Unsukuzouke; Unsukuzonke was Ubabazeleni's brother, that if Ubabazeleni should die, and his offspring should die also, there might be no dispute among Uzita's children, but it be known that Unsukuzonke would enter on the inheritance, and would enter on it with reason, it being his property.

na wa zala intombi ugemva kukan-sukuzonke ; ya kula, y' endela kuma*h*lanya. Kwa tiwa Uzita, " Lo 'mntwana okababazeleni." Wa pika Unsukuzonke ngokuti, " Umntwana wakwetu a d*h*liwe umuntu ngi kona, mina ngi zalwa naye na ?" Ngaloko ke Uzita wa mangala kakulu ngonsukuzonke, wa ti, " Uma u linga ukud*h*la izinkomo zalo 'mntwana, u ya 'ku-ba nekcala, ngokuba unyoko u zekwe ngenkomo zakwabo-babaze-leni ; owa kwabo ; abako aba-muva." W' ala, wa ti, " Kuna-loko ukuba umntwana wakwetu a d*h*liwe ngi kona, ku*h*le ngi buyise lezo 'nkomo, ngi zid*h*lele mina." W' ala Uzita ngokuti, " Uma u kipa lezo 'nkomo, wena ngokwako, u ya 'kuba u zikipile wena ebuko-sini ; a u sa yi 'kwelamana noba-bazeleni ; a ngi sa yi 'ku kw azi lapa u ng' owakona ; se u ya 'kuba umuutu nje o nge nagama kulo 'muzi. Se u zikipile njalo, a ngi sa kw azi mina."

Wa pika njalo ke, wa za wa k*q*inisa ngoku zi kipa izinkomo ; wa kitshwa ke ekwelamaneni no-babazeleni. Kwa ngeniswa Unsi-lane o yena e sesikund*h*leni sikan-sukuzonke, se ko ze ku kule umfana kababazeleni, a m dedele ke, a buyele ebu*n*aweni, a be umnawe wenkosi. Ku te uma ku

After Unsukuzonke his mother had a girl ; she grew up, and mar-ried Umathlanya. Uzita said, " The child is Ubabazeleni's." Unsukuzonke objected, saying, " Shall a child of our house be eaten by another whilst I am living, I who was born of the same mother as she ?" Uzita therefore wondered very much at Unsuku-zonke, and said to him, " If you try to eat the cattle of that child you will commit an offence, for your mother was taken to wife by the cattle of Ubabazeleni's house ; this child belongs to his house ; those who are born after belong to you." Unsukuzonke refused, and said, " Rather than that a child of our house should be eaten whilst I am alive, it is proper that I pay back those cattle, and I eat for myself." Uzita would not agree, but said, " If you take out[18] those cattle of your own accord, you will take yourself out of the chief-place ; you shall no longer come next in order after Ubabazeleni ; I will no longer know to what place you belong ;[19] you shall be a mere man without a name in this village. You have now taken yourself out for ever. I no longer know you for my part."

So Unsukuzonke refused, until at length he ended by taking out the cattle ; and so he was taken out from holding the position second to Ubabazeleni. And Unsilane was placed in the posi-tion of Unsukuzonke, until Uba-bazeleni's son should grow up, and then he would give place to him and return to the position of a brother, and be the brother of the head of the house. But when

18 That is, from your own herd, to pay back the dowry of your mother to Ubabazeleni. There is a play on the word *kipa*, " take out," which it appears best to preserve in the translation.

19 That is, I will not acknowledge you as having any position amongst us.

bube Ubabazeleni, Umatongo, ow' elama Unsukuzonke, wa ko-*h*lwa ukuba umne wabo kade u zikipa ebukosini, wa tanda uku-ngena a pate umuzi; kepa amadoda a m kumbuza ngokuti, "Wena, matongo, ku se nandawo lapa; u kona Unsilane o za 'upata umuzi." Wa yeka ke.

Ku njalo ke abantwana bonke baleyo 'nd*h*lu aba zalwa 'muva kwaleyo 'ntombi yokuk*q*ala, aba-ntwana bayo leyo 'nd*h*lu. E ku pume kuyo intombi a ba sa yi 'ku i landela; se kw anele end*h*lu-nkulu ngentombi leyo. Kodwa bona abantwana ba se ifa njalo lasend*h*lu-nkulu, uma be file bonke. Kodwa uma be se kona, ind*h*lu-nkulu a i d*h*li 'luto lwabo; ba pansi kwayo ngokuba unina u isi-tembu sasend*h*lu-nkulu ngezinko-mo zasend*h*lu-nkulu. A ku tshiwo ukuti, loku izinkomo se za buya, a ba se pansi kwend*h*lu-nkulu; ba se njalo, ugokuba uma ind*h*lu-nkulu i pela, i bona be nga d*h*la ifa layo lonke. Li d*h*liwa ilifa ngokula-ndelana kwezind*h*lu ekuzekweni. A li pambaniswa ukuba li nikwe o nge si ye wesitembu sasend*h*lu-nkulu, ku ze ku pele bonke aba landela ind*h*lu-nkulu; a li fumane ke ukugcina umntwana wokugcina o lunge naso isitembu. Uma be

Ubabazeleni died, Umatongo, who was next after Unsukuzonke, for-got that long ago his brother took himself out of the headship, and wished to enter on the government of the village; but the men re-minded him, saying, "You, Uma-tongo, have no longer any position here; there is Unsilane, who will assume the headship of the vil-lage." So he yielded.

So, then, all the children of a particular house, which are born after the first girl, belong to that house. The children from whose house a girl has departed, will not follow her [to become the property of the great house]; the chief house is satisfied with that girl. But the children are still the heri-tage of the chief house if all the heirs of that house die. But if they are still living, the chief house can touch nothing belonging to them; they are under the chief house, because their mother be-longs to the polygamic establish-ment of the chief house, because she was taken to wife by its cattle. It is not said, since the cattle [with which the mother was taken to wife] have now returned to the chief house [by the first girl], they are no longer under the chief house; they are under it still, for if the chief house come to an end, it is they who will enter upon the whole heritage. The heritage is taken in the order of the houses as regards the times of marriage. The heritage is not allowed to pass by any house, so as to be given to one who does not belong to the polygamic establishment of the chief house, until all are dead who follow the chief house in order; at last the last male child which belongs to the great house enters on it. When all are dead who

nga se ko bonke abafanele uku li
d*h*la, li d*h*liwa umdeni, ku landwe
ind*h*lu e be i *h*lin*h*lisana nend*h*lu
yasend*h*lu-nkulu uma ku *h*latshwe
inkomo. Li njalo ke ukud*h*liwa
kwalo. Ifa li landa izind*h*lu zonke
zangakwabo-lifa. Uma be nga se
ko bonke aba fanele lona, iponsakubusa li li d*h*le ke; ngokuba li li
d*h*la ngakona; se kw elalo ilifa; a
li sa yi 'kubuzwa 'muntu, ngokuba
ind*h*lu yonke i pelile; se li ngena
ngakona, ngokuba naye uyise wabo
munye, ka kude nefa likayise.
Uma ind*h*lu se i pelile, konke se
ku okwake.

Futi, ukukitshwa kwomfazi wo-
kuk*q*ala ebukosikazini, u kitshwa
ngezinto ezimbili, ezona zi fanele
ukuba a pume ngazo. U kitshwa
ngokupinga; uma e pinge e nga
ka zali umntwana, ku tiwe ka
fanele ukuba ind*h*lu yake i me
en*h*la nomuzi. Ku ti uma e zele
umfana a kitshwe end*h*lini esen*h*la,
a buyele esangweni noma o*h*lango-
tini lwomuzi; ku pindwe ku funwe omunye umfazi o zekwa-'bu-
tsha, ku nge si bo aba landela o se
kitshiwe; a zekwe ke lowo e intombi; a tshelwe lo o pingile, ku

can properly enter on the heritage,
it is taken by those who are of
'kin;[20] the heritage is taken by the
house which used to participate[21]
with the great house when cattle
were slaughtered. Such, then, is
the mode of inheriting. The heritage falls to all the houses in order
of their inheritances.[22] If all are
dead to whom the inheritance belongs, the iponsakubusa takes it,
for he takes it with good reason;
it is now his; no one will call him
in question, for the whole house
has come to an end; and he takes
possession with reason, because his
father and the father of those of
the chief house was one; he is not
far removed from his father's estate; when the chief house comes
to an end, the whole belongs to
him.

Further, as regards the ejection
of the first wife from the chief
place, she is ejected for two reasons
for which it is proper that she
should be ejected. She is ejected
for adultery; if she has been
guilty of adultery before she has
had a child, it is said that it is not
proper that her house should stand
at the head of the village. If she
has had a boy, she is removed from
the house at the head of the village, to the gate, or to the side of the
kraal; and another wife is sought
who is a virgin, and not one of
those who were under her who has
been ejected; and so she who is a
virgin is taken to wife; and she
who has been guilty of adultery is

[20] *Umdeni*, those who are of kin,—those belonging to the polygamic establishment of the great house, in the order in which the several wives have been
taken in marriage.

[21] All the houses under any particular house, whether the great house, or
the secondary great house, participate in the meat of all cattle slain by any one
house.

[22] That is, if the chief house fails of heirs, the heritage falls to the second
house; if that too fails, it falls to the third, and so on. If all the heirs of the
great house fail, the next heir is the iponsakubusa.

tiwe, "Ngokuba igama lako lobu-
kulu u li susile, ku za 'uzekwa
intombi kabani, i me esikund/leni
sako, i be unina kabani lo," ku
tshiwo indodana ey a/lukauiswe
nonina ngokupinga kwake, i ngeniswe kwalowo 'mfazi omutsha.
Uma nembala leso 'sikund/la sake
'cmi ka/le kuso, u yena o inkosikazi impela; u yena e se unina
womfana lowo o kitshwe kunina.
Nabantwana aba zalwa u lowo
'mfazi o ngenisiwe a ba busi; ba
landela inkosana le e ngeniswe
kwake; umntwana wokukqala walo 'mfazi u yena e ya 'kwelamana
nenkosana le; ku ti nezinto zakwabo zi tatwe kwabo, zi ngeniswe
kule ind/lu-nkulu, zi landele umfana lapa i ye koua; ku sale izintwana nje lapaya kwabo okudala
ezi lingene ukupilisa unina.

Ku /laliwe ke ngaloko, se kw a-
ziwa ukuba wa kitshwa njalo,
'eme lo omutsha a be inkosikazi.
Uma e lungile, lo 'mntwana e m
bambisisa kakulu, a ko/lwe unina
lowa, a zinge e se hambela nje
kunina lapaya, e nga se jwayele
kakulu, e se jwayele lapa kwabo.
Ku njalo ke ukukitshwa kwake.

Futi u kitshwa uma e nga b' azi
abantu basemizini; ngokuba kwabamnyama ind/lu e sen/la i yona
ku ind/lu yezihambi zom/laba
wonke, zi patwe ka/le kuleyo 'n-
d/lu, ngokuba ukupata abantu
basemizini ikcala lenkosikazi ya-
lowo 'muzi. Uku ba pata, si tsho
uku ba pa ukud/la, a nga katali

told, "Since you have destroyed
your great name, the daughter of
So-and-so will be taken to wife and
fill your place, and become the
mother of So-and-so," that is, the
heir, the son who is separated
from the mother on account of her
offence, and placed with the new
wife. If, then, she fills well that
office, it is she who is the chief
wife indeed; it is she who is the
mother of the youth who has been
taken away from his mother.
And the children of the new wife
are not chief; they come in order
after the young chief who has been
introduced into her house; the
first child of this wife comes next
in order after the young chief; and
the property of his house is taken
from his mother's house, and is
taken to the chief house; it follows
the boy to the place where he
goes; there is left behind in the
old house[23] only such little things
as are necessary for his mother's
existence.

So they settle down as regards
that matter, it being now known
that she was ejected for ever, and
that the new wife is established as
chief. If she is a good woman
and treats the boy with the greatest care, he forgets his real mother,
and habitually goes to the new
mother, no longer using himself to
the real mother, but now using
himself to the house of the new
chief wife.

And she is ejected if she does
not know strangers: for among
black men the head house is that
to which strangers from all parts
go, and are treated well there; for
the treatment of strangers is an
obligation resting on the chief wife
of the village. When we say to
treat them, we mean to give them

---

[23] The old house,—the house of the displaced chief wife.

uku ba pata ; uku nga b' azi ukuba a ba ncitshe ukud*h*la, a ku
landule, noma ku kona a ku fi*h*le,
a ku d*h*le ngasese kwabo ; a ba
tetise, a ba kipe ngolaka. Lowo
'mfazi kwiti u ya puma ; ka fanele
ukutwala umuzi ; u fanele 'euke a
buyele esangweni, ku ngene ona-
mand*h*la okuma ka*h*le kuleso 'si-
kuud*h*la. I loko ke ukukipa
umfazi ebukosikazini.

UMPENGULA MBANDA.

food, and to give it without weari-
ness ; not to know them is that
she should grudge them food, de-
nying that she has any, and if
there is any, concealing it, and
eating it secretly unknown to
them ; scolding them, and turning
them out of her house in anger.
Among us such a wife goes out ;
she is not fit to bear the village ;
it is proper that she go lower and
take her position at the entrance ;
and another take her place, who is
able to fill it aright. Such, then,
is the ejection of a wife from the
chief place. Such, then, is her
expulsion.

UNTHLANGUNTHLANGU.[24]

All the wives of the king have children except the chief wife.

Kw' esukela, inkosi ya tat' abafazi.
Ya ti, " Okabani u ya 'kuzala inkosi." Ba mita ; za pela izinyanga, sa fika isikati sokubeleta, ba
baleta. Wa salela o mit' inkosi e
se miti. Ba kula abantwana, ba
hamba, ba suswa emabeleni. Ba
pinda b' emita ; za pela izinyanga,
sa fika isikati sokubeleta, ba beleta. Ba kula abantwana, ba suswa emabeleni, ba kula, ba za ba
ba 'zinsizwa, e nga ka beleti.

IT is said in children's tales that a
king took several wives. He said,
" The child of So-and-so[25] shall be
mother of the future sovereign."
They became pregnant ; their
mouths were completed ; the time
of childbirth arrived, they had
children. But she who was to be .
the mother of the future sovereign
remained still pregnant. The
children grew, they walked, they
were weaned. Again the wives
became pregnant ; their months
were completed, the time of childbirth arrived, they had children.
The children grew, they were
weaned ; they grew until they
were young men, the chief wife
not having as yet given birth to a
child.

[24] *Unthlangunthlangu,* One who, when charged with an offence, denies every
thing in the charge. *Umuntu o zihlanguzayo,* One who excuses himself.
   [25] *Okabani.*—It is the custom of persons who are not related to call married
women by the names of their respective parents, and not by their proper
names.

The chief wife gives birth to a snake.

Kwa pela iminyaka eminingi; wa za wa kœatuka; wa beleta; ba butana abafazi, ba ti, "U zele inyoka." Ya puma amasuku amaningi, i nga peli esiswini; ya gcwal' indhlu. Ba baleka, b' e-m' emnyango. Ba memez' abantu, ba ti, "Ake ni zo'ubona umhlola." Kwa butan' isizwe: ba memeza kuyena, ba t' "I sa puma ini esiswini na?" Wa ti, "I sa puma." Ya ti inkosi, "A kw alukwe intambo." Wa ti, "Se i pelile."

Many years passed away; at length the skin of the abdomen peeled off;[26] she was taken in labour; the women assembled and said, "She has given birth to a snake." The snake took many days in the birth, and filled the house. They fled, and stood at the doorway; they called the people to come and see the prodigy. The nation assembled. They shouted to her, and enquired if the snake was still in the birth. She replied that it was still in the birth. The king told them to make a rope. At length she said, "The snake is now born."

The snake is cast into a pool.

Kwa ngeniswa umuntu; ba m nikela umgodo, ba ti, ka peny' i-kanda. Wa li peny' ikanda, wa hlangana nalo; ba m ponsela intambo, wa i bop' entanyeni, wa puma nayo. Ba wisa iguma lwakwabo, ba ti, "Inyoka ni na?" Ba ti, "Inhlwatu." Kwa funwa isiziba, ba i hhudula abantu abaningi, ba i pons' emanzini. Ba geza imizimba, ba kupuka, ba fika ekaya.

A man was made to enter the house; they gave him a pole, and told him to turn the snake over till he found its head. He turned it over and over till he found the head; they threw him the rope; he fastened it on the neck, and went out with it. They broke down the enclosure[27] in front of the house. They asked, "What snake is it?" They replied, "A boa constrictor." They found a pool, and many people dragged the snake along, and threw it into the water. They washed their bodies,[28] and again went up to their home.

[26] The natives believe in *fœtus serotinus*, that gestation may exceed the usual number of months or 280 days. When this is the case, they imagine that the skin of the abdomen presents a peculiar appearance, here called *ukukxatuka*, to peel or cast off as a snake does its skin. When therefore they say that a woman thus casts off the skin (viz., epidermis) of the abdomen, they mean that it is a prolonged gestation, and that she has passed beyond the natural period.

[27] The enclosure here spoken of is a small enclosure, generally made of reeds, made in front of the doorway to shield the house from the wind.

[28] They wash their bodies to get rid of the supposed evil influence which would arise from touching the snake, which they regard as an *umhlola*, a prodigy, or evil omen.

The king and his people fly from the place, leaving the mother of the snake behind.

Inkosi ya ti, " A ku balekwe." Kwa tiwa, " Ka sale unina wayo ; u zel' umlingo." Ba muka, ba bheka kwelinye ilizwe. Kw' akiwa ; za pela izind*h*lu. Ba kula kakulu abantwana, ba za ba tata abafazi. Z' enda izintombi ez' elama labo 'bafana. Kwa za kw' endiswa abanta babo.

The king gave directions for them to fly from that place, but said, " Let the mother of the snake remain ; she has given birth to a monster." They departed, and went to another country. They completed the building of their houses. The children grew up, and took to themselves wives ; and the girls, who were born after the boys, were married also. And at length their children were married.

After many years she follows them.

Wa hamba unina wenyoka ; wa *h*langana nabantu ; ba buza ba ti, " U ya ngapi ? " Wa ti, " Ngi landela inkosi." Ba ti, " U ini nayo ? " Wa ti, " Ng' umyeni wami." Ba ti, " Wa u sele pi ? " Wa ti, " Ya ngi shiya en*x*iweni." Ba ti, " Wa w one ngani ? " Wa ti, " Ng' ona ngokuzala isilwane." Ba ti, " Isilwane sini ? " Wa ti, " Iu*h*lwatu. Nga i mita iminyaka eminingi." Ba ti, " Ya bekwa pi ? " Wa ti, " Ya la*h*lwa emanzini. Ba baleka, ba ti, ngi nom*h*lola, ngi zele isilwane."

The mother of the snake set out ; she met with some people. They enquired where she was going. She replied, " I am following the king." They said, " What connection have you with him ? " She answered, " He is my husband." They asked, " Where have you been staying ? " She said, " He left me at our old village." They said, " What offence had you been guilty of ? " She said, " My offence was that of having given birth to a beast." They asked, " What beast ? " She replied, " A boa constrictor. I was pregnant with it for many years." They asked where it was placed. She said, " It was cast into the water. And the people fled ; and said there was a prodigy with me, for I had given birth to a beast."

She reaches the king's village.

Wa hamba wa buza emzini, wa ti, " Un*h*langun*h*langu w ake pi ? " Ba m yalela umfula. Wa hamba,

She went and enquired in a village where Unthlangunthlangu lived. They told her the name of the river on which he had built.

wa fika kona ; wa m bona umfana, wa ti, " Nang' okabani e fika." Wa ngena end*h*lini e sesangweni. Wa m bingelela umninind*h*lu ; wa m buza wa ti, " Se kwa ba njani esiswini ? " Wa ti, " Ku polile." Wa ti, " Be ngi buza ngi ti lo kwa ku *h*lezi isilwane na." Wa ti, " Ku lungile nje." Wa ti, " Inkosi ya ti ni ngami na ? " Wa ti, " Ku ya *h*lekwa. Ba ti, ' Lo wa fa, i ya jabula inkosi.' Ba ti, ' W' enz' a shiywe en*x*iweni, kona e pilile. Wa e ya 'kuzala omunye um*h*lola futi.' "

She set out and reached the place. A boy saw her and said, " There is the daughter of So-and-so coming." She went into the house at the gateway. She saluted the owner of the house, who asked after her health. She told her she was quite well. The other said, " I was asking because there used to be a beast within you." She replied, " It is entirely right." She asked, " What does the king say about me ? " She replied, " He laughs ; they said, ' The king is happy because she is dead ; ' they said, he would have done well in leaving her at the old village even though she had got well. She would again give birth to another prodigy."

The king summons her to his presence.

Wa puma umfazi o *h*lezi kwake, wa ngena enkosini ; wa fik' inkosi i lele. Wa buza kumntwana, wa ti, " Inkosi i lele na ? " Ya ti, " Ngi bekile." Wa ti, " Nang' u-nina wenyoka e fika." Ya vuka inkosi, ya *h*lala, ya ti, " U puma pi ? " Wa ti, " U ti u puma en*x*iweni." Kwa tiwa, " Hamba u m bize." Wa puma, wa m biza, w' eza naye, wa ngena end*h*lini." Ya ti, " Sa ku bona." Wa vuma. Ya ti, " Ku njani esiswini ? " Wa ti, " Ku polile."

The woman in whose house she was went out and entered the king's house ; when she arrived, the king was lying down. She enquired of a child if the king was asleep. The king replied, " I am lying down." She said, " There is the mother of the snake come." The king sat up and asked, " Whence has she come ? " She replied, " She says she comes from the old village." He told her to go and call her. She went and called her ; she returned with her and entered the house. He saluted her, and she returned the salutation. He asked after her health. She replied she was quite well.

She is jeered for her misfortune.

Wa *h*lala, wa piwa ukud*h*la, wa ku d*h*la. Ba ti, " U nga b' u sa kuluma naye, u fun' 'engeze omu-

She remained ; she was given food ; she ate. The people said to the king, " Do not be any longer talking with her ; it may be she

nye um*h*lola." Ba m akel' ind*h*lu ; ba i bek' esangweni. Wa *h*lala kona. Wa kœabana nabanye abafazi. Ba ti, " U zigabisa ngokub' u ini ? loku wa zala isilwane nje ? " Wa jaba ke. " Kwa ku tiwa u za 'uzala inkos', i buse abantwana betu. U s' u inja manje. U nga b' u sa si kulumisa tina. Tina si zele umuzi. Wena u inja nje. A u-buyeli ini esizibeni, lapa ku *h*lezi umntanako na ? " Wa ti, " Ni ya ngi *h*leka ini ? " Ba ti, " Si bona u si fikela ngobugagu." Wa tula.

will add another prodigy to the first." They built her a house near the gateway ; she dwelt there. She quarrelled with the other women. They asked, " What are you, that you exalt yourself ? Is it because you gave birth to a beast ? "[29] So she was ashamed. They said, " It used to be said that your child should be king, and rule over our children. You are now a dog. Be not making us talk for ever. We have given birth to this village. You are a mere dog. Why do you not go back again to the pool, where your child lives ? " She said, " Why do you laugh at me ? " They replied, " Because we see that you come to us with boasting." She was silent.

The king mediates, and she humbles herself.

Ya ti inkosi, " Mu yeke ni. Nga ngi ti u ya 'u ngi zalela inkosi. Wa zala umlingo. Musa ni uku m *h*leka ngawo. Naye ka

The king said, " Leave her alone. I used to think she would give me a child who should be king. She gave birth to a monster. Leave off laughing at her on that account. She too did not

[29] The notion so common in Zulu tales of women giving birth to animals has probably some connection with the curious custom called "Roondah," among the Western coast negroes ; it appears to be something like the Taboo of the Polynesians, that is, it is a system of prohibition relating to certain articles of food. It is thus spoken of by Du Chaillu :—

" It is roondah for me," he replied. And then, in answer to my question, explained that the meat of the Bos brachicheros was forbidden to his family, and was an abomination to them, for the reason that many generations ago one of their women gave birth to a calf instead of a child.

I laughed ; but the king replied very soberly that he could show me a woman of another family whose grandmother had given birth to a crocodile—for which reason the crocodile was roondah to that family.

Quengeza would never touch my salt-beef, nor even the pork, fearing lest it had been in contact with the beef. Indeed they are all religiously scrupulous in this matter ; and I found, on inquiry afterwards, that scarce a man can be found to whom some article of food is not "roondah." Some dare not taste crocodile, some hippopotamus, some monkey, some boa, some wild pig, and all from this same belief. They will literally suffer the pangs of starvation rather than break through this prejudice ; and they very firmly believe that if one of a family should eat of such forbidden food, the women of the same family would surely miscarry and give birth to monstrosities in the shape of the animal which is roondah, or else die of an awful disease. (*Op. cit., p.* 308.) See Appendix (A).

zenzanga." Ba ti, "U ini po kitina? Ka tule ke, a nga be e sa
kuluma, loku e se za 'kuzenza inkosi, ngokuba wa zala inyoka."
Wa ti, "Ngi yeke ni; a ngi se yi
'kupinda. Se ngi bonile uba ni
ngi tolile ngaloko, ngokuba nga
zala isilwane. Ba tula.

make herself." They replied,
"What is she to us then? Just
let her hold her tongue, and speak
to us no more, (since she will
make herself chief,) for she gave
birth to a snake." She said,
"Leave me alone. I will say nothing more. I now see that you
have taken me as a dependent into
your village, because I gave birth
to a beast." They were silent.

Ten children come out of the snake.

Ya *h*lala inyoka emanzini. Wa
*h*luba umntwana isikumba senyo-
ka; o pambili wa veza isand*h*la, e
umfana; wa susa isikumba senyo-
ka. Kwa vela abantu abaningi,
be landelene ngokwelamana. Ba
k*q*ed' ukuzala kukanina. Wa kuluma Un*h*latu-yesiziba, wa ti,
"Ntombintombi, si y' elamana."
Ba *h*lala kona esizibeni. Wa ti,
"A si pume, si kupukele ngapezulu." Ba puma emanzini. Wa ti,
"A si k*q*ond' ekaya." Ba ishumi
—abafana ba isi*h*lanu, izintombi
za isi*h*lanu futi.

The snake lived in the water.
The child which was in front of
the rest turned aside the snake's
skin; it was a boy; he put out his
hand and took away the snake's
skin. There appeared many children, who followed each other in
order. They were all the children
their mother bore. Unthlatu-yesiziba[30] spoke, saying, "Ntombintombi,[31] we are brother and
sister." They remained there in
the pool. He said, "Let us go
out, and go up to the land." They
went out of the water. He said,
"Let us go towards our home."
There were ten children—five boys
and five girls.

They obtain oxen, and set out in search of their mother.

Ba k*q*onda en*x*iweni. Ba ti,
"A si fune amatambo eziukabi."
Ba tola amatambo a ishumi. Ba
ti, "A si wa lungise, si w' enze
izinkabi." Ba wa beka 'ndawo
nye, ba vusa izinkabi. Ba ti, "A
si kwelcle." Ekan*h*latu-yesiziba
kwa ba Umpengempe. Wa ku-

They went to the old village.
They said, "Let us look for the
bones of oxen." They found ten
bones. They said, "Let us prepare them, and make oxen of
them." They placed the bones
together; they brought the oxen
to life again; they said, "Let us
mount on them." The name of the
ox of Unthlatu-yesiziba was Umpengempe.[32] He spoke, saying,

---

[30] *Unthlatu-yesiziba*, Boa-of-the-pool.

[31] *Untombintombi.*—The reduplication of *intombi* in this proper name is to
be understood as intended to magnify the sister; or, as the native says, to mean
that she is not a damsel "by *once*, but by *twice*." It may be represented by
"Damsel-of-a-damsel."

[32] *Umpengempe*, a perfectly white bullock.

luma, wa ti, " Kala kanjalo ke, mpengempe. Si fun' umame. Wa zala wa shiya ; sa d*h*la 'm*h*laba, sa kula. Si ng' abakalubundubundu-a-ba-lu-vume." Ba hamba bonke, be kwele ezinkabini. Ba d*h*lula emzini.

" Umpengempe, cry after your usual manner. We are seeking for our mother. She gave birth to us only ; she did not nourish us ; we ate earth and grew ; we are the children of Ulubundubundu-a-ba-lu-vume."[33] They all set out, having mounted on the oxen. They passed a village.

They enquire at a village. The people tell them to go forward.

Ya ti inkosi Un*h*latu-yesiziba, ya ti, " A si buye ; a si s' uku-d*h*lula umuzi." Ya kala inkomo. Wa ti, "Kala kanjalo ke, mpe-ngempe. Si fun' umame. Wa zala wa shiya ; sa d*h*la 'm*h*laba, sa kula. Si ng' abakalubundubundu-a-ba-lu-vume." Ba ti, " D*h*lulela ni pambili."

Unthlatu - yesiziba, the king, said, " Let us go back again ; let us not pass a village." The ox cried. He said, " Cry, Umpenge-mpe, after your usual manner. We are seeking for our mother. She gave birth to us only ; she did not nourish us ; we ate earth and grew ; we are the children of Ulu-bundubundu-a-ba-lu-vume." The people said, " Go forward."

They enquire at another village, and are told to go forward.

Ba hamba, ba fik' emzini. Ba finyana zi buyile inkomo. Wa i tshaya udade wabo inkabi. Wa ti, " Kala kanjalo. Si fun' uma-me. Wa zala wa shiya ; sa d*h*la 'm*h*laba, sa kula. Si ng' abakalu-bundubundu-a-ba-lu-vume." Ba ti, " D*h*lulela ni pambili."

They went forward and came to a village. They found the cattle come back from the pasture. His sister struck her ox, and said, " Cry after your usual manner. We are seeking for our mother. She gave birth to us only ; she did not nourish us ; we ate earth and grew ; we are the children of Ulu-bundubundu-a-ba-lu-vume." They said, " Go forward."

They reach Umkuzangwe's village, and are told to go forward.

Ba fik' enxulumeni likamkuza-ngwe. Ba ti, " Ni ng' abakabani na ?" Ba ti, "Si ng' abakan*h*la-ngun*h*langu." Ba ti, " Na sala pi

They came to the large village of Umkuzangwe.[34] They asked them whose children they were. They told them they were the children of Unthlanguthlangu. They said, " Where have you

---

[33] *Ulubundubundu-a-ba-lu-vume.*—Ulubundubundu is anything that is well mixed so as to be free from lumps, &c., as morter, or arrowroot. The meaning of the name therefore is, She-is-a-well-ordered-woman,-let-all-approve-of-her.
[34] *Umkuzangwe,* He who drives away leopards by shouting.

na?" Ba ti, "Sa sala emanzini." Ba i tshay' inkabi. Ba ti, "Kala kanjalo ke, mpengempe. Si fun' u-ina. Wa zala wa shiya; sa dhla 'mhlaba, sa kula. Si ng' abakalubundubundu-a-ba-lu-vume." Ba ti, "Si fun' umamo. Wa zala wa shiya; sa dhla 'mhlaba, sa kula." Ba ti, "Dhlulela ni pambili."

staid?" They said, "We staid in the water." They struck the ox, and said, "Cry, Umpengempe, after your usual manner. We are seeking our mother. She gave birth to us only; she did not nourish us; we ate earth and grew. We are the children of Ulubundubundu-a-ba-lu-vume." They said, "We are seeking our mother. She gave birth to us only; she did not nourish us; we ate earth, and grew up." They said, "Go forward."

They arrive at their grandmother's village.

Ba fika emzini lapa ku zalwa unina; b' em' esangweni; ba i tshay' inkabi, ba ti, "Kala kanjalo, mpengempe. Si fun' umame. Wa zala wa shiya; sa dhla 'mhlaba, sa kula. Si ng' abakalubundubundu-a-ba-lu-vume." Sa puma isalukazi endhlini, sa ti, "Ni ya ku zwa loku na? Ungani umntanami wa zala isilwane na, sa shiywa?" Kwa tiwa, "I pinde ni, ni tshaye." Ba i tshaya, ba ti, "Kala kanjalo ke, mpengempe. Si fun' uma. Wa zala wa shiya; sa dhla 'mhlaba, sa kula. Si ng' abakalubundubundu-a-ba-lu-vume."

They came to the village where their mother was born; they stood at the gateway; they smote the ox and said, "Cry, Umpengempe, after your usual manner. We are seeking our mother. She gave birth to us only; she did not nourish us; we ate earth and grew. We are the children of Ulubundubundu-a-ba-lu-vume." An old woman came out of the house and said, "Do you hear that? Did not my child give birth to a beast, which was cast out?" They said, "Strike the ox again." They struck it and said, "Cry then, Umpengempe, after your usual manner. We are seeking our mother. She gave birth to us only; she did not nourish us; we ate earth and grew. We are the children of Ulubundubundu-a-ba-lu-vume."

Their grandmother acknowledges them.

Kwa tiwa, "Yehlikela ni pansi." B' enqaba. Kwa nqandwa izinkomo; kwa tatwa inkabi ezimbili; kwa buzwa, kwa tiwa, "Ni ng' abakabani?" Ba ti, "Si ng' a-

They told them to get down from the oxen. They refused. They fetched the cattle; they selected two oxen,[35] and asked them saying, "Whose children are you?"

[35] This is for the purpose of inducing them to dismount. See Note 97, p. 247.

bakanhlangunhlangu." Kwa tiwa, "Na sala pi na?" Ba ti,
"Umame wa e zele inyoka. Kwa
tiwa, a i lahlwe. Umame wa
shiywa enxiweni. Kwa tiwa, u
ya 'ubuye a zale omunye umhlola.
Kwa hanjwa, wa shiywa." Kwa
buzwa, kwa tiwa, "Unyoko u zalwa iutombi yapi na?" Wa ti,
"Kalubundubundu-a-ba-lu-vume."
Wa vela uninakulu, wa ti, "Ng' o-
wami ke lo 'mntwana owa zal' inyoka, e kwa ku tiwa, 'U ya 'uza-
l' inkosi.' Wa zal' isilwane. Ba
m shiya."

They said, "We are the children
of Unthlangunthlangu." They
said, "Where have you staid?"
They said, "Our mother had given
birth to a snake. The king commanded it to be cast away. Our
mother was left at the old village,
for they said, 'She will give birth
to another monster.' The king
and his people set out, and she was
left behind." They asked, "In
what nation was your mother
born?" They said, "In that of
Ulubundubundu - a - ba - lu - vume."
Their grandmother stood forth and
said, "She who gave birth to a
snake is my child; of whom it
was said, 'Her child shall be king.'
She gave birth to a snake. And
they forsook her."

They set out with their grandmother, and reach their father's village.

Kwa hlatshwa izinkabi eziningi;
kwa butw' abantu; kwa tiwa,
"Ake ni ze 'kubona abantwana
aba puma enyokeni." Kwa tiwa,
"A ba kqutshwe." Ba kqutshwa.
Ba hlangana nabantu. Ba ti abantu, "Laba 'bantwana abakabani
na?" Kwa tiwa, "Abakanhla-
ngunhlangu." Ba dhlula. Ba
hlangana nabantu. Ba ti, "Laba
'bantwana ng' abakabani na?"
Ba hamba nesalukazi esi zal' unina. Kwa tiwa, "Ba be hlezi pi
na?" Kwa tiwa, "Ba be hlezi
esizibeni." Kwa tiwa, "Ba be
hlalele ni na?" Kwa tiwa, "Ba
be inyoka." Ba ti, "I bo Unhla-
ngunhlangu a e ba tsho, e ti ba
penduka izilwane na?" Ba ba
kombis' umuzi kanhlangunhlangu.
Ba kqonda kuwo. Ba fik' ekaya.
Kwa tiwa, "Ake ni pume ni bone

Many cattle were slaughtered;
the people were assembled; they
said, "Just come and see the
children who came out of the
snake." They said, "Let them be
directed on their way." They
were directed. They met with
some people who said, "Whose
children are these?" They replied, "Unthlangunthlangu's."
They went forward. They met
other people, who asked whose
children they were. They went
with the old woman, their mother's mother. They asked, "Where
did they live?" They answered,
"In a pool." They asked, "Why
did they live there?" They answered, "They were a snake."
They asked, "Is it they whom
Unthlangunthlangu used to say
became beasts?" They pointed
out to them the village of Unthlangunthlangu. They went to it.
They reached their home. The
people said, "Just come out and

abant' aba*hl*e. Kungati ba zalwa 'muntu munye." B' em' esangweni. Wa pum' unina. Ba i tshay' inkabi, ba ti, "Kala kanjalo ke, mpengempe. Si fun' uma. Wa zala wa shiya ; sa *dhl*a 'm*hl*aba, sa kula. Si ng' abakalubundubundu-a-ba-lu-vume."

see these beautiful people. They appear to be the children of one man." They stood at the gateway. The mother went out. They struck the ox and said, "Cry, Umpengempe, after your usual manner. We are seeking our mother ; she gave birth to us only ; she did not nourish us ; we ate earth and grew. We are the children of Ulubundubundu-a-ba-lu-vume."

Their mother recognises them.

Wa kal' unina, wa ti, "Laba 'bantu ba ya ngi dabula." Wa ti, "Ungati ba tsho kimi ; ba za ba pata nebizo likamame." Kwa tiwa, "I pinde ni." Ba i tshaya, ba ti, "Kala kanjalo ke, mpengempe. Si fun' umame. Wa zala wa shiya ; sa *dhl*a 'm*hl*aba, sa kula. Si ng' abakalubundubundu-a-ba-lu-vume."

The mother cried saying, "These people distress me. It is as if they spoke to me ; and they mention the name too of my mother." They said, "Strike it again." They struck it again and said, "Cry then, Umpengempe, after your usual manner. We are seeking our mother ; she gave birth to us only ; she did not nourish us ; we ate earth and grew. We are the children of Ulubundubundu-a-ba-lu-vume."

Kwa butw' abantu, kwa bizwa inkosi, kwa tiwa, ake i ze 'kubona. Ya fik' inkosi, ya *hl*ala pansi. Ba ti, "I ti inkosi, ake ni i tshaye." Ya kala. Ba ti, "Kala kanjalo ke, mpengempe. Si fun' uma. Wa zala wa shiya ; sa *dhl*a 'm*hl*aba, sa kula. Si ng' abakalubundubundu-a-ba-lu-vume."

The people were assembled, and the king was called to come and see. The king came, and sat on the ground. They said, "The king commands you to smite the ox." The ox cried ; they said, "Cry then, Umpengempe, after your usual manner. We are seeking our mother ; she gave birth to us only ; she did not nourish us ; we ate earth and grew. We are the children of Ulubundubundu-a-ba-lu-vume."

Their father makes many enquiries of their grandmother.

Kwa buzwa kuninakulu, kwa tiwa, "Laba 'bantu u hamba nabo nje, u ba tata pi ? " Wa ti, "Ba

They said to the grandmother, "Since you go with these people, where did you find them ? " She said, "They have just come to me,

fikile, be ti, ba vela pi. Ba ti, ba vela esizibeni. Kwa tiwa, esizibeni ba be fakwe ini? Ba ti, 'Kwa ku inyoka.' Ba ti, 'Uyise wayo kwa ku ubani?' Ba ti, 'Un*h*langun*h*langu.' Ba ti, 'Na bona ini uba na ni inyoka na?' Ba ti, 'Sa bona.' Ba ti, 'Ni zalwa kamabani na?' Ba ti, 'Si zalwa okabani.' Kwa tiwa, 'Ye*h*lika ni enkabini.' B' en*q*aba."

and when the people asked whence they came, they said they came from a pool. The people asked if they had been placed in the pool. They said, 'It was a snake that was put into the pool.' They said, 'Who was the snake's father?' They said, 'Unthlangunthlangu.' They said, 'Did you see that you were a snake?' They said, 'We saw.' They said, 'Who is your mother?' They said, 'The daughter of So-and-so.' They were told to come down from the ox. They refused."

The king asks them many questions.

I ti inkosi, "Ni k*q*onda ka*h*le ini ukuba ng' uyi*h*lo wenu Un*h*langun*h*langu na?" Ba ti, "Si k*q*onda ka*h*le." Ba ti, "A ba ko ini abantwana abanye kunyoko na?" Ba ti, "A ba ko." Ba ti, "Unyoko ukuzala kangaki na?" Ba ti, "Ukuzala kanye; wa zala inyoka." Ba ti, "Inyoka inyoka ni na?" Ba ti, "In*h*latu." Ba ti, "Ya zalwa ya bekwa pi na?" Ba ti, "Ya zalwa ya ponswa esizibeni." Ba ti, "Inyanga zayo zingaki i mitwe na?" Ba ti, "Iminyaka eminingi." Ba ti, "Wa e nga miti nabantu unyoko na?" Ba ti, "Wa e miti nabantu; ba za ba zala, ba m shiya. Ba za ba buya, ba pinda b' emita okunye; ba buya ba m shiya. Ba za ba zala kaningi, é sa miti umame. Wa za wa k*x*atuka, wa zala in*h*latu. Ya zalwa insuku ezi-

They said, "The king asks, 'Do you understand fully that Unthlangunthlangu is your father?'" They answered, "We fully understand." They said, "Has your mother no other children?" They replied, "She has none." They said, "How many times did your mother give birth?" They said, "Once only; she gave birth to a snake." They said, "What snake was it?" They said, "A boa." They said, "When it was born, where did they put it?" They said, "When it was born, they cast it into a pool." They asked, "How many months was the woman pregnant with the snake?" They said, "Many years." They said, "Was not your mother pregnant at the same time as others?" They said, "She was pregnant at the same time as others; at length they had children, and left her still pregnant. At length they became pregnant again; again they left her pregnant. At length they gave birth to many children, our mother being still pregnant; at length the skin of her abdomen peeled off, and she gave birth to a boa; it

ningi; ya gcwal' ind/ilu, ba pumela pand/ile abcsifazana. Kwa menyezwa, kwa tiwa, 'U s' ezwa na?' Wa ti, 'Ngi s' ezwa.' Kwa tiwa, 'A i ka peli na?' Wa ti, 'Se i pelile.' Kwa ngeniswa umuntu end/ilini, wa ti, a ba m ponsele ugongolo, a fune ikanda; wa li penya, wa ti, 'Se ngi li bonile.' Wa ti, "Ngi ponsele ni nentambo.' Wa i kunga emkqaleni."

Kwa' tiwa, "Na ni ku zwa ini konke loku na?" Wa ti Un/ilatu-yesiziba, "Nga ngi ku zwa. Kodwa nga ngi nga boni." Kwa tiwa, "W' ezwa ngaui na?" Wa ti, "Nga ngi zwa ukukuluma." Ba ti, "Ku kuluma ubaui?" Wa ti, "Ku kuluma Un/ilangun/ilangu." Ba buza, "Wa ti, a i bekwe pi na?" Wa ti, "A i yoponswa esizibeni." Kwa tiwa, "Wa ba bona abantu aba be i pete inyoka na?" Wa ti, "Nga b' ezwa." Ba ti, "Ba be i pakamisele pezulu ini na?" Wa ti, "Ba be i hhusha pansi, ba i ponsa emanzini." Ba ti, "Wa ba bona na?" Wa ti, "Nga b' ezwa." Ba ti, "Po, wa puma kanjani na?" Wa ti, "Nga kupukela ngapezulu." Ba ti, "W' enze njani ngapezulu?" Wa ti, "Nga kup' isand/ila." Ba ti, "Wa s' enze njani na?" Wa ti, "Nga susa isikumba." Ba ti, "Wa s' enze njani isikumba na?" Wa ti, "Nga si /ilubula." Ba ti, "Kwa vela ni pakati na?" Wa ti, "Kwa vela abantu aba ishumi. B' ema ngokulungelelana ngokwelamana kwetu." Kwa tiwa, "Abantu abangaki na?" Wa ti, "Abantu

took many days in the birth; it filled the house; the women ran out. They shouted, and asked our mother if she was still alive. She replied, 'I am still alive.' They asked, 'Is not the snake yet born?' She replied, 'It is now born.' A man was made to go into the house; he told them to throw him a pole, that he might search for the head; he turned it over, and said, 'I now see the head.' He said, 'Throw me also a cord.' He fastened the end on the neck."

They asked them if they heard all that. Unthlatu-yesiziba said, "I heard it; but I could not see." They said, "How did you hear?" He replied, "I heard them speak." They said, "Who spoke?" He replied, "Unthlangunthlangu." They asked, "Where did he command the snake to be put?" He said, "He commanded it to be cast into the pool." They said, "Did you see the people who took the snake?" He replied, "I heard them." They said, "Did they raise it from the ground?" He replied, "They dragged it on the ground, and cast it into the water." They said, "Did you see them?" He replied, "I heard them." They said, "But how did you get out?" He said, "I went up to the mouth of the snake." They said, "What did you do there?" He said, "I put out my hand." They said, "What did you do with your hand?" He said, "I removed the skin." They said, "How did you take away the skin?" He said, "I slipped it off." They said, "What came from inside?" He said, "There came out ten persons. They stood one after the other according to the order of their birth." They said, "How many persons?" He

aba ishumi." Kwa tiwa, "Komb' o kw elamayo." Wa m komba. Kwa tiwa, "Nawe, komb' o kw elamayo." Wa m komba. Kwa tiwa, "Nawe, komb' o kw elamayo." Wa m komba. Kwa ba njalo kubo bonke.

said, "Ten." They said, "Point out the one which followed you." He pointed her out. They said, "And you, too, point out the one which followed you." She pointed him out. They said, "And you, too, point out the one which followed you." He pointed her out. They all did so.

They recognise and point out their mother.

Kwa tiwa, "Komb' unyoko." Wa m komb' unina. Kwa tiwa, "I pi indhlu yakwenu?" Wa ti, "Nansi esangweni." Kwa tiwa, "Kw enza ngani indhlu yakwenu ukuba i be sesangweni na?" Wa ti, "Kw enza ngokuhlupeka, ngokub' a zala inyoka."

They said, "Point out your mother." He pointed her out.[36] They said, "Which is your mother's house?" He said, "There at the gateway." They said, "How happens it that your mother's house is at the gateway?" He replied, "It happens because of affliction ; because she gave birth to a snake."

The father acknowledges them, and gives them cattle.

Wa ti nyise, a ku butwe izinkabi zake izwe lonke. Kwa fika izinkabi ezi ishumi. Kwa tiwa, k' ehle Unhlatu-yesiziba. W' ehlela pansi. Kwa fika izinkabi ezi ishumi ; kwa nikwa udade wabo o m elamayo. W' ehlela pansi. Kwa tiwa, abanye a ba zehlele, se ku nikwe amakosi.

The father commanded the whole nation to collect his cattle. Ten oxen were brought. He told Unthlatu-yesiziba to come down. He dismounted. Ten other oxen were brought ; these were given to his sister who was born after him. She dismounted. The others were told to dismount of their own accord, for the chief children had received presents.

He makes Unthlatu-yesiziba king, and gives everything into his hands.

Wa jabula unina. Uyise wa m pata ngengalo Unhlatu-yesiziba, wa ti, a ba kqonde endhlini esenhla. W' ala Unhlatu-yesiziba, wa ti, "Ngi za 'ngena kweyakwetu." Wa t' uyise, "Mntanami,

The mother rejoiced. The father took the arm of Unthlatu-yesiziba, and said, "Let us go to the house at the head of the village." Unthlatu-yesiziba refused, saying, "I will go into my mother's house." The father said, "My child, what can I do, since

36 See Appendix (B).

ng' enze njani, ind*h*lu i senzansi uje?" Wa ti, "Ngi ya bona ukuba umame wa e *h*lupeka." Wa ti, " Mutanami, nga ngi bona ukuba e zele isilwane. Kwa se ku panyiswa inkosikazi e sen*h*la e b' i kuyo; se ku inkosikazi." Wa ti, "Nga ng' enza ugokuba lo wa e nga zalanga, wa e zele inyoka. Nga ngi te u yena o ya 'uzala inkosi." Wa ti ke, " Nam*h*la i fikile inkosi yami ; nonke se ni ya 'ubuswa Un*h*latu-yesiziba."

Kwa busa yena ke; abanye ba ba abake. Wa tata uyise konke oku okwake, wa ku nika yena. Wa ti, " Nengcozana se ngi ya 'unikwa u yena." Wa ti, " Bonke abami se ku ng' abake, ne ngi nako okwake."

Se i pelile.

UMATSHOTSHA (UMKAMAFUTA).

her house is at the lower part of the village?"[37] He replied, " I see that my mother was troubled." He said, " My child, I saw that she had given birth to a beast. And the chief wife was removed from the superior house where she lived ; and there is another chief wife in her place." He said, " I did this because this one had no child, but gave birth to a snake. I used to say, it is she who shall be the mother of the future king." He said, " And to-day my king has come ; and all of you will now be governed by Unthlatu-yesiziba."

So he reigned ; the others were under him. His father took all that belonged to him, and gave it to his son. He said, " I will now be given even the least thing by him. All my people are now his, and all I have is his."

This is the end of the tale.

APPENDIX (A).

SUPERSTITIOUS ABSTINENCE FROM CERTAIN KINDS OF FOOD.

THE following superstitions in abstaining from certain food resembles the Roondah of the West coast Africans :—

Ku kona kwabammnyama indaba ngokuzila ukud*h*la okutilo. Inkomo uma i kaatshelwe inkonyana, ya fela esiswini, kwa za kwa fa uonina wayo, i nga ka pumi, leyo 'nkomo i ya zilwa abatsha aba nga ka zibuli. Izintombi zona ngi nga zi pete zona ; a ku ko namkcabango wokuti, " Zi nga i d*h*la na?" ngokuba ku tiwa leyo 'nkomo i ya 'kwenza ufuzo olubi kwabesifazana,

THERE is among black men the custom of abstaining from certain foods. If a cow has the calf taken from her dead, and the mother too dies before the calf is taken away, young people who have never had a child abstain from the flesh of that cow. I do not mean to speak of girls ; there is not even a thought of whether they can eat it ; for it is said that the cow will produce a similar evil among the

---

[37] The king, being accustomed to live in the chief house, could not condescend to live at the gateway.

omunyo a be njalo ngam*h*la e bele-
tayo, a vinjelwe njengayo, a fe ne-
sisu. I zilwa ngaloko ke iukomo
onjalo.

Futi ingulube a i d*h*liwa izintombi nakanye ; ngokuba isilwane
esi mile kabi ; umlomo mubi, mude ngombombo wayo ; ngaloko ke
izintombi a zi i d*h*li ngokuti uma
zi i d*h*la ku nga vela ufuzo olu-
njalo euzalweni. Zi i yeka ngaloko ke.

Kuningi oku zilwayo abantu
abamnyama ngokwesaba ufuzo olubi ; ngokuba ku tiwa u kona umuntu owa ka wa zala ind*h*lovu ne-
hashi ; kodwa a s' azi ukuba ku
isiminya ini loko ; se zi zilwa ngaloko ke ngokuti zi nga veza ufuzo
ngokud*h*liwa ; nend*h*lovu ku tiwa
i veza ufuzo, ngokuba uma i bulewe, ukuma kwayo kwezinye izindawo zomzimba i umuntu wesifazana, njengamabele manye nowesifazana. Ngaloko ke i y' esabeka
kwabancane ukud*h*liwa ; 'kupela i
d*h*liwa ngezwe-'kufa, ku nge ko
'kud*h*la, ngokuti i lowo na lowo
kwabesifazana aba izintombi, " A
ku 'kcala uma ngi i zala ngi pilile,
ku noku nga i zali ngokubulawa
ind*h*lala." I d*h*liwa ngokunyinye-
ka nje.

Okunye oku zilwayo amatumbu
enkomo. A wa d*h*liwa amadoda
ngokwesaba ukuti, " Uma si wa
d*h*la, impi i ya 'ku si *h*laba oma-
tunjini." Abatsha a ba wa d*h*li ;
a d*h*liwa a se be badala.

Okunye oku nga d*h*liwa uvoko-

women, so that one of them will
be like the cow when she is in
childbirth, be unable to give birth,
like the cow, and die together
with her child. On this account,
therefore, the flesh of such a cow
is abstained from.

Further, pig's flesh is not eaten
by girls on any account ; for it is
an ugly animal ; its mouth is ugly,
its snout is long ; therefore girls
do not eat it, thinking if they eat
it, a resemblance to the pig will
appear among their children. They
abstain from it on that account.

There are many things which
are abstained from among black
people through fear of bad resemblance ; for it is said there was a
person who once gave birth to an
elephant, and a horse ; but we do
not know if that is true ; but they
are now abstained from on that
account, through thinking that
they will produce an evil resemblance if eaten ; and the elephant
is said to produce an evil resemblance, for when it is killed many
parts of its body resemble those of
a female ; its breasts, for instance,
are just like those of a woman.
Young people, therefore, fear to
eat it ; it is only eaten on account
of famine, when there is no food ;
and each of the young women say,
" It is no matter if I do give birth
to an elephant and live ; that is
better than not to give birth to it,
and die of famine." So it is eaten
from mere necessity.

Another thing which is abstained from is the entrails of cattle.
Men do not eat them, because they
are afraid if they eat them, the
enemy will stab them in the
bowels. Young men do not eat
them ; they are eaten by old
people.

Another thing which is not

tana wenkomo ; ngokuba ku tiwa omutsha a nge mu d/ɦle, u ya 'kwenza ufuzo olubi kumntwana ; umlomo womntwana u ya 'kututumela njalo, ngokuba udebe lwenkomo olu ngenzansi lu ya zamazama njalonjalo. A ba lu d/ɦli ke ngaloko ; ngokuba uma ku bonwa umntwana womuntu omutsha umlomo wake u tutumela, ku tiwa, " W' oniwa uyise, owa d/ɦla udebe lwenkomo."

Futi okunye oku nga d/ɦliwa abatsha umtala wenkomo, ufu ; ngokuba umtala a u naboya, a u namsendo ; u gwadula nje. Ngaloko ke ku tiwa uma u d/ɦliwa abatsha, abantwana ba ya 'kupuma be nge nanwele, amakanda e idolo nje. U yekwa ngaloko ke.

Futi ku kona oku zilwayo embuzini. Uk*q*ubu[38] lwembuzi a lu d/ɦliwa umuntu omncinane ; ngokuba ku tiwa imbuzi i namand/ɦla kakulu, i 'bukali ekubebeni. Ngaloko ke nomuntu omnciuane a ng' onakala ngofuzo lwayo, a be 'bukali kakulu, a pinge. Lu yekwa ngaloko ke.

Futi umtila wembuzi a u d/ɦliwa abatsha ; ngokuba imbuzi into e snza futifuti. Ku tiwa umuntu e d/ɦla wona, u ya 'kufuza imbuzi, a nga zibambi, a t' e /ɦlezi nabautu a be e zi/ɦleba njalonjalo ngokusuza ; ai ngamabomu, e punyukwa. U yekwa ngaloko ke.

Futi inkomo a i d/ɦliwa abatsha i nga ka boboswa ngapakati ; b' esaba ukuba aman*x*eba empi e ba /ɦlabayo, a ya 'kuvimbana, a ng' o-

eaten is the under lip of a bullock ; for it is said, a young person must not eat it, for it will produce an evil resemblance in the child ; the lip of the child will tremble continually, for the lower lip of a bullock moves constantly. They do not therefore eat it ; for if a child of a young person is seen with its mouth trembling, it is said, " It was injured by its father, who ate the lower lip of a bullock."

Also another thing which is abstained from is that portion of the paunch of a bullock which is called umtala ; for the umtala has no villi, it has no pile ; it is merely smooth and hard. It is therefore said, if it is eaten by young people, their children will be born without hair, and their heads will be bare like a man's knee. It is therefore abstained from.

*   *   *   *

*   *   *   *

*   *   *   *

*   *   *   *

Further, the flesh of a cow is not eaten by young people until it is eviscerated ; they fearing that wounds received in war will close and not bleed externally, but

---

[38] This word is not derived from *ukukqu̱ba*, to drive or push, but from *ukukqu̱ba*, to contract or draw in. The click in the former is pronounced with a slight expiration ; in the latter with a decided drawing in of the breath, producing a marked difference in pronunciation, which would prevent a native ear from confounding the two words. We have at present no means of distinguishing them in writing.

pi, 'opele ngapakati, umuntu a fe. Kw esatshwa loko ke.

Futi ku kona okunye oku ngenisa um*h*lola ngoku*h*leka. Ingulube isilwane esibi kakulu ngekanda. Uma i bonwa, i ya *h*lekwa kakulu isifazana, abadala ba m tulise o *h*lekayo, ngokuti, " U nga i *h*leki iuto embi; u ya 'kuzala yona, u jambe." Ba tuliswa ngaloko ke. Nesilima a si *h*lekwa, ngokuba ku tiwa o *h*lekayo u zibizela um*h*lola.

Kuningi okusele okunje okufuzisayo, nako ku ya zilwa njalo.

UMPENGULA MBANDA.

within, and the man die. It is dreaded on that account.

There is, besides, another thing which causes a prodigy through being laughed at. The pig is a very ugly animal as regards its head. When it is seen, women laugh at it exceedingly; but old people silence the one who laughs, by saying, "Do not laugh at an ugly thing; you will give birth to something like it, and be ashamed." So they are silenced. And a deformed person is not laughed at; for it is said the woman who laughs at the deformed person calls down an omen on herself.

There are many other such things which bring about things resembling themselves, and they too are abstained from.

APPENDIX (B).

UKUZWANA NGENKABA.

(SYMPATHY BY THE NAVEL.)

UNTHLATU-YESIZIBA is here supposed to recognise his mother, whom he had never seen, by what the natives call "sympathy by the navel," that is, the sympathy which is supposed to exist between blood-relations, who feel a mutual, undefined attraction towards each other without being able to assign a cause.

The belief in the existence of such a sympathetic power is common. Thus, Raynburn is travelling with Heraud, and falls in with an unknown champion keeping a mountain pass. Raynburn determines to put his prowess to the test; and after a long combat, in which neither gains any advantage, Heraud interferes, and advises the strange knight to yield:—"The young man then condescends to ask their names, observing, that at the sight and voice of Sir Heraud, he feels an *affray* of which he had never before been conscious. Heraud now, in his turn, refuses, and the young knight consents to speak first. The reader will perhaps hear with some surprise that this was no other than Aslake, Sir Heraud's son, concerning whose birth and education we have no information whatever, and that the *affray* occasioned by the sight of his father was the instinctive voice of filial affection." (*Ellis. Specimens of Early English Metrical Romances. Vol. II., p.* 90.) But the instinct of the horse Arundel detects his master Bevis, whilst Josyan his wife does not recognise him. (*Id., p.* 131.)—So our own Keble:

> " No distance breaks the tie of blood;
> Brothers are brothers evermore;
> Nor wrong, nor wrath of deadliest mood,
> That magic may o'erpower;
> Oft, ere the common source be known,
> The kindred drops will claim their own,
> And throbbing pulses silently
> Move heart towards heart by sympathy."

(*The Christian Year.*)

INDABA ngenkaba nkuzwana kwabo ngayo, ukuba ku ti uma umntwana o se kulile, e nga ka bi umfana noma intombazana, e se mncane kuloko, ku ti uma e nga vumi ukutatwa abantu abaningi, 'ala ukuya kubo, e jwayelene noyise nonina nabcnd*h*lu yakwabo; ku ti m*h*la ku fika owakubo o umdeni naye, a m bize; abazali ba ti, " Si za 'uke si bone, loku e nga vumi ukupatwa abanye 'bantu." Lowo o umdeni e m bizela uku m anga, umntwana 'esukele pezulu, a ng' esabi, a ye kuye; a m auge, a m singate. Ba tsho ke abazali ukuti, " Nembala! Kanti umntwana lo umuntu wakubo u mu zwa ngeukaba, ukuti ngi ng' ale kulo, owetu." Ku njalo ke ukuzwa ngeukaba.

Futi ku ti kumuntu omdala e hambile ezweni eli kude, e ng' azani namuntu wakona, a tshonelwe ilanga, a ti, " O, loku ilanga se li tshonile, a ngi nga u d*h*luli lo 'muzi, loku se li tshonile nje." A ye kuwo, e ng' azani namuntu, e yela ukulala nje, ukuba ku se a d*h*lule, a ye lap' e ya kona. Ku ti ngokufika kwake kuwo, a kuleke, a ngene, a *h*lale; a bingelelwe, e njengomfokazi kulowo 'muzi, ame*h*lo e ng' azani. Ba m buze lap' e vela kona; a ku tsho. Ba m pe ukud*h*la uma ku kona; ba m pate ka*h*le njengomuntu wabo, ba nga zibambi ngaluto kuye. A d*h*le, 'esute, a ncibilike, ba buzane izindaba; ba hambe ba hambe endabeni, ba ze ba fike ekuzalweni ukuti, " Wena, u ng' okabani na

THE sympathy which men feel with each other through the navel is this: When a child, who is now grown, but is not yet called a boy or a girl, being too young for that, will not be taken by many people, but refuses to go to them, being sociable with its father and mother and the people of their houschold: but when there comes one who is a blood-relation, and calls the child, the parents say, " We shall now see, for he will not be taken by other people." When that blood-relation calls the child to kiss it, it jumps up, and goes to him without fear; so he kisses it, and places it in his lap. So the parents say, " O, truly! Forsooth the child knows a blood-relation by the navel, that it must not object to him; he is one of us." This is what we mean by "to know by the navel."

Again, it happens with an elder person, when he has gone to a distant country, and has no acquaintance with any man there, he may be overtaken by night, and say, " O, since the sun has now set, let me not pass this village, for the sun has really set." He goes to it, being unacquainted with any one, going there just to pass the night, and in the morning pass on to where he is going. When he comes to it he salutes the householder and enters and sits down; he is saluted in return, being like a stranger in the village; the eyes having no sympathy. They ask him whence he comes; he tells them. They give him food, if there is any; they treat him kindly, as if he belonged to them; they refuse him nothing. He eats and is satisfied; he loses all reserve; they ask each other of the news; they proceed with the news till they come to birth, and ask, " What is your father's name in

ekutini?" be tsho isibongo sakona.
A mu tsho uyise. O buzayo a ti,
"U ng' okabani kabani," e tsho
uyise-mkulu. 'Etuke lo o buzwa-
yo, a ti, "Hau! Ubaba-mkulu u
m azi ngani na?" 'Ezwe e se m
pendula ngokuti, "U ti ngi nge
m azi ngani, loku ngi ng' okabani
kabani na?" Uyise-mkulu a be
munye wabo bobabili. Lapo ke
ku be se ku ba ukukala kubo bobabili. Ku tshiwo, ke abantu
ukuti, "Umuntu u mu zwa ngenkaba owabo. Si maugele ngoku-
patwa kwalo 'muntu, e patwa
ubani. Sa ti u ya m azi; kanti
ka m azi; u mu zwa ngenkaba nje
'kupela."

I njalo ke indaba ngenkaba. A
si ku zwa kwabadala ukuti, ukuzwa ngenkaba loku, ukuba inkaba
y enze njani ukuze umuntu 'azi
ngayo, ukuti owetu lo 'muntu,
loku inkaba yami ngi i zwa y enza
nje. A si fiki kuloku 'kukqonda
oku tshiwoyo ngayo. Kepa a ku
ngabazwa; ku ya kqiniswa njalo.

Futi ku kona kwabamuyama
ukukciteka kwezwe; abantu b' a-
hlukane nabantwana babo be se
bancinane; omunye umntwana a
tolwe umuntu e se zihambela nje,
e ng' azi lapa e ya kona; kanti
igama likayise u ya l' azi, nesi-
bongo u ya s' azi. Ba kciteke;
nabanye abantwana ba tolwe izindawo ngezindawo; ku be i lowo a
ti okababa wa fa, nomunye a tsho
njalo, be tsho ngokuba be ng' ezwa
lapa omunye e kona.

such a nation?" mentioning the
surname of the nation. He gives
the name of his father. He who
enquires says, "You are the son
of So-and-so, the son of So-and-
so," naming his grandfather.
The man who is asked starts and
asks, "O, how do you know my
grandfather?" And he hears him
say in reply, "Why do you say I
ought not to know So-and-so, since
I am the son of So-and-so, the son
of So-and-so?" The grandfather
of both of them is one. Then
both begin to cry. So the people
say, "A man knows one of his
blood-relations by the navel. We
have been wondering at the treatment of the man by So-and-so.
We thought he knew him; yet he
did not know him; he sympathised
with him by the navel only."

Such, then, is the case of the
navel. We do not hear from the
old men that to sympathise by the
navel is this or that, or how the navel acts that a man should know by
it that such a man is his relation,
because he feels his navel acting
thus. We have not attained to
such an understanding of what is
said about it. But there is no
doubt about it; it is confirmed
constantly.

Further; among black men there
is a desolation of the country; and
parents separate from their children
when quite young; one child is
taken by a person who is going
about objectless, not knowing
whither he is going; but he knows
his father's name and the family
name also. They are scattered,
and the children are provided for
in different places; and each thinks
that the child of his father is dead,
saying thus because neither knows
where the other is.

Ku ti ngokuzinge ku sukwa kulezo 'ndawo umuntu e se diniwe, a
ze a fike lapa kwa tolwa umnta
kayise kona ; uma ku intombazana
a in *h*lobouge nje, e ti intombi nje,
ngokuba se kwa la*h*loka igama
lake, likayise, li la*h*lwa ngoba ku
tiwa i kona abakubo be nga yi
'ku m tola ; noyise e nga sa patwa
ukuti, u umntakabani ; se ku tiwa,
"Okabani," ku tshiwo umtoli. A
ze a ti owesifazana, "Bani," e m
biza ngegama lake lokutolwa, "ngi
nge *h*lobonge nawe ; kungati u
umne wetu ; a ngi ku kcabangi
nakanye." Omunye a pikelele
ngokuti, "Nakanye ! u ya ng' ala
nje. Ng' owasekutini mina ; u ya
ng' ala nje. Musa ukwekcatsha
ngaloko." B' a*h*lukane nembala
ngokwala kwowesifazana.

Ku ze ku ti ngokuhamba kwesikati lapa umlisa e se jwayele, e
s' azana nabantu balo 'muzi, ba
buzane izindaba ; ba ze ba m tshele
labo aba *h*langene naye ka*h*le, lo
'milisa be ng' azi ukuba munye nowesifazana, be ti, ba ya *h*leba nje
indaba kumuntu aba kolana naye,
ukuti, "Lo 'mntwana okabani,
nyise. Kodwa la la*h*lwa igama
likayise ukuze ku d*h*liwo ngaye."
Ngaloko ke 'czwe owabo, a ng' e-

It happens because a man continually quits one place after another as he tires of them, he at
length comes to a place where a
child of his father is received into
the household ; if it is a girl, he may
begin to court her, regarding her
as any other girl, for her name
which she received from her father
has become lost ; it is concealed
because they suppose that then her
people will be unable to find her ;
and the name of her father is no
longer mentioned, by calling her
the daughter of her own father ;
but it is now said, "She is the
daughter of So-and-so," naming
the person who has taken charge
of her. But at length the woman
says, calling him by the name he
has received from those with whom
he has lived, "So-and-so, I cannot
associate with you ; it is as though
you were my brother ; I do not
think of it for a moment." The
other perseveres, saying, "Not at
all ! you refuse me, that is all. I
am of such a place. You merely
refuse me. Don't hide your feelings by such an excuse." So they
separate through the woman's re-
fusal.

At length in the course of time
when the man is getting accustomed to the place, and has a fellow feeling with the people of the
village, they begin to ask each
other respecting the news ; and at
length those with whom he is on
good terms, not knowing that the
man is one with the woman,
thinking they are merely telling a
matter of history to one whom
they love, say, "That child is the
daughter of So-and-so ; he is her
father. But the name of her father was lost, in order that we
may get cattle by her." So, then,
he hears that she is his sister ; he

tuki, a zibe nje ; a ze a *h*laugane nowesifazana ; a buzise ka*h*le kuye ukuti, "U lapa nje ; kwini u sa kw azi na ?" A ti, uma e kw azi, "Ngi ya kw azi." A buze igama lake ukuti, "Leli 'gama o bizwa ngalo manje u ya l' azi na ? ela pi na ?" A ti, "Elokutolwa." A buze omunye 'likayise ukuti, " Elikayi*h*lo u ubani na ?" A ti, "Ngi unobani." A buze abantu bonke bakubo. A ba tsho a b' aziyo ; a nga b' aziyo a nga ba tsho. A buze ua ngaye ukuti, " U ya m azi ubani na ?" A ti, " Ngi ya m azi." A ti, "U nga in komba manje na, uma u *h*langana naye na ?" A ti, "A ng' azi, ngokuba ukuku*l*a ku ya pendula." 'Ezwe ekupeleni kwamazwi e se gedeza umlisa, e bonga Amatongo akubo ; ekupeleni a ziveze ngokuti, " Nanku mina ke, nobani kababa. Ngi ti itongo lakwiti li s' emi. U ya bona uga ponsa 'kwenza amanyala. Kanti u ng' okababa."

Ba kale bobabili. Ba tsho ke ukuti, "Inkaba le oy enza nje le. Si be si ng' azaui." Leyo 'ndaba i ze i vele kubatoli. Abatoli, lapa e se bizwa umne wabo, ba linge uku m fi*h*la ; kepa b' a*h*luleke

does not start, but merely turns away their attention from himself ; at length he communicates with the woman, and enquires thoroughly of her, saying, " As you are living here, are you acquainted with your own people ?" If she knows them, she replies, " I know them." He asks her name, saying, " The name by which you are now called, do you understand it ? Where did you receive it ?" She says, " It is the name of the place where I have been taken care of." The other enquires the name she received from her father, saying, " What name did your father give you ?" She says, " My name is So-and-so." He asks the names of all her people ; she mentions those she knows ; she is silent respecting those she does not know. He asks also as regards himself, saying, " Do you know So-and-so ?" She replies, " I know him." He asks, " Could you point him out now, if you met with him ?" She says, " I do not know ; for growth changes a man." At the end of her words she hears the man rejoicing, and praising the Amatongo[39] of their people ; and at last he reveals himself, saying, " Behold, here I am, daughter of my father. I say the Itongo of our house is still mighty. You see I was nearly committing uncleanness. All the time you are my father's child forsooth."

Both weep, and say, " It is the navel which has brought about such a thing as this. We had no knowledge of each other." At length the real facts of the case are related by those who have taken charge of her. When her brother first claims her, they endeavour to conceal her ; but they are not

---

[39] That is, the ancestral spirits.

ngokwazana kwomntwana nama-
gama abantu bakubo a tshiwo umntwana, abatoli be nga w' azi.
B' a*h*luleke eku m fi*h*leni kwabo;
ba bize isond*h*lo; a ba nike; a
buyelc kuye. Naloko ke ku tiwa
indaba yenkaba.

Futi ku kona indaba e njengayo
le yenkaba, kodwa yona indaba
ey aziwayo; i fi*h*lekile ngokukci-
teka kwezwe.

Kwa ti ekukcitekeni kwetu
kwazulu, si kcitwa ukwa*h*luleka
kukadingane ngokulwa namabunu,
kwa ku kona obabekazi be babili
aba landela ubaba ekuzalweni;
owokugcina Umagushu, ibizo lake.
Wa tata umfazi se ku za ukukciteka izwe, udade waomanjanja
kan*h*lambela. Ku te e s' audu m
tata inyanga zi se ne e fikile
Umanjonga umkake, sa kciteka ke
kulelo 'zwe, si za lapa esilungwini.
Kwa ti end*h*leleni wa *h*lubuka, wa
buyela kwabakubo; e muka ku sa
tiwa u se niu*h*le, ku nga ka k*q*o-
ndeki. Wa la*h*leka njalo ke; i
ya m funa indoda yake; a i sa m
boni; ngokuba abautu ngaleso 'sikati ba se be nyakaza uje njenge-
zimpetu ezind*h*leleni, be ng' azi
lapa be ya kona uma ba ya ugapi
na.

Sa fika ke tina lap' esilungwini;
kanti naye u fikile kwezinye 'zin-
dawo esi ng' azani nazo. Si zinge
si kuluma ngaye, si ti, " Umakazi

able to do so through the knowledge the children have of each
other, and by their knowledge
of the names of their people,
which they do not themselves
know. They are unable to conceal her, and so they demand re-
payment for having brought her
up; he gives it them, and his
sister returns to him. That, too,
is called a case of the navel.

Further, there is a matter which
resembles this of the navel, but
this is something which is really
known, but it is indistinct through
the desolation of the country.

It happened when our family
was scattered when we lived with
the Zulus, in consequence of Udi-
ngane having been unable to contend in battle with the Dutch, we
had two uncles which were younger than our father; the youngest
was called Umagushu. When the
country was about to be desolated,
he married the sister of the Man-
janjas, the children of Unthlam-
bela. When they had been married, and his wife Umanjonga had
been with him now four months,
we were scattered from that country, and came here into the country of the whiteman. But in the
way she deserted, and returned to
her own people; when she went
away she was already beautiful,[40]
but they were not yet sure about
it. So she was lost; her husband
continually looked for her, but saw
no more of her; for at that time
people were in confusion like maggots in the path, and did not know
whither they were going.

So we came here into the country of the whiteman; and forsooth
she too came, to a different place,
with which we were not acquainted. We continually talked about
her, saying, " Where could the

---

[40] An euphemism, meaning she was pregnant.

umfazi kababekazi ow' emuka ne-sisu wa ya ngapi na ?" si funa si ḥlezi. Kwa za kwa ti, lapa nati se si kulilo, sa ḥlangana naye, si mu zwa ngegama, e sa si m biza ngalo. Sa buza masinyane, si ti, "U lapa nje, isisu ow' emuka naso s' enza njani na ?." Wa ti, "Sa puma." Sa dela ke ngokuti, "Po, loku sa puma njalo, si za 'uti ui na ?"

Ya i kona intombazana e si i bona, si mangale, si i bona i fana nabantwana bakiti ; impela uma si i bheka si bone ukuti, "Umntwa-na wetu lo." Kepa si nga bi nabo ubufakazi, ngokuba ku tiwa wa fa ; kodwa inkaba yona i ya mu zwa, a i tandi ukuba si dele ; si ya dela uma si nga m boni ; ku ti si nga m bona si kolwe impela ukuba umntwana wetu lo. Ku ze kwa ti ngesikati esinye, w' enda e fiḥliwe njalo ; ku ze ekwendeni wa buzwa igama likayise, wa ti, "Ubaba Umagushu." Kwa tiwa ke ewake,[41] ukubizwa kwake Uma-magushu. Sa li zwa lelo 'gama ; na manje leyo 'ndaba a i ka peli ; si y' azi ukuba umntwana wetu lo ngenkaba e si zwana ngayo naye.

UMPENGULA MBANDA.

wife of our uncle, who left us pregnant, have gone ?" We asked about her, whilst remaining at home. Until at length, when we too had grown up, we met with her, hearing her mentioned by the name by which we used to call her. We at once enquired, "Since you are really living, what became of the child with which you were pregnant when you went away ?" She replied, "I miscarried." So we were satisfied, saying, "Well, then, since she miscarried, what have we to say to it ?"

There was there a girl which when we saw we wondered, seeing that she resembled one of our own children ; in fact, when we looked on her, we saw that she was one of our own. But we had no evidence, for it was said the child of our uncle died ; but the navel felt her, and would not allow us to be satisfied ; when we were not look-ing on her, we were satisfied ; but when we looked on her, we fully believed that she was one of us. At length in time she married, being still concealed. When at her marriage she was asked the name of her father, she replied, "My father is Umagushu." So she was called Umamagushu at the kraal into which she married. We heard the name ; and even now the matter is not settled ; we know that she is our child by the navel, which causes us to have a sympathy with her.

---

41 *Ewake.*—This is a locative form, and is equivalent to *emzini wasewake,* that is, the kraal or village into which a girl has married.

INYOKA ENKULU E NOMLILO.

(THE GREAT FIERY SERPENT.)

In connection with the monstrous serpent mentioned in the foregoing tale, we insert the following, which may be regarded as a recent "myth of observation." The immigration of the Dutch to Natal began in 1836. All it requires as its historical basis are a large water snake, or eel, and firearms; imagination and frequent narration would readily supply the rest. The man who related it first mentioned this snake in connection with the rainbow, which some imagine is a large snake, and enquired whether this snake which the Dutchman killed was not a rainbow, which lived in the river? The native notion respecting the rainbow is added.

Kwa ti lapa ngi umfana, ng' ezwa amadoda, ngesikati sokufika kwamabunu, e ti, "I kona inyoka, e puma emanzini, e nomlilo; i ya gijima, i gijima kakulu; umuntu a nge i shiye, e hamba pansi; i z' i shiywe abamahashi."

Ya fika; kwa vela abasemangwaneni; ba i lalela; i puma esizibeni, ba i nqamula enhlokweni; wa buyela umzimba wenyoka pakati esizibeni; sa tsha isiziba, a nqamuka amanzi ukupuma esizibeni. Ba buza abantu, ba ti, "Amanzi lawa a nqamulwa ini na?" Ba ti abanye, "Izolo si i bulele inyoka kona lapa." Ku tsho basemangwaneni. Ba ti, "Ni bulele inyoka; i njani na?" Ba ti, "Si bulele inyoka; i b' i nomlilo enhloko." Ba ti, "Si funyanise i nelitshe lekcoba." Kwa tiwa, "Ake ni ye emabunwini, ni bone uba a ya 'ku y azi le 'nyoka

It came to pass, when I was a boy, I heard men say, at the time of the arrival of the Dutch, there is a fiery serpent, which comes out of the water; it runs very fast; a man cannot run away from it, if he goes on foot; horsemen can leave it behind.

It happened thus about this serpent: There came some of the Amangwane; they lay in wait for it; when it was coming out of the pool, they cut off its head; the body of the serpent went back again into the pool; the pool dried up, and the water ceased to flow from the pool.[42] Some of the men asked, "Why has this water ceased?" The others said, "Yesterday we killed a serpent at this place." They of the Amangwane said this. They said, "You killed a snake: what was it like?" They said, "We killed a serpent; it had a fiery head." They said, "We found in it a soft stone."[43] They said, "Just go to the Dutch, and see if they will

[42] This notion is similar to a superstition existing among the Bechuana:— "In the fountains in this country, there is a species of large water-snake. The Bechuanas consider these creatures *sacred*, and believe that if one of them is killed, the fountain will be dried up." *(Philip's Researches in South Africa. Vol. II., p. 117.)*

[43] *A soft stone*, probably alluding to some kind of bezoar, or intestinal concretion.

na ?" Kwa fika Amabunu, e ti, "Le inyoka ni i bulele nje ; ni i bulele kabi ; inyoka e nga bulawa. Le inyoka, tina 'mabunu si ti si i bulala, ku be se ku vele enye, ukuze si nga tshi isiziba ; ngokuba ka si i bulali nxa i vele i yodwa ; ngokuba no za ni bone, nina 'bantu abamnyama ; loku ni bulala inyoka i yodwa, ku ya 'kuze ku tshe amanzi, ngokuba i ya 'ku wa vimba, a nga b' e sa puma ; ngokuba nina, 'bantu abamnyama, na ku tshelwa ubani, ukuba inyoka leyo i ya bulawa na ?" Ba ze 'kuti abamnyama, "Tina si bona isilwane, si puma, s' alukela ngapandhle kwamanzi." A ti Amabunu, "Kona nga si bonwa isilwane njalo, a s' enziwa 'luto, nxa si ng' oni 'luto." Ba ze 'kuti abamnyama, "Tina ngokwakiti, a si kw azi, nxa si bona isilwane, si si yeke." "Ku zo'uvela," Amabunu a ti ; "isilwane si nga bo si bulala emini. Ni ya 'kuboua e ni nga bonanze[44] ni ku bone." Ba ze 'kubuza abamnyama, ba ti, "Into ni na e si nga bonanze si i bona na ?" A ze 'kuti Amabunu, "Ni ya 'kubona ! Isiṅqamu lesi senhloko ni si se ngapi na ?" Ba ze 'kuti abamnyama, "Tina si be si zifunela umuti nje wokuzelapela." A buza Amabunu, a ti, "Ni ze n' enze njani ngalowo 'muti, loku ni bulele isilwane nje, e ni nga s' aziko na ?" Ba ze 'kuti abamnyama, "Tina si bulala nje uba ku isilwane si nga bonanga si si bona ; si ya 'u si hlanganisa nemiti eminye yetu." A ze 'kuti, "A

know the serpent." The Dutch came, and said, "You have killed this serpent indeed ; you killed it wrongly ; it is a serpent which ought not to be killed. We Dutch kill this serpent, only when another comes with it, in order that the pool may not dry up ; for we do not kill it if it comes alone. For you black men will see something ; since you killed a serpent which was alone, the water will immediately dry up, for it will obstruct the water, and it will no longer flow. For, you black men, who told you that it is proper to kill that serpent ?" The black men answered at once, "We see an animal coming out of the water, and feeding outside." The Dutch answered, "Although an animal should be seen again and again, nothing is done to it, if it does no harm." The black men said, "As for us, if we see an animal, we do not know how to leave it alone." "Something will happen," said the Dutch ; "we must not kill the animal by day. You will see what you never saw before." The black men immediately asked, "What is that which we have never seen before ?" The Dutch answered, "You will see ! The head, with the piece attached to it, what have you done with it ?" The black men answered, "We were wanting medicine to doctor ourselves." The Dutch said, "What then will you do with that medicine, since you killed an animal with which you are not acquainted ?" The black men answered, "For our part, we just killed it because it is an animal which we never saw before ; we shall mix it with other of our medicines." The Dutch said,

---

44 For bonanga.

no 'nza ka*h*le. A ku bonanga ku
ze kw elape loko, loku nani ni ti a
ni kw azi."

A ya ukuba a buye kubantu
abamnyama, e ya ngamahashi ; a
fika ebusuku esizibeni, a *h*lala, a
ti, "Si za 'ubona ukupuma kwayo." A t' uba a *h*lale, a *h*lale, ya
puma inyoka ; za puma zambili ;
enye ya puma ngenzansi, nenye ya
puma ngen*h*la. Ya t' i sa puma e
ngenzausi, ya puma ku vuta umlilo. Ba t' ukwenza kwabo, ba i
bona ba ti, be sa i bona, ba i tshaya ngezibamu ; ba i tshaya, ba i
tshaya ; a ba i tshaya lapa i za
'kufa kona. Ya puma, ya puma,
ya ba·k*œ*otsha ; ba kwela emaha-
shini, ba baleka ; ba baleka, amahashi e tobangalolunye. Ba t' u-
ina ba baleke, ya k*q*oma amahashi
amabili a pakati. A t' amahashi
a pambana kabili ; amanye a bheka en*h*la nomfula, amanye a bheka
enzansi nomfula. A t' amahashi
amabili, la za la kcatsha elinye ;
inyoka ya za ya tshaywa Ibunu.
La i tshaya k*q*ede, la penduka
ihashi e be li pambili ; la penduka
k*q*ede, la se li buza, li ti, "I ye
ngapi ?" Uba se li bona ihashi, li
zwe ukukala kwesibamu, ilangabi
li nga sa li boni. La penduka, la
ti, "U ti, ku sa i boni nje ; u ti
lowa umlilo u baswe ini ?" La ti,
"Hamba, si hambe ke, si yo'bheka." Wa ti, "K*q*a. A pi amanye na ? Kepa wena u tsholo ni
ukuti, 'Ake si yo'ubheka' into e
kade i si katazile na ? Ba pi
abanye na ?" Li vele elinye Ibunu, li ti, "A si yo'funa abanye ; se
si li bonile ilangabi, lapa li vuta
kona." A ti omunye, "Si za 'u
ba funa ngani na ?" A ti omunye,
"Si za 'u ba funa ngezibamu ; si
za 'udubula pezu kwentaba uba si

"Take care. No one ever used
that as a medicine, for you too say
you are ignorant of it."

They went away from the black
men on horseback ; they came by
night to the pool ; they waited,
saying, "We shall soon see it come
out." When they had waited and
waited, the snake came out ; two
came out, one at the bottom and
the other at the top of the pool.
As soon as the one at the bottom
came out, there blazed up a fire.
They did thus when they saw it.
As soon as they saw it, they hit it
with their guns ; they hit it again
and again ; they did not hit it in a
mortal spot. It came out, and
pursued them. They mounted
their horses, and fled. They fled,
there being nine horses. When
they fled, the serpent selected two
horses which were in the middle.
The horses divided into two parties ; some went up the river, and
others went down. At length one
of the two horses hid away, and
the Dutchman at last hit the
snake. As soon as he hit it, the
horse which was in front turned
back ; as soon as he came back,
the Dutchman asked where it was
gone. When he saw the horse,
and heard the report of the gun,
he no longer saw the flame. The
other replied, "Do you say, you
no longer see it ; what do you say
the fire yonder was kindled by ?"
He said, "Let us go and look."
He said, "No. Where are the
others ? And why do you say,
'Just let us go and look' at a thing
which has just troubled us ?
Where are the others ?" The
other Dutchman said, "Let us go
and find the others ; we have now
seen the place where the flame is
burning." The other said, "How
shall we find them ?" He said,
"We will find them by our guns ;
we will fire them on the hill, when

pumele." Ba t' uba ba pumele, ba dubula, ba *h*langana namabunu a shiyangalombili. A buza, a ti, "N' enze njani? Ni sindile ini na?" Ba ti, "Si sindile. Ku ze elinye ihashi la kcatsha; la lamulelwa elinye; sa i dubula ngesibamu. Nakwa lapa i fele kona, ku vuta." Ba ti, "Hamba ni, si hambe, ke si yo'bheka lapa i fele kona, uba i file na?" Ba kamba. Ba t' uba ba fike, ba funyanisa se ku tunya intutu yodwa. Ba fika, ba funyanisa inyoka, inkulu; se ku vuza amafuta. Ba ti, i ngangomuntu, ubukulu bayo; ubude, inde impela, i nga i fike lapaya kwakcitwa. Ba buya, ba ti, "A ku yo'tatwa inqwelo, si zo'wolela le 'nyoka e ngagomuntu."

UJOJO SOSIBO.

we get out." When they got out, they fired, and met with eight Dutchmen. They enquired, saying, "What have you done? Are you safe?" They replied, "We are safe. At length one horse hid; it was helped by the other; we fired at the snake with the gun. And where it died, a fire was kindled." They said, "Go on, and we will go, and just see the place where it died, if it be really dead." They went. When they arrived, they saw nothing but smoke. They came, and saw the snake; it was great, and its fat was running out. They said, it was as big as a man, as to its size; as to its length, it was very long, perhaps it would reach from here to Ukcitwa's.[45] They went back, saying, "Let us go and fetch the wagon; we will carry away this snake which is as big as a man."

UTINGO LWENKOSIKAZI.

(THE QUEEN'S BOW.)

UMA izulu li suke li na, ku bonakala utingo lwenkosikazi. Be se be t' abantu, "Li za kusa; ngokuba ku bonakala uti lwenkosikazi, utingo;" li se: noma izulu li na kakulu, ku bonakala utingo, li se; li nga be li sa na, li se; no-

WHEN the heaven happens to rain, on the appearance of the rainbow men say, "It is going to clear up; for the rod of the queen, the bow, is seen;" and it clears up: even though it rains much, on the appearance of the bow, it clears up; it rains no more, but clears up; even though it has rained two

[45] A distance of more than 500 yards! But this is a very modest exaggeration, compared with the Scotchman's eel:—"An old man in Lorn used to tell that he went one summer morning to fish on a rock; he was not long there when he saw the head of an eel pass. He continued fishing for an hour, and the eel was still passing. He went home, worked in the field all day, and having returned to the same rock in the evening, the eel was still passing, and about dusk he saw her tail disappearing behind the rock on which he stood fishing." (*Campbell's West Highland Tales. Vol. II., p. 370.*) We may also not unaptly compare the Mussulman's exaggeration of the size and characteristics of Moses' serpent:—"Moses flung his staff on the ground, and instantly it was changed into a serpent as huge as the largest camel. He glanced at Pharaoh with fire-darting eyes, and raised Pharaoh's throne aloft to the ceiling, and opening his jaws, cried, 'If it pleased Allah, I could not only swallow up thy throne, with thee and all that are here present, but even thy palace and all that it contains, without any one perceiving the slightest change in me.'" (*Weil's Biblical Legends of the Mussulmans, p. 116.*)

ma li n' insuku zombili, ku bonakala utingo, li se.

Ba ti lu umnyama o *h*lala esizibeni, o fana nemvu. Ba ti, lapo u
*h*labe kona, u suke u puze esizibeni.
Isiziba esikulu abantu ba y' esaba
ukugeza kuso, ba ti, si nomnyama;
uma umuntu e ngena kuso, a banjwe umnyama, u mu d*h*le. Kodwa ba ti, esizibeni esi nomnyama
ku ngena isanusi es' etasayo, si
*h*lale nomnyama esizibeni, umnyama u nga si d*h*li, u si kcombe
ngombala; si ti si puma esizibeni,
se si pambe ngeziuyoka emzimbeni
waso, si ye nazo ekaya. Isanusi
izindaba e si zi kulumayo, abantu
ba kolwa i zo.

UGUAISE WASEMADUNGENI.

days, on the appearance of the
rainbow, it clears up.

The people say the bow is an
umnyama, which dwells in a pool,
and is like a sheep. They say,
that where it touches the earth, it
is drinking at a pool. Men are
afraid to wash in a large pool;
they say there is an umnyama in
it; and if a man goes in, it catches
and eats him. But they say that
a man who is being prepared to be
a diviner goes into a pool which
has an umnyama in it, and the
umnyama does not eat him, but
bedaubs him with coloured clay;
and he comes out of the pool with
snakes entwined about his body,
and goes home with them. Men
believe in the tales they talk about
the diviner.

UTSHINTSHA NOMNYAMA.

(UTSHINTSHA AND THE RAINBOW.)

NGA ngi lindile ngi linde ensimini,
izulu li na. La t' uba li se, kw' e-
*h*la umnyama, ow' e*h*lela emfuleni.
Wa puma emfuleni, wa ngena
ensimini. Nga baleka, mina tshi-
ntsha, umninisimu, ugi bona umnyama u s' u fika pansi kwami, se
ku beje emc*h*lweni ami; wa ngi
k*x*opa ngombala obomvu. Nga
baleka, nga pumela ngapand*h*le
kwensimu. Nga baleka ngokwesaba, ngokuti, "Ukufa loku; ini
uba ku ze kumina na?" Abantu
ba ti, "Umnyama ukufa; u ng' eze
wa *h*lala kumuntu." Ngoba ke
umnyama ngemva kwawo wa ngi
k*x*otsha ensimini, umzimba wami
wa nje, ukuti, wa nesi*h*lungu. Se

I HAD been watching in the garden when it was raining. When
it cleared up, there descended into
the river a rainbow. It went out
of the river, and came into the
garden. I, Utshintsha, the owner
of the garden, ran away when I
saw the rainbow now coming near
me, and dazzling in my eyes; it
struck me in the eyes with a red
colour. I ran away out of the
garden. I ran away because I was
afraid, and said, "This is disease;[46]
why does it come to me?" Men
say, "The rainbow is disease. If
it rests on a man, something will
happen to him." So, then, after
the rainbow drove me from the
garden, my body became as it is
now, that is, it was affected with
swellings.[47] And now I consider,

---

[46] Or death, that is, a cause of death or disease.
[47] He was suffering from a scaly eruption over the whole body.

ngi kcabanga ngokuti, "Ngu wo
ini na?" Ba ti, "U ya mu d*h*la
kambe umuntu, a penduke umbala
o nge wake."

Ba ti umnyama lo utingo lwen-
d*h*lu 'nkulu olu vela pezulu, ub' i-
zulu li nile; ku ti ku nga vela
lona, li buye li se. Ukuzwa kwami kambe, ba ya tsho, u hamba
nenyoka, ukuti lapa u kona, nenyoka i kona. Kepa mina a ngi i
bonanga. Nabatshoyo ukuti u
hamba nemvu. A ngi i bonanga.
Ba ti izanusi, ukutasa kwazo, zi
ngena emanziui esizibeni; zi pume
se zi kcombe udaka, lapa ku ngena
umnyama; zi pume ke se zi tasile
ke, uba se zi izinyanga ke.

UTSHINTSHA MGUNI.

saying, "Is it the rainbow" [which
causes the disease]? They say, it
injures a man, and his body assumes a colour which is not natural
to him.

Men say the rainbow is one of
the rods of the great house, which
appears in the heaven when the
heaven rains; when it appears, it
agaïn becomes fine. As to what I
have heard, they say it lives with
a snake, that is, where the rainbow
is, there also is a snake.[48] But, for
my part, I did not see any snake.
And others say, it lives with a
sheep. But I did not see any
sheep. They say that diviners,
when they begin, enter into a
deep pool of water; they come out
bedaubed with red earth, from the
place where the rainbow enters;
so they come out, being now fully
prepared to be diviners.

UMNYAMA.

(THE RAINBOW.)

UMUNYAMA nami uma ngi zwa
ngabantu abadala, umnyama u
imvu, o puma ezizibeni ezikulu.
U suk' u suka esizibeni, u *h*lale
ngapand*h*le ematsheni; u puma
n*x*a izulu li suka li *h*loma; ukuze
ke umnyama u pume, u puma
njalo. Ku ze ku fike umuntu o
puma kusasa; a t' ub' e zokufika,
u m sole; ba ze 'kuti abantu, "Lo
'muntu u nezilonda nje; w enziwe
umnyama." Ku zo'utiwa, "Nga
e funelwa inyanga yomnyama, i
m elape; u soliwe."

UJOJO SOSIBO.

As regards the rainbow, I too
hear old men speaking about it,
and they say, the rainbow is a
sheep, which comes out of great
pools.. It comes out of the pool,
and rests outside on the rocks; it
comes out when the sky is clouded; when, then, the rainbow comes
out, it comes out under these circumstances. And there comes a
man, who goes out in the morning; when he has arrived, it poi-
sons him; and men say, "This
man has an eruption; he has been
poisoned by the rainbow." And
then it will be said, "A rainbow-
doctor must be found for him, to
treat him; he has been poisoned."

[48] It is worthy of note that among the Dahomans, the word Danh is a
snake or rainbow, which is an object of worship. Burton says:—"Aydo-whe-do
—commonly called Danh, the Heavenly Snake, which makes Popo beads and
confers wealth upon man—is the rainbow." *(Mission to Gelele. Vol. II., p.
148.)* And there is a pool near the capital called Danh-to-men, Snake-or-Rain-
bow-water-in. *(Id., p. 242.)*

UNTOMBI YAPANSI.

The chief's three children.

Kwa ku kona inkosi etile; ya i lime insimu enkulu. Be ku ti ngesikati abantu abaningi ba ye 'kulima leyo 'nsimu. Kepa leyo 'nkosi ya i nabantwana abatatu nje; omkulu ku Usilwane; omunye ku Usilwanekazana; omunye ku Untombi-yapansi. Kepa ba be tandana Usilwane nosilwanekazana.

There was a certain chief who had dug a large field. At the proper season many men went to dig the garden. That chief had only three children; the eldest was called Usilwane;[49] the second Usilwanekazana;[50] and the other Untombi-yapansi.[51] But Usilwane and Usilwanekazana loved each other.

The chief's son tames a leopard.

Kwa ti ngesinye isikati w' emuka Usilwane, wa ya 'uzingela; wa buya e pete isilo; wa ti, "Inja yami le; ni ze ni i pe amasi, ni vube ngenkobe zamabele, n' enze isitubi;[52] ku ti lapa so ku polile ni i nike, i d*h*le; ngokuba i ya 'kufa uma ni i nika ku tshisa." B' euza njalo njengokutsho kwake.

It happened at a certain time that Usilwane went to hunt; he returned carrying in his hand a leopard; he said, "This is my dog; give it milk; mix it with boiled corn, and make porridge; and give it its food cold, that it may eat; for it will die if you give it hot." They did as he directed them.

The people suspect him.

Ya ze ya kula, kwa ba inja enkulu; kepa abantu b' esaba kakulu ngokuba ku isilo, be ti, "Si za 'kud*h*la abantu." Abantu be ti, "U za 'kuba umtakati Usilwane." Ba ti, "Ini ukuba a fuye isilo, a ti inja yake na?"

At length the leopard grew; it was a great dog; and the people were very much afraid because it was a leopard, saying, "It will devour the people. Usilwane will become an umtakati.[53] Why does he domesticate a leopard and call it his dog?"

---

[49] *Usilwane*, The beast-man.

[50] *Usilwanekazana*, The little-beast-woman. *Usilwanekazi*, The beast-woman. *Usilwanekazana*, the diminutive.—There is another version of this tale in which the names are different. Usilwane is called Unkoiya; Usilwanekazana, Ulukozazana,—Little-hen-eagle; and Untombi-yapansi, Umabelemane,—Four-breasts. Other differences will be mentioned in their proper place.

[51] *Untombi-yapansi*, The damsel-of-beneath, or of-the-earth. It may have reference to three things:—1. To poverty or distress; 2. To origin,—from the earth; 3. To her having travelled underground.

[52] *Isitubi*, porridge made with milk.

[53] A wizard,—secret poisoner.

Kepa Usilwanekazana, e *h*lupeka ngokuba e zwa abantu be ti
umnta kwabo u za 'kuba umtakati,
wa kcamanga e ti, "Konje ngi si
bulala ugani lesi 'silo na?"

But Usilwanekazana being troubled because she heard the people
say that a child of her family
would become an umtakati, said,
"With what can I kill this leopard?"

His sister kills the leopard.

Kwa ti ngolunye usuku kw' e-
muka abantu bonke ba ya 'kuvuna
insimu yenkosi. Kwa ti Usilwane
yena wa ya ezintombini; Usilwanekazana wa sala yedwa. Kwa ti
kusasa wa peka ubisi, lwa za lwa
bila; wa tela umkcaba, wa i nika
inja kasilwane. Ya *dh*la ya *dh*la;
ya ti lapa se i k*q*edile ya fa, ngokuba kwa ku tshisa.

It came to pass on another day
that all the people went to harvest
in the garden of the chief; and
Usilwane for his part he had gone
to visit the damsels; and Usilwanekazana remained alone. In the
morning she cooked milk till it
boiled, and added to it some
pounded corn, and gave it to the
dog of Usilwane. It ate and ate;
when it had finished it died, because the food was hot.

Usilwane kills his sister.

Kwa ti emini wa fika Usilwane,
wa bona inja yake i file. Wa ti,
"Silwanekazana, inja yami i bulewe ini na?" Wa ti, "I *dh*le ku
tshisa, ya fa." Wa ti Usilwane,
"Ini u bulala inja yami na? loku
kade nga ui tshela nga ti, ' Ni nga
i niki ku tshisa, i ya 'kufa.' U i
bulele ngamabomu inja yami."
Wa tata umkonto Usilwane, wa ti
kusilwanekazana, "Pakamisa umkono, ngi ku gwaze." Wa ti
Usilwanekazana, "Ngoba ng' enze
ni na?" Wa ti, "U bulele inja
yami." Wa ti Usilwanekazana,
"Ngi i bulele ngokuba abantu be
ti, 'U za 'utakata ngayo?'" Wa
ti Usilwane, "K*q*a! u i bulele nje
ngokuba u nga i tandi." Wa ti,
"Tshetsha, u pakamise umkono,
ngi ku gwaze." Kepa Usilwanekazana e *h*leka e ti Usilwane u ya
laula nje; kepa Usilwane e tukutele kakulu, wa m bamba, wa m
pakamisa umkono, wa m gwaza
pansi kwekwapa.

Usilwane returned at noon, and
saw his dog dead. He said, "Usilwanekazana, what has killed my
dog?" She replied, "It ate food
whilst still hot, and died." Usi-
wane said, "Why do you kill my
dog? for long ago I told you not
to give it hot food, for it would
die. You have killed my dog on
purpose." Usilwane took an assagai, and said to Usilwanekazana,
"Raise your arm, that I may stab
you." Usilwanekazana replied,
"For what evil that I have done?"
He said, "You have killed my
dog." Usilwanekazana said, "I
killed it because the people said
you would practise witchcraft by
it." Usilwane said, "No! you
killed it because you did not love
it. Make haste, raise your arm,
that I may stab you." But Usilwanekazana laughed, thinking
that Usilwane was merely jesting;
but he, being very angry, laid hold
of her, raised her arm, and stabbed
her below the armpit.

He lays her out in an attitude of sleep.

Wa tata Usilwane ukamba, wa tela kona ububende bukasilwane-kazana. Wa buya wa m esula ka/ɫle, wa m geza, wa m lalisa okcansini lwake; wa tata isikcamelo sake, wa m kcamelisa ngaso; wa m lungisa ekanda, e m tela ngamaka, e m kɋelisa; wa m gɋiza ezand/ɫleni na sezinyaweni; wa m gcoba ngamafuta, wa m embesa ingubo yake. Kwa nga ti u lele nje.

Usilwane took a pot, and put in it the blood of Usilwanekazana. He then wiped her carefully, and washed her, and laid her on her mat; he took a pillow and placed it under her head; he set in order her head, putting scents on it, and placing a fillet on her brow; he put armlets on her arms, and anklets on her legs; he anointed her with fat, and covered her with a blanket. It was just as though she was asleep.

He mixes his sister's blood with sheep's blood, and cooks it.

W' emuka Usilwane wa ya 'kutata imvu yake; wa buya nayo, wa i /ɫlaba; wa tela ububende bayo okambeni lapa ku kona obukasilwanekazana; wa bu /ɫlanganisa 'ndawo nye. Wa /ɫlinza imvu, wa sika ipapu nen/ɫliziyo nesibindi; wa kɋobela 'ndawo nye namatumbu nomhlwehlwe; wa peka 'ndawo nye kona loko; kwa vutwa, wa beka enzansi kweziko; wa geza, wa /ɫlala.

He then went out and took one of his sheep, and brought it home and killed it; he poured its blood into the vessel which contained that of Usilwanekazana, and mixed it together; he skinned the sheep, and cut out the lungs, the heart, and the liver, and chopped them up, with the entrails and the caul; he cooked it together; when it was done, he placed it at the lower side of the fireplace; and washed himself and sat down.

He offers it as food to Untombi-yapansi.

Ku ti lapa ilanga se li muka wa fika Untombi-yapansi. Wa ngena end/ɫlini kwabo, wa funyana Usilwane e /ɫlezi; Usilwanekazana e lcle. Wa ti Usilwane, "Tata, nampo ububende,[54] ntombi-yapansi, u d/ɫle." Wa ti Untombi-yapansi, "Usilwanekazana u lalele ni na?" Wa ti Usilwane, "A ng' azi. U lele nje." Wa ti Untombi-yapansi, "O, ububende yalobu bu vela pi na?" Wa ti Usilwane, "A u i boni imvu leyo

When the sun was declining, Untombi-yapansi came. She entered her mother's house, and found Usilwane sitting, and Usilwanekazana lying down. Usilwane said, "Take; there is food, Untombi-yapansi, and eat." Untombi-yapansi said, "Why is Usilwanekazana sleeping?" Usilwane said, "I do not know. She is merely sleeping." Untombi-yapansi said, "O, whence did this food come?" Usilwane replied, "Do you not see that sheep?"

---

[54] *Ububende* here means the food made of blood, and viscera; it is something like "sausage meat" or "black-pudding."

na?" Wa ti Untombi-yapansi, "I *h*latshelwe ni na?" Wa ti Usilwane, "I *h*latshiwe nje."

Untombi-yapansi said, "Why was it killed?" Usilwane replied, "It was merely killed."

She is prevented from eating it by a fly.

Wa puma ke Usilwane, wa ya elawini lake, wa ya 'ku*h*lala kona. Wa tata Untombi-yapansi ububende; wa ti lapa e za 'kud*h*la, kwa fika kuyena impukane enkulu, ya banga umsindo, i ti, "Bu! bu! ngi pe, ngi ku tshele." A i kape ngesand*h*la. A ti, lapa e za 'kud*h*la, i fike masinyane, i ti, "Bu! bu! ngi pe, ngi ku tshele." Kwa ti lapa i pinda ngokwesitatu Untombi-yapansi wa memeza wa ti, "We, silwane! We, silwane! Nansi impukane i ti, 'Bu! bu!' a ngi i pe, i ngi tshele." Wa ti Usilwane, "I bulale; i ya ku ko*h*lisa; u nga i pi."

Then Usilwane went to his own house, to wait there. Untombi-yapansi took some food; when she was about to eat, there came a large fly to her and made a great noise and said, "Boo! boo! give me, and I will tell you." She drove it away with her hand. When she was again about to eat, the fly came immediately and said, "Boo! boo! give me, and I will tell you." When it did thus the third time, Untombi-yapansi shouted, saying, "Here, Usilwane! Here, Usilwane! There is a fly which says 'Boo! boo!' and asks me to give it, and it will tell me." Usilwane replied, "Kill it; it is deceiving you; do not give it."

She gives the fly food, and it tells her of the murder of her sister.

Wa pinda futi Untombi-yapansi wa ka ububende; ya banga umsindo omkulu impukane, i ti, "Bu! bu! ngi pe, ngi ku tshele." Wa i kapa ngesand*h*la. Ya buya ya pinda futi, ya ti, "Bu! bu! ngi pe, ngi ku tshele." Kwa ti lapa i pinda futi okwesitatu, wa i pa; ya kota, ya ti, "Bheka; u nga bu d*h*li lobo 'bubende, ngokuba Usilwane u bulele Usilwanekazana. Wa ti, 'U be d*h*lala ngesilo sake.' Bheka, Usilwanekazana u file; ububende bake lobo; nesilo si file."

Again Untombi-yapansi took some of the food; the fly made a great noise, saying, "Boo! boo! give me, and I will tell you." She drove it away with her hand. Again it said, "Boo! boo! give me, and I will tell you." When it did so the third time, she gave it; it licked the food and said, "Take care; do not eat this food, for Usilwane has killed Usilwanekazana. He said, she killed his leopard without cause. See, Usilwanekazana is dead; this is her blood; and the leopard is dead."

She runs away, and is pursued by Usilwane.

Wa suka masinyane Untombi-yapansi; wa tata ingubo ey embetwe Usilwanekazana, wa m embula; wa bona igazi li puma pansi

Untombi-yapansi at once arose; she took off the blanket with which Usilwanekazana was covered, and saw the blood flowing from

kwekwapa. Wa puma ngamand*h*la Untombi-yapansi, wa gijima e ya lapa ku kona aoyise naonina. Ku te lapa e seu*h*la kwomuzi, wa puma Usilwane end*h*lini, wa bona Untombi-yapansi en*h*la kwomuzi. Wa memeza Usilwane e ti, "Mina lapa, ntombi-yapansi! u ya ngapi na?" Wa baleka ngamand*h*la Untombi-yapansi. Wa m landela Usilwane e pete umkouto, e ti lapo e ya 'ku m bamba kona, u ya 'u m gwaza ngomkonto.

beneath the armpit. Untombi-yapansi rushed out, and ran away to her fathers and mothers.[55] When she was at the upper part of the village, Usilwane left his house and saw her. He called her, saying, "Here, attend to me, Untombi-yapansi, where are you going?" Untombi-yapansi fled with haste. Usilwane pursued her, taking an assagai in his hand, thinking when he should catch her, he would stab her with it.

Untombi-yapansi escapes.

Wa ti lapa e seduze kakulu Usilwane, Untombi-yapansi wa ti, "Dabuka, m*h*laba, ngi ngene, ngokuba ngi za 'kufa namu*h*la." Wa dabuka um*h*laba, wa ngena Untombi-yapausi. Wa ti lapo Usilwane e se fika lapo, wa funa, e nga m boni lapo e tshone kona Untombi-yapansi; wa ti Usilwane, "Hau! hau! u tshone pi, loku ngi te ngi lapaya wa e lapa na?" A ka be e sa m bona. Wa buyela emva Usilwane.

When Usilwane was very near her, Untombi-yapansi said, "Open, earth, that I may enter,[56] for I am about to die this day." The earth opened, and Untombi-yapansi entered. When Usilwane came there, he sought, but could not see where Untombi-yapansi had descended; he said, "Hau! hau! where did she descend! for I thought when I was yonder, she was here." He was no longer able to see her. He went back again.

She goes near the chief's garden and gives an alarm.

Wa hamba Untombi-yapansi; kwa ti lapa so ku *h*lwile wa lala, e nga pumanga pansi. Kwa ti kusasa wa vuka futi, wa hamba. Kwa ti lapa se ku semini kakulu wa puma pansi, wa ye w' ema egangeni, wa memeza e ti, "U so ya yiyayiya[57] yedwa kwela nonyaka;

Untombi-yapansi went on; when it was evening she slept, not having come out from the earth. In the morning she awoke, and again went on. When it was midday she came out of the earth, and went and stood on a small elevation, and shouted, saying, "There will be nothing but weeping this summer.[58] Usilwanekaza-

---

[55] The brothers of the father are called fathers; and the father's polygamic wives, mothers.

[56] See Appendix.

[57] Yiyayiya *for* lilalila; in Isikqwabe dialect.

[58] The *u* here does not refer to any particular person, but to the people of the chief in general. The natives say on such occasions, "U ya 'kuba Umayemaye kwela nonyaka," "There will come Umayemaye this summer," Umayemaye being a name personifying mourning. "The woe-woe-man will come this summer."

Usilwanekazana u bulewe Usilwane ; u ti, u be d*h*lala ngengomende yenkosi." Sa ti isalukazi esi lapo embutisweni, " Kungati ku kona oku lengezayo, ku ti Usilwanekazana u bulewe Usilwane ; u be d*h*lala ngengomende yenkosi." Ya ti inkosi, " Si tate ni, ni si ponse emnceleni." Ba si tata, ba si bulala, ba si ponsa emnceleni ; ngokuba be ti, " Si *h*lolela umntwana wenkosi."

na has been murdered by Usilwane ; he says, she has killed the prince's leopard[59] without cause." An old woman which was in the royal garden said, " It sounds as though some one was shouting afar off, saying, ' Usilwanekazana has been killed by Usilwane ; she has killed the prince's leopard without cause.' " The king said, " Seize her, and cast her outside the garden." They seized her, and killed her, and cast her outside the garden ; for they said she was prophesying evil against the king's child.

She goes to another place and shouts again.

Wa pinda wa d*h*lula lapo Untombi-yapansi, wa fika kwelinye iganga, wa ti, " U so ya yiyayiya yedwa kwela nonyaka. Usilwanekazana u bulewe Usilwane ; u be d*h*lala ngengomende yenkosi." La ti ik*xx*eku, " Ku kona oku lengezayo ; ku nga ti ku ti, ' U so yiyayiya yedwa kwela nonyaka. Usilwanekazana u bulewe Usilwane ; u ti, u be d*h*lala ngengomende yenkosi.' " Ya ti inkosi, " Li tate ni, ni li ponse ngapand*h*le kwomncele." Ba li tata, ba li ponsa emnceleni.

Again Untombi-yapansi passed onward from that place, and went to another small elevation, and cried, " There will be nothing but weeping this summer. Usilwanekazana has been murdered by Usilwane ; he says, she has killed the prince's leopard without cause. An old man said, " There is some one shouting afar off' ; it is as if it was said, ' There will be nothing but weeping this summer. Usilwanekazana has been killed by Usilwane ; he says she has killed the prince's leopard without cause.' " The chief said, " Seize him, and cast him outside the garden." They seized him, and cast him out.

All the people run to her when she shouts the third time.

Kwa ti, lapo w' esuka futi Untombi-yapansi, wa ya eduze nabo, wa memeza e ti, " U so ya yiya yedwa kwela nonyaka. Usilwanekazana u bulewe Usilwane ; u

Untombi-yapansi then again departed and went near them, and shouted, saying, " There will be nothing but weeping this summer. Usilwanekazana has been killed by Usilwane ; he says she

---

[59] *Ingom'-ende*, the name here given to the leopard, means a *long wedding song.*

ti, u be d*h*lala ngengomende yenkosi." Kwa ti lapo bonke abantu
b' ezwa ukutsho kwake, ba kala
bonke, ba baleka, ba ya kuyena,
ba ti, "U ti ni na?" Wa ti,
" Usilwanekazana u bulewe Usilwane ; u ti, u be d*h*lala ngengomende yenkosi."

has killed the prince's leopard
without cause." When all the
people heard that, they all cried,
and ran towards her, and said,
"What do you say ?" She replied, " Usilwanekazana has been
killed by Usilwane ; she has killed
the prince's leopard without cause."

Usilwane is seized and bound.

Ba buya abantu bonke, ba ya
ekaya. Ba fika, wa baleka Usilwane ; ba m biza, ba ti, " Buya
wena ; u s' u ti ku kona abantu
aba fa bonke na ?[60] Wena u se
z' 'ubulawa."[61] Wa buya Usilwane, wa ngena end*h*lini. Ba m
bamba, ba m bopa, ba ti, "U za
'kwenziwa njani na ?" Ya ti inkosi, "Vala ni emnyango, ni tshise
ind*h*lu, ku ze ku tshe tina soba-
tatu. Kepa wena, ntombi-yapansi,
hamba u ye kodade weuu, u ye
'ku*h*lala kona ; ngokuba mina no-
nyoko si za 'kutsha nend*h*lu ; ngokuba a si tandi ukuhamba, ngokuba Usilwanekazana u file, nati
si za 'kufa kanye naye."

All the men went home. When
they arrived, Usilwane fled ; they
called him, saying, " Come back ;
do you think that there is any
reason why all the people should
be killed ? You are not about to
be killed." Usilwane came back,
and went into the house. They
laid hold of him, and bound him,
and said, "What is to be done
with him ?" The king said,
"Close the door, and set fire to
the house, that we three may be
burnt.[62] But you, Untombi-yapansi, go to your sister,[63] and live
with her ; for I and your mother
shall be burnt[64] with the house ;
for we do not wish to live, because
Usilwanekazana is dead, and we
too will die with her."

Usilwane pleads in vain.

Wa ti Usilwane, " Mina ; musa
ni uku ngi tshisa nend*h*lu ; ngi
gwaze ni ngomkonto." Ya ti inkosi, " K*q*a, mntanami ; ngi za 'ku

Usilwane said, " Attend to me ;
do not burn me with the house ;
stab me with an assagai." The
chief said, " No, my child ; I will

---

[60] U s' u ti ku kona abantu aba ka ba fa ngako bonke na ?—This would be
the full form of the sentence. It is meant by the question to say, that he need
not imagine that one murder—namely, his own—will be added to the murder
already committed.

[61] Wena, u se z' ubulawa, *for,* a ku se z' ubulawa.

[62] We three—namely, himself, wife, and Usilwane.

[63] The name of this sister in the other tale is given. It is Umkindinkomo,
—Cow-hip-dress ; because the hip-dress she wore was made of a cowhide.

[64] In the other version the father is represented as arming and fighting
with Unkoiya, who also arms. Unkoiya first hurls his lance, but it falls short ;
the father's pierces Unkoiya with a fatal wound. But subsequently, without
any reason being given, the father, mother, and village are burnt.

ku zwisa ubu*h*lungu obukulu ka-kulu, ngokuba u wena o bulele umntanami."

cause you to feel very great pain, for it is you who have murdered my child."

The chief sends Untombi-yapansi to her sister.

Wa ti Untombi-yapansi, "Ngi za 'kuhamba nobani na?" Wa ti uyise, "Tata inkabi yakwenu, u kwele pezu kwayo, u hambe. Kwo ti lapo u pezulu okalweni u ya 'kuzwa ukuduma okukulu kwoku-tsha kwomuzi; u nga bheki ngase-muva, u hambe nje."

Untombi-yapansi said, "With whom shall I go?" Her father replied, "Take your ox, mount it and go. When you are on the top of the hill, you will hear the great roaring of the burning vil-lage; do not look back, but go on."

She meets with an imbulu, who deceives her.

Wa hamba e kwele enkabini. Kwa ti lapa e sokalweni w' ezwa ukuduma kwomlilo. Wa kala, e ti, "Konje lolo 'ludumo olungako ku tsha uma nobaba." Wa hamba wa ye wa fika emfuleni omkulu. Wa fika lapo, kwa vela inubulu; ya ti, "Dade, ntombi-yapansi, ake w e*h*like lapa enkabini yako, ngi kwele, ngi bone uma ku nga ngi fanela ini na?" Wa ti, "K*q*a; a ngi tandi ukwe*h*lika." Ya ti, "Ku nani na?" Kepa Untombi-yapansi wa e kw azi ngapambili ukuba imbulu i za 'uvela lapo; ngokuba unina wa e m tshelile, wa ti, "Uma inkabi i nyatele pezu kwelitshe, imbulu i ya 'upuma kona." Ngaloko ke w' esaba ukwe*h*lika enkabini. Wa ti lapo, "Suka, ngi d*h*lule." Ya ti im-bulu, "Hau! Ngi tsheleke, ngi bone uma ku ya 'u ngi fanela ini na?" W' e*h*lika. Ya ti, "Leti izinto zako, ngi fake, ngi bone uma

She went, riding on the ox. When she was on the hill, she heard the roaring of the fire. She wept, saying, "So then I hear this great roaring; my mother and father are burning." She went on, and came to a great river. When she came to it, there appeared an imbulu, and said, "Princess, Un-tombi-yapansi, just come down here from your ox, that I may get up, and see if it becomes me or not?" She replied, "No; I do not wish to dismount." The im-bulu said, "What is the matter?" But Untombi-yapansi knew[65] be-forehand that an imbulu would appear at that place; for her mo-ther had told her, saying, "If the ox treads on a stone, an imbulu will come out at that place." She was therefore afraid to dismount from the ox. So she said, "Get out of the way, and let me pass on." The imbulu said, "Hau! Lend me the ox, that I may see if it is suitable for me?" She dis-mounted. The imbulu said, "Hand me your things, that I may put

---

[65] The words with which she is warned before setting out are given in the other version :—"Ba ti, a nga li tinti itshe eli send*h*leleni." "They told her not to tread on a certain stone which was in the path." This is much more precise, and gives us the idea not distinctly brought out in the above, that there was a certain stone known as being the haunt of some magical evil power.

ku ya 'u ngi fanela ini na?" Wa i nika zonke izinto. Ya binca imbulu, ya kwela enkabini, ya ti, "We, kwa ngi fanela!"

them on and see if they are suitable for me?" She gave the imbulu all her things. The imbulu put them on, and mounted the ox, and said, "Oh, how they become me!"

The imbulu gives her a new name.

Wa ti Untombi-yapansi, "Yehlika ke, u lete izinto zami, ngi kwele." Ya ti, "A ngi tandi. U ngi tshelekele ni na?" Wa ti, "Ku tsho wena, ukuti, a ngi ku tsheleke." Ya ti imbulu, "A ngi tandi." Ya ti imbulu, "A s' ekqe lapa ematsheni, si bone o ya 'kuba nenyawo ezi 'manzi." Y' ekqa imbulu; kepa yena Untombi-yapansi wa hamba emanzini, ngokuba a ka kweli 'ndawo.

Kwa ti lapa se be welile ya ti imbulu, "Ezako inyawo zi 'manzi; manje wena igama lako Umsila-wezinja. U mina manje Untombi-yapansi." Kepa Untombi-yapansi a ka pendulanga 'luto, wa tula nje. Ya hamba imbulu, i kwele enkabini, 'eza ngeniva Untombi-yapansi.

Untombi-yapansi said, "Dismount now, and give me my things, that I may get up." The imbulu said, "I do not wish to get down. Why did you lend it to me?" She replied, "You asked me to lend it to you." The imbulu said, "I do not wish to get down. Let us leap here on the stones, and see which will have wet feet." The imbulu leapt; but Untombi-yapansi walked in the water, because she was not mounted on any thing."

When they had passed across, the imbulu said, "It is your feet that are wet; now your name is Umsila-wezinja.[66] And I am now Untombi-yapansi." But Untombi-yapansi made no answer; she was silent. The imbulu went on, riding on the ox, and Untombi-yapansi coming after on foot.

They reach the sister's village.

Ba ya ba fika lapo w' endela udade wabo kantombi-yapansi. Ba ngena ekaya, b' enyuka, ba ya ngasenhla. Ya fika ya ngena imbulu, naye Untombi-yapansi wa ngena. Ya ti imbulu, "Musa ukungena. Bamba inkabi yami." Wa i bamba Untombi-yapansi; ya hlala imbulu.

They went on, and came to the place where the sister of Untombi-yapansi was married. They entered the village, and went to the upper part of it. The imbulu went into a house, and Untombi-yapansi also went in. The imbulu said, "Don't come in. Hold my ox." Untombi-yapansi held the ox; the imbulu sat down.

[66] *Umsila-wezinja*, Dogs'-tail.

The imbulu deceives her.

Wa buza udade wabo kantombi-yapansi, wa ti, "U ubani na?" Ya ti imbulu, "U mina, mnta-kwetu. Hau! a u ngi boni ini na?" Wa ti, "K*q*a; a ngi ku boni; ngokuba owakwetu um-ntwana nga m shiya emncinane; ngi ya l' azi kodwa igama lake. Kepa futi umzimba wake wa u kazimula, ngokuba wa u itusi." Ya ti imbulu, "Mina nga gula kakulu. Igama lami ng' Untombi-yapansi. Umzimba wami so wa pela lowo o itusi." Wa kala udade wabo, e ti, "Hau! Kanti umnta-kwetu lona na?"

Wa ti udade wabo, "Kepa lona o semnyango u vela pi yena na?" Ya ti, "Into nje; nga i tola lapa emfuleni, i hamba pansi nje." Wa ti, "Ngi ku pe ukud*h*la na?" Ya ti, "Yebo; ngi lambile." Wa i pa isijingi. Ya d*h*la. Wa ti, "Biza umuntu wako lowa, ngi mu pe; nangu umlaza." Ya ti, "Mu nike kona emnyango lapaya." Wa ti umyeni wake, "K*q*a, musa uku mu pa umuntu pand*h*le; u m nge-nise end*h*lini, a d*h*lele kona." Wa m biza, wa ti, "Ubani igama lake na?" Ya ti imbulu, "Um-sila-wezinja." Wa ti udade wabo, "Ngena, u zokud*h*la, msila-we-zinja."

The sister of Untombi-yapansi asked, "Who are you?" The imbulu replied, "It is I, child of our house. Hau! do you not recognise me?" She said, "No; I do not recognise you; for the child of our house I left when she was still young; I know nothing but her name. But, besides, her body glistened, for she was like brass." The imbulu said, "I was very ill. I am Untombi-yapansi. I no longer have that body of mine which was like brass." Her sister wept, saying, "Hau! Forsooth is this the child of our house?"

Her sister said, "And she who is at the doorway, whence does she come?" The imbulu said, "It is a mere thing. I fell in with it at the river; it was merely going on foot." She said, "May I give you food?" The imbulu replied, "Yes; I am hungry." She gave it porridge. It ate. She said, "Call your servant yonder, that I may give her; here is some whey."[67] The imbulu said, "Give it to her there in the doorway." Her husband said, "No, do not give food to the person outside; bring her into the house, that she may eat here." She called her, saying, "What is her name?" The imbulu replied, "Umsila-we-zinja." Her sister said, "Come and eat, Umsila-wezinja."

Untombi-yapansi wastes the food.

Wa ngena end*h*lini; wa tata ukamba lwabantwana udade wabo, wa m nika ngalo umlaza. Ya ti imbulu, "K*q*a! k*q*a! Musa uku

She went in; her sister took a child's vessel, and gave her some whey in it. The imbulu said, "No! no! Child of our house,

<hr>

[67] The story makes it clear however that we are not to understand simple whey, but whey mixed with ground mealies. Poor people and dependents only eat ground mealies mixed with whey; superiors use amasi.

m nika okambeni lwabantabako, mnta-kwetu; u m telele pansi nje, a d*h*lele kona." Wa ti umkwenya wabo, "K*q*a, musa uku m telela pansi umuntu, u m kangeze ezand*h*leni." Wa ka ngokezo udade wabo, wa m kangeza. Kepa Untombi-yapansi wa pa*h*la insika ngezand*h*la zake, wa m kangeza udade wabo; ku ti lapa e se k*q*edile uku m kangeza, a yeke izand*h*la, a kcitcke amasi; a tete a ti, "Ini ukuba ngi ku kangeze amasi ami, u wa kcite na?" A ti, "Kw' enza, ngokuba ngi kangeza, ngi pa*h*le insika." Wa mu pa inkobe; wa d*h*la. Ba lala.

do not give it to her in the vessel of your children; pour it for her on the ground, that she may eat it there." Her brother-in-law said, "No, do not pour food for a person on the ground; give it to her in her hands." Her sister dipped it out with a spoon, and poured it into her hands. But Untombi-yapansi put her hands round the pillar of the house, and her sister put it into her hands; when she had finished, she separated her hands, and the amasi was spilt. Her sister scolded, saying, "How is it that I pour my amasi[68] into your hands, and you throw it away?" She replied, "It is because, when I stretched out my hands, I placed them on each side of the pillar."[69] She gave her boiled mealies; she ate; and they retired to rest.

She is sent to watch the garden.

Ku te kusasa wa ti udade wabo kantombi-yapansi, "Ngi ya *h*lupeka ngokuba ku nge ko 'muntu o ngi lindelayo; zi ya ngi *h*lupa iziuyoni ensimini kwami." Ya ti imbulu, "Nangu Umsila-wezinja; a ka hambe naba ya 'kulinda naye, a ye 'ku ku lindela." Wa ti, "Hamba ke." Wa hamba Untombi-yapansi kanye nodalana.

In the morning the sister of Untombi-yapansi said, "I am in trouble because there is no one to watch for me; the birds trouble me in my garden." The imbulu said, "There is Umsila-wezinja; let her too go with those who watch, that she may watch for you." She said, "Well, go." Untombi-yapansi went with Udalana.[70]

[68] The sister here magnifies her gift by calling the whey amasi. Untombi-yapansi acts thus because it was not proper for her to eat the milk belonging to her brother-in-law. See Note 95, p. 164. The Imbulu has no regard for such customs.

[69] In the other version, it is groundnuts which are given to her. She takes but one out of the vessel, and all the rest disappear. It is thus, and not by dropping whey, that she fixes attention on herself. The chief exclaims, "Lolu udodovu lwenkosikazi lu tate yanye ind*h*lubu, za pela zonke csitsheni." "This skinny one of the queen has taken one groundnut, and no more are left in the dish." She thus also manifests her magical power, which is brought out so much afterwards.

[70] *Udalana*, Little-old-one.

Ba fika ngapandhle kwomuzi, w' ema Untombi-yapansi, wa ti, "Dhlula wena, dalana." Wa dhlula Udalana; ba hamba, ba fika emasimini. Kepa Udalana e ya kwabo insimu, ya i ngasenhla; kepa leyo e lindwa Untombi-yapansi ya i ngenzansi, amakxiba e bhekene. Inyoni ziningi kakulu; kwa ti be sa fika, za fika. Wa zi ponsa Udalana, wa ti, "Nazo, msila-wezinja." Wa ti Untombi-yapansi, "Tayi, tayi, lezo 'nyoni ezi dhla insimu kadade, kona e ngo 'dade ngasibili, ngoba se ngi Umsila-wezinja. Nga ngi nge 'msila-wezinja ngempela; nga ngi Untombi-yapansi." Z' esuka masinye izinyoni njengokutsho kwake. Ba hlala imini yonke izinyoni zi nge ko. Kepa Udalana wa mangala kakulu ngokuba e bona izinyoni zi nge ko, loku zi m hlupa kangaka youke imihla.

When they came outside the village Untombi-yapansi stopped and said, "Do you go before, Udalana." Udalana went on; they reached the gardens. Udalana went to the garden belonging to her house, which was high up; and that which was watched by Untombi-yapansi was low down, and the watch-houses were opposite each other. The birds were very numerous. As they were entering the garden the birds came; Udalana threw stones at them, and said, "There they are, Umsila-wezinja." Untombi-yapansi said, "Tayi, tayi, those birds which devour my sister's garden, although she is not my sister truly, for I am now Umsila-wezinja. I was not really Umsila-wezinja; I was Untombi-yapansi." The birds went away immediately in accordance with her word. They remained the whole day without any birds coming. And Udalana wondered much when she saw that there were not any birds, since they troubled her so much every day.

She is visited by strange guests.

Wa ti Untombi-yapansi lapa se ku semini kakulu, wa ti, "U ze u ngi ponsele, dalana; ngi sa ya 'kugeza." Wa hamba wa ya emfuleni; wa fika wa ngena pakati esizibeni, wa geza; wa puma umzimba wonke wake u kanya itusi, e pete induku yake yetusi. Wa tshaya pansi, wa ti, "Puma ni nonke, bantu bakababa nenkomo zikababa, nokudhla kwami." Kwa puma abantu abaningi nenkomo eziningi, nokudhla kwake. Wa

When it was midday Untombi-yapansi said, "Do you throw stones at the birds for me, Udalana; I am now going to bathe." She went to the river; when she came to it, she went into a pool and washed; she came out with her whole body shining like brass, and holding in her hand her brass rod. She smote the ground and said, "Come out, all ye people of my father, and cattle of my father, and my food." There at once came out of the earth many people,[71] and many cattle, and her food.

---

[71] In the other version, the dead,—her father, mother, and Ulukozazana, — are among the company.

dhla. Kwa puma nenkabi yake, wa kwela pezu kwayo, wa ti,

"Enkundhleni kababa sa si ti
    E-a-ye;
Kwezi-matshoba amhlope sa si ti
    E-a-ye."

Kwa vuma abantu bonke kanye nezihlahla, zi in vumela. Kwa ti lapa e se kqedile konke loko, w' e-hlika enkabini yake; wa tshaya ngenduku yake pansi, wa ti, "Da-buka, mhlaba, ku ngene izinto zikababa nabantu bake." Nembala umhlaba wa dabuka, kwa ngena izinto zonke nabantu.

She ate. Her own ox also came out; she mounted it and said,

"In my father's cattle-pen we used
    to sing E-a-ye;
Among the white-tailed cattle
    we used to sing E-a-ye."

All the people, together with the trees, took up the song, singing in unison with her. When she had done all this, she descended from her ox; she smote the ground with her rod, and said, "Open, earth, that my father's things and his people may enter." And truly the earth opened, and all the things and men entered.

She returns to the garden and Udalana wonders.

Wa buya wa tata umhlaba omnyama, wa zibekca ngawo em-zimbeni, wa ba njengaloku e be njalo. Wa kupuka, wa ya ensi-mini, wa ngena ekxibeni. Wa ti, "Kade zi kona ini izinyoni na?" Wa ti Udalana, "Au! we ba-ndhla! u bona ngoba e ngi shiye nezinyoni eziningi ngedwa na?" Ba ti be sa kuluma wa fika um-hlambi omkulu wezinyoni. Wa ti Udalana, "Nazo, msila-wezinja." Wa ti Untombi-yapansi, "Tayi, tayi, leziya 'nyoni ezi dhla insimu kadade. Kona e nge 'dade ngasi-bili; kona se ngi Umsila-wezinja; nga ngi nge Umsila-wezinja ngasi-bili; nga ngi Untombi-yapansi." Z' esuka masinya izinyoni njengo-kutsho kwake.

Again she took some black earth and smeared her body with it, and was as she was before. She went up from the river to the garden, and went into the watch-house. She said, "Have the birds been here some time?" Udalana said, "Au! by the council! does she see because she left me alone with many birds?" As they were still speaking a large flock of birds came. Udalana said, "There they are, Umsila-wezinja." Untombi-yapansi said, "Tayi, tayi, you birds yonder which devour my sister's garden. Although she is not my sister truly; although I am now Umsila-wezinja; I was not truly Umsila-wezinja; I was Untombi-yapansi."[72] The birds at once went away in accordance with her word.

[72] In the other version it is very different; she does not protect the garden, but gives it up to the birds. "Za fika izinyoni, za wela ensimini. Wa ti, 'Tai, tai, tai; insimu kadade. Kona zi wa dhla, a zi wa kqedi.' A kwa sala nanxa li linye. Kwa ti nya. Ba ti, 'Insimu yenkosi u i nika izinyoni.'" "The birds came, and dropped into the garden. She said, 'Tai, tai, tai; it is my sister's garden. Though they eat the corn, they do not eat it all up.' They ate it all; there did not remain one ear of corn; the garden was utterly desolate. The people said, 'She gives the king's garden to the birds.'"

Kepa Udalana e mangala kakulu u loku 'kutsho kwake, a ti, "U ti ni, yebuya, msila-wezinja, na?" A ti Untombi-yapansi, "A ngi ti 'luto." W' enka Udalana kwelake ikæiba, wa ya kwelikantombi-yapansi, wa ti, "Hau! wena u d/lela pi, msila-wezinja, na?" Wa ti Untombi-yapansi, "U tsho ngani na?" Wa ti, "Ngi tsho ngoba ngi nga boni izala laƙo lapo u d/lela kona." Wa ti Untombi-yapansi, "Ngi ya d/la nje."

But Udalana wondered much at that saying of hers, and said, "I say, Umsila-wezinja, what are you saying?" Untombi-yapansi replied, "I say nothing." Udalana descended from her watch-house, and went to that of Untombi-yapansi, and said to her, "Hau! where have you eaten, Umsila-wezinja?" Untombi-yapansi said, "Why do you ask?" She replied, "I ask because I do not see the refuse of the sugar-cane where you have eaten." Untombi-yapansi said, "I have eaten?"

Kwa tshona ilanga, ba buya ba ya ekaya. Ba fika, ya buza inkosi ya ti, "Be zi kona inyoni, msila-wezinja, na?" Wa ti Untombi-yapansi, "Ehe; be ziningi kakulu." Ya ti imbulu, "Ukuma kwake yena. Umsila-wezinja u za 'ku/lala pansi nje, i ze i d/liwe izinyoni. Ku ti lapo se i pelile, u ti w a/lulwe izinyoni." Ba /lala; ba lala.

The sun set; they returned home. When they arrived the chief asked, saying, "Were there any birds there, Umsila-wezinja?" Untombi-yapansi replied, "Yes; there were very many indeed." The imbulu said, "This is her custom. Umsila-wezinja will just sit on the ground, until the garden is utterly destroyed by the birds. And when it is all gone, she says she has been worsted by the birds." They sat; they retired to rest.

Udalana makes a discovery.

Kwa ti kusasa ba hamba ba ya 'kulinda. Kwa ti lapa be sesangweni w' ema Untombi-yapansi, wa ti, "D/lula." Wa ti Udalana, "Hau! wena u nani uma u d/lule na? Zonke insuku ku hamba mina pambili." Kepa Untombi-yapansi wa e saba ukud/lula ngokuba umbete u ya m esula umuti lowa a u gcoba emzimbeni ukuze itusi li nga kanyi, ba m bone abantu. Wa d/lula Udalana. Ba fika emasimini, ba /lala. Wa ti Udalana, "Nazo, msila-wezinja." Wa ti Untombi-yapansi, "Tayi, tayi, lezo 'nyoni ezi d/la insimu kadade; kona e nge 'dade ngampela; kepa kwa ku udade."

In the morning they went to watch. When they were at the gateway Untombi-yapansi stood still and said, "Go on." Udalana replied, "Hau! what happens to you if you go first? Every day I go in front." But Untombi-yapansi was afraid to go first because the dew wiped off that with which she smeared her body, that the brass-colour may not glisten, and people recognise her. Udalana went on. They came to the garden and sat down. Udalana said, "There they are, Umsila-wezinja." Untombi-yapansi said, "Tayi, tayi those birds which devour my sister's garden; although she is not my sister truly; but she was my sister."

Wa ti, " Hlala, u bhekile wena, dalana ; ngi sa hamba ngi ya 'kugeza." Wa hamba. Kwa ti lapa e se hambile Untombi-yapansi, wa landela ngasemuva Udalana, wa ye wa fika emfuleni naye. Wa fika Untombi-yapansi, wa ngena esizibeni, wa puma umzimba wake u kazimula, e pete induku yake yetusi. Wa mangala Udalana ngokubona loko. Kepa Untombi-yapansi wa e nga m boni Udalana, ngokuba wa e kcatshile. Wa tata induku yake Untombi-yapansi, wa tshaya pansi, wa ti, " Dabuka, mhlaba, ngi bone izinto zikababa, zi pume zonke nabantu bakababa, nezinto zami nezinkomo." Kwa puma konke loko njengokutsho kwake. Kwa vela nokudhla ; wa dhla. Wa tata ingubo yake i kqatshelwe ngezindondo, wa i binca, wa kwela enkabini yake, e hlobile. Wa ti,

" Enkundhleni kababa sa si ti
        E-a-ye ;
   Kwezi-matshoba abomvu sa si ti
        E-a-ye."

Ba vuma bonke kanye nezihlahla ngaloko. Udalana w' esaba, wa tutumela ngokuba kwa ku nga titi nomhlaba u ya zamazama.

Kwa ti lapo Untombi-yapansi e s' ehlika enkabini, wa buya pambili Udalana, wa fika kukqala ensimini. Kepa Untombi-yapansi wa ti, " A ku tshone konke loko pansi." Kwa tshona konke. Wa zibekca ngomuti emzimbeni wake, wa buya wa ya ensimini. Wa fika wa ti, " Kade zi kona ini izinyoni, dalana, na ?" Wa ti Udalana, " Kade u hlalele ni emfuleni wena na ?" Wa ti Untombi-yapansi, " A u boni ini uma inina a ngi kw azi ukugeza masinya, ngoba umzimba wami mubi, umnyama kakulu na ?"

She said, " Stay and watch, Udalana ; I am now going to bathe." She went. When Untombi-yapansi had gone, Udalana went after her, and she too went to the river. When Untombi-yapansi came to the river she entered the pool, and came out with her body glistening, and carrying in her hand her brass rod. Udalana wondered when she saw this. But Untombi-yapansi did not see Udalana, for she had concealed herself. Untombi-yapansi took her rod and smote the ground and said, " Open, earth, that I may see the things of my father ; that all may come out, and my father's people, and my things and the cattle." All these things came out in accordance with her saying. Food also came out ; she ate. She took her garment which was ornamented with brass balls, she put it on, and mounted her ox, having adorned herself. She said,

" In my father's cattle-pen we used
        to sing E-a-ye ;
   Among the red-tailed cattle we
        used to sing E-a-ye."

All the people and the trees took up the song. Udalana was afraid, and trembled ; for it was as if the very earth was moving.

When Untombi-yapansi was getting down from her ox, Udalana went back before her and came first to the garden. And Untombi-yapansi said, " Let it all sink into the ground." Every thing sank into the ground. She smeared her body, and returned to the garden. When she came she said, " Have the birds been long here, Udalana ? " Udalana said, " Why have you staid so long at the river ? " Untombi-yapansi replied, " Do you not see that I cannot wash quickly, for my body is dirty and very black ? "

W' esuka Udalana wa ya ekæibeni lapa ku kona Untombi-yapausi, wa hlala kuyena, e m buka emzimbeni wonke ; kepa a nga boni lapo ku kona ibala eli kazimulayo. A mangale uma u zibekce ngani na.

Udalana arose and went to the watch-house where Untombi-yapansi was ; she sat by her, looking earnestly at the whole of her body ; but she did not see anywhere a glistening spot. She wondered what she had smeared herself with.

The chief visits the garden.

Ya fika inkosi emasimini, ya ti, "Sa ni bona, msila-wezinja ; zi kona izinyoni na ?" Wa ti, "Yebo, nkos', zi kona." W' ehlika ekæibeni Untombi-yapansi, 'esaba ngoba ku kona inkosi pezulu ekæibeni. Ya ti inkosi, "W ehlikela ni, msila-wezinja, na ?" Wa ti, "Kqa ; ngi y' ehlika nje, nkos'." Y' ehlika inkosi, ya hamba ya ya ekaya. Ba buya nabo outombi-yapansi. Ba fika ba dhla ba lala.

The chief came to the garden and said, "Good day, Umsila-wezinja ; are there any birds here ?" She said, "Yes, sir, there are." Untombi-yapausi descended from the watch-house, being afraid because the chief was ou it. The chief said, "Why do you get down, Umsila-wezinja ?" She replied, "No, I merely get down, sir." The chief got down from the watch-house, and returned home. Untombi-yapansi and Udalana also went home. On their arrival they ate and lay down.

Udalana tells the chief what she has discovered.

Kwa ti kusihlwa Udalana wa ya enkosini, wa ti, "Nkos', wo vuka kusasa kakulu, u ye 'kuhlala ekæibeni lami, kona ku ya 'kuti emini lapa Umsila-wezinja e se hambile ukuya 'kugeza, si m landele. U ya 'ubona umzimba wake u ya kazimula. A fike a pume nenduku yake yetusi pakati esizibeni, a tshaye ngayo pansi, a ti, ' Dabuka, mhlaba, ku pume izinto zikababa zonke.' Ku pume nezinkomo nabantu nokudhla nezinto zake zokuhloba. A kwele enkabini yake, a hlabele, ku vume abantu nenkomo nemiti ; konke ku m vumele." Ya ti inkosi, "Uma ngi hamba nje kusasa ngi

In the evening Udalana went to the chief and said, " O chief, wake very early in the morning, and go and stay at my watch-house ; then at noon when Umsila-wezinja has gone to bathe we will follow her. You will see her with her body glistening. She comes out of the pool with her brass rod, and smites the ground with it, and says, ' Open, earth, that all the things of my father may come out.' And there come out cattle and men and food and all her ornaments. You will see her mount on an ox, and sing. And the men and the cattle and the trees take up the song, and every thing sings in unison with her." The chief said, "If I go in the morning shall I

ya 'u ku bona loko na?" Wa ti Udalana, "Yebo, nkosi, u ya 'u ku bona." Ba lala.

see that?" Udalana said, "Yes, O chief, you will see it." They retired to rest.

The chief watches in vain.

Kwa ti lapa ekuseni ya vuka inkosi, ya ya ekxibeni likadalana. Kwa ti lapa se ku sile ba hamba Odalana nontombi-yapansi. Kwa ti lapo be sesangweni wa ti Untombi-yapansi, "Dhlula, wena, dalana." Wa ti Udalana, "Ini wena u nga hambi pambili na? W e-saba ni ukuhamba pambili?" Wa dhlula Udalana, wa hamba. Wa ti Untombi-yapansi, "Hau! Ku ngani namuhla umbete u nga bi ko na?" Wa ti Udalana, "Kumbe nga be ku hamba impunzi." Wa ti Untombi-yapansi, "Kepa w ome kangaka umbete na?"

Ba hamba ba ye ba fika emasi-mini. Ba hlala. Za fika inyoni. Wa ti Udalana, "Nazo, msila-we-zinja." Wa zi kuza njengabantu bonke; kepa a zi sukanga; za ba hlupa kakulu. Ya ti inkosi, "Ku ngani ukuba zi ni hlupe namuhla izinyoni na?" Wa ti Udalana, "Emihleni u ya zi kuza ngokunye Umsila-wezinja. Kepa namuhla a ng' azi uma u yekele ni na."

Kepa wa ti Udalana, "Ku nga-ni ukuba namhla u nga yi 'kugeza na?" Wa ti, "Kqa; ngi y' enqe-na namuhla." Kepa Untombi-yapansi 'ezwa ukuti u kona umu-ntu o kona emasimini, ngokuba e bona umbete u nge ko. Kwa ze kwa tshona ilanga. Y' ehlika in-kosi ekxibeni, ya ya ekaya. Kwa ti ngasemuva ba buya nabo Onto-mbi-yapansi.

When the chief arose in the morning he went to the watch-house of Udalana. When the sun was up Udalana and Untombi-yapansi set out. When they were at the gateway Untombi-yapansi said, "Do you go on, Udalana." Udalana said, "Why do not you go first? Why are you afraid to go in front?" Udalana went on. Untombi-yapansi said, "Hau! How is it that to-day there is no dew?" Udalana said, "Perhaps a deer has passed." Untombi-yapansi said, "But why has the dew dried up so much?"

They went on and came to the garden. They sat down. The birds came. Udalana said, "There they are, Umsila-wezinja." She scared them in the same way as all other people; but they did not go away; they troubled them very much. The chief said, "How is it that the birds have troubled you so much to-day?" Udalana replied, "On other days Umsila-wezinja scares them in a different manner. But to-day I do not know why she has departed from her usual method."

Udalana went to Untombi-ya-pansi and said, "Why do you not go to bathe to-day?" She said, "No; I am lazy to-day." But Untombi-yapansi perceived that there was some one in the garden, because she saw that there was no dew. At length the sun set. The chief went down from the watch-house and returned home; and Untombi-yapansi and Udalana also returned after him.

Kwa ti lapo se be fike ekaya wa ti Untombi-yapansi, "Zi ya si *h*lupa inyoni." Wa ti udade wabo, "U zi bheke kakulu izinyoni, msila-wezinja, zi nga k*q*edi ama-bel' ami." Ba lala.

When they reached home Untombi-yapansi said, "The birds trouble us." Her sister said, "Watch the birds with great care, Umsila-wezinja, that they may not destroy my corn." They retired to rest.

The chief watches a second time, and hears Untombi-yapansi's charm.

Kwa ti ekuseni inkosi ya puma, ya hamba ngenye ind*h*lela, ya ye ya fika emasimini, ya kcatsha pakati kwamabele. Kwa ti lapa se ku sile ba hamba Odalana, ba ya 'kulinda. Ba fika esangweni, wa ti Untombi-yapansi, "D*h*lula." Wa ti Udalana, "K*q*a; a ngi tandi nami. D*h*lula wena." Wa d*h*lula Untombi-yapansi. Kwa ti lapa be hamba Untombi-yapansi wa bheka ezitweni zake, wa bona ukuba umbete u ya k*q*ala ukususa umuti. W' ala ukuhamba, wa ti, "D*h*lula, dalana." Wa d*h*lula Udalana. Ba fika emasimini. Wa ti Udalana, "Na namu*h*la a u zokuya ini ukuya 'kugeza na?" Wa ti, "Ngi za 'kuya." W' e*h*lika ek*x*ibeni Untombi-yapansi, wa ya kudalana ek*x*ibeni; wa fika wa *h*lala kona. Za fika izinyoni; wa ti Udalana, "Zi kuze, msila-wezinja." Wa ti Untombi-yapansi, "Tayi, tayi, lezo 'nyoni ezi d*h*la insimu kadade; kona e nge 'dade ngasibili; se nga ba Umsila-wezinja; nga ngi nge Umsila-wezinja ngampela; nga ngi Untombi-yapansi." Z' emuka izinyoni masinyane. Kepa inkosi ya mangala ngokubona loku.

In the morning the chief left home and went by another way to the garden, and hid himself in the midst of the corn. When it was light Udalana and Untombi-yapansi went to watch. When they came to the gateway Untombi-yapansi said, "Go on." Udalana replied, "No; I too do not like to go first. Do you go in front." Untombi-yapansi went first. As they went Untombi-yapansi looked at her legs, and saw that the dew was beginning to wash off that with which she had smeared herself. She refused to walk first, and said, "Go on, Udalana." Udalana went on. They came to the garden. Udalana said, "And to-day too are you not going to bathe?" She replied, "I am going." Untombi-yapansi got down from her watch-house, and went to that of Udalana; she sat down there. The birds came; Udalana said, "Scare them, Umsila-wezinja." Untombi-yapansi said, "Tayi, tayi, those birds yonder which eat my sister's garden; although she is not my sister truly; since I became Umsila-wezinja; I used not to be Umsila-wezinja indeed; I was Untombi-yapansi." The birds went away directly. And the chief wondered when he saw it.

He watches her at the river.

Kwa ti emini wa ti Untombi-yapansi, "Ngi sa ya 'kugeza ma-

At noon Untombi-yapansi said, "I am now going to bathe, Uda-

nje, dalana; u ze u ngi bhekele izinyoni ensimini." Wa hamba Untombi-yapansi. Wa ye wa fika emfuleni. Kepa inkosi nayo ya hamba nodalana. Ba fika emfuleni, ba kćatsha esi*h*la*h*leni. Wa ngena emanzini esizibeni Untombi-yapansi; wa puma umzimba wake u kazimula itusi nenduku yake; wa tshaya ngayo pansi, wa ti, "Dabuka, m*h*laba, ku pume izinto zikababa, nabantu bakababa, nenkomo zikababa, nezinto zami." Kwa puma konke loko noku*h*dla kwake. Wa *dh*la, wa binca ingubo yake, wa *h*loba ngezinto zake, wa kwela enkabini yake, wa ti,

"Enkund*h*leni kababa sa si ti
   E-a-ye;
Kwezi-matshoba am*h*lope sa si ti
   E-a-ye;
Kwezi-matshoba abomvu sa si ti
   E-a-ye."

Ku vuma abantu bonke nezi*h*la*h*la.

| | |

The chief wondered on seeing it. He said to Udalana, "I will go out and lay hold of her, that she may no longer be able to hide herself again." Udalana assented. When all those things had again sunk into the ground, the king went out. When Untombi-yapansi saw the chief, she feared greatly. The chief said, "Do not fear, my sister-in-law. For for a long time you have been troubled without ceasing, for since you came here you have concealed yourself."

lana; do you watch the birds for me in the garden." Untombi-yapansi departed, and went to the river. And the chief too and Udalana went to the river and hid in the underwood. Untombi-yapansi went into the pool, and came out with her body glistening like brass, and with her brass rod; she struck the ground with it and said, "Open, earth, that my father's things may come out, and my father's people, and his cattle, and my things." Every thing came out, and her food. She ate; and put on her garments and her ornaments, and mounted the ox and said,

"In my father's cattle-pen we used
   to sing E-a-ye;
Among the white-tailed cattle
   we used to sing E-a-ye;
Among the red-tailed cattle we
   used to sing E-a-ye."

All the people and the trees took up the song.

He surprises Untombi-yapansi.

Kepa inkosi ya mangala ngokubona loko. Ya ti kudalana, "Ngi za 'uvela mina, ngi m bambe, a nga be e sa zifi*h*la futi." Wa vuma Udalana. Kwa ti lapa se ku tshone izinto zonke ya vela inkosi. Wa ti Untombi-yapansi, lapa e bona inkosi, w' esaba kakulu. Ya ti inkosi, "Musa ukwesaba, mlamu wami. Ngokuba kade u *h*lupeka isikati sonke, loku wa fika lapa u zifi*h*lile."

The chief wondered on seeing it. He said to Udalana, "I will go out and lay hold of her, that she may no longer be able to hide herself again." Udalana assented. When all those things had again sunk into the ground, the king went out. When Untombi-yapansi saw the chief, she feared greatly. The chief said, "Do not fear, my sister-in-law. For for a long time you have been troubled without ceasing, for since you came here you have concealed yourself."

She is made known to her sister.

Ya m tata inkosi, ya buya naye nodalana, wa ya ensimini. Ya ti inkosi, "Ku ze ku ti lapa se ku *h*lwile kakulu, u buye naye, dala-

The chief took her and went with her and Udalana to the garden. The chief said, "When it is quite dark, come back with her,

na, u fike, u m beke end/Llini kwako; ngi ya 'kuza mina uodade
wabo lapa se ni fikile." Ya buya
inkosi, ya ya ekaya. Kwa ti lapa
se ku /Llwile ba fika Odalana, ba
ngena end/Llini kwake. Y' eza
inkosi, ya biza udade wabo. Ba
ngena end/Llini, ya m veza Untombi-yapansi. Wa kala udade
wabo e ti, " Kade nga tsho nga ti,
' Ku ngani ukuba a nga kanyi
umzimba wake na?'" Ba buza
kuyena Untombi-yapansi uma ini
leua na. Wa ba tshela ukuba imbulu; wa ba landisa konke ukwenza kwayo imbulu.

Udalana, and put her in your
house; I will come with her sister
when you are there." The chief
went home. When it was dark
Udalana and Untombi-yapansi returned and went to Udalana's
house. The chief came, and called
the sister of Untombi-yapansi.
They went into the house, and he
brought forth Untombi-yapansi to
her. Her sister cried, saying,
" Long ago I said, ' How is it that
her body does not glisten?' " They
enquired of Untombi-yapansi what
that thing was. She told them it
was an imbulu; and gave them a
full account of what the imbulu
had done.

The imbulu is destroyed.

Ya ti inkosi, " Hamba, dalana,
u tshele abafana, u ti, a ba vuke
kusasa, b' embe umgodi esibayeni
omude; ku ti abafazi ba peke
amauzi ekuseni kakulu." Wa ba
tshela konke loko Udalana. Ba
lala.

Kwa ti ekuseni kakulu ba vuka
abafana, b' emba umgodi omude;
kwa telwa ubisi okambeni; lwa
ngeniswa ngomkcilo pakati emgodini. Ya ti iukosi, " Hamba ni,
ni bize bonke abafazi, nomakoti
'eze lapa." Ba bizwa bonke, ba ya
ba fika. Ku tiwa, " Yekqa ni lo
'mgodi nonke." Ya ti imbulu, i
y' esaba ukwekqa. Ya ti inkosi,
" Kqa; yekqa nawe." Y' ala imbulu. Ya futeka inkosi ngolunya,
ya ti, " Yekqa, yekqa masinyaue."
B' ekqa abanye abafazi; kepa imbulu, kwa ti lapa i ti nayo i y' e-
kqa, umsila wayo wa bona amasi,
ya ngena pakati, ya ziponsa nga-
mand/Lla. Kwa tiwa kubafazi,
" Gijima ni, ni tate amanzi atshi-

The chief said, " Go, Udalana,
and tell the boys to awake in the
morning and make a deep pit in
the cattle-pen; and the women to
boil water early in the morning."
Udalana took the message to
them. They retired to rest.

Early in the morning the boys
arose and dug a deep pit; they
put some milk in a pot, which they
let down by a cord into the hole.
The king said, " Go and call all
the women and the bride[73] to come
hither." All were called and went.
He said, " All of you jump across
this hole." The imbulu said it
was afraid to leap. The chief said,
" No; do you too leap." The imbulu refused. The chief boiled
over with anger and said, " Leap,
leap immediately." The other
women leapt; and when the imbulu too was leaping, its tail saw
the milk, it went into the hole,
throwing itself in with violence.
The chief said to the women,
" Run and fetch the boiling water

---

⁷³ That is, the imbulu.

sayo, ni tele pakati."　Ba wa tata, ba tela pakati emgodini amanzi. Ya tsha.　Ba i gqiba emgodini.

and pour it into the hole."　They fetched it and poured it into the hole.　The imbulu was scalded. They covered it up with earth in the hole.

The chief marries Untombi-yapansi.

Kwa ti lapo inkosi ya tshela abantu, ya ti, "Hamba ni, ni tshele isizwe soṅke, ni ti, a si ze lapa; ngi ganiwe; ku fike umlamu wami."　Sa tshelwa soṅke isizwe, sa fika.　Kwa ngena umtimba.　Wa sina Untombi-yapansi nabantu bakubo.　Wa *hlala* e jabula nodade wabo.　Kwa *hla*tshwa izinkomo, ba *dhla* inyama. Ba *hlala* 'ndawo nye bonke ka*hle*.

Lydia (Umkasetemba).

Then the chief told the people, saying, "Go and tell the whole nation to come here, for I am a chosen husband; my sister-in-law has come."　The whole nation was told; the people came.　The marriage company entered the village. Untombi-yapansi danced together with her people.　She lived in happiness with her sister.　Many cattle were killed, and they ate meat.　They all lived together happily.

APPENDIX.

In several of the Zulu Tales we have allusions made to persons descending into the *water*, remaining there, and returning, as quite a natural thing.　Water is not destructive to them.　In a tradition of the origin of the Amasikakana, the tribe descended from the unkulunkulu Uzimase, they are said to have come up from below, but to have first revealed themselves to some women, whilst still in the water.　In another tradition we hear of a *heaven*-descended unkulunkulu ; and there is, so far as I know, every where, among the people of all tribes, a belief in the existence of *heavenly* men (abantu bezulu); and of a king of *heaven*, whom they suppose to be the creator of lightning, thunder, and rain. The two following tales give an account of men who descended to the *lower regions*, and returned to relate what they had seen, not quite after the manner of Virgil or Dante, but strictly in accordance with their own earthly imaginings. They have a notion then,—or rather the fragments of their traditions clearly show that their ancestors believed,—that not only earth, heaven, and water have their man-like inhabitants, but that also underground there are those who are still occupied with the busy cares and necessary labours of life.　They are supposed to be the departed dead, and lead a very material kind of existence. A more full account of the *abapansi*—subterraneans, or underground people— will be given under the head, "Amatongo."

Who can doubt that we find here the relics of an old belief, clothed after a new fashion, different from that to which we have been accustomed, coarse and unattractive, in accordance with the habits and unintellectual condition of the people ; but of a common origin probably with that which in other countries, whose inhabitants have been in different circumstances, and had a different development, has formed the basis of more exact theologies ; or of such fanciful tales as that of "Jullanár of the Sea," in the *Arabian Nights ;* or of such pleasing conceits as have been clothed with so much poetical beauty by the pen of La Motte Fouqué in his Undine ?

UMKATSHANA.

Kwa ti Umkatshana wa vuka e ya 'uzingela nezinja zake; wa vusa iza; izinja za li kxotsha; la ya la ngena emgodini, nenja za ngena, naye wa ngena. W' emuka w' e-muka nalo, wa za wa fika kubantu aba ngapansi, lapa kw akiweyo. Wa bona izinkomo; wa fika ku sengwa. Wa ti, "Kanti, kw aki-we lapa." (Ngokuba ku tiwa in-komo lezi e si zi hlabako, ku tiwa ku fuyiwe zona ngapansi, zi buye zi vuke.) Kepa ba ti, "Inja yetu le i kxotshwa ubani na?" Ba ti, ukubheka, "A, nangu 'muntu." Wa e se hlangana nezake izihlobo. Ba ti, "Goduka! Musa ukuhlala lapa." Wa buya wa goduka ke.

Insuku za se zi dhlulile zake lapa ekaya; se be ti, "Wa ya ngapi na lo 'muntu? U file," ba m bona e fika. Ba ti ke, "U vela pi na?" Wa ti, "Ngi be ngi mu-ke nenyamazane; ya ya ya fika pansi kwabapansi, i ngena emgo-dini. Nami nga ngena ke. Ka-nti ke i ya lapa kw akiweko." Ba buza ke ba ti, "U ti ng' abantu nje na?" Wa ti, "Yebo; nobani nobani ba kona. Ngi buyiswe i bo."

Leyo 'ndawo lapa a tshona kona kulabo 'bantu ku tiwa Usesiyela-mangana, kwelasemahlutshini, ela l' akiwe Ubungane, uyise kalanga-libalele, uyisemkulu. Ezimbutwi-ni, uma e nga tsho ezimbutwini, a ti Usenhlonga. Amagama aleyo 'ndawo.

Once on a time Umkatshana arose in the morning to go to hunt with his dogs; he started a rheebuck; his dogs drove it; it went and en-tered a hole, and the dogs went in too, and he too went in. He went on and on with the buck, until he came to the people who are be-neath, to the place where they dwell. He saw cattle; when he arrived the people were milking. He said, "So then there are peo-ple who live here." (For it is said that the cattle which we kill be-come the property of those who are beneath; they come to life again.) They said, "This dog of ours, who is driving it?" They said when they looked, "Ah, there is a man." And then he met with his own friends. They said to him, "Go home! Do not stay here." So he went home again.

The days in which he was ex-pected to come home had already passed away; and when the people were saying, "Where has the man gone? He is dead," they saw him coming. They enquired of him, "Whence come you?" He said, "I had followed a buck; it went until it reached the people who live beneath, it going into a hole. And so I too went in. And the buck went to the place where they live." So they asked him, saying, "Do you say they are men like us?" He replied, "Yes; and So-and-so and So-and-so were there. I was sent back by them."

The place where he descended to those people is called Usesiyela-mangana, in the country of the Amathlubi, where Ubungane lived, the father of Ulangalibalele, that is, his grandfather. In the Izim-butu, if it be not said Izimbutu, it is called Usenthlonga. These are names of those places.

Ku tiwa nma umuntu e file lapa em*h*labeni, wa ya kwabapansi, ba ti, "Musa ukuk*q*ala u *h*langane nati; u sa nuka umlilo." Ba ti, ka ke a *h*lale kude nabo, a ke a pole umlilo.

UMPONDO KAMBULE (AARON).

It is said that when a man dies in this world, and has gone to the people who live beneath, they say to him, "Do not come near us at once; you still smell of fire." They say to him, "Just remain at a distance from us, until the smell of fire has passed off."

INDABA KANCAMA-NGAMANZI-EGUDU.

(THE TALE OF UNCAMA-NGAMANZI-EGUDU.[74])

UNCAMA wa lima insimu yombila; kwa t' uba i k*q*ale ukuvutwa, ya ngena ingungumbane, ya zing' i i d*h*la njalo; e zing' e vuka kusasa, a fike i d*h*lile. Wa za wa linda usuku olu namazolo. Kwa ti ngam*h*la e bona amazolo emakulu, wa vuka, wa ti, "Nam*h*la nje ngi nga i landa ka*h*le, uma i d*h*lile ensimini, ngokuba lapa i hambe kona amazolo a ya 'kuvutuluka; ngi ze ngi i fumane lapa i ngene kona." Nembala ke wa tata izikali zake, wa puma, wa fika ensimini; i d*h*lile; wa i landa ngomkondo, u sobala lapa i hambe kona, amazolo e vutulukile. Wa hamba wa hamba, wa za wa i ngenisela emgodini. Naye ke wa ngena, ka b' e sa buza, ukuti, "Loku i ngene lapa nje, ngi nge nanja, ngi za 'kwenze njani na?" Ngokutukutela ukuba i k*q*ede ukud*h*la kwake, wa hamba pakati, e ti, "Ngo ya ngi fike lapa i kona, ngi i bulale." Wa ngena nezikali zake. Wa hamba wa hamba, wa za wa fika ek*c*ibini; wa ti, isiziba;

UNCAMA dug a mealie garden; when the mealies had begun to get ripe, a porcupine entered it, and continually wasted it; and he continually rose early, and arrived when the porcupine had devoured his mealies. At length he waited for a day on which there was abundance of dew. On the day he saw much dew he arose and said, "To-day then I can follow it well, if it has eaten in the garden, for where it has gone the dew will be brushed off. At length I may discover where it has gone into its hole." Sure enough then he took his weapons, and went out to the garden; it had eaten his mealies; he followed it by the trail, it being evident where it had gone, the dew being brushed off. He went on and on, until he saw where it had gone into a hole. And he too went in, without enquiring a moment, saying, "Since it has gone in here, and I have no dog, what can I do?" Because he was angry that the porcupine had wasted his food, he went in, saying, "I will go till I reach it, and kill it." He went in with his weapons. He went on and on, till he came to a pool; he thought

---

[74] He-prepares-for-his-journey-by-smoking-*insangu*. Instead of eating, he strengthens himself with the *igudu*, or insangu-horn.

wa tulis' ameⱥlo, wa za wa bona ukuba ikcibi nje. Wa hamba ekcaleni, wa dⱥlula. Kwa ba mnyama emgodini, e nga bonisisi kaⱥle; ameⱥlo a za e jwayela umgodi, wa bona kaⱥle. Wa za wa lala, e nga fiki 'ndawo; kwa ti ku sa wa e vuka, e hamba njalo; e hamb' e lala, wa za wa fika emfuleni; wa u wela, wa hamba. Lapo ka hambi ngokuba e bona amasondo ayo; u se hamba ngokuba imbobo inye a ngena ngayo; u pike ngokuti, "Ngo ze ngi fike ekupeleni kwomgodi, anduba ngi dele."

Wa za wa bona pambili ku kꝗala ukukanya; w' ezwa ku kuza izinja, ku kala abantwana; wa dⱥlula; wa vela pezu kwomuzi; wa bona ku tunya umusi; wa ti, "Hau! u pi lapa? Nga ti, 'Ngi landa ingungumbane;' nga fika ekaya." Ukubuya kwake e ⱥleⱥla nyovane, e se buyela emuva; wa ti, "A ngi nga yi kulaba 'bantu, ngokuba a ngi b' azi; ba funa ba ngi bulale." Wa bona izwe elikulu. Wa baleka, wa hamba imini nobusuku, e ti, "Kumbe ba ngi bonile." Wa za wa wela lowo 'mfula a u wela e sa landa; wa dⱥlula kulelo 'kcibi a dⱥlula kulo kukꝗala; wa za wa puma.

Wa mangala ekupumeni kwake, ngokuba lapa a vela kona, wa ku bona konke oku fana noku ngapezulu, izintaba namawa nemifula. Wa goduka ke, wa fika ekaya endⱥlini yake. Wa ngena, wa biza

it was deep water; he looked carefully, until he saw that it was only a pool. He went by the edge, and passed on. It was dark in the hole, he not seeing clearly; at length his eyes became accustomed to the hole, and he saw well. At length he lay down to sleep before he had reached any where; and in the morning he awoke and set out again. He went and slept until at length he came to a river; he crossed it and went forward. He now no longer went forward because he still saw the footprints of the porcupine; he now went because the hole was the same as that by which he entered; he persevered, saying, "I shall at length arrive at the end of the hole, whereupon I shall be satisfied."

At length in front he saw it began to get light; he heard dogs baying, and children crying; he passed on; he came upon a village; he saw smoke rising, and said, "Hau! what place is this? I said, 'I am following the porcupine;' I am come to a dwelling." Whereupon he returned, walking backwards, and returning on his path, and said, "Let me not go to these people, for I do not know them; perhaps they will kill me." He saw a great country. He fled, and went day and night, saying, "Perhaps they have seen me." At length he crossed that river which he crossed whilst he was pursuing the porcupine; he passed the pool which he passed at first; at length he went out of the hole.

He wondered on coming out; for at the place from which he came, he saw all things resembled those which are above, mountains, precipices, and rivers. So he went home, and came to his own house. He went in and asked his wife for

ukcansi kumkake. Umkake wa m
bheka, wa tshay' izandhla, wa kala; abantu b' etuka, ba ti budu-
budu, be buza, "Ini na?" Wa ti,
"Nang' Uncama e fika!" Abantu
ba mangala, ba buya ba pinda ba
kala isililo. Umfazi wa ti, "Ikca-
nsi lako nengubo zako nemintsha
yako nesikcamelo sako nezitsha
zako, konke nga ku lahla, ngi ti, u
file; izingubo namakcansi nga ku
tshisa."

Wa i zeka ke indaba, wa ti,
"Ngi vela kude; ngi vela kubantu
aba ngapansi. Ngi be ngi lande
ingungumbane; nga fika, kw akiwe; ng' ezwa ku kuza izinja, ku
kala abantwana; nga bona abantu
be nyakazela; ku tunya umusi.
Kwa ba ukubuya kwami ke, se
ng' esaba, ngi ti, be za 'u ngi bulala. Ni bona ngi fika nje."

Leyo 'ndoda ihhwanqana elifu-
tshanyana, lisinindoiwana; umzimba wonke u pelile uboya; li-
bana; lizigejana, amazinyo a wa sa
pelele. Nami ngi ya l' azi. Nga
li bona ngi se umfana. Ku zinge
ku tiwa, "Nang' umuntu owa fika
kwabapansi." S' esaba ukungena
emgodini wesambane ngokuzwa
leyo 'ndaba, ukuti, "U ye u fike
kwabapansi."

UMPENGULA MBANDA.

a mat. His wife looked at him;
she smote her hands and cried;
the people started; they hurried
in and asked, "What is it?" She
said, "Behold Uncama is come!"
The men wondered, and again
shouted the funeral dirge. The
woman said, "Your mat, and your
blanket, and your kilt, and your
pillow, and your vessels, every
thing I have buried, saying, you
were dead; your blankets and
mats I burnt."

So he told the tale, and said,
"I am come from a distance; I am
come from the men who live underground. I had followed a porcupine; I came to a village; I heard
dogs baying, and children crying;
I saw people moving backwards
and forwards, and smoke rising.
And so I came back again. I was
afraid, thinking they would kill
me. It is because [I feared and
returned] that you see me this day."
That man was a very little
whiskered man, who was hairy all
over; his whole body was covered
with hair; very ugly; he had
many gaps in his mouth, his teeth
being no longer complete. And I
too know him. I saw him when
I was a boy. It was continually
said, "There is the man who went
to the underground people." We
were afraid to go into an ant-bear's
hole from hearing that tale, to wit,
"He went till he reached the
underground people."

In Pococke's *India in Greece*, pp. 308—311, we read a legend of the priest
Sónuttaro, who performed a feat similar to that ascribed to Untombi-yapansi.
A shrine had been prepared for the reception of relics. Sónuttaro being anxious
to obtain a casket of especially valuable relics to deposit in the shrine, "dived
into the earth and proceeded subterraneously to the land of Nágas." The Nága
king, on discovering the object of his visit, determined to keep possession of
the casket, if possible. This he effected by means of his son, who swallowed
it together with its contents, and then extended his dimensions to a most monstrous magnitude, and calling forth thousands of snakes similar to himself, en-
circled himself with them and remained coiled up in fancied security. But the
priest's power and subtlety were too great for the serpent's magic. He "miraculously created an invisibly attenuated arm," by which he extracted the precious casket, unperceived, from the stomach of the Nága. When he had done
this, "rending the earth" *(dabula umhlaba)*, he again returned to the upperworld.

U M A M B A .

A king marries two sisters.

Kwa ku kona inkosi etile e zeka abafazi abaningi. Kwa ti lapa se be baningi ya zeka intombi ezimbili zenye inkosi. Kwa ti enye intombi ya i beka inkosikazi ; kepa enye intombi ya i nomona omkulu ngokuba nayo ya i tanda ukuba i be inkosikazi. Kwa ti, lapa se zi kǫediwe ukulotsholwa, za sina zombili.

There was a certain chief who married many wives. Whcu his wives wero very many he married two damsels, the daughters of another king. One of these he made the chieftainess ; and the other was very jealous because she too was wishing to be the chieftainess. When the dowry was paid, both danced the marriage dance.

The queen's first infant dies.

Kwa ti ngesinye isikati b' emita bonke abafazi baleyo 'nkosi. Ba beleta abanye, kepa inkosikazi y' epuza yona ukubeleta. Kwa ti lapa se be zwile ukuba i belete, wa puma udade wabo, wa ya kona end/lini ; wa fika wa ti, "Leta ni umntwana, ngi m bone." Ba m nika. Wa m tata, wa m buka. Kepa e sa m pete wa fa umntwana. Ba ti bonke abantu, "U m pete kanjani umntwana na ?" Wa ti, "Kǫa. Ngi te ngi m tata, wa e se file." Ba mangala bonke abantu.

It came to pass in process of time that all the chief's wives were pregnant. They gave birth to their children, but the chicftainess was long in giving birth. When they had heard that she had given birth, her sister went to her house ; on her arrival she said, " Bring me the child, that I may see it." They gave her the child. She took it and looked at it. But whilst it was in her arms it died. All the people said, " How have you handled the child ?" She said, " No. As soon as I took it, it died." All the people wondered.

And her second and third.

Ba ze ba buye b' emita futi, ba baleta. Wa ti omunye futi umntwana wa m tata naye, wa fa futi. Kwa ze kwa fa abantwana abatatu. Kepa bonke abantu ekaya ba ti, " Ba bulawa udade wabo."

Again they had children. And the queen's sister took the second child also, and it too died. And three children at length died in this way. And all the people said, " They were killed by the queen's sister."

Ba buye b' emita futi. Wa ti

Again they were pregnant. The

unina wendoda, "Uma abantwana laba abafayo a ka ba pati udade wenu, nga be nga fi. Kepa ngokuba u ya m nika bona u ya ba bulala."

mother of the chief [75] said, "If your sister had not touched the children which are dead, they would not have died. But she kills them because you place them in her hands."

She gives birth to a snake.

Wa beleta futi, a ka ze a tshela 'muntu ukuti u ya beleta. Kwa ti kusasa bonke abantu b' ezwa ukuti, u se belete. Ba ya 'kubona umntwana. Ba fika ba ti, "Ake si bone umntwana." Wa ti, "Kqa. Namhla a ngi belete 'mntwana; ngi belete isilwane nje." Ba ti, "Isilwane sini na?" Wa ti, "Imamba." Ba ti, "Ake u i veze, si bone." Wa i veza. Ba mangala ngokuba be bona imamba.

Again she gave birth to a child. But she told no man that she was in labour. In the morning all the people heard that she had a child. They went to see it. When they came they said, "Just let us see the child." She replied, "No. I have not given birth to a child this time; but to a mere animal." They said, "What animal?" She replied, "An imamba." [76] They said, "Just uncover it, that we may see." She showed it to them. They wondered when they saw an imamba.

Her sister gives birth to a boy.

Omunye futi lowo udade wabo wa beleta umfana. Wa jabula ngokuba yena e belete umuntu, kepa lo e belete inyoka nje. Ba kula bobabili. Ya ti inkosi, "Laba 'bantwana bami, omunye igama lake Umamba, omunye Unsimba." Ba kula bobabili. Kepa Umamba wa e hamba ngesisu nje.

Her sister too gave birth to a boy. She rejoiced because she gave birth to a human being, and her sister had given birth to a snake. Both grew up. The chief said, "As regards those children, the name of one is Umamba, [77] and of the other, Unsimba." [78] But Umamba went on his belly.

The queen's sister is suspected.

Wa ti uma a zale Umamba, yena wa kula, a ka fa; ba ti abantu, "Bheka ni ke manje, ngokuba lo 'mntwana a ka fanga ngokuba yena e inyoka. Abanye be be bulawa u yena unina kansimba, e tanda uma ku buse Unsimba."

When she gave birth to Umamba, and he grew up and did not die, the people said, " "See now then, for this child did not die because he is a snake. The others were killed by the mother of Unsimba, because she wished that Unsimba should be king." But

---

[75] The mother of the chief, lit. of the husband.
[76] The *imamba* is a deadly snake.
[77] *Umamba*, The-imamba-man.
[78] *Unsimba.—Insimba* is a wild cat.   The-cat-man.

Kepa wa ti uyise kansimba, "Uma ni u bona umuti a bulala ngawo abantwana, u lete ni kumina, ngi ze ngi u pate, ngi pate yena ngezand/la zami, nayo u ya 'kufa; ngokuba ni ti, 'Abantwana u ba pata ngesand/la, ba fe.' Nami ngi ya bona, ngokuba abantwana aba abantu ba ya fa; kepa inyoka a i fanga. Kodwa mina a ng' azi uma ba bulawa ini na?"

the father of Unsimba said, "If you see the medicine[79] with which she killed the children, bring it to me, that I may take it in my hand, and touch her with my hands, and she too will die; for you say, 'She touches the children with her hand and they die.' And I too see that it is so, for the children which are human beings die; but the snake is not dead. But for my part I do not know if they were killed."

Damsels come to marry the princes, bnt they fear Umamba.

Kwa ti, lapa se be kulile, ku fike izintombi zi ze 'kugana. Ku ti lapa be buza be ti, "Ni ze 'kugana kubani na?" zi ti, "Kunsimba." Ezinye zi ze 'kugana kumamba. Kepa ku ti lapa se zi m bonile ukuba inyoka, zi baleke, zi ti, "Be si ti umuntu nje."

Uyise e /lupeka kakulu, ngokuba e m tanda Umamba. Kepa intombi zonke zi m esaba ngokuba e inyoka. A ti uyise, "Nawe, nsimba, a u yi 'kuganwa, e nga ka ganwa Umamba; ngokuba u yena omkulu kunawe." Kepa Unsimba a /leke ngokuba e bona intombi zi m ala Umamba; a ti Unsimba, "Loku intombi zi ya m ala Umamba, mina zi ya ngi tanda, ku ya 'kwenziwa njani na?" A ti unina kamamba, "U ya /leka nje uyi/lo, wena nsimba. U kona umuntu ow' alelwa ukuzeka, ku tiwe u ya 'upikanisana nesilima na?"

It came to pass when they were grown up, damsels came to choose their husbands. When the people asked them whom they came to choose, they replied, "Unsimba." But others came to choose Umamba. But when they saw that he was a snake, they fled, saying, "We thought he was a real man."

The father was greatly troubled, for he loved Umamba. And all the maidens were afraid of him because he was a snake. The father said, "And you too, Unsimba, shall not be married before Umamba; for he is your superior." But Unsimba laughed because he saw that the damsels rejected Umamba, and said, "Since the girls reject Umamba and love me, what is to be done?" And the mother of Umamba said, "You, Unsimba, your father is merely laughing. Was there ever any one who was prevented from marrying because it was said, he rivals one who is deformed?"

[79] This is the first and only instance which we meet with in these stories in which "medicines" are mentioned as a means of revenge. There is nothing in the action of the sister at the time of taking the children which would lead us to suspect she was using poison. The account there given seems rather to point to magical power, or to what is called the "influence of the evil eye." One is therefore inclined to ascribe this remark of the chief to some modern interpolation. If not it is probable that the tale itself is of a comparatively recent origin. But excepting this mention of "medicine" it bears the same stamp of antiquity as the rest.

A damsel comes to choose Unsimba, accompanied by her sister.

Kwa ti ngasemva kwalòko kwa fika izintombi ezi vela kwelinye ilizwe, z' eza 'kugana kona ; enye ya i pelezela enye. Kwa buzwa uma i ze 'kugana kubani na. Ya ti, " Kunsimba." Za ngeniswa endhlini. Wa vuma uyise ukuba a ganwe Unsimba.

Kwa hlatshwa inkomo, kwa butana abantu abaningi, ngokuba ku ganwe umntwana wenkosi. Kwa ti kusihlwa kwa ngena izinsizwa eziningi zi ze 'kukqomisa izintombi. Kwa ti lapa se zi ngena izinsizwa wa ngena Umamba. Za ti zonke izintombi za baleka zi kala, za ya emsamo. Ya ti inkosi, " Ba tshele ni ukuti a ba muse ukubaleka, ngokuba umntwana wami lowo." Ba ti abantu aba sendhlini, " Hlala ni pansi ; musa ni ukubaleka, ngokuba umntwana wenkosi lo." Wa tata ukcansi lwake, wa hlala pezu kwalo. Za ti izintombi, " Kepa w' enziwa ini ukuba a be inyoka na ? " Ba ti, " Unina wa e bujelwa ; wa ze wa zala yena." Ba mangala kakulu.

It came to pass after that, that two damsels came from another country to choose a husband ; one was the companion of the other. They asked whom she came to choose. She replied, " Unsimba." They placed them in a house. The father agreed that Unsimba might marry.

Cattle were killed, and many people assembled, because the king's child was an elected bridegroom. In the evening many young men came in to get the damsels to point out those they liked best. When the young men had come in, Umamba also came. And the damsels fled, screaming, to the upper end of the house. The king said, " Tell them not to run away, for that is my child." The people who were in the house said, " Sit down ; do not run away, for this is the king's child." He took his mat and sat upon it. The damsels said, " But how did he become a snake ? " They said, " His mother lost her children by death ; and at last he was born." They greatly wondered.

The sister chooses Umamba.

Za kqomisa izinsizwa ezintombini ; za kqoma izintombi. Kepa udade wabo kamakoti wa kqoma Umamba. Kepa Unsimba e nga tandi ukuba umlamu wake ukuba a kqome Umamba, e tanda ukuba a kqome yena. Ba buya ba buza ba ti, " Wena, u kqome 'bani na ? " Ya ti intombi, " Ngi kqome Umamba." Kepa izinsizwa za ti, " Ansimba. " Ya ti intombi, " Kqa amamba." Za ti izinsizwa, " Ansimba. " Ya ti intombi,

The damsels were made to point out their favourites among the young men. But the sister of the bride pointed out Umamba. But Unsimba did not like his sister-in-law to point out Umamba, wishing her to point out himself. They asked her again, " Who do you point out as your favourite ? " The damsel replied, " Umamba." But the young men said, " You mean Unsimba." The damsel said, " No ; Umamba." The young men said, " You mean Unsimba." The damsel replied, " No ; Uma-

"Kqa amamba." Wa ti Unsimba, "Kqa; i yeke ni nje, ngokuba noma i kqome yena Umamba, i za 'ku m ala ngokuba inyoka."

Wa ti Unsimba, "Nina ni aobani, amagama enu na?" Za ti izintombi, "Lona o ze 'kugana, igama lake Unhlamvu-yobuhlalu. Udade wabo lo, igama lake Unhlamvu-yetusi." Kepa Unsimba wa e nga m tandi Unhlamvu-yobuhlalu kakulu, kepa wa e tanda Unhlamvu-yetusi.

mba." Unsimba said, "No; just leave her alone, for although she has chosen Umamba, she will soon reject him because he is a snake."

Unsimba said, "What are your names?" The girls said, "She who has come to marry is Unthlamvu-yobuthlalu.[80] And her sister's name is Unthlamvu-yetusi." But Unsimba did not love Unthlamvu-yobuthlalu very much, but he loved Unthlamvu-yetusi.

One goes to Unsimba's house, the other to Umamba's.

Kwa ti lapa se zi kqedile ukukqoma, w' emuka Unsimba wa ya elawini lake, nomamba wa ya elawini lake. Kwa tiwa izinsizwa, "A si tate umakoti si mu yise elawini likansimba." Wa hamba Unhlamvu-yobuhlalu. Za ti kunhlamvu-yetusi, a ka ye elawini likamamba. Wa ya, wa fika, wa ngena, wa hlala pansi.

When they had ended pointing out their favourites, Unsimba went to his house, and Umamba went to his. The young men said, "Let us take the bride to Unsimba's house." Unthlamvu-yobuthlalu went. They told Unthlamvu-yetusi to go to the house of Umamba. She went and entered the house and sat down.

Unthlamvu-yetusi is asked if she will be Umamba's bride.

Wa bona Umamba e hlezi okcansini lwake, ku kona udade wabo kamamba elawini likamamba, e hlezi naye. Wa ti udade wabo kamamba, "Loko zi ti intombi zi kqoma, kepa wena wa kqoma inyoka, u ya 'kuvuma ukuba w e-udele kuyo na?" Wa hleka Unhlamvu-yetusi, wa ti, "Ku tiwa u dhla abantu ini na?" Wa ti Umamba, "U kona umuntu o kqoma inyoka na?" Wa ti Unhlamvu-yetusi, "Loko u nga dhli 'bantu, mina u ya 'ku ngi dhla ngoba ngi nani na?"

She saw Umamba resting on his mat; and Umamba's sister was also sitting there in Umamba's house. Umamba's sister said, "Since the damsels pointed out their favourites, and you pointed out a snake as yours, would you agree to be his wife?" She laughed and said, "Is it said that he devours men?" Umamba said, "Is there any one who chooses a snake?" Unthlamvu-yetusi said, "As you do not devour men, what is there in me that you should devour me?"

---

[80] *Unthlamvu-yobuthlalu.*—*Inthlamvu* is a berry, and here applied to *ubuthlalu*, means a *single bead*, of glass or some inferior substance; as distinguished from *inthlamvu-yetusi*, brass-bead. *Unthlamvu-yobuthlalu*, Bead-woman. *Unthlamvu-yetusi*, Brass-bead-woman.

Ya buye ya puma leyo 'ntombazana. Wa ti Umamba, "Sukuma u vale." Wa ti Un*h*lamvu-yetusi, "Ini wena u nga vali na?" Wa ti Umamba, "A ngi nazo izand*h*la zokuvula." Wa ti Un*h*lamvu-yetusi, "Emi*h*leni u valelwa ubani na?" Wa ti Umamba, "Ku va'la umfana wami e ngi lala naye." Wa ti Un*h*lamvu-yetusi, "Kepa u ye ngapi namu*h*la na?" Wa ti Umamba, "U pumele wena, ntombi yami." W' esuka Un*h*lamvu-yetusi wa vala.

Wa ti Umamba, "Ng' end*h*lalele." Wa ti Un*h*lamvu-yetusi, "Emi*h*leni w end*h*lalelwa ubani na?" Wa ti Umamba, "Umfana wami." W' esuka Un*h*lamvu-yetusi wa m end*h*lalela.

Wa ti, "Tata umfuma wamafuta, u ngi gcobe; kona ngi za 'kulala ka*h*le." Wa ti Un*h*lamvu-yetusi, "Ngi y' esaba ukupata inyoka." Wa *h*leka Umamba. Ba lala.

Umamba's sister went out. Umamba said, "Arise, and close the doorway." Unthlamvu-yetusi said, "Why do you not close it?" He replied, "I have no hands with which I can close it." Unthlamvu-yetusi said, "Who closes it every day?" He replied, "The lad who sleeps with me closes it." Unthlamvu-yetusi said, "And where has he gone?" Umamba answered, "He has gone out on your account, my love."[81] Unthlamvu-yetusi arose and closed the doorway.

Umamba said, "Spread the mat for me." Unthlamvu-yetusi said, "Who spreads it for you day by day?" Umamba replied, "My lad." Unthlamvu-yetusi arose and spread the mat for him.

He said, "Take the pot of fat and anoint me; then I shall sleep well." Unthlamvu-yetusi said, "I am afraid to touch a snake." Umamba laughed. They went to sleep.

The people wonder at her courage; and Umamba's mother rejoices.

Kwa sa kusasa ba vuka; kepa abantu bonke ekaya ba mangala ngokuba be ti, "Sa ze sa m bona umntwana o nesibindi kangaka u*k*ulala nenyoka end*h*lini."

Kwa ti kusasa unina kamamba wa keta ukud*h*la okumnandi kakulu, wa ku peka, wa ku yisa entombini, e kuluma yedwa, e ti, "Uma nami nga ngi zele umuntu ngempela, u be za 'ku m zeka lo 'mntwana wabántu."

They awoke in the morning; and the people wondered, for they said, "We never met with a child possessed of such courage as to sleep in a house with a snake."

In the morning Umamba's mother took some very nice food, and cooked it and took it to the damsel, talking with herself and saying, "If I too had given birth to a real human being, he would have married this child of the people."[82]

---

[81] Lit, my damsel, but meaning, my sweetheart or love.

[82] Child of the people, a title of great respect. The natives address their chiefs and great men by "Muntu wetu," Man of our people.

Unthlamvu-yetusi anoints Umamba.

Kwa ti kusi*h*lwa b' emuka futi ba ya 'kulala; ya ngena leyo 'ntombi; ba *h*lala nayo; ya buye ya puma. Wa ti Umamba, "Hamba u vale." W' esuka Un*h*lamvu-yetusi wa ya 'kuvala. Wa ti Umamba, "Kambe na izolo w a-lile uku ngi gcoba. A u boni ukuba ngi ya hamba kabu*h*lungu, ngi hamba ngesisu? Ku tanda uma ku ti lapa se ngi lala ngi gcotshiwe; kona umzimba u ya 'utamba, ngi lale ka*h*le. Ake u ngi size, u ngi gcobe namu*h*la. A ngi d*h*li 'muntu; nomfana wami u ya ngi gcoba nje, ngi nga mu d*h*li." Wa tata umfuma Un*h*lamvu-yetusi, wa tata uluti. Wa ti Umamba, "K*q*a; awami amafuta a a kiwa ngoluti; a ya kcatazwa nje; a tambile." Wa ti Un*h*lamvu-yetusi, "Zigcobe wena; a ngi tandi uku ku gcoba mina." Wa ti Umamba, "K*q*a. A ngi d*h*li 'muntu. Ngi gcobe nje." Wa tata Un*h*lamvu-yetusi amafuta, a kcatazelwa esa-nd*h*leni sake, wa m gcoba Umamba. Kepa ku ti lapa e m gcoba 'ezwe umzimba wenyoka u banda kakulu, 'esabe. A ti Umamba, "K*q*a; ngi gcobe nje; a ngi d*h*li 'muntu." Wa m yeka e se m k*q*edile uku m gcoba.

In the evening they again went to retire to rest; the sister of Umamba again went into the house; they sat with her; again she went out. Umamba said, "Go and close the doorway." Unthlamvu-yetusi arose and closed it. Umamba said, "So then yesterday you refused to anoint me. Do you not see that I move with pain, for I go on my belly? It is pleasant to lie down after having been anointed; then my body is soft, and I sleep well. Just help me, and anoint me to-day. I devour no one; and my lad only anoints me; I do not devour him." Unthlamvu-yetusi took the pot of fat and a stick. Umamba said, "No; my fat is not taken out with a stick; it is just shaken out into the hand; it is soft." Unthlamvu-yetusi said, "Anoint yourself; I do not like to anoint you for my part." Umamba said, "No. I devour no man. Just anoint me." Unthlamvu-yetusi took the fat, and poured it into her hand, and anointed Umamba. But when she anointed him and felt the body of the snake very cold, she was afraid. But Umamba said, "No; just anoint me; I devour no one." When she had done anointing him, she left him.

Umamba transformed.

Wa *h*lala Umamba isikatshana, wa ti kun*h*lamvu-yetusi, "Bamba lapa kumina, u k*q*inise kakulu, u ng' elule, ngokuba umzimba wami u finyele." Kepa Un*h*lamvu-yetusi wa ti, "Ngi y' esaba." Wa ti Umamba, "K*q*a. A ngi z' 'u kw enza 'luto. A ngi d*h*li 'mu-

Umamba waited a little while, and said to Unthlamvu-yetusi, "Lay hold of me here very tight, and stretch me, for my body is contracted." But Unthlamvu-yetusi said, "I am afraid." Umamba said, "No. I shall do you no harm. I devour no one. Lay

ntu. Bambela ensikeni, u bheke emsamo; u nga ngi bheki mina; u donse ngamand*h*la; ngokuba ukuhamba kwami ku ya ng' apula; ngako ngi tanda ukuba ku ti lapa se ngi lala umuntu a ng' elule." Wa bambela ensikeni Un*h*lamvu-yetusi, wa donsa ngamand*h*la. W' ezwa e buya nesikumba. Wa si la*h*la ngamand*h*la, w' etuka, e ti, "Inyoka." Kepa wa pendula ame*h*lo, wa bheka wa bona Umamba e mu*h*le kakulu, umzimba wake u kazimula. Wa jabula kakulu, wa ti, "Wa u nani na?"

hold of the pillar, and look at the upper end of the house; do not look at me; and drag with all your might; for my mode of going hurts me; therefore I like when I am lying down that some one should stretch me." She laid hold of the pillar, and dragged with all her might. She felt the skin come into her hand; she threw it down quickly, and started, thinking it was the snake. And she turned her eyes and looked, and saw Umamba very beautiful, and his body glistening. She rejoiced exceedingly and said, "What was the matter with you?"

Umamba tells Unthlamvu-yetusi his history.

Wa ti Umamba, "Uma kade e bujelwa; kepa be ti abantu abantwana bakwetu ba bulawa udade wabo, kama. Kepa kwa ti uma e nga ka ngi beleti, wa ya kubo, wa tsho kumue wabo ukuti, ak' a zingele imamba eucane, a tate isikumba sayo. Kwa ti lapa se ngi zelwe nga fakwa kuso isikumba leso. Kepa bonke bakwiti a b' azi uma ngi umuntu; ba ti ngi inyoka impela, ngokuba una a ka ba tshelanga ukuti ngi umuntu; u ze u nga tsheli 'muntu nawe."

Umamba said, "My mother had for some time lost all her children by death; and the people said that the children of our house were killed by my mother's sister. Before giving birth to me my mother went to her people, and told her brother to catch a small imamba and to take its skin. And when I was born I was put into the skin. But none of our people knew that I was a human being; they thought I was truly a snake, for my mother did not tell them that I was a man; and do not you tell any one."

Wa ti Un*h*lamvu-yetusi, "Ngezinye izinsuku u ke u si kumule ini isikumba lesi na?" Wa ti Umamba, "Ehe, umfana wami u ya ngi gcoba ngamafuta, a buye a ngi kumule nje." Ba lala.

Unthlamvu-yetusi said, "On other days do you take off this skin?" Umamba said, "Yes, my lad anoints me with fat and takes it off." They retired to rest.

The damsels return to their fathers, accompanied by their lovers.

Kwa ti kusasa wa ti Un*h*lamvu-yobu*h*lalu, "Se ngi tanda ukubuyela ekaya manje." Kwa *h*la*h*lwa izinkomo za ba 'mashumi 'mabili.

In the morning Unthlamvu-yobuthlalu said, "I now wish to go home." They picked out twenty head of cattle. Umamba said, "I

Wa ti Umamba, "Nami, baba, ngi ya tanda ukuba ngi kipe amashumi amabili, ngi ye 'kukqoma le 'ntombi kuyise." Wa vuma uyise; wa hamba nenkomo eziningi nensizwa ez' endayo. Ba hamba.

Kwa ti lapa be puma ekaya Umamba wa ti, a ku patwe umfuma wake; wa u pata Un*h*lamvu-yetusi. Kwa ti lapa be senkangala, wa hamba kancane Umamba emva. Wa ti kun*h*lamvu-yetusi naye a ka hambe kancinane. Ba hamba abantu bonke pambili, kepa bona bobabili ba hamba emva. Wa ti Umamba, "A si *h*lale pansi, u ngi gcobe ngamafuta, u suse isikumba, ngokuba ngi ya *h*lupeka; bu ya ngi bulala utshani uma ngi hambe ngesisu nje." Ba *h*lala; wa m gcoba ngamafuta, wa m donsa; isikumba sa puma. W' esuka Umamba, wa hamba. Ba hamba emva bona. Kwa za kwa ti lapa se be ya eduze nabantu, wa faka isikumba futi Umamba.

too, father, wish to take twenty, that I might go and choose this damsel at her father's." The father assented, and he went with many cattle and young men to make the marriage settlement. So they set out.

When they were leaving home Umamba told them to take his pot of fat; Unthlamvu-yetusi carried it. When they were on the high land, Umamba went slowly after the rest; and told Unthlamvu-yetusi also to go slowly. All the people went on in front, but they two went in the rear. Umamba said, "Let us sit down, and do you anoint me with fat, and take off the skin, for I am troubled; the grass hurts me when I go on my belly." They sat; she anointed him with fat, and dragged him; the skin came off. Umamba arose and walked. They went behind the others. And when they were near the people Umamba put on the skin again.

Umamba causes alarm.

Ba ya ekaya bonke, ba ngena. Kepa abantu bakona ba baleka, b' esaba inyoka. Ba ti, "Nampa abayeni bakan*h*lamvu-yobu*h*lalu be fika nenyoka." Za ti intombi, "Musa ni ukutsho njalo. Umyeni kan*h*lamvu-yetusi." Ba mangala abantu, be ti, "Ku ngani ukuba u ng' esabi, loku ku inyoka na?"

They reached the damsel's home and went in. But all the people of the place fled, being afraid of the snake. They said, "There is the wedding party of Unthlamvu-yobuthlalu coming with a snake." The damsels said, "Do not say thus. That is the bridegroom of Unthlamvu-yetusi." The people wondered and said, "How is it that she is not afraid, since it is a snake?"

Preparations for the marriage.

Ba *h*latshiswa inkomo ezimbili. Kwa ti uma se i pelile inyama ba buyela kubo abayeni. Kwa ti

They had many cattle killed for them. When the meat was eaten the bridegrooms' party returned to

ngesinye isikati ba tuma umuntu ukuba a ye 'ku*h*lalela umtimba. Wa bizwa umtimba; kwa gaywa utshwala, kwa tiwa a ku hanjwe ku ye 'kutatwa umtimba. Ba fika nawo.

Kwa ti kusasa kwa butana abantu abaningi, kepa abanye be *h*leka ngokuba Umamba e nga kw azi 'kusina, be ti, " Loku e inyoka u ya 'usina kanjani na ?" Lwa ngena udwendwe, ba sina omakoti neziutombi namadoda akubo.

Kwa ti lapa umtimba se u k*g*edile ukusina, kw' emuka abayeni ba ya 'ku*h*loba. Umamba wa ngena elawini lake, nomfana wake wa m g*c*oba ngamafuta, w' esusa isikumba. Wa ti, " Hamba u ye 'kubiza uma, a lete izinto zami." W' eza unina nezinto zake. Wa binca konke okwake Umamba, wa ti kumfana, " Bheka uma Uusimba u se pumile ini end*h*lini na ?" Wa ti umfana, " Ehe, u se pumile."

their people. After a time they sent a man to wait for the marriage party.[83] The marriage party was summoned; much beer was made, and they were told to go and bring up the marriage company. They came with it.

In the morning there assembled many people, but some laughed because Umamba did not know how to dance, saying, " Since he is a snake how will he dance ?" The line of wedding guests entered, and the brides and the damsels and men of their people danced.

When the marriage company had left off dancing, the bridegrooms' party went to adorn themselves. Umamba went to his house, and his lad anointed him with fat, and took off the skin. He said, " Go and call my mother, that she may bring my things." His mother came with his things. He adorned himself, and said to the lad, " See if Unsimba has already left his house." The lad replied, " Yes, he has already left it."

Umamba reveals himself at the wedding-dance.

Wa tata Umamba esikulu isikumba, wa faka sona, wa puma e hamba ngesisu. Kwa ti bonke abantu aba m bonayo ba ti, " Manje u se mkulu kakulu, ngokuba e g*c*obe amafuta." Wa ya esibayeni, wa *h*lala pansi. Kwa ti lapa abayeni bonke se b' emi, Umamba wa nyakaza, w' eza umfana wake, wa m bamba ekanda, w' esusa isikumba. Kepa bonke abantu b' a*h*lulcka uku m bheka ukukazimula kwake.

Umamba took a great skin, and put it on and went out, going on his belly. When the people saw him they all said, " Now he is very great, because he has anointed with fat." He went to the cattle-pen and sat down. When all the bridegrooms' men stood up, Umamba wriggled himself, and his lad came and laid hold of his head, and took off the skin. And all the people were unable to look on him because of his glistening appearance.

---

[83] The man who goes to wait for the marriage party is called Umkongi or Um*h*laleli. His office is to urge on the friends of the bride to hasten the marriage ; he stays at the bride's kra'al, and there is guilty of all kinds of mischief until they get tired of him, and the wedding party sets out.

Unsimba fears, and the people rejoice.

Unsimba w' emuka wa ya end/ilini, 'esaba ngokuba e bonile ukuba Umamba u umuntu; wa tukutela kakulu. Abantu bonke ba mangala ngoku m bona e se umuntu. Ba m bamba be ti, "Kade w enziwe ini na?" Uyise w' ala ukuba ku sinwe ngalolo 'lusuku. Wa ti, "Ku ya 'usinwa ngomso, ngokuba ngi tanda uku m bona namu/ila."

Unsimba went away to his house, being afraid because he saw that Umamba was a human being; he was very angry. All the people wondered when they saw that he was now a man. They laid hold of him, saying, "What has been done to you all this time?" His father refused to allow them to dance on that day. He said, "You shall dance to-morrow, for I wish to look at him to-day."

Umamba marries, and is happy.

Kwa ti lapo unina wa jabula ngokuba umntwana wake e zekile. Kwa buyelwa ezind/ilini, kwa /ilalwa. Kwa ti kusasa kwa sinwa; kepa Unsimba e /ilupeka ngokuba e bona Umamba e umuntu. Ba /ilala bonke, uyise e jabula kakulu e bona Umamba ukuba u umuntu. W' aka owake umuzi, wa /ilala nabantu abaningi aba tanda ukwaka naye. Wa ti lapa e se tungile wa zeka abafazi abaningi. Wa busa nabo.

Lydia (Umkasetemba).

Then the mother rejoiced because her child had taken a wife. The people returned to the house and sat down. In the morning they danced; but Unsimba was much troubled because he saw that Umamba was a human being. They all remained, rejoicing; the father rejoiced exceedingly when he saw that Umamba was a human being. Umamba built his own village, and lived there with many people, who wished to live with him. And when he had sewn on the headring he married many wives; and lived happily and prosperously with them.

UNANANA-BOSELE.

Unanana builds in the road.

Kwa ku kona umfazi owa e nabantwana ababili abancane, be bakulu kakulu; kepa kwa ku kona omunye umntwana owa e sala nabo. Kepa lo 'mfazi ku tiwa wa

There was a woman who had two young children; they were very fine; and there was another child who used to stay with them. But that woman, it is said, had wil-

y ake end*h*leleni ngabomo, e temba ubuk*q*a nobung*q*otsho.

fully built her house in the road, trusting to self-confidence and superior power.[84]

Various animals visit her house in her absence.

Kepa ngesinye isikati w' emuka wa ye 'kuteza; wa ba shiya bodwa abantwana. Kwa fika inkau, ya ti, "Abakabani laba 'bantwana aba*h*le kangaka na?" Wa ti umntwana, "Abakananana - bosele." Ya ti, "W' aka end*h*leleni ngabomo, e temba ubuk*q*a nobung*q*otsho."

Kwa buya kwa fika impunzi, nayo ya tsho njalo. Wa ti umntwana, "Abakananana - bosele." Zonke izilwane zi fika zi m buza njalo, wa za wa kala umntwana ngokwesaba.

On a certain occasion she went to fetch firewood, and left her children alone. A baboon came and said, "Whose are those remarkably beautiful children?" The child replied, "Unanana-bosele's."[65] The baboon said, "She built in the road on purpose, trusting to self-confidence and superior power."

Again an antelope came and asked the same question. The child answered, "They are the children of Unanana-bosele." All animals came and asked the same question, until the child cried for fear.

An elephant swallows the children.

Kwa fika ind*h*lovu enkulu kakulu, ya ti, "Abakabani laba 'bantwana aba*h*le kangaka na?" Wa ti, "Abakananana - bosele." Ya pinda ya ti, "Abakabani laba 'bantwana aba*h*le kangaka na?" Wa ti, "Abakananana-bosele." Ya ti, "W' aka end*h*leleni ngabomo, e temba ubuk*q*a nobung*q*otsho." Ya ba gwinya bobabili; ya shiya leyo 'ntombazana. Ya hamba ind*h*lovu.

Kwa ti ntambama wa fika unina, wa ti, "Ba pi abantwana na?" Ya ti intombazana, "Ba tatwe ind*h*lovu e nopondo lunye." Wa ti Unanana-bosele, "I ye ya ba beka pi na?" Ya ti intombazana,

A very large elephant came and said, "Whose are those remarkably beautiful children?" The child replied, "Unanana-bosele's." The elephant asked the second time, "Whose are those remarkably beautiful children?" The child replied, "Unanana-bosele's." The elephant said, "She built in the road on purpose, trusting to self-confidence and superior power." He swallowed them both, and left the little child. The elephant then went away.

In the afternoon the mother came and said, "Where are the children?" The little girl said, "They have been taken away by an elephant with one tusk." Unanana-bosele said, "Where did he put them?" The little girl

---

[84] *Ubung*q*otsho* is any thing by which a man trusts to attain superiority, wordiness, craftiness, bodily strength, a name, passion, power; all this in one is *ubung*q*otsho*.

[85] *Unanana-bosele.—Isinana* is a batrachian reptile, nearly globular, with very short legs, and exuding a milky fluid when touched. It is frequently found under stones.—*Bosele*, of the family of frogs.

"I ba d*h*lile." Wa ti Unanana-bosele, "Ba file ini na?" Ya ti intombazana, "K*q*a. A ng' azi."

replied, "He ate them." Unanana-bosele said, "Are they dead?" The little girl replied, "No. I do not know."

She goes in search of the elephant.

Ba lala. Kwa ti kusasa wa gaya umkcaba omningi, wa tela okambeni olukulu kanye namasi, wa hamba e pete nomkonto wake. Wa fika lapo ku kona impunzi; wa ti, "Mama, mama, ngi bonisele ind*h*lovu e d*h*le abantabami; i 'lupondo lunye." Ya ti impunzi, "U ya 'uhamba u fike lapo imiti yakona imide, na lapo amagcaki akona em*h*lope." Wa d*h*lula.

Wa fika lapo ku kona isilo; wa ti, "Mama, mama, ngi bonisele ind*h*lovu e d*h*le abantabami." Sa ti, "U ya 'uhamba, u hambe, u fike lapo imiti yakona imide, na lapo amagcaki akona em*h*lope."

They retired to rest. In the morning she ground much maize, and put it into a large pot with amasi, and set out, carrying a knife in her hand. She came to the place where there was an antelope; she said, "Mother, mother, point out for me the elephant which has eaten my children; she has one tusk." The antelope said, "You will go till you come to a place where the trees are very high, and where the stones are white." She went on.

She came to the place where was the leopard; she said, "Mother, mother, point out for me the elephant which has eaten my children." The leopard replied, "You will go on and on, and come to the place where the trees are high, and where the stones are white."

The elephant attempts to deceive her.

Wa hamba e d*h*lula kuzo zonke, zi tsho njalo. Wa ti e kude wa bona imiti emide kak*u*lu, namagcaki am*h*lope pansi kwemiti. Wa i bona i lele pansi kwemiti. Wa hamba; wa fika, w' ema, wa ti, "Mama, mama, ngi bonisele ind*h*lovu e d*h*le abantabami." Ya ti, "U ya 'uhamba, u hambe, u fike lapo imiti yakona imide, na lapo amagcaki akona em*h*lope." W' ema nje umfazi, wa buza futi,

She went on, passing all animals, all saying the same. When she was still at a great distance she saw some very high trees and white stones below them. She saw the elephant lying under the trees. She went on; when she came to the elephant she stood still and said, "Mother, mother, point out for me the elephant which has eaten my children." The elephant replied, "You will go on and on, and come to where the trees are high, and where the stones are white." The woman merely stood

wa ti, " Mama, mama, ngi bonisele indhlovu e dhle abantabami." Ya buya ya m tshela i ti, ak' a dhlulele pambili. Kepa umfazi e bona ukuba i yona leyo, ya m kohlisa ukuti ak' a dhlulele pambili, wa tsho futi e ti, " Mama, mama, ngi bonisele indhlovu e dhle abantabami."

still, and asked again, saying, " Mother, mother, point out for me the elephant which has eaten my children." The elephant again told her just to pass onward. But the woman, seeing that it was the very elephant she was seeking, and that she was deceiving her by telling her to go forward, said a third time, "Mother, mother, point out for me the elephant which has eaten my children."

The elephant swallows her, to her sorrow.

Ya m bamba, ya m gwinya naye. Wa fika pakati esiswini sayo, wa bona amahlati amakulu, nemifula emikulu, nezinkangala eziningi; ngenxenye ku kona amadwala amaningi; nabantu abaningi ab' ake imizi yabo kona; nezinja eziningi, nezinkomo eziningi; konke ku kona pakati; wa bona nabanta bake be hlezi kona. Wa fika, wa ba pa amasi; wa ti, " Kade ni dhla ni na?" Ba ti, "A si dhlanga 'luto. Sa lala nje." Wa ti, "Ini uma ni ng' osi inyama le na?" Ba ti, "Uma si si sika isilo lesi, a si yi 'ku si bulala na?" Wa ti, "Kqa; si ya 'kufa soua; a ni yi 'kufa nina." Wa basa umlilo omkulu. Wa sika isibindi, w' osa, wa dhla nabanta bake. Ba sika nenyama, b' osa, ba dhla.

The elephant seized her and swallowed her too. When she reached the elephant's stomach, she saw large forests, and great rivers, and many high lands; on one side there were many rocks; and there were many people who had built their villages there; and many dogs and many cattle; all was there inside the elephant; she saw too her own children sitting there. She gave them amasi, and asked them what they ate before she came. They said, " We have eaten nothing. We merely lay down." She said, " Why did you not roast this flesh?" They said, "If we eat this beast, will it not kill us?" She said, "No; it will itself die; you will not die." She kindled a great fire. She cut the liver, and roasted it and ate with her children. They cut also the flesh, and roasted and ate.

Ba mangala abantu bonke aba kona lapo, be ti, " Wo, kanti ku ya dhliwa, lapa tina si hlezi si nga dhli 'luto nje na?" Wa ti lo 'mfazi, " Ehe. I ya dhliwa indhlovu." Ba sika bonke labo 'bantu, ba dhla.

All the people which were there wondered, saying, " O, forsooth, are they eating, whilst we have remained without eating any thing?" The woman said, " Yes, yes. The elephant can be eaten." All the people cut and ate.

The elephant dies.

Kepa yona ind*h*lovu ya zi tshela ezinye izilwane, ya ti, "Seloku nga gwinya lo 'mfazi, ngi ya fa; ku 'bu*h*lungu esiswini sami." Zi ti ezinye izilo, "U nga be, nkosi, kw enza ngokuba abantu se be baningi kakulu esiswini sako." Kepa kwa ti lapa se ku isikati esikulu, ya fa ind*h*lovu. Wa i dabula ngomkonto, e genca imbambo ngombazo. Kwa puma inkomo, ya ti, "Mu, mu, sa za sa li bona ilizwe." Kwa puma inbuzi, ya ti, "Me, me, sa za sa li bona ilizwe." Kwa puma inja, ya ti, "Sa za sa li bona ilizwe." Nabantu ba puma be *h*leka, be ti, "Sa za sa li bona ilizwe." Ba mu pa lowo 'mfazi; abanye inkomo, abanye nezimbuzi, abanye nezimvu. Wa hamba nabanta bake, e fuyile kakulu. Wa fika ekaya, wa jabula ngokuba e buye nabo abanta bake. Wa fika i kona leyo 'ntombazana yake; ya jabula ngokuba ya i ti unina u se file.

LYDIA (UMKASETEMBA).

And the elephant told the other beasts, saying, "From the time I swallowed the woman I have been ill; there has been pain in my stomach." The other animals said,[86] "It may be, O chief, it arises because there are now so many people in your stomach." And it came to pass after a long time that the elephant died. The woman divided the elephant with a knife, cutting through a rib with an axe. A cow came out and said, "Moo, moo, we at length see the country." A goat came out and said, "Mey, mey, at length we see the country." A dog came out and said, "At length we see the country." And the people came out laughing and saying, "At length we see the country." They made the woman presents; some gave her cattle, some goats, and some sheep. She set out with her children, being very rich. She went home rejoicing because she had come back with her children. On her arrival her little girl was there; she rejoiced, because she was thinking that her mother was dead.[87]

UMNTWANA WENKOSI OHLAKANIPILEYO.

(THE WISE SON OF THE KING.)

The king's daughters bathe. A strange thing happens to the youngest.

KWA ti inkosi yasempumalanga ya b' i nesizwe esikulu; ya i nezin-

A KING of the east reigned over a large nation; he had many daugh-

---

[86] In another narration the elephant is represented as uttering a loud and prolonged groan, when the woman began to cut slices from the liver, and as the operation proceeded, the groans became so terrible and reached so far that the animals were startled where they were feeding, and attracted to the place where the elephant was.

[87] Compare this Tale with the account of the Isik*q*uk*q*umadevu, p. 56—60. And with Ugung*q*u-kubantwana, p. 176.

tombi eziuingi, zi nesiziba sazo.
Kwa t' emini za puma za butana
za ya esizibeni, za ya 'kubukuda.
Ya puma encinyane, ya ngena esizibeni. Za tukulula ke impaƕla
yazo, za ngena ke zonke, za bukuda. Za bukuda, za bukuda. Ya
puma encinyane, ya puma ya kala
ngapezulu kwesiziba, ya ti, "Puma
ni, ni zo'ubona mina, ukuba ngi
nani. Buka ni, amabel' ami a se
kukumele e nganga omfazi, a nganga wenu futi, nina zintombi."

Za puma ke zonke esizibeni, za
ti, "A, si buye si ye kubaba, si ye
'ku m bonisa lo 'mntwana wake,
ukuba u nani na." Za fika ke
ekaya enkosini e ng' uyise, za ti,
"Baba, a u bone loku; nangu
umntwana wako. Si be si ye 'kubukuda; sa m bona e se puma esizibeni e se amabel' ake se makulu
nje." Wa ti uyise, "A p' amadoda?"

ters; they had their own pool in
the river where they bathed. At
noon on a certain day they left
their homes and joined company
and went to the pool; they went
to sport in the water. One little
one started out from among them
and went into the pool. So they
all took off their dresses, and went
into the pool and sported. They
sported and sported. The little
one went out and shouted on the
bank of the pool, saying, "Come
out, and see what is the matter
with me. Look, my breasts are
swollen, as large as a woman's, as
big as yours too, ye maidens."

They all went out of the pool
and said, "Let us go back to our
father, and show him what is the
matter with this child of his." So
they came home to the king their
father, and said, "Father, look at
this; there is your child. We
went to sport in the water; we
observed, when she came out of
the pool, that her breasts were as
large as this." The father said,
"Where are the men?"

The king calls a council to consider the matter.

A fik' amadoda, wa ti, "Linganisa ni lo 'mƕlola, nokuba ukufa
ini na? Linganisa ni, nina badala,
ukuba kwa ka kw' enza ini loku
na? Na ka ua ku bona ini na?
Umntwana engaka a be nje amabel' ake na? Loku e be nga ka
fanele njeua ukuba amabel' ake a
ngangaka, e ng' umntwana nje
na?"

La ti ibandƕla, "Kqa; si nge
ze sa kw azi loku. Umƕlola. A
ku kulume wena, wena umntwana
e ng' owako." Ya ti inkosi,
"Kqa! Ka pume lap' ekaya.

When the men came he said,
"Consider this wonderful thing,
and whether it is disease or not?
Consider, ye old men, if there ever
was such a thing as this? Did you
ever see it before? The breasts of
a child of this age to be as big as
this? Since it is not proper that
her breasts should be so large, she
being so young a child?"

The council answered, "No; we
have never known of such a thing.
It is a prodigy. Do you speak,
you whose child she is." The king
said, "No! Let her depart from
her home amongst us. For I do

Ngokuba lesi 'silo esi ngapakati kwake umntwana a ng' azi ukuba si ya 'kupuma s' enze njani na. Ngi ti mina, isilo esi lapa esiswini somntanami. Ngi ti, ka si ye 'kupuma e nge ko lapa ekaya, nakuba e fa, a fe ugi nga m boni ukupuma kwalesi 'silo."

not know what the beast with which the child is pregnant, will do when it is born. I say, there is a beast inside the child. I say, let it go to a distance and be born, at a distance from this home of ours, even though she die, that she may die without my seeing her when the beast is born."

The little one is driven from her home.

Wa kala ke umntwana. Za kala ke zonke izintombi, uma e se puma, za ti, "Umnta kababa kaz' u za 'kuya ngapi na?"

The child wept. And all the maidens wept when she left her home, saying, "Alas, whither will the child of our father go?"

She wanders, not knowing where to go.

Wa hamba ke, wa puma ekaya; wa dinga nje; emzini woyise wa puma. Wa dinga, wa dinga, wa dinga. Kwa ku kulu ukudinga kwake e miti leso 'sisu.

· So she went, leaving her home; she knew not where to go; she quitted her father's village. She wandered hither and thither without an aim. Her wandering in uncertainty was great whilst thus pregnant.

She gives birth to a boy.

Wa za wa fika kwomuny' umuzi o nga si wo woyise. Wa m zala umntwana; umntwana wa m zalela esizweni esinye. Wa ti, "Be ngi ti ngi mit' isilo; kanti ngi mit' umuntu." Kwa fik' abakubo e se m zele aba m funako; ba m funyana, ba ti, "Si funa wena. Uyiẖlo u ti, a si hambe si funa wena lap' u fele kona, amatambo nje. Kanti u lapa na?" Wa ti, "Ngi zele. Ngi zele umuntu, umfana wami."[88] Wa ti, "A

At length she came to another village, not belonging to her father. She gave birth to a child; she gave birth to it among another people. She said, "I thought I was pregnant with a beast; and forsooth I have given birth to a human being." When she had given birth to the child her friends came who were seeking her; when they found her they said, "We are seeking you. Your father told us to go and seek for the place where you died, and find if it were but your bones. And in truth are you here?" She replied, "I have become a mother. I have given birth to a human being, my own boy." She said, "Let us go home

[88] Comp. what is said by the mother of Ukcombekcansini, p. 116.

si buye. Ngi ya vuma, ngi zele umuntu. A ng' azi ukuba wa ngena ngapi. Ngokuba ni ya ng' azi ukuba ngi be ngi nga ka faneli ukuba ngi nga nesisu. Na odade ba ya ng' azi e ngi hamba nabo uba a ngi bonanga ngi kuluma nandoda. Ngi kqinisile. Nami ngi m pete ngokuba ngi bone ku ng' umuntu; ngi be ngi ya 'ku m la*h*la in*x*a ku be ku isilwane. Ngi bone ku umuntu nje."

again. I am willing, for I have given birth to a human being. I know not how he entered within me. For you know that I was not yet of sufficient age to become pregnant. And my sisters with whom I went know that I never spoke with a man. I speak the truth. And I myself have taken care of my child, because I saw it was a human being; I would have forsaken him if it had been an animal. I saw that it was a real human being."

She returns to her home.

Ba hamba ke ba buya ke ukuya enkosini yasempumalanga. Ba fika ke ekaya enkosini. Ya jabula inkosi'; ya but' isizwe, ya ti, "Woza ni nonke;" ya ti, "Bonga ni nonke. Lo 'mntwana m bonge ni. Bonga ni, jabula ni, ngokuba umntwana womntwana nje wami, ngokuba ka si ye wandoda; ngokuba u be nga k' endi; umntwana wami nje."

So they set out and returned to go to the king of the east. They reached the king's home. The king was glad; he told the whole nation to assemble; he said, "All of you give praise. Praise this child. Praise and rejoice, for he is the child of my child only, for he is not the child of a male; for she had not married; he is my child only."

The child becomes a great doctor.

Wa kula ke; w' elapa, wa inyanga, wa siza, w' a*h*lula izinyanga. Wa bizwa ngokuti, Umntwana wenkosi o*h*lakanipile. Wa mkulu kubo bonke abantwana benkosi ngokutandwa.

Ku gcwale abantu emzini wenkosi aba ye 'kwelatshwa; wa z' a*h*lula izinyanga zonke. Abantu ab' a*h*lula izinyanga ngokufa kwabo wa ba siza kakulu kuso sonke isizwe soyise. Wa puma, wa hamba kuzo zonke izizwe, e hamb' 'elapa, e *h*lala nje 'elapa, e siz' abantu.

So he grew up; he treated diseases, he was a doctor, he alleviated suffering, and excelled other doctors. He was named, The wise son of the king. He was greater than all the king's children as regards being beloved.

The king's town was full of people who went there to be healed; he excelled all other doctors. People whom the doctors could not cure of their diseases, those he helped much throughout the whole nation over which his father reigned. He left his country and travelled among all nations, going about healing diseases, and merely staying in a place to heal diseases and to help the people.

He goes about with his mother doing works of mercy.

Naye unina nabanye abantu a hamba nabo nonina, ba hambe b' e-lapa nabo ; e nga nikwa 'nto ; e ti, " Ngi umntwana wenkosi mina ; ngi ya ni siza nje. Ubaba u in-kosi, u nako konke. Ngi ya ni siza njc ngomsa." Za ti nezizwe za hambe zi ti, " Nati se si ng' a-boyiħlo, ngokuba ku si funi 'luto umvuzo ; se si ng' aboyiħlo nati. U inkosi."

His mother too and others who went with him and his mother, also treated diseases. He was not given any reward. He said, " I am a king's child ; I have no other object than that of helping you. My father is a king, and possesses all things. I help you from pure mercy." The nations too said con-tinually, " We too arc the children of your father, because you seek nothing of us as a reward ; we arc now the children of your father. He is king."

Ka be s' aziwa ke kwabo-nto-mbi. Wa hamba njalonjalo. Uku-pela kwayo.

So he ceased to be known among the people of that maiden. He went about without ceasing. That is the end of the matter.

Nga i tola le 'ndaba kumamħle-kwa wakwandħlovu ; uyise ng' U-zikisa, ngesikati ku sa busa Uzi-ħlanħlo, uyise kasingela, notshaka kasenzangakona.

Umpondo kambule (Aaron).

I received this account from Umamthlekwa Wakwandhlovu ; Uzikisa was her father, at the time when Uzithlanthlo, the father of Usingela, was king, and Utshaka, the son of Usenzangakona.[89]

UFUDU OLUKULU.

(THE GREAT TORTOISE.)

Kwa ti ngendħlala, (kwa se ku busa Ugobinca, umfo wabo biħla, owa bulawa Umdingi,) omame ba be yokuka imfino, be hamba no-makulu, be batatu, ku ng' umakulu 'wesine. Ba fika emtshezi umfula. Ba ti, nxa be pakati, kˣwa vuka kwa ku nga ufudu olukulu olu ngangesikumba senkabi, lw' ema pakati kwamanzi ; amanzi a gcwa-la, ngokuba lwa vimbele. Ba

It happened in the time of the famine, (Ugobinca was then king, the brother of Ubithla, who was killed by Umdingi,) our mothers went to gather herbs ; they went with our grandmother ; they were three, and grandmother was the fourth. They came to the river Umtshezi. When they were in the midst, there arose as it were a great tortoise, which was as big as the skin of an ox. It stood in the midst of the water ; the river fill-ed, because it had obstructed the water. The three passed over ;

---

[89] There can be little doubt that this is a legend of some perverted tradition of the history of our Lord. It was probably obtained through the Portuguese.

wela abatatu ; wa tshona owesine, o 'mamekulu ngokugewala kwamanzi. Lwa m tata ke, lwa m bamba ngomlenze, lwa ya esizibeni ; lwa m veza nje ; wa vela nje, ba za ba pelela abantwana bake, ba kala pezu kwesiziba. Lwa tshona nayc.

Kwa ti ngelinye ilanga b' alusa abafana emtshezi. Inkomo za hamba za fika emtshezi. Umfana wa ponsa itshe esizibeni. Inkomo za buya ke, za fik' ekaya. Wa ti unina, "D/iluna, nank' ukud/ila kwako." Wa ti umfana, "A ngi ku tandi ukud/ila ; ngi ye esizibeni mina." Wa t' unina, "U za 'kwenza ni ?" Wa ti, "Ngi tanda ukuya 'kuzifaka kona." Wa ti, " Ini e kona esizibeni na ?" Wa tsho, e se kala umfana izinyembezi, wa puma end/ilini, wa gijima kakulu. Wa puma unina end/ilini, wa ti, " Majola, gijima ; nank' umntwana e ti, u ye esizibeni ; m bonise ni ; u ya kala." W' esuka uyise neband/ila ; wa gijima ; iband/ila la m landela. La fika e se pakati esizibeni, e se vele ngekanda. Uyise wa tanda ukuzila/ila kona esizibeni ; la m bamba iband/ila ; ba ti, "Musa ; u se e file lo 'mntwana." Wa ti uyise, " Ngi koke inkomo zonke ; umuntu u ya 'kuziketela inkomo en/ile o ya 'ku m koka umntwana wami ; u ya 'kuziketela inkomo en/ile. Ngi ya fa ; ngi jiyelwe ukuba ng' enza njani ngomntanami." La za la tshona ilanga, e vele umfana

[90] See Appendix, p. 342.

the fourth, which was the grandmother, sank, because the river was full. The tortoise took her, and held her and went with her into the deep water ; it just raised her above the water ; she was just apparent, until all her children had come together ; they lamented on the bank of the deep water. The tortoise went down with her.

It happened on another day some boys were herding on the Umtshezi. The cattle went till they came to the Umtshezi. A boy threw a stone into the pool. The cattle returned home. His mother said to him, " Eat ; there is your food." The boy said, " I do not wish for food. I am going to the pool for my part." The mother said, " What are you going to do ?" He said, " I wish to go and get into it."[90] The mother said, " What is there in the pool ?" The boy now shedding tears went out of the house, and ran fast. His mother went out of the house and said, " Umajola, run ; there is the child, saying he is going to the pool ; look to him well ; he is crying." The father started up with a company ; he ran, the company followed him. When they arrived the child was already in the midst of the pool, his head only appearing. The father wished to throw himself into the pool ; the company held him back ; they said, " Don't ; the child is already dead." The father said, " I set forth all my cattle ; the man shall select a fine bullock who takes out my child ; he shall select for himself a beautiful bullock. I am dying ; I am at a loss to tell what to do for my child." At length the sun set, the boy still appearing in the

emanzini esizibeni. Kwa za kwa
fika abantu bonke bemizi. Kwa
za kwa *h*lwa, ku *h*leziwe pezu
kwesiziba, ku kalwa kona. Wa
za wa tshona. Ebusuku se ku
baswe umlilo e se bonwa ngesi-
bane, e kuluma e ti, "Ngi banjiwe
ngenyawo." Wa tshona naye.
Ba goduka, ba buya ke ba y' ekaya, ba *h*lakazek' abantu, be ti, " U
d*h*liwe ufudu." Kwa tshaywa
inkabi; ya ya 'kubika kungonya-
ma, uyise kabi*h*la.

water of the pool At length all
the people of the village came.
When it was dark they sat down
on the bank of the pool and
lamented there. At length he
sank. At night they lit a fire, he
being still visible by the light, and
speaking said, " I am held by the
foot." He too sank. They went
home, and the people separated,
saying, " He has been devoured by
the tortoise." An ox was selected,
and went to tell Ungonyama, the
father of Ubithla.[91]

Kwa ti abafana ba ya 'kud*h*lala
emfuleni kuwomtshezi; ba ti be
fika ba ti, "Nanti idwala eli*h*le;
a si biye izibaya zetu ngobulo-
ngwe." Ufudu ke. Ba buye ke
ba pinda ba ya kona. Wa ti umfana omncinane, "Leli 'dwala li
name*h*lo." Ba ti abanye, "K*q*abo;
u namanga." A ti, "Li nawo
ame*h*lo." A tule; a tate intonga
yake, a *h*labe esweni lofudu, a ti,
" Ini leli 'li*h*lo na ? Nanti ili*h*lo
li bhekile." Ba ti, "A li ko ili-
*h*lo, mfana," be biya izibaya ngo-
bulongwe. Wa fika ekaya umfana
omncinane, wa ti, " Li kona idwala eli name*h*lo." Wa pendula
uyise, wa ti, "Ame*h*lo anjani a
sedwaleni na ?" Wa ti, "K*q*a; a
kona ame*h*lo."

It happened that some boys
went to play on the banks of the
river Umtshezi; on their arrival
they said, " There is a beautiful
rock; let us make our cattle-pens
upon it with cowdung." But it
was a tortoise. [They fetched
some cowdung] and went back to
it again. A little boy said, " This
rock has eyes." The others said,
" No; you are telling lies." He
said, " It has eyes." He was silent; and took his stick, and thrust
it into the tortoise's eye, saying,
" What is this eye ? See, the eye
stares." They said, " There is no
eye, child," they making their pens
with cattle-dung. The little boy
came home, and said, " There is a
rock which has eyes." His father
answered, " What kind of eyes are
in the rock ?" He said, " Indeed,
there are eyes."

Kwa ti ngelinye ilanga lwa ba
sibekela ufudu; wa wela kude
lapaya omunye omncinane; wa
hamba e kala e y' ekaya; ba buza
ekaya, ba ti, " U nani na ?" Wa
ti, "Abanye ba sitshekelwe 'li-
dwala; la ngeua nabo esizibeni."

It happened on another day the
tortoise turned over with them;
one little boy crossed the river at
a great distance; he went crying
home; they asked, "What is the
matter ?" He said, " The rock
has turned over with the other
boys; it went with them into the

----

⁹¹ That is, in accordance with native custom, the messengers who go to re-
port to the chief, do not go empty-handed; but take a bullock, which is said to
go and tell the chief.

Ba pela bonke; kwa sinda omunye, yena lowo owa ya ekaya e
hamb' e kala. A puma amadoda,
a ti, "Hamba u ye 'ku si kombisa
lapo idwala li be li kona." Ba
fika ; wa ti, "Nanku ke lapa
idwala li be li kona." A ti amadoda, "Inganti ufudu njo na?
Kanti ba d*h*liwe njo na abantwana?" A ba sa ba bonanga. Kwa
kalwa ke. Kwa bikwa ke, ku
bikelwa abantu bonke.

UMPONDO KAMBULE (AARON).

pool." They were all lost ; there
escaped that one only, who went
home crying. The men went out
and said, "Go and point out to us
the place where the rock was."
They arrived ; he said, "There is
the place where the rock used to
be." The men said, "Was it then
a tortoise? Have then the children been devoured?" They saw
them no more. They mourned for
them. And all the people were
told the history.[92]

APPENDIX.

NGALOKO 'kukumbula isiziba kwake umfana, e nga sa d*h*li nokud*h*la,
ku kona iudaba ngaloko 'kwenza
okunjalo. Ku tiwa, ku kona isilwane emanzini es' azi ukutata isitunzi somuntu; lapa e lunguzile
si si tate ; lowo 'muntu a nga be e
sa tanda ukubuyela emuva, a tande
kakulu ukungena esizibeni ; kuyena ku nga ti a ku ko 'kufa kulawo 'manzi ; ku njengokuba e ya
ebu*h*leni nje lapa ku nge ko 'luto ;
a fe ngokungena e d*h*liwa isilwane,
esi nga bonwanga kukgala, ku
bonwe ngoku m bamba ; ku tshiwo
ke ukuti, "Kanti si tate isitunzi
sake ; ka sa boni ; u se 'meh*l*o
'mnyama ; ka sa boni 'luto ; i yo
le 'nto e m enze ukuba a be nje."
I leyo ke indaba e ngi y aziyo uma
ku tshiwo.

As regards the boy recollecting
the pool, and no longer eating any
food, there is an account about a
notion of this kind. It is said
there is a beast in the water which
can seize the shadow of a man ;
when he looks into the water it
takes his shadow ; the man no
longer wishes to turn back, but
has a great wish to enter the pool ;
it seems to him that there is not
death in the water ; it is as if he
was going to real happiness where
there is no harm ; and he dies
through going into the pool, being
eaten by the beast, which was not
seen at first, but is seen when it
catches hold of him ; and so it is
said, "Forsooth it has taken his
shadow ; he no longer sees ; his
eyes are dark ; he no longer sees
any thing ; it is that which causes
him to be as he is." This is the
tale which I hear people tell.

Kw' aliwa futi ukuba umuntu a
lunguze esizibeni esimnyama, kw e-
satshwa kona loko ukutatwa kwesi-
tunzi sake.

Ku kona ngasemak*x*oseni indaba
e njenga le yokuti ku kona isilwane esi bamba isitunzi somuntu.
Kwa ku njalo ke nasemak*x*oseni,
iziutombi zimbili, enye kweyen-

And men are forbidden to lean
over and look into a dark pool, it
being feared lest their shadow
should be taken away.

Among the Amak*x*osa there is
a tale like this which states that a
beast seizes the shadow of a
man. So it was then among the
Amak*x*osa, two damsels, one was

---

[92] Have these tales any connection with the Tortoise-myths of other countries? See *Tylor's Early History of Mankind*, pp. 332 –336.

kosi, za lunguza esizibeni. Za donseka, za ngena kona ; ku nga ti zi biziwe. Kwa *h*latshwa umkosi enkosini ; inkosi ya putuma kona nezinkomo ukuya 'u*h*lenga umntwana wayo. Kwa fakwa ezi nombala nezibomvu nezim*h*lope. K*q*a, a sa m yeka, kwa za kwa fakwa izinkabi ezimbili zimnyama, zi 'nsizwa ; sa m yeka, sa d*h*la zona ; wa kitshwa. Emva kwaloku ka banga e sa ba njengoku-k*q*ala ; wa penduka isipukupuku nje esi nga sa k*q*ondi 'luto. Ku tshiwọ njalo indaba yakona. Ko-dwa eningi i la*h*lekile.

UMPENGULA MBANDA.

the daughter of a chief, looked into a pool. They were drawn, and went into it ; it was as though they were called. The alarm was given to the chief ; he hastened thither with cattle to redeem his child. They cast in spotted cattle, and red, and white. But the beast did not let her go, until they cast in two black, hornless oxen ; then it left her and ate them ; and she was taken out. After that she was no longer as she was before ; she became an idiot, no longer understanding any thing. Such then is the tale among the Ama-k*x*osa. But much of it is lost.

FABULOUS ANIMALS.

THE following account of fabulous animals,—which bear a strong resemblance to the domestic and other sprites of Northern Nursery Tales,—the Fables, &c., are introduced here in order to give the Reader a more general idea of the native mind, as it may be a year or more before we shall be able to enter on the Second Volume of the Nursery Tales, much of the materials for which is already collected, and which is quite as striking, if not more so, than any yet published.

ISITWALANGCENGCE.

The Isitwalangcengce described.

KU kona indaba e si i zwa ngabadala ; ba ti, kwa ku kona isilwane esi tiwa Isitwalangcengce, si fana nempisi ; kepa ikanjana laso lisi-devezana, libanzana ; si twala izinto zonke, ikanda laso li ik*q*oma lokutwala. Ku ti uma izwe li file, a si be si sa *h*lala end*h*le, si *h*lala eduze nomuzi njalo. Ind*h*lebe

THERE is a tale which we hear from the ancients ; they say, there used to be an animal called the Isitwalangcengce ;[93] it was like an hyena ; but its little head was rather spread out, and broadish ; it carried all things, its head being a basket for carrying. If there was a famine it no longer lived in the open country, but remained constantly near a village. Its ear

---

[93] Basket-bearer.

yaso ibukali ngalapa ku *h*latshwe inkomo ; ngokuba ngomkuba wabantu abamnyama, uma omunye e *h*labile, u kumbula abangane bake bonke ngoku ba pa inyama; kakulu owesifazana. Uma inyama se i d*h*liwe yezitebe, ya pela, ku sale eyasend*h*lini, owesifazana a zinge e y a*h*lukanisa, e kumbula abangane bake, e ku ti nabo uma be i pete ba m kumbule; ngokuba ku tiwa, " Imikombe i y' enanana ;"[95] ngaloko ke a zinge e ba vczela amakqata abesifazana, e tuma abantwana. Isitwalangcengce si *h*lala ematameni ezind*h*lu, ekcaleni lomnyango, ukuze ku ti lapa umntwana e ti u ya ngena, si be se si m tata kanye nenyama leyo, si m ponsa ekanda ; u ya kala se si gijima naye. Ku tiwa, a si mu d*h*li umuntu, si d*h*la ubukcopo bodwa ; si ye naye edwaleni, si m etula kona, si tshaye ikanda, si kote ubukcopo, si shiye isidumbu.

was sharp in the direction where a bullock was slaughtered ; for according to the custom of black men, if one has slaughtered, he remembers all his friends for the purpose of giving them meat ; especially the women. When the meat of the mats has been all eaten, and the meat of the houses[94] remains, a woman customarily divides it, remembering her friends, that they too when they have meat may remember her ; for it is said, " Meat-baskets mutually exchange;" therefore she makes a habit of bringing out for the women pieces of meat, which she sends by the children. The Isitwalangcengce remains at the sides of the houses, at the side of the doorway, that when a child is going in, it may lay hold of him together with the meat, and throw him on its head ; the child cries when the Isitwalangcengce is already running away with him. It is said it does not eat a man, but only his brains ; it goes with him to a rock, and throws him down there, and knocks his head, and licks up the brain, leaving the body.

The Isitwalangcengce outwitted.

Ngaloko ke sa vusa umuntu e lele, sa m tata, sa m faka ekanda, sa puma naye lowo 'muntu, sa hamba. Wa buza lowo 'muntu, wa ti, " Si ya ngapi na ?" Sa ti, " Si ya ngeyamadwala ind*h*lela," ngokukumbula lapo ku kona inda-

So then it awoke a man who was asleep, and took him, and put him on its head, and went out with the man, and departed. The man enquired, saying, " Where are we going ?" It replied, " We are going by the path of rocks," remembering where there was a

[94] The meat is distinguished as, *Eyezoso,* the meat of the roasting ; that is, the pieces cut off and roasted on the day the bullock is killed ; *Eyezitebe,* the meat of the mats, that which is boiled and brought out on mats the second day ; and *Eyezind*h*lu* or *Eyasend*h*lini,* the meat of the houses, that which is set aside for the use of the village.

[95] This is a proverbial saying, equivalent to "Love begets love," or "Kindness begets kindness." Those who send meat to their neighbours, when they have slaughtered a bullock, have meat sent to them when their neighbours slaughter. So, "Imikombe a i pambano,"—Let our meat-baskets cross each other,—is equivalent to "Let us be on terms of good fellowship."

wo yokubulala ikanda. Ba hamba ke, ba za ba fika e*h*lauzeni, lapa ku kona imiti. Sa hamba si d*h*lula naye ngapansi kwemiti ; 'apule amagaba emiti, e wa beka ek*q*omeni lelo, 'enzela ukuze ku ng' ezwakali ubulula, uma e se pumile. A za a ba maningi ama*h*lamvu emiti ; wa wa shiya ngapansi, wa *h*lala pezu kwawo. Ngaloko ke sa hamba si sindwa ; sa d*h*lula emtini ; w' elula izaud*h*la, wa bamba umuti ; sa d*h*lula sa ya edwaleni. W' o*h*la masinyane, wa gijima wa ya ekaya. Sa fika, sa tulula edwaleni ; a sa bona 'muntu, ukupela ama*h*lamvu lawo wodwa. Sa buyela ekaya, si ya 'ufuna lowo 'muntu.

place for breaking the head. So they went until they came to a bushy country, where there were trees. It passed with him under the trees ; and the man broke off some branches of the trees, and put them in the basket, doing so in order that the lightness may not be noticed if he got out. At length there were many branches ; he put them at the bottom, and sat on the top of them. Thus it went with a heavy weight ; it passed by a tree ; he stretched out his hand, and caught hold of the tree ; it passed on towards the rock. He got down directly and ran home. The Isitwalangcengce came, and emptied the basket on the rock ; it saw no man, but only the branches. It went back to the house, to find the man.

Many escape by a stratagem.

Wa i dumisa leyo 'ndaba, loku abantwana be be pela. Umntwana a bizwe kwenye ind*h*lu, ku tiwe, "We, nobani !" A sabele. Si be se si gijima pambili, si ya lapo e bizwa kona, se si m amukela, se si d*h*lula naye. Ku ya bizwa ; se ku tiwa, "Kade e pumile lapa." A pike lowo o m bizayo, a ti, "Ka fikanga lapa." Kanti u tetwe Isitwalangcengce. Lowo 'muntu wa veza ikcebo lokuba izind*h*lela a zi be mbili ; a i nga bi nye ; "Loku sona Isitwalangcengce si tanda eyamadwala, kepa mina nga sinda ngend*h*lela ye*h*lanze." Ngaloko ke lelo 'kcebo la siza kakulu leso 'sizwe. Noma umntwana si m bambile, si buze si ti, "U ti a si ye nga i pi ind*h*lela

The man reported the matter, for the children were coming to an end. A child may be called from one house, it being said, "Wey, So-and-so !"[96] The child attended. And the Isitwalangcengce ran forward to the place where she was called, and caught her, and went off with her. The people call her, and it is now said, "She went out from here a long time ago." The one who called her says, "She did not come here." In fact she has been taken by the Isitwalangcengce. That man devised the plan of having two ways, and not one only ; he said, "Since the Isitwalangcengce prefers the path of rocks, but," said he, "I escaped by the bush-path." So that plan was of great assistance to that tribe. And if the Isitwalangcengce caught a child, and asked it, "Which way do you say we shall go?" it

---

[96] *Nobani* means So-and-so, a female. *Bani*, So-and-so, a male.

na?" a ti, "O, nkosi, ind*h*lela en*h*le eye*h*lanze," 'enzela ukuze endaweni yake a beke ama*h*lamvu, a goduke yena; si hambe ngoku-jabula, si ti si za 'kusuta ubukco-po; si tulule ama*h*lamvu. Kwa za kwa ba ink*g*waba *y*ama*h*lamvu edwaleni; abantu ba goduke.

Lesi 'sitwalangcengce indaba e insumansumane, indaba endala. Manje se ku tuliswa ngayo aba-ntwana uma be kala, ngokuti, "U za 'kutatwa Isitwalangcengce."

UMPONDO KAMBULE (AARON).

answered, "O, sir, the good way is that of the bush," saying thus in order that it might put branches in its place and return home, and the Isitwalangcengce go on re-joicing, thinking it is about to get a fill of brains; but it pours out branches only. At length there was a great heap of branches on the rock; and the man went home.

The Isitwalangcengce is a fabu-lous accouut, an old tale. Now children are silenced by it when they cry, by saying, "You will be carried off by the Isitwalangce-ngce."[97]

INDABA KADHLOKWENI.

(THE HISTORY OF UDHLOKWENI.)

KWA ti uba ku *h*lwe kwa fika impisi, ya m tabata Ud*h*lokweni, inkosikazi yomuzi omkulu; ya m twala, ya hamba naye; ya fika e*h*latlni, ya ti, "D*h*lokweni, si za 'kuhamba nga i pi ind*h*lela na?" Wa ti, "A si hambe ngeyentuba ind*h*lela." Ba fika ke nayo impisi. Wa bambela emtini pezulu. Ya m bona, ya ti, "D*h*lokweni, wa ha-mbela pezulu na? Woza." Ya buya ya m twala. Ya ti, "D*h*lo-kweni, isililo sako si duma pansi. U be u ngakanani na, ukuba isi-lilo sako si be ngaka nje!" Wa ti, "Ngi be ugi mkulu, ngi inkosi-kazi enkulu; ngi be ngi ba pata ka*h*lc bonke abantu bomuzi wami." Sa buya sa pinda futi, sa ti,

WHEN it was dark there came an hyena,[98] and took Udhlokweni, the chief wife of a great village; it took her on its head and went away with her; it came to a forest, and said, "Udhlokweni, by which path shall we go?" She replied, "Let us go by the path of the narrow pass." So she and the hyena arrived. She lay hold of a tree overhead. It saw her, and said, "Udhlokweni, do you climb into the tree? Come along." So it carried her again. It said, "Udhlokweni, your funeral la-mentation makes the ground thunder. How great a person were you, that your funeral la-mentation should be so great!" She said, "I was great, being the great queen; and I used to treat kindly all the people of my vil-lage." Again it said, "This is

---

[97] So the American Indians silence their little ones, by "Hush! the Naked Bear will get them." (*Hiawatha, p.* 559, and Note 55.) The Naked Bear, like the Isitwalangcengce, is a fabulous animal. In other countries they are frightened by the Wolf.

[98] Isitwalangcengce, or Isidawane.

"Isililo sako lesi. U b' u ngakanani na! Abantu ba ya dabuka
ukukala. U b' umkulu, dhlokweni. Nami ngi y' ezwa ukuti u
b' umkulu. U b' u ba lungisa
abantu." Sa pinda futi njalo, sa
ti, "Se ku kala nabantwana manje
ke." Wa ti, "Yebo, abantwana
ngi be ngi ba tanda kakulu bonke;
na onina ngi be ng' aba izinto, ngi
ba pa, na onina na oyise; ngi be
ngi nga buki 'luto; zonke izinto
ngi be ng' epana nje." Sa ti,
"Yebo, dhlokweni, nami ngi y' e-
zwa ukuba ba ya dabuka abantu
ngawe. Kodwa mina se ngi ku
tabete njalo kubo abantu labo bomuzi wako." Wa bambela emtini
futi, w' enyuka; sa hamba sodwa
ke Isidawane; sa fika emfuleni, sa
zilahla, sa kala sa ti, "Maye, dhlokweni! Kazi n ye ngapi na? Nga
zibulala, nga ti, ngi lahla Udhlokweni." Kanti Udhlokweni u se
balekile; u se buyele kubantu
bake aba m kalelako.

Umpondo kambule (Aaron).

your funeral lamentation. How
great a person were you! The
people are distressed by your
funeral lamentation. You were
great, Udhlokweni. I perceive
you were great. You used to
order the people well." Again it
said, "Now the children are crying." She said, "Yes, I used to
love the children much; and I
gave the women many things, both
the women and the men; I regarded nothing; I used to give
them every thing." It said, "Yes,
Udhlokweni, I too perceive that
the people are grieved for you.
But I have now taken you from
the people of your village for
ever." Again she caught hold of
a tree, and climbed up. The Isitwalangcengce went on alone; it
came to the river, and threw itself
down, and cried, saying, "Woe is
me, Udhlokweni! I wonder
where you are gone. I have killed
myself, thinking I was throwing
down Udhlokweni." But in fact
Udhlokweni had fled, and had
already returned to her people,
who were mourning for her.

ISITSHAKAMANA.

Kwa ti indoda ya tata umsundu,
ya hamba ke ya ya 'kutiya izin-
hlanzi elutukela, inxa ku sa busa
Usenzangakona; ya bamb' isilwane, Isitshakamana; sa teta sa ti,
"Mntakabani, kabani, kabani," sa
kquba njalo amabizo aoyise-mkulu
kwa za kwa ba eshumini amabizo,
a nga w' aziyo naye. Sa ti, "U
ng' enze 'lunya lwani, uku ngi

It happened that a man took a
worm, and went to catch fish in
the Tukela, at the time when Usenzangakona was king; he caught
an animal, the Isitshakamana; it
spoke, saying, "Child of So-and-
so, of So-and-so, of So-and-so."
It went on thus repeating the
names of his grandfathers, until it
had mentioned names up to ten,
names which he did not himself
know. It said, "Why have you
treated me so unmercifully as to

kipa esizlbeni, ngokuba mina a ngi pumi esizibeni ? ngi *h*lale esizibeni njalo ; ngi ya l' esaba ilanga." Kwa *h*langan' ame*h*lo ake nawaso, wa baleka ke wa y' ekaya, wa ti, " Ngi zibekele ni ; ngi fi*h*le ni ; ngi bone 'lukulu ; ngi bone isilwane lapa be ngi ye 'kutiya izin*h*lanzi ; ame*h*lo aso a kimi lapa nje ; ngokuba ame*h*lo aso a 'ndawo nye nezimpumulo nend*h*lebe nomlomo. Kepa si ya ngi d*h*la ke noma ngi lapa nje ; ku nga ti si kwimi lapa nje." Kwa vela indoda, ya ti, " Ngi za ngi ni tshela, ngi ti, ' Ni ya 'uze ni kipe Isitshakamana.' I so ke njalo leso o si kipile namu*h*la, es' azi abantu abadala bonke." Wa fakwa ke embizeni, wa zitshekelwa. Wa ti, " Ngi kipe ni, na manje si sa ngi bhekile." Wa kitshwa. Wa ti, " Ngi fulele ni ngengubo zonke zomuzi." Wa ti, " Ngi kipe ni, si sa ngi bhekile. Ngi se ni emgodini wamabele." Ba ti, " Umgodi u ya 'ku ku bulala ; u ya tshisa." Wa ti, " U mbulule ni, w oz' u pole." Ba u mbulula ke, wa pola. Ba m faka ke ingcozana. Wa ti, " Ngi kipe ni ; si sa ngi bhekile futi, nokufudumala futi ku ya ngi bulala." Ba m kipa ke. Wa puma, wa ti, " Ngi se ni end*h*lini." Wa fika ke end*h*lini. Wa fa ke ngako loko ngokubona kwake Isitshakamana. Wa ti, " Ngi dabuk' uvalo, isilwane si ngi biza ngobaba, na ngobaba-mkulu, na ngobaba-mkulu waobaba-mkulu ; si k*q*ed' abantu bonke nezizukulwane nezi ng' aziwa na ubaba na ubaba-mkulu. Ngi fa ngaloko kc." Wa fa ke, wa pela.

take me out of the pool ? for I do not quit the pool ; I live in it constantly ; I am afraid of the sun." His eyes met the eyes of the beast ; and he fled and ran home. He said, " Put a pot on my head ; hide me ; I have seen a great thing ; I have seen a beast, when I went to catch fish ; its eyes are still staring at me ; for its eyes and nostrils and ears and mouth are altogether in one place. But it is destroying me though I am here ; it is as though it was here with me." A man came and said, " I continually am telling you, ' You will one day catch an Isitshakamana.' It is that animal which he has caught to-day, which knows the names of all the old people." He said, " Take the pot off my head ; even now it is still looking at me." They took off the pot. He said, " Cover me with all the blankets which are in the village." He said, " Take them off from me ; it is still looking at me. Carry me to a corn-hole." They said, " The hole will kill you ; it is hot." He said, " Take away the stone, that it may cool." So they took away the stone, and it cooled. They put him in a little while. He said, " Take me out ; the beast is still looking at me even here ; and besides the heat is killing me." They took him out. When he came out he said, " Take me into the house." He came into the house. So he died on that account, because he saw the Isitshakamana. He said, " I am torn to pieces by fear, when the beast calls me by the name of my father, and of my grandfather and my grandfather's father ; mentioning all people without exception and generations which were unknown both to my father and grandfather. I die on that account." So he died.

Kwa ku tiwa Isitshakamana si-mbulungwana; si hamba ngesinqe, si liugana nomntwana o nga ka hambi.

Kwa ti emva kwaleyo 'ndaba ngalo 'nyaka kwa zalwa umntwana Ujobe, na manje u se kona lowo 'mutwana owa zalwa ngalowo 'nyaka, o tiwa Usitshakamana. Nam*h*la nje u se nabazukulwane, u se mpunga manje.

UMPONDO KAMBULE (AARON).

It was said that the Isitshaka-mana was small and round; it walked on its buttocks, being the size of a child which does not yet walk.

It happened after that, even in the same year, Ujobe had a child, and the child is still living which was born in that year, who is named Usitshakamana. He has grandchildren now, and is grey.

UTIKOLOSHE.

UKU mu zwa kwami ngi mu zwa ngabantu aba vela ebuuguni; ngo-kuba ngokwazulu a ku ko Utiko-loshe. Kepa kutina bakwazulu umuutu e se ngi ke nga mu zwa e ti u m bone ngame*h*lo yena; k' e-zwa ugandaba nje; wa ti, isilwane, si lala esizibeni; kepa ngasebu-nguni. Wa ti lowo umfo wetu, isilwanyazanyaua si futshane, si noboya. U si bone eketweni; ku ketwa, naso si keta.

Kepa kakulu ku tiwa isilwane esi tanda abafazi; ku tiwa kakulu abafazi bangalapa ba pinga naloko. Ku tiwa abafazi bonke bangakona ba vame ukuba ku ti lowo 'mfazi a be notikoloshe wake, indojeyana e ngapansi kwendoda yake. Ku ti uma umfazi e ya 'uteza, a buye nayo e twele nezinkuni. Amadoda akona a ya zi bulala njalo lezi 'zi-lwauyana, e ku tiwa Otikoloshe. Ku tiwa abafazi bangalapa ba tanda Otikoloshe kunamadoda.

UMPENGULA MBANDA.

I HEAR of this creature from men who come from the Amak*x*osa; for among the Amazulu there is no Utikoloshe. But among us Amazulu I heard a man say that he had seen it with his eyes, and not heard a mere report; he said it was an animal which lives in a pool; but it is found among the Amak*x*osa. This brother of mine said, it was a short little animal, and hairy. You may see it at a dance; when the people dance, it too dances.

But especially it is said that the beast is fond of women; it is said that the women of those parts co-habit with it. It is said that all the women of those parts have usually her own Utikoloshe, a little husband which is subject to her husband. And when a woman goes to fetch firewood, she returns with the Utikoloshe carrying the firewood. The men of those parts kill these animals which are called Otikoloshe. It is said the women love them more than their hus-bands.[99]

[99] Shaw, in *The Story of My Mission*, p. 445, thus alludes to this monster: —"The people universally believe that aided by some mysterious and evil in-fluence, the nature of which no one can define or explain, bad persons may enter into league with wolves, baboons, jackals, and particularly with an ima-ginary amphibious creature, mostly abiding in the deep portions of the rivers, and called by the Border Kafirs Utikoloshe."

Ukukqala kwami ukuba ngi ti nga ngi kqonda ka*h*le, ngi te nga senga inkomo zikazilinkomo. Uzima, umkake, wa ngi nika iselwa elikulu, wa ti, "Wo li ta, li zale." Kwa za ku ya sa kusasa, umuntu ka sa tsho ukuba li ke l' etiwa; ku se se lize, li d*h*liwe Utikoloshe.

Umfana wake, Un*x*atshe, wa ti ukuba e k*hh*eza kulezi 'nkomo, wa ngxama Utikoloshe, wa ti, "Ngi ya ba 'ungena enkomeni, ngi fikane kuze!" W' apuka lo 'mfana owa e zi k*hh*eza, e umuntu omu*h*le. Izintambo zonke zokusenga ku fikwe zi la*h*lekile; namatole a wa vulele ebusuku, a ncele.

———

Omunye umfazi. Kwa ti ku yiwa emjadwini. Ba m biza abanye abafazi; wa ti, "Ai. Ngi sa gcoba imbola." Ba se be hamba ke. Ba hamba, ba hamba, ba ti be send*h*leleni indoda kanti se i lalele, i solile. Wa puma ke umfazi, wa fika ke Ugilikak*q*wa, wa tata isikaka seula, wa s' embata, wa ti, "Ngi ya 'ufika emjadwini ng' enze njc ke, mina mfana kagilikak*q*wa wasemlanjeni," e linganisa ukud*h*lala a ya 'ud*h*lala ngako e se fikile ukutshuluba ngokwamakxosa.

When I first began to look about me and to understand things well, I milked the cows of Uzilinkomo. Uzima, his wife, gave me a great calabash, and told me to fill it with milk. On the following morning no one would think that any milk had been poured into it; it was always then empty, the milk having been eaten by the Utikoloshe.

When his boy, Un*x*atshe, milked the cows into his own mouth,[1] the Utikoloshe was angry, and said, "I continually pass from cow to cow, and find no milk!" And the boy, who was a beautiful fellow, who milked the cows into his own mouth, became deformed.[2] And when they went to milk, all the milking cords were lost; and the Utikoloshe let out the calves by night, and they took all the milk.

———

Another woman I knew. The people were going to a wedding dance. The other women called her; she said, "No. I am still ornamenting myself with coloured earth." So they set out without her. They went on and on, and whilst they were in the way, the husband was laying wait, thinking he had a reason for complaining of his wife. So the wife quitted the house, and Ugilikak*q*wa[3] came, and took a garment made of the skin of the oribe and put it on, saying, "I will come to the dance and do this,[4] I the child of Ugilikak*q*wa of the river," imitating the play which he would play when he got there, after the manner of the Amakxosa.

---

[1] It is a custom among native boys when herding cattle to steal the milk by milking into their own mouths. When this is suspected, the father will give them a calabash, saying, "Since you know how to milk, milk into the calabash!"

[2] Lit., Broke,—had spinal curvature.

[3] Utikoloshe.

[4] Imitating the native dance.

Ya vuka ke indoda, ya m kaẞlela pansi ngomkonto nomfazi bobabili. Ya ba lalisa 'ndawo nye endẞleleni; y' esula umkonto igazi; y' emuka ya ya emjadwini. Kwa ti nxa be buyayo ba bona ukuti, "A, kanti ubani lo u m bulele umkake." Ba ti, "Kanti u m bulele nje u be s' azi ukuba Ugilikakꞇwa u kekxeza nomkake."

———

Kwa ti umfazi e Umtshakazi wa ti, "Ngi y' aliwa." Wa ti omunye, "W' aliwa kanjani na?" Wa ti, "Ngi y' aliwa, mnta kwetu." Wa ti, "Kꞇa; u nge ze w' aliwa." Wa ti, "U tsho ukuba u ng' enze njani na?" Wa ti omunye, "A ke w enze ke." Wa mu pa imbola namafuta, wa ti ke, "Ngi ku pe nje, u z' u tambise; u z' u vuke u peke inkobe zamabele amẞlope; se u zi pekile, ke u fune isitshana, u zi tele, u hambe ke; u ya 'kuti u semfuleni u ti, 'Wa, gilikakꞇw—o!'" Wa puma ke Umakꞇutsha-zinduku-zomlambo; wa kꞇala ke umfazi kaloku ukuti, "Hau! kanti, i le into. Betu!" Wa baleka. Wa tsho ke Ugilikakꞇwa ukuti, "U nge ngi bize, u ngi bize u buye u bayeke. U be 4 ngi bizeya ni na?"[6] Wa baleka imfazi wa za wa fika ekaya. Utikoloshe wa ti ukubona ukuba u lilikelwa abantu, wa buyela esiziɔeni.

So the husband started up and dashed him to the ground, stabbing him with an assagai, and the wife as well. He placed them together in the path; he wiped the blood from the assagai; and went to the dance. And when the people were returning they saw and said, "Ah, so then that So-and-so has killed his wife. He has killed her forsooth because he knew that Ugilikakꞇwa cohabited with her."

———

It happened that a woman whose name was Umtshakazi said, "I am rejected by my husband." Another asked, "Why are you rejected?" She said, "I am rejected, child of my people." She said, "No; it is not possible for you to be rejected." She said, "Tell me how you can help me?" The other said, "Just do so." She gave her coloured earth and fat, and said, "I give you this that you may supple yourself; and tomorrow morning boil some white amabele; when you have boiled it, just take a little vessel, pour the corn into it, and go to the river; when there you shall say, 'Wo, Ugilikakꞇw—o!'" Umakꞇutsha-zinduku-zomlambo[5] came out of the river; and now the woman began to say, "Hau! forsooth it is that thing I have summoned. Our people!" and ran away. So Ugilikakꞇwa said, "You cannot call me, and when you have called me run away. Why have you called me?" The woman fled till she reached her home. When the Utikoloshe saw that he was pelted with stones by the people, he went back again to the pool.

———

[5] He who uses in dancing the rods (i. e. reeds) of the river.
[6] The Utikoloshe speaks the dialect of the Amakꞇwabe, clearly suggesting that these tales are not indigenous to the Amakxosa.

Kwa ti indoda i ngena end*h*lini yayo ya *h*la i pambana nesitunzana si puma. Ya za ya nga i ya hambela kudo. Umfazi wa *h*langana ke nekek*x*e lake leli. Indoda ya buya ebusuku. Ya fika be lele 'ndawo nye. Ya gwaza Utikoloshe ; ya shiya umfazi. Ya ti indoda kumfazi, " Tata izitungu zotshani, u bope." Kwa lalwa ke. Kwa sa kusasa ya ti, " Tata ke, u twale." Wa tata ke, ya pelezela, wa ya kubo. Ba fika enkund*h*leni lapa amadoda e butene kona emziui wako wabo, ya ti, " Yetula." W' etula. Ya ti, " Tukulula." Wa n*q*aba. Ya tata insutsha ; ya ti k*q*in k*q*in intambo ; ya penya. Ba ba sa ku ti gaga, ba ti, " A !" Ba se be tata intonga, be nga sa kulumanga, ba keta inkomo zayo zonke, ba i nika. Ya buya nazo ke.

UNOKO MASILA.[9]

A man one day when entering his hut just saw the small shadow of something pass out as he went in. At length he pretended that he was going to a distance. So his wife had the company of her sweetheart,[7] the Utikoloshe. The husband came back by night, and found them sleeping together. He killed the Utikoloshe ; but left the wife. He said to his wife, " Fetch some bundles of grass, and tie him up in it." They then lay down. In the morning he said to her, " Take that up and carry it." She took it up ; and he went with her to her people. When they came to the cattle-pen, where the men were assembled, iu the village of her people, he said, " Put it down." She put it down. He said, " Untie it." She refused. He took an assagai ; and the cord was cut with a kin, kin ;[8] he unfolded it. They then looked over it, and said, " Ah !" They then took a rod, without saying a word, and selected all his cattle,[10] and gave them back to him. And so he went home with them.

THE ABATWA.

ABATWA[11] abantu abafutshane kakulu kunabo bonke abafutshane ; ba hamba ngapausi kwotshani, ba lala ezidulini ; ba hamba ngenkungu ; ba sen*h*la nezwe, lapa be

THE Abatwa are very much smaller people than all other small people ; they go under the grass, and sleep in authills ; they go in the mist ; they live in the up-

---

[7] The word here used is only applied to improper intercourse between people ohe or both of whom are married—Ikek*x*e, Ikek*x*ezakazi.

[8] The cord used would be dry hide ; the " kin, kin," is intended to imitate the sound which is occasioned by cutting the hide.

[9] This man is of the tribe of Amangwane. He has lived with the Ama-k*x*osa, and heuce many K*x*osisms.

[10] Which he had paid as the woman's dowry.

[11] *Abatwa* is the name given to the Bushmen. But they are not Bushmen which are here described. But apparently pixies or some race much more diminutive than the actual Bushmen. Yet the resemblance is sufficiently great to make it almost certain that we have a traditional description of the first intercourse between the Zulus and that people. I have not succeeded in getting auy details about them. The singular is Umutwa.

ⱡlala kona emaweni ; a ba namuzi lapa u nga ti, "Nanku ke umuzi wabatwa." Umuzi wabo u lapa be bulele kona inyamazane ; ba i dⱡle, ba i kꝗede, ba hambe. Ba pila ngaloko.

Kepa ku ti uma umuntu e hamba a kꝗabuke e ⱡlangana nomutwa, Umutwa a buze ukuti, " U ngi bonaboue pi na ? " Kepa kwa ti ngoku ng' azaui kukꝗala nabatwa, umuntu wa kuluma isiminya, wa ti, " Ngi ku bonabone kona lapa." Ngaloko ke Umutwa a tukutele ngokuti u ya delelwa u lowo 'muntu ; a be se u ya m tshaya ngomkꞔibitshelo, a fe." Kwa za kwa bonwa ukuba ba tanda ukukuliswa ; ba ya zonda ubunꞔinane babo. Ngaloko ke umuntu wa ⱡlangana nabo, a m bingelele ngokuti, " Sa ku bona ! " A ti Umutwa, " U ngi bonabone pi na ? " A ti umuntu, " Ngi ku bonabone ngi sa vela lapaya. U ya i bona leya 'ntaba ; ngi ku bonabone ngi kuyo ke." A tokoze ke Umutwa, a ti, " O, kanti ngi kulile." Ku be se ku njalo ukubingelelwa kwabo.

Ku tiwa uma Abatwa se be hamba, lapa be be ⱡlezi kona uma se ku pelile inyamazane, ba kwela ehashini, ba kꝗalele entanyeni ba ze ba fike esinꝗeni, be landelene. Uma be ngu fumananga 'nyamazane, ba dⱡla lona.

UMPENGULA MBANDA.

country in the rocks ; they have no village, of which you may say, " There is a village of Abatwa." Their village is where they kill game ; they consume the whole of it, and go away. That is their mode of life.

But it happens if a man is on a journey, and comes suddenly on an Umutwa, the Umutwa asks, " Where did you see me ? " But at first through their want of intercourse with the Abatwa, a man spoke the truth, and said, " I saw you in this very place." Therefore the Umutwa was angry, through supposing himself to be despised by the man ; and shot him with his bow, and he died. Therefore it was seen that they like to be magnified ; and hate their littleness. So then when a man met with them, he saluted the one he met with, " I saw you ! " [12] The Umutwa said, " When did you see me ? " The man replied, " I saw you when I was just appearing yonder. You see yon mountain ; I saw you then, when I was on it." So the Umutwa rejoiced, saying, " O, then, I have become great." Such, then, became the mode of saluting them.

It is said, when Abatwa are on a journey, when the game is come to an end where they had lived, they mount on a horse, they beginning on the neck, till they reach the tail, sitting one behind the other. If they do not find any game, they eat the horse.

[12] The Zulu salutation is, " Sa ku bona," We saw you. Hence the play on the words.

ABATWA UKWESABEKA KWABO.

(THE DREADFULNESS OF THE ABATWA.)

B' ESATSHWA abantu; a b' esabeki ngobukulu bemizimba, nokubonakala ukuba ba amadoda; ai, ubudoda a bu bonakali, nobukulu a bu ko; izintwana ezincinane ezi hamba pansi kwotshani. Kepa indoda i hambe, i bheke pambili, ngokuti, "Uma ku vela umuntu noma inyamazane, ngi ya 'ku ku bona loko." Kanti Umutwa u se kona lapa ngapansi kwotshani; indoda i zwe se i ħlatshwa umkcibitshelo; i bheke, i nga boni 'muntu o u ponsayo. I loko ke oku kǫed' amandħla; ngokuba umuntu u ya 'kufa e nga lwanga nendoda e lwa naye. Ngaloko ke izwe labatwa li y' esabeka; ngokuba a ba boni 'muntu a ba ya 'kulwa naye. Abatwa ba amazenze, ona e nga bonakali lapa e puma kona; kepa a ħlupe indoda, a i buse, a kwcle pezu kwayo, i ze i putelwe ubutongo, i nge nakulala, i nga gǫulisi inħliziyo; ngokuba izenze lincinane: isandħla sendoda sikulu; ku sweleka ukuba si bambe into ezwakalayo. Ba njalo ke Abatwa; amandħl' abo njengamazenze a busa ngobusuku, nabo ba busa ngesikota, ngokuba si ya ba fiħla, ba nga bonakali. Nanko ke amandħla Abatwa a b' aħlula abantu ngawo, ukukcatsha, be kcatshela abantu; ba ba bone nganħlanye, bona be nga bonwa.

THEY are dreaded by men; they are not dreadful for the greatness of their bodies, nor for appearing to be men; no, there is no appearance of manliness; and greatness there is none; they are little things, which go under the grass. And a man goes looking in front of him, thinking, "If there come a man or a wild beast, I shall see." And, forsooth, an Umutwa is there under the grass; and the man feels when he is already pierced by an arrow; he looks, but does not see the man who shot it. It is this, then, that takes away the strength; for they will die without seeing the man with whom they will fight. On that account, then, the country of the Abatwa is dreadful; for men do not see the man with whom they are going to fight. The Abatwa are fleas, which are unseen whence they come; yet they teaze a man; they rule over him, they exalt themselves over him, until he is unable to sleep, being unable to lie down, and unable to quiet his heart; for the flea is small; the hand of a man is large; it is necessary that it should lay hold of something which can be felt.[13] Just so are the Abatwa; their strength is like that of the fleas, which have the mastery in the night, and the Abatwa have the mastery through high grass, for it conceals them; they are not seen. That then is the power with which the Abatwa conquer men, concealment, they laying wait for men; they see them for their part, but they are not seen.

---

[13] That is, a thing must be felt before the hand can lay hold of it.

Umkcibitshclo wabo a ba *h*laba ngawo into noma umuntu, a u bulali wona ngokwawo ; u ya bulala ngokuba isi*h*loko somkonto wabo s' ekatwa ubu*h*lungu, ukuze ku ti u sa ngena u veze igazi eliningi ; li gijime umzimba wonke, umuntu a fe masinyane. Kepa lobo 'bu*h*lungu babo, imvamo yabo i y' aziwa amapisi ezind*h*lovu. Nako ke ukwesabeka kwabatwa a b' esabeka ngako.

UMPENGULA MBANDA.

The bow with which thcy shoot beast or man, does not kill by itself alone ; it kills becausc the point of their arrow is smeared with poison, in order that as soon as it cnters, it may cause much blood to flow ; blood runs from the whole body, and the man dies forthwith. But that poison of theirs, many kinds of it are known to hunters of the elephant. That then is the dreadfulness of the Abatwa, on account of which they are dreaded.

FABLES.

IMBILA YA SWELA UMSILA NGOKUYALEZELA.

(THE HYRAX WENT WITHOUT A TAIL BECAUSE HE SENT FOR IT.)

Ku tiwa, imbila ya swela umsila ngokuyalezela ezinye. Ngokuba ngam*h*la kw abiwa imisila, la li buyisile izulu ; za puma ke ezinye ukuya 'utata imisila lapa i tatwa kona ; y' a*h*luleka enye ukuba i hambe nazo, ya yaleza ezilwaneni zonke ezi nemisila, ya ti, " O, nina bakwiti, a no ngi patcla owami umsila ; ngi ko*h*lwe ukupuma emgodini, ngokuba izulu li ya na."

Za buya ke ezinye nemisila ; leyo yona a i banga i sa ba namsila ngokwen*g*ena ukupuma, izulu li buyisile. Ya la*h*la konke oku*h*le ngomsila ; ngokuba umsila u ya siza ekuzipungeni ; ngaloko ke imbila a i sa zipungi ngaluto.

IT is said, the hyrax went without a tail because he sent other animals for it. For on the day tails were distributed, the sky had become clouded ; other animals then went out to fetch their tails, to the place where they were given away ; but another, the hyrax, was prevented from going with them, and he exhorted all the animals who have tails, saying, " O, my neighbours, do you bring back my tail for me, for I cannot go out of my hole, because it is raining." So the others returned with tails, but the hyrax himself never had a tail because he was disinclined to go out in the rain. He lost all advantages of a tail ; for a tail is useful for driving away flies ; the hyrax then has nothing to brush them off with.

Se ku izwi elikulu loko 'kulibala kwembila kubantu abamnyama; ba kuluma ngaloko 'kutsho kwembila, ku tiwa kwaba nga zikatazi ngaloko oku tandwayo abanye, naba tshoyo kwabanye, ku tiwa, " Bani, a w azi ukuba loko 'kutsho kwako kwokuti, ' A no ngi patela,' —a w azi na ukuba umuntu ka patelwa omunye, uma into leyo i lingene abakona? O! imbila ya swela umsila ngokuyalezela. Nawe, musa ukwenza njengembila; ku yi 'kuzuza 'luto ngokuyalezela; zihambele ngokwako."

I njalo ke indaba yembila. A i kulumanga yona ngomlomo, ukuti, "A no ngi patela;" kwa vela izwi kodwa ngokuba izilwane zi nemisila, kepa yona a i namsila; kwa nga ya swela umsila ngokuyaleza, na ngokuba izulu imbila i ya l' esaba uma li buyisile; a i pumi emgodini uma li ng' enzi izikau zokusa.

I njalo ke indaba yembila. Ya kqondwa abantu ab' enqenayo ukusebenza ngamhla izulu li libi; ba kcela ukupatelwa abanye. Ku tshiwo njalo ke ukupendulwa kumuntu o ti, "Wo ngi patela," u ti, oku tshiwo kuye ukwelandula kwake, e landula ngokuti, "Imbila ya swela umsila ngokuyalezela. Bani, musa ukutsho njalo." A hambe ke lowo o kcelwayo, 'enzela ukuze ku ti noma e nga m patelanga, a nga m buzi kakulu, ukuti, "Ku ngani pela ukuba u nga ngi pateli, loku ngi ku yalezile na?" A m pendule ngembila leyo.

Umpengula Mbanda.

That loitering of the hyrax is now a great word among black men; they use the words of the hyrax, and say to those who do not trouble themselves about that which others like, and who tell others [to act for them], " So-and-so, do you not know that that saying of yours, ' Do you bring it for me,'—do you not know that another does not bring a man any thing, when there is only enough for those present? O! the hyrax went without a tail because he sent for it. And you, do not act as the hyrax; you will not get any thing by asking others; go for yourself."

Such then is the tale of the hyrax. He did not actually speak with his mouth, saying, "Do you bring it for me;" but the word arose because other animals have tails, but the hyrax has none; and it was as though the hyrax went without a tail because he sent for it; and because he is afraid of a cloudy sky, and does not go out if there are not gleams of sunshine.

Such then is the tale of the hyrax. It was understood by those who were disinclined to work when it is foul weather; they asked others to bring for them. So it is said in answer to a man who says, "O, bring for me," one says when he refuses him, " The hyrax went without a tail because he sent for it. So-and-so, do not ask me to fetch for you." So he who asks goes away. He acts thus that when he returns without it he may not ask many questions, saying, "How is it then that you have not brought it for me, since I asked you to do so?" He answers him by the hyrax.[14]

[14] Other people have other fables to account for the tailless condition of certain animals; but none of them are equal in point to this Zulu myth of the Hyrax.

In the Norse tales the Bear, at the instigation of the Fox, fishes with his

IMPISI NENYANGA.

(THE HYENA AND THE MOON.)

KWA ti ngolunye usuku impisi ya fumana itambo; ya li bamba, ya li pata ngomlomo. Lokupela inyanga i pumile unyezi omuhle, amanzi 'cmi, ya li lahla itambo, i bona inyanga emanzini, ya tabata inyanga, i ti inyama emhlope; ya tshona nekanda, a ya fumana 'luto; kwa dungeka amanzi; ya buyela emuva, ya tula; a kcweba amanzi, ya gxuma ya bamba, i ti i bamba inyanga, i ti inyama, i bona emanzini; ya bamba amanzi; a puma amanzi, a dungeka; ya buyela emuva.

Enye impisi ya fika, ya li tata itambo lelo, ya i shiya. Kwa za kwa sa, inyanga ya nyamalala ngokukanya. Y' ahluleka impisi leyo. Ya buyela ngolunye usuku, kwa za kwa vutwa lapo a i bambanga 'luto.

Ngaloko ke leyo 'mpisi ya hlekwa kakulu, uma ku bonwa i zinge i gijimela emanzini, i bambe amanzi, a vuze, i pume-ze. Nga-

IT happened once on a time that an hyena found a bone; he took it up, and carried it in his mouth. Since then the moon was shining with a beautiful light, the water being still, he threw down the bone when he saw the moon in the water, and caught at the moon, thinking it to be fat meat; he sank head over ears, and got nothing; the water was disturbed; he returned to the bank, and was still; the water became clear; he made a spring, and tried to lay hold, thinking he was laying hold of the moon, thinking it flesh, when he saw it in the water; he caught hold of the water; the water ran out of his mouth, and became muddy; he went back to the bank.

Another hyena came and took the bone, and left the other still there. At length the morning arrived, and the moon became dull through the daylight. The hyena was worsted. He returned on another day, until the place, where he could get nothing, was trampled bare.

Therefore that hyena was much laughed at, when it was seen that he ran continually into the water, and caught hold of the water, and the water ran out of his mouth, and he went out without any

tail through a hole in the ice, till it is frozen; when he attempts to escape he loses his tail.—The story from Bornu represents the Weasel as fastening a stick to the tail of the Hyena, instead of the meat which was to have been fastened on as a bait for fishing; and the Hyena loses his tail by pulling.—In others, with less point, the Wolf loses his tail either by fishing with it at the instigation of the Fox, or by covering the reflection of the moon on the ice, which Reynard persuades him is a cheese.—Whereas in Central-America the Stag and Rabbit had their tails pulled off by the princes Hunahpu and Xbalanqué. (*Tylor. Op. cit. p. 355.*)

loko ke ku tiwa, uma ku laulelwa umuntu, ku tiwe, " Bani, u njengempisi ; yona ya la*h*la itambo, ya bamba ize, ngokubona inyanga i semanzini."

UMPONDO KAMBULE (AARON).

thing. Therefore when a man is laughed at, it is said, " So-and-so, you are like the hyena ; it threw away the bone, and caught at nothing, because it saw the moon in the water."[15]

IZIMFENE NENGWE.

(THE BABOONS AND THE LEOPARD.)

KU tiwa imfene ya *h*langana nengwe e*h*latini ; ya biza ezinye izimfene, ukuba zi zoku i libazisa ingwe, ukuze zi i bulale i nge nasu.

IT is said a baboon fell in with a leopard in the forest ; he called some other baboons. He came and bamboozled the leopard, that they might kill him, when he was left without resource.

Za fika ke kuyo, za i kcoba. Kepa kukqala ingwe y' ek*x*waya, ngokuba ku ya zondwana ingwe nezimfene, ngokuba ingwe i bulala amazinyane ezimfene. Ngaloko ke izimfene zi ya *h*lupeka endaweni lapa ku kona ingwe ; a zi hambi nganye, zi hamba nganingi. Ngaloko ke ingwe y' ek*x*waya, ya bona ukuba i za 'kufa. Kepa izimfene za i pulula ; ngaloko ke ya za ya tamba, ya jwayela ngokuzwa izand*h*la zezimfene zi nga kqinisi ; y' ezwa ukupenya, ya kw azi, ngokuba nazo zi ya kcobana ; ngaloko ke ya tamba, ya bekela.

So they came to him, and caught and killed the vermin which were on him. But at first the leopard was on his guard, for the leopard and baboons hate each other, for the leopard kills the young baboons. Therefore baboons are troubled in a place where there is a leopard ; they do not go alone there, they go in company. The leopard then was on his guard ; and he saw that he was about to die. But the baboons stroked him ; therefore he at length became gentle and accustomed to them, because he felt that their hands were not pressed hard on him ; he felt the separation of his hair ; he understood it, for leopards also kill vermin one for another ; therefore he was gentle, and lay quiet.

Za i penya ke zi funa izintwala, za za za i ti nghu, a ya b' i sa bonakala ; ezinye z' emba umgodi omude, ngokuba umsila wayo ingwe mude ; z' enza loko ngokuba

So they turned aside the hair, hunting for vermin, until they surrounded him, and he could no longer be seen ; some dug a long[16] hole, for the leopard's tail is long ; they did that because they knew

---

[15] This is precisely similar to our " The Dog and the Shadow," or to " The Hibernian Moon-rakers."

[16] The same word means *deep* and *long*.

z' azi ukuti, " Ingwe ilula kunati;
uma si ng' enzi ikcebo, i za 'ku si
bulala." Za u kqeda ke umgodi
lowo, za u faka ke umsila, za u
gqiba ke kakulu, zi u gqiba njalo
se zi i pata kakulu ngoku i funa
izintwala, ukuze i ng' ezwa ubuhlungu bokugqitshwa. Ku t' uba
zi kqede uku u gqiba umsila, ezinye za ti kwezinye, " Hamba ni,
ni gaule izagitsha manje." Za zi
gaula ke, za buya nazo; zi lingene
zonke izimfene. Za kqala ke ukutata izagitsha zazo, za i yeka uku i
kcoba; za i tshaya; i ya kqala
ukutukutela, i jama; se zi i tshaya kakulu; i se i zinge i bukuzeka,
i nga se nakusuka, za za za i bulala, ya fa. Za i shiya.

Umpengula Mbanda.

that the leopard was more active
than they, and if they did not devise something, he would kill them.
So they finished the hole, and put
the leopard's tail in it, and rammed
the earth down tight around it;
they rammed it continually, at the
same time handling him very
much in searching for vermin, that
he might not feel the pain of being
rammed down. When they had
made an end of ramming down the
tail, some said to others, " Go and
cut sticks now." So they cut
them, and brought them; they
were sufficient for all the baboons.
So they began to take their sticks,
and left off catching vermin; they
beat him; he began to be angry,
staring about; and they beat him
excessively; and he continually
rolled on the ground, being no
longer able to get up, until they
killed him, and he died. So they
left him.[17]

INDABA YOMUNTU OWA LAHLA ISINKWA; WA PINDA WA SI FUNA, KA B' E SA SI TOLA.

(THE TALE OF A MAN WHO THREW AWAY SOME BREAD; HE LOOKED FOR IT AGAIN, BUT NEVER FOUND IT.)

Indaba yendoda eya i hamba i
pete isinkwa; i puma se i dhlile

The tale of a man who was going
on a journey carrying bread with
him; he set out, having already

[17] This fable bears a strong resemblance in meaning to that of the Boar and
the Herdsman, one of the tales told by the " Seven wise men."
There was a boar of unusual size and ferocity which was the terror of all
who lived in the neighbourhood of the forest which he frequented. The cattle
of a herdsman unfortunately wandered into this forest, and the herdsman,
whilst searching for them, found a hawthorn tree, covered with ripe fruit; he
filled his pockets, and when about to proceed on his way, was alarmed by the
boar. He climbed the tree, but the boar detected him by the scent of the fruit
he had in his pockets. The man propitiated the beast not only by emptying his
pockets, but also by plucking fruit from the tree, and casting it to his formida-
ble enemy. The beast, being satisfied, lay down to rest; "the artful herdsman
now lowered himself so far as to reach with his fingers the back of the animal,
which he began to scratch with such dexterity that the boar, who was hitherto
unaccustomed to such luxury, closed his eyes, and abandoned himself to the
most delicious slumbers; at which instant the herdsman drew his long knife
and pierced him to the heart." (Ellis's Specimens, &c. Vol. III., p. 39.)

ekaya ; i ng' azi ukuzilinganisela ngokutata isinkwa esi lingene ukuba i si k*q*ede ; ya tata isinkwa esikulu ; kwa nga i ya 'u si k*q*eda. Kepa end*h*leleni ya d*h*la, ya za y' a*h*luleka. Ya ko*h*lwa uma i za 'u s' enze njani na. A ku banga ko ukuti, " A ngi si pate ; kumbe ngapambili ku lanjiwe, ngi ya 'kudinga ukud*h*la ; kumbe ngi nga *h*langana nomuntu e lambile." Konke loko a kwa ba ko. Kwa ti ngokwesuta kwayo, kwa fi*h*leka umkcamango wokulondoloza isinkwa leso ; ka tandanga ukuba a si pate, ngokuba wa se e suti ; wa bona kunye oku ya 'kwenza a hambe kalula. Wa si la*h*la ngenzansi kwend*h*lela, wa d*h*lula ke e se lula. Kwa za kwa d*h*lula izinsuku e nga buyi ngaleyo 'nd*h*lela. Izimpuku za si tata, za si d*h*la, sa pela.

Ku te uma ku fe izwe, li bulawa ind*h*lala, e hamba ngaleyo 'nd*h*lela, e hamb' e mba imiti, (ngokuba amabele e se pelile ; se ku d*h*liwa imiti,) ind*h*lela ya m kumbuza leso 'sinkwa. Wa si bona si se kona ; unyaka wa ba njengokungati usuku lwaizolo. Wa bizwa masinyane i leyo 'ndawo ngoku i bona nje, ukuti, " I yo le 'ndawo e nga la*h*la isinkwa kuyo." Wa fika kona ; wa bona lapa isiukwa sa wela kona ; wa ti, " Sa wela lapaya." Wa gijima ukuya 'u si tola. Kepa ka si fumana. Wa k*q*ala ukubhekisisa esikoteni, lokupela kw enile ; wa funisisa ngokunga u za 'u*h*langaua naso, lapa e putaza ngezand*h*la ekweneni ; kwa za kwa d*h*lula isikati. Wa

eaten at home ; and not knowing how to allowance himself by taking bread which was equal to his consumption, he took a large quantity of bread ; he thought he should eat it all. But by the way he ate, until he could eat no more. He could not tell what to do with it. He did not say to himself, " Let me carry it ; perhaps in front there is hunger, and I shall want food ; perhaps I may meet a man who is hungry." There was no such thought as that. But through being satisfied, the thought of taking care of that bread was hidden ; he did not wish to carry it, because he was then full ; he saw one thing only which would enable him to go easily. He threw the bread on the lower side of the path, and so went on no longer burdened. He did not return by that path for many days. Mice took the bread, and ate it all up.

It came to pass when the land died, it being killed by famine, as he was going by that way, going and digging up roots, (for there was no corn left ; roots only were now eaten,) the path made him remember the bread. He saw it still there ; a year was as it were a day of yesterday. He was at once summoned by the place by merely seeing it, and said, " This is the very place where I threw away my bread." He arrived at the place ; he saw where the bread had fallen ; he said, " It fell yonder." He ran to find it. But he did not find it. He began to look earnestly in the long grass, for it was very thick ; he searched thinking he should fall in with it, as he was feeling with his hands in the thick grass ; until some time had elapsed. He rose up, and

sukuma, wa kcabauga, wa ti,
"Hau! Kwa buya kw enza uja-
ni? Loku ngi ti, a ngi ka ko*h*lwa
nje indawo e nga si pousa kuyo.
K*q*abo; a i ko enye; i yo le."
Wa toba wa funa. Lokupela u
funa njalo, namand*h*la u se wa
tolile, u se k*q*inile ngokwazi ukuti,
"Noma ngi lambile nje, ku za 'u-
pela; ngi nga tola isinkwa sami."
Wa za wa jamba, wa kupuka, wa
buyela end*h*leleni, wa funa indawo
lapa a k*q*ala koua ukuma, wa ti,
"Nga hamba konke lapa ngi nga
ka si ponsi." Lokupela lapa a si
ponsa kona, kwa ku kona isiduli;
wa bona ngaso, wa ti, "E! nga ti,
uma ngi lapa, nga ti!" Wa tsho
e linganisa ngengalo; i ya ya ingalo lapa a si yisa kona. U se
gijima ngejubane, e landela ingalo.
Wa fika, wa putaza masinyane;
ka z' a si tola. Wa buyela kona,
wa ti, "Hau! s' enza njani? loku
nga si ponsa lapa uje, ngi nga bonwa 'muntu, ngi ngedwa nje."
Wa gijima. Wa za wa d*h*lulelwa
isikati sokumba imiti; wa buya-
ze; imiti a nga i mbanga. Wa
buya e se pele amand*h*la, ngokuba
e uga zuzanga leso 'sinkwa.

Na manje u se kona lowo ngalapa ngaselwand*h*le. Leyo 'ndaba
wa i zeka se li tulile izwe, ind*h*lala
i pelile. Kwa ba 'ligidigidi loko
'kwenza kwake kubo bonke aba
ku zwayo, be ti, "Bani, nembala
ind*h*lala y enza umuntu a be 'me-
*h*lo 'mnyama. Wa ka wa si bona
ini, wena, isinkwa esi la*h*lwa ngomunye unyaka, si tolwe ngomunye,
si sa lungile na?" Wa ti, "Madoda, ind*h*lala a y azisi. Nga ngi
ti ngi funa ka*h*le, ugi za 'u si tola.

thought, saying, "Hau! What
happened after I threw away the
bread? For I say, I do not yet
forget the place where I threw it.
No surely; there is no other; it
is this very place." He stooped
down and searched. For whilst
he is thus seeking he has gained
strength, and is now strong
through knowing, to wit, "Though
I am hungry, my hunger will end;
I may find my bread." At length
he was confused, he went up again
to the path, he found the place
where he first began to stand, he
said, "I passed over all this place
before I threw it away." For
where he threw it away, there was
an ant-heap; he saw by that, and
said, "Ah! when I was here, I
did thus!" He said this, imitating
with his arm; the arm goes in the
direction in which he threw the
bread. And now he runs quickly,
following the direction of the arm.
He came to the place, and at once
felt about; he did not find the
bread. He went back again, and
said, "Hau! what has become of
it? since I threw it exactly here;
for no man saw me, I being quite
alone." He ran. At length the
time for digging roots had passed
away; he went home without any
thing; he dug no roots. He now
became faint again, because he had
not found the bread.

And that man is still living,
yonder by the sea. The man told
the tale when the country was at
peace, and the famine at an end.
It was a cause of laughter that
conduct of his, to all who heard it,
and they said, "So-and-so, sure
euough famine makes a man dark-
eyed. Did you ever see bread,
which was thrown away one year,
found in another, still good to
eat?" He said, "Sirs, famiue
does not make a man clever. I
thought I was seeking wisely, and

Ind*h*lala i ya k*g*eda uku*h*lakanipa.
Mina ngokulamba kwami nga ko-
lwa impela ukuba ngi ya 'ku si
fumana; loku nga ngi ngedwa, ku
nge ko umuntu. Kanti loko i
kona kwa ngi bangela ind*h*lala,
nga za nga pons' ukufa."

UMPENGULA MBANDA.

should find it. Famine takes away
wisdom. And for my part, through
my hunger, I believed in truth
that I should find it; for I was
alone, there being no man with
me. But in fact that was the
means of increasing my want,
until I was nearly dead."

SPEAKING ANIMALS.

INDABA YEKWABABA.

(THE TALE OF A CROW.)

KWA ti kwazulu ku *h*leziwe ku
buswa, ku ng' aziwa 'luto olu za
'kwenzeka. Ngoluny' usuku ikwababa la biza umuntu wakwazulu,
induna, ibizo lake Unongalaza,
la ti, "We, nongalaza! We,
nongalaza!" Kwa lalelwa, kwa
tiwa, "A ku bonakali 'muntu o
bizayo, 'kupela ikwababa leliya."
La ti, "Ni *h*lezi nje. Le 'nyanga
a i 'kufa. Ni za 'ubulawa kwazulu; uma ni nga hambi, ni za
'kufa ngayo le 'nyanga. Hamba
nini nonke." Nembala ke a ba
*h*lalanga. Umawa kajama, inkosi
yalabo 'bantu, w' esuka, w' eza
lapa esilungwini. Aba salayo ba
bulawa.

UMANKOFANA MBELE.

IT happened that among the Zulus
men were living in perfect prosperity, not knowing what was
about to happen. One day a crow
called one of the Zulus, an officer,
whose name was Unongalaza, and
said, "Wey, Unongalaza! Wey,
Unongalaza!" The people listened and said, "No one can be
seen who is calling; there is only
that crow yonder." It said, "You
are living securely. This moon
will not die [without a change].
You will be killed in Zululand; if
you do not depart, you will be
killed during this very month.
Go away, all of you." And in
truth they did not stay. Umawa,[18]
the daughter of Ujama, the chief
of the people, set out, and came
here to the English. Those who
remained behind were killed.

ENYE YEKWABABA FUTI.

(ANOTHER TALE OF A CROW.)

KWA ti abafazi be bahili be
sen*h*le, be pumile, kwa fika

THERE were two women in the
fields. A crow came and pitched

<hr>

[18] That is, she and a part of the people.

ikwababa, la *h*lala pezu kwomuti, b' ezwa li kala li ti, "Maye, maye, mnta kadade o nga zaliyo. Umakazi yena o ze 'enze njani na loku e nga zali nje na?" B' esuka, ba baleka, ba y' ekaya. Ba fika, ba i zeka leyo 'ndaba. Kwa tiwa um*h*lola. Lowo 'mfazi o nga zaliyo intombi kasipongo wakwad*h*lanimi kona lapa emakuzeni. Emva kwaloku indoda yake ya gula kakulu.

ULUHOHO MADONDA.

on a tree, and they heard it crying and saying, "Woe, woe, child of my sister, who hast no children. What will she be able to do since she is childless?" They started up and ran away. When they reached home they told the tale. The people said it was an omen. The woman who had no child was the daughter of Usipongo of Idhlanimi here among the Amakuza. After that her husband was very ill.[19]

INDABA YENJA EYA KQAMBA IGAMA.

(THE TALE OF A DOG WHICH MADE A SONG.)

KWA ku te 'nyakana kwa fa ilizwe ku lwa Umatiwane nompangazita, kwa kxokozela amakuba ku linywa abantu ; ba bheka pezulu, a ti, "Ni bheka ni? I tina." Ya se i tsho ke inja esitshondweni, umuzi wenkosi, ya ti kqa ngesinqe, ya ti,

It happened long ago when the country was desolate, during the war between Umatiwane[20] and Umpangazita,[21] the hoes rattled as the people were digging ; they looked up, and the hoes said, "What are you looking at? It is we." Then a dog sat down on his buttocks at Isitshondo, the king's town, and said,

"Mad*h*lad*h*la ; a ni namhhau
Ngomkelemba wame.[23]
Ngi vumele ni, baba wame,
Ngomta kad*h*lakad*h*la yedwa
    kcatsha."[25]

"Madhladhla![22] you have no pity
For my treasure.[24]
Sing with me, my father,
About the son of Ukadhlaka-
    dhla, his only son !"

Abantu ba ti ngaloko 'ku*h*labelela kwenja, ba ti, "Li file izwe."

The people said, on hearing that song of the dog, "The country is dead."

Lelo 'gama la li igugu kakulu ezintombini, la li *h*latshelelwa ngezinyembezi.

This song was a very great favourite with the damsels, and used to be sung with tears.

UNOKO MASILA.

[19] Comp. these tales with those given, p. 131—133.
[20] *Umatiwane*, a chief of the Amangwane.
[21] *Umpangazita*, a chief of the Amathlubi.
[22] *Umadhladhla*, the name of Ungaloukulu, the son of Ukadhlakadhla, who was killed by the Amangwane during the war. *Amadhladhla*, his people.
[23] *Wame* for *wami*, or *wam'*—e, to prolong the word for the sake of the rhythm.
[24] The dog rebukes the people for not weeping for their dead chief.
[25] *Yedwa kcatsha*, (Zulu, *kcoko*,) emphasizing yedwa, *his only son, only indeed.*

RIDDLES.

1

KQANDELA ni inkomo e nga lali pansi nakanye. Ku ti ngam*h*la i lalayo i be se i lele umlalela wafuti; a i sa yi 'kupinda i vuke. Ukulala kwayo ukufa. Inkomo e dumile kakulu, isengwakazi; abantwana bayo ba ya londeka i yo. I ba nye njalo kumniniyo, ka i sweli eyesibili, i yo yodwa 'kupela.

Guess ye a cow which never lies down. When it lies down it lies down for ever; it will never rise up again. Its lying down is death. It is a very celebrated cow, and one which gives much milk; its children are preserved by it. The owner possesses only one; he does not want another; he only requires one.

2

K*q*andela ni upuzi; lu lunye, lu neminyombo eminingi; kumbe amakulu; u *h*lanze izinkulungwane eziningi ngeminyombo yalo; uma u i landa iminyombo yalo a ku ko lapa u nge fumane 'puzi; u ya 'ku wa fumana amapuzi. Umnyombo umunye a wa balwa amapuzi awo; u nge ze wa fa ind*h*lala; u nga hamba u ka u d*h*la; futi u nge pate umpako ngokwesaba ukuti, "Ngi ya 'kud*h*la ni pambili na?" K*q*a; u nga d*h*la u shiye, w azi ukuba loku ngi hamba ngomnyombo, ngi za 'ufumana elinye ngapambili njalo. Nembala ku njalo. Iminyombo yalo i k*q*ede izwe lonke, kepa upuzi lunye olu veza leyo 'minyombo eminingi. Ku ba i lowo a lande omunye, a li ke ipuzi, bonke ba ya ka eminyonjeni.

Guess ye a pumpkin-plant; it is single, and has many branches; it may be hundreds; it bears many thousand pumpkins on its branches; if you follow the branches, you will find a pumpkin every where; you will find pumpkins every where. You cannot count the pumpkins of one branch; you can never die of famine; you can go plucking and eating; and you will not carry food for your journey through being afraid that you will find no food where you are going. No; you can eat and leave, knowing that by following the branches you will continually fiud another pumpkin in front; and so it comes to pass. Its branches spread out over the whole country, but the plaut is one, from which springs many branches. And each man pursues his own branch, and all pluck pumpkins from the branches.

3

K*q*andela ni inkomo e *h*latshelwa 'zibayeni zibili.

Guess ye an ox which is slaughtered in two cattle-pens.

4

Kɋandela ni indoda e nga lali; ku ze ku se i mi, i nga lele.

Guess ye a man who does not lie down; even when it is morning he is standing, he not having lain down.

5

Kɋandela ni indoda e nga zama-zami; noma izulu li vunguza ka-kulu, i mi nje, i te puʰle; umoya u wisa imiti nezindʰlu, kw enakale okuningi; kepa yona ku njengo-kungati li kɔwebile nje, a i zama-zami nakancinane.

Guess ye a man who does not move; although the wind blows furiously, he just stands erect; the wind throws down trees and houses, and much injury is done; but he is just as if the sky was perfectly calm, and does not move in the least.

6

Kɋandela ni amadoda amaningi 'enze uʰla; a ya sina ijadu, a vu-nule ngamatshoba amʰlope.

Guess ye some men who are many and form a row; they dance the wedding dance, adorned in white hip-dresses.

7

Kɋandela ni indoda e ʰlala ezi-teni ngemiʰla yonke, lapa ku ʰla-selwa njalonjalo; kepa i ba nevuso ku nga puma impi, y azi ukuba konje namuʰla ngi sekufeni; a i naʰlati lokubalekela. Ukusinda kwayo ukuba ku pele impi. I dʰle nomfino, ngokuti, "Hau! nga sinda namuʰla! Ngi be ngi ng' azi ukuba ngi za 'upuma em-pini." A i nabantwana, ngokuba y ake pakati kwezita, ya ti, "Kɋa; kuʰle ukuba ngi be nge-dwa, kona ko ti ku sa ʰlatshwa umkosi, ngi be ngi lunga."

Guess ye a man who lives in the midst of enemies every day, where raids are made without ceasing; and he is alarmed when the army sets out, knowing that he is then in the midst of death; he has no forest to which he can escape. He escapes only by the enemy retiring. He then eats food, saying, "Ah! escaped this time! I did not think that I could escape from the midst of the army." He has no children, be-cause he lives in the midst of ene-mies, saying, "No; it is well that I should live by myself, and then when an alarm is given, I may be ready to escape."

8

Kɋandela ni indoda e nga lali ebusuku; i lala ekuseni, ku ze ku tshone ilanga; i vuke, i sebenze

Guess ye a man who does not lie down at night; he lies down in the morning until the sun sets; he

ngobusuku bonke; a i sebenzi emini; a i bonwa ukusebenza kwayo.

then awakes, and works all night; he does not work by day; he is not seen when he works.

9

Kqandela ni amadoda a hamba e ishumi; uma ku kona eyomuvo, lawa 'madoda a ishumi a wa hambi; a ti, "Si nge hambe, loku ku kona um*h*lola." Ku ya mangalwa kakulu a lawo 'madoda; a libale ukuteta ikcala ngokuti, "Ku ngani ukuba si ve, loku kade si ng' ëvi na? Um*h*lola." A nga tandani naleyomuvo.

Guess ye some men who are walking, being ten in number; if there is one over the ten, these ten men do not go; they say, "We cannot go, for here is a prodigy." These men wonder exceedingly; they are slow in settling the dispute, saying, "How is it that our number is over ten, for formerly we did not exceed ten?" They have no love for the one over the ten.

10

Kqandela ni indoda e ku nga tandeki ukuba i *h*leke kubantu, ngokuba i y' aziwa ukuti, uku*h*leka kwayo kubi kakulu, ku landelwa isililo, a ku tokozwa. Ku kala abantu nemiti notshani, uako konke ku zwakale esizweni lapa i *h*leke kona, nkuti i *h*lekile indoda e nga *h*leki.

Guess ye a man whom men do not like to laugh, for it is known that his laughter is a very great evil, and is followed by lamentation, and an end of rejoicing. Men weep, and trees and grass; and every thing is heard weeping in the tribe where he laughs; and they say the man has laughed who does not usually laugh.

11

Kqandela ni umuntu o zenza inkosi, o nga sebeuzi, o *h*lala nje; ku sebenza abantu bake bodwa, yena k' enzi 'luto; u ya ba tshenisa loko a ba ku tandayo, kodwa yena ka kw enzi; a ba boni abantu bake, ba bonelwa u ye, bona ba izimpumpute, isizwe sonke sake; u yena yedwa o bonayo. Ba y' azi ukuba noma be nga boni bona, ngaye ba ya bona; ngokuba a ba lambi konke a ba ku swelayo; u ya ba tata ngezand*h*la, a ba yise lapa ku kona ukud*h*la, ba buye

Guess ye a man who makes himself a chief; who does not work, but just sits still; his people work alone, but he does nothing; he shows them what they wish, but he does nothing; his people do not see, he sees for them, they are blind, the whole of his nation; he alone can see. They know that though they cannot see, they see by him; for they do not go without any thing they want; he takes them by the hand, and leads them to where there is food, and they return with it to their

nako; kodwa yena ka pati 'luto, ngokuba u zenz' inkosi; u sa za wa ba inkosi, ngokuba abantu bake ba pila ngaye.

Kuqkala kwa ku kona umbango ngokuti, "U nge buse tina, u ng' enzi 'luto; si nga wa boni amandhla obukosi bako." Wa ba pendula ngokuti, "Loku ni ti a ngi 'nkosi, ngi za 'uhlala ke, ngi tule nje, ngi bheke pansi. Ngaloko ke ni ya 'ubona ukuba nembala ngi inkosi, ngokuba ngokubheka kwami pansi izwe li za 'kufa; ni za 'kuwela emaweni na semigodini; ni dhliwe na izilo, ni nga zi boni; ni fe na indhlala, ukudhla ni nga ku toli; loku ni banga nami, ni izimpumpute."

Nembala ba bona ukuba u inkosi, ba ti, "A ku vunywe obala, a si buse, si ze si pile. Uma si fa indhlala, lobo 'bukosi betu bu ya 'kupela. Si amakosi ngokupila." Wa vunywa ke, wa busa ke; izwe la tula.

Kepa umuntu o nga gezi nakanye; u hlala nje. Kepa ku ti mhla e gula isifwana esincane nje, isizwe sonke sake si hlupeke, ku fiwe indhlala; abantu b' esabe ukupuma ezindhlini, ngokuba ba ya 'kuwela emaweni, b' apuke. Ku fiswe ukuba nga e sinda masinyane; ku tokozwe lapa e se sindile.

homes; but he touches nothing, for he makes himself a chief; he remains a chief for ever, for his people are supported by him.

At first there was a dispute, and his people said, "You cannot be our king and do nothing; we cannot see the power of your majesty." He answered them, saying, "Since you say I am not a chief, I will just sit still, and look on the ground. Then you will see that I am truly a chief, for if I look on the ground the land will be desolate; you will fall over precipices and into pits; you will be eaten by wild beasts through not seeing them; and die through famine, being unable to find food; because you dispute with me, you are blind."

So they see that he is a chief, and say, "Let us acknowledge openly that he is our king, that we may live. If we die of famine, that majesty which we claim for ourselves will come to an end. We are kings by living." So he was acknowledged a chief, and reigned; and the country was peaceful.

And he is a man that never washes; he just sits still. And when he is ill even with a slight illness all his nation is troubled, and dies of famine; and the people are afraid to go out of their houses, because they would fall over precipices and be dashed to pieces. They long for him to get well at once; and the people rejoice when he is well.

12

Kqandela ni inkomo e nge nanyama; a ku sikwa 'ndawo kuyo; ingulukukqa nje; a i hambi uma i

Guess ye a bullock which has no flesh; no one can cut into it any where; it is a mere hard mass; it does not go unless it is

nga kqutshwa, i ma njalo, i ze i sunduzwe umuntu. A i vumi ukusunduzwa uma y enyuswa ngomango ; i ze i vume uma y e*h*la. Inkomo e nga tandi ukwenyuka ; i tanda ukweuswa njalo, i vume ke.

Futi, a i u weli umfula, i ma nganeno ; uma umuntu e tanda ukuba i wele, nga e i sunduza ngamand*h*la amakulu ; kepa uma amanzi e tshonisa, a i vumi ukuwela, i ya m kcatshela emanzini ; ngokuba i y' azi ukukcatsha emanzini amakulu, a nga b' e sa i bona. I ketelwa izindawo ezi bonakalayo pansi, ukuze umuntu a i bone, a i kqube kona ngoku i sunduza.

Uknd*h*liwa kwayo kunye 'kupela, ukukoka ngayo ikcala, uma umuntu e nekcala eli nga kqedwa ngayo. 'Kupela ke i lowo umsebenzi e w enzayo.

Kepa inkomo e nolaka kakulu ; uma i sunduzwa i bekiswa endaweni e ngasen*h*la, ku yu *h*lakanitshwa abantu aba i kqubayo, omunye a tsho kubo ukuti, " Hlakanipa ni ; le 'nkomo ni ya y azi ukuba a i tandani nokwenyuka ; bheka ni i nga si *h*labi ; uku si *h*laba kwayo ku ya 'kuba kubi kakulu, ngokuba si ngenzansi, yona i ngen*h*la ; si ya 'uko*h*lwa ukuvika, ngokuba indawo imbi, a i si lungele ; si ya 'kuti lapa si ti si ya vika, si we, i fike i si kqcdcle." I kqutshwa ngoku*h*lakanipa okunjalo ke, ukuzc ku ti lapa se y ala ukwenyuka, i funa ukubuya, ba i dedele, i d*h*lule ; kumbe ba nga be be sa i landa, ngoba i ya 'kubaleka, i ba shiye, i ze i fike endaweni e lungele yona, abantu i nga sa ba lungele ; b' a*h*luleke.

UMPENGULA MBANDA.

forced, but always stands still, until it is pushed along by some one. It will not be pushed along if it is driven up a steep place ; but it allows itself to be pushed down. It is a bullock which does not like to go up hill ; it likes always to be made to go down, and then makes no opposition.

Further, it does not cross a river, it stands still on one side ; if any one wishes it to cross, he must push it with great strength ; but if the water is very deep, it will not cross, but hides itself from him in the water ; for it knows how to hide in deep water, and he can see it no more. One chooses for it a place where he can see the bottom, that he may see it and drive it forward by pushing it.

There is only one mode of eating it by paying a debt, if a man has a debt which can be paid by it. That, then, is the only work it can do.

And it is a very fierce bullock ; if it is pushed up hill, the men who drive it are on their guard, and one says to the others, " Be on your guard ; you know that this bullock does not like to go up hill ; take care that it does not gore us ; if it gores us it will be very bad indeed, for we are below, and it is above us, and we shall be unable to shield ourselves, for it is a bad place, and is not advantageous for us ; and when we think we are shielding ourselves, we shall fall, and it come and make an end of us." It is driven with such care, that when it will not go up, and wishes to come back again, they may make way for it and it pass on ; aud perhaps they will not follow it any more ; for it will run away, and leave them behind, till it comes to a place which is good for it, but bad for the men. So they are beat.

KEY TO THE RIDDLES.

1

Si tsho ind*h*lu ukuti inkomo e isengwakazi; ukusengwa kwayo ku ukutokoza ngayo pansi kwayo, ngokuba i *h*lala isikati eside, abantu be londekile, be nga zinge b' aka. Ku ze ku ti ngam*h*la i wayo, i be se i wile njalo; a i sa yi 'kupinda i vuke. Si ti "i inkomo" ukuze umuntu a nga kcabangi ngend*h*lu, a zinge e funa ngasezinkomeni, e landela igama lokuti "inkomo," 'esabe ukuti ind*h*lu; u ti, "Ngi ya 'kuti ind*h*lu kanjani, loku ku tiwa inkomo nje na? Ngi ya 'kuba ngi y' eduka."

We mean a house by the cow which gives much milk; the milk is the joy a house affords those who live beneath it, for it remains a long time, the people being preserved, and not continually building. But when it falls it has fallen for ever; it never rises up again. We say "cow" that a man may not think of a house, but seek about continually among cattle, following the name "cow," and fearing to say house, saying, "How can I say that a house is a cow? I shall make a great mistake if I say house."

2

Umuzi, nezind*h*lela ezi puma kuwo zi iminyombo e *h*lanzayo; ngokuba a ku ko 'nd*h*lela i nge namuzi; zonke izind*h*lela zi puma emakaya, zi ya emakaya. A ku ko 'nd*h*lela e nga yi 'kaya. Ind*h*lela si ti i umuyombo o *h*lanzayo, ukuze imfumbe i be n*h*le ngobulukuni. Amatanga imizi e ku puma kuyo izind*h*lela.

A village, and the paths which pass from it are the branches, which bear fruit; for there is no path without a village; all paths quit homesteads, and go to homesteads. There is no path which does not lead to a homestead. We say the path is a branch which bears fruit, that the riddle may be good because it is hard. The pumpkins are villages from which the paths go out.

3

Intwala, ngokuba umuntu u ya i tata engutsheni, ka namand*h*la oku i bulala ngesitupa si sinye; uma e nga *h*langanisi izitupa zozibili, a i kciudezele, i fe; nesinye isitupa si be bomvu, nesinye si be n*h*jalo, zi lingane zombili ngobubomvu. Si ti "inkomo," ukuze

A louse, for a man takes it out of his blanket, but he cannot kill it with one thumb; but only by bringing the two thumbs together, and squeezing it between them that it may die; and both nails be bloody, and one equal the other in being red. We say "ox," that the

imfumbe leyo i be lukuni uku i kqandela; emuva, uma se b' a*h*lulekile, u ba tshele o ba kqandelisayo, u ti, "Intwala ni ti a inkomo ngani na, loku i *h*latshelwa ezibayeni ezibili?" u tsho izitupa. W enza uku ba dukisa, ngokuti, izibaya.

riddle may be difficult to guess; afterwards when they cannot tell, you say to the persons who are guessing, "Why do you say that a louse is not an ox, for it is killed in two cattle-pens?" meaning the thumbs. You do thus to lead them wrong, by calling them cattle-pens.

4

Insika a i lali, ngokuba i y' ema njalo, i linde ind*h*lu. Uma insika i lala, ind*h*lu i nga wa. Kodwa lapa e ti "indoda," u ya pambanisa, ukuze imikcabango yabantu i nga fiki masinyane ezintweni; kodwa ba zinge be kcabangela kubantu njengegama lokuti indoda. Lapa se b' a*h*lulekile, a ti, "Ni ti insika a indoda ngani, loku ni i bona nje i pase ind*h*lu ingaka? Kepa i nga wi."

A pillar does not lie down, for it stands constantly and watches the house. If the pillar lies down, the house may fall. But when one says "a man," he entangles the matter, that the thoughts of the men may not reach the things at once; but continually have their thoughts running on men in accordance with the word, man. When they cannot tell, one replies, "Why do you not say that the pillar is a man, since you see it upholding so great a house as this? But it does not fall."

5

Ind*h*lebe. U ba tshela lapa se b' a*h*lulekile, a ti, "Ubani owa ka wa bona ind*h*lebe yomuntu ukuzamazama kwayo, i zamazamiswa umoya na? Si ya bona imiti notshani nezind*h*lu zi zamazama; kepa ind*h*lebe, kqa; ku zamazama umuntu yedwa; noma 'emuka nomoya, a ku muki yona, ku muka yena; uma e wa, yona i se mi; noma e baleka, i mi njalo."

The ear. One says to them when they cannot tell, "Who ever saw the ear of a man move, it being moved by the wind? We see trees and grass and houses move; but not the ear; the man only moves; if he is carried away by the wind, the ear is not carried away, it is he who is carried away; or if he falls, it still stands erect; or if he runs away, it still stands erect."

6

Amazinyo. Si ti abantu ab' enze u*h*la ngokuba amazinyo a mise kwabantu be lungela ijadu, ukuze ba sine ka*h*le. Lapa si ti, ba

The teeth. We call them men who form a row, for the teeth stand like men who are made ready for a wedding-dance, that they may dance well. When we

"vunule ngamatshoba am*h*lope," si ya ngenisa, ukuze abantu ba nga kcabangi masinyane ngokuti amazinyo, ba kitshwe ngokuti, "Abantu ba faka amatshoba," ba zinge be funa ngakubantu; ngokuti, loku amatshoba a fakwa abantu be y' ejadwini, b' eza 'usina, noku*h*lela abantu, ba zinge be tsho ukuti, "Amadoda lawo abantu." Kepa a ti o ba kcandelisayo, "Kepa ba ya 'kusina kanjani uma se be *h*langene ngemizimba na?" A zinge e ba kipa ngamazwi kuloko a ba ku tshoyo. Ka piki nje ukuti, "Kca; a si ko loko. Imfumbe a y enziwa njalo." Umuntu u ba kipa ngamazwi, ba kolwe nembala ba bone ukuti, "A si ka fiki lapa e tsho kona." A ti ngokutsho ukuti, "A ni wa boni amazinyo; uku*h*lela kwawo njengabantu; amatshoba am*h*lope a ni wa boni amazinyo?" Ba ti, "U s' a*h*lulile."

say, they are "adorned with white hip-dresses," we put that in, that people may not at once think of teeth, but be drawn away from them by thinking, "It is men who put on white hip-dresses," and continually have their thoughts fixed on men; for since white hip-dresses are put on by men when they are going to a wedding to dance, and to set men in order, they say continually, "The men of the riddle are men." And the man who is making them guess says, "But how can they dance if their bodies touch?" He continually draws them away by words from that which they say. He does not merely deny that they are right by saying, "No; it is not that. The riddle is not explained in that way." He draws them away by words, and they really believe that they see that they are not near the meaning of the riddle. At length he says, "Do you not see the teeth; their order like that of men; the white hip-dresses do you not see they mean the teeth?" They say, "You have beaten us."

7

Ulimi lu umuntu o *h*lupekayo ngokuba lu pakati kwempi; amazinyo a impi; ngokuba uma amazinyo e d*h*la ukud*h*la, ulimi lu zinge lu tola ingozi ngesikati amazinyo e lwa nokud*h*la, ukuze a ku gayise. Ngaloko ke lapa si ti "umuntu," si ya pambanisa, ukuz' abantu ba nga kumbuli masinyane ngolwimi, ba zinge be funela ngakubantu, ngokuti, "Loku indaba i ti umuntu nje na, i nga tsho ukuti ulimi, so ba si ya ponsi-

The tongue is a man which is in affliction because it is in the midst of enemies; the teeth are the enemy; for when the teeth are eating, the tongue is often injured whilst they are fighting with the food, that they may grind it. Therefore when we say "a man," we entangle the subject, that men may not at once think of the tongue, but continually have their search directed to men; and they say, "Since the riddle says a man only, and says nothing about the tongue, we shall be wrong if we

sa uma si ti ulimi." Ngaloko ke nembala a lu tokozi, ngokuba lapa amazinyo e *h*lafuna ukud*h*la ulimi lu zinge lu nyakanyakaza emkatini wamazinyo, lu vika, ku nga bulawa ukud*h*la, ngokuba ukud*h*la ku ya bulawa njalonjalo amazinyo; kepa lona a lu bulawa amazinyo, ngokuba lu y' aziwa, umuntu wakona; kepa lu zinge lu tola ingozi, ngokuba ku liwa esikund*h*leni salo, lapa lw ake kona; lu tokoze uma ukud*h*la ku nga ka d*h*liwa; lapa ku d*h*liwa ukud*h*la, lw azi ke ukuba konje namu*h*la se ngi sengozini, ngi za 'kubulawa, ku nga kcetshwa mina; ngi fa ngokuba ku liwa pambi kwami. Nango ke umuntu o pakati kwezita, ulimi.

say the tongue." The tongue, then, is not happy, for when the teeth are chewing food, the tongue continually moves from side to side between the teeth, and is on its guard when the food is killed; for the food is constantly killed by the teeth; but the tongue is not killed by them, for it is known, it is a man of that place; but it continually meets with an accident, for there is fighting in the place where it dwells; it is happy before the food is eaten; but when the food is being eaten, it knows that it is in the midst of danger, and is about to be injured, without having had any charge made against it; it dies because the battle is fought in its presence. There, then, is the man who is in the midst of enemies, the tongue.

8

Imivalo. Ukusebenza kwayo ebusuku ukulinda izinkomo ngokuvala esangweni; ku *h*langane ukuze inkomo i nga toli 'ndawo yokupuma; noma i linga ukupuma y a*h*luleke ngokukqina kwemivalo; ku ze ku se izinkomo zi nga pumanga; ekuseni zi pume ngokuvulelwa, imivalo i lale ke.

The closing-poles of the cattle-pen. Their work by night is to watch the cattle by closing the gateway; they are close together that the cattle may not find a place of escape; though one try to get out it may be unable to do so through the strength of the bars; and when it is morning the cattle have not got out; in the morning they go out because the gateway is opened for them, and so the closing poles lie on the ground.

9

Iminwe. Ukuma kwayo i ishumi 'kupela; i lingene, i hamba ngamibili. Ngaloko ke uma ku

The fingers. Their proper number is only ten; they are matched, going in pairs.[26] Therefore, if

[26] He means, the index and middle fingers,—the ring and little fingers,—and the thumbs.

kona womuvo, a i sa lingani na sekuhambeni na sekubaleni ; kubi ukubala kwayo ; a kw aħluki, ku isipitipiti nje. I loko ke e si ti i libala ukuteta ikcala, ngokuti, uma ku y' enzeka, a ku ko 'buħlungu, u nga suswa umunwe ngezwi nje, impela ku nga tshiwo ukuti, "Suka ; a u fanele lapa."

there is a supernumerary finger, they are no longer fit either to go together in pairs or to count with ; their counting is bad ; there is no argument, but only difference. This is what we mean when we say they are slow in settling the dispute, that is, if it could be done without pain the supernumerary finger could be taken off with a word, truly it would be said, "Away with you ; you are not fit for this place."

10

Umlilo. Ku tiwa u indoda ukuze loko oku tshiwoyo ku nga bonakali masinyane, ku fiħlwa ngendoda. Abantu ba tsho okuningi, be funa ngokupikisana, be geja. I b' enħle imfumbe ngaloku ngoku nga bonwa masinyane. Si ti "indoda," ngokuba umlilo a ku tandeki na sendħlini u basiwe ukuba u kçatshe izinħlansi zawo zi wele ezingutsheni. Ku ya kalwa umninizo ngokuba i ya 'kutsha ; a bone se i bobokile, a kale. Noma ku pekiwe ukudħla, uma umlilo umkulu, ku nga bekwa imbiza, i ya 'kutshiswa umlilo, yona i tshise ukudħla. I ħlekile ke indoda, ukuti umlilo. So ku kalwa. Futi uma inħlansi i ponseke etshanini bendħlu, i nga bonwa, ku bonwe ngokutsha ; ku ya 'uħlangana abantu bonke lapa ku bonakale ilangabi lawo, i tshe indħlu nezinto zonke ; ku kalwe kakulu ; nezimbuzi zi tshe namatole ; nabantwana ba tshe. Ku kale izinkomo, zi kalela amatole azo e file ; ku kale abantu, be kalela izimbuzi zabo ; ku kale umfazi nendoda, be

Fire. It is called a man that what is said may not be at once evident, it being concealed by the word, "man." Men say many things, searching out the meaning in rivalry, and missing the mark. A riddle is good when it is not discernable at once. We say "a man," because it is not liked that the fire, even indoors where it is kindled, should cause its sparks to start out and fall on the clothes. The owner of the clothes cries because it burns ; and when he sees a hole in it, he cries again. Or if food is being cooked, if the fire is large the pot may be put on, and be burned by the fire, and the pot burn the food. So the man laughs, that is, the fire. And the people cry. Again, if a spark is cast into the thatch of the hut, it is seen by the fire ; all the men will come together when the flame of the fire appears, and burns the house with the things which are in it ; and there is a great crying ; and the goats are burnt, and the calves ; and the children are burnt. The cows cry, crying for their calves which are dead ; men cry, crying for their goats ; the wife and husband cry, crying for their

kalela abantwana babo be tshile;
nabantwana ba kalele uyise e tshile, wa fa e ti u landa impa*h*la yake
e igugu, ind*h*lu i dilikele pezu
kwake ; ku ka*l*a nendoda, i kalela
umfazi wayo e tshile, wa fa e be ti
u landa um̄ntwana pakati kwen-
d*h*lu, wa fa naye ; ku kale nemiti,
i kalela ubu*h*le bayo obu nga se
ko, se bu tshiswe umlilo, se i
sbwabene imiti, se i bunile, ubu*h*le
bayo bu pelile ; ku kale nezinkomo, zi kalela utshani, ngokuba a zi
sa d*h*li 'luto, se zi fa ind*h*lala. I
loko ke uku*h*leka kwomlilo.

children which are burnt ; and the
children cry for their father who
has been burnt, having died whilst
fetching his precious things from
the burning house, and the house
fell in on him ; and the husband
cries, crying for his wife who has
been burnt ; she died when she
was fetching her child which was
in the house, and was burnt together with it ; and the trees cry,
crying for their beauty which is
lost, being now destroyed by the
fire, and the trees are shrivelled
and withered, and their beauty
gone ; and the cattle cry, crying
for the grass, because they no
longer have any thing to eat, but
are dying of famine. This, then,
is the laughing of fire.

11

Iso.

The eye.[27]

12

Itshe. Lapa si ti " ukukoka
ik*c*ala," si tsho ukubiya indawo e
ku sweleke ukuba i vinjwe ngetshe ; noma ukugaya ngalo. Uku-
k*g*eda ik*c*ala ke loko, i kona si ti,
" Li ya d*h*liwa ngako," ngokuba
nalo i kona imisebenzi e ku swele-
kele ukuba y enziwe ngalo lodwa.

A stone. When we say " paying a debt," we mean when it is
wanted to stop up the gateway of
an enclosed place with a stone ; or
to grind with it. That is to pay a
debt ; and therefore we say, " It is
eaten," for it too has its work
which can be done by it alone.

UMPENGULA MBANDA.

[27] This riddle bears a curious resemblance to our fable of " The Belly and
the Members." It is as much a fable as a riddle.

ERRATA.

		FOR	READ
Preface to Vol. I., P. 3, Liue 16,	reflection	refraction
PAGE 9, Note, Line 3,	Jamsaxa	Jarnsaxu
15, Note 16, L. 7,	been	seen
23, 19,	wati	wa ti
30, 17,	Whoever	Who ever
35, 3,	umninikazind*h*lu	umnikazind*h*lu
44, 26,	natiou	nation
54, Note 54, L. 1,	Kabib	Kabip
62, 32,	umnyeni	umyeni
63, 34,	vutele	" Vutela "
71, 5,	their	there
76, Note 99, L. 2,	Abbousset's	Arbousset's
84, Note 12, L. 6,	natives	nations
95, Note 25, L. 2,	traditiou	tradition
105, Note 36, L. 13,	Mary Loft	Mary Toft
113, 17,	rogal	royal
118, 1,	are	is
123, Note 58, L. 13,	Snend	Svend
149, 8,	'ug*q*ushuka	'ug*q*ashuka
149, 9,	'uk*q*abuka	'ug*q*ashuka
153, 10,	who descended	who, having des.
159, 9,	Gleddon	Gliddon
163, 22,	king-medicine	king's medicine
188, Note 31, L. 3,	Amanzi	Ananzi
199, Note 43, 15,	has	have
204, Note 47, 33,	Langfellow	Longfellow
205, Note 47, L. 4,	Mira	Miranda
212, 13,	k*x*ak*q*aza	kcwabaza
226, 26,	enkabeni	enkabini
234, Note 76, L. 12,	Jain	Iain
244, Note 92, 10,	Ihhoboshi	Uhhoboshi
252, 31,	iziutomhi	izintombi
294, 19,	Men believe iu the tales they talk about the diviner	Men believe in the tales the diviner tells them
317, 47,	In the Izimbutu, &c.	It is at Izimbutu or Usenthlouga These are the names of the place
346, 10,	man	men
346, 29,	lay	laid

CONTENTS OF THE FIRST VOLUME.

CONTENTS.

END OF VOL. I.

Printed at Springvale Mission Station, Natal.

OPINIONS OF THE PRESS.

(From the *Saturday Review*.)

" By this time the study of popular tales has become a recognised branch of the study of mankind.
It is highly creditable to Dr. Callaway, Dr. Bleek, and others to have made a beginning in a field of research which at first sight is not very attractive or promising. Many people, no doubt, will treat these stories with contempt, and declare they are not worth the paper on which they are printed. The same thing was said of Grimm's *Mährchen;* nay, it was said by Sir William Jones of the Zendavesta, and, by less distinguished scholars, of the Veda. But fifty years hence the collection of these stories may become as valuable as the few remaining bones of the dodo."

(From the *Spectator*.)

" We shall look with great interest to the remaining parts of this series."

(From the *Kentish Gazette*.)

" This is in every respect a most interesting work."

(From the *Mission Field*.)

" The student of ethnology, or of that interesting branch of knowledge which is now entitled comparative mythology, will find rich materials in this book, and will be grateful to the large-minded missionary who, amid more serious occupations, and many harassing cares, has opened a new intellectual field to European explorers."

(From the *Natal Witness*.)

" Some portions of the tale of Ukcombekcansini are as beautiful and graceful as a classic idyll. Once more, then, we heartily commend this work to our readers, wishing we may be able to persuade them to procure it for themselves, and so fully to enjoy a rich store of interest and amusement, of which they will otherwise have little conception. The work decidedly improves, in every respect, as it proceeds, and this is high praise."

" We must leave unnoticed many interesting portions of the book before us, trusting that we shall have succeeded in whetting the appetites of our readers sufficiently to procure it and read for themselves. It is impossible to open it anywhere without alighting upon either some curious analogue of our own nursery tales, or upon some strange phase of our common human nature. To the student of man, it is a book of singular interest."

" The part before us of Dr. Callaway's most interesting collection of Zulu traditions, contains three tales that will yield the palm to none that have preceded them for the strange and startling variety of their incidents. Indeed, we cannot remember that in the legends or fairy tales of any people we have met with adventures of a more wild and imaginative cast than in the story of Umkxakaza, combined, too, with a broad genial humour, that reminds us of the rough old tales of the Norse Thor, and not unrelieved by touches of tenderness and pathos."